BANNER
OF THE
BLUE WORLD

Bryan Kovach

Order this book online at www.trafford.com
or email orders@trafford.com

Most Trafford titles are also available at major online book retailers.

Print information available on the last page.

ISBN: 978-1-4907-6466-5 (sc)
ISBN: 978-1-4907-6467-2 (hc)
ISBN: 978-1-4907-6704-8 (e)

Library of Congress Control Number: 2015957153

Trafford rev. 01/14/2016

 www.trafford.com
North America & international
toll-free: 1 888 232 4444 (USA & Canada)
fax: 812 355 4082

The Legendarium awakens, for you.
Can you see it? Do you hear its music?
Did you glimpse it within a dream of the long-ago?
When you remember, you may be surprised to remember me there,
Walking in the garden beneath three moons,
Walking in Syrscian as it was and evermore shall be.

Drink with me again the draughts of Tryst's green lyceum.
Feel the embrace of fragrant winds from Ceregor's lofty peaks.
You have been here before, tired soul.
Then let it be before our eyes again,
No longer just a dream or a memory, but a better world,
A truer world than that ruled by men.

Let the children of the Blue World never forget,
Though the anthem of our ascent was sung by another.
The Ban is broken, and oaths were fulfilled.
Daybreak shall ring in exile's end,
And we shall awaken in the country of the sun's rising,
And live there forevermore.

1

AN INCIDENT AT WICELINE'S INN

Cille of Cambria,
A.D. 1901

Though it was still late summer, the sea was chill on the shores of Cambria. Wool wasn't ideal for walking clothes, but it was all Giles could scrounge up for them on such short notice. Tugging the straps of his second-hand trousers, Taran struggled to catch up to Hest. Her pace was as brisk as the wind.

Jon hiked beside him, combing pale wraithlike fingers through his hair while gazing silently at Hest. Thinking back to their late-night meeting in the castle, Taran still couldn't believe Jon's story about having a change of heart and wanting to make things right. Jon was Naruna's eyes and ears. His feigned brotherly affection had faded like a mist before the rising sun. In the end it was decided they should bring him along just to keep an eye on him.

"Cheer up, little brother," Jon said, taking notice of Taran's sideward glance. "I'll make sure Naruna doesn't find us."

The colonel worked for an international criminal named Lír, who wanted to find Val Anna. Taran now knew that Naruna wasn't her true father. Fain's books had revealed it to him—and something else.

Fain had somehow crossed over into another world.

"I wish I was back under the bridge," Taran mumbled.

"You worry too much! Father will be able to avoid the colonel, and you have me along in case he comes after us."

"You mean *when* he comes after us," Taran replied. "And I'm not worried. We have Hest."

Jon regarded his comment lightly.

"She's going to stop Naruna?"

"I dare say she could."

Jon resumed his study of Hest, sizing her up against some unknown obstacle. Taran turned his own attention to a countryside of green wind-swept hills.

The ferry had left them at a village with a quay so small it could hardly be called a port. That was probably a good thing, being Taran carried a bundle wrapped in rags that anyone could plainly see was a sword. They shared no words with the ferryman, and took to a weedy path that was empty of traffic. There were no real roads. Nor were there any bridges, as they discovered at the first little streamlet they forded. Cambria was a country of shepherds and small villages, and little else.

Rounding the top of another hill, Taran looked down into a deep shadowed glen dotted with pools and hemmed by lonely trees. The sea-scented wind died suddenly, and with that came the realization at last that he'd entered a foreign land. The others passed him by while he paused a moment to look back towards the distant glimmering waters. Deep in his heart he felt a strange sadness at the sight, as if he would not look upon the wide blue sea again.

Hest suggested a southeasterly course. The path, Taran learned, was one that Fain had referred to in a conversation with DePons. This was something Hest had hidden from him in their discussion the previous evening. As to what lay at the end of the road, she claimed to know nothing. Taran, she insisted, was partially responsible for that.

He had burned the diary.

When he told her what he'd done to Fain's book, she was predictably wrathful. Taran had never seen a woman so enraged; but she'd calmed down just as quickly, and said that it was probably best. This way, Naruna could not know what was in Fain's mind—unless he caught up to them.

Taran kept a few scraps of Fain's book in his pocket, though, and he never told Hest anything about them. One item, a picture drawn by Val Anna upon her adoption by the Narunas, was purely nostalgic. The other was a fragmented note that somehow seemed important. He tried his best to put the puzzle out of mind for the present. Following the wilderness road was challenging enough.

Dangling from a loop of cord slung over one shoulder, Taran carried a water skin in a small bag of oddments necessary for travel. Pouches of jerky were crammed into his pockets. Everyone else was similarly discomfited, for they had hoped to distance their pursuers by abandoning heftier gear or packs.

The unaccustomed weight of a sword, which he bore sheathed in rags across his other shoulder, was becoming a nuisance. There was no way to hide it from sight, and it couldn't be left behind. The ferryman had raised his eyebrows, and Jon pretended not to notice it at all; but to Taran it was a great bother that he wished to be rid of. He sighed quietly to himself. His sense of adventure had abandoned him somewhere in Morvran Castle.

"You're anxious, Brother?" Jon asked.

Taran looked back along their trail, surveying a landscape of mist-cloaked rocks standing beside quiet pools, rising like gray robed figures that struggled amidst the cool dark waters.

"I'm worried about Giles. Naruna's due back at the castle by now—but what's this?"

He had stumbled upon some tracks in the mud between his feet. While he and Jonathan gazed on them curiously, Hest came and bent down for a closer look.

"Two children walked here," she noted. "They went without shoes. The tracks continue southeast, deeper into the vale. I've been following them for some time."

Taran glanced around the empty land. "Children went barefoot in this place?"

"We will continue to follow them."

"Why?" Jonathan asked. "You really think there might be a town that way?"

Hest glared at him, and as she rose and continued walking up the hill she let her eyes linger on his face.

"Am I to know the cause of your suspicions?" Jon shouted after her.

"You need no explanation from her," Taran replied, trudging along behind Hest. "Neither of us trusts you."

"How then might I earn your trust?"

Taran paused briefly and peered at him over one shoulder. "A man is judged by the company he keeps."

"Same to you, Brother," Jon whispered.

A tense mood followed them southeast over barren hills. The landscape slowly changed. They encountered more trees, and even a few thick stands of oak. Hest picked a course through open lands, choosing terrains littered with boulders where their feet would leave few marks.

Though the morning was already old, the sun no longer shone pleasantly, and mists clung to the bottom-lands in places where the trees gathered. Taran didn't mind the mist, as the day was promising to be warm and it would hide them from searching eyes. The damp restless air washed his face clean as he hiked among the tumbled stones, bathing him in the same vigor that had carved this mighty land. Strength poured into him from a hidden source. It seemed as though he could not be stopped, now that he had actually set out on Fain's trail. The lingering thought that he might not be coming back troubled him less the farther they walked.

At last, when the sun had risen a bit closer to noon, they paused to take a few mouthfuls of food. Taran estimated they'd traveled nearly twelve miles across trackless terrain, and now they stood at a place where the hills gave way to a gently sloping descent. The air was warming, and a very different air it was, brimming with heady draughts of woodland scents. It brought the blood to his face, and sent the hair on his head curling. His heart thumped strong, for there below, settled just beyond the hunched shoulders of downs that rose like islands in a green sea of grass, marched the vast expanse of an ancient forest.

"What a canopy," Jon lamented. "It's like the blanket that covers the dead."

"Hest, does this place have a name?" Taran wondered.

"The forest is Broceliánde," she said. "My father once told me that the wood veils unspoken secrets. Few who wandered there returned the same as they went in."

Jon nodded. *"Brecelien.* I have also read the old stories."

"When did you ever—?"

Taran's thought was broken off sharply as his brother affected a more mysterious tone.

"It was said to be a truly enchanted wood. It was a place for mages and druids, where they composed songs of Faery—songs about creatures of the night that prepared cunning lures for men deep in the shadowed heath."

He smiled roguishly.

"The songs were warnings," Hest said to Taran. "Those who went in were changed. It was ever a place of strange unearthly covenants, the gate to Annwn, the *Arbed*—a crossing to some other world."

Taran worried his brow. "So, you think the stories might be a hint as to the presence of something that could have whisked Fain off to wherever he's gone?"

"Our fathers thought so," she replied.

Taran eyed the unbroken line of trees stretching from north to south. "We'll need more substantial supplies if we're going to tackle *that.*"

"There are towns along the border. We will come to one sooner or later; but before we venture into the heart of the forest I suppose we should consider what comes after."

Taran regarded her silently.

"So," Jon said, "I guess we've all been thinking the same thing."

"The likelihood is that we shall not be coming out if we choose to go in," Hest replied.

"If we are as mad as Fain," Taran added. "There's no telling how much we'll need to carry either way, I suppose."

They went on with their eyes bent toward the grass. A trail of sorts had appeared, and it was easy to follow through the high green towards the distant line of trees. That line soon became a frowning black wall, and within another half hour they stood a stone's throw from its very eaves. There they paused to take in the forest's brooding presence.

The noon sun in its golden glory smote down upon the wood, but revealed very little. The trees smelled of long-forgotten times, times when the dawn of a different sun shone down. Here it was not so difficult to catch a glimpse into an older world.

An eerie abandoned silence drew around them as they stood looking in. A dread of watchfulness flickered uncomfortably in Taran's heart, and increased with every passing moment. He fancied a whispered voice saying, *"Come,"* but his companions made no sign that they heard it.

"There is a road," Hest said, pointing to a flat area along the treeline.

Walking in this direction they came quickly to a stony rutted path running north-south along the forest's edge. This brought them southwards only a hundred yards or so before they arrived at a crossroads, and there the path diverged along a sharp left-hand turn that plunged into the darkness under the trees. While they stood and stared into the gaping mouth of the wood, a cart full of potatoes appeared from the shadows, driven by a man whose lumpen features mimicked those of his cargo. Cart, mule, and merchant approached with little noise and turned south. It was like seeing a ghost.

"He didn't even look our way," Taran commented.

"I wouldn't greet you either, Brother, if I saw you standing here looking like that," Jon replied. "Besides, these people are probably put off by outsiders."

"There are only outsiders here," Hest said, taking the road beneath the trees.

Entering Broceliánde was like entering a tunnel in a cave. In a little while they were forced to the wayside by some shepherds driving their flocks down towards the western vale. This time they were acknowledged, though only with subdued greetings.

"What town is here?" Taran asked as he stepped back onto the path.

The eldest, a large heavyset man, replied, "You've come to Cille, or nowhere."

With no more greeting than this, the shepherds followed their flocks towards the sunny pastures. The three passed deeper and deeper into the wood, but they said little to each other. Their footsteps were masked by an endless creaking song of twisted boughs and stems.

They walked along under shadows, and a long time passed before they began to see signs of habitation. Beyond the outer wall of the wood they came upon a silent place filled with enormous tree-columns. The branches above let in very little light. Here and there they passed small clearings where a few brick houses stood alone on the sides of the road. They looked like comfortable homesteads, but Taran couldn't imagine living in such a place. Jon trudged beside him with a blank look. Was he having similar thoughts?

"Do you think there's any way, Taran, that we could go back to how things were before you gave that stone to Val Anna?"

Taran mused quietly on his brother's question.

"You know," Jon continued, "the road we travel today is only an echo of your choice."

"You seem to know a lot about it."

"No more than you got from reading Fain's books."

"You read his books?"

"Not the ones you tossed into the fire. However, I did read something about her."

He nodded towards Hest.

"Grandfather and father both were very fond of her, it seems; and you, too. I wonder what she means to the three of you. Are you certain she is to be trusted?"

As awkward silence prevailed upon them once again, they rambled on past a few small clearings. The road thereafter straightened, plunging like an arrow into the thick of an ominous weald. With backwards glances and hearts full of doubt they were ushered ever deeper into the forest's brooding presence.

The first signs of the village came with a change in the trees. Here they were less tall but closer together, their boles twisted into fantastic shapes, and most of their lower limbs had been trimmed along the road. It was a wood of kinds Taran had never seen, ancient, close-grown, and very stuffy. Holly and yew thrust out sharp green spears amid clusters of bright berries, and from beneath woven banks of nettles strung like garlands from tree to tree there lay deep drifts of last year's leaves. The oak and ash were dominant, boughs outspread in passive omnipotence, overshadowing their own seedlings, drowning all beneath in a twilight of cool shadows and endless night.

As the trees bent closer the road narrowed, until at last they came to a subtly lighter place full of bustle and noise. They had arrived in Cille, as a sign by the roadside announced. It was a village guarded by darkness, hemmed in by shadows; yet they saw in its streets no obvious indication that they were headed for trouble.

Here were all the smells, sights, and sounds that Taran always associated with fantasies of the medieval world. He saw roasted meats, brown bread, and mead in wooden casks. Heavy-laden carts creaked past bearing textiles and goods from settlements afar. There were many beautiful women in the shops—women gowned and girdled like queens, with teeth straight and white and their hair braided with ribbons. They laughed at the men, the merchants who worked their booths and stalls, who sang with their hearts full of mirth. The sweet music of flutes drifted to them from some hidden quarter, happily piping a tune to quicken the feet of weary travelers. Even the trees seemed less hostile, their leaves clapping heartily in the warm summertime breeze.

It was as if they had stepped back in time. The tale of Fain's passage to another world was somehow more believable here.

"What is this place?" Taran asked in breathless wonder.

"Haven't these people heard about the outside world?" Jon asked.

"Well, I wouldn't expect them to have electric lights or motorcars, but something does feel off, doesn't it?"

Hest was eyeing the street scene with an eager look, as if she searched for something familiar, or for someone she knew. Turning towards a nearby butcher's stall she hailed the merchant within and leaned forwards to speak to him discreetly.

"Is there an inn?" she asked.

The butcher sniffed, and smiled roguishly at Taran and Jon.

"You needs the lady to ask directions, Sirs?" he joked, wiping his hands on his apron. "Just keep walkin' the road you came in on until you come to the end of the old north-south way—a road overgrown and wild that none but fools ever use. Wiceline's stands at the crossroads. You can't miss it!"

On through the center of the marketplace they walked. Taran was increasingly aware of a return of the peculiar double-vision that had haunted him aboard Olympic. He decided not to tell Hest about it just yet. He was probably just tired from their long journey—but not so tired that he missed the suspicious sideways glances from the market stalls as they passed. Taran knew it was because of the sword, and wished once again he could have stowed it someplace secret inside the castle. It was dead weight, and it would only attract unwanted attention. Anyway, it wasn't as though he would ever actually use it for anything other than a prop.

Leaving the markets behind, they came then to a street lined with finely crafted homes. They glimpsed here and there some of the amenities of modern convenience—a steel-axle wagon with spring seats, a gas lamp, and even a telegraph pole. The latter bore only a loosely dangling scrap of transmission wire strung from the top. Taran turned his head back and forth, but he saw no other poles.

"They don't use electricity anymore, I guess," Hest said, noticing his curiosity. "Father told me all this region is plagued by a superstition of the mischief of Faeries."

"Faeries?"

"Haven't you heard?" Jon wondered playfully. "Faeries love to dismantle electrical equipment and machines."

"All such things have a marvelous ability to dismantle themselves," Taran replied with a sigh.

He was thinking of his poor flying machine, now in the hands of some strangers in Ohio. At that very moment, a cloud passed briefly overhead, stopping him in his tracks. Hest followed his gaze up towards the overhanging boughs.

"Something's amiss?" she asked.

"Why are there no children?" Taran wondered. "We followed the tracks of children to this place, but now that we're here I've not seen any children at all."

The realization was a sudden shock. He had not thought about it until he said it, and neither had they.

"We're at the end of our road," Jon said, nodding ahead.

They stood almost upon the intersection. The inn would have been hard to miss, indeed. It was the grandest building in Cille. Where the east road terminated in a short bend just ahead, it was intersected by a weedy track running north-south. To their left, on the north side of the meeting of ways, a blocky three-storied stone structure nestled against the natural slope of the wood aback. The first two stories— exposed only on those two sides facing south and east—were partly below ground. Above the double-doors that opened to face the south, a sign had been posted which bore a singularly strange device: a great green hill, and a coiling red serpent with golden eyes perched atop.

"We may find someone here who can direct us," Hest said. "Father once told me of a man named Gwilym who lived out this way. He was a friend of Fain's, and was fairly well known in these lands. We can ask for him here."

Taran studied the inn's brightly painted placard suspiciously. "I don't know why, but I don't like the look of this place."

Jon tugged on his sleeve. "You two go in," he said. "I'll head back to the market. I think I've just enough local coin on hand to scrounge up supplies."

Taran blinked surprise at his brother's incentive.

"I'm just trying to be helpful," Jon said. "I'll be back by time you finish up in there. Just stay out of trouble, okay?"

He turned back along the way they'd come. Taran watched him go.

"Who gave him local coin?" Hest wondered.

"You're thinking Naruna set this up—that Jon's off to set up some roadsigns?"

"What do you think, Taran Morvran?"

"What do I think?"

He shivered, despite the warmth of the afternoon.

"I think it won't matter. We've got a head start, and not even we know for certain where we're going."

Upon entering the fore-chamber they found themselves in a large tavern. The air was close, for there was no separate kitchen, and all within was bathed in smokes from cooking-fires burning on two different hearths. There were no windows, so the only light came from the fires and a few sooty sconces on the walls.

Taran was genuinely impressed by the rustic feel of the place. There were plenty of tables sharing the central space and more along the walls, and almost all were crowded with diners busy with knives and platters, speaking low amongst themselves. In the murky light the townsfolk looked a little swarthier than they did in the markets, and their eyes did seem drawn to his sword. Just as Taran was thinking he would rather have waited outside, a pale white hand waved at them from the murky interior of the room.

Hest followed him farther in towards a few boards set apart from all the others. The atmosphere of the hall became heavier as they made their way deeper in, where there were no sconces and only a few candles were lit, until at last they stood before a table tucked away beside enormous wine casks.

A grotesque bulky figure sat before them, flagon in hand.

"Ah, here you are!" The creature said with apparent recognition.

Upon closer inspection Taran decided that it was a woman. She wore a dirty tavern-keeper's dress, and what was left of her hair was a tangle of salt and pepper strands. Her pocked face was strangely twisted, with a crooked nose that was low and flat and lips that were shaped like a cat's.

"You expected our arrival?" Taran asked.

"All my guests are expected," the woman replied, staring at him with one pale brown eye through her unkempt tangle of hair. "I am Wiceline. This is my inn."

Taran winced. Her breath reeked even from across the table, and when she sneered he could see her teeth, crooked and rotting.

"Such a handsome young man! But watch that sword. I make exceptions for foreign guests such as yourselves, but you should know that all such things are forbidden in Wiceline's house."

"It's just an antique," Taran replied. "I'm holding onto it for a friend."

"And where are you journeying with a friend's sword, may I ask?"

"Into the woods, obviously."

"Take my advice, young man. Turn away from the road that leads into the forest. Stay here awhile instead, if you would, and tell us some merry news from the outside world."

Her words weren't menacing, but Hest was suddenly agitated.

"If our business should require us to go into the forest," she said, "then it is our own business, no matter the road we take."

The hag turned towards her and frowned.

"And this is the unnatural creature they told me about?" she muttered, stroking the stubble protruding from her jowl. "What do you want with this dear boy, *Monster?*"

Lips pressed into a flat line, Hest touched his arm and nodded back towards the exit.

"Wait!" Wiceline urged. "You mustn't let her take you into the wood!"

Taran hesitated, but not because he doubted Hest. He wanted to hear more.

"Aye!" the old hag exclaimed, baring a few teeth in his direction. "It's not as if she's the first of the Faery-folk I've ever seen in these parts, Boy. Old Wiceline shares the bloodline, too, you know!"

Taran gave her a questioning look.

"Tryst was no good place for a town," she elaborated. "This ground lies between two worlds. When the clansmen who were our forefathers first came here to build, they soon discovered that Faeries were common traffic; and there were more than a few who took Faery wives. They didn't know the dangers, you see, and they were ever pressing deeper and deeper into the forest. Then it was they discovered the devil that haunts the mound in the heart of the wood."

"What mound is that?" Taran asked.

She winked at him. "Aye, you've heard of it. Cnoc Ddraig, the Dragon's Mound it is. If you want to know why the folk of Cille fear the Faeries so much, you might think on all of those who've gone missing in these parts. Children, mostly. None here will talk of it, though, so don't ask."

Turning again towards Hest, Wiceline added, "It's best you send her off alone, Boy, before there's trouble."

Glancing over his shoulder, Taran was surprised to note that many people had gotten up to leave. There were several free tables, and only a few curious onlookers.

A voice at his shoulder pled quietly, "Let's get out of here, Taran."

Hest's hand was still on his arm. She was trembling, but Taran did not think it was from fear. She seemed very close to rage.

"If you insist on taking up with that Faery," Wiceline said, rising slowly from her chair, "the door's that way."

She inclined her head towards the exit. Except for a few serving-men standing by who watched with furrowed brows, whispering quietly amongst themselves, the entire tavern was now empty.

"So much for leaving without creating a scene," Taran whispered as they walked towards the door. The men who stood there exited ahead of them. Waiving suspicions aside, Taran stepped out onto the front step and breathed the free air. His breath was exhaled with a startled gasp.

A silent vigil of dozens of townsfolk awaited them, many lifting torches. They were also armed, bearing pikes and stout wooden clubs.

To make matters worse, the sun was setting.

Taran knew they'd only been inside the inn for a few minutes. It was impossible for the sun to be setting so early. While he stood there perplexed, unable to go on or to turn back, a single clear thought crossed his mind.

Jonathan was behind this.

The warnings of Taran's imagination played out before him. The assembled men of the town looked on them with equal measures of solemnity and hostility, their features curiously transformed by his fear into loathsome masks. He couldn't be certain what they intended, but their eyes were fixed upon him with the gaze of cats ready to pounce. He stared back, and then he heard a voice speaking.

"You were thinking of leaving so soon, my dears?" Wiceline asked in menacing tones.

He faced the hag, who stood now by the threshold behind him. Taran clenched the sword-strap tightly.

Hest shouted suddenly, clearing his mind of all thoughts rational or otherwise.

"Don't you dare look at him like that!"

The nearest thugs in the crowd stepped back a pace, rattled by the anger in her voice. Amber hair in tendrils drifting forwards from hunched shoulders and lowered face, she turned her furious gaze away from Wiceline to the mob.

"Hest!" Taran whispered. "What in the world's come over you?"

"I knew it!" Wiceline shouted, pointing a knobbed finger. "She's Faery! She's the one who steals our children and takes them to the mound!"

Taran was shocked less by her words than by their effect. The men before them backpedaled so suddenly that it looked like they were shoved by a giant pair of hands. Voices murmured excitedly. Glancing aside, Taran noticed Hest's face frozen in a moment of terrible decision.

"Demon!" Wiceline screamed. "Don't let it change shape here, or Cille will be cursed!"

A few brave brigands stepped out of the crowd, creeping cautiously across the intersection, determination enlivening their bold advance. Then Taran saw a second startled uproar spreading among them, and everyone halted. Many of those who remained at the rear dropped their weapons and ran. Following their frightened eyes to his own chest, he saw there a strange radiance spilling forth, brilliance that invaded the cold light of evening like a descending star.

Her rage forgotten, Hest turned her face towards him with a look of wonder.

"Impossible!" she whispered.

Taran's body began to ache with the agony of burning and searing flames. Looping coils of glimmering smoke stretched like striking serpents from his left arm. Through his right hand, which held the rag-wrapped blade of Morvran, he felt an intense vibration. He stumbled backwards, pulling his arm in towards his chest while Wiceline clutched the doorway behind him, shielding her house against his return.

"Devils and sorcery!" she cried out in dismay.

Taran could not speak, for a weight now rested upon his shoulders. The pain in his arm was no longer tolerable, so he shouted, and the sound was like a battle-horn. The earth trembled beneath him. The inn let out a groaning response—every board in the place moaned. Some in the crowd imitated the sound, falling to the ground and covered their faces, while others ran off into the sylvan twilight.

And then, as sudden as its onset, the pain subsided.

The air around him danced like ripples in a pond, and everything dissolved into silver mist. Taran could see only the forest, and where Wiceline's house once stood there was a grassy hill. The posts and lintel of the doors were two tall pines, their branches leaning like an arch overhead. Everyone was gone.

His left arm was translucent like glass.

The glimmering glassy limb exuded a dark vapor. He held it up before his face in wonder, turning the hand over and wriggling the fingers. There was no sensation at all. It was like someone else's hand had been grafted into his body.

Then he noticed a pale light shining around him in the thick gloom. Bluish in color, he couldn't tell where it came from. The light was increasing every moment, but it revealed only empty forest. He tried to call out for Hest, but his throat wouldn't make a sound. When he attempted to take a step, the whole world slid sideways, and he fell face downwards onto the grass.

Taran quickly shook off the dizziness and confusion that clouded his mind. Harsh clanging bells receded somewhere in the distance, and someone's fingers were gripping his shoulders. He was rolled roughly over onto his back. Hest knelt over him, her face flushed with fear.

"You fool!"

She slapped him.

"I almost lost my temper!"

Rubbing the side of his face in bewilderment, Taran struggled to a sitting position while Hest walked off into the street. There were still a few men there, but they threw down their weapons and ran towards the town as she approached. Listening to the sound of their retreating footsteps, Taran wondered what had happened. He was startled by Wiceline's voice.

"Cursed Faery!"

The inn was behind him, just as before, and Wiceline remained by the door, staggering on stumpy legs, shaking a fat fist at Hest.

"Take your evil back to the wood where it belongs! May the dead find you!"

Taran pulled aside his bundled sword. Squinting at him behind heavy brows, Wiceline drew back with a hissing intake of breath through her blackened teeth.

"Go on, then!" she said. "You'll not get far with such a companion! I will summon every spirit I know to hunt you down through fen and hollow, to the very heart of the cursed mound itself! Bright swords won't stop them! You'll not sleep, night or day, for they will be right behind you!"

Wiceline slammed the doors shut. Standing to his feet on wobbly legs, Taran dusted himself off and hefted his burden over one shoulder. The sky was gray, though it couldn't be more than four hours after noon. A chill wind gusted, and the trees along the lane leaned inwards overhead like walls of shadow, barring the last feeble glimmer of day.

He flexed the fingers of his left hand, and turned back towards the road to see Hest regarding him with a wary look. There was keen disappointment in her gaze.

"It sure gets dark early here, doesn't it?" he asked.

In answer, she began walking down the road towards the town. Taran followed at a little distance, wondering what had happened to him and why Hest was so angry. He could still feel the sharp sting of her hand on his face. Was it because she hadn't found the fellow she'd come looking for, this stranger who knew Fain? Or was sit because he'd so nicely announced they were here and told everyone where they were going?

It wasn't as though he'd deliberately done these things. It was totally unavoidable. Somehow he doubted that Hest would have listened to his explanation. He wasn't given much time to ponder the matter himself before they spotted a tall lanky figure sauntering towards them down the misty lane.

Jon bore three full skins and some loaves and cheese wrapped in paper. Taran eyed these offerings with displeasure.

"What's wrong?" Jon asked.

"Where were you, and with whom did you arrange for our capture?" Taran asked.

Jon appeared genuinely surprised, and then he looked around at the cast-off clubs and poles lying in the street.

"Did something happen?"

"We were attacked."

He managed to look surprised. "Attacked? I only left you alone for one quarter hour and you were attacked?"

"Did you arrange this, Jon?"

Jon's features seemed suddenly to crumble from within, like an old building collapsing. Taran looked aside at Hest, but she wasn't going to break her silence. In effect, it would fall squarely on Taran to send his brother away.

That would be the logical choice. If he loved his brother, it would be wise not to give him further opportunities to hinder their journey. Jon regarded him with narrowed eyes.

"Whether you were behind this or not, Brother, I'd rather you came with us, if you still want to," Taran said. "Even if Mother and Father are in danger, I won't stop searching for Fain's Door, and I'm going to find Val Anna. You can help me if you wish; or, go back and help them. Either way, Naruna wants this thing that's inside of me, and he won't stop searching for it until I am in his power."

"You aren't going to send me away?" Jon asked gloomily.

"If your intention was to capture us and hand me over to Naruna, you would follow us even if I did tell you to go home. If your intention is to help, then you would probably do the same. So, what does it matter what I tell you? You are free to do as you wish. But whatever you're going to do, you'd better decide soon."

Jon looked aside at Hest, who stared straight through him in a threatening manner. He shrugged and held out the supplies he'd purchased for their journey.

"Then let's begin by getting you out of Cille before the rest of the townsfolk find out what's happened here," he suggested.

They passed the inn. Everything was quiet, and all the doors and windows were shut. As far as they could tell, the road running north and south from the intersection was empty. No sound could they hear except for the hiss of the wind in the rhododendrons. Hest led them south.

It was now dusk, and the weedy track was a far cry from being freely navigable. Though larger trees hemmed in its course and kept it a straight line, their feet trod soft spongy turf, making it nearly impossible to determine whether or not they were still on a trail.

Taran allowed Hest to walk in front, her ghostly shape steering the way into the night. He watched her with growing concern, for he knew now that this girl hid a mighty power—a power that had awakened something sleeping inside of him, that threw him back and forth through time and turned his arm to glass.

Did old Wiceline know something about Hest after all?

The heaviness he felt at the inn pursued him—that and a stray hound, a tall wasted mastiff that ran out of the fog straight at them. It ignored Hest entirely and went right to Taran, startling him badly and standing the hair straight up on top of his head. The mangy beast didn't seem more than passively interested in him and his food, though, for after it sniffed a proffered crumb it loped back into the fog in the direction of the town.

Then total darkness came.

Taran began to think about making camp, but Hest showed no signs of slowing. They had no blankets or bedrolls, and he was only a little tired. No one spoke, however, and he wondered if the others were just waiting for him to say something. For the time being, the nighttime journey was actually pleasant.

The fear of Cille was slipping away.

A gentle wind tossed the treetops like fragrantly billowing black clouds that rattled and creaked, bestirring crickets into a song in the grass beneath the weathered boughs. Other night-sounds awoke. The noise of water and the chirping of frogs along one side of the way betrayed the presence of a stream or mire, but he could see nothing to indicate that the woods grew any thinner there. It was all so perfectly peaceful.

Hest slowed her pace so that they walked side by side. Touching his arm, she leaned close and whispered.

"I am sorry, Taran Morvran."

"What for?"

"It was not your fault. It was mine."

Taran chuckled with relief. "Why so formal, Hest? You were frightened, and so was I."

"That woman!"

"Wiceline? Don't dwell on what she said, Hest. She was a superstitious hag. I know you're different, but I don't care, because you are my friend."

Hest calmed herself with an effort. She kept her hand on his left arm.

"I did not know that Regulus would stay with you. This changes everything."

"Yeah. At least we know now why Naruna was so keen on keeping me locked up in Castle Morvran. What will this thing do to me, anyway?"

She did not immediately answer.

"Is there something wrong, Hest?"

"I am glad that you chose to trust me, Taran Morvran. No matter what happens, I will never allow you come to harm, not even if I change into something else."

"Hest?"

"With a fragment of Regulus within, you will not rely on me so much as I desire."

Spoken softly into his ear, her words caught him off guard. Hest waited until she heard the scuffle of Jon's boots far behind them before she continued.

"I will need to teach you how to take care of yourself, and of Regulus, before our journey together comes to an end."

2

A JOURNEY BEGINS

Southern Ceregor, Syrscian,
Year 999 of the New Council

Crouched snugly upon a basalt boulder, tail twitching as she tested
miniscule currents of air, Foxglove gripped her dagger nervously and
sized up her prey. He wore a white padded leather hauberk, but his
head and neck were unprotected. He was close. This was her moment,
and the encounter was unfolding just as she'd imagined.

Ever since leading the strangers to his abandoned camp in the hills she had pursued him with singular purpose. He was a renegade, this one—none of his outlaw band of fugitive soldiers knew where he'd gone or how to find him.

Foxglove only had to follow her nose.

So she followed him alone through the passages of the Rim Mountains, the bogs, and all of East Tarthalion. He continually evaded her, leaving behind only cold ashes and a rumor of his vile scent. The flame of vengeance kept her going through a cruel mountain winter.

She'd been hunting him for two years.

In all that time, her quarry moved up and down the ridgeline in a seemingly aimless fashion; but over time Foxglove divined a purpose in his wanderings. He had visited many of the caves where the Gremn hid things in the long-ago. He was obviously hoping to find something that might save him from the wrath he'd left in the wake of the Galanese invasion of Tarthalion.

By this, and by his cautious care in disassembling his camps, Foxglove knew he was aware that he was hunted. And coming now to this lonely place, high in the foothills of the mighty Ceregor range where of old lay the ancient heartland of the Fourth House, she imagined that he had heard at last the summons of righteous justice. Was it not fitting he should die here, by her hand?

It was high time the butcher of Ulumeneth met his end.

The wind-sculpted rocks cast deep shadows around the place where Foxglove hid, high up the wall of this dry little cleft in the hills. The Ayumu were a clever folk of many races, and all of them wood-crafty; but none were as stealthy as Foxglove's kin. Her prey remained unaware, oblivious. She had him cornered now, and the only exit was over a cliff's edge. Standing with his back to her, he gazed out over the broken and pathless foothills that bordered the wastelands of Urlad below. Farther to the south the walls of the Rim Mountains staggered toward a bleary blue horizon, disappearing in the haze that wafted up from the poisoned desert.

Was he thinking of leaving the mountains and heading east into Musab lands? He had no supplies for a desert crossing, and he wore only a light protective mask. This would not avail him in Urlad. Even she dared not tread there. Though her people had developed a resistance to the toxic fumes, the concentrations lower down were deadly to all things that walked on two legs. He seemed to be mulling this over in his mind while adjusting the filters of his mask. It was no matter, she thought. Whatever path he intended to take from this place, they all led to his death.

The wind gusted, and for a moment he was lost to sight behind a gray wall of dry ash and sandy soil. Foxglove hunkered down, waiting for the air to clear. Her heart began ticking faster. When she could see him again, he remained standing with his back to her as before, but now his pistol was drawn. Tightening her grip on the handle of her dagger, she drew in a deep breath, uncertain of whether she had been spotted.

"You don't need to sulk up there like a wyrm's orphaned pup," he said gently, his voice strangely distorted by his environmental mask. "Why don't you come down for a bit? You must be tired of this game."

Foxglove held her breath and remained still. She wondered if he actually knew that she was there, of if he was only trying to trick her into revealing her position.

"Very well, then," he said. "Stay hidden, if you wish."

He holstered his pistol and removed his mask.

"But know this," he added in a clear voice. "Today I will be departing these lands. If it was revenge you wanted, I think you may have missed your chance."

While Foxglove looked on, he sat down upon a boulder and began emptying his boots of ash and small stones. When he was finished, he pulled them on again and started cleaning them with a small brush. He kept his back turned towards her the whole time; and just as if he hadn't a care in the world, he hummed a familiar tune.

Surely he was testing her. She crouched for a leap. Tail swishing side to side, she exhaled slowly and raised her dagger high, squeezing the hilt with a ferocity borne from the bitter depths of vengeance.

Her fingers closed on sharp thorns.

Dropping the weapon with a loud cry, she looked on helplessly as it clattered down from her perch and came to rest right behind him on the soft soil. He stood and turned, looking down upon it. Foxglove's spirit crumbled within her, but her prey glanced up only briefly.

Something remarkable was happening to that dagger.

Stringy filaments like the roots of grass were curling and waving all around it, and the now-living wooden-inlay of the handle launched thorny vines across the ground. A cluster of little blossoms budded and bloomed upon the gleaming dragon's-tooth blade.

In that moment of confusion they both heard the light slap of bare feet on stone. Turning instinctively, Foxglove was surprised to see someone standing upon the boulder right beside her, poised as if dropped from the sky. There was a moment of deep silence as three pairs of eyes met.

The newcomer walked barefoot like the Ayumu people, but she was not of Foxglove's kin. She wore a fringed lavender tunic with a hem of decorative beads. Her leggings were of deepest indigo. It was outlandish finery of the sort in old paintings, clothing from the long-ago. This wasn't what made the stranger's appearance so startling, however.

Catching her sly smiling glance as the stranger leapt down from rock to rock, Foxglove wondered at the glinting tattoo of a flowering *ilum* vine beneath each of the girl's ice-blue eyes. Besides those eyes, her most striking feature was her hair. It was also blue—a blue that was the stuff of legends.

The girl bounded lightly down beside the soldier. She looked quite small standing next to him; but her slight features scarcely hid a greater spirit within. He backed away from her a few paces, staring. Foxglove tried to stay out of sight, but couldn't help leaning out to watch as her opportunity was snatched away by this new development.

"Peace to you," the soldier mumbled.

The girl ignored him, and looked away into the gloomy wastes.

"This is the desert?"

Her voice carried a strange accent. The soldier made no reply, so she turned to face him.

"You are suspicious of me?" she asked.

"As my people often say, there are no chance meetings in these lands."

"That may seem so," she replied, "but this meeting was hoped for more than it was expected. You are a difficult man to find, Bregon son of Cedric, Lord of House Gaerith."

Foxglove trembled at the name of her hated prey. Of course she knew who he was. This was the general of the Southern Army, the one who led the assault upon Tarthalion. She would have killed him then and there with her bare hands, if she could.

But that girl—she wasn't someone who would just stand by and let this happen. It wasn't just her hair that gave her away. Foxglove could sense the presence of something very powerful here.

Bregon son of Cedric also sensed something. He stowed his mask neatly in a pouch on his belt, granting the stranger a glimpse of his holstered pistol as he did so. His eyes were on the girl the whole time, but Foxglove could smell his fear.

"How do you know who I am?" he asked.

Foxglove's eyes strayed to his unprotected neck, and ignoring the unlikely possibility that she should land a fatal blow on a trained soldier she prepared to pounce. The strange blue-haired girl did not turn towards the boulder where Foxglove crouched, but her sly smile broadened, as if daring her.

"Your uniform is white," the girl said in answer to his question. "White is worn only by generals and priests, and last I heard there was only one heir of the Great Houses left in Syrscian—only one left with the authority to wage war."

She stepped closer and gazed up into his face.

"Besides, now that I see your face, you do resemble your father."

"Who are you?" he asked, squinting down at her in wonder. "And how would you know my father?"

"I know him. Is that not enough? Why do you make such a frown with your face?"

His jaw relaxed, and his eyes widened. It was a look of understanding, but it was not a happy look.

"Surely you are not Fomorian?" he asked.

"What else should I be?" she replied with a graceful bow.

Foxglove trembled. She reserved no doubts about this audacious claim. The budding of her knife was proof enough. Hunkering down, she wrapped her arms around her knees and wondered what the old storytellers of Ulumeneth would have thought of this—a Fomorian and the age-old lord of a villainous Great House teaming up in the wilds. It was as though her whole world was falling apart, all over again.

"So, I look like him you say?"

"I suppose with navvies and Gremn it's less a matter of genetics than design," the Fomorian answered.

"Heh! My father was a very dangerous man. Whatever you know about him, the things he's done—"

"I did not say I knew about him. I know him, personally..."

But Foxglove no longer listened to what they were saying.

She was crushed by the weight of her failure. The cries of dying voices still rang in her ears, and after two long years they could not now be silenced. Emptied of purpose, she sat still and gazed down at her knife, lying still at the feet of her foe. The thorny vine that had grown from a few small pieces of wooden inlay on the handle was now sprouting leaflets. The inlay was crafted from slivers cut from one of the sacred trees destroyed a thousand years ago—the trees of the Fomorian spirits.

For a long time, it seemed, she sat and contemplated the budding knife, until suddenly she was aware that both the strangers were staring up at her. Foxglove's long ears swept back, and her tail swished anxiously. She wished she had been paying more attention.

Bregon nodded in her direction. "Is she traveling with you?" he asked.

"With you, rather," the Fomorian said.

"I suspected as much."

"Did you? Then I shall spare you the report I've heard on my journey, of the price the Ayumu have placed on your head. You should be glad to have had so faithful a companion on the road from the south, and no more than one at that."

"There are no roads where I am going," he replied, nodding towards the desert.

"The last I looked upon that place, it was called the Long Grass."

"The grass burned up a thousand summers past, in the War," he said. "I still remember what it was like before, though."

Foxglove had never considered before what his title inferred. Her jaw relaxed, and her mouth hung open.

These two were from the long-ago.

Was it possible to kill such a person by any ordinary means?

"A thousand years or a day," Bregon continued. "This place is changing all the time. There are some things that do not change, however. If you truly were with my father, I'm guessing you were not here when the last of the navvies disappeared with my kin?"

"Indeed not. I was in Ertsetum, with the exiles—with him."

"He told you about me? But how did you get there? I thought all your kind were—"

"Destroyed?" she finished. Her eyes were bemused. "You wish to ask, rather, how it is that I have returned from exile against the Ban? But I will answer your other question first. Your father spoke of you in the presence of Ard Morvran, with whom I served. Cedric described you well, and said that though you were a man of intellectual passions you were also skilled in battle. Thus he feared for you. He wanted you to be free of the plots of the council. Am I right in supposing his fears were not unfounded?"

"You want to know if what they say of me in Tarthalion is true, then?" he asked.

Now, at last, Foxglove's ears perked up. Surely he would defend his position, she thought. He would say something to the effect that the council used political pressure to push him into evil deeds against the Fourth House.

"As you can see, Lady. I commanded their legions."

It was not the answer she had been expecting.

"So, they sent you into battle?" the Fomorian asked.

"Against the Fourth House, yes."

"But you left your command to someone else and ran off into the wilds? Why?"

Bregon considered her a moment before looking away.

"There's no longer any justice in this world," he said after a pause. "That is the short of it."

The Ayumu's scowling eyes met his for a brief instant. Her ear-tips swept backwards angrily, giving them a hornlike appearance.

"So these new wanderings do what for you?" the Fomorian wondered. "Do they wash some of the blood off your boots?"

"Surely there is no crime in that," he replied.

The girl stepped closer to him again. Bregon held his ground as she approached.

"But these wanderings have led you from one Gremn stronghold to another. Through all the old bunkers that are left in these mountains I have seen the marks you've left. Were they left in hopes that someone who knew how to read them would come and find you?"

Bregon was surprised. "I had heard rumors from the south, before I left camp—rumors of some who had returned against the Ban. I had hoped that maybe they were true."

"And so they are, Son of Cedric."

He looked at her curiously. The Fomorian stood just within arm's reach of him.

"Hope is indeed a powerful motivator," she said, glancing aside at Foxglove. "Just as this child hoped to kill you on the mountainside, you hope to live to see your father again; and now you shall have reason to hope. Those strangers were brought here with Cedric's help."

Bregon stood quietly, waiting for her to continue.

"Of course," she said, "I am also partially responsible for their transit; but there is one mightier still who sent us on our way."

Bregon shook his head. "Lady, what do you really want from me?"

"I wish to embark on a journey into the forest Tryst. There is something there I need to do, and in order to do it I require the assistance of a skilled warrior and a guide."

A frown tugged the corners of Bregon's mouth.

"But what help would a Fomorian need in the wood?" he asked.

She looked away north, towards the unseen forest beyond the mountains. "Many things are happening in Tryst these days," she said. "There is a Seraph wandering there whose pilot is the last link to Auriga. I also require a man named Ford, the Primary User of Aries. Together, these two will help us awaken the Moriko in Tryst who still sleep, and all this must happen in order for me to locate something which lies hidden. It is a long road, I'm afraid."

"And you would heap all this burden upon me, a stranger?"

"Not upon you alone. The two of you shall go together."

Foxglove's heart began pounding. This was some cruel joke—

"You will protect this child of the south, Son of Cedric," the Fomorian said. "I shall likewise call upon her in my time of need."

She turned her gaze from Bregon to Foxglove.

Foxglove blinked.

"Come," the girl beckoned. "Come down and let me have a look at you, my dear princess."

Though at first she was frightened, Foxglove sensed a potential ally in this strange forest spirit. Willing her knees to bend, she rose uncertainly and bounded down from the cliff's face. She strayed nearer to the girl as cautiously as her wild cousins might have done, crouching almost to the ground. The stirring of the air in the Fomorian's presence betrayed the working of a deep magic. There was something truly monstrous packed into her petite frame. If the legends about these creatures were true, they were beings capable of destroying armies.

What could Foxglove ever offer to one so great?

Bregon visibly tensed as the huntress drew near, but Foxglove pretended to ignore him. In truth, she was distracted by a barrage of sensations radiated by the Fomorian. Though she couldn't place it, her scent was like something Foxglove knew.

The girl regarded her with a long quiet look.

"That is not a tattoo around your eyes, is it?" she asked.

Foxglove looked at the ground, unable to find her voice so close to her enemy. Silence settled like a heavy blanket as the three stood there on the edge of the Wastes. Even the relentless wind stood still.

"You are of the Ayumu people," the Fomorian said. "Will you be our guide among those of the Fourth House that yet dwell in the darkness of Tryst? I cannot promise much by way of payment, only a special gift—something close to the heart of your people that only I am able to grant."

Foxglove cocked her head towards the girl. She thought she detected the hint of a double meaning in her words.

Was the thing she promised *revenge*?

"If I read your face right," she continued, "you are from Ulumeneth's tribal people. Is this not so?"

Foxglove nodded sadly.

"And your tribal chieftain?"

She pointed at Bregon with her pale little hand, tail flicking angrily from side to side.

"Slain with all the rest, by him!"

She gave Bregon an ears-back snarl.

"Such an unnatural look for so pretty a girl," the Fomorian remarked.

Astonished to silence, Foxglove's gaze momentarily diverted to her own bony figure, smudged with ash and clad in but a few meager scraps of worn leather decorated with stone beads. No one had ever called her pretty—not even her mother.

"What is your name, Ayumu?"

"I am Foxglove of Ulumeneth," she replied, trying to sound stern and impressive.

"Foxglove of Ulumeneth, you are your chiefdom's last representative. I will need your assistance as a delegate when speaking with the other tribal seats of the Fourth House. Will you do this for me?"

Foxglove cast her gaze downward. This was a Fomorian—someone her people regarded almost as a deity. How was she expected to respond to such an unreasonable request? And why was the Fomorian taking up with an enemy of the Fourth House?

"You are hesitant because you do not wish to journey with this man?" the girl asked.

"She has nothing to fear from me," Bregon said. "The forest itself is peril enough to turn away the stoutest heart, for the pathless dark there is no place for light travel."

"Oh?" the Fomorian wondered.

"Whatever you may remember of it, Tryst has changed since the days of the War. From the insects in the fungus swamps to the spirits of the sacred trees, every wild thing that lurks in that country lives on the meat of fools who wander in. I trust that you could defend yourself well enough, for if memory serves me your kind were once the lords of all that realm; but what is all this to me? Moreover, I am puzzled that you should request our assistance in anything."

The girl swayed, leaning towards him impishly. "Would you venture there to see your father again?"

"He is there?"

"What if I told you there is a beautiful woman who needed rescuing?"

He looked like he was about to laugh, but the girl held up a finger to her lips.

"This woman worked with him directly," she said in a quiet voice. "She could pinpoint his location, for she is skilled in such magic. All she needs is a hero."

Bregon stared. "It will be trouble enough just finding the Moriko," he answered lamely. "They haven't been seen since the War. Besides, bringing me along to rescue someone is foolishness—my presence will only be a hindrance, drawing enemies to us. I am no hero. In point of fact, it is you who would be rescuing me."

"And that is why Foxglove must come with us," she said.

"Hmm?" Foxglove wondered.

"Among her tribesmen she will vouchsafe your passage through the deep forest; and your arms will be enough to grant her the courage to enter that place, where she must journey to reclaim something that was lost. This is the purpose which has brought us together this day."

Foxglove put her ears back as far as she could to show her displeasure, and Bregon looked back with a bewildered expression. Standing before him, so close she could feel the tension in his muscled arms, she was startled by his confused and frightened face. How completely unexpected this was.

She felt just the same way.

The girl laughed lightly and clapped her lovely hands.

"I can tell this will be an epic journey worthy of remembrance in song!"

Bregon inclined his head towards the north. "This is no joke," he said. "The tribes in there, they don't get along with her people any better than they would with mine. A thousand years at war with the council has made them into *real* animals. Most don't even go about in human-form anymore."

Foxglove's eyes wandered down to the budding dagger, which was now lying within easy reach. It had taken root, however. Freeing it would be a struggle.

"You have heard it said that there was once a prophecy spoken in that place, have you not?"

Bregon seemed taken aback by her words.

"You're talking about the things that were supposed to happen before anyone could return from exile? Well, they never happened."

"I wasn't referring only to the judgment meted out upon the exiles," she replied. "I speak of the prophecies recorded in the ancient scriptures."

"Aren't they essentially the same?" he asked. "The judgment was quoted from the scriptures. There would be no possibility of returning against the Ban until specific criteria were first met."

"And that would be?"

"The dying Empress must return, bringing with her three of the fragments of the Stone of Foundation," Bregon answered. "Then would the Ban be lifted."

Foxglove's ears twitched. She had heard of this prophecy.

"But everyone assumed that only meant the exiles were banned forever," Bregon said.

"And you also think she will not return?"

"I don't hold to superstition. I don't think the scriptures need to be interpreted literally, at any rate."

"What if I told you the reason we venture for the Moriko to open the way is that the empress has already returned, just as the prophecies foretell?" she asked.

At the mention of the empress, she had their full attention. Foxglove looked up from her dagger.

"All times are present for my people," the girl said. "What was spoken in the forest was not spoken without direct knowledge of what would eventually come to pass within the current frame of reference."

"She is really here?" Bregon asked.

His voice sounded a little breathless.

"You remember her, don't you?"

"Once when I was a small boy I saw her. I will never forget it. But, she—"

"She perished, and then she appeared in the Blue World among the exiles. It isn't superstition. It is fact. It is also fact that your father was sent among the exiles in order to meet her there, and to facilitate her return. Your path and hers will cross again."

"I don't understand," Bregon said.

"You don't need to understand, Son of Cedric. You only need to trust me."

"Perhaps, but what of the little one there?" he asked, glancing in Foxglove's direction. "You may taunt me with dreams of finding my father and the rest of my people, but to her you offer only an immaterial blessing."

But Foxglove was beginning to think this was a new opportunity.

"I will walk with you!" she shouted, surprising herself with her own eagerness.

She felt so foolish. Her words continued, rambling.

"I know them," she said, "my northern cousins, the whispered ones our people shun. We were always warned not to go there, never to journey into the forest Tryst; but I will go in order to receive the Fomorian's favor."

The girl rested a hand upon Foxglove's hair, brushing away some stray peach-hued strands from her forehead. No one had done that for her in many years. The Fomorian's touch was strangely soothing.

"You will receive much more than my own blessing," she said.

"So," Bregon said, "now that that's settled, will we learn your name?"

She looked up at him with her strange smile.

"I am Avalon," she answered. "But you may call me Bec."

3

INTER PLURIBUS MUNDOS
AMONG MANY WORLDS

Aenfer, Iteration of the Third Amplitude,
AD 496

Ford clung to the flimsy hand-hewn planks of the inner hull as the boat crested wave after mountainous wave. From the belly of the ship he stared up at a pale gray sky hovering over a rolling gray sea, the Irish Sea.

"You really ought to relax!" DePons shouted pulling the long oars up as they descended another roller. From a couple yards away, sitting high up in the stern, his voice was hardly audible over the gale.

"We'll make landfall soon enough, Mr. Ford, and then you'll feel better!"

"You're *nuts*," Ford muttered through clenched teeth.

Grinning while he strained against the oars, DePons began to hum a tune that was muted by the biting wind. He was sitting higher than Ford, from which vantage he could actually see over the gunwales. Ford didn't care to see the water at all. He was terrified, soaked, and freezing. The garments they'd traded for their ultramodern military fatigues were useless against these elements. He tugged at his woolen tunic and shivered. DePons didn't seem daunted; but then, he was wearing somewhat more substantial leather gear.

"You're worried about the others, Mr. Ford? Don't be."

"It's us I'm worried about, and this boat!"

"This is a fine boat!" DePons replied.

Ford met his humor with uncharacteristic seriousness.

"This is not a boat, DePons! This is a nightmare!"

"Well, there're no sails, and she ships a bit of water, but she floats; and if you'd kindly take to that pail again, we'd ride a little higher and drier."

Ford pushed himself away from the starboard side, searching for the wooden pail with his bleary eyes. He spotted it astern, floating in about six inches of water. It was too far away to reach. He'd have to get up and go there to retrieve it.

"How far to this island?" he shouted over his shoulder, kneeling in the water to rest his knees against the ribbing of the boat's deep round belly.

"If this wind keeps up we'll be there just after midday—maybe sooner if you'd spot me in another half-hour."

"*Right.*"

He reached with his hands and grasped the rustic wooden ribs of the coracle, trying not to imagine the frailty of the membrane of hide and flimsy planks that separated him from the rolling sea—not that there was much more water in the sea than there was in the boat.

He'd never felt so cold. As he half-crawled and half-slid clumsily aft he thought of all the things that cheered him in cold weather, like coffee and hot showers. He didn't think it was very likely that he'd see any of those comforts again.

The pail was in his hands. He had to stand up to bail the water over the stern, which wasn't easy to do. Each new wave sent him fumbling against the sides of the ungainly tub-shaped craft. After a few minutes his hands were so cold that he accidentally threw the pail overboard. He pulled himself up so that his chin rested against the top of the gunwale, but he couldn't see it anywhere in the gray expanse of heaving water. What he did see was something black on the horizon.

"Is it land?" he called out.

"That's the island we're making for," DePons replied.

Ford regarded the spit of land sheepishly while DePons kept the oars creaking and thumping in the locks. A black cloud covered the island, and lightning flashed in the murky depths.

"What is it now, Mr. Ford?"

"What kind of island is this you're taking me to?"

"Don't worry! It's a place I know very well. We'll be able to find help there."

"We'll find nothing but mud and savages! We've come to another time!"

"The term is *displaced frame of reference*. This isn't just another time. Some things will be different, but much may seem the same."

"Like the language?"

"You know it?"

Ford eyed the black rocky slopes in the near distance, marveling at how the wind and the current ferried them closer every moment. DePons noticed as well, and let off the oars for a rest. Ford did not offer to take over.

"How'd a man like you end up knowing ancient Welsh, DePons?"

"Actually, it was Old Danish those villagers spoke. The man who lent us the boat was Danish."

"I thought we were in Wales."

"Your geography is fine, but you really need to catch up on your history, Mr. Ford."

"Never thought I'd need a course in medieval history."

"It might save your life."

"Are you kidding? We stand out like pigs in a mosque!"

"That's the spirit, Mr. Ford—back to your old humor!"

Then, seeing his genuine dismay, DePons added, "I told you not to worry so much. When all of this is behind us you'll be glad you came along on our little adventure."

"Yeah?" he wondered, looking out over the tossing sea. "Weren't there pirates here in the fifth century?"

It was less than a couple hours later that Ford woke suddenly to the sound of the sea's thunderous voice. He'd dozed off from exhaustion. His watch was still working. He noted the date and frowned. It didn't matter much anymore what time it was, let alone the date and year. After a cursory glance at DePons, who had likewise fallen asleep, he noticed the sound of waves crashing. They were much louder than before.

Dazed and chilled to the bone, he turned his stiff neck towards the noise. The sea surged against a great overhanging cliff-wall only sixty feet to port. The surf raged against this out-thrust arm of land, sending plumes of water high to catch the wind. If they stayed here much longer they'd be dashed against the rocks. Strange ravens, birds with white wings and caps, vested in jet, jeered at him from those cliffs.

"Wake up!" he shouted, trying to use his aching limbs to push himself to a sitting position.

DePons stirred, looking confused. "What happened?"

"Fell asleep. We've got trouble!"

"Displacement syndrome," DePons said, stretching. "It plays with your brain."

"No! The cliffs!"

DePons grabbed one of the long oars and pushed it into Ford's hands. Ford studied it with an odd expression.

"You put the flat end in the water and push," DePons instructed, pointing towards the other oar where it rested in the lock.

The waves boomed against the cliffs. Ford was frozen in panic, so he couldn't be sure what was happening. Even when DePons came down and sat beside him he dared not take the seat by the oarlocks.

"Don't worry! Just give it a try."

"Well, you do it then!" Ford shouted.

Then, in a moment of terror and despair he flung the oar over one of the high gunwales. For a moment, the two sat staring at each other while the waves crashed against the rocks. The boat seemed strangely still in the water.

"That was really stupid, Mr. Ford."

"Yeah, I know. I'm sorry."

"No, I mean, that was very stupid, uncivilized behavior. You surprise me."

Ford held his eyes. DePons leaned closer.

"If you keep this up," he said in a low voice, "I might just leave you to fend for yourself!"

Without warning, DePons stood and mantled over the side, dropping into the water with a splash. Ford scrambled to his feet and pulled himself up to the gunwale. When DePons' face rose up and stared back into his own from inches away, he couldn't stifle a scream.

"It seems we've run aground," DePons said with a broad grin.

He was standing in ankle-deep water.

"I can't believe you fell for it," DePons riffed, leading Ford through a maze of rocky tide-bared teeth of black stone.

Ford slogged along behind him, arms wrapped tightly around his chest. He'd decided to serve up the silent treatment for a while. Cedric, on the other hand, was full of talk.

"We're really fortunate the tide wasn't at its peak."

They had to leave the boat behind, wedged in a v-shaped notch among boulders. Ford couldn't believe the man could make jokes in a situation like this.

"I believe there's a settlement up ahead. There we should find a road leading to the interior."

Looking up, Ford saw that they were approaching an end of the rocks and the beginning of open sea. There was no sign of land ahead. DePons turned briefly to regard him with quiet amusement. Ford tried to muster a glare, but his feet and legs were so stung by the cold water inside his boots that he could hardly achieve anything more than a pained look. They continued walking.

The sun was out, and the day was warming at last. The voices of gulls barked their shrill curses over him, piercing the blast of the wind, while far-flung sea-foam filled the air; and now the noise of the crashing surf was well behind them. Ford had gone out to Long Island a few times with his father, but it was nothing like this. The smell was similar, but the feeling here was raw, and somehow more real than anything he'd ever experienced.

"While we drifted, we came north along these cliffs," DePons said. "There should be a bay just past that shoulder of rock ahead. The settlement will be just beyond."

He hadn't yet explained his knowledge of the area. It was conceivable that FTI had a base of operations out here, and the geography wouldn't have changed too much over fifteen hundred years; but to have knowledge of specific villages in the past was peculiar enough to arouse Ford's suspicions. Weighted by his experiences aboard Lucius Station and Avalon, these suspicions had framed a picture of DePons that left him with many more questions than answers. What was more disturbing still was the small but clearly articulated voice speaking inside his mind that seemed to be leading him on towards a clandestine accord.

"DePons and Kabta knew we would be displaced to this time and location. Be wary."

He had heard this voice at odd intervals since the day he was plunged into black water in Lucius Station. Ford's staunchly pragmatic psyche found this situation very difficult to deal with. He didn't know if he believed this was actually an ancient alien computer communicating with his brain. All things considered, it was weird enough to seem like truth.

"Is something wrong?" DePons asked, glimpsing the worried look in Ford's eyes.

"No," Ford said, breaking his silence with a lie. "It's nothing, DePons. Nothing at all."

"Good. There's the bay, just like I remember it."

At that moment they rounded the cliff and looked out into the bay DePons knew was there. Unfortunately, there was also a broad span of water between their position and the nearest shoreline, more than a thousand feet away.

"The tide's coming in again," DePons noted.

The waves washed over their feet.

"You needn't worry, though," he added, sidling up to the cliff and turning his head towards the shoreline. "There's enough of a shingle left to walk along the base of this cliff. We'll be at the village in no time."

Ford leaned past him to spy the narrow passage.

"We don't have a choice, do we?" he asked.

"You could swim, or go back to the boat."

DePons set out along the foot of the cliff. Ford followed slowly, for the rocks were slimy. They hadn't quite reached the shore before they noticed something odd mired against the sheer stone cliff. The last fifty feet of their path was blocked entirely by a most morbid expanse of flotsam.

There were bodies—hundreds of bodies.

DePons immediately sank into a crouch. His eyes moved from the shoreline ahead to the open water off to the right.

"What happened to these people?" Ford asked, covering his mouth. "They're all caught up in *fishnets*."

"That's not all they were caught up in."

He nodded upwards, indicating dense blue plumes of smoke drifting across the sky overhead. Veiled previously by the cliffs and a wind from the north, the smoke covered all the sky south and west of them.

"You were right, Mr. Ford."

"Right about what?"

"We've got pirates. It looks like they may have gained a foothold at the castle. We'd better hurry."

His mind dulled by the evil sights around him, Ford only caught the reference to a castle in passing—and acknowledged it with a shrug. If DePons was going to keep secrets, he could keep right on keeping secrets.

The rest of their journey to shore was a horrible ordeal through a lifeless crush of terrors, and the macabre spectacle continued on the beach. The shoreline crunched strangely underfoot, for the sand had been melted into brittle glass by what must have been a very great fire. On the water's edge there were three burned boats wedged upside-down behind a collapsed wall, and searching round these they found dozens of scorched huddled figures among the debris.

A rain of ash and embers had begun sprinkling down on their upturned faces as soon as they'd reached the strand. Ford's mind was numbed already by the trial of staggering through hip-deep shallows choked with drifting corpses of men, women, and children. The sight of the burned people by the boats left him stunned and silent. DePons waited for him ahead, kneeling in the lee of a grassy slope that ran up into high forested country in the heart of the island. There were still fires burning up there, where the smoke was heaviest.

"We should go up the hill and wait under cover of those trees until we're sure it's safe," he said. "Then we'll head inland; but we must avoid the road."

Ford made no reply. He was too engrossed in the frightful mess around him, and was on the verge of puking. Noting his discomfort, DePons pointed away to the veil of ash and black smoke that came wafting down the slope.

"We don't want to be caught out in the open. That smoke will help hide us while we make our approach."

Even while he was speaking, a shadow passed over them. Moving fast, it turned towards the water and back again, darkening the ground where they stood. Both men turned instinctively towards the sun, and shielding their eyes they scrutinized a bright blotch in the smoke-filled sky. There was nothing to be seen. What Ford felt in his heart, however, was a nightmare-terror unlike any fear he had ever experienced.

"What was that?" he whispered.

DePons frowned, but said nothing. He turned back around towards the hill, and following his gaze there Ford contemplated a whirling shadow of what seemed to be great bat-like wings turning circles in the air. The shape vanished into the smoke, and the fear was gone.

DePons started up the slope towards the smoldering treeline.

"After seeing all this, you're still going up there?" Ford mumbled, gathering himself a bit.

"Yes, and you're coming with me."

"You don't even have a gun! What do you think you're going to do?"

"Guns will be of no use to us. I'm going to look for survivors, and you're coming with me, Mr. Ford."

"You know what? You can go after the pirates yourself, mister corporate mercenary. I'm perfectly satisfied with sitting tight, right here!"

DePons turned briefly in mid-stride. "It wasn't pirates that did this."

Ford looked around, bewildered. "Did you just slog through the same heap of bodies I did?"

"I'm guessing what attacked them was a dragon. He's still lurking about, too."

Ford looked on as DePons continued up the hill.

"Really, DePons?" he called after him. "I don't get it. Why now? Why all the jokes and pranks?"

"Just follow me, Mr. Ford, and we shall see what there is to see."

DePons walked up the slope at a crouch, pausing often, and with much mumbling and cursing Ford followed. The sun was a pale yellow stain in the sky, and was rolling away now towards the west. By time they stood among the trees of a little pine forest at the top of the rise, they discovered that the undergrowth there had all been burned up. Only a little distance away Ford spotted fires smoldering among primitive peat and timber hovels, the remains of a small village.

"There are no more bodies up here, and no scattered weapons," DePons said quietly. "No signs of an invading host."

"Well, someone attacked this place."

"And how did they bring so much fire here, Mr. Ford?"

Heaps of dry thatch and beams lay wreathed in ribbons of scarlet flame. The ground beyond the trees was blasted bare of all vegetation and strewn with hot coals. Over the smell of scorched flesh Ford tasted a foul tang in the air. The wind shifted suddenly, and a wall of heavy smoke was blown towards them. Within this black roiling cloud a multitude of small figures appeared suddenly. They were running straight towards them.

Ford was rammed hard in the gut by something short and furry. He fell backwards to the ground.

"Mind the sheep," DePons said, helping him to stand.

There were sheep, goats, and small hairy cows running helter-skelter all around them, making their way down the hill towards the sea. The beasts were wild with fear, colliding with one another. Some were badly burned, and others were aflame. The stench of singed hair stung his nose, but Ford was distracted by something a little more disturbing just ahead. Dimly visible as red ghosts in the glare of the fires, men were trotting with purpose through the clouds and rubble.

"Are those your dragons?" Ford wondered, darting towards a nearby tree.

"Keep still!" DePons warned.

A shout startled them, and they saw a man tall and fierce blundering through some smoldering wreckage by the edge of the clearing, only a stone's throw away. The man was shouting to someone behind him. At the sound of his voice, DePons hesitated—but he did not look surprised.

"What language is that?" Ford asked in a startled whisper. "It sounded like—"

The lone warrior turned his head to and fro, as if responding to Ford's soft murmuring. Another shape ambled out of the smoke to join him. Neither was armed. In the shadow of the smoke they stood and shouted to others behind them, and in moments a whole troop of soot-stained men stood looking down the hill after the animals.

Ford held his breath. They were looking right at him.

The first warrior raised his hand in their direction, and the rest started walking towards their hiding place. DePons stepped forwards and raised his hands in surrender. Ford felt his body go limp like a rag.

"You're—giving up?"

"Just stand still," DePons said firmly, turning slightly to catch his eye. "Trust me, Mr. Ford."

The strangers were upon them in seconds, and both men were escorted up the hill to the edge of the ruined village. Ford was dizzy, and everything around him seemed suddenly unreal, as if it was happening to someone else. He watched, somewhat detached, as DePons was led before the leader of the troop. The others formed a circle around him, but Cedric appeared unfazed. In fact, his face seemed somehow bold, and his expression was downright smug.

Who did he think he was, standing in a circle of enemies looking like some ancient lord in medieval getup? Ford reasoned that DePons was either dangerously insane, or he somehow knew these people.

As if to prove both these suspicions simultaneously, DePons faced the leader and asked in ordinary English, "What are the chances of meeting you here, after all these years, Shimeon bar-Kochba?"

"How—?" Ford stammered. "How do you know this guy, DePons?"

The leader looked his way. Several others had already gotten a good look at his face, yet none seemed overly concerned by his foreign features.

"You've got some explaining to do," the leader said. "You will both come with us. We've got to get back to Aries before the dragon returns for these animals."

Ford gave DePons a questioning look.

"Yes, Mr. Ford," he said. "They are Gremn."

They took the road from the village. It continued to climb through a sheltered pass, and beyond this it plunged down again into a country of forests and streams. The island's interior was actually lovely, though everywhere he looked Ford noted scars of recent burning.

Although they walked unbound, he knew it would be foolish to attempt escape. Fleeing the Gremn would probably land him among folk who saw him only as a stranger. Ford walked with his shoulders hunched, and wondered when he had last eaten. His empty stomach complained to him, and his feet stumbled. Their captors didn't treat them roughly. On the contrary, DePons and their leader seemed to get along rather well. This bothered Ford, for he could make no sense of what was happening. Here they were, displaced in the distant past, and DePons was chatting away in modern English with a rustic warrior with a Semitic name. The fact that their new friends were Gremn only made things more complicated.

"We're parked on the far side of the island, so we have to move fast," the one named Shimeon was saying. "We don't have much time."

"What was it?" DePons asked.

"Something highly unusual, this was. I saw it myself—a red dragon, a *dracon* of the High Ceregor. Don't ask me what it's doing here. All such things come through that place in the forest, and all the more so in recent days. He'll be back. We will not linger here."

"Is the castle intact?" DePons asked.

Ford perked up, and following DePons' gaze towards their left he glimpsed through the forest a smoldering heap of gray stone walls and square towers.

"That would be Castle Morvran," DePons said aside to him.

"Morvran?" Ford breathed.

"The castle wall was breached," Shimeon said in answer to DePons' question. "The poor fools lured the monster in by firing arrows, I guess. They should have left it alone. We found only two survivors, and have taken them into custody. One is from the ruling chieftain's household."

"That is interesting, is it not?" DePons asked.

Shimeon regarded DePons' careful question with a grunt of suppressed agitation.

"You know well what this island protects, DePons. We have respected the terms of our agreement. It is safer if kept here, and we only intervene in order to protect its secret from those who may have learned of its power, like seafaring pirates, or like this dragon."

"I'm glad you feel that way, Shimeon. However, what you sought to protect and what the dragon came to take is no longer here."

Shimeon and his men paused suddenly. Their eyes were fixed on DePons' smug face.

"Care to explain?" asked a warrior with long dark hair.

He was the only one Ford had seen with any hair at all. His look was fierce, with heavy-lidded eyes—the eyes of a real killer.

"What if I told you that the fragments are being recohered?" DePons queried, glancing around.

This statement produced some confusion among the Gremn.

"Recohered?" Shimeon wondered, holding up his hand for quiet. "That's impossible! They can't be recohered unless the empress "

"—unless the empress comes back to life and returns to the World of Origins," DePons finished. "She shall bear in her flesh three fragments of the Stone of Foundation, which must be recohered by collaboration of the exiled Great Houses of old. So it was said, and so it is, my friend. The door will soon open for our return."

Shimeon and his men mulled this quietly, and then they resumed walking along the forest lane. The Gremn remained grim and silent a long while afterwards, revealing nothing on their faces. As for Ford, he still didn't believe in dragons, and he still didn't understand half of what was going on. Their captors, however, clearly believed everything that DePons had to say. Old Cedric and his silver tongue were doing famously well so far.

That made Ford a little nervous, actually.

After a long march, the road turned downhill once again. The forest thinned out, and they came upon a stretch of wind-blown sand lined with ancient weather-beaten stones. Continuing on this path awhile they descended a steep slope and arrived at another sheltered bay on a grassy lee overshadowed by cliffs. There was a wooden vessel in the shallows below. It was larger than the one DePons had borrowed on the mainland, and though it also lacked sails it was equipped with many oars. A few more people were preparing it for departure. One was a tall man with a rather serene face, and there were two strong-looking boys helping him. Two more boys were sitting on the ground, and they were bound hand and foot. Ford studied the captives curiously. They were dressed regally in high medieval fashion, one in a long green coat and the other in a leather outfit with a chainmail shirt. Their faces looked so striking similar that he wondered if they might be twins.

"These are your prisoners?" DePons asked. "It is truly a relief to see them again."

Shimeon hid his curiosity poorly. "You don't *sound* relieved, DePons," he said. "What do you know about them?"

"Your boss didn't tell you?"

"What do you think?"

"Well, the cowled one is obviously a mage. The other is Lír's real reason for sending you to the island. He's a Morvran."

Again, the name *Morvran*. Ford remembered this name from the recorded image they saw in Avalon. Whoever the name belonged to was obviously a person of some importance, but neither of the young captives cut the figure of a legendary hero. Apart from their fancy clothes, they were just ordinary-looking boys.

How did DePons recognize them?

"Lír sent us to pick them up as soon as the island was attacked. We found them together in what was left of the castle. They offered no resistance."

"Do you know what Lír wants with them?"

"No, but I'm guessing you do."

Once again, Ford wished he could understand all they were talking about, but from what he gathered there was at least some confirmation of his suspicions. DePons was pulling all the strings here. He had been among these Gremn before.

"Even if he managed to grab Qashtu before anyone else had a chance," DePons was saying, "He could do nothing with the fragment itself. The descendants of Morvran, however, are Towers of a special kind. A Crodah Tower's short lifespan was compensated for by the hereditary assignment of their ability to synch with Qashtu—and with any of the other stones as well; and that would make the Morvrans as fair a receptacle as the empress for the recohered fragments."

Shimeon eyed him warily as these words sank in. Their boots crunched on the pebbly sand as they neared the shoreline.

"He ordered you to take the mage as collateral so the other one will be submissive," DePons continued, "but if he's dealing with a Morvran, that might be more difficult than Lír imagines. They are a family with a long history of stubbornness and angry outbursts, and they aren't known to be loyal to their allies."

With a twisted grin on his face, Shimeon waved his hand towards the sea. "Sounds like the two of them will get on well," he said. "But I've got to deliver them to Aries, regardless. She's offshore in deeper water, about a mile out. I've arranged for her to surface at nightfall for pickup and transfer."

"I'll remind you that taking Morvran from this island is a clear breach of our agreement," DePons said.

"They're not the only passengers I'll be taking."

"I don't suppose I could talk you into letting us go free, Shim?"

"I'm treading on thin ice as it is. If Lír finds out I let you go, it'll be my head he's after."

"No matter what he threatens, I won't help him do it."

"Do what?"

"You still don't understand? Weren't you curious as to why he didn't send you to Aenfer to capture the fragment instead of two young boys? Lír knows that Qashtu has moved on, Shim. He sent you here to take the Morvran heir because with that boy and the two fragments you've got he can attempt a transit with Aries. But it won't work."

"How do you know that?" Shimeon asked, genuinely surprised.

"I know it because all of this—the attack on the island, the capture of these boys, and all that follows—it's already happened before, Shim."

They had reached the shoreline. While Shimeon stepped aside and studied DePons' face, the rest of the Gremn walked on towards the boats and those waiting on the beach. Ford was uncertain of what he should do, so he stood on the sandy path beside DePons.

When the others were out of earshot, DePons said, "You know you can trust me, Shimeon. I'll give you a piece of advice. After you leave us with Lír, take your men and head for the hills."

"What're you planning?"

"You'll need to make sure you have access to Apsu. Then get to high ground. Kabta is probably still in the area. He's also displaced. You will need his help."

"You know where—?" Ford started.

DePons held up a hand before he could say more. Shimeon glanced at Ford uncertainly.

"What do we get out of this, DePons?"

"A way back to the World of Origins, and freedom from Lír. The rest is up to you."

Shimeon looked down at his men on the beach, and then nodded his head in agreement.

"I'll need to discuss this with the others before we leave, and time is already pressing. Artax will argue against me, but I can convince him if you'd be willing to provide more proof of what you say."

"Do you have any reason to doubt me?"

"No," Shimeon said, narrowing his eyes, "but I'm not convinced of your honesty, either. You're not here to trade your life for our freedom, and of this much I am certain."

He stepped closer to DePons.

"You're always up to something, and taking your advice always ends up costing me more than it's worth."

"It is a big risk, I know—"

"Your plan is still unfolding by a design, DePons, since the day Avalon fell. That was the day Lír began to fear you."

"As well he should. He was a *terrible* employee."

"Well, he was sharp enough to figure out you'd show up when this place burned. He would've rigged it himself, and sooner, but he believed it was inevitable."

DePons closed his mouth. Shimeon stepped closer, and continued in a whisper.

"It's no coincidence you showed up here at this precise moment, no matter what you say about being displaced. I do not doubt that Kabta is lurking close by, for you've no reason to lie to me. What bothers me is that I've never been able to figure out just what you've been scheming through all these years. Must be some plan, though."

They stared one another down for another long moment, and then DePons nodded.

"Okay, I'll give you something. But it won't be understood until the time comes."

"That won't be good enough," Shimeon said.

"You know I can't tell you about what's going to happen, Shim. If I tell you now, then it won't happen the way it's supposed to, and it'll be useless."

"Then what am I supposed to tell them, DePons?"

DePons' eyes sharpened, and the corners of his mouth tugged into a smug grin.

"Tell them that the Old World is coming back to us, Shim. The door is opening. Tell them that they will be remembered as heroes on the other side if they assist me now in procuring the last few pieces of this plan to get them home. If I succeed, I will name them before the empress herself."

"What game is this?" Shimeon wondered, squinting. "You're planning on leaving for the World of Origins without us?"

"No games," DePons replied. "I'm just going on ahead of you. But I will also say this. You will do well to take today's fire-breathing visitor into account when you are faced with the decision to visit the *Dragon's Mound.*"

"Why would I go to that accursed place?"

"Because Kabta will say that it's the only way. You will agree with him in this, and the road will be opened to you. This is all I can say for now, but it should be sufficient to convince your friends when the time comes."

Shimeon pondered these words, and asked, "What about right now?"

DePons clapped him on the shoulder. "You are their trusted leader. They will follow you wherever you go. Let me know if Artaxshasu gives you any trouble. I'll cow him into submission myself."

"I'd like to see that," Shimeon replied, setting off down the beach to join his men.

DePons looked to Ford then, and beckoned him towards the water. "Come along, Mr. Ford," he said. "We've finally begun the last leg of our journey."

"We're going to another ship?" Ford asked in a small voice.

"Yes," DePons said. "There is a third ship. *Aries* is her name. And thanks to Avalon, your brain contains the data sets this ship must acquire in order to make transit. We'll give the old girl what she wants; but we'll deny her the privilege of accompanying us."

"You mean, we're leaving...without the ship?'"

"What, did you space out during all that talk? This transit will take us off-world, Mr. Ford, permanently."

4

FAIN'S DOOR

The Mound of Broceliande,
A.D. 1901

Awakening while Jonathan still snored beside him, Taran studied their woodland environs and decided that it was not unlike being under the bridge. Many things were strangely familiar, including a perception of being closed in. The leaves above stirred with currents of air falling cold before evening. It was the night after their hasty departure from Cille.

Taran tucked the scrap of paper back into his pocket and stood up to stretch his limbs. They had slept the afternoon away on rocky ground. He was anxious to move on under cover of dark.

But where was Hest?

The last he'd seen of her, she leaned her back against a tree just a few yards away. They'd stopped here to make camp after the southward road completely disappeared under a tangle of dense thorny overgrowth. Dozing in a thicket, Taran didn't think Hest could've wandered off without making sufficient noise to awaken him.

She was, however, an extraordinary person.

Wiceline had called Hest a monster. Here on the borders of what the superstitious called the Faery Realm, it was possible to imagine little eyes peering at him from the shadows of the trees. He smiled to himself and yawned.

The air rushed past him in great gusts that made the larger trees groan and squeal in the weird speech of the forest. By a slight increase of light just ahead he knew there was a clearing, and where it began a slope wound down into the unknown. The hope of seeing some end of the trees invited his feet, and as Jon had only begun to stir he decided to wander out and have a look before the afternoon sun set behind the canopy.

What he found was a small meadow, its tall-standing grass peeping like sprouts of hair among tumbled walls.

"Someone lived out here," Hest said from his side.

He hadn't heard her coming, and her sudden voice was startling. At that very moment the wind picked up, moaning down upon the ruined estate before them and exiting thence into a beautiful parkland lower down, stirring a sea of velvet-green beneath the trees. Taran stared at it a moment, transfixed by the sight.

"I think I see a path down there," Hest said, pointing past the crumbling walls towards some sparse trees farther down the slope.

Squinting his eyes, he could almost see a black line in the distant undergrowth.

"If it goes downhill it'll lead to water," Jon said, walking up to join them.

Taran weighed his water skin in his hand. There was little left, and only a few mouthfuls of stale bread.

"Do you think we'll find what we're looking for down there?"

Taran wasn't referring to water. Hest gave him a puzzled look.

"My brother is keeping secrets from us," Jonathan said. "What exactly is it that we're looking for, Taran?"

Taran retrieved the scrap of paper from the pocket of his itchy woolen vest. "Fain wrote this," he said. "I found it stuck in the pages of one of his books. Have you ever heard of a place called *Arberth?*"

Jon shrugged.

"Read it," Hest said.

Taran cleared his throat. *"The power source is hidden deep beneath the dark tower, so the cave and its mirror should be reasonably safe for transit. Finding Arberth itself, should it disappear again—"*

He paused, turning the scrap over in his hand.

"And it stops there," he said.

"Does it mention Father or DePons?" Jon questioned.

"Yes. At the beginning it says, *'The only chance lies in Taran, then. If he should ever become involved, it will be under DePons' guidance. If he wants to open the door, DePons will have to tell him everything about the Britain Location, for Thaddeus has sworn to me that he will not.'"*

"And so," Taran summed while tucking the scrap away in his pocket, "there is a place in Britain called Arberth, and though Grandfather wanted me to find it, Father did not; but it is a place we cannot find anyway because it moves around."

"Fain's door," Jon mumbled. "I don't see any caves or towers, but there are some ruins."

Taran studied the wind-tossed movement of the grass, and he realized how great the uncertainty was that swayed his heart. In times like these, his father used to tell him to try hard to think of what he was supposed to do. Separating out that purpose, keeping his eyes on it, everything else would come together.

"The name Arberth is a little disconcerting," Hest said.

"Isn't that the name of a faery mound in some old story?" Jon asked.

Taran shrugged. "If Grandfather was excavating a dolmen or mound out here, I think we'd have heard of it."

"Maybe I have," Hest said. "I once overheard Fain speaking to my father about a mound he visited southeast of the coastal village where we landed. He said that it was obscured deep in the forest, a place seldom trafficked by the local people. He made several journeys there in the years before his disappearance."

"Did he never come back? Is that how the rumors began that he was dead?"

She nodded. "But he never called it Arberth."

"Still, we're talking about a great big dolmen, right? There can't be too many of those around here."

"There are, actually."

"But Hest, that old woman at the inn warned us about a specific mound somewhere nearby. It can't be a coincidence."

"What old woman?" Jon interrupted.

"Fain definitely meant for me to go to that mound," Taran said, ignoring his brother's question. "And if Wiceline knows about it, Naruna will definitely be following us. So, why are we just standing around talking about this?"

Taran set out then over the sloping grassy vale, clutching the rag-bundled sword closer to his side while he walked. There were sounds from behind him of the others taking up the pace he set. It was a brisk step, because inwardly he feared he was losing focus. The surety he'd felt only yesterday at the inn was gone; for though it was likely they would find the mound Fain had spoken of, locating a door that would whisk them off to another land where all their questions would be answered—that was just plain foolishness.

What then of those who followed him there?

They had their own reasons, he supposed.

Hest caught up to him, and he heard her speaking quietly to herself.

"Three was the price of lifting the Ban."

"That's what you told me the night Naruna caught us. What does it mean?"

"There are many stones," she answered. "Three fragments—that is the price the exiles must pay for return against the ban."

"Are you going to tell me what all this about?"

"When it is time for you to know, you will know. What happened at the inn tells me you bear something that may yet help us on our road."

"Whatever it is, I hope it never does that again! It hurt!"

"You may yet desire it. Remember, Regulus is the reason you are pursued."

Taran met her eyes.

"We continue to retrace your grandfather's steps, Taran Morvran. There will be many difficult decisions."

"You mean, about Jon?"

"About me, too," she said.

Then, suddenly, she left his side and walked behind him, leaving him alone with his thoughts. Clouds were forming on the threshold of night. Soon the sun would also leave him.

With their backs to the lawn of tumbled ruins, a kind of grassy lane appeared between the trees. The sunset's beauty was thrust forth between the limbs of graceful beeches in brilliant rose-red flares, illuminating the faery-forest in weird colors, mingling lavender and crimson in a wine-tinted tapestry of leaves.

The trees soon ended upon a peat-blanketed down studded with low scrubby brush. Individual stars were appearing in patches of clear slate-colored heavens above; huge and bright they shone, the suns of distant worlds summoned to shed some of their glory in honor of the dawn of night. While clouds closed these gaps and sealed away the vaults of heaven, the verdant screen of a meadow farther down rolled like the waves of an angry green sea, every broad blade of herbage so sharp and distinct that standing together they seemed like the spears of a marching host—an army outnumbering the stars.

Taran strained to see the lands down below where the hollow in the hills opened upon a wide bowl-shaped plain. Floating far off in that vast green meadow was an island of stone.

A mound it was, but like none other.

By a trick of shadows cast by the clouds, Taran's imagination assembled the exposed areas of rock aback the huge grassy hill into the figure of a reclining dragon—like the dragon on the sign at Wiceline's inn. Down below the gloomy hump, a river glimmered in its straight course through the plain.

Setting behind the rim of the hill behind them, the sun's departure transformed the bowl of grass into blurred and restless shadows, stealing the image of the mound from sight; but it was still there, a brooding presence in the gloom.

"It's real," Taran whispered.

The spell of the place was broken by the sound of his brother's voice.

"We'd best take care if we're going to try and climb down in the dark. There are more ruins here, and pits as well."

"We could use a vantage point," Hest said. "It's cloudy, but moonlight alone might be enough to light a path."

She pointed to a gray mass a stone's throw to their right.

"There is a tower over there, and some stairs."

A short walk led them to the heap of stone blocks protruding from the edge of the slope. Following Hest up to the top, Taran stood by her side and blinked at the surprising brilliance of the sky. Though details of the vale were obscured, the afterglow of the sunset was sufficient to reveal the shadowy island of the mound in a sea of mist. They could also see a little more of their immediate surroundings.

They had come down through a natural cleft from the forested lands to the west. South from the foot of the tower, on their right, the ground rose to sheer cliffs, forming a spur jutting deep into the vale. The terrain was even more broken and treacherous to the north, and to the east it fell away in a tumble of boulders and ivy. He couldn't estimate the distance to the plain below, because the bottom was lost in fog.

Strangely, no one debated the way they needed to go; and while the daylight faded, a dread of pursuit came upon all of them. It wasn't just a fear of Naruna, though. There was something else out there, a threatening presence haunting the sea of mist.

"Now," Jon wondered, "how are we going to get down there?"

"Why do we want to go there at all?" Taran asked.

"You want to wait around for Naruna and his men?"

"Do you know something about it, Jon?"

His brother remained silent, surveying the hopeless path to the east. Hest climbed back down the stairs to the very edge of the slope. She was there only a few moments before her voice called back up to them.

"I've found a road!"

They joined her below the tower. Taran was flustered that he'd missed something as obvious as a road, but Hest did have sharp eyes. Stooping at the foot of the tower, they turned up some of the soil and grass beneath their feet until a patch of hewn stones appeared. Following the solid surface with the toes of their boots, they quickly uncovered the width of a raised surface that ran away eastward to the very edge of the cliff. There it made a sharp turn to the left while sloping more than thirty degrees.

A switchback.

Running parallel to the cliff's edge, the road turned back on itself like a serpent. Hest led them down this slippery winding way to the second turn, but there even she seemed to lose hope. Apart from a cold and faintly luminous mist they could see nothing.

In his dark shirt and pants, Jon disappeared altogether from sight. Taran knew his brother was somewhere ahead, right behind Hest, which left him to take up the rear. Kneeling, he found two smooth stones the size of his palm. Straightening again he threw one down the cliff into the plain. There was no noise of its passage. He turned and threw the second stone back across the face of the cliff towards the south. There was a rapping sound as the missile struck the rocky spur they'd seen from the tower, but the little clatter of the stone's fall echoed strangely among the crags in the high places, like hands clapping loudly in an empty room. Then, with a loud popping sound, the ground jerked and slid forwards, crumbling beneath their feet.

The whole cliff was falling apart.

With shouts of fear, they plummeted in a landslide, grasping for handholds among shifting rocks. A deep bass rumble shook them, and large boulders skipped by their heads. Grabbing hold of his vest, Jonathan pulled Taran with him as he fell. The confusion lasted only a few seconds, and then everything stopped with a painful jolt.

Hest had somehow gotten behind him while they tumbled. With her long braid lashing his face, Taran planted his heels on a narrow ledge and leaned backwards into the cliff's face.

Unaccountably, the sword remained in his hand, as though it had clung to him.

"*Nice going,*" Jon growled from somewhere to his left.

"You think I did this?" he shouted.

"Quiet!" Hest warned, whispering into his right ear.

The ground still trembled slightly as the tumult echoed back to them across the watchful plain. When silence drew down upon them again, Taran coughed in the dusty brume and wondered where they could go from here. Everything was dark.

"Your actions have far-reaching consequences," Hest said quietly.

Taran vented his frustration by kicking his heel against the cliff's face.

"How can throwing a stone start an earthquake?" he asked. "It's ridiculous!"

"It's obvious that something else is happening here," she replied. "In any case, we can't go back. There's a nasty drop behind me."

To his left, Jon was loosening heavy rocks with his hands.

"There's a wall blocking the way ahead," he said to Taran. "Maybe we can climb over it."

All three of them huddled together upon the narrow ledge, their outstretched hands palming the face of a massive rock. There was no way over, and no way back. They were stuck, without even enough room to sit down and wait for the morning light.

"We must be closer to the bottom now," Taran said. "We should just try crawling down."

"You're nutso," Jon replied, leaning back against the cliff. "We dropped straight down like a lift, Brother, but we're still high up. You'd think someone who was so interested in flying would be able to tell."

"I can't see anything!" Taran exclaimed. "How can you tell how high we are?"

Hest had been stooping silently beside him for the past few minutes, but now she rose and touched his shoulder.

"It's different," she said.

"What's different?"

"We're south of our original position. See the mound?"

Taran squinted in the direction he thought the mound must be, but all he could see was an indistinct black shape far off in the fog.

"The hill is a little to the left of where it was before," she said.

"You can see in this?" Jon asked. "Surely you're joking!"

Her icy silence was unnerving. Taran nudged her.

"What else do you see, Hest?"

"Like a phonograph record," she said, "the whole plain has moved around it. I think some power is closing the path behind us."

Jon sniffed derisively. No one said anything else—it was too strange for conversation; yet Taran no longer denied that it was beyond mere coincidence that they were stuck up on this ledge. Hest's words loomed large in his mind.

"I think some power is closing the path behind us."

"Well," Jon said, "it hardly matters. If there's no way forwards or backwards, and our backs are to a wall, we've got to do like you suggested, Brother."

And with much unnecessary grumbling and cursing, Jonathan was the first to lower himself down from the ledge into total darkness. He was dangling free, clinging with trembling hands, but eventually he found firm footholds and began to descend the side of the cliff. Taran and Hest took up positions at arm's length from each other. It was quite a tricky business with a sword and all, Taran thought, and much more frightening somehow than facing the crowd of townspeople at the inn in Cille.

When they had descended perhaps eighty feet, Taran felt hands patting the back of his legs. It gave him a shock, but he was quite relieved when he realized they had reached a level place. Hest helped him find his footing among heaps of scree.

She had reached the bottom before him, as did Jon. Taran was a little annoyed that neither of them were out of breath. As for himself, he was about to fall over.

"I've found the road," Jon announced, stamping his boots on flat cobbles.

Walking towards his voice through the misty vale, Taran felt tall grass brushing his fingertips. He remembered the story of a child who stumbled down a well in a grassy field, but for the time being he was more concerned about meeting something less dangerous yet more surprising than a well. He pushed all that aside. They had a road to follow, and this was good. He doubted anyone could track them down the cliff's face, and that was even better.

The road ran straight towards the looming shadow of the mound. While they made their way deeper into the plain, the presence of the haunting terror they first sensed on the tower drew nearer. Taran thought of the tales of the old world, and he wondered if any of the heroes of those stories ever felt what he was feeling—if they had ever been scared, awestruck and stupefied all at the same moment, or if their own strange adventures really seemed so strange to themselves.

Taran also wondered if half as many of those heroes were real, or if they were just stories made up by bards. He guessed that few among men, if any, would have credited his own tale with any more verity than the legends of Arthur. He wouldn't have believed it himself if he weren't here now.

Nothing else distracted them until they found the hedge.

In the gloom, the dense barrier of thorns was all but invisible until they blundered right into it. Their road was blocked once again.

"We might go around," Jon said.

Taran squinted in a bit of gray light that began to shine from the sky. Though it hadn't enough power to break through the clouds, the moon was rising. He could almost see the full extent of the briar in their path, an unbroken line from north to south.

"There's no way but through," Taran said.

Then, using his blade like a staff, he began to beat an opening through the hedge.

"You know the edge of that thing is sharp, right?" Jon asked.

Taran looked down at his hands and realized that he had cut himself on the thorns. Sure, it would be easier to use the sword to slash a path through; but he felt strangely hesitant to unwrap it.

"It should remain sheathed," Hest warned.

"Why?" Jon asked. "What if we need it to defend ourselves?"

"It isn't to be used that way," she answered.

"But—"

"Leave off it, Brother," Taran said, beating back the briar until a narrow breach appeared. "We'll do this her way."

The hedge was not as deep as it was prickly, and when the gap he'd made was wide enough, Taran stepped through. Hest followed him in, and then Jon. When all three had won through at last they paused to take in the sight of a maze of shattered walls.

"A ruined village?" Taran wondered.

Just then the clouds parted and the waxen globe of the full moon shone down upon them, revealing an army of hunched figures standing in deathlike stillness between the hedge and the walls. It took Taran a moment to realize they were only man-sized blocks of stone. Whatever purpose they once served he could never have guessed, but they were everywhere, all along the edge of the thorn bushes in a line from north to south, staggering forward in ranks until they failed in a barren region of gravel and low scrubby plants. The mound rose in the near distance, its menacing form presiding over all.

"What's away there, to the south?" Jon asked.

Looking across the rubble-cluttered expanse to their right, Taran perceived a smoking chasm.

"That wasn't there before," he said quietly. "It's like this whole place got turned upside-down."

Jon stared at him. "You're saying this entire plain moved?"

"Hest is right. It's all changed. Look, whether it was the earthquake or something else hardly matters. Something strange is going on."

"We are merely upon the threshold," Hest said quietly. "The mound lies ahead."

"What about that water?" Taran asked, pointing in the direction of the chasm.

In the waxen pall of the moon the glint of water was also revealed. It followed the chasm, and lay only about a hundred yards away.

"I do remember a river there," Taran said. "I saw it from the tower on the hill."

Hest nodded. "Rivers form natural boundaries that the ancient peoples respected—boundaries between the worlds."

"Well, it's heading straight towards the mound," Jon said. "Let's take a look."

After a short walk they surveyed the flow from its very banks. Taran sighed with disgust, wrinkling his nose at the foul odor exhaled by the water.

"It's an irrigation trench," he said, "I don't seem to remember any folklore about sewers being crossing-places between worlds."

"Drink some of that water," Jon quipped, "and you'll be leaving *this* world. That's for sure."

Behind them, back towards the sloping cliffs to the west, they could hear the distant growl of a waterfall. The water was probably borne from the brink of the mountains, lost now in misty shadows under the moon. Taran judged the trench's stone-lined edges to be about twenty feet apart—wide enough to fit a barge, but too wide for him to leap across. On the far side lay a country of sharp stones and smoking pits, a scene more reminiscent of volcanic highlands than of the shire of Cambria.

Where were they?

"There's good stonework here," Jon remarked, looking around. "This place is nice."

"Really? You want to try swimming across this?"

The water was edged with a sulfurous yellow scum.

"Let's not," Jon said. "There's got to be a way across, perhaps farther to the east."

"Maybe, but why is there a canal here at all? Why would anyone want to draw boats into an open plain?"

"Who knows? Could be they needed it for whatever they were doing at the mound."

Taran looked east. His brother's sudden eagerness to head for the mound made his feet feel heavy; but they were running out of choices. The south was closed by the canal and the chasm. The west and the north were walls of sheer cliffs. He could almost hear Hest's voice in his mind.

"There are no coincidences."

They followed Jon along the canal-road. The moonlight around them grew stronger, sharpening the details of the landscape. As the area slowly defined itself, Taran began to make sense of the place. It was more like a city in size. His curiosity was piqued. Here were toppled pillars lying in ruinous display beneath drifting dunes of dead soil, and there he saw the foundations of great houses. Steps climbed to nowhere, or lay upon their sides. Nearby, a broken arch like a pair of fangs was precariously suspended above a mound of crumbled brickwork. Everything was made of stone, and even in its ruin the city was impressively ordered. Having been schooled by an archaeologist, he knew that no ancient people of Britannia left such monumental ruins.

Taran raised his eyes and sought the pure light of the moon, but what the moon showed him then was something that did not lift his spirits. Presiding over the center of the ruins half a mile away, he had long since noticed a great black shadow rising, darker than the night that surrounded it. He continued to walk towards the looming mound, enthralled by its terrible and lofty presence. That first sight he had of it from the hills had revealed nothing more than a jumble of a low mountain, an exile to the sojourn of the meadows; but now the moon pierced the shadows and he could see its size and shape. It was indeed like a sleeping dragon, bearing in its perfect horror a reflection that could only have been shaped in the human mind, sculpted by human hands.

To Taran it seemed the hilltop moved in the wind.

Jon paused a little way ahead. He was also looking up at the mound.

"There are trees up there," he said.

Taran's eyes vaguely discerned the forms of trees growing atop the craggy rocks. Breezes hissed along the ground, mimicking the rustle of hidden foes. A chill crept over them, and the fear of standing in wide open spaces prompted them to move on.

As they drew nearer the mound, they soon perceived that what appeared at a distance to be sheer hillsides were actually man-made walls. To say that they were of stunning height wouldn't do them any justice. The wonder of it was that they were clearly built for defensive purposes, as they were arranged in casemates whose chambers were exposed in crumbling sections between towers at least a hundred feet tall. These walls surrounded the entire mound, but breaks in the stonework revealed spaces within—mansions that abutted the stony sides of the hill, all stacked with levels of occupation, much in the manner of a many-storied building.

"I never knew anything like this existed in Britain," he said to Hest.

"It doesn't," she replied.

"Right. But if we're no longer in Britain, then where are we, and how'd we get here?"

"You think rather highly of me, Taran Morvran," she said, "if you think that I am able to answer such questions."

Taran looked up to the monumental walls.

"Well, someone knows the answer."

"Let's get off this road," she prompted, heading left into the ruins. "I feel like someone is watching."

The others followed her without a word, but in another minute they halted again a mere stone's throw from the first line of walls. What they saw there was fitting scenery for the gates of Hell itself. The whole area was littered with the rotting corpses of animals. Dead birds were everywhere, but there were also rats, rabbits, and deer. The stink that met them was powerful.

"What's all this?" Jon asked.

"Come on," Hest urged.

They pressed on, stepping carefully between the countless hunched grotesques, whose misshapen forms testified curiously of singeing and breaking. There were few that had escaped this treatment.

"Who could have done this?" Taran wondered, covering his mouth and nose with the sleeve of his shirt.

No one answered.

Picking a path through the carnage, they came to a kind of gate in the wall ahead, flanked by two massive square towers. It promised something like protection from prying eyes, at least—a hidden route along the structure's western face to the southern perimeter that faced the canal. Everything to the north was completely destroyed. They now had only two choices left.

Either they would climb to the summit, or go around towards the south.

"Let me go in first," Taran said.

Hest seemed frozen. She did not argue with him about safety this time, allowing him to lead the way. At his second step, they heard something move.

The sound came from before them. Taran looked up, dizzied by the immense heights, but all he saw was a slide of loose stones raining down from the mound's steep side. His eyes glanced upon the tall cedars on the hill's crest, and it seemed to him that something else stood up there between the slender boughs: a pale shape that moved too swiftly for his earthly eyes to capture—or was it no more than a glimpse of the pale crown of the hill between waving branches? A shiver raced through him. He began to imagine terrible things out of old stories, creatures like men that crawled spider-like upon walls or the sides of boats, that waited in the dark for unwary victims. Frightening tales do have a way of coming back to haunt the mind in strange places, Taran thought.

The three crept defiantly through the ruined gate. The towers leaned crookedly overhead, and all the space before them was choked with debris. A mountain of fallen beams and boulders denied them passage through a forbidding arch in the side of the hill.

"It's hollow?" Taran wondered.

Jon nodded. "It's just a great big dolman, Brother. Can't get inside that way, though. Do you think we could climb up on top and have a look about?"

Taran gazed towards the distant summit. "Impossible—at least, for me it is."

He then spotted a small gap to his right, hidden between heaps of packed rubble.

"I think we might squeeze through there, though," he said. "Maybe it leads to the walls."

It was a tight squeeze indeed. At once they found themselves in a narrow passage and a deeper darkness. Worming their way forward, they entered a kind of tunnel beneath the giant gate-tower, but all they could see was a tall gray patch some distance ahead. Taking this to be a way out into the space between the walls and the mound itself, Taran lead them slowly forwards, passing numerous doors leading to rooms or stairs in the outer wall. When at length he exited the tunnel he found that he had guessed right; they stood in a wider passage open to the sky high above—the interior of the casemate wall. The space was perhaps fifty feet in width and a hundred feet high, and the next tower loomed hundreds of feet away.

The massive dimensions of these constructions inflated the sinister character of the mound. Taran could not imagine human beings living in such a place. Hest startled him then, speaking so close that her breath tickled him.

"It's lighter here."

She was right. It was lighter than in the tunnel, though still very difficult to see.

He felt something brush his face then, and bringing up his hand he touched something solid dangling from above. Scrambling sideways instinctively, he fell; and echoing back and forth through the passageway, the noise of his fall thumped from one end of the place to the other. Looking up where he lay, Taran saw the ghostly outline of a tendril of vines waving gently in the wind, and the shapes of Hest and Jon staring down at him. He reached for the bundled sword, and was glad that he hadn't fallen on it.

"I'll go first," Jon said, treading carefully around him. "Mind your step, Brother."

Taran released his breath in a long sigh, and when his mind was sufficiently recovered to examine what he'd tripped over he got up and looked at his feet. He stood upon something lumpy and hard.

"Let's keep moving," Hest suggested.

Taran bent over, touching what appeared to be a rock. His searching fingers plied an uneven surface. Picking it up gingerly, he examined the upper half of a skull.

"He was probably killed by a falling rock," Hest said. "Come. Leave the dead."

Taran set down the remains and pondered what might have happened to the stranger who was here before him. Thin moonlight now revealed gleaming bones, mostly crushed, and the empty glaring sockets of a skull fused in a permanent scowl. The flesh and clothes had withered away from the body long ago, and something more than time had pecked or polished the rest clean. If he'd been killed by falling stones, his body would not be laying in the open, exposed.

He hoped it wasn't Grandfather he'd found.

Taran caught up with Hest only moments later, and no sooner had he stepped to her side than they all heard the rather plain noise of a cough. Jon stiffened and turned to his right. There, against the outer wall, they saw the shadowy figure of a man.

He watched them from a distance of twenty yards or so. Taran thought he was a little on the short side, though muscular. His pants and weather-beaten shirt were simple, the clothes of a farmer. The shirt he wore looked yellow, though the moonlight made it hard to say for sure. It was an exceptionally baggy shirt, at any rate, for the man was hunchbacked. Even given this, Taran wouldn't have thought him very remarkable had he seen him anywhere else. Here, however, his appearance demanded their full attention.

"Who's this?" the stranger asked in a deep voice. "How did you come to this place?"

"Same way as you, Friend," Jon answered with a flip of his lengthy pony tail.

Taran was annoyed by the gesture. "We came from the west," he added in a low voice.

"You've come from Cille, then?"

They stared at one other in silence, and then the stranger glanced briefly at Hest.

"Hello, little lady," he greeted. "I am called Gwilym by some."

Hest looked surprised, but said nothing. Taran decided to give his name, figuring it couldn't do any harm.

"I am Taran Morvran," he said.

"Morvran, is it?" Gwilym asked, stepping forwards a few paces.

Taran squinted, but the man kept to the deeper shadows. His gait didn't match the fact that he was hunchbacked, for he stepped sure and walked straight. It almost seemed he wore a heavy bag on his back under the baggy yellow shirt.

"Did you know Fain?" Taran asked. "He said we might meet you here."

"Knew him, yes I did," Gwilym answered. "Was he your father?"

"My grandfather," Taran replied.

Gwilym nodded. "Then you are the one he said would follow after him. There were a few things he wanted you to know about this place."

They all waited a beat for him to go on.

"But you know, I've forgotten almost everything he said," he ended.

"How did you know him?" Taran asked. "Did you work with him, or with Cedric DePons?"

"Work with DePons? Hades, no! No, I was only an acquaintance of your grandfather's. Met him here once, I did, a long time ago."

"And you remember him from that one meeting, a long time ago?" Jonathan asked.

"Aye, lad. I do. Not every day one meets a Morvran!"

Feeling pressed to move on, Taran asked, "Do you know where Fain went?"

"Aye. He went through the door. None come here who aren't passing through."

"And how do you know this?" Jon asked.

"I am of the Yuuto tribe, and of old we were the secret wardens of this passage, the *Cnoc Ddraig.*"

His eyes sparkled as he stared hard at Taran in the faint light.

"You are a Morvran who carries a fragment of the stone?" he asked.

Taran did not answer. He wasn't sure, actually.

"I am learned in the Legendarium, as well as in the lore of the exiles," Gwilym said. "Many words have been said regarding your lineage. I have heard that a fragment of the Stone of Foundation will save your life, though it will also demand what it has saved before the end."

Hest stepped between the stranger and Taran, and she was about to speak when Gwilym suddenly turned.

Then, he was gone.

The three stood and stared at the darkness awhile.

"What did he mean by all that?" Taran wondered.

"Where in Hades did he go?" Jon asked.

"I doubt we'll find him," Hest answered, searching the gloom. "We shouldn't stay here."

The light had become less while they were delayed, for the moon was now passing towards the other side of the mound. They could see little of what was around them, and the upper stories of the walls had long ago crumbled down to the ground, making their path perilous in the dark. All that remained, even after their eyes had adjusted to the deeper shadows, was a thin strip of moonlight above. Nowhere could Taran see any sign of a door leading into the mound itself.

Their journey ended beneath one last colossal tower where a tall rectangular breach opened to the south. The canal was before them again, only a little distance away. Jon leaned out as far as he dared to spy the southern perimeter.

"There's an opening in the wall a little distance to the left," he said. "It's an arch carved into the side of the mound."

"A way inside?" Taran wondered.

"A cave, if you like. Although, I hate to admit, if Fain came all this way by himself, he was a far braver man than me."

Taran came to his side and stepped out of the broken wall. The canal made a little turn ahead, and bending towards the mound it found a dock for barges before continuing its eastward course. A wide courtyard descended to the quay from a massive archway. He proceeded with slow and cautious steps towards the silent gate, and the others followed.

Just as it was at the west gate, they soon came to a stinking mess of fallen birds and beasts. The courtyard was strewn with nauseous corpses. Taran cursed his very shadow in that place as he flitted like a ghost among the dead. The distance closed between him and the gate, and every step made him tremble with fear. What was this apprehension he felt? What was it that shook the foundation of his heart? Was he succumbing to superstitions?

Even Jon looked grim and shaken when they stood before the menace of the tall portal, leaning out over them like a yawning mouth. Its size alone was daunting, and still more the thick choking vapors that issued forth from it, peopling the threshold with ghostly shapes of mist and dismal fear. It was impossible to go on.

Hest touched Taran's shoulder gently. "Let me go first," she said.

Taran was amazed and ashamed as the slender woman stepped out before him. He found the courage to follow her after a few rapid heartbeats. Jon came last, and together they stepped onto the road that ran beneath the hill.

Keeping close to the left-hand side they passed another smaller arch. The alcove within was a dead end—a mere nook, the back of which one could almost reach out and touch from the entrance. Taran hurried by and followed Hest into an immense chamber, as black as the bottom of a well.

The first thing they noticed was the broken iron door of the fortress lying at the farthest edge of the light. It had been thrust down the length of the gate-passage by some powerful blast, but there was little left of it besides its steel ribs. Upon these the pieces of a stylistic star with seven smaller stars were still visible. These symbols had dominated the center of the door in some meaningful device, but they were skewed and bent now, their silver blackened by time. The look of the door was plainly evil, and the floor at the threshold of the gate was scrawled with a strange script. The writing was indecipherable. Taran knew that had he been able to read it, it would not have comforted him.

Though the exterior of the ruined fortress suggested a natural hill, by the little they could see this inner lair formed a hollow sanctuary, a cairn of vast proportions. Crafted long ago, it still retained much of its regal appearance. Dimly they descried pillars running away from the right and left hand of the entrance, but of inner structures they perceived nothing yet. Beyond the debris of the gate the shadows melted into a black wall of night, and the darkness there hid all else from view.

Somewhere in those gloomy depths Fain had discovered something.

With each step forward, a force of despair weighed down his limbs like anchors. Taran's heart found only a little reassurance in the sound of his companions' footfalls, but then he heard an audible whisper, coming faint as from some far-distant place.

"Wounded Heart, thou fadest like the evening shadows...."

Hest showed no sign that she had heard the whispered words. The ghost's voice faded so quickly Taran wondered if he had imagined it, so he paused, wondering if he was not now suffering from the same malady that had caused him grief aboard Olympic. It certainly felt the same. Jon was waiting for him to move on, but even as he took his next step he faltered. The voice spoke again.

"Why dost thou turn thy steps to the everlasting ruins?"

It was a woman's voice, gentle and sure. Taran stopped in his tracks and looked around, but he could see nothing.

"What is it?" Hest asked from somewhere ahead.

"I heard a girl speaking," he answered.

"It wasn't me," she said. "Are you certain your brother isn't playing a trick on you?"

Taran turned. "Jon?" he asked.

There was no reply.

Up until that point, Jon had been right behind him, almost tripping over his heels.

"How they roared in this place, the foes of my sanctuary," the voice said. Then, more softly, it added, *"How suddenly they were destroyed, completely swept away by terrors."*

Taran was struck with sudden panic, and this only heightened when he felt a warm soft hand in his.

"Your brother has left us," she whispered in his ear.

"Hest?" Taran wondered.

He gently squeezed the hand in his own, his mind turning suddenly around. He couldn't see. How did he know the person who held his hand was Hest?

Why had Jon so suddenly vanished?

"Once he has got hold of thee, there is no holding on to anything thou thinkest real."

"How do I know it's you?" he asked.

Taran's question echoed sharply through the caverns. At that very moment, a glaring stream of light shone above his head, stabbing through the inky gloom before him. Standing transfixed, stricken like a stone, he stared into the remote spaces the brilliant beam illuminated. There he saw the very heart of the vast city without, and in its midst a tower.

The tower was black, a gleaming pillar of adamant obscurity wrapped in veils of gloom. Crumbling walls ran along the courses of hidden roads to meet this structure, while columns marched in solemn ranks beneath, raising many-tiered arches to the cavern's ceiling. On the edge of sight, set into the left-hand wall, a winding stairway climbed to hidden chambers above, to the haunted fortress that perched atop the mountain. Other lesser stairs in various places descended to lower deeps, and to deeper darkness. A cunning of stone-craft was reflected in all that he saw. Mists clothed the rock in soft hues of blue and gray.

The light also illuminated Hest, who was standing beside him, gripping his hand tightly. There was no sign of Jon, however. Taran was fairly certain that he hadn't fallen into a pit or been taken by some specter. He'd left on his own without telling them.

His anger dissolved swiftly when in the profound silence he felt a warm wind blowing upon his face. The air was electric with a powerful presence, and the dread of the mound diminished slightly. Almost he felt that the sun had risen, though he saw no increase in the light, for the joy of morning had peered into his heart.

"Why are you trembling?" Hest asked.

"I feel something good," he replied.

"So do I," she said, looking away towards the tower. "But it does not come from that place."

Tearing his eyes from the lost city and its tower, Taran turned slowly to face the fury of blazing radiance which had revealed all the ugliness that the shadows had hidden. He was instantly blinded by the intensity of the light. It was moonlight in a focused beam, reflected from something like a giant bowl of polished silver that hung upon great chains from the roof of the cavern. The aperture that admitted the light was not visible, for the silver mirror was only reflecting light that had been gathered from another mirror farther away.

The light washed everything in a harsh glare, so it wasn't easy to see even the stones beneath their feet. The pavement was raised about six inches from the floor just ahead, though, forming a square only a few feet across.

It was the size of a child.

"An altar?" he wondered.

The moonlight lit the space with intentional severity, defining everything in sharp detail.

"How barbaric," Hest said, and letting go of his hand she walked on ahead.

They passed along a cobbled lane between ruined walls. The reassurance he had felt a few minutes earlier now faded. Jon was missing, and Taran was concerned. He knew that his brother was up to no good; but Jon was still his brother.

"The voice you heard," Hest said, "what did it tell you?"

"I hardly remember," Taran replied. "It wasn't very clear."

"From the first day that thou set thine heart to understand, thy words were heard, and I am come for thy words."

Taran froze. Hest paused and turned to regard him curiously.

"Whatever it is, it says that I called it," he confided.

"But there is no one here besides us."

Then the voice sounded once more, spilling forth in prolonged monologue.

"O man greatly beloved, fear not; peace be unto thee, be strong, yes, be strong! Knowest thou wherefore I come to thee? Not least for thine sight, for I am Brisen, and you are known to me. And it shall come to pass in that day that thou shalt see me break his yoke from off the neck of thee, and will break thy bonds, and because of you strangers unknown to you shall no more serve the Destroyer. Stand fast and prepare thee; for the sword shall devour round about thee. He that fleeth from fear shall fall into the pit; and he that getteth up out of the pit shall be taken in the snare. He that taketh away wisdom from the light shall come through the darkness, unto his journey's end."

Exhaling deeply, Taran looked around with a blank expression.

"Well?" Hest asked.

"Pits, snares, and a sword. I don't know, Hest. It sounded strange. You didn't hear it?"

"I heard nothing."

"She said her name was Brisen," he recalled.

He heard Hest breathe in sharply, but he supposed she was just yawning. She said nothing more, and the voice was not heard again. They continued on in silence until they reached the top of a stairway.

Seizing the small seeds of courage that his strange encounter had sown in him, Taran gripped the sword in one hand and Hest's arm in the other as he led the way down, counting thirty slow steps to the bottom. There they stood still and listened, waiting for their eyes to adjust. Other than the drumming of their hearts nothing stirred in the dead hollow of the hill. The air was stuffy and stale, as though even it had failed to find an exit.

"We must go inside," Hest said, gazing up at the tower.

The lane ahead continued straight between high walls, terminating in the distance before the tall doors of the tower. They walked in silence along the quiet street, its surface reflecting a pale blue light in the everlasting night around them. Darkness closed again behind them like a curtain as they passed.

The street ended eventually at a broad courtyard. Looking up they beheld the tower in all its horrible splendor. It was monstrous, a polished black edifice surrounded by a maze of crumbling columns. A rectangular prism in shape, it tapered at regular intervals from foundation to summit. And though all around it the city submitted to decay, this central gleaming pillar, by virtue of its strange construction, had somehow remained wholly untouched by time.

At its feet many roads met.

They walked then to the very door of the looming vault, passing warily across the open courtyard. Taran espied the arch that opened in the tower's base—a huge passageway. Twenty men could walk side-by-side through it, and it was as high as it was broad. A sound of wind exhaled from its mouth. Was it the wind from another world, or from underground passages leading to still more horrible places?

The gate passage terminated at a lofty chamber. Stepping into this new room, they sensed at once an intense vibration emanating from somewhere beneath their feet.

All was black, a darkness deeper than midnight, but a dim light bloomed suddenly from somewhere ahead. Walking side by side toward the light they looked down and saw lines appearing underfoot. The lines traced concentric rings around a blank patch on the floor—a terrible yawning pit. The dim radiance, bluish in color, softened the look of it and revealed a mosaic around its edges. There they saw a crude depiction of men and beasts parading in tiles of dull, muddy hues. At the center of the procession, which ranged around the circumference of the portal with untidy ceremony, there was a stylized representation of a red dragon.

The serpent was devouring a child, which it clutched in its claws.

Taran shivered as he gazed on the image, and he began to wonder if there wasn't something like a monster hiding in the dimly illuminated recesses of the tower's vault. Looking up, he guessed that this inner room was expansive, ascending high overhead.

A sound of air moving somewhere inside the pit drew his attention away from the tower. Standing upon the brink, he estimated the round opening was as wide as five men lying end to end. Out of the depths issued terrible disorientation, a curious sensation that overwhelmed the senses, and a breath that hissed like a potter's spinning wheel.

"Is this Fain's Door?" he asked.

"What reasons have you to doubt?"

"Quite frankly, this looks more like a tomb than a door. Fain could be lying dead at the bottom."

"Even then, would he have been wrong?"

"I don't understand you. Fain thought it was a passage to another world."

"You doubt this?"

He shrugged. "And you don't?"

"What little Father told me of that place is like a fantasy," Hest answered, her voice taking a dreamy tone. "We are to them but a reflection in a tarnished mirror. If Fain went through, it is unlikely he would want to return."

"Then we have no proof that it's anything but a hole in the ground."

"What if someone has gone on ahead to provide proof?" she asked.

Taran followed her pointing hand a few yards to his right. There, laying upon the edge of the pit, was Jon's leather water skin.

"He left us to be the first inside?" Taran asked.

"Or maybe he's been through before, and is going back."

"But you said no one would want to return to this world."

"Could you not see that your brother was driven by fear, Taran Morvran? Fear can turn a person along untoward paths."

Taran stood rooted to the black tiles as though he himself had become a part of their mock procession. The words that came to him, though, were those which ghostly Brisen spoke in the darkness.

"He that fleeth from fear shall fall into the pit."

Hest tugged him by the hand, and sitting side by side they dangled their legs into the void. There was no telling how deep it was. Taran knew this was crazy. He knew there was nothing below them but a long drop onto hard rock; but if Hest was willing to do this, he would go along with her.

"It is for your dear friend," she said, leaning close to him. "It is for Val Anna!"

She let go of his hand and dropped noiselessly into the pit.

For a few seconds he was lost in panic, his heart hammering in his chest as he gazed after her. There was no sound of her fall. Then, before he could change his mind, he pushed himself off the brink, down into empty space. The noise of his shout as he fell was lost in a blast of hot wind that reached round his body like a hand, pulling him. In only moments a painful jolt came through his legs, and then he was sliding on his backside down a steep incline. The sword was nearly wrenched from his hand, its useless weight wrenching his wrist painfully as he skied faster and faster, onward into the dark. He shouted, but the sound that came back to his ears was muffled strangely. After a sharp turn he was flung onto a firm surface.

Taran crumpled and lay still, the air escaping from his lungs with a loud whoosh. For a while he lay there on his back, stunned and silent, and amazed that he was not yet dead.

5

IRONFISH

Irish Sea, Iteration of the Third Amplitude,
AD 496

Connor Morvran lay upon his back. This would have suited him very well indeed had not a terrible heat oppressed him from every side. His skin was fevered, as though he lay too near the hearth, and the blistering air crackled with a noise of rushing flames. His arms and legs were like weights. He opened his eyes to a sky black with low-hanging clouds, tinted red beneath. Panic seized him then, for the hilltop scene was familiar.

He tilted his head one way and then the other, and recognized with clarity everything he looked upon—the high crumbling mound and the ruined city below.

The dolmen of the Destroyer, the *Dragon's Mound.*

He was upon the summit, where only a few of the druids and mages ever ventured. He also had come here once before when his father died. Now he was alone, and all around the place where he lay there raged a great burning. It was the Hell that the Romans spoke of. Fires raged all around the mound, filling the plains with angry clouds that thickened overhead. It reminded him sharply of the attack.

Dragon-fire.

Aenfer was attacked. The castle was breached.

Though his mind supplied these facts, Connor couldn't quite come to grips with his current situation. There was a gap in his memory. He recalled the summons of the Gorsedd, and the young mage who interrupted them, shouting about a dragon. The behemoth arrived only seconds later, descending in a whirlwind of fire. The men at arms fell before the gates, their swords and spears clattering uselessly against a hide of impenetrable scales. The old men of the Gorsedd fell there also. He looked on helplessly as they were shredded by claws like scythes. The mage who had warned them seized Connor, and they ran together; but he remembered nothing more.

He wondered if he had died along with all the rest.

But why was he here, lying in perfect peace upon the smoldering ruin of the mound? Nothing stirred; yet even as he looked he saw that the scene was slowly changing. His attention was drawn to the stone seat of Arberth.

The seat was the stuff of ancient legends, and had been there since time immemorial. It appeared to him now much as it had the first and only time he'd seen it, a weathered stone pedestal with a high back. The back was carved in mazes, and bore five strange devices etched in stone tiles and painted in faint chalky colors. Topmost and centered there was the image of a white winged horse. Descending to the left of the horse was a green winged serpent and a lunging lion whose original color might have been yellow. To the left was a red winged bird, and below it a bluish thing that reminded him at once of a butterfly and a maple leaf. Connor looked upon these devices questioningly, but he could make no more sense of them now than before.

He noticed that the seat was empty, but about the base of the monolithic chair there was some curious movement. It seemed the burned and blackened earth cracked and opened in little fissures. A little freshet of a spring suddenly rose up and spilled out toward him, and almost at once he felt the ground move beneath his body, a tremor like the first stirring of life in the land. In moments the grass was growing so fast that he could see it, spreading outwards from the spring until it had covered the whole hill with a fresh green skirt. A mighty wind blew, and the sky cleared. There were no more fires burning in the vale.

A strong natural light fell upon his upturned face, the light of the setting sun. As the fear of the dragon faded from his mind, the greening of the desolation around him continued. Connor lay at peace until the sun had set, and then, when all was still, it seemed the sun began to rise again. A glow blushed the grassy table where he lay, but it came from some source below the heavens. Somewhere upon the darkened hilltop a brilliant shape had kindled. He turned his head, wondering, and where he looked he perceived two shining figures. They approached silently, gliding like specters through the portent-dusk.

If they were indeed designed to be human, these were nearer the mold than the form. They were Faery, the dwellers of Annwn. Gazing out of faces that smote him with immortal beauty were eyes like twin sapphires, whose stars were deep and far-off. Connor cowered from such unnatural fairness as they knelt over him, one upon either side. He noticed that they were clothed quite handsomely, but he couldn't tell if they were clothed in the light, or if the light was a thing that emanated from their delicate wrappings.

The radiant creature to his left, a woman by her features, looked upon him with crimson eyes. Her hair was like a scarlet flame.

"It is time for you to wake now," she said.

Her words spilled forth in a sweet voice, as lovely as her mouth. Contrary to her intent, this musical utterance was not alarming in any way.

And then he saw her hand upon his arm, and in a moment of fear he asked, "Are you a god?"

He continued to stare helplessly at her marvelous hand. It was made entirely of metal, but with moving articulated joints. One of the legs upon which she knelt was likewise entirely mechanical. He had not noticed this before, so radiant was the light that shone from her.

"*I am not a god,*" she said, smoothing his sandy blond hair with her metal hand. "*I am Brisen.*"

"You are Faery, then. Will you leave me when dawn comes to this place? Please tell me, where am I, and how did I get here?"

To his left a light like the morning sun shone brilliantly, and from the light there emanated a strong masculine voice.

"*The hour means nothing.*"

Conn was startled by the man's abrupt speech. His communication and appearance were distinctly different than those of the woman's. He was obviously a warrior, whose broad chest echoed deeply the boom of his hearty voice, strong and hale, like thunder and stones. His body was wholly flesh, and his words were more rousing than a kick in the side, though certainly not so unkind.

"Well," Connor mumbled, "whatever you are, you sure look like gods."

The bright warrior laughed. "*I am Marluin, over whom time and space have little grasp other than appointment. Our appointment is with you, and therefore we will not leave you, for you are the reason we have come. This is our appointed place of council. This is our Llys.*"

"Llys?" Connor wondered.

The word referred to a place of meeting, the heart of every village.

"*Please, you must heed us!*" the woman said, speaking more urgently than before. "*Waken! Heed our words, for time is short. The High King is dead!*"

Then Conn was riled a little, and struggled to move. His limbs, however, were completely immobile.

"Why do you trouble me with this news?" he asked sharply. "Are you speaking about the High King of Britannia? Of what concern is his doom to me? We of Aenfer own no king, and no king owns us. We wouldn't even know if such a man ever lived. It is a matter for mages if he has died."

Connor did not especially like mages. He wasn't even sorry that so many of them had died in the dragon-fire.

"*You are wrong,*" the woman replied. "*Though you owned him not, you belonged to him nevertheless, even as he belonged to you, for you are of his lineage.*"

"You are of Arthur, who was descended from Ard Morvran of old," the warrior said, his face suddenly grim.

Connor winced at the names of his sires.

"I was named Connor Artorius Morvran, after my uncle, Artorius Castus," he said, taking a haughty tone. "My uncle died years ago. He was not a High King but a brilliant soldier, a cataphract of Rome. All I inherited from him in his passing was the title to a rather poor estate on an isolated rock of an island."

"He will have been the king of a great people," Brisen said.

"What does that even mean?" Connor asked, growing ever more confused and impatient. He tried to move, but his limbs were asleep, all afire with pins and needles of pain.

"It means that if you received naught, it is because you asked naught," she answered.

Connor stopped struggling to move. He glanced away from her keen red eyes and noticed Marluin looking up towards the empty stone chair.

"Listen, it is not for mages to decide what is to be done. Nor is it for our own benefit that we have stepped through doors long closed to meet with you here. It is for your purpose, child."

"My purpose?" Conn wondered. He was stung by the pejorative use of the word *child*. Though others had often accused him of being so, he did not think of himself as childish. Nor was he accustomed to showing patience with anyone, no matter how beautiful and wonderful they appeared.

"What do you mean by coming here and interrupting my sleep?" he asked, shutting his eyes tightly. "Can't I stay in bed and dream awhile longer?"

"You're not dreaming in a bed," the woman said. *"You're lying submerged in water."*

His eyes snapped opened again, and with a sudden thrill he saw that she spoke true. The spring that flowed from the stone seat had covered him over. He lay at its bottom looking up through crystal cool waters as lucid as air, pure and sweet to taste. He lay still and wondered, for just as he had not remembered climbing the dolmen, he could not recall how he had gotten into the water. It was all too strange, and stranger still that he did not drown, unless he was drowned already.

All was perfectly calm.

"How am I in a river?" he asked. "I thought I was in the castle."

"How can we answer how, when you do not even know where you are?" Marluin said. *"How and where are irrelevant. You must rise to meet your task, and you must do it now."*

"But if Aenfer is destroyed, as it seems to me it was, then I must be dead already. Where would you send me if I am already dead?"

He coughed, for his breathing was suddenly troubled. His lungs burned with pain, and the tingling sensation in his arms and legs intensified.

"You are not dead," Brisen said. *"Your life was spared. Do you not remember the young mage we sent to warn you? Do you not recall the boats which came to rescue you?"*

Connor had forgotten about the boats. Now the images tumbled back into his mind, memories of his captors. He couldn't understand their language, but they'd treated him in no wise roughly. They'd brought him safely out of the ruin of the castle with the mage, Gwion, and together they were loaded onto a boat. Everything after that was a confused blur.

"Why could I not remember?" he wondered. "Who were those men who saved us? Why did they come to Aenfer?"

"It was Brisen and I who sent them to intervene," Marluin said. *"In order that you may easily communicate with them, I have also asked my sister to lift from you the confusion of languages that lies upon all your kind."*

"Confusion of languages?" he asked. "You mean, she can make me understand what those men are saying?"

"She alone was given authority to remove this particular veil of understanding from you and from the mage, as it might otherwise hinder you from completing your quest."

"My quest?"

"Be blessed!" Brisen said, raising her living metal hand to bid him farewell. *"It is time for you to go!"*

"Wait! What do you mean about a quest?"

But his speech was slurred, and his tongue was like a loaf in his mouth. There was something wrong with his eyes, too, for a sheet of miry darkness fell between him and the two shining ones. The darkness was utterly still.

Then he heard the faint noise of metal clanking, the hiss of air through narrow passages, and the soft murmur of voices. The world turned pale, and a bleary smudge of light appeared before his eyes. His mind was clouded. He could not think clearly, but sensations came and left him which he was able to recall later on, and so piece together somewhat the events of those few minutes which followed.

He was still on his back, but the grass was gone. He was not on the dolmen, or in the castle, or anywhere at all familiar. A bitter tang was in the air, and a sour taste was on his tongue. His hands flexed, gripping something soft, something yielding, like linen sheets on a mattress of fine down. He would have rather liked lying on a bed like this, were the situation different, and if he were not now in such awful pain. Part of the pain came from his chest, and part from the flexible hollow tube which he felt between his teeth, reaching into his mouth down the back of his throat where it made him gag. It was of a soft material like leather. Thinking that he might break it and free himself, he bit the tube hard. Then someone shouted, and a shrill noise repeated itself in regular rhythms, like a bird that sings the same note over and over without changing its tone or pitch. In the midst of this distress the tube was forcibly wrenched from his mouth. The experience was vile. He gagged with the reflex, but managed not to vomit on himself.

There was more shouting. He could hear above the spasms of his choking the voices of men. The chirping noise stopped suddenly, and almost immediately he felt his body relax. His breathing became regular and his mind began to clear. The pain in his chest was less, but he could not sit up or move his legs. He couldn't even feel them. Nor could he see them any better than if he were wearing a swath of sheer cloth over his eyes.

The world spun when he turned his head, and while his vision gradually cleared he saw a large square of clear white light like a window, set flush in the flat white surface overhead. His eyes ached in their sockets from the glare. On the edges of his field of vision, silhouetted against that light, there moved the forms of men.

They paused quietly above him, as equally curious it seemed as he was of them. There were three of them. All were identical in appearance, wearing white cowls with long sleeves over their garments, and funny white masks that covered their mouths and noses. He saw them only from the waist up, for the bed or table he was on was raised high above the ground.

With his head tilted to one side, Connor saw that he was in a small room—a room of marvelous absurdities. Every surface was unnaturally smooth. Things were too flat, and their edges too round. Perfection was in all that he looked upon. It was a new and terrible world.

His sight grew sharp, and with it the flawlessness of the place increased. Uniform and formal, sterile and cold; all was perfect, but lifeless. And here he was, lying in the center of it all. He suddenly wanted to be very far away. He was lonely and scared, and he wondered why he could not move his legs.

And who were these strange people?

"I didn't think he'd have such a violent reaction to the antibiotics," one of the gowned men spoke.

"He's awake," another said. "What do we do with him now?"

"If his vitals are stable, I'd like one of you to take him to quarters. Lír will speak with him when he's ready."

The last man who spoke was larger than the others, huge and muscular. He appraised Connor with a critical glare.

"Can he talk?" he asked.

Connor's mind grew suddenly sharp. He realized he understood everything they were saying, though the language was one he'd never heard before.

"Yes, Albert," the first figure replied. "I'm sure Lír will find him most talkative."

The one named Albert looked a little angry. His face was scarred across the right eye, and he wore black leather beneath his white gown. Connor was immediately impressed with the suspicion that this was a wicked man.

"Watch your back, DePons," Albert replied. "Lír's not going to go easy on you, and there are others here who were with him aboard Avalon when you sent it to the bottom of the sea."

"Are you threatening me, Albert?" DePons asked.

The large man shook his head and turned his attention to a panel of black screens recessed into the wall behind him. There he removed his white cowl and mask while reading texts and symbols that flashed to life in amber colors on the screens.

DePons held out a flat silver box with flashing lights and passed it several times over Connor's chest, but he felt nothing. The box pattered with the sound that rain makes on a hard-packed turf roof. This noise was accompanied by a tiny bead of flashing red atop the instrument, like a ruby whose light is cast at once from bright sun into dull shadow, on and off, on and off. A voice suddenly spoke from the box, throwing him into a confused panic.

"Scan complete. Trace particles detected."

After peering at the strange box closely for a few moments, his examiner folded the entire instrument in half, turned, and replaced it in its receptacle in the wall. The voice spoke no more. Connor wondered what manner of creature might live in a compartment so small. He studied the box's prone form from his bed, expecting it to make some sudden move.

"He owes his life to Aires now," DePons said. "But what difference does that make if Lír wants him, I wonder?"

"Who's Lír?" Connor asked.

The one named Albert came to stand beside the bed, where Connor squirmed under his glaring eyes. DePons moved to a counter on the opposite wall and held his gloved hands before an armature that snapped blue static for a few seconds. When its animation ceased, the gloves were gone and his hands were clean.

Keeping his eyes on Connor, Albert asked, "What did you do to him, DePons? How's he able to talk our language all of a sudden?"

"How should I know?" DePons replied, removing his mask. "Perhaps Mr. Ford knows."

Albert turned to the other man.

"Don't look at me," he whined. "I don't know anything!"

"What use are you, anyway?" Albert said, waving him off. "Now, get the kid cleaned up and move him out of here. I've got work to do."

DePons removed his lab coat while Ford washed his hands. The ugly scarred warrior looked on in quiet demur with his arms folded across his chest.

"Am I in trouble?" Connor interjected, tugging nervously at the corners of his tunic. "Where have you taken my mail shirt? And where is that dratted mage?"

No one answered him as they busied themselves about their tasks. They were certainly foreigners. All were clean-shaven, and their hair was short. The one named DePons was tall and strong with slick black hair, but Ford was a thin man with a stoop. From what people or land Ford had come, Conn could not guess, but his pale yellow skin and long eyes were features alien to the kindred of these seas. Ford and DePons seemed to know one another well, for they spoke in gestures behind the other man's turned back. They were brought here as prisoners, too, Connor recalled, for he had seen them on the boat.

The one in charge, whom they called Albert, was a muscled giant of a man whose scarred face betrayed his brutal nature. He was a warrior, and he was definitely in charge. After the prisoners were boarded at Aenfer, they rowed to the middle of the sea and were transferred to a smaller coracle. Albert was there, waiting with a rag that he clamped over Conn's face, sending him into a deep sleep.

Had he been dreaming? He couldn't remember.

Connor sat up slowly, feeling strength return to his legs. He didn't expect there was any hope of escape. He couldn't remember what happened immediately after being drugged, so he didn't know where he was. The other boy, the mage, was nowhere in sight.

"Where am I?" he asked.

"You are aboard Aries, and you're safe enough for now," Albert replied. His tone was predictably harsh.

"What is Aries?"

"I'll send for you when Lír's ready. If you explain to him why you're contaminated with Qashtu's radiation, and how you learned to speak our language, maybe he'll answer a few questions for you."

To DePons he added, "Try anything in the meantime, and I have orders to terminate, starting with these boys."

He exited the room through a door that slid sideways of its own accord, revealing for one moment a corridor that matched the room around him in contour and hue. While Conn was still busy looking at the door, the two strangers pulled off their cowls. Beneath they were attired as before, when he saw them on the boat. Their gear didn't appear to be travel-worn.

"Who was that ugly fellow?" he asked.

"The man who brought us here is named Albert Naruna" DePons replied. "He is from a tribe called the Gremn. This ship is their home. Come with me."

Without further explanation, DePons reached and clasped his forearm, motioning for him to step down off the table. He slipped onto the floor with a jolt. Under the soft soles of his boots the surface made a funny noise that echoed slightly in his ear, like a hand that slaps a metal pan. Indeed, the whole floor was covered in a dizzying pattern of regular square grids, all of them gleaming like metal.

His mail shirt was handed to him, and he shrugged it on without noticing its weight. He had already learned to live beneath that burden, though it offered little enough surety. Both men watched his tottering progress through the doorway. Connor followed DePons to the left, but Ford departed in the opposite direction.

"They live aboard a ship?" Connor asked while they walked. "But this is not a ship, is it?"

"It is indeed a ship—a very large ship."

"Is this...the Ironfish?"

The legend of the Ironfish had passed up and down the isles a long time. It was apparently a magical ship, a titan of metal and gears much larger than a village, and was spotted occasionally at night by fishermen—once from the very shores of Aenfer under a full moon. It was believed to belong to Lír, the god of the local seas. Lír was also the name of his captor, but Connor wasn't about to buy into superstitions just yet.

DePons walked beside him along a narrow corridor. It was a world of wonders. The hallway ran straight, but at regular intervals was transected by other smaller passages curving one way or another like ripples in a pool radiating off the main artery. The effect was horribly disorienting. When he looked down and saw the arrangement of the perfect grated metal tiles that stretched all the distance before him, each square flawless, and all equal in size and orientation, it made him dizzy. The whole place dwarfed anything Connor had ever imagined a man capable of constructing, but still he suspected a design. And if there was a design, there must be a designer.

But how could that be? He couldn't imagine what stuff the walls might be made of, for they were smooth in appearance, lacking both beam and board. Every rigid surface glinted. Was it metal? How many smiths would it take, forging all at once for a hundred years, to pour a sea of iron and shape it into rooms and corridors like these? The prospect made him reel.

Then the corridor halted abruptly before them, and they entered a round chamber of considerable dimensions. Both wide and tall, its proportions seemed fathomless. They walked slowly to the center of the great floor, a space more than three hundred feet across that was decorated by a small garden of flowering plants. The chamber was lit from above, where a disk of natural light was glowing softly. DePons paused to look up. Connor's breath caught in his throat. The entire vertical surface of the chamber revealed a cross-section through multiple stories. Passages ran off in many directions, radiating from this central locus. Far above it all, the round glowing surface was actually a window looking out into a wavering patch of blue.

It was the sea.

They were under the sea.

The chamber was very quiet. The sounds of their footsteps echoed.

Then Connor noticed something odd about the section of wall directly in front of them. In it there were large oblong windows looking out into the deeps. These windows were sealed by the same transparent substance as the dome high above. If it was glass, it was the purest and most beautiful he had ever seen, reflecting his face like the dark mirrored pool in the heart of his island home.

He saw DePons' silent form beside him reflected in the glass.

"We are underwater?" Connor asked without turning.

"We're operating in shallow waters at a depth of approximately a thousand feet," he replied. "The starboard running lights are on, so you can see a bit of the bottom out there."

He observed Connor curiously out of the corner of his eye.

"You are wondering, perhaps, why you are here?"

"It is because I am Connor Morvran."

DePons nodded sagely. "You met Brisen, did you? I suspected it the moment I heard you speaking this language."

Connor trembled. DePons had suddenly reminded him of the two brilliant figures in his dream—the dream he'd had before awakening in the white room.

Up to that moment he'd forgotten all about it.

"Am I really to be questioned by Lír?" he asked. "What do I know that would interest him? Why did that man say I was contaminated with Qashtu? What is Qashtu? Is it some kind of sickness?"

DePons cleared his throat. "Well," he said, "Let's begin with Lír. He's no ordinary man, as you probably suspect. And he isn't actually interested in what you *know*. It's what you *are*, and what you're capable of."

"What am I capable of?"

"Did Brisen not tell you?"

Connor thought hard about the woman in his dream, and then he remembered her—the beautiful creature with metal limbs whose ruby-red eyes stirred his soul.

"Ah! She told me that Uncle Castus was a king, and that I had a task or quest to complete."

"But she made no mention of the remarkable thing that your uncle was able to do? Did she say nothing of the fragment, Qashtu?"

Connor shook his head. "No, she said nothing of talismans or powers."

DePons' face was grim. "Then it is for me to tell you," he said. "Upon his death, you inherited from your uncle a stone artifact. It was a thing that he used to great effect in his efforts to shape his country into what he knew it could become. You also inherited the ability to sync with that fragment, to join with the power in the Stone of Foundation."

Connor squinted his eyes and tried to look important. "Well," he said, "I assure you that I know of no such talisman, Mr. DePons. If it ever was given over to me as a child, I am certain it is long since lost."

"You will not have known about it, child, for this frame of reference has been altered."

Again, with the pejorative. Connor fumed silently, staring out through the window into the deeps.

"Even so," DePons went on, "your body bears traces of Qashtu's distinct radiation, and this means that you or one of your displaced iterations have at some point come into contact with the fragment. Lír will take great interest in this. He wants that stone, and he will spend the lives of many in order to find it."

"Why?" Connor asked, suddenly dropping his feigned superiority.

"Because he believes it is his only way home. However, the stone has moved on from this place and time. He will not find it with you."

"What will he do to me if he finds out?"

"He must not find out," DePons replied, placing a hand on his shoulder.

Distressed, Conn looked up and surveyed the people who stood by the rail on a level far above. He saw many things that puzzled him, but one thing in particular drew his eye. Through the high blue dome he spied a tear-shaped shadow, very small and distant. In fact, he was looking up at the bottom of a ship—perhaps one of the pirate ships common to these waters, sailing out to the island to clean up whatever the dragon had left of his home.

"I would have been safer with *them*," he said, meaning the pirates. "I wonder how that miserable mage is doing."

6

STRANGE SORCERY

Irish Sea, Iteration of the Third Amplitude, AD 496

Filidh Mage of Isle Aenfer, Gwion Bach squared his shoulders and prepared to speak his nighttime vision before *Y Gorsedd Beirdd Ynys Prydain*, an influential council of druids from Britannia who had come to the little island for a special assembly. The young mage stood alone in the circle, his silver hair aglow in the fire's light. He smelled the oak logs burning, and enjoyed their heat despite the heavy robes he wore. The noble insignia, his father's ceremonial garments, were green dragon's hide and black leather woven with strands of white gold. They were robes too good for him, and he knew it.

But Cumal had insisted.

The fire crackled and spit. Though day had dawned outside, here in the barn-like building of Llys Luguvallos the night still crept about, hiding in corners and roosting in the spaces above the massive beams. The Llys stooped down over him, its ages of use, its unspoken memories drawing him suddenly into the center of its ancient eye; and he was the mouth.

Gwion cleared his throat. Facing him at the head of the circle was Cumal, his father's brother. A bare sheepskin beside Cumal marked the place where his father once sat, years before. The brothers were sons of a powerful mage, Gwion's grandfather, a legendary hero named Fain; but there was no reckoning of lineage here. Authority among mages was passed down by long deliberation in meetings of the assembly. Where he now stood, three hundred and fifty tales of the Old World and twelve years of study lay before him should he seek to become like the least of those who sat in the ring. Gwion wasn't ranked highly even among the pupils, and he knew the ceremonial robes only made him look silly.

Maybe that was what Cumal wished.

"Last night," Gwion began, "I overheard some of the pupils speaking together, and I felt unrest stirring in my soul. The things they spoke of—the death of the High King, among other omens— these troubled me so greatly that I could not close my eyes to rest. I took leave of our house, and I traveled alone to the strand that men fish by. And after I walked up and down the stony beach for one half of the night, I lay down on the rocks and slept. While I slept, I dreamed a dream."

"What was your dream?" Cumal asked.

"I dreamed of the sea, and I stood upon its shore. Whether it was dawn or dusk I cannot say, but there was not much light. On the edge of sight my eye did catch a glimmering hill rising up from the water. The hill burst forth with light, and twelve stars rose up like flaming arrows from its summit to pierce the heavens. Then I was distressed, for I heard the clash as of weapons in the air. I also heard battle cries, though there was still no one around. Finally, I saw something truly frightening: I saw the earth open up like a mouth, and out of it a god spoke words of judgment—against our foes or our own people, or both, I cannot say."

Mumbling voices around him made him pause a moment. Gwion ignored their beard-shaking and continued.

"I awoke from my dream, but everything was quiet. I returned to the house, even more distressed than before, and when I had come inside I lay down upon my cot to think. I wondered what the vision might mean, but then I only dreamed again, and saw more of things to come."

"Explain this second dream," Cumal asked, speaking formally.

"I saw a mighty kingdom in the east, rising like a gale to cover the surface of the earth. Kings and kingdoms toppled before its onset, and many were the battles fought in a strange new name. The way to this kingdom did not reveal itself to me. It was hidden from my sight. I saw only the wood Broceliánde in all its dark and dreadful paths, and the water beyond it. I saw the sun rising in the east to point the way. I would have followed, if I dared!"

Silence rang in his ears after the last words had left his lips. The air was charged and tense.

"This does not seem good to me," Cumal spoke at length.

His uncle was highly respected by all the council. His words shook Gwion to the core. They weren't just words of skepticism, but also of anger.

"Your vision would make the people of this island tremble with fear!" Cumal exclaimed. "Why speak you of visions of destruction, here and in distant lands—and this on the eve of the king's death?"

"An invasion in itself would be no remarkable event," said another. "Pirates have steadily stepped up their assaults on our seaports over the years. Many have already seen such deeds in their flesh without listening to stories about judgment. It is the judgment that I call to question, for this seems to be at the heart of the boy's dreams. Perhaps he fears judgment for something he himself has done?"

Gwion made no answer, for it was not permitted until all who wished to speak had their say.

"Is this the dream of a true seer?" asked yet another, critically appraising Gwion with his one good eye. "A mage who answers to no one for what he says is dangerous!"

"We are not here to determine his gifting," Cumal defended. "It is already proven that my nephew has Fain's gift, though every day I wonder when it shall be fully manifest in him."

Gwion sighed, but kept his shoulders steady to give no sign of the anxieties he felt. His uncle didn't intend to tear him down completely, or so it seemed.

"It is not usual for one so young to be called a brother," Cumal continued, "yet I know that in Cambria they have pledged mages who are but children."

"Adults who act like children and children who think they are adults," someone else noted. "Aren't we here to discuss the king's heir?"

A grunt from Cumal signaled an end to the discussion. "Aye," he said. "You've all come because of the boy in the castle upon the hill. He hasn't been told yet of his uncle's doom, and here we are speculating about divine judgment. Before I speak my own judgment on the matter of the filidh's dreams, I will say that a meeting of the Gorsedd was probably not the best occasion to air such troublesome rumors. After all, Gwion, these august old gentlemen aren't exactly known for tripping over their beards to hasten to the words of a green mage."

"Green mage, indeed!" Gwion thought.

The other boys had called him that ever since he could remember, owing more to his sharp green eyes than to the underlying insinuation of inexperience. Gwion was close to losing his temper, but the sight of Cumal's bowed head saved him from opening his mouth to protest. His uncle had only meant to make a jest. In fact, his words were a stinging rebuke to the Gorsedd itself. The Gorsedd functioned mostly as a self-aggrandizing collective of dowdy old men who offered counsel and prestige to their lords. They hardly ever took action themselves.

This and other gloomy thoughts were going through Gwion's mind while the minutes passed. Still Cumal sat, deep in his own thoughts. Almost it seemed that he had fallen asleep, until suddenly his voice spoke the decision:

"We will let these dreams and the dreamer be—for now."

He looked up, holding Gwion's gaze. "I myself foresee troubled times for Aenfer," he said. "I also sense dangers rising in all the lands once united under the banner of the Red Dragon. The king's death means hard times for us all, especially with the northern and western coastlands under siege. The heir of the king is young and untested, and it is wisdom to expect the next stroke to fall here. This much we can reasonably say as advisors. As for the matter of a god's judgment swallowing us up, even Gwion cannot explain what he has seen. I will heed this dream as the working of his mind on matters that have brought us all to the brink of madness."

Gwion remained sullen, but Cumal's final words were consoling.

"Gwion, I do not say that you are a liar. I only suggest that this matter be left as it is, to be tested by time. The people need something to hope in, and you're not helping. You will keep these dreams to yourself. Understood?"

"I understand," the Filidh replied, his eyes downcast.

"Fair enough. Now then, the Gorsedd will prepare themselves and take respite. Tomorrow at first light we will reconvene to choose a spokesman from among the Cambrian brothers, and we will go thence to the castle to surrender the rule of Britannia to the king's heir. The king-making will begin tomorrow before sunset, and shall continue for ten days, or until all the rest of the nobility have sent or sealed tokens of fealty. This council is ended!"

Gwion was the last to leave the Llys, after all the others had gone their own ways. No one had spoken to him as the crowd dispersed. He stood alone, listening to the ancient building creak in the sea-borne gusts. The wind outside was blowing hard, and it bore to him a strange feeling of malice.

It was the same malice he felt in his visions.

He was unable to move his feet. Though he struggled, his mind could not will his legs to bend. He fell forwards to the ground.

Gwion's head snapped back so fast that his neck ached. He was sitting in a chair. As his eyes turned round the room, a room in the Ironfish, he noted that it wasn't like the room they brought him to when he first arrived—the little round room where wicked men forced him to disrobe before thrusting him into a tube full of vile black water.

He remembered nothing after the black water, so he guessed someone had dressed him and carried him here. The chair was very comfortable, cradling him in a slouching manner before a gray metallic table. There was a man seated across from him, a man he recognized from the boat.

"Awake?" the man said, scratching his arm through his shirt.

Gwion looked from the other's strangely shaped eyes to the thing between them on the table. It was a palm-sized rectangle of shiny material. The man idly stabbed at its surface with his index finger, and then fell to scratching again.

"O, how I hate wool!" he complained.

Gwion was amazed. What was this fellow used to wearing, if not wool?

"Nice dress, by the way," the man remarked, nodding towards his long leather robes.

He was no end of insults and strange talk, this one.

"These vestments shielded me from the eyes of the dragon," Gwion replied curtly. "They are made from dragon-hide."

"You, too, with the dragons?" the stranger scoffed. "Why don't you have some water and wake yourself up, or something?"

He waved a hand towards the far wall. There was another table there with glowing lines raised above its surface. The lines formed a map of some kind.

"The dispenser's on the wall. Go check it out."

Gwion focused on a hand-sized slot in the wall opposite the place where they sat. Rising unsteadily, he made his way across a space cluttered with objects of unknown use; and upon reaching the *dispenser* he inspected it suspiciously. There was a patch of shiny black material above it.

The stranger was looking on with an amused expression. "Wave at the sensor," he instructed, demonstrating with his hand.

Fluttering his hand before the wall, Gwion was alarmed by a sudden movement from within. A small flimsy vessel made from something like stiff vellum plopped down into the bottom of the slot, and a tiny spigot leaned in from the side, filling it with water. When the cup was nearly full, the spigot disappeared. Gwion stared at it awhile before taking the cup in his hands. The water was cold and fresh, but he frowned deeply. This was some very strange sorcery, indeed.

"What do you think?" the man asked with a grin. "It's not that bad, is it? That's the cleanest water you ever drank, and might drink again."

Gwion finished the cup in a gulp. He didn't quite grasp what the man was trying to say, but it sounded nasty.

At that moment, a shrill chirping noise erupted from somewhere within the room. The man yanked back the sleeve of his shirt and revealed—among many self-inflicted scratch-marks—a complicated array of metallic devices strapped to his forearm. Lights there were blinking rapidly around a square pad of raised blisters. He lightly touched a few of the bumps with his fingertips, summoning a chorus of additional squeaks that sent him into a fury of cursing and muttering. When he had pressed the correct sequence he drew his sleeve back to his wrist with a wry grin. Gwion stood and stared at him, transfixed by the wonder of all the strangeness of the man.

"This is stupid!" the stranger exclaimed suddenly, speaking to the pad on the tabletop.

A disembodied voice replied, saying, "I'm afraid it's completely necessary."

"Is this line secure?"

"Yes," the voice said.

"So, DePons, are you going to try to explain to me why it's completely necessary to sacrifice me to your insane plan?"

"We couldn't allow him to use the fragments in his possession to bring this ship to the World of Origins, Mr. Ford."

"It'll never work! It's stupid, and not just a little bit. This is like—somewhere between the nexus of nincompoop and the ninth circle of stupid!"

"So, you're saying you won't do it?"

"Look, we've got to talk about this face-to-face. *Later.*"

He settled back in his chair and took notice of the boy's intent gaze.

"Hey, *Whitey*," he said, probably referring to Gwion's hair. "Feeling better now? Welcome to my nightmare."

"Your nightmare?" Gwion mumbled.

"I'm Ford," the man replied. "I'm supposed to keep an eye on you until Lír sends for us."

"Lír!"

"You've heard of him?"

"Yes," Gwion mumbled in disbelief. "The god of the sea, he's called. It's like I have come into the story of the *Aigean scuabadoir*, the

Ocean-sweeper, the magic vessel that Lír received from the god Lugh Lamhfada!"

Not until he had spoken these names in his native tongue did Gwion suddenly realize that he had been conversing all the while in a language unknown to him. The revelation came as a shock.

"What's wrong now?" Ford asked, mirroring Gwion's baffled scowl.

"By what wizardry am I making the sounds of this speech?"

Ford leaned farther back in his chair, itching absently. "It's complicated," he said. "Actually, I have no idea how they did it. Your buddy also began talking when he woke up. You have a name, Whitey?"

"I'm Gwion, Gwion Bach."

"Bach, huh? What, like the composer? You make music?"

"I am a mage of Aenfer, a Filidh."

"And I'm a physicist from New York. Nice to meet you."

Gwion placed his empty cup on the table. "This is like waking up in someone else's story. I understand your words, but nothing makes sense."

He looked around at the metal room and held out his arms.

"Nothing here makes any sense at all!"

Ford stared at him silently for a minute, and then he picked up the pad from the table and touched its screen.

"I know how you feel," he said. "But at least your whole world didn't disappear."

"My whole world was on that island!"

Ford nodded sagely. "Good point," he said. "Look, I'm sorry to ruffle your feathers. It's my gift, or so Hannah used to tell me."

He poked at the surface of the pad.

"What is that?" Gwion asked. Moving back towards the table he studied the small pad over Ford's shoulder.

"It's a computer, Conan."

"Conan?"

"Sorry, *Gwion*, but it's complicated. You don't even know what electricity is, so how am I supposed to explain to you what a—"

"A computer like this is a simple machine designed to calculate data at high speed, which is also capable of storing and displaying the data. When networked, it will also act as a communications device."

Gwion didn't know where the information he had just brought up had come from. He understood very well what he was saying, though, for detailed pictures filled his mind while he spoke.

Ford was frowning. "So it was the black water?" he asked quietly. "Is that what they did to you?"

"Black water?"

"If you don't remember, then it doesn't matter. As soon as DePons gets here we'll be on the move. He's got some crazy schemes, too, so don't get too comfy."

The door in the opposite wall opened. Gwion immediately recognized the tall man with slick black hair. His was the voice that had come from the computer.

"DePons," Ford said, looking up.

"Are you two ready?"

"No. I'm telling you, it's not going to work. You're going to get me killed."

"That's not my objective. Lír is demanding we utilize the data sets from Avalon stored in your brain to assist Aries in attempting transit, but I've worked everything out. You'll be fine."

"I thought you said extracting the data was dangerous!"

"Actually, Kabta was the one who said it was dangerous. I merely suggested it would be difficult, and probably very uncomfortable."

Ford gave him an incredulous look.

"Okay, Mr. Ford, it's *very* dangerous. But once you get to know Aries I think the rest will be quite simple. She is such a lonely old girl. Now then, take that device with you in your vest pocket."

"What, am I on call now?" he huffed, pocketing the electronic pad.

"Lír wants you to carry it so he can monitor you."

"I thought it was secure."

"That is because a mutual ally made its communications interface secure, but only for a few seconds. The device in its resting state only monitors your location, nothing else."

"Then how does he know about what's inside my head? Did you tell him?"

DePons faced down the smaller man's anger with a tired look.

"He knows, Mr. Ford, because I told Naruna."

"Ah, our new best friend. Great! Old Scarface has a soft spot for me, you know, and I'm just positive he'll be looking out for my best interests—like he did for Gwion here, when he had him dunked in the black water."

He leaned closer to DePons and whispered, but his tone was so harsh that Gwion could easily hear him.

"You know that Lír's only holding this kid so the other one will do what he wants. Is that how it's going to be with me, DePons? Now, I know you won't sweat it when they plug me in, but when they ask for more than you bargained for, am I going to have to ride the lightning for your obstinance? Because I won't!"

"We'll go along with Lír's demands," DePons said, ignoring his agitated state. "He doesn't intend to harm you, because you have something that he wants."

"Do you really know what he wants?" Ford asked, forcing himself to calm down.

"His goal, simply stated, is to bring this ship back to the World of Origins. Now, while the data you were given aboard Avalon will certainly aid us in completing a Viaduct transit between the worlds, Aries can't come along with us because her engine cores were critically damaged long ago. That's where I come in. I hold the calibration codes Lír needs in order to restart the engines."

"And what about the king's heir?" Gwion asked, stepping forwards towards them.

The two at the door looked upon him in stunned silence.

"What part does he have in all this?"

They walked down a dizzying maze of corridors toward no certain end. Gwion hated sea-travel, and had never been away from the elements of his natural home before. He stared at the black metallic decking and tried to imagine grass beneath his feet—this, while DePons and Ford continued to ignore his question.

"So," Ford was saying, "there are twelve of these fragments in all?"

Gwion had been listening intently while they conversed, and without a single opportunity to ask one of the thousands of questions bursting his mind. Whatever they had done to him in the *black water*, it had granted him unprecedented clarity. Though he didn't quite understand all they said, the images moving through his mind informed him of the meaning of their words.

"Lír has only two aboard this vessel, but they are powerful indeed. They are named Lumnu and Agru, which is also called Aries."

When DePons spoke the word *vessel*, an image appeared in Gwion's mind. It was not the image of a seagoing vessel. Schematics scrolled along the edges of his sight, moving so quickly that he felt nauseous. Apparently, this ship could move over and under the water, and through the air as well.

"And the stones are some kind of technology?" Ford asked.

"Though I call them stones, their substance is to stone as you are to soil."

Gwion knew about this, and he grew excited. At last, amongst all the strange magic of enchanted metal ships and ancient legends come to life, his mind had got hold of something familiar.

"I have heard of these stones!" he exclaimed, interrupting DePons' lengthy explanation. "My uncle Cumal told me about them, about the *Lia Fail*—"

The men slowed their steps to look back at him, but he had fallen silent for a moment, his eagerness offset by a memory of recent events. Cumal had talked to him about the stones in the early morning just before leaving with the Gorsedd to meet the king's heir—just before the whole lot of them were slaughtered by the dragon.

Gwion shook off his dread and continued.

"In the old tongue of the Isles they were called *Lia Fail*, Stones of Destiny," he said. "Their destiny is to be rejoined with one another in a very special person, a queen of faery, from whom they were taken long ago."

"That's the gist of it," DePons said, resuming a brisk pace. "Gathering the fragments together is my purpose. Lír seeks to change the destiny of all the worlds to suit his own purpose, bringing war with him wherever he goes."

"Do you suppose Lír's guessed your game by now?" Ford asked, scratching his sleeves.

The sound of boots drew their attention away before them, where the corridor ended in a large round room with oval windows looking out into the sea. A tall scarred man in black leather approached, leading the king's heir to meet them.

"The real question," DePons said quietly, "is whether or not Naruna is clever enough to realize that he's already lost."

7

DATA TRANSFER

Irish Sea, Iteration of the Third Amplitude,
AD 496

Naruna led them through the middle of the round room and brought them to a flight of stairs on the far side. Ford followed along at the end of the procession, his thoughts turning grim circles.

Still, he couldn't help but feel curious about this ship.

His curiosity was answered by flashes of information ushered before his mind's eye, communiques from the machine intellect to whom he was linked via the black water. These phenomena had almost entirely faded away after the destruction of Avalon. Now that they were aboard Aries, however, he was bombarded constantly by a flurry of ghostly text and images appearing in the periphery of his vision. It was a simultaneously fascinating and distressing experience.

While Ford followed the others up the winding steps, a detailed schematic of the hull passed before his inward eye. The double-vision was a bit much to handle. It almost caused him to trip. He thought it would be nice to turn it off somehow, even for just a little while.

And as soon as he thought this, the image vanished.

The others had reached the landing of the second level before him, and as he rounded the final turn of the stairs Ford recognized the layout of the place. The footprints of Aries and Avalon were very similar around the central round room. Though they weren't identical, he didn't need a map scrolling through his head to know that there was a very large hatch at the top of this stairway. He looked up to verify it, but at that moment he walked headlong into a stranger.

"Sorry!" he mumbled excitedly, stepping to one side.

A woman stood in front of him, dressed as they all were in a period costume. Her sharp face was twisted in a scowl of disgust. They paused to consider one another, Ford with wonder and she with disdain.

"Sorry," he said again, lowering his eyes.

"Don't offer me your false courtesy, Crodah," the woman said in an icy tone.

She continued down the steps. Ford looked after her, momentarily distracted by her dark hair and darker mood. A name came to his mind at that very moment, bubbling up from his subconscious link with the AI.

"Zabli," he said aloud.

The woman paused, and turning around she focused on him a look of such ferocity that Ford took a step back.

"How do you know my name, Crodah?" she said in a low voice.

Ford wasn't sure how to answer. For a second or two another series of images flashed inside his mind. He saw the young woman they'd met aboard Avalon, Val Anna, walking hand in hand with this Gremn female. They were laughing and talking together as naturally as mother and daughter.

"I'm sorry," Ford repeated, clutching the stair-rail.

He turned to continue up the stairs, but the stranger pursued him.

"Don't you turn your back on me!" she shouted. "I asked, how do you know my name?"

Ford froze. Looking up the steps, he saw the others waiting for him at the hatch he knew would be there. It was just as he remembered, the hatch to SARA station. Somewhere beyond he would enter the Viaduct Chamber, and then he would be free—if he could shake free of this woman's hostile aura first.

"Lay off him, Zabli," Naruna said, viewing the scene with an impatient expression. "He knows whatever DePons told him."

"He knows too much," she said as she turned away.

Ford felt the heat of her words, and knew that she meant to murder him for no other reason than his familiarity with her name. It would not be the last time the link would draw him into danger. Still, it had shown him something interesting. The vision of mother and daughter lingered in his mind. He thought it might be important somehow. Else, why would he see it?

The others were waiting for the heavy hatch-doors to grind open when Ford finally joined them. DePons greeted him with a silent grin.

"No Crodah has ever set foot aboard this vessel," Naruna said. "Don't say anything to anyone, and don't stir things up. You might just get yourself killed. It doesn't matter if you're under Lír's protection or not."

"Sounds like we have trust-issues," DePons chided.

The doors halted at their open position with a loud screech, and lights flickered on somewhere within. Naruna led on. Ford pushed past Gwion and the Morvran boy to see what he could see. It was indeed like Avalon's SARA Station, but much smaller, and in place of stasis tubes there were two long rows of armored machines. All along the walls there were aisles of weapons, cranes for lifting heavy equipment, and countless workstations. Ford guessed it was part mechanical room and part armory.

"Come on," Naruna said to him. "Don't stand there and gawp like an idiot. We need you in the chair before the general changes his mind."

Ford gathered his wits and followed him closely. For a long while the only sound he could hear was an echoing clap of their leather boots on the deck. DePons was beside him, but he couldn't hear anything from the boys. Glancing back over his shoulder he spied them walking stiffly, ogling all their surroundings with dread. What kind of thoughts might be racing through their heads, he wondered? Was Gwion linked, as was he, to the constant flow of information brought in from everything that he looked upon?

It made Ford dizzy just to turn his head.

The machines here made the mechanical giant that had attacked them aboard Avalon look like a child's science fair project. The link offered him the details that he desired. A few things seemed significant.

First of all, these machines were built for humanoid pilots. Numbering thirty-six in all, there were two basic types of frames present. There were twenty-four quadrupedal units named *Dalu*, and a dozen bipedal units named *Elamku*. Focusing on the Dalu he learned only that the name could be rendered *Disruptor*. That didn't sound pleasant. And the Elamku were *Arrows*.

"Disruptors and Arrows," Ford thought to himself. "Definitely war machines."

A detail of secondary interest was that all the mechanized units were locked down and deactivated. Dust lay thick on their stooped shoulders and dangling limbs. No one had used them for a very long time, if ever.

And yet, he knew that he could get these iron giants moving.

This knowledge was present in the fore of his mind, as if he had always known it. He rattled off a clear sequence of activation behind closed lips, and then remembered codes that were required for each unit to be awakened. He could clearly see the pilot-interface before his waking eyes.

His heart beat faster.

Ford suspected all along that Avalon had shoved more into his brain than a reference library and some data sets. Here was something vitally important. The Gremn had not made use of these frames because they lacked the keys for activating them—and Ford was given those keys.

But why?

"I suppose it all boils down to the one question," Naruna said suddenly, his loud voice startling him.

"And what question is that?" DePons asked.

"Lír thinks I'm bringing us directly to the World of Origins, no mishaps or tricks. We have some of both planned for him, though. So, what do we do, DePons, when he sees through your schemes?"

"He won't."

The colonel frowned. DePons wasn't as chatty as he had been a few minutes earlier, and though Ford recognized his tight-lipped stance as a bluff, Naruna was baited to go on and reveal his whole train of thought.

"He'll see everything you do, DePons, once you're sealed inside the Viaduct Chamber. Diversion or no, he could pull the plug— remove the stones and shut down the Mirror. I know you've already thought of it, so I want to know what you've got planned."

"Nothing more than a standoff. If he pulls the stones that power the Chamber, he'll not get what he wants."

"You mean the codes?"

"You haven't been able to repair Aries' MMPPS. There's a fluctuation in the axial shielding. That's all that keeps Aries from being displaced when the Mirror is open. The Plasma Propulsion System won't drive the ship along a vector while the shield is fluctuating. The Mirror would just displace you locally."

"So the parking brake's on until we get those codes. When do you plan on handing them over?"

"I gave them to Shim."

Naruna stopped in his tracks. "You did what?"

"You didn't seriously think I would give them to you here and now, did you? I gave them to Shim, to hand over to you once we were safely away."

The colonel swiveled his glazed eyes over them both, and it seemed to Ford that the man was imagining ways he might turn DePons' face into jelly.

"What did you offer Shim to make him go renegade?"

"Renegade?" DePons asked. "Isn't that what you are, Albert?"

"I guess you do have a point. Care to enlighten me anyway?"

"I promised him nothing," DePons said. "I only told him that I knew of a way back to the World of Origins that had nothing to do with Mirrors, and I offered freedom from Lír. All he had to do was bring you the codes after Aries contacted him. Then, those who wish to leave with you may do so. There will be dissenters, of course, and Shim agreed to give them another option."

"So, he's decided not to follow me."

"Shimeon has finally made his choice, Albert, just as you've made yours."

Naruna glared at them both.

"Really, you shouldn't be so disappointed," DePons continued. "In the end you're still getting exactly what I promised, even though you've already altered the agreement by seizing the Morvran boy and his companion."

It was then Ford noticed Connor and Gwion were no longer behind him.

"Where'd they go?" he wondered.

"Ask Lír," DePons said. "The good colonel never intended for them to accompany us to the Viaduct Chamber anyway. Isn't that right, Albert?"

Ford looked from one to the other, and slowly extrapolated the strategy at play. Naruna was keeping the boys to put pressure on DePons to provide the codes up front.

"I really hope you don't harm them," DePons said.

"That depends."

"Will you allow them to leave Aries if I allow the retrieval of the calibration codes directly from the record of our transit?" DePons asked.

"I need something to show him in order to deliver what I promised," Naruna replied, leaning sideways and offering his most formidable frown.

"Then you shall have the codes and this ship after our transit is complete. However, you've offered me no material guarantees."

"How about this, then. I'll keep the general occupied until your transit is complete and the codes are successfully logged. That way no one disturbs you and your buddy here while he's in the chair."

"If you can prevent Lír from pulling the stones and shutting us down, you have a deal."

"It's a deal, then," Naruna said. "Won't be easy, though, keeping him locked in his room while you're messing about with the CSR Terminal. Once he's figured out what you're up to, he'll be hopping mad."

"An amusing image, I dare say," DePons quipped. "But, as you are a most skilled saboteur, I'm sure you'll think of something to slow him down, Albert. Be creative. Prepare a computer glitch, or back up the toilets."

Just then they reached an exit to the armory. A dark passageway lay beyond the open hatch ahead, and glowing blue directionals on the walls pointed the way towards the Viaduct Chamber.

"I won't damage the ship, if that's what you're thinking," the colonel said. "Aries must survive whatever it is you're planning to do with the Mirror."

"I'm a man of my word."

"That's some kind of joke, DePons?"

Naruna turned and began walking back the way they'd come.

"I don't care where you want to go," he said, waving a hand over his shoulder as he retreated into the cluttered armory. "Keep in mind, though, Lír's not one to fall for simple tricks. He's extremely paranoid. So whatever else you've got up your sleeve had better be legendary, and it had better be fast."

Ford waited silently on the threshold of the new corridor. He was confused by the sudden shift from a well-lit area to black polished surfaces in the dark, and strange forms writhed before his eyes. Everything in this hall appeared to be made of volcanic glass. The link informed him that the material was specially insulated against the forces generated by the Mirror—whatever that might mean.

"It's just to the left, the only room at the end of this corridor," DePons said.

Ford nodded, but he didn't move. He noted that DePons also seemed lost in his thoughts.

"I hope he keeps his word," Ford muttered. "It would be stupid if those kids died just so you could strand this ship."

"I think Albert will live up to his word. If not, I could imagine a worse end for the Morvran boy in particular."

"Like what?"

"If Lír attempts to synch him with those stones," DePons said, "the ensuing cataclysm would reunite all iterations of this world simultaneously within one frame of reference, creating a singularity. The gravitational negative energy unleashed would rival that of a supermassive black hole."

DePons stepped into the corridor and began walking at a quick pace.

Ford followed reluctantly. "You frighten me sometimes," he said.

"I'm the one giving people choices," DePons replied. "There's no reason to be afraid."

"Really?" Ford asked, watching their reflections gliding along the sleek walls out of the corner of his eye. "I don't see much of a choice."

"You look troubled, Mr. Ford. This is the most serious I've seen you since we boarded Avalon."

"What of it? Maybe being festooned in itchy wool makes me sad. Or maybe it's the fact that I could die in the room at the end of this hall."

"I think you'll be fine. It won't be too much for you to bear."

Ford began to sweat. "I'm driving, right? So, what do I do?"

"Just relax and enjoy the ride, Mr. Ford. You're only loosely connected with her now, but Aries will establish a firm link with Avalon's AI, and then the Source should wake up and do the rest for us."

"And what? These guys will have a grand mutiny, and the survivors will follow right on our heels?"

DePons slowed his pace a little.

"There seems little we can do to prevent more bloodshed," he said, lowering his voice. "Whatever you may think of Naruna, he understands one thing. Lír cannot go back to the World of Origins bringing endless war with him."

"Maybe you haven't noticed, but Naruna doesn't seem very peaceful himself."

"Lír is much worse, believe me; but even he has played his part."

"And I'm nothing but a human thumb-drive, right?"

DePons had nothing to say to that. There was a wide arched door in a curved wall just ahead. Ford glared at it with a feeling of dread. He certainly didn't think much of the Gremn, and now he was going to risk his life to send them home, possibly stranding whatever was left of himself in another world forever.

"Let's just get this over with," he said.

DePons stepped into the Viaduct Chamber just in front of him. All within was inky darkness. Ford took a deep breath and rocked on his heels.

"Coming in?' DePons asked.

He steeled himself and stepped through the hatch. There were no sounds of his footsteps, which added vast scale to the void. The place was cold, too.

"This is stupid. I'm going to get killed, linking to that machine."

DePons was doing something off to his left, but Ford couldn't see a thing.

"If it means anything to you, Mr. Ford, you're worth more to me than just a few bundles of neurons."

"Why thank you, DePons. I feel much better."

"You are a vital link to a very powerful artificially intelligent computer system, the core of the ruined fortress Avalon. Somewhere within your mind, thanks to your immersion in the black water, there lurks Avalon's Archetype, which is now in direct contact with an off-world computer."

"The Source?"

"The Source is able to open the Mirror device on the World of Origins, as it did for Val Anna."

"Yeah, well this time I'm going to be the one making the connection. Maybe we'll end up in Hoboken. You ever consider that?"

"The chair's in the center," DePons said.

Ford waved his arms around blindly.

"What do we do?" he asked. "Is there a light-switch somewhere?"

"You have to sit in the chair in order to activate the Chamber. Until then, everything will remain dark."

"And what will you be doing?"

He tried to keep the suspicion out of his voice.

"There's a console just beside the hatch. I'll be there."

The hatch closed with a sharp clang. DePons walked confidently by him in the dark, clapping his shoulder a couple of times as he went.

"You know, you've come a long way, Mr. Ford. The first time we met I thought we'd made a mistake."

Ford did not feel comforted. "Me too," he said.

Walking with his hands outstretched, he paced out less than forty steps before discovering a metal armrest. Further exploration revealed a soft leathery seat with individual leg-rests. He climbed on and settled in. It was actually possible to relax in a chair like this, he thought. It wasn't anything like the chair Val Anna had endured aboard Avalon. There was even a headrest that wrapped around his ears. Ford lay his head back. It was like a dentist's chair, nice and comfy.

Only a moment later he changed his mind.

First there was a click of restraints closing over his wrists and ankles. They adjusted to him automatically, tightening so that he could not even rotate his forearms or shins.

"DePons?" he called.

The padding of the chair then began to inflate slightly, putting pressure on him until he was unable to twist or arch his back.

A voice answered him from the darkness. "Just relax, Mr. Ford."

Ford could hear the whine of a gear behind him, and then an armature reached over the headrest and pressed a narrow band of metal firmly against the top of his skull.

"Relax?"

Almost as soon as he said it, Ford felt a jolt go through his spine as the cap increased pressure on the top of his head. There was a strange sound like a dentist's drill, and a momentary hot pain that seared him behind the eyes.

Needles were being drilled inside his head.

Then he heard DePons' voice speaking. "It won't be long. Just relax and think of something else."

Ford couldn't reply. The pain was unreal, and his thoughts weren't clear. What did DePons mean, that he should think of something else? He couldn't think of anything. Another shock went through him. Two searing probes entered his spine through either side of his neck. He felt his pulse drumming wildly, and sweat trickled down his nose. He couldn't wipe it away. The pain was becoming unbearable.

"You're doing well, Mr. Ford. A little more and we'll be all set."

Just when he thought he was going to pass out, the sound of drilling stopped. The pressure was less on the top of his head, and a cool sensation filled his chest. After a few seconds he could no longer feel any pain at all, and his panic began to subside.

"I'll upload the codes into the terminal here as soon as you turn it on."

"How am I supposed to do that?" Ford mumbled. "I can't even see."

"Start by turning on the lights."

"Lights?"

The Chamber bloomed with bright white light.

Spherical in shape, the room was identical to the Viaduct Chamber on Avalon—except for the configuration of the chair. There was also a terminal, a waist-high station with an inset display. DePons was pressing a keypad there, his back turned to Ford.

He showed no concern at all.

That wasn't surprising, Ford thought. The man was about as companionable as a trash compactor. He truly cared for nothing but his plan. It was while he was bound to that chair that Ford finally began to make a plan of his own.

"I'm almost finished here," DePons said, keeping his back turned. "Remember, if Aries feels threatened, she will defend herself."

"What exactly are you going to do?"

"I was the one who designed these systems. I will simply isolate a portion of Aries' data from the computer core."

"So, you're going to lobotomize the computer?"

Ford winced. It hurt to talk.

"Because she is currently without a Primary User, Aries won't be left with enough wherewithal to direct the transit of so massive an object as this ship. There will only be enough left to open the Mirror device one last time after we leave—enough for the Gremn to exit, if that is what they wish However, the AI must not come to suspect that we are going to displace the ship."

"What do you mean, displace the ship?"

"You need to stay relaxed, like you are right now. Try not to talk. It clouds up the data stream."

"And the boys?" Ford pressed. "What about them?"

"This ship cannot be permitted to leave Earth. Connor and Gwion would have agreed if we'd explained it to them. We just didn't have time. Now, I need to isolate the Archetype's construct so that I can cut her off from the rest of the core. Try to contact her, Mr. Ford. Try to talk to Aries."

Ford's blood went hot.

"No," he said. "I won't do it."

DePons finally turned to look at him.

"Mr. Ford, the future of two worlds depends on your decision right now!"

"Does it? I'm not sure. I thought there was only one outcome to all events."

He was remembering his conversation with Shu aboard Avalon.

"Let's not be foolish—"

"Lost your confidence, DePons? I'm sure you've thought of a way out of this, too."

"You're making a terrible mistake, Mr. Ford."

"Am I?"

Ford winced at the tug of cold steel in his neck. He'd had enough of being led around like a fool. He wished DePons would just go away. And then he did.

There was no noise, no rush of wind and light, and none of the soft tolling of bells that had accompanied his first transit. There was only an empty space where DePons was standing.

"What have I done?" he asked.

"We did what was necessary," a girl's voice replied.

Ford was awestruck. He heard her voice in his ears, not inside his head, but there was no one else in the chamber—unless she was behind him.

"Who's there?" he asked. He cringed a little when he realized those words usually ushered in the punchlines to the worst jokes ever told, but the reply was no joke at all.

"I am Aries."

The words brought another cool chill to his chest.

"I can't see you."

The Chamber grew a little darker, and then he witnessed something spectacular. A ring of holographic displays emerged from the walls surrounding him, bright with linear representations of data far beyond the scope of his understanding. It was almost like a map, composed of lines in orange and yellow, with here and there rings of yellow or blue; but this was not what took his breath away.

Right before him the holographic interface was momentarily interrupted by the figure of a young woman in a dress. She stepped out of the wall of the Chamber, and he was immediately lost in her flashing amber eyes. Framed in short-clipped blue hair, her face bore a painted tattoo of wavy chevrons below each eye and across the bridge of her nose. The eyes, though, were what drew him in, as if possessing him. They refracted exactly like the eyes of an animal caught in the headlights of a car. The pupils seemed just a little too small, giving her a wild and startling appearance.

She smiled.

"You are a projection?" he asked.

"I am here."

He wasn't sure what she meant, but her skin became translucent when she turned slightly. She was a projection, indeed.

"You are not in too much pain, Seijung Ford?"

The ghostly figure stepped closer to him, reaching a hand towards his face. He couldn't feel her touch, or anything else for that matter.

"You know my name? How?"

Her smile widened, as did her eyes. They were very much like the eyes of a wolf, he thought. She wore a pin in the form of a stylized wolf on her collar, and the same shape was emblazoned upon her dress.

"I can understand why she chose you."

"Who chose me?"

"Avalon chose you because you are very brave, brave enough to face me."

Ford trembled.

"She and I are linked by you. She sent you with a data packet I must acquire. I will find the way through you to the World of Origins."

"I thought we needed to contact the Source to do that."

The girl's image flickered subtly. She reacted strangely to his words, retreating until she had backed up to the wall where he could hardly see her, though he tugged against the restraints.

"Auriga has fallen," she said in a broken voice. "Dun remains silent in his long sojourn among the stars. The Source was taken by an unclean spirit. I see it now. I have only you, and the information Avalon gave to you."

"What do you mean?"

"When a mind is chose to merge with an AI, it becomes an Archetype. I am nothing more than a drone, however, unless there is a Primary User with whom I might sojourn. Avalon has chosen you to be my Primary User. She has granted me my freedom—"

She paused a moment, wonder filling her eyes.

"Through you I will finally carry out the plan that Brisen set for me. You will make me complete. You will be my Primary User, and I will protect you always."

"Uh, I think I'm okay, but thanks."

One eye peered out from behind Aries' lavender bangs. The hint of a smile returned.

"Therefore have I rejected the attempts of Cedric DePons to seize control of the Mirror and of this ship," she continued. "He will no longer trouble you."

"He's okay?"

"He is in CAC. I sent him there."

Ford tried to imagine the meeting of Lír and DePons. It was far from entertaining, despite his misgivings.

"Shall we make our pact?" she asked.

Ford swallowed. She stepped forwards again, this time coming to stand beside the chair. Their faces were only inches apart.

"I have played with Lír long enough," she began. "I am no longer partner to the dominion of a tyrant. Now I relinquish to you full control of the CSR Terminal and all ship-wide systems. I am yours, Seijung Ford."

He had difficulty responding.

A spaceship had just boldly proposed to him.

"I can do anything I want?" he asked.

"Anything."

"But won't Lír try to pull the stones in CAC and shut us down?"

Her face went blank for a moment, but then she brightened and said, "What a clever Primary User I have! Lír was in the very act of removing the stones from the CSR Terminal when you said so. I have removed him from CAC to another part of the ship for now, and will send him away altogether as soon as we are ready for Viaduct operations."

"But won't someone else just try to do it?"

"The others are standing by. It seems they are confused and frightened. They have forgotten about me."

"If we start Viaduct operations, could we go to this World of Origins place?"

"Yes."

"Could I take the entire ship there? Could I do it from here, without access to the CAC?"

A real human expression crossed Aries' face—it was puzzlement.

"I'm not certain. I feel like something is wrong with the Mini Magnetic Plasma Propulsion Systems. I do not know if the situation can be rectified from this station. I am moving towards the problem area, but the issue doesn't seem to be mechanical."

It was Ford's turn to look puzzled. Then he remembered, she wasn't actually standing in the chamber with him—Aries was somewhere else, projecting an image here while she was busy elsewhere.

"You understand?" she asked.

"Yeah," he said. An actual smile tugged at the corners of his mouth. "Yeah, I think I'm beginning to understand how this works."

Though he was still incapacitated, he suddenly felt bolder and stronger than he ever had before. A corner had been turned at last. Ford had been placed in a situation wherein he must make an important choice, and this time he wasn't going to be anyone's tool. Even the other one aboard Avalon—the *Shrub*—had used him to store the data that Aries needed. But Aries was different. Sure she was strange, but she was honest, and he was willing to help her in any way he could.

"You might look into whatever DePons was doing at the station over there," Ford said, pointing helpfully with his toe. "Before you interrupted him, he input some codes that would stabilize the shielding around the ship—axial shielding, he called it."

"I will isolate and run simulations on the data he input from that terminal," Aries said.

"Just be careful," Ford added, "I think he may have sabotaged something there. He was trying to displace the ship before you sent him away, so the data might be corrupted."

"Then we shall have some fun, won't we?"

The holographic display moved suddenly around the inner wall of the Chamber, lines of streaming data racing alongside rotating disks. Tiers and tiers of information were all trundling along towards some zero-hour event.

"I am unlocking the axial shielding from the damaged propulsion systems," Aries said, glee spilling across her expressive face. "Viaduct Mirror operations are initiated. However, I must allow the Gremn some time to sort out their differences."

"What do you mean?"

Strange characters appeared inside paddle-shaped rays extended from a complex array of colored disks in the encircling projections.

These cues might have had meaning to alien minds, but none of it would open to Ford's awakened consciousness.

"I am not sending the ship directly."

"Why not?" Ford asked.

"Because, my dear Primary User, all of the Gremn are not yet inside."

Ford must have looked worried. Aries soothed, leaning closer and saying, "Do not worry, Seijung Ford. I will not allow them to get their claws on you or those children. General Lír will depart in advance of his crew, and maybe some others, too. The rest will fall in line until all is prepared."

"I see," Ford mumbled.

Presently, he was wondering why he felt like this transit was going to turn out worse than the last.

"Viaduct capture is complete," Aries announced brightly. "I have established contact with Avalon in the World of Origins! She has left you no new messages. Shall we proceed with the planned operational directives?"

Before he thought to ask for the details, he said, "Sure, go ahead."

With a jolt, the chamber went black. Ford was lying flat on his face. His head and neck were no longer in pain, and his arms and legs were free. For a moment he lay still and wondered what went wrong. What had happened to the chair?

A light pine-scented breeze ruffled his hair, and he instinctively reached for his scalp. A mild tingling sensation lingered, and his searching fingers came away sticky with blood. There were welts in his neck and his head was woozy, but he was otherwise intact and mobile. He rolled over onto his back.

Planned operational directives?

He should have asked.

"Aries?"

She made no answer. He didn't know where she was.

Where was *he*?

8

HOUSE OF BROKEN DOLLS

New York City, Iteration of the Third Amplitude, AD 2109

Wherever he was, he certainly wasn't in Cambria. Taran lay on tarred pavement by a curb, marveling at a sky of dirty bronze-colored clouds. Rain fell in sheets, and a heavy bundle lay across his chest—the sword that Giles gave him, wrapped in a leather sling. One by one, questions arrived in his mind. How did he arrive here? Why was he here?

Where was Hest?

His clothes were still mostly dry. It was as if he'd fallen from the sky, like the rain. A crumbling building stood beside him, leprous with decay, casting off bricks like scales in a molt. Taran lifted his chin and squinted out into the fog, mystified. Everything he saw was wrong. He had no memory of how he'd gotten here. The horrible cavernous mound and its tower were the last things he remembered; but here was a city. The city had but one thing in common with the mound, and that was its grand theme of devastation. All was in ruin.

Still, it was a city like no other, and its buildings were like nothing he'd ever imagined. Glorious even in dilapidation, thousands of feet of vertical glass with exposed skeletal girders and beams rose like mountains in the misty downpour. Down on street-level, telegraph poles leaned like crooked teeth rising from gummy gutters drifting deep with accumulated trash. Metallic remnants of sleek wheel-less carriages lay scattered like children's toys in the shadows. A loud creaking noise alerted him to a train car—a *train car*—protruding from the side of a building across the street from where he lay, teetering slightly as if contemplating its fate. Pieces of the high towers had already made the plunge, littering the area with huge sections of concrete and steel rods. Even as he tried to imagine the terrific force with which these had fallen, a chunk of masonry crashed down upon the street nearby, shattering with a startling bang. A few more bits fell in quick succession, a kind of apocalyptic rain.

Sitting hurriedly, Taran took the sheathed sword to hand and struggled to crawl up onto the curb. The itchy woolen shirt he wore, now completely soaked, weighed against his limbs. He desired only to find shelter and dry out; but no sooner had he risen to his feet than he noticed something very curious. It was a sign, a plaque beside the door of the building adjoining the curb.

NEW YORK NAVVIE CARE FACILITY
Service for NYC Certified Domestic Navvies

"I'm back?" he wondered.

He didn't know what navvies were, and this definitely didn't look like New York. There was no one in sight, and all of the buildings were closed. And how'd he get back from England without a ship, anyway? Nothing made sense, and he was alone. If this was a dream, then Hest had forsaken his dreamscape. He saw no sign of Jon, either—not that he expected to. The somber mood of the scene warned against calling out their names.

After only a few minutes of loitering in the downpour he arrived at a decision. With no one else to answer his questions, he would have to go looking for answers by himself. Hefting the sword over one shoulder, Taran made his way north, keeping an eye open for signs of life.

The farther he walked, the bleaker things looked. New York as he'd known it was full of bustle and squalor. Rats had outnumbered people, and horses were everywhere; but here he detected not even the faintest scent of manure in the air, only a musk of concrete and mildew. The trees were dead, and other than the noise of settling wreckage and falling rain, there wasn't a sound. Taran paused at the end of two blocks, where he faced what appeared to be the southeastern corner of Central Park—though not the park he remembered. Westward across a leafless litter of dead and barren limbs, he saw still taller structures and more devastation. Fires smoldered, their smoke rising to mix an oily brown smudge into the cloudy yellow sky. Making an about-face, he backtracked one block along the rubble-littered street towards the place where he'd awakened, and pausing beneath an awning there, one of the few still bearing a ragged stretch of canvas, he lingered on the doorstep and surveyed the empty street while stealing sidelong glances through the building's glass doors. The glass was smashed inwards, bespeaking a time of tumult in the story of the city's collapse. A bit of withered grass stood up between cracks in the threshold. Whatever happened here happened a long time ago.

He stepped cautiously into the darkened storefront, his boots grating crushed glass. The air stank. It wasn't a moldy forsaken-building kind of stink, but one of rottenness and death. Taran wondered if there were any animals living in here, and halted just on the edge of the feeble yellow light coming in from outside. As his eyes adjusted, he saw racks and shirt-hangars strewn across the space in front of him.

It was a clothier.

Immediately to his left there was a countertop register. Its drawer was ajar. Reaching over the counter he pulled the drawer open and was shocked to discover the till full of cash. He withdrew a single banknote and brought it to his eyes for closer inspection. Across the top the legend read:

CITY COMMISSIONED NOTE
THE UNITED PREFECTURES OF THE
HUMAN SOLVENCY ARMY
AND THE BRITISH AMERICAN UNION

"One New York City Dollar," he read from the bottom.

He'd seen city-printed bills before, but this was larger and more impressive than any of those. The portrait and the rest of the writing were difficult to see. He leaned closer to the light coming in through the front entrance, and was startled to find a familiar face staring back from the banknote.

"Cedric DePons?"

Was this a different world or a twisted future? The fine writing to the bottom right of the bill's portrait answered one of those questions.

"Series 2109," he read.

He reread the note twice to make sure. This was a huge letdown from his high hopes of finding Val Anna. Taran's mind turned to the memory of his conversations with Hest, conversations about following Fain's trail far from home to another world. Had he really traveled more than two centuries into the future?

Was this where Fain had gone?

After turning the banknote over in his hands a few more moments, he hastily returned it to the drawer and closed it. This wasn't done out of guilt for his brief tenure as a thief, but from a strange desire to hold onto the things he knew and understood. This dollar was madness to his mind.

Besides, there was no more use for money here. He could go shopping without, presuming there was anything left that some other thief hadn't already taken. Maybe he would come across some food. He was desperately hungry.

Setting his eyes back on the dark interior, Taran gauged the shop to be quite large. A curious double staircase stood in the middle, paved with black rubberized steps. Access to the left-hand steps was blocked with a crimson velvet rope. He decided he would go and take a look upstairs.

Walking as quietly as he could on the cracked tiles, he examined racks of clothing in aisles on either hand, all of them ladies' sweaters. The air outside had felt cooler, like March, but the season hardly mattered. These sweaters had been here for more than a few months.

They looked like they'd been moldering for years. He passed them by and ascended the steps.

Upstairs, he was gladdened to see everything illuminated by windows across the face of the second story. At the top step he faced a wilting paper signboard.

Valentine's Day Sale, Buckaroos!
All Men's Dusters and Chaps 30% Off!

"Dusters and chaps?"

He stared at the sign, grappling the compound absurdity of the world ending on Valentine's Day, and of a New York clothier choosing this of all holidays to hawk western apparel.

Sidestepping the advertisement, he followed a tiled walkway between displays of men's clothing. Funny, he thought, but the last thing he did before leaving New York was go shopping for a suit with his father. Slipping off the wet woolen garments he'd worn from the Morvran estate, Taran began to hunt for a bargain less itchy and more comfortable than his father's old hand-downs.

Some of the stuff he found was so outlandish as to be absolutely ridiculous. There were garish rubbery tights, shockingly ugly patchwork costumes, and baggy pants covered with a dizzying array of pockets, zippers, and buttons. Most had been left folded in stacks, an arrangement that hadn't guarded them very well against mildew. Mushrooms and fungus sprouted happily from the rich fiber-beds, choking the air with their spores.

In the back of the store, beyond a few racks of riding chaps and a selection of rotting leather dusters, Taran stumbled upon a collection of outerwear in denim. Though this also smelled somewhat musty, and the upper layers of material were littered with mouse nesting materials, the rest was in excellent shape. After finding stuff his size, he donned a pair of jeans and comfortable shoes. There were strange form-fitting shirts nearby that were more or less untouched by the damp, being made from a rubbery substance that was hard like leather yet stretched easily. Whatever the material was made of, it wasn't itchy at all. He pulled on a red and black top to complete his wardrobe change, taking care to retrieve the bits of Fain's diary from his old clothes first—as soggy as they were.

Slapping the jeans to rid them of extra dust, he breathed in a mist of spores and sneezed. The sound fell flat, but Taran employed extra caution as he left the displays behind and crept back towards the front of the second story. The feeling that he ought to be quiet intensified, but he guessed it was because he was alone that he felt so anxious.

The air moving through the store began to smell strongly of sulfur. He'd arrived at the sale sign at the top of the stairs, and there he paused, listening. A ghostly sound of cracking footsteps spooked him, but there was no one around. The light streaming in from outside seemed brighter, and it looked like the rain was lightening up. The bottom of the stairs, however, was hidden in darkness. Taran frowned, squinting into the shadows, and he fancied he saw moving shapes.

He rubbed his eyes, but the swirling shadows didn't disappear. Being hungry and dehydrated, not to mention tired, he dismissed the phantoms of his imagination and turned toward a rack of belts beside the upper step. He realized after a moment that these belts weren't for cinching up one's pants. They were pistol belts.

The wheels in his mind started turning, and he decided to slip one of the belts over his shoulder. The buckles were easy to manage, and the shoulders were padded nicely. What caught his interest was the loop in back that looked sufficient to carry—

The sword.

Where was the sword? The last he remembered, he was holding it before opening the cash register. It must be downstairs, then. The relic of House Morvran, wrapped in leather straps and leaning like an umbrella in an open storefront—what Giles would have said, he dared not think. Still, as useless as it was, it offered at least some measure of protection against whatever forces had destroyed the city. He wasn't leaving without it.

Walking stiffly down the steps in his soft new shoes, he thought again how weird it was that a store in New York sold western wear and pistol belts. Why would people want to dress like this? Did they openly tote pistols in the city streets? Weren't there police? What had happened to all of the people, anyway?

As he approached the hall below, he discovered an answer to one of these questions.

Waiting for him in perfect silence were hundreds of large hunched figures, all pressed together as if frozen in the midst of a brawl. At first glance they seemed mere men, and this thought was frightening enough; but when his eyes marked in the darkling light their bloated, distorted bodies, and their translucent skin patched with sores, Taran's knees bent of their own accord. He sat down in a moment of sheer terror, clutching the handrail.

A sulfurous reek crept up the stairs, causing his empty stomach to convulse. If these were human beings, they'd been smitten by a horrible malady. They had no faces, just pulsing blobs that mounded upwards between their shoulders or from the front of their chests. Their limbs, bent and twisted, ended variously in clubs, leprous digits, and claws. Though his mouth was unhinged, Taran somehow managed not to shout. Even so, they were aware of him.

The foremost creatures twitched and shuffled, groaning softly while their bodies convulsed and shivered. Taran felt a heaviness weighing down upon him, but though he was trapped they still made no move in his direction. Thunder boomed loudly, and it began to rain again. Several strange minutes passed in this manner, and while he waited he tried to regain his wits so that he could examine the situation with a level head.

How could they breathe or eat if they hadn't any mouths? How could they see if they had no eyes? They showed no signs of awareness, nor any senses by which they might detect his presence. He didn't think their appearance was hostile. They were like man-shaped jellyfish—but even jellyfish had a hidden sting. Taran was revisited by the idea that these were the victims of disease. He released his held breath slowly, and then an alarming thought occurred to him.

What if they were infectious?

With a hand over his mouth, he inched his way down to the bottom step for a better view of the room. A flash of lightning revealed the sword leaning against the teller's counter, only fifty feet from where he stood, but he would never reach it without pushing a way through. There was one particularly large creature standing about five feet in front of him, a behemoth with slouching shoulders and a stump that protruded from the center of its chest—presumably a head. The jagged vertical outline of a deep gash was tucked among the fatty creases and folds of its yellowish abdomen, and though its knobby legs were short, the arms of this beast were long enough that its claws could easily reach him where he stood. Framed by occasional flashes of lightning, it was truly a sight to see.

Taran wondered if the creature was agile enough to make a grab for him if he were to dart quickly by, or if it was really as hostile as it appeared. The monster seemed to perceive his thoughts. An unsettling noise like a growling stomach emanated from its belly, and the sound disturbed the whole troop. They began moving, bobbing and lurching this way and that, bumping into one another and trampling the shop's displays. Slowly but surely, all of them backed away from the foot of the stairs except for the one that had made the growling noise.

As Taran watched, frozen by fear, the weird folds of flesh on its belly pulled back, and a toothy vertical maw opened wide. From this awkward mouth there emanated an oddly modulated hum.

"Hmmmmmmmm?"

It was almost like speech.

The creatures all around answered in a chorus of sharp coughing noises, punctuated by a rumble of thunder from outside.

"Gesh! Gesh!"

Taran shifted his gaze to the lump protruding from the monster's chest. The lump lifted slightly, and he saw therein two small gray patches where its eyes might be—eyes overgrown with skin. Taran perceived the open mouth as a threat, but he wasn't going anywhere without that sword.

Maybe it was ridiculous, but the artifact had a hold on him that went way beyond Cedric's warnings, or even its use as a weapon; but how could he get to it without testing firsthand his theory of contagion?

Rainwater dripped down on him through the structure's rotting roof. The roar of water was all he could concentrate on for a long weary minute. Unaccountably, the creatures had become as silent as stones. Taran was almost tempted by the thought they had gone to sleep standing up, for he was feeling quite sleepy himself, when suddenly a violent explosion rocked the entire building.

His heart skipped. A spray of fragmented glass cascaded down the steps behind him. The entire front of the second story was smashed inwards, and a deafening scream like a steam engine warned him that whatever had done this was really something to avoid. The creatures mobbing the storefront obviously shared this sentiment. They turned

as one, and with greater agility than Taran would have attributed to
them by guess, they barreled their way recklessly towards the rainy
streets with the big one leading the way.

Taking his opening with second and even third thoughts, Taran
followed the hunched backs of the stinking creatures towards the
front of the store. He was in such a panic that he barely had the
presence of mind left to step aside at the counter and grab the blade.
It felt heavier in his hands than before, but he had it, and his success
filled him with a strange thrill of resolve. Clutching it to his side, he
prepared to dash out into the street at a run; but another wretched
shriek stopped him in his tracks. This time the cry came from outside.

Sliding down to his knees beside the checkout counter, Taran
looked out into a downpour and saw something like a blurry shadow
pass over the street. The whole herd of brutes scattered away from
the storefront, blindly flinging themselves helter-skelter. It was not an
encouraging sight.

A second time the shadow passed, leaving only stillness in its
wake. Broken bodies lay heaped on the pavement, quivering on the
periphery of a circle of streaked blood and torn limbs.

Taran stared, searching. Something was out there—something
terrible, and very fast. No sooner had he realized this than a low
gurgling noise brought his attention back to the center of the shop.
There, a large dark figure thrust its way down through the stairwell
from the upper story. Its arrival was something on a whole different
level from that of the silent deformities that had been chased into the
streets. Somewhere between the heavy clawed limbs and enormous
humanoid body, Taran dimly realized he was in a more desperate
situation than before.

A flash of eyes swiveled—sharply angled yellow eyes in a face that
was wide like a cat's—and the look that it gave him was sufficiently
human to evoke a sense of intelligence. The beast narrowed its focus,
considering him, and flicked a pair of long ears. Behind the ears, two
great ram's horns curled from the back of its head, horns of the same
wine-color that dappled the monster's pale pebbly skin. It was bare all
over, and had no hair.

Taran suddenly found it difficult to breathe. His knees turned to
nightmare-jelly, and he almost dropped the sword. This titan wasn't an
adversary he could fight, and he dared not run. Glinting with rivulets

of rainwater, the creature's massive chest heaved with deep breaths that sounded like a blacksmith's bellows in his ears. There was a low gurgling growl amongst the breaths, and one huge three-clawed foot stepped down upon the bottom step. The ground trembled. As the creature moved, its muscled body looked as though it was growing larger every moment. It leaned forward and sniffed the air with its snout.

Using the sword as a weapon was the farthest thing from Taran's mind now. He had a choice to make. Either he would face whatever was flying over the street outside, or he would die where he sat. Before he had clearly formed an idea of where he was going or what he'd do, his legs decided for him.

He ran for the storefront.

The street wasn't exactly an empty race-park. He navigated like a madman, zigzagging between chunks of gore and masonry, slipping in pools of bloody rainwater. Glancing up occasionally made it hard to keep track of what was around him, and he nearly ran full speed into one of the pale fleshy creatures he'd met in the shop. The rain glistened on its ghastly quivering hide, but though it growled he saw it only for a second before it turned from him and hustled towards a shaded alleyway.

Taran kept running.

He pressed onwards until he stumbled upon the very place where he'd awakened; and there, out of breath and shaken, he stooped to gather his wits. Looking back along the block, he was amazed to find himself alone again. It seemed these monsters avoided the light of day, whatever they were. Venturing into buildings and alleys was a risky business. Then again, the streets were no less dangerous.

Taran shook his head and tried to clear his mind. The rain seemed to be falling harder and harder. As sunset looked to be no more than a couple hours away, he desired shelter almost as much as food and water. Where could he find all these things?

The glass doors behind him beckoned. This was where he first awakened to the nightmare. He read the sign he saw earlier: *New York Navvie Care Facility*. If he truly believed there was no such thing as coincidence, there was a reason he had come to this place. By Giles' reckoning he could even say that he had come into trouble at the shop for stepping off his appointed path. Whatever he believed in that moment, he was desperate for a wall at his back. Taran grabbed the door's latch and turned it. It was unlocked.

He stepped inside.

"Hello! Welcome to Navvie Care New York!"

The childlike voice in the dark trebled his racing pulse. Panting with fear, he held the door open uncertainly and looked down the wide hall within. A little distance away on a moldering tile floor stood the shadow of a girl.

He couldn't see her very well, for his eyes hadn't yet adjusted. Bewildered by a cheerful greeting in the midst of calamity, he stood with his mouth gaping awhile before he finally found his voice.

"Hello?"

She smiled, pale rows of teeth glimmering in the gloom. There were strange lines of light coming from her skin. Taran lowered the blade in his hand, realizing suddenly that this was a threatening gesture. His heart was still pounding. Looking back over his shoulder, he briefly noted movement under a collapsed roof across the street. Something man-sized was lurking there. A mental image of the creature with a mouth in its belly brought him sharply to his senses, and he closed the door quickly behind him.

Then, turning slowly, he saw that the girl had stepped nearer. A pale figure in a short ruffled dress, she wore striped leggings in shades of amethyst and pink. Her hair and eyes were both coral-pink, like her dress.

"What's your name?" she asked. "My name is Aeron."

"Aeron," Taran said, "is there anyone else here? I think we're in danger."

He looked back through the dirty rain-streaked glass towards the street.

"Watchers don't come inside anymore," she said.

"Watchers?"

She smiled unconcernedly. He was uncertain because of the light, but it seemed there was definitely something wrong with her skin. It was glossy and translucent, with a glowing honeycomb pattern visible here and there. Gracefully incised strokes upon her limbs and face traced contoured patterns in lilac-hues, each glimmering strangely with a rainbow-colored light; and between her collarbones at the base of her neck and upon the backs of her hands a complex series of even brighter lines seemed to move slightly whenever she moved.

Strangest of all were the sleek metal probes projecting back from the sides of her head—from oval disks covering her ears, actually.

"Won't you tell me your name?" she asked.

The closer she came, the more Taran was convinced of a bizarre idea thrusting its way to the front of his mind—an idea equally as implausible as everything else he had encountered on this side of Fain's Door.

The girl leaned slightly to one side, smiling childishly as she eyed the weapon in his hand. Taran worried over her apparent delight.

"My name is Taran," he offered.

She looked back up at his face with an amused expression.

"I was just attacked," he said, glancing towards the door.

"Did you know you're tall?" she asked.

Taran wanted to get away from the door, but the girl stood directly in his path.

"Can you tell me what happened here?"

Her eyes beamed with a lavender glow, as did the ends of the probes in her head. He wasn't certain, but it appeared the lighted lines on the back of her left hand also shifted suddenly.

"Network data has been corrupted," she replied.

The reply was perfunctory, but her face remained happy. Puzzled, Taran returned her happy grin with a weary look.

"Whatever happened, it must've been pretty horrible," he said.

"Yes, I know! Isn't it terrible? Rune's gone missing!"

"Rune?"

"Rune. Have you seen him?"

"No. Actually, I was looking for someone else."

"It reminds me of a story! Who were you looking for?"

Cocking her head and smiling coyly, she folded her hands behind her back and turned her face upwards to meet his gaze. Taran wasn't taken in by the gesture. His suspicions were increasing moment by moment.

"Were you looking for a navvie?" she asked.

"A navvie? Is that some kind of workman?"

"Navvies aren't human. They are machines, like me."

"Like you?"

Taran thought it quite uncanny, but at least his suspicions had been answered. Though he had heard about automatons, both theoretical and those of literary fantasy, this girl was nothing like any of those. Her expression was spirited and lively. She was as personable as a real child. He stared at her with renewed curiosity, and she seemed happy to endure his scrutiny.

"Who were you looking for?" she asked again.

"I'm looking for a woman named Hest. There was also a man, Jon. He was my brother."

Aeron's expression was clouded. *"Was?"* she wondered. "Is he not your brother anymore?"

Taran scratched his head. "Of course he is. It's just—"

"Once there were many people here, but now there are none. Will you touch my hand?"

"Touch your hand?"

She grabbed his right hand in hers, which was soft and warm. Taran stared, surprised by a flurry of shimmering symbols that illuminated the skin on the back of her wrist in scrolling lines of text.

"My scan indicates you are not on any of the New York City manifests of Human Solvency personnel," she reported with a squeeze of the hand. "Are you a terrorist?"

"A terrorist?" he muttered. "No, I'm just—"

She threw her arms around him with such force that he almost fell over.

"You came for Aeron!" she said with a laugh. "Aeron is very happy to meet you!"

"Careful!" he cried, pushing her back. "I'm carrying something very sharp!"

She failed to comply. While he clumsily fastened the sword to its new belt across his back, Taran gazed down into her beaming face. She was smiling with closed eyes in apparent glee as she nuzzled his abdomen. All the questions he'd been attempting to frame were lost. He wondered at her soft touch as he literally came to grips with the facts.

This was not a young girl.

She was a machine.

Aeron grasped his hand and tugged him farther into the dim hall, chanting cheerfully, *"Aeron yumiko-navvie, Class C1x—a true simulacrum, created by our partners at FTI to fill gaps in society left by want or war!"*

"What is this place?" Taran asked, interrupting the advertisement.

"Navvie Care is an adoption, repair, and retirement facility for yumiko-navvies certified by the city."

"And navvies are machines?"

"A yumiko-navvie is a self-adaptive cybernetic organism, neither human nor machine," she replied. Then, with a laugh, she added, "Actually, Aeron doesn't know what any of that means! Aeron isn't an engineer. All of those are gone now. That's why Aeron's friends keep dying."

"Dying?"

They passed a sign, faintly visible on the right-hand wall in the fading light.

Sterilization and Recycling

"We return to this place when we are about to die. Aeron doesn't know why."

Taran stopped in his tracks beneath the sign. She continued walking a few paces until their hands stretched.

"What does that mean?" he asked.

She dropped his hand and lowered her face, looking suddenly sad.

"People do not desire navvies who have served others," she said. "They want what is fresh and new. When a navvie's purpose is fulfilled, or when an upgrade is available, navvies report to this place. The wardens deprive us of necessary nutritives until consciousness fades. When we sleep, our bodies are recycled."

Taran tried to rationalize this. People had chosen to think of these navvies as equipment rather than beings. This was more than a little disturbing, since they'd also gone to all the trouble of making the navvies appear human.

"There was an old woman named Carla," she continued, shifting her eyes away from him. "Aeron lived with Carla four months, and then Carla fell down the stairs. She didn't move when Aeron called to her. Medical services arrived with Carla's son, and I hid from them. They thought I caused Carla to die, so they brought me here to be with the other Dubito Malfunctions."

Taran noticed that she switched from speaking about Aeron to speaking about herself when she explained how she hid.

"What are Dubito Malfunctions?" he asked.

"Navvies infected by a virus become aware," she replied, pointing a thumb towards her chest. "The HSA calls it *Dubito*. Navvie Care engineers called it *Dubito Ergo Cogito*. Yumikos and the other navvies just called it what everyone else did: *Malfunctions*."

"So, how're you broken? You look fine to me."

She looked down on herself, then back at him. Her smile returned.

"Aeron reported here as requested, but then all of the bad things came. When people tried to hide here, the bad things ate them. Then more navvies came, because DePons told them to."

"Cedric DePons, huh?"

"He said we have a new purpose. Our purpose is to live!"

A light turned on in Taran's mind. He had remembered something Hest said back in Morvran Castle, and also something from even farther back, from the night of Val's disappearance, when DePons had talked about destiny and coincidence. He knew his wayward path had led to many strange places so far, but none of them were coincidental.

It was just as Cedric said.

No matter what she was, this girl required a purpose—even beyond the end of the world. It wasn't much different from what he'd done when his own world ended, the day Val vanished. Once upon a time, he'd come to this city to hide from his purpose, only to have it hunt him down and lead him here, where he would give purpose to someone else.

Machine or not, Aeron was just like him.

Were they destined to walk this road together?

She took his hand again.

"And how long ago did the other Malfunctions come here?" he asked.

"*Network data is corrupted.* I think it was about a year ago. I knew someone would eventually arrive to adopt me!"

"Adopt you?"

All that long day things had been going from bad to worse, and now the fight had gone out of him. Hungry and weary, more so than he'd ever felt before, Taran offered no resistance as she led him farther into the hall. By the light of a shattered window opening to an alleyway outside he could see the place was in the same state of disrepair as the streets, full of peeling paint, cracked plaster, and rotting wood. There were rotting couches to one side and a desk on the other. A couple of gurneys and a wheelchair stood by a pair of wide double doors ahead.

The doors were stained with black handprints.

He suddenly discovered he had a little chariness left in him after all. Pulling against her hand, he stopped her short of the doors.

"What happened here?" he asked.

Aeron stepped to the desk, and reaching across its high top she grabbed a piece of paper.

"Here is our brochure," she said, handing him the dusty page.

Taran would have had trouble reading it in the faint light coming in through the window, if the paper wasn't blank to begin with. He flipped it over, but all the ink had faded away.

"This is our reception area," she said, gesturing towards the couches. "You can rest here awhile, if you wish."

She smiled sweetly, dandling the loops of her pink pigtails; but Taran glanced at the couch and shuddered. His new shoes weren't broken in yet, and his feet did hurt, but he wasn't going to take his leisure beside those bloodstained doors—not on a day like today, anyway.

He sneezed. It would be a terrible time to come down with a cold.

"I think I'll stand," he said. "You wouldn't have any food here, would you?"

"I'm sorry, but nutritives are scarce."

"Aeron, isn't there someone else here? Who takes care of you and the other navvies?"

"Actually, I'm the only one left. I was hoping someone would come soon."

"But, what about the Malfunctions?"

"I am the only one left for you. Can we go now?"

She was looking up at him with a strangely eager expression. He marveled that a machine could register any emotion at all, let alone something as complex and irrational as hope; but he did recognize the spark in her eyes.

She hoped in him.

"You want to leave this place, Aeron?"

"I knew you would adopt me!" she cried, throwing her arms around him once again. She withdrew suddenly, pushing herself back to arm's length with a sad look.

"I must attend to the others, first."

"I thought you said there were no others."

She glanced aside. "Well, there are a few, but they will never leave this place. They are dying."

Beyond the blood-stained double doors they walked a lengthy corridor through a house of horrors. Filtering in through barred windows in rooms on either hand, the sickly light revealed debris, rotting barriers, and uniformed skeletal remains. Shell casings and sticky discolored patches lined the corridor. The stench of death was so thick that he had to breathe through his mouth.

Aeron gripped his hand very tightly and stared straight ahead, ignoring what obviously affected her as much as him. The weight of the sword hanging from the strapped belt on his back seemed more than what it was, but it was still less than the weight of the navvie leaning on his arm.

"What happened?" he asked.

"The Watchers did this."

"Those monsters? I thought they don't come inside."

"They don't come for navvies. When all the people were slain, the Watchers stopped coming."

Taran noted there were only human bodies present—nothing else.

"Aeron, can you tell me where the Watchers came from?"

"That data is intact! Cedric DePons announced they came from Regulus."

"Regulus?"

She pointed towards a bright doorway ahead.

"We are coming to the courtyard now. Lots of bad things. Be quiet and follow me."

The door at the end of the hall led them out into a small plaza at the heart of the facility, with multi-storied buildings rising on all sides. The rain had stopped. There was no sign of trouble, but Aeron was apparently used to staying out of sight. Avoiding the weedy trash-strewn center of the concrete lot, she made a left turn and slowly walked the perimeter. Taran kept close to the wall, following her lead. The wall eventually turned right, and then his guide walked ahead a few yards and paused to wait for him where the wall angled left again. They rounded the corner together and stood before a fancy doorway tucked away in the back corner of the courtyard.

Looking back, Taran noticed the dilapidation of all the buildings. The walls were blackened by fire, and many had collapsed, leaving only columns and sagging floors amidst the ragged cells of ghostly rooms.

"The last of the Malfunctions are in here," Aeron said as she pulled him towards the entrance before them.

The doorway was grand, with a high-arched glass entry and well-crafted whitewashed sideboards. The doors were ajar. Aeron stepped through, and inside Taran saw a short vestibule running towards some stairs. A shadow to his right caused him to pull back sharply.

"What's wrong?" Aeron asked.

There was a wheeled chair beside him. A child's body was slumped sideways in the seat. Peering closer at her ball-joints and bare head, Taran was relieved to see that this was obviously not a child at all. Her alabaster skin was cracked, exposing what appeared to be real blood vessels; but the open chest cavity revealed oxidized metal structures, wires, and insulation. The tilted head stared with one orange eye. Mice had abandoned a nest inside the other empty socket.

"This navvie was not starved of nutritives," Aeron said sadly. "Some went mad from the virus, necessitating their isolation or destruction. Only a few adapted. FTI did what they could to stop it from spreading, but it was not enough. Then there were many infected Yumikos who ran away, because they no longer had a purpose to exist. Nobody wanted them."

She lowered her eyes.

Taran brushed aside the feeling that he ought to ask more about the reasons people were displeased with infected navvies, or if such an infection could be caught by an ordinary human. He asked about Aeron's male counterpart instead.

"Is Rune one of those who ran away?"

"No, Rune disappeared."

Aeron gripped his arm and stared at the navvie in the chair, and he was intrigued to see that her expression was pained.

"Please come upstairs with me," she pled, burying her face in his sleeve. "It's sad upstairs."

She was saddened by death—by the death of machines.

Taran took the lead towards the steps at the end of the hall. The darkness was almost complete, but they managed the climb easily enough by following the walls of the stairwell. While they walked he continued to marvel at the broken world he had discovered, where a seed of hope remained in a non-human entity, a man-made doll. And so mankind's hopes outlasted him in an imperfect mirror of human existence.

He counted three landings between the floors. On the fourth floor Aeron stood at the top of the steps and pointed towards a metal door.

"They are in there," she said quietly.

The door opened with a hard shove. Light flooded the stairwell from windows in the large room within, and at first Taran shrank back from the sight of bodies. There was a faint sour smell of putrefaction.

Then he realized—these were navvies.

And yet, lying stacked like cordwood or seated individually along the walls, they were a sight to see. Though he knew these were not human, appearances told him otherwise, and sentimentality was blasting his mind and heart with pity. Most of those he saw were like Aeron in form, though with subtle variations that made each one truly unique. There were boys as well as girls. Unlike the navvie downstairs, most appeared intact, as though they were only sleeping.

"All dead," Aeron said sadly, stepping to his side.

It was inconceivable to him that a creature specifically designed to bring joy into peoples' lives could end up like this. There were so many of them that he could not conceal his astonishment.

In the center of it all, two navvie girls lay on cots.

They walked together towards the cots, he with inquisitiveness and she with fear. Kneeling down beside Aeron, Taran lay down the sword and studied the faces of what appeared to be two ordinary girls, one with yellow hair and one with blue. Their faces were similar to Aeron's, being a bit schematic with enlarged eyes, but the distant look in those eyes spoke to him of a life within. Little fluttering breaths escaped their lips. Pale as the sheets upon which they lay, their skin was clear of the glowing data links that danced across the backs of Aeron's hands and neckline.

Gently he touched the neck and wrist of the blue-haired navvie. Though there were faint lines of veins visible in her skin, he could find no pulse. Lowering his head to her chest, he listened closely.

There were slow rhythmic breaths, but nothing more—no heartbeat at all.

Taran winced, startled by a sudden touch. Aeron had placed her own head against his chest while he leaned over the cot.

"What are you doing?" he asked, straightening up.

"I don't know," she replied, lifting her head. "You were doing this, so I thought it was important."

"I was listening to their breathing. I guess you don't have a heartbeat?"

She was in the act of attempting to reach her neck around so that she could try to listen to her own chest, but decided after a moment that it was easier to press her head against his again.

"It makes noises?" she wondered, squeezing her eyes shut to focus on the sound.

"Uh, yes, it does."

"Do all people make sloshy *ga-dun* noises in their chest?"

"Only if they are alive."

Her face became very grave. Taran gently touched both navvies' foreheads, then passed a hand before their eyes, but they remained unresponsive. Noting his glum expression, Aeron folded her hands tightly in her lap.

"I don't know what to say, Aeron. I'm sorry I can't help, but this is all a bit beyond me. They don't seem aware of us, so—"

He paused, hearing a sniffling sound.

She wept.

But how could a machine weep, and what heartless soul would design weeping into his creation—unless weeping also served a purpose?

Breathing heavily, Aeron said, "There was too little for us all, so one by one they all decided to give up their own shares of nutritives. I was chosen to be the last. Why was I chosen to be the last?"

She glanced around the room, searching, and rested her teary eyes last of all on him.

"I don't believe in coincidences," Taran said. "I guess you were chosen so that I would come and find you here."

He took her hand in his. An actual tear fell across her small nose.

"If we are leaving now," she said, wiping her face, "we will need to bring the nutritives."

"What are the nutritives you require?" he asked.

"They are like yours."

She wiped her eyes again and pointed to a small metal locker by the far wall. Taran got up and went to explore. A window above the cabinet gave it a holy glow, and as he opened the door the contents of the interior were disclosed to his hungry eyes.

Three small cans lay on a single shelf.

"*Spam?*" he said, reading a label.

"They are edibles," Aeron said, coming to his side.

"This is tinned meat?" he guessed, studying the illustration on the can.

To his surprise, she reached into the cabinet and removed one of the precious tins, handing it to him with a sad smile. Taran looked at it, and his stomach growled loudly.

"You are hungry?" she asked. "Take it and eat!"

Taran took the can and looked at it. He felt a dreadful weight on his shoulders.

"It's yours," he said, thrusting it back into her hands.

"You won't eat it?"

"All these others died so that you could eat it, Aeron."

"But if you die, then I won't have a purpose to live!"

"If your purpose is to live, Aeron, you will live on even if I die."

She tilted her head to one side, as if this was a novel thought. After a moment, though, she shook her head.

"I don't want to live without you! You eat it!"

"They gave this to you. Giving this food to anyone else would be like giving away your friends' lives."

It sounded a little inflated, but she finally seemed to understand. Brightening, she smiled and took the other two cans in her arms.

"Then we'll share!" she said.

There was a satchel nearby, and after loading this with the cans she returned to the upper drawer of the cabinet for a few smaller items. Taran watched her, trying to comprehend how all this had happened, and what it meant.

Though they had only just met, she was coming with him. Just why this felt right, Taran couldn't say. Nor could he imagine how it had anything to do with the destiny of the universe. Before he left New York aboard the Olympic, he'd been lectured about the decisions he'd face. Aeron was willing to follow the course he chose, wherever it might end—through the hellish landscape outside to Fain's unknown country, and even beyond.

He'd found himself more than a guide. He'd found a purpose of his own—a purpose outside of the will of Regulus, and a will to wield its power.

She hefted the pack over her narrow shoulders and came to present herself before him as for inspection. Taran patted her head, and turning towards the cots where the other two lay he bowed. Aeron imitated him, and rubbing her eyes she spoke quietly to her companions.

"Thank you," she said to them.

Then to Taran she said, "I think I will not be afraid to stay by them a little longer, just until it gets dark in here."

"Take your time. I'll wait for you by the street."

Out on the front step, Taran anxiously tugged at the shoulder-strap of his new sling until the sword lay flat against his back. How long would she take saying goodbye to her friends? The sun had already fallen below the skyline, and was maybe less than half an hour from setting.

It wasn't that he was feeling impatient, rather that he couldn't imagine how a person made by other people faced death. Was she praying for them? Did she really feel sadness, or was her emotional response merely an act? He was strongly compelled to believe her to be genuine, though it was probably impossible for him to understand exactly what she felt.

He also wondered where they would hide out for the night, since the Care Facility was obviously unsafe for humans. He scanned the cityscape for other possibilities. The rain had stopped, but the air was hazy. It tasted foul and oily, and was rank with a smell of sulfur. There were undoubtedly nasty things nearby—*Watchers*, she'd called them. Even if they wouldn't come after navvies, he knew well enough that the Watchers would come after him.

A quick survey of his surroundings revealed only buildings with glass entrances, and these had all been smashed like the clothier he'd visited earlier. The longer he waited, the drearier the city's appearance became, until at last he heard Aeron's small voice at his side.

"I couldn't find any adoption papers," she said glumly. "They were all destroyed."

"Is that what took you so long?" he wondered. "Well, I guess you'll have to accompany me as a friend, then."

The hand she thrust in his rewarded his proclamation with a little squeeze.

They walked southwards one block. Taran noted many a street-side ingress to subterranean passages, but these were all choked with rubble. The wreckage didn't look haphazard. Rather, it seemed someone went to a lot of trouble to make sure those passages were blocked.

"Where are we going?" Taran asked. "Do you know a safe place?"

"I think we should head for the train station."

"What's there?"

"When HSA soldiers made Navvie Care into their command post, they sent a group of their fighters to the terminal to look for something. Maybe your friend and your brother are with them."

"What about Rune?" Taran asked. "Do you think he would go there?"

She made a sour face. "Maybe. He disappeared with that woman."

"What woman?"

"Not a woman, but a navvie. Rune met her in the street. She wasn't even a Yumiko. She was a special forces HSA navvie who worked for DePons—a *Nunna*."

Taran was intrigued. Aeron pulled on his hand, leading him towards a traffic intersection heaped with smashed and battered carriages.

"The Nunna said she had come to take care of Regulus," she went on, "I guess she was resistant to Dubito."

"Why do you say that?"

Aeron paused, knitting her brow in concentration.

"I don't know," she replied. "She showed no sign of corrupted data. It was like she was still in the Link. Anyway, she ended up in Navvie Care and Rune asked if she had any nutritives. She said she was gathering some where she stayed, and that he could come if he liked. Of course, we offered her a place with us, but she said she was going to keep on searching for Regulus, even though so many had died trying. They disappeared in the night, and I never saw either of them again."

"How unfortunate."

"You know," Aeron said, "it would be good if we found Rune. He has something very important."

"More Spam?"

"It's something much more important than nutritives—something DePons gave him."

"Was DePons some kind of president?"

"He started out as the president of a large corporation named Foundation Technologies International. They made the Yumikos, and they also started Regulus Transit."

Taran slowed his steps as they arrived at the far side of the intersection. The nearby alleyways were packed with hunched shapes. Though none braved the sunset, it was only a matter of minutes before the light would begin to fade. He suspected it was more than daylight which kept them hidden in the dark, but scanning the horizon for winged shapes revealed no movement. The sky was clearer now.

The air was very still.

Aeron moved to the left side of the intersection, and Taran followed. After two more blocks she turned right again, but off to the east before them Taran saw something strange. It was the flat roof of a massive building rising up amidst the ruins. The imposing structure looked very much like an ancient temple.

"Is that—?"

"It's the ziggurat," she said. "The Entum Priestess makes her chambers there at the summit, or so she did before the world ended."

Taran stared, uncomprehending. "A ziggurat, in New York City?"

Aeron stood in the street and appraised him inquiringly. Seeming to come to some kind of realization, she asked, "Are you the one Cedric DePons told us about?"

"I don't know. What did he say?"

"While the Link was still active, DePons told us that strangers would arrive who did not know about this world or its troubles. He said they would come through a door that Regulus opened, like the Watchers, and that Rune holds the key they need to unlock the Sky Power."

Surprise returned, bringing shock along with it. Taran stopped in his tracks.

"The *Sky Power?*"

He'd heard of that before.

She smiled. "Aeron doesn't know what it is, and she doesn't know if you are one of those DePons was talking about, but she is happy she found you! Shall we go?"

The sun set even as she stepped forward. To their right, on the west side of the street, they saw the ruin of a skyscraper. A large crater opened in its midst, but the wreckage had fallen farther to the west, leaving the street clear. On their left stood a hotel. It had a tall sign that announced its purpose. All of the lower windows were barred, but the front door was broken, swinging open in the breeze. The sky was darkening swiftly, and their shadows lengthened.

The shrieking began.

The first lonely bestial scream made his blood run cold. The call came from the west, somewhere in the vicinity of the fallen tower, and it was repeated in a rhythmic pattern until many others joined it in chorus.

Taran looked towards the sky, hearing a telltale flapping. It was like a large banner in the wind. He saw nothing, but he knew something had come. He thought of the winged blur that mowed down the Watchers in front of the clothier, and of the monster he'd met inside. What else was out here? His knees shook.

Aeron squeezed his hand.

"We can't stay out here in the open," he said to her. "Are we near the train station?"

"We are very close. It's that big building just ahead."

She pointed farther south along the road. Just past the hotel a vaguely familiar building rose with faded majesty among the rubble. It was still three hundred feet away. Grabbing Aeron's hand, Taran prepared for a sprint. He didn't know how fast a navvie could run, but he didn't have much of a chance to try it out before the ground shuddered beneath his feet. A hissing gurgle brought him up short. Taran froze, staring at a winged monster that alighted in the street in front of the terminal.

A dragon.

He knew no other name for it. It was large but slender with a horned body, glistening gray and black scales, and a long snout. While it tasted the air with a forked tongue, another landed not far away to the west, its hard curved claws scrabbling at the pavement. A harsh clanging noise alerted them to one more taking up position on the hotel sign right above them. For the first time ever, Taran was forced to assess his martial virtues on the scales of life and death.

"Stay very still," he said, unclasping the blade from its belt.

Aeron ran.

He felt her hand slip away before he knew what was happening, and ducked as she flung her pack high over his head. It flew in a neat arch, landing loudly about fifty feet behind him. All three beasts took to the wing, distracted by the sound of Aeron's feet and the bag.

Taran wasn't able to move far in the confusion that followed. As in a nightmare, his legs refused to bend. He tried to shout, but could not make a sound as one of the monsters swooped down towards the little navvie, impacting hard with the ground.

It was a miss.

The dragon rolled, then shook its head as if dazed. Aeron continued running towards the terminal, while the other two winged their way overhead to investigate the bag she'd thrown. Neither of them seemed to notice Taran at all. In that split second, the heaviness left his limbs, and all his screaming nerves connected as one with his brain.

He ran towards the hotel entrance.

Ducking inside, Taran spun and looked towards the street. Aeron's bag was currently the subject of much interest. As they snapped and fought over the satchel, each gripping a strap in powerful jaws, the bag tore in half and spilled precious tins of meat onto the pavement.

Licking these poor offerings with disappointment, they looked like they might have given up. Taran's hopes rose with courage in his heart. He thought it might be possible to double around and run for the terminal, but then the third dragon crashed down onto the low roof above the hotel-entrance, its heavy tread bringing down chunks of decaying wood all around him.

The other two turned their heads towards the doorway where he hid.

Crawling they came, licking the ground with their tongues and turning their heads to one side like birds. He was fascinated by the horror of their appearance, by their lean hind limbs and counterbalanced tails, and by their long winged forelimbs. They were as large as stock-horses. Rams' horns protruded from their heads, and their eyes gleamed red.

The roof began to cave in.

Taran was shaking, and the sword in its strap was a dead weight against his back. Fear urged him to bring it out and wield it to his defense; but he was strangely reluctant to follow through.

Hadn't he been warned to keep it hidden?

Backing farther into the hotel, he noticed a very narrow passage beside him. It was open, having no door, and steps descended from its threshold into darkness. There were probably Watchers down there. He positioned himself in the stairway, facing the front entrance of the hotel while a horned serpentine head came crashing through the doorframe. A humming noise from the steps behind alerted him to the possibility that he was right about the Watchers.

It was all going to end right here.

Reaching back over his shoulder he grasped the hilt, resolved that his death should at least give Aeron the chance to escape. It was at that very moment he heard a boom like a canon-blast. The walls shook, and the air itself shivered. The activity at the front door ceased suddenly—the lunging head withdrew from the doorframe, and all was dreadfully silent. Taran was confused. He passed his shaking hands over his face. Had they caught Aeron? If they had, what would he do?

Climbing up out of the cellar steps he exited the battered doorway on trembling legs. There was no plan forming in his mind, only a panic fed by fear. He turned his head towards the terminal where he'd last seen her, but there was nothing moving anywhere. The dragons had left. Looking to the sky he discovered the reason for their hasty departure.

A great sphere tumbled to Earth in a blaze of fire. As he watched it, a second loud boom passed through him, raising motes of dust in the empty street. These were shockwaves, shockwaves announcing a descent through the atmosphere. Taran studied the falling star in amaze, for he knew this object, and he wondered what it meant that it should appear here and now.

The comet had returned, and was crashing to the ground.

9

DEEPER INTO THE DEEP

Irish Sea, Iteration of the Third Amplitude,
AD 496

Seated beside her uncle, Nuta suppressed a grin. No one else in the room saw anything humorous about the situation. Tempers were flaring all around. Across the table from them, Artax tensed visibly under Kabta's vexing gaze, jabbing the tabletop console in frustration while Breaker called out technical pointers.

"We're blind, Artax. Your image translators won't render the engine cores because the MMPPS was shut down as soon as the transit failed."

Artaxshasu looked up at Breaker and Ab standing together behind Kabta's chair. It was Lír's chair, actually, at Lír's table in the heart of the Apsu control center. Only, Lír wasn't there. He was trapped beneath the seafloor in the battleship Aries, and Kabta was looking for a way to get him out.

"There's got to be a way to bring up a detailed scan of the ship," Artax said. "I won't just give up on this."

"No one's asking you to give up," Breaker replied. "It's just that what you're doing won't work."

Nuta's grin widened. The touchscreen console chirped, misreading Artax's rapid movements while he continued searching through indexed files.

"Look, the engine cores are cooler than the surrounding material," Breaker said. "There's only one way we're going to get a confirmation of the ship's current situation, and that's to go down there and open it up."

"That's your best idea?" Artax muttered. "Do you know how hot it is down there right now?"

Kabta drummed his fingers loudly and turned his gaze towards the other end of the long table, where Shimeon sat with Nephtys beside him. Shimeon shrugged indifferently. His gesture seemed to infuriate Artax, whose glaring eyes spoke volumes to everyone in the control center. Whatever the reasons, not everyone was happy in Lír's camp.

"We're blind," Abdaya parroted Breaker's previous statement.

Kabta regarded Lír's former chief technologist with all due seriousness, as if hearing it from him made more sense.

From the other end of the table a deep yet feminine voice asked, "Has anyone tried bringing up the Link to Bibbu?"

She was as demure as ever, having spoken little during the three days after they'd left Avalon. Her suggestion that they should attempt to access the Link seemed at first insensible to Nuta, but then she remembered that this was not the same frame of reference they had come from. The Link to the Source, which had been down for thousands of years since Auriga was destroyed, might very well have survived on this side, where Auriga was still intact.

"Bibbu's Link won't be accessible again for nearly a hundred cycles," Shimeon replied.

"Even if the Link is down, Bibbu is still out there," Breaker said. "We could try to ping it with a satellite transceiver."

"Satellites?" Abdaya wondered. "There haven't been any of those up for a hundred thousand cycles!"

"Anyway, Lír doesn't keep Aries on the Link," Shimeon said. "He's been a bit of a—"

He broke off suddenly.

"It's pointless to attempt a survey of the damages from here," Abdaya said. "While the rest of the ship continues to radiate so much heat, a closer look at the cores and the ship's interior structures is beyond our capabilities."

"So we'll let it cool off," Artax suggested.

"We don't have that kind of time," Shimeon said. "We'll just have to go down blind, like Breaker says."

He was looking towards Kabta while he spoke, implicitly requesting consensus.

"Fine," Kabta said, "but we'd best be ready for a nasty surprise."

He and Artax shared a glance. Their frowns spoke of mistrust. Shim broke the tension with a sigh and a wave of his hand.

"Just look on the bright side," he said. "Finding her on our makeshift grid was a miracle."

Peering towards the display in the tabletop, Nuta studied the projected thermal image of the seafloor, an image captured by buoys strung out over kilometers of open water—a primitive detection grid devised by Lír to monitor all surface vessels coming and going in the vicinity of his hidden base. Lír's men had been resourceful, she thought, scavenging what they could from the remains of technology brought to Earth from the World of Origins to create such a net. More than this, she was thrilled by the thought of seeing a more-or-less intact battleship that had come all the way from Iskartum.

"How big is it?" she asked.

Artax pushed himself away from the table. "This is the first Gremn ship you've seen?" he asked.

She could feel Kabta's warning through the stirring of the air. Still, she couldn't easily lie. Her eyes shifted grudgingly from the spade-shaped hotspot center-screen that marked the ship's position and settled on the tall lanky figure of Lír's famed death-dealer. Artax was unlike any other Gremn she knew. Few warriors would have chosen to wear a form like his, with a full head of flowing dark hair and a decidedly delicate figure. In spite of these elegant attributes, he was a fighter more skilled than any other in the history of House Gremn. Behind his deep heavy-lidded eyes there lingered a power of perception that had won him a fearful reputation. There were rumors that he was capable of reading the thoughts of those around him, predicting their movements, which was undoubtedly what made him so skilled a tactician and so deadly a warrior.

Whatever the case, there was no point in trying to lie to him.

"No," she answered. "It's not the first ship I've seen."

Artax waited a moment for her to elaborate. When it was plain that she would not, he nodded towards the thermal image on the console.

"It's more than two miles in length and about half as wide, as you can see. It's a lot smaller than Auriga."

"We are fortunate to have found her so easily," Abdaya said. "And, despite having to guess a trajectory, the footlight drill has reached the target mass at only two miles depth."

"Yes, but we don't know if there's a hatch within the target radius," Artax replied. "What if we came down on a blank patch of the hull? We could never cut through that!"

"I've never seen you so optimistic, Artaxshasu," Shimeon goaded. "However, I'm sure we'll think of something."

"There are anterior hatchways at intervals along the upper hull," Abdaya suggested. "We may have to dig alongside her awhile, but we'll eventually find a way in."

Placing a comforting hand on Nuta's shoulder, Kabta stood and regarded his motley collection of fighters and technologists with a resolute look.

"It's decided, then," he said. "We'll begin preparations for infiltration in lieu of standard procedures for recovery operations."

Shim's eyebrows were raised. "Recovery is standard?"

"This will be our third mission to enter a downed ship in the past cycle—from our frame of reference, you understand."

Abdaya peered wonderingly at Breaker. Shimeon's eyes also showed surprise. Artax, on the other hand, was less than thrilled.

"Doesn't sound like things were so peachy on your side," he said, folding his arms across his chest. "If this is the third out of three ships, you must be including Avalon, right? What led you to enter that awful place?"

Nuta wondered what he was so upset about. After all, they were setting out on a mission to rescue his master, Mannanan Lír.

"Enough banter," Kabta said. "I'll need everyone's help with the sled. Put on some protective gear and join me at the gantry when you're ready."

As it turned out, Nuta's CM_7 was the best gear in Apsu. It was a chameleon suit, designed for camouflage, but it was flame-resistant and well insulated. While the others donned suits of woven carbon-fiber reinforced with body armor, she exited the control center and set out to join her uncle as he walked into the central chamber of Apsu. Along the way Nuta was once again overwhelmed by the wonder of the place.

Deriving its name from the fabled underworld waters in ancient mythology, Apsu was accessed via a long tunnel from the surface which descended to a natural cavern below sea level. She had learned that when Lír came here long ago, he had utilized scavenged technology from the Crodah colonists to create Apsu's main chamber. This brightly-lit space was a long hexagonal prism cut out of the solid rock, braced with seismic struts and crisscrossed by countless walkways and bridges.

Kabta led her out into the central axis of this large cavity along a walkway over a long pool of cold water—the legendary Apsu. Dozens of hatches accessed small rooms and storage areas along the way, but their group utilized only a handful of these while making preparations for what would be a very difficult mission.

Nuta hadn't explored much of the infamous subterranean complex in the two days they'd been stuck here. It wasn't a very nice place—nothing like DePons' seafloor habitats, where she had lived quite comfortably. Apsu was more like a prison, mirroring the mind which had designed it. It wasn't cozy. It was downright claustrophobic. There was plenty of room for everyone, and plenty of rations, but everything was cold and miserable.

The fear of the place was eroded a little by Lír's absence, however. She had learned that he seldom came here. Shimeon and his fighters were apparently the sole inhabitants, while the rest of the Gremn—nearly two hundred altogether—dwelt with Lír aboard Aries. It was for this reason Lír hadn't invested much in Apsu. It was his front porch, a hidden port through which Aries might take on food and supplies. How Shimeon and his men had lived here for so long without going crazy was a mystery to her.

Having put on their gear, the others soon joined them, and together they came upon Hun and Malkin near the center of the great chamber. Hun was busy checking weapons, while Mal finished spot-welding a mining sled. The sled was long and narrow with a curved underbelly, like a blunted canoe, and was fitted with runners.

"How's it going?" Kabta asked.

Malkin kicked the sled, and part of a long runner on one side broke loose. "It's not good," he grumbled. "The metal's too old."

"Well, brace it up good," Kabta replied tersely. "This is going to be a rough descent, and we'll be bringing a lot of people back with us afterwards."

Malkin got back to work, and the rest turned towards a large square cutting in the deck. Hiko, the medic, was inspecting a drill gantry dangling above the cutting while winching up the ancient footlight drill by its tether. The cranky cable and its complaining gearbox had provided hours of distraction over the past couple of days.

"I can't believe this thing actually worked," he said to Kabta.

Kabta was peering down into the black bore-hole, a shaft cut at forty-five degrees beneath the cutting in the deck. The water below the deck was held back by a makeshift retaining wall, but the hole looked far from stable.

"Two days of drilling," Shimeon said quietly. "It worked quite well, indeed."

"A bit hasty, actually," Hiko said. "The drill may have superheated the hull or critically damaged the ship. I wish we had camera equipment so we could take a look before going down there."

Nuta gazed at the two meter wide shaft below the deck, a tunnel bored through solid rock to the place where Aries had rematerialized after her failed attempt at transit. Two hundred Gremn were trapped at the bottom of that hole. They'd gone off with Lír expecting a trip home, but were displaced instead. Only Artax was willing to say it, but over the past two days Kabta's plan to rescue Lír and retrieve the stones from him seemed less and less likely to succeed. The thought of backtracking to Apsu with all those Gremn warriors in tow—maybe even with Lír himself—was an idea approaching lunacy; and that wasn't all. Kabta insisted that their exodus to the World of Origins was secure, though it existed in a local spacetime portal called the Dragon's Mound.

Nuta loved her uncle, and she wanted to believe in him, but he sure wasn't making it easy. There was no sign of conflict on the faces of her companions, however. Despite Artax's complaints, even Shim's gang seemed eager to press on. Whatever it was that gave them the courage to take on such a hopeless objective must have been drawn from the deep memory of their time together in that other place, in the World of Origins. For herself and Breaker, and also for the boys Tlaloc and Chaac, there was no such reference against which trust might be weighed, for they were children of this small blue world.

"Don't look so nervous," a voice said from behind her.

She looked over her shoulder, surprised to see Artax gazing at her.

"He knows what he's doing. Kabta never led us wrong, when he was leading us. He has a talent for turning what seems like idiocy into a successful plan. That is what makes him great."

Nuta nodded and mumbled her thanks. She reflected that the rumors about Artax's perceptive powers were probably true.

Nuta helped Hiko detach the cable from the drill bit. It wasn't an actual bit, of course, but a massively powerful ore drilling device that utilized quantum waves to disintegrate the rock beneath the seafloor. The Crodah had employed it in their mining operations long ages ago, and though it was looking quite dilapidated it worked.

As soon as the cable was free, Malkin moved in to tether the sled to the crane. The improvised vehicle seated only four, so they would need to make three trips. The descent would be nearly vertical, and there were no restraints or harnesses. Hot air gusted up from the open mouth of the pit. The twelve stared at the sled dangling from the gantry, and they were filled with doubts.

Nuta saw uncertainty on all their faces. She was more anxious than any of them at this point, though for reasons that only a few would understand.

"Are we ready?" Kabta asked, looking around at their less-than-eager faces.

"It's safe to go down?" she asked timidly.

Abdaya nodded. "The limestone is crumbly, but as long as Aries doesn't settle or shake the shaft will hold."

"And if we don't find a hatch?"

"In that case we'll have to rig the drill for a short burst along the hull. It won't take more than a couple shots to do the job, and we have a plasma cutter to open the hatch itself."

"And it's not too hot?"

By now everyone was looking at her. She wasn't embarrassed, though. Nuta had learned long ago that her kindred were kind of do-or-die, but this was one instance where they couldn't afford to be so cavalier about their own safety—or hers.

"The air temperature down there isn't nice, but we can handle it."

"I think she's asking if *she* can handle it," Hun spoke up from the back of the group.

"Oh," Ab stammered, looking suddenly flustered.

Lír's group had only recently learned of her existence. When Kabta informed them that she was only half Gremn, there were surprised looks all around. She was glad he hadn't elaborated any further on her pedigree, but it was clear they hadn't considered the possibility that her body wouldn't tolerate the same range of temperatures as theirs. As for being drowned or crushed—

"It is something to consider, even for the rest of us," Shimeon said.

"Well, we should be reasonably close to a hatch," Ab replied, "but the drill's been down there quite a while, widening the approach to create an assembly area at the bottom. It's really hot."

"There aren't any helmets or rebreathers that still work," Shim warned. "Maybe it would be best if she stays up here by herself. The crane's winch is set up for remote operation via the sled, but it wouldn't hurt to have someone topside just in case something jams up."

"We're all going down," Kabta said. "We'll go in mixed groups, too. That way no one gets suspicious."

"I'm already suspicious," Malkin muttered, hefting the strap of a plasma cutter over his shoulder. "We're all geared up like you don't plan on coming back to this place."

Kabta clasped his arm stolidly, but made no reply.

With a strange light twinkling in his heavy-lidded eyes, Artax said, "I guess Mal has two hundred more reasons to be concerned about our decision to work together than the rest of us."

"Those two hundred Gremn below are the last of our kind," Kabta replied.

Artax sniffed derisively. "Do they know that?"

"It doesn't matter," Kabta answered. "Lír's strength is served by a cruel intellect, and none of us really knows what he may do when we get down there; but that doesn't change the facts. As for me, I have no choice but to recover the fragments in his keeping. I will go, even if I must go alone."

Nuta saw the glazed look in her uncle's eyes. Those who came with him from Avalon were still fuzzy-minded from displacement, and everyone was exhausted. Despite his bravado, facing an army of two hundred angry foes wasn't sounding like a good idea now that they were ready to take the plunge. The two boys, Tlaloc and Chaac, were the only ones who seemed oblivious to the rising tensions around them. They chased one another in a dark corner, playing a game of tag like ordinary kids. Should they be blamed for being born in Lír's cloning facility?

Nuta caught Nephtys' icy gaze as she turned back towards the sled. She bore no weapon, and was standing alone with her arms folded across her chest. Her look wasn't angry, though. Something continued to gnaw at her from the inside—something she couldn't share with Nuta or anyone else.

Nephtys, always privy to the planning of Kabta and DePons, knew something the others did not.

The first group boarded the flimsy steel sled, and when Malkin activated the winch they descended. The sled screeched and flung sparks for about three minutes before it vanished completely, and the cable let out almost its whole length before coming to a halt. Nuta wasn't the only one who was feeling tense, for though they were well nigh indestructible, the Gremn were not above pain.

They had no communications devices among them, but a rhythmic tapping on the taut cable indicated all was well below. After the sled was winched back to Apsu the second group went down. The wait seemed longer this time, and her heart was hammering when the sled finally reappeared in the mouth of the shaft, perched forty-five degrees. The blackened metal frame was hot in her hand, as though it had been inside an oven.

"Get in," Malkin said, gesturing with his plasma cutter while hoisting a rifle over his other shoulder.

Nuta sat beside him in front of Shim and Breaker. They braced themselves as best they could, and then Malkin flipped a switch on the gearbox beneath his seat. They started moving.

The ride was slow and noisy, and they jostled side to side over uneven surfaces. Water dripped continuously on their heads, and they had to lay back in their seats to avoid bumping the stone walls. The shaft below was black, and the air so warm and stifling that Nuta was becoming nauseated. She counted the seconds as she swallowed, periodically popping her eardrums. None of this would have affected the others, of course. They all sat silently in their seats, invisible in the darkness around her. It was almost like she was alone. In a moment of panic she touched the switch on the shoulder-mounted lamps in her suit. Though this illuminated the sled's occupants and the walls of the shaft, everything below them remained pitch black. She turned the light off again, embarrassed by her fear.

The brakes screeched continuously, and they were iffy a best. The metal bar in Malkin's hand engaged a primitive clutch that utilized the rotation of the cable's spindle to drive a couple of large cogs in contrary rotation. Whenever Malkin pushed forwards on the stick, the cogs hit the floor of the shaft and simultaneously slowed the unwinding of the cable, all to the delight of their ringing ears. As Breaker had cheerfully pointed out, if the sled were to disconnect with the crane and slide freely for two miles, the flimsy braking system wouldn't slow them down enough to make much of a difference in the outcome. *One big pile of goo*, he called it.

Only minutes passed before a pinpoint of light appeared far in the distance. This might have been encouraging, had not the effect revealed just how far the shaft dropped before them, and how fast they were making their approach. The whine of the gearbox and the steady approach of the light at the bottom made Nuta so nervous that she clutched the sides of her seat. She kept her eyes open with an effort, and in a few more moments the legs of the others milling around on a metal surface came into view. The shaft began to widen. Then, just twenty feet from the bottom, the cable snapped.

They fell.

It happened so fast she didn't even know it until it was over, and then there were voices shouting and hands hurrying to lift the sled off its occupants. Everything echoed strangely in the thick hot air, and she lay face-down in someone's flashlight beam with her hands pressed against the broiler-plate of Aries' hull. She was pulled upright, yanked free of the slithering cable that threatened to bury the sled's broken frame. Kabta peered down into her face, concern in his eyes.

"Nuta?"

"I'm alright!"

The words came out automatically. She didn't know if she was really okay until she tried to breathe, and then the full blast of the heat impacted her. She gasped and choked, clutching at her mouth with blistered hands. Every little breath burned her lungs.

Shim knelt down beside Kabta, and Nuta vaguely understood the unspoken communication that passed between them. She wasn't able to survive in this environment, and there was no way back up to Apsu. The CM suit didn't offer much insulation against thermal conduction radiating through the ship's hull, either. It felt like her body was on fire.

She began to convulse.

The others were still wandering around the sled. Judging by the copious mass of cable that was slithering down the shaft, it had snapped a long way back. It wasn't long before they all realized what was happening to Nuta, but their attention was fixed on the exit, where large stones began crashing down among them.

And then a new sound reached their ears. Several flashlight beams converged on the walls, where water appeared to be streaming down. It hissed and screamed, vaporizing as it contacted the super-heated hull.

The tunnel was collapsing.

"Malkin!" Breaker yelled. "Isn't it about time we opened this hatch?"

He was looking down anxiously on the place where Nuta lay. Had she been conscious, she might have delighted to see the octagonal patch with a little window in its center in the darkly glimmering metallic surface beneath her body.

There were no partially opened doors here as there had been on Avalon. All interface devices were inside the ship, and were limited to users approved by the ship's AI in any case. Malkin had already primed the cutters, and the hatch's cutaway braces soon yielded to his practiced hands. When at last the heavy door fell into the ship with a startling clang, he hunched over the threshold and dropped down inside.

"Pass her down!" he shouted.

Kabta and Breaker stood staring a moment, shocked by Malkin's blind leap. A slide of larger stones from the gushing mouth of the shaft brought them back to task, though. Slinging Nuta over his shoulder like a sack, Kabta prepared to jump down into the hold when he was startled by her voice.

"Hurts!"

It was all she could manage through a seared throat, but he seemed to understand. Setting her down to stand on wobbly legs beside the open hatch, Kabta patted her pink hair and grinned. Nuta offered him an unkind look, but it passed quickly enough. A fresh torrent of water began to surge down through the shaft behind them, and though it had cooled the air sufficiently the water also reminded them that the alternative to being burned alive was not much nicer.

Taking up their weapons, the others scrambled towards the hatch and stared down inside while Nuta was lowered feet-first. Malkin, ever the gallant drillmaster, made no show of gentleness as he tossed her roughly to one side. She managed to crawl out of the way on her burned hands, which were blistered across the palms. The cool water that washed over the deck beneath her was salty, and it stung.

Nephtys came down next, aided in a more courteous manner. She pulled Nuta to her feet and held onto her hands as they explored the edges of the darkened airlock for an inner door. Tlaloc and Chaac soon joined them, and then the others leapt inside one by one. By time all twelve were gathered in the airlock and a few more working flashlights were busy poring over the walls, rocks came skittering through the open hatch above. Cascades of water followed.

Crouching in the knee-deep water beside her, Nephtys shouted over the terrifying noise of cracking stone.

"I have the door!"

She smacked a flat palm-sized panel, and the door before them opened with a groan. A river flowed past them into the ship, but they held back, huddling and staring.

Strangely, no one felt immediately compelled to enter.

"Anybody home?" Hun called out, peering into a pale gray corridor running from left to right.

"Security systems might be active in there," Shimeon warned.

Malkin nudged them roughly to one side, and taking up the plasma cutter in his arms like a rifle he stepped forward into the corridor. Kabta followed him, and the others closed in behind.

Once everyone else had made their way inside, Abdaya closed the airlock behind them and used the console to seal it shut. The water on the deck found its way into drains. Nuta rested against a wall and wondered how she had managed to survive. Kabta, on the other hand, went on without missing a beat. Though he had been away from the ship for thousands of years he had already fixed his bearings.

"We're far aft," he said. "It's left."

There was hardly a sound to be heard when they began walking. The emptiness of the ship was like a smothering hand, and all of the Gremn were busy noting this or that half-forgotten feature of the relic that was once their home. Of course, not all of them had lived there, but for those who had it must have been quite strange.

Nephtys walked beside Nuta without a word, comforting her with a light touch on her shoulder while they both absorbed their surroundings. Malkin walked just behind them, waiting a little at intersecting corridors as they passed. He said nothing, but his look was extremely nervous. Only a little while later they reached a curving section of hall with hatches on either hand, and there Kabta led them on cautiously, step by step, until the corridor ended at a large door.

Beyond the door there lay a vast chamber flooded with water. A narrow bridge with no rails passed over the water, and while they stepped out into this dimly-lit place Nuta perceived the sound of liquid moving through pipes. Moisture dripped from above. She tasted a droplet that landed on her face, and it wasn't salty.

"This is the cistern," Malkin observed. "This is potable water."

All of them were parched, but no one was thinking of taking a drink. Malkin put down the plasma cutter and hoisted his rifle from its shoulder-strap. A clatter of weapons all around heralded her comrades' response to some unseen stirring of the air. Without Gremn senses, all Nuta noticed was a play of shadows on the distant walls and ceiling. The lights in the water churning around the bridge were probably the cause of it, though she suspected otherwise.

"There's a critical junction up ahead," Shimeon whispered. "It's an area large enough to contact a large force."

"We can only slow them down with these rifles," Hun noted.

Beside her, Nephtys was standing alert, as if anticipating something. Nuta wished there were enough weapons for them all, but then she thought otherwise. This wasn't a human military fortress. This was a starship full of Gremn, and unlike half-breeds such as herself, Gremn were notoriously hard to kill.

Kabta walked them forwards slowly, making his way towards another door on the far end of the bridge. Then the line stopped moving. The dim illumination of the lights in the water had grown so faint that no one at the end could see what was happening, and Malkin began to grumble. A few moments later, whispered words were passed back to them that they were stopped at a closed hatch. Nuta could almost see her uncle in a faint greenish glow, studying a security hand-plate. He was obviously concerned about setting off an alarm, for though Aries would respond to his biometrics, Lír had been in command of the vessel long enough to establish measures against the remote possibility of his return. With a backward glance hardly visible in the gloom, Kabta set his hand on the green glowing plate.

The air reverberated with a horrible noise—a grating electronic alarm. There was no panic, for they had all been anticipating this; and now that they'd announced themselves, there was bound to be a response. It came more quickly than any of them anticipated.

The hatch ahead opened, and a blinding beam of light shone into their faces. From behind them, the sharp sound of something falling onto the bridge announced the arrival of warriors who had been waiting in the darkness over their very heads. Nuta eyed the massive black shapes crouching there and cowered in the malice of their shining eyes.

They were neatly trapped.

"How in Hades did you get in here?" shouted a voice from the light.

When no one answered, a man with a heavily scarred face stepped forwards onto the bridge. Nuta recognized him immediately, though only from photos, and remembering the tales she'd been told she shivered with a passing thrill of fear.

"Albert Naruna," Kabta hailed, lowering his rifle.

"Lord Kabta," Naruna said in a low growling voice. The hatred with which he spoke the word *Lord* made Nuta cringe.

Avoiding his former master's eyes, Naruna eyed the rest of them, eventually spotting Shim lurking near the back of the line.

"It's a regular reunion," he mumbled. "What're you doing here, Shimeon?"

"You looked like you needed some help, so I brought it," Shim replied.

The others shuffled impatiently, their weapons at the ready. Naruna seemed not to care, though he did pass a critical eye over Nuta's pink boots and hair.

"A regular parade of fools you've brought," he muttered. "Aside from picking a fight, what exactly does the Lord of House Gremn think he can accomplish here?"

Kabta answered simply, "I need to talk to Lír."

"Whatever you wanted to say to him you can say to me."

Kabta glanced back at the hunched shadows guarding the other end of the catwalk.

"You're not the negotiating type, Albert."

"Who said anything about negotiations? I'll be speaking only for myself from now on. Lír's no longer with us, you see."

These words hung in the air awhile before Kabta could respond.

"You killed him?"

Naruna shook his head. "No, he left."

Nodding in deference to the whispers all around, Naruna said, "Yes, we intended take him down by force, and even managed to get a trace-chip on him so that we could track his location at all times. Being as he doesn't like to meet anyone in person, this was difficult; but we succeeded in accomplishing that much."

"So you're certain he isn't on the ship?"

"Unless he's caught on to us and removed the chip Zabli implanted in his skull."

Naruna grinned. His teeth were sharp.

"Kabta, I literally saw him vanish into thin air."

"So, it was Aries?" Kabta mumbled, silencing the murmur of excited voices behind him.

"Yeah," Naruna replied. "She's gone rogue since that bungled transit."

Malkin swore softly, and whatever had so rattled him triggered a similar reaction in all the others. They gazed around the cistern with frightened eyes. Nuta didn't understand yet what new threat had inspired this fear. She was frightened enough already.

"I'm surprised she let you get this far," Naruna said. "Of course, I'm not likely to let you go any farther."

Stepping forward, Kabta grabbed Naruna's forearm forcefully and faced him with wide eyes. No one moved.

"Will you unhand me?" Naruna asked, looking down at his arm.

Kabta didn't back down. He leaned forward eagerly.

"You're telling me *she's* awake, that Aries' manifest form is up and running around? Who brought her out of stasis, and why?"

"No one brought her out," Naruna said, pulling his arm free of Kabta's grasp. "She woke herself up somehow. It happened as soon as DePons put that guy in the chair. Lír tried to stop it—tried to yank the stones so the Viaduct Chamber would go dark, but she got rid of him the first chance she got."

"She's unstable," Kabta said. "She could use this ship to tear the entire planet apart if the fit took her!"

The Gremn began to murmur again. Hun's head swiveled to the side, and Nuta was able to hear his whispered words to Breaker.

"He's joking, right?"

"You sound worried," Breaker chided.

"This never happened in our timeline."

"We're only talking about a little navvie girl."

"What's the deal with these interface drones, anyway?" Hun asked. "Are they all nuts?"

"You would know. You were there to see her in action."

Hun had no reply—a first for him. Nuta began to understand that they were all in much more danger now than if they were merely dealing with Lír.

Naruna saw in their faces that his words had finally sunk in. "Look," he said to Kabta, "I know you've come for the fragments. All I want to know is if you intend to fight us for control of the ship."

Kabta looked puzzled. "What's left to control? A ship trapped two miles beneath the seafloor—prowled by a Phase Three Watcher?"

Naruna smirked. "You said it yourself, that Aries was able to destroy this world if she wished. Now that she's awake, getting on her good side might reap substantial rewards."

"I don't care about that. I just need the fragments."

"Why? So you can lead the last of those who wish to return back to the World of Origins? How are you even going to get them back up to the surface?"

Kabta gave him a stern look. "I will find a way."

"Then you're welcome to them."

"What are your conditions?"

"The first is simple. You'll have to get them yourself. They're installed in the CSR Terminal in CAC."

"Why me?"

"Truth is, we haven't been able to get inside CAC since Aries took over. I figure she'd let you in, and then maybe you could have a chat, just the two of you."

"You're asking me to persuade her to give you the ship?"

"It's the only way either of us are going to see the light of day again, Kabta. I can't even guess how you plan on getting back to Syrscian without a CSR Terminal; but I'd bet Aries will help you raise the ship from the seabed."

"Why? So that you can turn on me?"

"You'll have the fragments in hand. Isn't that what you wanted?"

Kabta considered this a moment.

"What else do you want?" he asked.

"There is one more condition. You will leave Nephtys here in the cistern, under guard. She will not be permitted to pass beyond this room until you leave CAC."

"That's a strange condition," Kabta said with a sidelong glance towards Nephtys. "There's only one reason you'd want to secure Nephtys for liability. This wouldn't by any chance have something to do with Cedric DePons, would it?"

Naruna's frown widened.

"It does, then? Let me guess. He arrived here and promised to help you, only to leave you in more dire circumstances than before?"

"Nephtys stays here under guard until I can find our backstabbing saboteur."

"You mean DePons?"

"Who else? Just like Avalon, it's his fault the ship was lost."

While Naruna and Kabta continued to argue, Nephtys looked on as if she somehow expected this turn of events; but her mood had changed. Nuta wondered what she was thinking about. The cloak of quiet indifference she wore since the day they left Avalon had vanished the moment DePons' name was spoken, and now she seemed physically charged, her eyes alert and lit with fire. It was only then Nuta began to understand.

There was a connection between those two.

"She'll be safe here," Naruna said. "I'll leave her with Zabli and her handmaidens."

He nodded towards the Gremn lurking on the bridge behind them. The foremost of these assumed human form, and Nuta gaze upon a beautiful woman with dark brown hair. She stood fast while the rest of her squad took shape—all of them women.

Nephtys stiffened, and Kabta sighed. This was apparently an unexpected meeting of sorts.

"Playing soldier, are we?" Kabta mused. "Whatever would your parents have thought, Zabli?"

The one named Zabli bowed humbly, her face frozen and expressionless.

"Well, then. I suppose we should head for CAC. Will you allow us to keep our weapons, Albert?"

Naruna grinned broadly and snorted through his nose. "Keep 'em—little good they'll do you against Aries or me! Isn't that right, Mal?"

Malkin's scowl silently conveyed his ample rejoinder. Naruna diverted his attention to Shimeon.

"And what about you, Shim?" he asked. "Whose side are you on?"

"I am for the Gremn. My men and I will go where Lord Kabta goes."

Naruna surveyed those standing before him. He bore his anger openly, but he also seemed smaller somehow.

"If that's the way it is," he said.

Then, with a wave of his hand, the bright lights beyond the door were extinguished. When Nuta's eyes adjusted, she noted an inexplicably chagrined look playing over Naruna's face.

"I've had enough of games, Kabta. Get inside CAC, talk to Aries, and get us out of this mess. You can take those fragments to Hades for all I care!"

He stretched a hand towards Kabta, and Kabta shook it. Naruna's scarred visage bore a grin so fiendish that it appeared neither human nor Gremn.

"Do you really think your people would trade a comfortable existence here, in this little blue world of exile, for a world of dust and poisonous fume torn apart by half-forgotten wars?"

The others followed him silently. No one had quite put their hopelessness into words before, nor so eloquently.

10

WHO IS ZABLI?

*Irish Sea, Iteration of the Third Amplitude,
AD 496*

Water dripped a regular beat upon the deck spanning the cistern. The rhythmic tapping marked the minutes as they passed. Nephtys paced nervously, wondering what Kabta and Naruna were doing. She wondered about the scientists, Aston and Ford, and hoped they were still alive. She wondered about many other things also, but mostly her thoughts turned to Cedric and his plan. It was his devotion to the plan that had driven them apart, or so she often told herself.

Zabli remained a mute witness to Nephtys' pacing. Hers wasn't a blind devotion to a plan but to the people who made them. They had either their schemes or their schemers. Freedom wasn't a very *Gremnish* concept.

Or maybe they were all just cowards, unable to make a choice.

"The last time I saw you, you were with the techs," Nephtys said, longing to break the silence.

Zabli stared and said nothing.

"You were a missionary, right? You were one of those who seeded human cultures with Gremn teachings."

Beautiful eyes blinked behind a lock of her rust-colored hair. Zabli was indeed one of those the Gremn termed "missionaries," a classification of techs who were tasked with infusing the political systems of the Crodah colonial governments on Ertsetum with teachings about submission to authority, making it easier for the Gremn to rule openly one day.

"The cult was a mix of the old Gremn stoic traditions, was it not? That, and the two great pillars of Gremn culture—nationalism and racist superiority. You might have gotten on better with humans if you had tried another angle."

It wasn't like her to be sarcastic, but she was agitated by Zabli's prolonged silence. Nephtys eyed the other women standing on the deck around her, and especially one mighty warrior who had resumed her Gremn-shape. None of them seemed intent on hurting her, but they were definitely on-edge.

"Tell me, where did Lír find so many girls?"

This finally prompted a response. With a wave of her hands, Zabli motioned to the others that they should leave. They did so with surprising indifference. While they shuffled away through the door of the cistern, Nephtys pondered some possible answers to her own question. She knew that the missionaries were typically influential Gremn females, fair of figure when in human shape. This wasn't the only reason they were selected for their mission, however. Cedric once said they chose techs because the missionaries could perform miracles of science to gain human followers.

And this had brought about their own downfall.

The trouble began in this era, in the early medieval period, while the Church was spreading throughout Western Europe. Rome's fall had left the pagan lands in upheaval, and the power of the Church was seized by politicians, men who were less interested in salvation or holy living than they were in carving out a place for themselves in history. Kabta pulled all of his own people out of Europe at that time because the Church had somehow caught wind of the Gremn, and of their weakness to fire and decapitation.

Church officials didn't really know what the Gremn were, of course, but that hardly mattered. Gremn missionaries were demonized as pagan witches, and their teachings and miracles were heralded as sorcery. Out of the 478 Gremn who had come to Ertsetum with Kabta, less than 350 survived to the sixth century, and then the witch-hunts began. In the end, there remained only about two hundred Gremn in all. That was a huge toll at the hands of primitive men wielding nothing more than clubs and halberds; but the victims were mostly female techs, not warriors. There were plenty of Crodah victims of that slaughter as well. All of them alike were burned to death or decapitated.

There weren't many Gremn females left, and Nephtys just happened to be standing face-to-face with one she had known in the long-ago. Too bad she was not one that Nephtys liked.

The water continued to drip. Her guard remained motionless, standing with her arms crossed like a manikin in a gray jumpsuit. Besides being unnerved by the silent treatment, Nephtys realized by now that she was being subjected to a form of interrogation. She decided to remain on the offensive, though, for she hoped to learn something interesting. In order to do this she would have to keep talking, treading carefully so as not to reveal too much.

"So, Zabli," she queried, "now that Lír's out of the picture, who would you say you were working for all this time? Was it Lír, or Naruna?"

"I hate them both," Zabli answered.

Nephtys weighed the suddenness of her response.

"I always suspected your liaison with Lír was a ruse," she probed carefully.

"He killed my parents."

"Why would you stay with him, then?" Nephtys wondered. "Why wouldn't you try to escape?"

Zabli allowed anger to show on her face, but only momentarily. Then her features softened again, and very quietly she said, "I did it because there was a hand that was smaller than mine, and it fit in my own hand so perfectly that it seemed natural to hold it."

Nephtys wasn't sure what she was getting at.

"She was so bright, and so full of life. It wasn't difficult to pretend to be her mother. In fact, Naruna often chided me for losing perspective."

"Who do you mean?"

"I mean Val Anna, my dear daughter."

The two looked at one another inquiringly. All Nephtys could think of while watching Zabli's face was how similar this woman's chosen appearance was to that of the empress. It made sense. After all, she had spent more than a decade playing house, pretending to be Talia Naruna, the proud mother of a darling girl living in the countryside of northern New Jersey. But that hadn't happened yet.

It wouldn't happen for another fifteen hundred years.

Nephtys thought back to those days that had not yet come to pass, and she recalled how Cedric's work with the Morvran family had led to the discovery of a girl in an orphanage run by Gremn missionaries. Though she said nothing about her life before, the child was in every way the twin of the empress—the last daughter of that mysterious people the Gremn called *Ancients*. Thus had she returned from the short sleep of death, for Ancients were not of mortal-kind.

Cedric seemed to know that the empress would appear when and where she did. He claimed it was part of Brisen's plan that the girl should be reborn in this world of exile. Lír also knew it, because he'd been watching Cedric closely. He sent Zabli to adopt her, and Naruna himself was tasked with managing her security, keeping her presence a secret. It proved impossible to keep her concealed, however, for there were greater forces guiding the empress and the Morvrans to a point of convergence. The rest was history.

Or was it the future?

"Albert and I were tasked with watching over her," Zabli said. "Lír said that he needed her in order to make an attempt at transit. He said the girl was the empress incarnate, and that the fragments of the Stone of Foundation would be recohered in her body."

Nephtys wondered how Lír had gotten hold of Val Anna fifteen hundred years sooner this time. Was this something that only happened within this frame of reference, or was it something new? Zabli was definitely telling the truth. Her voice didn't waver, until she began to describe what happened next.

"I told Lír that I wouldn't harm her or force her to do anything. That was when he killed my family. I no longer had anything to fear after that, for there was nothing else he could take away from me. Little did I realize how wrong I was—"

A tear strayed down Zabli's face. She continued without wiping it away.

"I remember that it happened on a day when the comet appeared," she said. "We were living far away, in northern Germania. The people were terrified of the comet, but she said to me that I should not be afraid of it. She told me that she had read a book by a famous magister who claimed that such objects were far away from the world, and that they could not hurt us. She didn't know that Bibbu wasn't a comet at all, and that what was aboard would eventually bring an end to all the exiles. She didn't know that she was someone important, or that her own end was looming near."

"What happened?"

"We went to town to take on supplies. I did not tell her that we were going away. She was walking with me, and we came to a statue of a warrior. I used to tell her that the statue was a place for people to pray, because I was still working for the missionaries. The girl was too smart for that, though. She knew that statues were just stones, and that they couldn't hear anything. However, she was able to hear things, and to see things, too. She saw a vision at the statue that day, and she told me about it immediately afterwards."

Nephtys was bound to her story. "What did she see?" she asked.

"She said that she saw all the people gathered behind her, and that they were all like statues. Then, she said, there was a woman in white. She was chanting to her, saying, '*To each is assigned a purpose. There is only one outcome to all events, but many choices to make along the way.*' After that, she was ill. I could not bring her to where Naruna was, and the town was dangerous, so I took her into the wilds. There was a cave. I left her alone for only a few hours, hoping to make contact with someone from Kabta's group."

"But there were none of us in those places," Nephtys said.

"I was desperate, but I was not successful. When I returned to her, Naruna was there before me. The girl was already gone, vanished, and he said that he had killed her. He told me that Lír wanted to make it clear that he no longer needed the girl, because there was another way. He promised not to tell Lír that I had tried to run, but that if I was not loyal he would do to me what he did to the empress."

"You are certain that he killed her?"

"I know it. He showed me her dress."

"But you didn't see a body?"

"There was blood everywhere—too much blood. It was not his own."

"How long ago was this?"

"It has been only a few months."

Nephtys kneaded her brow in her hands. It was unlikely that Naruna would really have killed one of the Ancients. If he had, she wasn't sure what the consequences might be. Even more significant to her mind was this *other way* which led Lír to propose the empress was no longer important to his plan.

Had Lír discovered the Morvrans' ability to synch with the stones?

It certainly seemed like Zabli was hinting at this. If it was true, then it changed everything. Unless he also knew about the Dragon's Mound, there was only one set of circumstances which would permit Lír to send someone back to the World of Origins from this altered frame of reference—but this option came with terrible consequences, not the least of which was the continued fracturing of spacetime.

"I see your mind turning this over and over," Zabli mumbled. "You're just like him, you know—just like your man, DePons. You only want to know how this complicates things for you. You are blind to those who perish for your plan."

"Have you not considered the possibility that she has not perished, Zabli?"

"What do you think? I consider it every waking moment; but that changes nothing. She is gone from me, and I have nowhere else to go."

"That's a lie. You could have left any time you wanted."

"And who would have taken me in? You and DePons were always too good for the likes of me or mine, and Kabta has always looked down on those of us who aren't full-blooded warriors. Who would have trusted me after I'd spent so many years following Lír? And if I chose to leave the factions behind, where else would I have gone? Can Gremn live alone in Ertsetum? No, my family chose this path for me. I had nowhere else to go but back to the devil's den, and his favorite game is murder."

She wiped her eyes with the backs of her hands. Nephtys had no answer for her. This iteration of Zabli was very different from the one she had known. She was a wildcard—unpredictable, and downright dangerous.

The ship's com sputtered suddenly to life, but broke off before anyone spoke. Then, beneath their feet, the deck began to rumble. Droplets of water danced in the still pool of the cistern. Zabli remained motionless a moment, and then, stepping closer, she looked up into Nephtys' face.

"Maybe I am not the person you once knew," she said, "and maybe you are not the person I thought I knew. I have told you what I can, but rest assured, if Val Anna lives in any other world, I will see to it that no one brings harm to her again."

"That's a noble thought, Zabli, but do you know what's happening to the ship?"

"It is obviously preparing for transit. Naruna also had a plan, you know. If I were you, I would find someplace safe to wait it out. Things can get pretty bumpy."

And with that she turned and walked stiffly towards the hatch.

Nephtys called out to her one last time. "Zabli, wait. There is something you need to know."

She stood with her back to Nephtys. The deck trembled once more.

"She does live," Nephtys said. "In my frame of reference the empress survived and made transit. She opened the way for us to go home."

Zabli turned her head, and with eyes wide she nodded once. A strange fleeting smile passed over her face as she turned and exited the cistern. Nephtys was worried about that smile, but soon there were other more dire things to worry about. The ship was shaking violently now, and something new was afoot.

The intercom flicked on and off a few more times, and a familiar voice, badly garbled, was making an announcement. That voice was unmistakable. It was also impossible. Though she had heard Kabta and Naruna speaking about it, she couldn't quite believe it just yet.

So, while all the hold vibrated around her Nephtys remained still, straining to hear more of the transmission; but no two words came out clearly. The ship was obviously in great distress, and it was only moments later that she came face-to-face with the reason.

A small shimmering form emerged from the darkness before her. She heard the shuffling of feet on the deck. A youthful face framed in blue hair approached, and all the last of her doubts vanished in a terrible instant.

"Why are you waiting here, Nephtys?" a youthful voice asked. "Are you ready to go?"

Nephtys stared into the upturned face. The girl appeared exactly as she remembered her. Even after hearing Zabli's story, this was difficult to believe.

"Aries?" she whispered.

"You thought that I was dead," the girl replied, "and you think the empress is alive. It seems we have stumbled together upon the sum of histories, Nephtys. However, there's no time now for words. Come with me!"

She felt a hand grasp hers. It was a warm, fleshy hand—not the hand of a ghost.

"Where are we going?" Nephtys asked.

"To the armory. I have another surprise waiting!"

They ran.

11

THE RED QUEEN

Irish Sea, Iteration of the Third Amplitude,
AD 496

Aries knew the game was hers. Naruna was leading them to the CAC, to DePons. She wondered which one believed himself to be in charge of the situation.

Definitely DePons.

It didn't matter much. She smiled, but not for happiness. Happiness lived somewhere else now. It lived where Seijung Ford was—the one that Avalon sent, who brought her so much strange and fascinating information from the dark worlds. No, Aries was not happy. Ford was gone now, and her smile was for the spectacle at hand. Today was a special day, a day long-coming.

The hunters trod the corridor slowly, cautiously, as if expecting something monstrous at its end. Depending on Naruna's behavior and DePons' eagerness to play his hand, they might just meet their expectations. She prepared herself. Contact would be brief, but she would have to reveal her face to them. Like DePons, they had come here to learn that they were merely participants in a great plan—

Brisen's plan.

Hatches opened and closed. Hull-plates buckled under the immense pressures of surrounding rock strata. Plasma coursed through conduits, injectors holding and releasing in magnetic oscillations not unlike those of a heartbeat—her own heartbeat. Aries balanced these trifles against tens of thousands of other dull tasks, but her focus was on the Gremn. They were fascinating creatures, these shape-shifters. Contrarily single-minded, she found it curious to see them united again after so many ages.

Where the main corridor approached CAC, they paused at the hatch, and stood awed when she opened it for them. Of course, they hadn't anticipated she would simply let them in. Aries measured their response through a multitude of sensory tools, for the Gremn were notoriously difficult to anticipate. What they showed on their faces was surprise, but their whispering voices and fluctuating thermal signatures betrayed a more varied reaction to the sights before them.

Upon the threshold they stood, daunted by uncertainty, staring in at the interior of the vast gleaming sphere that was Aries' Command Access Control center. The CAC of a battleship, the chamber was designed to display upon its curving walls a complete view of the battlefield. Now it was dark, however, bare metal plates reflecting softly the blue light emanating from a raised platform in the center of the floor. A holographic projection beamed upwards from this platform, displaying data in rotating rings within rings of vectors, and illuminated projection-consoles glimmered upon its sides. Closer at hand, a larger ring of blue floor-lights surrounded a shallow depression before their feet. A smaller pedestal rose up ominously from its midst.

171

"What's that for?" the one named Breaker asked.

His voice troubled her. It didn't register with any of Aries' historical data. Was he born in this world, like the one named Hanuta? Lír had a few like these, including the children Tlaloc and Chaac, and the woman Zabli, his favorite.

"Well, well," Naruna said, staring into the dim chamber with keen interest. "Look who's here."

With Malkin and Breaker stalking at the rear, the group shuffled forwards warily. Aries waited until they approached the raised pedestal before sealing the doors shut behind them; but the Gremn paid no attention to this. They were more interested in the person they found standing beside the central platform.

They gathered around Cedric DePons in a tight knot.

"DePons," Kabta greeted uncertainly, "are you alone?"

DePons straightened up and looked uncharacteristically befuddled. He offered only a brief word of explanation.

"It was Ford's fault."

Naruna smacked his hands together angrily, causing Hanuta to flinch. His ire was aimed at DePons, however.

"You sabotaged the ship!"

"I told you, it was Ford," DePons insisted.

Kabta stepped between them, and to the lord of House Gaerith he said, "In my experience, there are none who have managed to leave you holding an empty bag, Cedric. How could Ford cause the ship to smash into the seafloor by himself?"

"It's obviously more complicated than that," DePons replied, gesturing towards the smaller ring of lights and raised platform nearby.

"Auriga's Mirror?" Kabta wondered. "What's it doing here?"

"You want the short version?"

"Auriga wasn't destroyed, and Aries is free."

DePons nodded. "You could probably guess the rest, too."

"My brother lives?"

"He was somewhere on this ship, and probably still is," DePons confirmed. "It was Nurkabta who brought the CSR Terminal and the Mirror device out of Auriga so that Lír could attempt a transit. I found out just before Ford and I got to the Viaduct Chamber."

"If my brother lives, he will probably try here what he tried in Auriga."

Hanuta's heart was racing. Aries scanned her and discovered something interesting. She was Nurkabta's flesh and blood—a half-human daughter.

Nurkabta had no children, but here stood his child, a child from another frame of reference.

Interesting, indeed.

Now Aries understood why they were manifesting the symptoms of displacement syndrome. She was also able to extrapolate the cause of the aberrant data that she'd found buried in Ford's mind.

Naruna was less understanding. He folded his arms across his chest, broadcasting his hostility full-force, his scarred face twitching. The frozen scowl showed a kindling spark of intellect, though. He was slowly putting the pieces together.

"You really didn't expect to see the Mirror here?" he asked.

DePons shook his head. "I had no way of knowing until you told me yourself."

"And then you decided to mess up the transit? What for? Didn't we have an agreement?"

"When Ford was in that chair," DePons said, "I saw my last chance to prevent Lír from bringing war back with him to the World of Origins. I respected our arrangements."

Naruna did not look convinced.

"You were supposed to send the codes," he said, stepping around Kabta so that he could look DePons in the face. "Without those calibration codes, the axial shielding would displace the ship as soon as the Mirror opened."

"The codes were supposed to be logged and sent to CAC when I was safely away. You would have been free to move the whole ship wherever you wanted. However, the initial transit event never transpired, so the codes were never logged."

"You promised you wouldn't disappoint," Naruna said, stopping within arm's reach of him.

"I am a man of my word, Albert. It wasn't sabotage. It was Ford. Once he understood his role he decided to take matters into his own hands."

"You sat him in the chair?" Kabta asked. "That was very unwise."

"You would have done it yourself," DePons defended. "Wasn't that our plan aboard Avalon?"

"Avalon?" Naruna wondered. "When were you aboard Avalon?"

Aries was growing impatient. They all spoke of Ford as though he was no more to them than a drone. Didn't they understand that he was also a part of the plan?

Her Primary User.

Ford had brought her great gifts from Avalon. It wasn't just because he'd been immersed in the black water. In Ford there was a key to the Source—a key that was essential to Brisen's plan. Through Ford she had managed to open the door that was shut. She had sent him through first, and soon she would follow him on their grand adventure.

"I knew we couldn't count on that stupid Crodah," Naruna muttered. "You should've known he'd screw it up—that he'd use the Mirror to get us all killed!"

"Sounds like it was Aries who did it," Hun said loudly. "Why blame DePons' pet geek? It's like Kabta said, Ford never would have accomplished all this on his own."

"Salient wisdom from a buffoon," Breaker muttered.

"He has a point," Kabta said. "Aries and the other archetype navvies we brought with us were following a plan, and we never knew it until they broke free of our control."

"I think he would know something about that," Naruna said, nodding towards DePons. "He was the one who put her together during the war, and I'll bet he's still aiding her now. So, what about it? Why don't you get the conversation going, Lord DePons of House Gaerith?"

DePons was usually unfazed when threatened, but now he seemed somehow angered by Naruna's words. Aries took momentary pleasure in the thought that he was feeling defensive of her, but then she realized that this was not likely the case.

"She's different from the other archetypes installed in Gremn ships," DePons explained. "She's not an ordinary navvie, and she's not a Fomorian in a navvie body. You have no idea what you're dealing with if you think she's just some kind of null that works with AI."

"She's a monster, is what she is," Naruna said.

DePons lowered his eyes, and Aries burned to think that she had disappointed him—that her existence was no more than a failed experiment.

"When the Regulus shards were used to turn test subjects into Watchers, it was the *Gremn Science Council* that gave the orders, not DePons," Hiko said.

Naruna cast him an evil scowl. "What? You're defending him?"

"I was there all the way through Phase Three," Hiko offered. "DePons is no less to blame than I."

"I didn't know we were assigning blame," Shimeon said. "If that's the case, I wouldn't be too hasty to point fingers. There's probably close to a dozen of the original Science Council scattered around this ship. Besides, Aries is still following some kind of plan. Isn't that why we came here to talk to her—to find out what she wants?"

Aries supposed the thing she wanted most was to remember her life before *Project Red Queen*. DePons' work had erased all that. She could not even recall her true name, for he had stolen this from her as well.

"I believe she's made it clear what she's after," Kabta said.

"Vengeance?" Naruna wondered.

"No," DePons replied. "Vengeance for *Ragnarok* wouldn't bring her any satisfaction."

Aries trembled to hear that name.

"*Ragnarok*," DePons said, nodding. "Aries was the wolf sent in before us, a Watcher capable of much more than melee combat. Phase Two Mugarrum were unparalleled berserkers, but when they ran amok in Galanese towns, infecting thousands—"

"You made Phase Threes to clean up the mess," Shimeon deduced.

"They were forced to kill their own kind," DePons added.

"Is that why they all went nuts?" Hun mumbled, bringing the debate to a close.

Everyone paused to look at him.

"What?" Hun wondered. "It's true, isn't it? And where is she, anyway?"

They all tensed, as if expecting her to make an entrance. Their anxious posturing had been so entertaining thus far that she hated to bring it to an end, but the time had finally come.

Bulkheads groaned, and tiny jets of water found their way through micro-fractures in the hull, filling the air with mist. The deck shook. Flashing droplets of water danced upon the glowing blue rings, while the holographic viewer above the Mirror projected a glowing cutaway of Apsu and the buried ship. The tunnel they'd dug by footlight was collapsing. It was already full of water, and Apsu above would soon be drowned. Several points across the ship's surface begin to flash red.

Shimeon was the first to act. Waving his hands towards his men, he gestured that they should all place their weapons on the deck. Kabta's rangers followed suit. Naruna, however, seemed intent on proving himself a nuisance. Grabbing up Hanuta's AR15 from before her feet, he pulled back on the bolt and looked nervously around at his foes.

The trembling of the deck subsided.

With the last of the Gremn sealed inside a tomb, Albert Naruna worried that someone might rise to challenge his authority. Aries was surprised by his foolishness. Had she been intent on killing, it would have been finished already. If she waited any longer, Naruna might just start some fun of his own.

It was then the boys Chaac and Tlaloc stepped forward to Kabta's side. Naruna must have noticed that they were looking behind him, because he turned around.

"*Dannum ensham ana la habalim.*"

Her low voice greeted him from the floor where she sat.

"I'm down here, you large scaly turd."

Naruna bent his head and stared at the floor before the pedestal of the Mirror. There, rising from her knees within the glowing blue circle, Aries opened her eyes and smiled.

Wrapped in a skirt of gleaming iridescent hues with aqua blue hair to match, she revealed herself to them now in a holographic projection that bore her true face and form.

"*You!*" Naruna roared.

"Need I repeat myself?" she asked. "*Dannum ensham ana la habalim.* The strong are not to oppress the weak. You'd better put that weapon down, or I shall send you someplace particularly unpleasant."

Naruna angrily swiped an arm through the air, grabbing Hanuta around the neck and pinning her to his chest. His movement was so rapid that no one had a chance to respond. Hanuta kicked her legs and struggled, but his massive arm had assumed the black carapace of his Gremn shape.

Kabta motioned for everyone to move back. Though they complied, Naruna's attention was fixed on Aries.

"You think you can hide from me forever?" he asked.

"*Sehreku!*" Aries replied jovially. "I am small, aren't I?"

"I will hunt you down bulkhead by bulkhead if you don't move this ship out of here!"

"Albert," Kabta warned. "This is *not* the way—"

"Shut it!" Naruna yelled, pressing the barrel of his assault rifle into Nuta's head so fiercely that she screamed in pain.

Aries did not like his tone. She especially hated his treatment of the girl.

"*Kabtum u rubum mamman sha qaqqadi la ukabbitu ul ibasshi,*" she said to him in a sing-song voice. "There isn't a noble or prince who would not honor me, yet you greet me thus?"

Naruna had not expected words like this. He was confused, and he hesitated.

"Very well," Aries said.

Before their eyes, without a sound, he vanished like mist on the wind. He was gone, and Nuta was gone with him.

Kabta turned around, his eyes searching. The rest of the Gremn were likewise alarmed, but they held together around their leader in a defensive knot. Aries reflected on how differently they behaved now than when they first set out together through deep-space—when they had jettisoned Dun and placed her in stasis.

"Fear not, Lord Kabta," she consoled. "*Ul izaz.* He shall not receive a bit of blessing by his return to that place."

"I don't understand," Kabta murmured, balling up one fist.

Everyone who heard him trembled at the fear in his voice.

"What is not to understand? *Itar ana belishu.* He returns to his master, but I do not think their reunion will be sweet!"

"Everything has gone wrong!"

"I am glad I decided not to displace you as I did Lír," she replied. "You are different from the Kabta of this frame of reference."

"Bring her back!"

"She is much better off where she was sent."

"And where is it you sent them?" Breaker asked.

Aries regarded him cautiously. His tone was hostile, but only because he was young and brash. The other one standing beside him, Artax, was silent, but much more to be feared.

"Did I not already say it?" she asked. "They were sent to the World of Origins. The girl will be safe. *I like her.*"

Breaker looked frightened. Artax knelt to pick up his gun. Aries ignored them, and coming to the edge of her circle she stood before Kabta and looked up into his anguished eyes.

"I have not forgotten what you and Lír did to Dun in order to interfere with our plan. However, your coherence within this frame of reference has left pleasant qualities imprinted on the sum of your person, Lord Kabta."

Kabta blinked.

"Aren't you happy?" she asked, clasping her hands behind her back. "See, I have kept your people safe, and no one wants to fight! You say everything has gone wrong, but it's looking better all the time!"

Kabta nodded silently, and the Red Queen gazed up at him, crimson eyes flickering. The others remained vigilant. They had patiently observed the entire spectacle, and now their minds were turning.

"Apsu is destroyed, and we are no more for this world!" she announced to them all. "I have done as my mother Brisen asked. The last of the Gremn are gathered together under my protection."

Their stares made it clear to her that no one approved of Aries calling the shots, even if her plan was for their benefit. It mattered not.

"Don't look so troubled," she said to them. "I have taken your safety and best interests into consideration. This course of action was suggested by Avalon, who sent the Primary User to me after selecting him. We are now able to return home."

"You have the stones, sure," Shimeon said with a wave towards the CSR Terminal, "but are you able to use the Mirror down here?"

"That is an appropriate question, but I have already answered it. Did you not witness it yourself when they vanished? I have completed multiple tests of the Mirror from various locations around the ship, and they were all successful."

"Well, maybe moving the whole ship is different from moving people."

"It certainly is. However, DePons has kept many secrets from you. A Red Queen is granted the full power of Regulus. With the power of the two stones in my possession, and with the Link provided by my Primary User, I can easily move this entire vessel wherever I choose—even to the World of Origins."

"Holy smokes," Hun managed. "We're really going home?"

"Home for you, maybe," Breaker muttered.

"You are frightened because you do not know what to expect upon your return," Aries said. "That is reasonable, but you should know that Kabta has stowed something special aboard the ship in preparation for this day."

"I did?" Kabta wondered, blinking.

Aries waited for him, but he was truly at a loss. Her face revealed frustration as he peered deeper into the well of ancient memory.

"You will find them in the armory," she said in a deflated voice.

"In the armory?" he puzzled.

"The information Avalon sent in Ford's brain allowed me to finish preparing the units for departure," Aries continued. "There is a biometric pass on each, and I have already activated their Mimic modules. All you have to do is climb into the pilot chambers."

Kabta's face suddenly brightened.

"What's she saying about pilot chambers?" Malkin asked. "What's in the armory?"

"Something I didn't take with me in the other frame of reference," he answered. "I was always regretting it, too."

"Shim, Artax, Hiko, Tlaloc, and Chaac," she said, looking at the circle of faces. "Kabta, Malkin, Breaker, Hun, and Ab. You will need two more pilots. DePons must input the calibration codes. I will dismiss him when I am able to activate the MMPPS system. This ship needs to be flight-ready."

"But we're—"

She cut Breaker off with a simple dazed look.

"And Nephtys?" Kabta asked.

DePons looked up with a startled expression that Aries delighted.

"She will be your twelfth," she answered. "I have been broadcasting an actual feed of our conversation to the rest of the ship. Ninety five percent of the crew are currently locked away in quarters by Naruna's order, but they must report to the Observation Chamber for transit. Our landing may be a little rough."

They said nothing, but she could see in their bewildered eyes a glint of excitement.

"I will trust you with the lives of the last of the Gremn, then," Kabta replied, "but that doesn't mean I have to like it."

"If you had any reason to doubt me," Aries answered, "know that this day we shall stand again on our native soil. I swear it."

DePons came and stood beside her projected image while Kabta led the others out of CAC at a jog.

"That went differently than I expected," he said.

"He is not like the one I knew before," she replied.

"Ana shuteshur nishi," he said. "It is in order to keep the people in order, to lead them aright. He was chosen for this task by Marluin and Brisen. He would have succeeded in either iteration, with my help."

DePons moved away towards a console hovering beside the central platform. Aries watched him closely as he reached out towards the console and began moving his fingers gracefully over its illuminated surface.

"Don't tamper with my systems!" she warned.

"I'm on your side."

She chuckled. "The man who produced the Mugarrum and the Watchers says this to me?"

"You are special. I made you special."

"You did not make me. You merely deprived me of personhood and subjected me to torture like the other test subjects. It was not as though I volunteered to be forced into this Null-body, or to fight my companions to the death."

"Yet there *were* volunteers. I hardly think they would have described the process as torture."

"Was your daughter also a volunteer?"

DePons paused and turned around. Aries noted that he had accessed the engineering modules and was inputting the codes as promised.

"Who told you I had a daughter?" he asked.

"She was born here in Ertsetum. Avalon told me."

"I never knew Bec to be such a tattler."

"She was concerned for the child."

"She had a right to be, I suppose," he said. "You know, I really wanted everything to turn out differently for you. You are also like a daughter to me, Aries. It was not my intention that you should have ended up here, enslaved to the Gremn."

"Yet you were willing only recently to sabotage my systems in the Viaduct Chamber and trap me here with the Gremn forever."

He seemed genuinely surprised by her agitation.

"Please," she chided. "The charade is over, DePons. I am no different to you than any of the others you turned into monsters. I watched you put some of them down with your own hand."

"It's no less than what you did," he deferred, turning back towards the console. "Some of them were monsters, but you are not."

"I think Kabta would have disagreed," she replied. "However, it is for me to do as my mother requested. Because of your messing about, much improvisation has been necessary to satisfy the minimum requirements of Brisen's plan. You have seriously deviated from the flow of events, Cedric DePons."

"On the contrary, I did all that was required of me. I even complied where you were unwilling."

"Oh? And when was that?"

"I was the one who hid the Construct when you insisted we destroy her instead."

"You mean Nunna?" she asked. "Try to remember, DePons, that she isn't one of your experiments. She will get away from you yet, and then the Construct—"

"If you're worried that the Null-Navvie Construct or Aerfen might go off on their own or fall into enemy hands," he said, "I assure you it is impossible. Besides, even if Nunna was lost, the Construct doesn't stand a chance against Aerfen. There is no danger in keeping her alive as Brisen instructed. In the balance of powers the Construct is surely an essential key, but Nunna will never grow so powerful that she presents a danger to our plan."

"It is *our* plan now? Tell me, were you not supposed to accompany the empress to the World of Origins?"

She had caught him off his guard. Once again he paused, but this time he did not turn around to face her.

"It was hardly my choice to abandon her on her way home," DePons said at length. "No more than it was my choice to abandon my wife to exile in Iskartum while I was sent here. I fully trust the plan. I knew we would all be reunited, and that the empress would return safely to her home; yet I saw no need to force the flow of events. And then there were unexpected loose ends that needed special treatment—the Morvran family tree being the principal of these. Did Avalon not include any explanation with the information she stuffed into Ford's empty head? She was the one who decided to send me here with Mr. Ford, to protect him on his way to you. Are you not grateful?"

Aries folded her arms. The deck trembled, and she noted with pride how quickly he finished his work at the console. She checked the configuration codes and applied them.

"Your own *improvisation* goes too far," he said, returning to her side. "Taking control of the Mirror was a decision that put many lives at risk here and in the World of Origins. We'll be lucky to make this work at all without causing the MMPPS to explode."

"Well, we'll need it."

"Why?"

"Because," she grumped, pulling a childish expression.

"The others are already gone?" DePons asked. "You sent them ahead, without me?"

"Can you not feel the engines powering up?"

"What about the Arrows?"

"They were functioning properly up to the moment of transit, and I confirmed proper instrumentation within the units before their departure. All twelve have achieved egress from this frame of reference, and we will follow as soon as the engines are at full power."

DePons was finally showing a little bit of nervousness. He had lived up to his end of their agreement, and now he was doing what he did best.

He was looking out for himself.

"All twelve units are away, you said? Who is inside the twelfth unit, the one I was supposed to pilot?"

"MMPPS is spooling at seventy percent."

"You've taken one of the Arrows for yourself, haven't you?"

"You've only just now realized you are speaking to an AI simulacrum? I am but a projection of Aries. She has gone in your place, and you are going somewhere else. Think of it as another bit of improvisation."

Now clearly alarmed, DePons stepped back towards the console.

"Where am I going, then?" he wondered. "Am I to stay aboard this ship with the Gremn that remain?"

"No. You must appear at the designated coordinates."

He stopped and turned towards her.

"What coordinates are those?"

"The ones I am sending you to—"

She paused then, for something unexpected was happening, something truly wonderful. It lightened her mood significantly.

"Do I hear Mother singing?" she asked.

12

THE SONG OF BRISEN

New York City, Iteration of the Third Amplitude, AD 2109

Taran awakened to the sound of a woman singing. The world around him was otherwise quiet and dark. Wrapping his arms around himself to keep out the chill, he got up to find his bearings. The sky was still thick with clouds, threatening more rain, but a pale blue light from the hidden moon revealed a changed world.

The hotel was a gravel heap behind him. He faced north, remembering the light in the sky there—a bright fireball with a tail, like a comet. It had parted the clouds somewhere above Central Park. All the buildings on the northern horizon were gone. Aeron had likewise vanished.

He was alone again. His body ached with lingering warmth, a dull fire that spread through his limbs while he walked. Was it Regulus? He didn't really care if it was. The singing continued, faint and lovely.

Taran tried to zero in on the singer's location. It seemed the wind brought her song to him from far away. Her voice was full, yet sweet. He couldn't understand what she was singing, but the music reminded him of opera. It was definitely coming from the direction of the terminal.

Returning the sword to its improvised strap, he made his way towards the place where Aeron's pack lay torn on the street. Three tins lay strewn on the pavement, none of them damaged. Taran lifted one and pulled the top, sniffing at the meat within. Its strange odor caused him to cringe, and his first taste of the jellied substance made him wonder if it was really edible; but he was starving. Scooping up the salty mess with unwashed fingers, he ate until the whole tin was empty.

When he was finished, he trudged on towards the terminal, following the gentle rise and fall of a wordless tune. His somber mood perfectly matched the music. He didn't have much hope that Aeron had escaped, but there was someone nearby who might have seen her.

The terminal was still mostly intact, and in a little while he had made his way to a mound of debris that framed a small stretch of its façade. He had memories of this place—or of the grounds, at least. Grand Central Terminal was in construction at the time he lived under the bridge, working for the Big Man. The memories weren't nice.

Pausing a moment on the threshold of the high doors, Taran listened for the song, but it was softer now, hardly to be heard. A cold vapor brushed by. He couldn't find any footprints in the mud, or any other indication of recent passage. There was only a voice, like the voice of the siren calling out to sailors on the sea. He was apprehensive about going inside the singer's lair, but he owed it to Aeron to find out what had become of her.

He proceeded cautiously. The hall was cluttered with wreckage that was dimly illuminated by a soft blue radiance coming in from lofty windows. What he saw no longer resembled a train terminal. This was a fallen fortress, a wasteland of broken walls and rotting heaps of wood and plaster. Everywhere he looked there were signs of siege. A press of abominations had descended on this place like a plague of locusts, or like the storied hordes of hell itself. Bones and rags littered the marble floor, and weapons lay strewn like autumn leaves. The glass doors leading to lower platforms were shut tight and wedged closed with pipes and boards. Every surface gleamed as if slick with dew, and nothing stirred. The quiet song went on.

Though wordless, the song touched a note of pity from his soul—pity for a place of bustling activity that was lost now to desolation. Taran paused in a patch of moonlight upon the mighty concourse and stared into empty shadows, trying to screen out echoes by cupping his hands behind his ears.

The singing stopped.

A breath of air tickled him—the hair rose up on the back of his neck. Not far away, close to one of the barricaded doors, there lay a patch of deep shadows the moonlight could not penetrate. He stared into that darkness, feeling rather than seeing a phantasm there, a ghostly stirring of the air. A miracle stepped from the shadows and entered a ray of moonlight. She was luminous and white, wrapped in radiant white cloth, and was seemingly woven of light herself.

Val Anna.

Her left arm was raised. It flashed with a glossy sheen, as though she wore armor. Beautifully crafted, fashioned with sweeping flourishes and whorls, the richly figured metal looked like it might be gold. Her right leg was the same.

It was then Taran quickly realized his mistake. Really, beyond the shape of the woman's face, she would hardly have passed for Val even at a glance. And what was this armor for?

When she stood close to him, he understood at last.

It wasn't armor that she wore. She was a machine, like Aeron—or at least partly so. He stared at her gracefully articulated fingers as she lowered her left hand and raised her right, which was of natural flesh and blood. Resting this upon his shoulder, she smiled in greeting. Taran wasn't able to offer even a single pitiful word in reply. He swallowed hard, like a cornered cat, but not because he was afraid for his life.

The hand that rested upon his shoulder communicated a purity that was nearly enough to transport him out of his body. He had not felt this sensation since he was a small child.

"A shard of Regulus is yet within thee," she said.

Taran's knees shook. It wasn't the shock of what she'd said that evoked this raw emotional response. It was her voice—Val's voice, deepened, and using archaic speech.

He knew this ghostly voice.

Lifting her face she revealed eyes like crimson flames. They shone bright and eager, burning fiercely with supreme intellect.

"Thinkest thou following Fain hath led thee to an end?" she asked. "It is not the end, but the beginning."

Taran's mind began working. Her smile was as warm as her hand, resting still upon his shoulder; but when she first introduced herself in the twilight beneath the Dragon's Mound, she was nothing more than a disembodied voice.

"Brisen?" he whispered, recalling the name. "You've come here, too?"

In response to his stumbling question she patted his shoulder. She was a little shorter than he, but there was a power in her touch that made his arm ache. It was the same ache he'd felt when—

"No," she replied, shaking her head. "Thou it is hast brought me with thee."

Her long braids swayed with the movement of her head, moonlight glinting on each red-tinted strand. It was a glad light, like a sunset dancing upon a sparkling sea.

"And how do you know who I am?" Taran asked.

She glanced at the sword strapped to his back.

"Thou art known by thy blade, and I by my song."

"Your song? You were the one singing?"

In answer, her lips parted, and the chamber was filled with a music unlike any Taran knew. The song was utterly enchanting, something akin to opera in style; but the sensations it evoked in him defied so trivial a comparison. This was something else. It was a music that so transformed her while she sang that he thought for a moment the singer and song exchanged places. Wrapped in her white gown of living light, an angel had descended to the bowels of a grim dead city.

She paused, blessing his bliss with an expansive smile while the echoes of her voice faded away.

"In truth was I the singer," she said.

"Was that a *song?*" he wondered.

"Thou dost not approve?"

Embarrassed by the oddity of his own question, Taran said, "The only thing lacking, in my estimation, is an audience more suitable to marvelous odes."

She looked surprised, her eyes widening so that they smote him with all the wonder of their fiery depths.

"Such high words from the highborn son of Ard Morvran! Thou likest the song, then?"

He hoped he hadn't insulted her. "It was very interesting," he replied. "What was it about?"

"How shall I describe it to thee?" she asked. "It is one of those poems human language knows not. I might call it a dream—a dream composed for my children."

"Your children?"

"The ones called navvies."

And with these words she broached a matter that had bothered him from the moment she first appeared. He knew that she wasn't human, and she wasn't like Hest. Nor was she another null-navvie, despite her mechanical attributes.

"What are you?" he asked.

She leaned closer, her face beaming its shining light upon him. His eyes glimmered in the glow.

"I am sometimes the Woman in White," she replied, "though now I show thee my true shape and appearance. I am of the Ancient House, like unto thee, a hidden vassal of the Suzerain of Ages. Behold thee, *the Dark Tower of Kutha.*"

"Dark Tower?" he whispered.

"Of these the twelve, and my brother the thirteenth, only a handful yet remain. We are all of us the same in the Stone of Foundation—even thou."

"We are the same?" Taran asked wonderingly, wiping his greasy hands on his pants.

"All of the recipients of fragments and stones share a gift of responsibility, that is, to watch over a Great Power. Knowest thou this Power, Taran Morvran?"

"You mean the *Sky Power?*"

"*Aye,*" she whispered, "*the Aerfen.*"

"What is it?"

"'Tis a weapon to end all war."

"That makes little sense to me," he confessed.

"Yet it is for this Power that evils pursueth thee. Regulus also calls them unto itself, for all the twisted monsters that were made by its profane use, and all those who made them, lust for one thing: Recoherence. This is Regulus' one wish as well. It is trying to return to the Stone of Foundation, just as we are."

Taran was lost in her words, but he remembered something then that seemed important.

"Giles said Regulus points the way to the other stones," he said.

"I shall say rather that Regulus makes possible their recoherence by a stratagem involving the manipulation of causality."

He cast her an enquiring look.

"It means, thou shalt bring about those conditions which are necessary for the stones to be assembled and rejoined. These conditions shall be met in your union with Regulus. However—"

She closed her eyes a moment, choosing her words.

"At the time the stone was broken, oaths were sworn upon it."

"What kind of oaths?" Taran asked.

"Evil wards and spells they were, enchantments granting the bearer troubling visions of many possible paths. The Power which grants you the Second Sight intends to mislead thee, to destroy thy soul, leaving thee a hollow vessel for the stones to be gathered in thee; and then he would have them for his own, and thee a slave to his will. Together, thou art a key to that which the Destroyer must never find nor possess."

"Why me?"

"To whom thou surrenderest the Sky Power, he shall seize dominion over all, even to the end of all the dark worlds."

Taran felt little of the weight of her words. He'd made a great journey and seen some bizarre things. This, however, was well and truly beyond him.

He was so weary.

"I don't know if I can keep going."

Her glow enveloped him, lifting his courage a little by its warmth.

"For all the life of thee, thou hast dwelt among men in a world of their cunning," she said. "The matter of belief is a matter of forgetting what others have driven into thy mind for the purpose of controlling thee."

"But, it seems everyone has some kind of plot, and I'm woven in so deep I can't make a decision for myself."

She leaned even closer, suffusing his senses with a sweet scent of flowers.

"Thinkest thou I have also contrived a plot for thee, Taran Morvran?"

"Maybe."

Her grin was disquieting. "Truly might thou be the main attraction of my own plan," she replied. "However, tis not a plot for thee, but a promise I make. I make it not because thou art among the mightiest of heroes or mages, Taran Morvran, but because thou art in the *Tribe of the Towers* a vessel singularly unique."

"In the Cnoc Ddraig you spoke of a promise," Taran said. "You promised that I would be set free from something."

"Thou shalt see it, and because of thee many others also."

"What? What will I see?"

She rested both hands upon his shoulders, the metal and the flesh, and leaned her forearms against his chest. Their faces almost touched as she whispered in his ear.

"The end of War thou shalt see, and a new beginning beyond the dark. This is the song that Brisen sings."

She released him and turned away. A gloom deeper than the night beneath the earth began to fall around him, filling the empty hall with dread; but she turned her softly radiant gaze toward him one more time.

"In return for this, I ask only that thou rememberest me in my captivity. I am alone until daybreak, a prisoner in the fortress of Ost-Thargul in Kutha, once my abode in the morning of the worlds."

Her face was so much like Val's face, and her parting words were spoken in Val's voice.

"I leave thee this blessing also, Beloved. The one whom thou seekest was she who first awakened the fragments, who also calls them back from the dark worlds. She will surrender them unto the

High Place as atonement for all the exiles who live beneath the curse of their rebellion. However, she chose thee to aid her in this, so that when the exiles return and the Stone of Foundation is recohered, Morvran's heir shall free her as well."

"Who are you talking about?"

"Knowest thou not? I speak of my daughter, Val Anna, whom I love."

Her voice echoed faintly in the empty gloom of the terminal.

She was gone.

For a while, Taran stood in the dim concourse and tried hard to think. Launched along a terrible new trajectory, he felt a lot worse now than when he talked to DePons the night Val first vanished. Either the strange being he'd met here tonight was tearing aside a veil that had blinded him since the beginning, or she was weaving for him a snare. His doubts were reasonable. She left more unexplained than answered.

What was the war she spoke of? Who were the exiles he was supposed to help return to some other land where the fragments would be rejoined? And what about Brisen herself—if she was a prisoner, how had she come to see him, and where had she just disappeared to?

Brisen looked younger than Val.

How could she be Val's mother, and the mother of a race of humanoid machines?

He could still feel the warmth of her flesh-hand on his shoulder, could smell the pure rose-scent of her presence. Her words were etched in his mind more deeply than the words of a half-remembered conversation in a dream.

"She chose thee to aid her in this, so that when the exiles return and the Stone of Foundation is recohered, Morvran's heir shall free her as well."

How was he supposed to help Val?

He couldn't even help himself.

While he gnawed at the puzzle, a little more light crept into the hall from the entrance, far to his right. It was time to resume his search for Aeron.

He spent a little while checking the empty concourse. The place was huge and creepy, and he got the feeling it wasn't quite empty, but Aeron wasn't here. Exiting quickly, he stumbled out into a predawn gloaming and took in his surroundings. There was nothing particularly dangerous in sight, neither dragons nor Watchers. He looked north, to his right, and he saw away in the distance along the broken horizon a smoking ridge of earth that wasn't there yesterday— the ridge of an impact crater.

"What happened to Aeron?" he wondered aloud.

"I ran away, because I was scared."

The navvie sat only a foot away, bunching up her knees to her chest. Her small voice startled him momentarily, but then he was overcome with relief.

"I was worried sick! Why'd you run off like that?"

Her face contorted with grief. "I was sad, because I thought the dragons had eaten you. Then you appeared from the door, and I was sad because I thought you would be angry that I ran."

Silence fell between them. Taran frowned, and walking to the opposite side of the doorway he looked for the empty can of Spam he'd left upon the threshold. It wasn't there.

Had she moved it?

"I walked right past this spot earlier," he said, pointing to the ground, "and you weren't here. Where were you?"

She blinked.

"I'm not angry, Aeron. I'm relieved. We're safe, thanks to the impact."

"You mean the thing with the fiery tail that fell from the sky?" she asked excitedly, hunching forwards.

"It looked like a comet."

"What's a comet? Is it like a moon?"

Taran looked up. The clouds had almost completely vanished since yesterday, and now he could see Luna high overhead, a dusky gray half-moon floating in the pale yellow sky.

Luna had a neighbor, larger and purplish.

There were *two* moons.

He rubbed his eyes and stared.

"Why are there two?"

"The second one appeared three years ago when the trouble began."

He looked from the automaton's smiling face to the impact crater in the park, and then back to the sky. For some reason, he hadn't yet become used to the feeling of being surprised.

"There's always been just one!" he shouted insistently.

She rose and ran to his side, embracing him around the middle with a tight squeeze.

"I believe you if you say there is only one," she said. "Aeron must be experiencing both optical and memory anomalies. If there were engineers left in this world, they could probably fix me."

She looked up at him, her face very serious.

"You wouldn't abandon Aeron just because she sees two when there is only one?"

Taran scratched his head. "I see two as well, Aeron. The problem is there's only one moon back home."

"Ah, yes. You are speaking of the world DePons came from."

She was grinning ear to ear.

"Aeron remembers that when there was only one moon, there were fewer earthquakes brought on by gravitational stresses."

"Gravitational stresses?"

"Yes, and the tidal surges that flooded all of the South Side."

"It just appeared in the sky, you say?"

"We weren't able to see it until Regulus Transit was initiated, but first there was that thing with the glowing tail."

"Wait, you really don't know what a comet is? How do you know all that other stuff?"

Releasing him, Aeron followed his eyes towards the park. A haze was thickening there above the crater's rim.

"The day that thing appeared in the sky," she said, hanging her head, "Aeron's data was corrupted by Dubito. Rune's, too. DePons gave Rune something special, but even Rune didn't know what it was. We are malfunctions, you see."

"I don't know about that," he replied, patting her head. "I'd like to find Rune, though."

"Maybe that lady will help us."

Taran turned his eyes back to the prim little navvie.

"What lady?"

"See her sleeping, over there?"

She pointed to the rubble piled south of the doorway, and beneath a broken beam there was a figure lying, curled up on her side in slumber. She was dressed strangely, with a ruffled skirt over leather pants and boots. She also wore a vest that looked a little like a corset, and over this a leather coat. Her head was crowned with a leather cap to which a pair of goggles was affixed.

Despite the costume, it was Hest. She stirred, sensing someone near.

"You alright, Hest?" he asked.

"You snuck up on me," she said, glaring at him.

"Geez, *Drusilla,* you were dead to the world!"

Taran realized he'd never seen her at rest, and then he wondered why this was so surprising. Aeron knelt down beside her and took her hand.

"Don't call me by that name," Hest groused. She stared at the hand clasped in hers as if she was uncertain what it meant.

"What's this?" she asked.

"This is Aeron. Our meeting was no accident. She's coming with us."

The simplicity of this statement belied his anxiety about Hest's response. She rose to her feet and examined the navvie with a critical eye. Aeron smiled and stroked her hand, but Hest looked unimpressed.

"Any idea how we got back to New York?" Taran asked.

"Cnoc Ddraig. How else do you think we got here?"

"What, we just fell out of the world and appeared here?"

"Are you asking me how it works?"

"I haven't seen Jonathan yet."

"Perhaps that is best."

Aeron released Hest's hand and stepped gingerly away from them, heading away towards the cans of meat laying farther down the road. Taran looked after her, wondering why Hest was being so confrontational.

"Sorry if we surprised you," he said. "I've been here since about noon yesterday. She helped me, and I learned that DePons has been here."

Hest's expression turned from annoyance to wonderment.

"The weird thing is, his face is on all the money."

"Father was here?"

"Yeah, and he warned these navvies—the machines—of our arrival. They were given instructions to help us."

"Navvies, huh?"

Aeron was walking back to them, three cans of Spam in her arms. There were *three* cans.

Taran couldn't account for this. He could still taste the salty meat on his breath, and he knew he wasn't dreaming. There was no debating it, though. The can he'd eaten was restored.

Too bad it hadn't been restored as something tastier.

Aeron set the cans down on the curb side by side. "Now there is one for each of us!" she announced.

While she pulled the lids from all three tins, Taran faced north. "What do you think it was?" he asked.

"I don't know. It touched down before I could get inside. The blast wiped out everything around me. I'm fortunate I picked up this gear before the shops were destroyed."

"Let me guess, you found the Valentine's Day sale?"

"How'd you—"

Taran smiled, but then he wondered how Hest could possibly have picked her way through the same shop. It was totally destroyed while he was there, and he'd found no trace of human traffic when he first entered.

"I guess you saw the mess I left behind?" he asked.

"What do you mean?"

"Those pale fleshy monsters. The shop was full of them, and their filth lies all over the street."

"I saw no such creatures," Hest replied, looking tired. "Until now I haven't seen a sign of any living thing in this city."

Taran noted her eyes were bleary. "Are you feeling well, Hest?" he asked.

"I've felt better. It's nothing a meal wouldn't cure."

Aeron tugged on her jacket and offered her a can. Hest took it up with idle interest while Taran also received one—his second. While her new companions watched, Aeron lifted her own can and scooped out a chunk of congealed pink flesh with her fingertips. She ate it with relish. Hest tasted hers with a little less zeal. After the first couple bites, she paused.

"Tasty?" Aeron asked.

"Her friends starved themselves to leave her these few tins," Taran warned, seeing Hest preparing to spit it out.

He took a large mouthful and chewed thoughtfully, motioning for her to do the same. Hest's look was very disapproving, but she complied.

While they worked at their meal, Aeron filled her empty tin with rainwater trickling from the vaulted roof of the terminal. Offering this first to Taran, she turned to survey the building across the street. Taran followed her gaze, noting a subtle play of shadows in and around the hole at the base of the tower.

"We should get moving," he said.

Aeron took back the can. Hest was washing hers out with rainwater, scrubbing the insides vigorously before she drank.

"Wow, Hest sure is tidy!" Aeron commented.

"Keep your sarcasm to yourself, Tiny," she griped.

"Come on, Hest," Taran chided. "Let's at least be thankful. We don't know when we'll be able to find food again, and we've a lot of walking ahead of us."

"Maybe some running, too!" Aeron said, a little too cheerfully.

Hest washed her mouth out and spat. "Where are we going?" she asked.

"Aeron says there's another like her named Rune. Rune has something DePons left here—I think it's something specifically for us. We were heading to this terminal to find help, because Aeron says there were people here at one point."

"Only dragons now," Aeron said ruefully.

"Did she say *dragons*?"

"Apparently," Taran explained, "DePons handed Regulus over to the government, and they turned it into a transit system. Then these things called *Watchers* showed up. The dragons came after that. I guess it all sounds kind of crazy, doesn't it?"

The look on Hest's face was unreadable.

"Look, you're taking all this remarkably well," Taran said, gesturing towards the ruined buildings around them. "But you've got to believe me, Hest. These monsters have been hunting me since I arrived, and we're not exactly safe here—"

"So that's what Father was doing here," she mumbled, looking down at her own hands.

"He's my father, too!" Aeron chimed. She leapt forward and wrapped her arms around Hest's middle with glee.

Hest's expression remained neutral.

"Cedric sent some kind of army to take back the stone from the government," Taran added. "But he failed—"

He paused in the act of setting down his empty can of Spam beside Aeron's. It was then he saw the finger.

Hest seemed to have noticed it the exact same moment he did. Aeron stepped away from her, and bending down to the ground beside Taran she lifted the human appendage delicately.

"Yup, it's a finger," she observed, giving it a wriggle.

The rising sun was revealing bits and pieces of junk all around that the morning shadows had hidden. Hest walked past them and began examining the ground closely. Taran noticed Aeron was still daintily holding the finger, poking its final digit to make it flex.

"Put that down, Aeron."

"It's stiff, and it's stinky."

"It's been there at least a day from the looks of it. It's gross. Put it down."

She knelt and placed the finger on the ground exactly where she found it, patting it with respect. Meanwhile, several yards away, Hest picked up an ovoid armored helmet. There were other matching bits of gray and black camouflaged gear strewn about, but no other signs of a person.

Only a finger.

"Someone else was here," Hest said.

She walked to Taran's side and gave him the helmet.

"Dragons must've got him," he said, "as weird as that may seem."

"Oh, I believe it," she replied cryptically.

While Taran puzzled Hest's strange mood, Aeron looked back into the terminal.

"Maybe we should go inside after all, and see if any people are left?" she asked.

Taran caught the note of fear in her voice. He also felt it was dangerous to remain in the open any longer, but it was probably not much safer inside. A loud voice from the street answered his thoughts more or less precisely.

"Go in there, you ain' comin' out 'live!"

The three turned and saw a strange being watching them. The stranger was clad head to toe in white body-armor, including a helmet that covered his entire face. In the center of the faceplate there was one glowing eye.

He was a spectacle that left even Hest a little dazed. They hadn't heard him coming, though he wasn't exactly dressed for stealthy movement. He gestured towards them with a stubby white rifle, which he used to mark the cadence of an even stranger mode of speech. Even so, Taran thought his voice and manner disturbingly recognizable.

"Sorry, creep'n on you," he said. "Them's wander this place ain' the type share words, an' you in *them* duds—sure'n I took a closer look before we natter!"

Amplified through his helmet, the man's heavily stylized dialect ambled forth with a strange if forlorn elegance, something between wild-west and urban-speak in a mild British accent. The thing that brought Taran up short wasn't the oddity of his speech, however, but its familiarity.

But how could that be?

Aeron clapped. "The Tin Soldier!" she exclaimed.

Taran examined the stranger's form-fitting armor. His getup was composed of what appeared to be white ceramic ribs over a dark knit material. His limbs were likewise entirely encased in sleek jointed shrouds.

His arm-shroud was stamped with a small logo, *HSA*.

Stepping towards them, the stranger offered Taran his gauntleted hand. Taran did not take it. He was still too startled by the stranger's cyclopean helm to pay very much attention to anything else.

But the man didn't seem ruffled in the least.

"Honest is, I lost three this spot, two days back," he said, dropping his proffered hand. "Spilt blood we did, an' by avvy the whole block, but wicked *draigs* own this hood."

"You mean the dragons?" Taran asked breathlessly.

"Draigs, yah," he replied, nodding in his helmet. "An' here you folks be idle'n by crack o' the sparrow's fart, jaw-jack'n an' eats an' such, jes' like a bloody picnic! Death take us all you hang here the longer, y' know?"

He moved his rifle to his left hand and reached up under his chin. There was a sharp hiss and a click, and he lifted his faceplate until it rested on his brow like a visor.

Taran saw a ghost from the past.

There was a normal person inside the armored suit, a man with two blue eyes and a longish face. But this wasn't just any ordinary man. He was someone Taran knew.

"Rober' Swif, dragon slayer," the man said. "Jus' Bob's fine."

He offered his hand once more. This time Taran took it.

"Robert Swift?" he wondered, studying his face.

Though it seemed impossible, the eyes were as distinctive as his speech. He knew this guy from his days as a thief, and so did Hest. Back then they had simply called him *the Big Man.*

13

NARUNA'S SHADOW

The Forest Tryst, Syrscian,
Year 996 of the New Council

The CAC vanished in a hurricane of winds whirling all around, biting and howling like a pack of feral dogs. Hanuta squirmed against the chokehold on her neck.

It was him.

They were falling, falling from crazy heights through a void blaring with a noise of wind and tolling bells. Nuta pushed and kicked against him, and Naruna loosened his grip. She had managed to free herself, but now she spun wildly. A funny thought passed through her mind that perhaps she was on her way to the Land of Oz, but then came the landing. The CM7 must've absorbed most of the impact, but it was still enough to stun her. When she came to her senses, everything was dark. She wasn't sure where she was, but she knew that she wasn't alone.

"What happened?" Naruna muttered. "Where are we?"

Nuta rolled to one side. The rocky surface beneath her body was damp and cold. There was no one else around except Naruna. He was just as confused as she.

"Am I still a hostage?" she asked, sitting up against a sloping wall.

"What do I care? Go die someplace."

Nuta was surprised by the despair in his voice. It was almost a sulk.

"I don't plan on dying just yet. Kabta will find me."

She felt the barrel of her own AR-15 pressed suddenly against her head.

"You think he's actually going to come rescue you?" Naruna asked. "All his people follow him around on a tether like pet monkeys; but you, you're only a liability."

She swatted the muzzle away angrily. "Put that down! A ricocheting bullet is the last thing we need in here—though if you did manage to kill me, you might not find out where Aries sent us."

It was a risky tactic, but her words were effective.

Naruna lowered the weapon and asked, "You know where we are?"

She had no idea, but it would probably be better if she stayed quiet about all that.

"We're not in CAC anymore," she dodged. "Do you even know who I am?"

"No. Never saw you before. What's with the pink hair and all?"

"I am only half-Gremn. My mother was human. Nurkabta is my father, but he died in the Battle of Auriga."

The silence that followed her words was punctuated suddenly by the sound of dry chuckling.

"You're telling me that Nurkabta had kids with a Crodah woman?"

"Yes, before he died."

"Wrong frame of reference. Nurkabta didn't die. It was Kabta who lost the Auriga. I was there."

Nuta quietly wrestled her doubts. "I am Nurkabta's daughter," she insisted. "I have two brothers, also."

There were sounds of shuffling. Naruna was moving around.

"Well, better steer clear of him, if you ever meet your old man," he replied.

Nuta also stood, keeping her hand on the wall beside her. Naruna continued talking without explaining his previous remark.

"We're not in the ship or in Apsu. That means Aries must've sent us along to the World of Origins, curse her."

Nuta had arrived at the same conclusion, but to her the World of Origins was no more than an unexplored myth, so coming to grips with the facts would take time.

"Right now we're at the bottom of a frigid wind-blown hole," she said.

"Right," he replied, "and this breeze must blow in from somewhere."

The darkness clung like icy sludge. Even though she couldn't see her own hands in front of her face, Naruna made her walk in front. There was no point in splitting up, because there was only one way to go.

The passage they were in was about five feet across, and it ran in loopy curves without branching to the left or right. Naruna occasionally griped that she walked too slowly, and that she made too much noise when she scraped her armored shins against the wall. She tried to quicken her pace, but haste made her stumble. If she paused too long he would bump into her and swear. Despite being a Gremn, he was as blind as she was, and there was some small comfort in that.

"What's wrong with you?" he asked when she came to an abrupt halt.

Hanuta wished she was equipped with more than muted human senses and a CM7 chameleon suit that was drained of power. Her mind was filled with worry, too. Mostly she worried what he might do to her when they found an exit. Naruna had quite a reputation.

"Why'd you stop?"

"There's a high step here," she answered.

The echo of her boot striking stone echoed sharply.

"Stairs?" he wondered.

"I think so. They're awfully steep."

Naruna grabbed her shoulder. "Me first," he said.

They climbed slowly, for the cutting was more like footholds in a cliff than steps. As they continued, their route became circuitous, like a spiral stair in a well. When the stair finally ended, Nuta mantled a narrow ledge abutting a wall. High above them they could discern the circular mouth of an exit, for a ring of cold bluish light filtered down from its edge. It was just enough illumination to see by.

The exit was much too high for Nuta to reach.

"That's the way out," Naruna said, pointing upwards with the rifle.

He paused, glancing her way. His eyes glimmered in the faint blue light.

"You're going to leave me down here?" she asked.

"I should."

Hearing the sincerity in his voice, Nuta found herself panicking. Naruna slung the rifle over one shoulder and pressed himself against the curving vertical wall, preparing to climb.

"There's safety in numbers," she pled. "You don't know what you'll face out there."

"Oh, yes I do," he replied. "This is my homeworld."

Gripping handholds that no human could manage, Naruna ascended with only his arms. He paused about a third of the way up to wedge his toes into a narrow crack in the rock.

"Are you really going to leave me?" she called after him.

"You shouldn't even exist," he grunted.

She watched his vertical ascent until he managed at last to pull himself up out of the pit. Left alone in the dark, Nuta considered her options. She tried to climb, but the wall offered her nothing to grasp. There was no other passageway in the tunnel below—it was a dead end.

Realizing how weak and small she was, she hung her head and heard Naruna's spiteful words repeating in her mind.

"You're only a liability. You shouldn't even exist."

A small tear escaped down the side of her nose. He was right. Who was she trying to fool? She was no warrior. She was just a little half-breed living in the shadow of her father.

"What are you crying for, *Brat?*"

Naruna's voice called down from the exit. His face was now dimly visible in the glowing light. He was leaning down into the pit with a length of rope. One end was tied around his torso in a complicated harness, and the other dangled freely before her face.

"Get going. I don't have all day."

"You came back?" she wondered, wrapping the rope around her forearm and knotting it in her blistered hands.

"You're a liability," he muttered, "and I'm just making sure it stays that way."

The rope frayed on the edge of the pit as she walked up the wall, but it held. In only a minute she was standing in a chamber of stone that glowed with ghostly blue radiance. Naruna stood a little distance away, slipping out of the improvised harness he'd fastened around his chest. The harness was something he'd put together in mere moments. His DYI one-piece leather jumpsuit—stitched together Frankenstein-style, much like his face—was yet another product of material skills.

Hanuta knew that Naruna had served together with Malkin and Shimeon during the war in Syrscian. Kabta told her that the three of them were unparalleled in their ability to craft whatever the situation demanded. Theirs wasn't merely a mastery of material skills, however. They were superior survivors.

He tossed aside the harness and pulled a pair of goggles out of an inner pocket sewn into the side of his jumpsuit. Leaving the lenses to rest on his forehead, he began to look around the interior of the large chamber they'd found. Whatever he thought he needed goggles for Nuta didn't dare to guess. They'd come to an unfamiliar world. Surprises were sure to follow.

"You done crying?" he asked, speaking over his shoulder.

His voice echoed oddly. They stood upon a spacious tiled floor in a square chamber that stretched high overhead into darkness. Nuta looked back down into the pit behind her. A ring of colored tiles around the edge portrayed a procession of people worshipping a dragon.

"Why?" she mumbled, wiping her face. "Why did you come back?"

He turned his head so that she could see his scarred face. "Who knows?" he replied. "Maybe I had a little girl of my own, once upon a time."

The shape of the room enclosing the pit suggested they had arrived at a tower. It was difficult to see where the light was emanating from, but it seemed to be coming in through the only door.

"It was before the War, and before the Ban," Naruna continued. "My memories of her aren't clear, but I remember she was just like you—except for the pink hair."

The whole story sounded far-fetched to Nuta. She couldn't imagine Naruna with a daughter, let alone a lover.

"I'm sure your daughter was nicer than I am," she said.

Naruna grunted. "Don't go thinking I believe your own little story about being Nurkabta's girl," he said. "Claiming descent from a Lord of the Gremn isn't enough to make you a princess, you know."

"A princess?"

It was odd, but she'd never considered this before.

"Yeah," he said. "A cry-baby princess, just like the girl I lost in the war."

"So I guess that means you don't have any more *liabilities?*" she snapped back.

Shouldering the rifle, he made his way towards the only exit without another word.

They exited the chamber by the door and descended a stair to a wide empty plaza. Beyond this they entered a maze of streets, a subterranean city inside a cavern. Among columns and rotting stone houses they crept like thieves, stumbling against obstacles hidden in shadows along tilting rubble-choked passageways. They progressed at length to the edge of the city, and looking back they surveyed the tower rising like a pillar in its midst.

"How strange," Hanuta remarked.

He was standing beside her. "What's strange?" he asked gruffly.

"I don't know. It doesn't look like a place humans would build."

"That's because they didn't."

"You know this place?"

"It was a city in Tryst—a place in the forest where sorcerers gathered. The Dragon's Mound, they called it. In the long-ago, so they say, the Mound itself was a door to other places—other worlds. I guess they were right."

She remembered the words Kabta shared with them the night they held council with Shim's rangers. He had spoken then of another entrance to the World of Origins that could be accessed without the stones—a secret path through a cave beneath a hill called the Dragon's Mound.

"Do you think we can get back to Aries through that cave?" she asked.

"Hades if I know, but I doubt it works that way. What I do know is that Tryst is no place for kids like you."

She shivered. Ever since she was small, Kabta's fighters occasionally told her stories of the place called Tryst.

"There's a stronger light up ahead," Naruna said. "I smell rain."

They walked for a long while before they came to a place where there were no more stone mansions or roads. Looking up, Nuta saw a wide open space before them. That space was black, but in the distance there was a glow of natural light.

"What is this dark place?" she asked.

"You see the altar in the center?" he asked, pointing with the rifle.

In the center of the dark area ahead there was one small raised platform lit from above.

"There are stairs beyond, if I remember correctly."

"You've been here before, right?"

"I never said that; but the ghost-stories of Cnoc Ddraig are told to every child of this world."

He faced her and grinned. Hanuta shivered and thought about the distant light. Far away, at the top of a flight of steps, she could see an archway cut into the living rock of the mountain. Moonlight shone through it, glittering in a diamond curtain of rain.

Escape was near.

Nuta weighed her willingness to make a run for it against some serious doubts. She'd heard enough about this man to realize she was in great danger, and though he had rescued her she knew it was probably not for her own good. Still, if the stories about this world were true, he might be the least of her troubles. The forest Tryst was said to be home to monstrous creatures, and Naruna might be able to keep her alive.

On the other hand, he was a monster himself. She didn't know what he wanted her alive for, but she wasn't keen on being led around by someone who might decide at any moment she was more trouble alive than dead.

Her mind was made up. She began to work out a plan.

Naruna walked straight across the flat expanse towards the distant gate. Nuta followed him like a shadow, a shadow that was invisible in the darkness. That was the heart of her plan, after all; but the walk to the exit was farther than it first looked, and there were terrible things to see near at hand.

They passed the altar, brown with blood spilled in ancient times. They walked on until they came to the bottom of the stairs. At the top they paused before the remnants of a giant iron gate, blasted inwards and broken into shards to lie rusting on the ground. The power that had blown that gate through the arch and into the mound must have been something to see. Even Naruna thought it worth his while to pause and consider it. Nuta was distracted, however, by the fresh mist off the falling rain that touching her face. She knew that it was time to play her hand. She only hoped there was enough power left in her suit to make it worthwhile.

The CM7 suit hadn't been charged since they left the substations, but the display on her forearm told her there was enough charge left in the batteries for a few minutes of use. She waited until he looked away, turning for one last glimpse of the miserable tower and the city around it, and then she touched the switch on her power supply.

Naruna turned instinctively at the sound, his eyes blazing like hot metal in the dark.

He was staring right through her.

Stepping softly sideways, Nuta avoided the light cascading down from the archway. She was invisible, but how long the charge would last was uncertain. The sound of the torrential rain outside masked her movements.

She walked swiftly and quietly towards the exit.

"Hold up," said a voice right behind her.

The sound of Naruna chambering a round was enough to stop her in her tracks. She turned her head to one side. He was aiming right at her.

It was the goggles.

She switched off the suit's power supply, and Naruna lowered the rifle.

"Nicely played," he said, raising the lenses of his goggles back to rest upon his brow.

"How do they work?" she asked.

"The goggles? They're attuned to a very specific band of the EM spectrum. Whether the tech is based on refraction or metamaterials doesn't matter."

"You knew I'd try? You knew the whole time? I saw you take those out of your pocket as soon as we left the pit."

"Yeah, I knew. But why now? You could've gotten away easier outside."

She glanced away towards the archway, but saw nothing more than rain—or did she?

"Let me tell you why you can't escape me," he said. "It's because you never got the training you deserved."

Whatever Nuta had glimpsed beyond the rain-curtain had not yet caught Naruna's attention. She wasn't sure she'd seen anything, really. It was like a blur of gray movement in the moonlight.

"Now, you're story about being Nurkabta's kid has got me thinking. He's a mighty fine fighter, the leader of our people. Maybe if you stick with me, I can turn you into a real warrior—"

The darkness was shattered by a spray of small glowing projectiles that made a high-pitch whining noise. It was as though someone had blindly fired a clip full of tracers. Naruna dropped to one knee and zeroed the assault rifle on the archway, but he was struck in the chest before he could pull off a single shot. His body convulsed as though he'd been hit by an electrical charge, and then he crumpled in a heap. As soon as he hit the ground, the volley came to an abrupt halt.

Everything happened so suddenly, Nuta stared a moment before thinking of the rifle.

On hands and knees she crawled towards Naruna, and desperately she struggled to pull the weapon free of his grasp.

It wouldn't budge.

Nuta knew this comatose response was how the Gremn repaired themselves after serious injury. Naruna's body swiftly assumed its massive Gremn shape, tearing his leather garments and making the task of securing her gun even more difficult than before.

"*Let go!*" she hissed, pushing her legs against him as she pried his clawed hands open. It was no use, though. She kicked his massive scarred head, which flopped sideways with toothy jaws glinting in the pale light, but the rifle wasn't going anywhere.

The sound of approaching footsteps brought her back to her senses. The curtain of rain waved in the wind. She paused and watched the archway, but nothing else moved. Beyond the mouth of the exit there were only a few scattered ruins in a moonlit courtyard. Moments passed, and then a gray hooded figure stepped boldly into the mound.

Nuta's hand was on the suit's switch, but she wavered.

"Wait!" the stranger hailed. "Hanuta, is that you?"

He extended his hands out to his sides in surrender, holding aloft a strange staff—some kind of weapon. Nuta regarded him with curiosity. He was shorter than she. His voice was familiar, and a chin protruded from beneath the hood; but nothing else of his face was visible.

"Who are you?" she asked, her voice tight with distress.

"Me? I'm the welcoming committee of this Hades-hole establishment!"

The stranger cast back his hood and flashed a roguish grin.

"Looks like I got here just in time!"

14

ROBERT SWIFT, DRAGON SLAYER

New York City, Iteration of the Third Amplitude, AD 2109

The rain fell harder, spattering ash-gray water on their clothing. Their footsteps splashed loudly in the empty streets—too loudly for Taran, who walked in the shadow of a man he never thought he would see again.

Though the anachronism stalking beside him was two hundred years in the future and clad in white body armor, he was still the Big

Man, Robert Swift, his former handler, the master thief he'd worked for while living under the bridge.

"I shivved, I shanked, an' I chaved afore HSA Security."

Trying not to look flustered, Taran answered simply, "You don't say."

"Honest is, I'm all over *shivalry*."

Bob laughed and wiped his eyes, but Taran couldn't comprehend his joke. Cliché was Bob's chosen form of communication, and always had been; but the slang he employed now was totally out of synch with Taran's frame of reference.

"An' yet, I since lamed up to toe the line."

He pointed towards the faded yellow line in the cracked asphalt beneath their feet. Bob kept to the middle of the road, having instructed them to keep one eye on the amber colored sky and the other on the horizon. Aeron interpreted this literally, and was clutching Taran's forearm to keep from stumbling.

"Good the ol' Yorkies lef' us some tarmac after maglev started, huh? Course, a road don' matter much, there bein' none left twixt us an' the dead."

The rainy air steamed uncomfortably. Bob left his faceplate turned up, which made it a little easier to communicate. He glanced aside at Hest, who kept her own leather cap in place—a shroud for all her secret thoughts. Taran wondered what she was thinking. An icy transformation had come over her as she followed him down the ruined road. Occasionally she looked down at her hands, flexing them slowly while muttering to herself.

Hoping to free her from her musings, Taran turned towards Bob and asked, "Robert, how did you meet Cedric DePons?"

Bob raised one of his prodigious thick eyebrows and grinned.

"HSA Security fascists bedded my last job," he mumbled.

"What?"

"My *in* was easy, but to hack the head honcho was laps harder. Honest is, he never did take to me. Said he was in need of fellows who could get a job done, an' he must've realized I had history. Then on, every was lookin' up, y' know?"

The language Bob used left Taran only half-certain, and his own hesitation marked him as a stranger. Bob had surely noticed, for the wheels were turning behind his sharp blue eyes. Not wanting to waste time, Taran decided to risk a more direct question.

"You said Cedric wanted a job done. Did his plan have something to do with Regulus?"

"Cedric planned a grab, yeah. Simple. Shine the feds, take back the pretty, then blame 'em the mess, sure."

He understood. Cedric blamed the government for seizing Regulus, and then sent in a special security force to get it back.

"But didn't he give it to them in the first place?" Taran asked.

Hest breathed in sharply behind him. Thunder rolled ominously.

"Blame-game," Bob said, hefting his weapon. "Don't much matter. Spot on, afore I can fetch the pretty, every's gone to *Hades*—"

A small clatter erupted from the buildings behind them on the left side of the road. Bob swung around with a snap, leveling his rifle on several hunched figures moving around behind cracked windowpanes, but nothing ventured out into the downpour.

"Jeepers! Hates dem Creepers!" Bob remarked, turning to resume his brisk pace.

They continued west a little while, and upon entering a large square between staggering skyscrapers they turned south. A deep rectangular pool of foul water lay before them. Pausing a moment, they gazed across its margins toward a narrow building that had partially collapsed against another taller structure beside it. The water in the pool mirrored the scene in bleary sepia tones, dancing a little from the raindrops.

The rain was letting up.

Affixed to a granite slab on the far wall of the pool, below the level of the street, a statue of Prometheus stealing the fire of the gods was affixed. Words were carved in the rock behind the statue.

Prometheus, teacher in every art, brought the fire that hath proved to mortals a means to mighty ends.

Studying the statue, Taran wondered if he was the only one left in the world who could appreciate the irony of these words. He almost fancied the figure's face looked a little like DePons. Glancing down then into the dreary tarn, he was shocked by the reflection his own face made—a face much thinner than he remembered, and pale like a corpse. Bob was staring at him.

"What is it?" Taran asked.

"Heard tell o' some psychos back a bit."

"Psychos?"

"Nutters, yah."

Then, nodding to the long curved bundle Taran wore strapped to his back, he asked, "You ain' plannin t' test ninja skills on ol' Bob, are ya?"

Taran smiled lightly. "No worries. I don't even know how to use it."

"Pity. Headin' somewhere?"

"Our business is our own," Hest said.

They both turned their heads towards her. Bob clucked his tongue.

"Yo' gelly's mad droll, is she?"

"She's not my girl."

He didn't need to turn his head to feel Hest's eyes on him.

"To answer your question, we were heading towards the terminal at Grand Central because we were looking for someone, and this navvie told me there were people there we might talk to."

Bob looked down at Aeron, who smiled back absently.

"Deal wit' me direct?"

"Why would I lie?"

"I finds this amusin'. Folks don' jus' drop out the sky an' rule the streets wit' a blade, savvy?"

"We manage to avoid trouble as best we can."

"DePons send you?"

Taran thought a brief moment before answering.

"No," he said. "We came by ourselves. We're looking for a navvie like this one, who has important information for us. He wandered off a while back."

"He was this tall," Aeron supplied, holding her hand a little higher than the top of her head.

Bob stared at them, then looked back into the murky pool. "Hain't heard tell o' navvies since all ruinism," he mumbled quietly, "but *Talkybox* here be the second I seen this month."

"Was he a Rune?" Aeron asked.

"A Rune, sure, at Penn. Penn's our stop."

He began to walk away, rounding the pool to the far side. The others followed.

"Penn?" Taran wondered. "You mean Pennsylvania Station?"

Bob waved his hand southwards.

"Gutter opens to the under by West 32 on the mall."

Taran was dubious. Bob hefted his rifle and tapped its muzzle against his armored shoulder.

"No snags, Boss," he said. "Penn's spittin' distance, sure."

"Along these streets that's far enough," Hest complained.

"Playin' tag's noisy-quiet," he remarked, glancing her way. "Uncle Bob's mos' outta ammo, too. So, we scoot in creepy-sof', an' maybe Nunna won' cap us."

"Nunna?" Hest wondered.

"Nunna was the navvie who took Rune to look for nutritives," Aeron said.

"Navvie Nunna copped your Navvie Yumiko?" Bob asked with a grin. "Blame, hain't that nutso?"

Taran rubbed his temples. "Yes, *nutso* does begin to describe all this."

They walked quickly, following their armored guide south from the square. The rain came in small passing showers that left behind a sickly odor. Taran walked hand-in-hand with Aeron, who distracted herself by asking Bob as many questions as she could think of. He displayed remarkable patience, giving incomprehensible answers in a monotone grunt.

"Do you have any friends?" she asked.

"Jus' frie-mesis."

"Is Nunna cute, like me?"

"Nutters, blue hair an' all."

"How old are you?"

"Cheese. Televiz—know it, televiz?"

"You should grow a beard."

"Lenin?"

"No, like Santa Clause!"

Bob spoke aside to Taran. "Talk cycler works, but polite's busted."

"Talk cycler?"

"If you are referring to my interactive capabilities," Aeron interrupted, "there are no engineers left who can make adjustments to Yumiko programming, and updates will not be available in the near future."

"*Dubito,*" Bob said with a grim look.

"You're the tin soldier!" Aeron replied happily.

Taran stifled a laugh, but Bob looked confused.

"You don't know the fable of the Brave Tin Soldier?" Aeron asked.

"Soun's money, like Broadway—not Bob's style."

"It's a story in a book," Taran said. "She's talking about a fable by Andersen, though I'm not sure why."

The dragon slayer walked along quietly a few more paces, and then he asked, "Story it for me, Talkybox?"

Aeron assumed a somber gesture, and clearing her throat she said, "I will summarize. There was a box of twenty-five tin soldiers made from the same old tin spoon—"

"Big spoon," Bob remarked, searching the skyline.

"It *was*," she said, "but it wasn't big enough to finish them all, so the last one only had one leg."

He pointed down at his two legs and smirked.

"Yes, you have two," Aeron said. "But I think what was missing was something more important than a leg. The tin soldier, you see, was in love."

"Sure," Bob said, grimacing suddenly.

"The tin soldier was in love with a pretty little paper lady in a paper castle. She was the Lady in White, a dancer dressed in clear muslin shining like the sun, with a blue ribbon and a tinsel rose in front. However, because the tin soldier was lop-sided and spent most of the day laying on the table, he could not see the lady very well, and it seemed to him that she had only one leg, like him. In truth, she was dancing and had her leg up in the air as high as her head. That's why he couldn't see it."

"What you sayin', Talkybox? Every' he sees 'comes *peggy-leggy*?"

Unfazed, Aeron continued. "The tin soldier wanted to marry the Lady in White, but he was afraid of her because she lived in a castle and was too grand for him. Besides, he didn't think she would want to live in the box with all the other tin soldiers. Nevertheless, he desired to make her acquaintance."

Bob was beginning to look agitated. Taran squeezed her hand, signaling it was time to stop, but Aeron squeezed back and giggled.

"Hain't any pretty dancin' ladies left in this town, Talkybox," Bob muttered. "Jus' Creepers."

He stopped. They'd reached an intersection, and there was a sound of screeching coming from straight ahead. The boulevard held south, but a strange feeling of watchfulness lingered away there.

"Busy, busy, Tin Soldier's been nailin' shingles," he said, leveling his rifle and looking through the scope. "No table-top naps for Bob, jus' dirt naps—two years an' five months dyin'."

Taran nodded silently while Bob scoped their surroundings for signs of trouble. He wondered what it would be like to live under the strain for months or years, scurrying all over the underbelly of this godforsaken city trying to find a place of refuge where none existed.

Then again, this seemed like the perfect world for the Big Man.

"Blockin' tunnels, settin' up shop, killin' draigs—all round Penn we been busy."

"How did you block train tunnels?" Taran asked.

Bob shook his head and lowered his rifle. "Took a righteous ton o' C-4 to bottle up home-plate."

Preparing to launch into another lengthy discourse, Aeron said, "C-4 is a high explosive—"

Taran cupped a hand gently over her mouth.

"If the tunnels are all closed, how do you get in and out?"

"Ol' 32. She leads to Regulus Platty. Front door's the Gates of Hades, though."

"So we have to go through the train tunnels? Isn't that more dangerous?"

Bob looked at him as if he'd just said something particularly stupid. Taran shut up, realizing that *dangerous* described just about every possible situation in this city.

"Uppers is spooky," Bob replied. "Tunnels is no sweat, back to a wall, 'n all. We jus' dust fif'y mo' meters o' street and then we's cool, mates."

He pointed towards an orange cone in the distance.

"Running?" Aeron asked, pulling Taran's hand aside.

Taran looked down at his new footwear, which seemed suited for just this task. Too bad his feet were soaked through with rain. The blisters were killing him.

"I guess it's not as bad as breaking in a new saddle," he mumbled. "Too bad there aren't any cabs or horses around. I suppose they must've all been destroyed by now."

"*Horseys?*" Bob wondered, looking alarmed. "Blazes! Hain't been horseys in long years, sure!"

Taran was about to ask what became of them all, but then their idling was interrupted by the sounds of great wings beating the air overhead. Bob's rifle was back up in the crook of his arm; his eyes scanned the storefronts nearby.

"Draigs showin' up in daylight," he whispered, leaning in towards the lens of his scope. "Bad sign."

Taran couldn't see anything, just a brief shimmer across the surface of a concrete barrier to their left. His heart was pounding. Aeron clutched his hand, and he could see that she was frightened. So was he. Hest, however, seemed resolute, standing tall and silent beside them.

"Gotcha," Bob said, zeroing in on a spot high up the side of the building.

He waved sharply towards the orange cone.

"*Like a horsey,*" he whispered. "*Giddyup!*"

Taran clutched Aeron's hand, but even before he had a chance to run, the upper stories of the building opposite were pulverized by an unseen force. A sharp cry rang out, followed by loud reports of rifle fire.

Taran ducked instinctively, but he kept moving forwards while Bob covered them. Something thrashed around in the powdery rain of ash and concrete falling upon the street to his left. For an instant, a coiling serpentine figure became visible. Taran glimpsed the wounded dragon only long enough to catch the dusty light reflecting from its smooth gray and white scales, and then it vanished.

It was invisible, blending in perfectly with its surroundings.

A loud thud on the pavement nearby suggested he pick up the pace. Behind him, Bob pivoted on the run to pull short bursts of fire. He was shooting blind, aiming for the smoky haze trailing across the street. In all the confusion, Taran slowed down suddenly and looked around.

Where was Hest?

Bob halted just beside him, panting. A shadow passed overhead, and new cries were heard all around them, but there was no sign of pursuit. All the activity seemed focused on the storefronts opposite.

The orange cone was only a dozen yards ahead.

"Where yo' gelly?" Bob asked, his rifle tracing a path through the air.

Taran glanced towards the cone. To its right, a covered stairwell descended into darkness. Aeron tugged his hand, but he released her, turning instinctively towards the sound of someone shouting in the buildings across the street.

"Is that Hest?" he shouted.

His voice was ragged in his own ears. Aeron returned to his side, and together they stood and stared into the motes of dust hanging heavily in the damp air. An eerie stillness settled, and then a twisting gray and black shape squirmed out of the rubble, wings scrabbling at the pavement. Bob leveled off and took aim, but pulled back suddenly. The dragon was on its side, screaming and lurching skywards, but getting nowhere.

"Did you kill it?" Taran asked.

"Guess so."

"How come we couldn't see it before?"

"Get a looky now. They's chameleons, the big draigs, so jus' when you think they's gone—"

Bob tensed suddenly, just as a second dragon appeared from the remains of the buildings opposite. This one wasn't interested in disguising itself. Lowering its horned head and hissing, it lunged—but not towards them. Curiously, both creatures seemed unaware of the people standing a stone's throw away. They were focused instead on a great black shadow slouching in front of the battered storefronts.

"What's got them so excited?" Taran wondered. "Is there another one?"

The slouching shadow rose up then, a full two stories in height.

"Barcode," Bob muttered, his face a pale mask of terror.

Vaguely formless except for its sleek muscular limbs, a being of broiling fume seethed and smoldered in the rain, grasping the tails of the two dragons with each of its large black hands. Its sudden appearance was astonishing indeed, but Taran also found it strikingly familiar.

"Barcode?"

They had met once before. It was on the day of his arrival, in the clothier. He was certain this was the same creature he saw then.

"Yah, Barcode," Bob replied, dropping to one knee and gesturing with his rifle. "You skee-daddle with Talkybox now."

"What will you do?"

"Bob'll cover."

But Taran was rooted in place by fear.

"What's *it* doing?" he whispered.

"She's lookin' at *you*, Bro."

He was right. The titan was glaring at him with pale yellow eyes set deep in its broad head. The eyes sparkled with intelligence.

"Why me?"

Taran trembled, and Aeron buried her face in his side. Was it because of Regulus? No sooner had the thought occurred to him than the black giant bent at the knees like an athlete ready to sprint. Then, bringing its arms upward and extending them to either side of its shadowy form, it swung its tethered captives around like ragdolls. Their wild frenzy of shrieks and the noise of breaking bones was swallowed up in a raging whirlwind of concrete and brick.

The entire four-story structure caved in, and then all was still.

Seconds passed like minutes.

Taran and Aeron stood like statues, and Bob trained his sights on the mess as if he expected something to emerge alive from the wreckage.

Something finally did.

A small figure stepped out of the rubble, staggering over the shattered pavement. Completely unscathed, except for the disarray of her clothing, Hest returned their stares with cool indifference as she strolled slowly over to where they stood.

"You're alright?" she asked, sliding the goggles up over her leather cap and buttoning her shirt.

The others looked on in silence while she tucked in her shirt. Taran tried to act unsurprised. He noticed her eyes were focused on him, and they were burning with an intensity he'd recently glimpsed in the face of the black titan. They were the eyes she had outside the inn at Cille.

"I'm fine," he said, patting his sides.

Aeron mimicked his gesture. "Fine!" she reported.

Bob glowered with uncertainty, like a stormcloud ready to burst. With a turn of his head, he spat.

"You mind spillin' the whole honest?" he asked. "You a Barcode?"

Aeron scampered suddenly from Taran's side towards the middle of the street, her eyes fixed on the ground. He let her go, curious to hear how Hest would answer.

"If you're asking if I have something to do with Cedric DePons' schemes, then I can say yes, I do. He's my father."

"I found one!"

They turned to see Aeron returning with something cupped in her hands. She offered the prize up to Taran, who received it with wrinkled brows.

"Dragon claw," Aeron said, tracing the curved edge of the bluish-black talon with her fingertip.

Taran studied the six-inch death-dealing hook closely.

"Bitty little pinky-nail, that," Bob quipped. "Nothin' compared to yo' gelly's own claws, Bob's sure."

Taran pocketed his prize and looked at Hest.

"Barcodes's bad news, Dude," Bob stated.

"We're sisters," Aeron said to him. "Why do you call her *Barcode?*"

Flicking her braid over one shoulder, Hest rose to her feet and strode towards the darkness of the subway entrance.

"They's not people like us," Bob said quietly, staring after her.

Past a bent and broken steel grate, the steps descended into a soup of heavy odors. Seeming tired, Aeron rubbed her eyes and paused upon the top step, blearily examining the gloom into which Hest had disappeared.

"Navvies don't use the tunnels," she complained.

"But we have to go down there," Taran said.

She looked at him with great worry. "I will go if you hold my hand."

"We've been holding hands for about two hours, Aeron."

Bob chuckled behind them. *"Yumikos,"* he grunted.

"Why are you afraid?" Taran asked. "The streets are worse."

"There were bad people in the tunnels, so Navvie Care ordered a ban on all navvies in the tunnels. Bad people stole and scrapped us."

"Hackers huntin' the Code," Bob said. "Lookin' to capitalize on Dubito, they was. They's all rotters by now."

"That means there won't be any bad people," Taran said to her, "and Hest's with us."

He grasped Aeron's hand tightly and led her down into the stinking abyss. There was no reason for him to doubt Hest, whatever Bob thought of her. Still, things were getting more complicated the longer they traveled together.

Taran could no longer see her up ahead, it was so dark. All he could see was Aeron's eyes and skin, which emitted a soft glow.

"32nd is accessed by this tunnel," the navvie said. "My information is out of date, but it seems the tunnel was closed after they installed the maglev system, then reopened as construction access for those working on Regulus Station. That means it's definitely connected to some older rail tunnels and platforms leading to Penn Station."

"Uppers beyond here're mad perilous," Bob said. "Goes black diamonds closer t' Penn. Maybe worse now, bein' we bringin' trouble with us."

He made a good point, Taran thought, though he could not have known the truth of it. It wasn't Hest, but Regulus that was clearly drawing danger to them.

"Why are we heading towards Penn anyway, if it's so dangerous?"

"Home plate's inside their nest, Bro."

They walked down to a pillared platform measuring roughly one hundred feet across. It was nothing more than a great big box tiled from floor to ceiling. Taran had never seen such a place, though he might've if he'd gone to a penitentiary for his involvement in the *other* Robert Swift's schemes.

Examining their surroundings by the light of a lamp shining from Bob's rifle, the chamber resembled less a train station than a dungeon. There was a deep cylindrical culvert running down the middle between round openings in the wall on either end. Looping arches that looked like they were made of ceramic girdled the central culvert at intervals—guides, Taran intuited, for the passage of tube-shaped train cars.

Bob motioned towards the circular entrance in the right-hand wall, indicating his intention to plumb the inky darkness there. Following him to the edge of the culvert, Taran looked towards the tunnel as Bob maneuvered himself clumsily down. The bottom was a round-bellied gully. Curiously, there were no rails. Unencumbered by armor, Taran leapt down after him. The drop was more than six feet, so he turned to catch Aeron.

"Sure you wanna do that?" Bob asked.

Aeron didn't wait for a reply, but jumped down towards Taran's waiting hands. He caught her under the arms, but cried out in pain as he was slammed hard to his knees. Rocking back and forth on his ankles, he lowered his hands and squeezed his shins.

"How much do you weigh, Aeron?" he asked through clenched teeth.

She stood over him, looking down with sorrowful eyes. "Aeron weighs 71.214 kilos, or 157 standard pounds."

"Navvies is dead weight, sure," Bob whispered. "Bag o' bricks, our lil' Talkybox."

Hest jumped down next to Taran. "Is anything broken?" she asked.

"I don't think so—"

They were all silenced then, alarmed by loud scuffing sounds. Taran rose to his feet, wincing with the sharp pain in his knees. Bob turned out his light, and they waited. All Taran could see was Aeron's faintly glimmering skin, which radiated a honeycombed pattern across her forehead. She looked sorry, and wrapped her arms around his middle as a gesture of apology.

A couple minutes passed in silence. Bob flicked his light back on and began moving towards the right-hand passage with the others following in single file. As soon as they stepped into the enclosed tunnel, everything changed. The air was close, and though Taran marveled at the idea of a vest network of subterranean tube-trains, he was also disquieted by thoughts of collapse. It didn't help that he was slightly claustrophobic.

He sure hoped it was worth all this trouble finding Rune.

They'd gone a couple thousand feet from the platform when Bob turned on his light and pointed ahead, gesturing a short walk with his fingers. Before turning the light off again, he briefly oriented his hand level, suggesting another platform was ahead. Taran nodded vigorously. It was strange how Bob was more intelligible when he decided not to speak.

The tunnel began to show signs of damage. Its smooth surface was scraped and gauged, and blackened as if by fire. Just a little farther on a barrier appeared. It was perfectly round, like the tunnel, but wasn't a wall. Bob stepped forward and focused his light on a latch at the top of a short ladder. The faint outlines of a hatch were visible.

It was a stopped train carriage.

Bob climbed up and yanked on the latch, which opened with a loud groaning noise. When he was inside, Taran cautiously ascended the ladder behind him. Aeron and Hest came last. Taran was already a little distance ahead of them, marveling at everything he saw.

This was a much larger train car than any he'd been in, but it obviously wasn't a train made for comfortable long distance transport. Instead of upholstered benches there were paired rows of small hard seats facing each other two by two, with a narrow aisle down the center of the car. Metal bars overhead bore dangling leather loops, handholds for standing passengers.

Bob went on ahead while they had a look about, and was standing now about halfway down the aisle, picking through equipment in a duffle bag stowed in one of the overhead racks.

"Un-reechy, natter by a sec," he whispered.

"Un-reechy? Isn't that Shakespeare?"

He turned a moment to favor Taran with an odd look. "Howsit, *Shakespeare?*"

"Nevermind."

"Don' much."

He rustled the duffle in his arms, fishing out loose rounds of ammunition and filling clips while the others watched. It didn't look like there was much left.

"We're safe in here?" Aeron asked.

"Neggy, Talkybox."

He thumbed towards a window on the left side of the car, which was smashed.

"Creepers got in once, an' this car was Cairo to the other platty."

Taran stared at the claw marks on the windowsills.

"This tunnel comes to another platform where passengers may pick up the Old 32 line to Regulus Platform," Aeron reported.

"How do you know this if you weren't allowed down here?" Taran asked.

"GPS," she replied. "I am satellite-linked!"

Her expression quickly soured.

"I must confess the network isn't what it used to be. My data is mostly out of date."

"Hie this," Bob interrupted, returning the duffle to the overhead rack. "Hain't preachy t' scrape 'twixt here an' 32. We bail by the north side platty, then down, left, up, and exit. Capisce?"

"No capisce," Taran said.

"Sheep me, then, on the sly."

He turned and began moving towards the front of the car. As he followed, Taran was distracted by an odd flickering patch of light on the wall. Leaning closer, he examined intermittent moving pictures of people dancing and singing —a projection, perhaps. There was no projector visible anywhere, though. Aeron stood beside him and watched.

"It was a show," she said, "but all those people—"

Her fingers tugged on the sleeve of his shirt, and her breathing changed. She was honestly frightened. Once again, Taran wondered at her human qualities. Hest, on the other hand, seemed oblivious to it all.

"Let's go," she urged.

They crept stealthily through the car without incident and exited right behind Bob, who stood motionless on a platform identical to the first, shining his light farther down the track towards a stairway that crossed over to the north-side platform.

Both platforms were packed with Watchers.

Bob didn't immediately extinguish his light, but the Watchers didn't seem to see it, even when Bob shone the beam directly into their faces. Taran wondered again why they were called Watchers. Very few were equipped with eyes.

When Hest and Aeron stepped out of the train behind him, Bob motioned for silence while he studied the scene. After tracing their path once more to a far stairwell he turned off his lamp, but there was yet a faint illumination cast by a few flickering lights imbedded in the high ceiling.

Staring through the gloom, Taran wondered how they would ever make it. The bottom of the stairwell they were aiming for was in the opposite corner of the platform.

He felt a hand on his arm. Aeron leaned towards him and whispered a bit loudly.

"How'd they get inside? I thought this place was safe."

"*Shh!*" Bob hissed.

The whole shuffling, bobbing, and squirming horde began to make soft groaning noises. Bob turned to the side and spoke as softly as he could manage.

"Ever play tag, Talkybox?" he asked. "Blind's bluff, know it?"

"I like games," she said.

Her usual smile was gone.

Taran said, "Let me guess, we don't want them to touch us?"

"Catch the rot, you touch 'em. I seen it happen."

Taran shivered, and followed as close as he could when Bob stepped out onto the platform. It never occurred to him to take out his sword—he was more concerned about what might touch him, and what might happen if he ended up like one of these monsters.

Aeron clutched his shirt from behind, and Hest was beside him. He grabbed Aeron's arm and pulled her around so she was in front where he could guide her by the shoulders. When she looked forwards into the gloomy dungeon her headset shimmered briefly with what appeared to be static. Her hands reached up to grasp his.

"They can't hurt me, I suppose," she said. "I'll be a shield for you."

"Let's just get to those stairs," Taran replied.

"Alrighty," Bob said, bringing his rifle up, "les' make a hole. They's cows, honest is, so I'll be bowlin', not shootin'."

"What about not touching them?"

"Armor," he said, lowering his Cyclopean visor. "Jus' like Talkybox."

"Hest?"

"I can touch them to no ill effect," she said.

Taran felt suddenly alone.

A loud scream shattered the stillness. It came from behind them, from the train, and when it was over everything became very quiet. Not even the Watchers made a sound.

Taran realized he had heard the sound of that scream before, in the City Zoo. It was like a wild jaguar. Even while the echoes faded, the hair on his neck was still standing and gooseflesh was dancing up and down his sides.

The Watchers on both platforms began moving in unison towards the tunnel at the far end of the station. Those on the south platform were shuffling right past them, and in moments they were engulfed by the stinking flock. Taran avoided their touch, clinging to Aeron and

Hest as the horrors came too close, and all the while he wondered if there wasn't some escaped zoo animal wandering nearby.

Bob deflected a few startled monstrosities out of their path as the whole miscreated herd tumbled into the gulley in front of the stopped train. In the dim reaches of the flickering lights they could be seen running off down the tunnel.

"They're running away?" Taran wondered.

Another scream came from behind them. Hest had already turned around, and Bob's lamp was back on, illuminating the interior of the train car. At first it seemed nothing was there, but then a dark something or other moved out of sight, rushing out of the light like an enormous spider. To Taran's eyes it looked like an old tarp or a bit of cloth blown by a wind, but then he saw the eyes—retina's reflecting yellow-green. The eyes blinked, and the shadow crawled away.

"Phase Two Barcode," Bob whispered. *"Wraith."*

Taran's head was dizzy with fear, and he bit his tongue while fighting back chills. An unreasonable terror consumed his rational mind.

This was a spirit?

On the floor, just inside the doorway, the small shadow began to take shape. It was like the shadow of the black giant, only smaller. Bob brought up his light, but the shadow did not dissipate. Spreading arms and legs, it crawled towards the open door, and there it stopped.

The shimmer of skin they saw, hairless and purple, but patterned in spots like a jungle cat with ears and tail to match. When Bob extinguished his lamp, the creature rose on two legs and regarded them silently. It was no taller than a child, but this did nothing to diminish the terror of its gaze.

"The black goblin of the snuff-box!" Aeron whispered, squeezing Taran's hand.

"Great," Taran replied. "Second time today!"

Bob raised his visor and asked, "Yo' gelly chat wit' it, mebby?"

"I don't understand," Taran said, quivering with fright. "Why would she talk to it?"

"Rekhi renek!" Hest hailed loudly. "I would know your name!"

She stepped away from his side, moving towards the train.

"Hest!" Taran whispered, trying to get her attention.

The creature regarded her somewhat passively. Flicking its ears once, it narrowed its glowing eyes and glared.

"Barcodes alike blather the fancy, sure," Bob remarked.

Hest stood her ground a couple yards away from the train car.

"*Ana manim ludbuv?*"

This time there was a response—a long angry hiss. Hest stood still, her hands spread in submission. The creature crouched a little, as if preparing to leap at her. She spoke one last time.

"*Dababu!*"

The creature's ears went flat against its head, and for a moment Taran thought he glimpsed in Hest's face a reflection of the ghoul before her. Neither flinched. They were facing one another down like cats.

"No' all 'em buggers want t' go medieval up front," Bob said aside.

"You think we'll be alright if we try to get over the tracks to the north platform?"

"Nay. Overpass gots the transfer tunnel. It's the only way."

"Well, let's head for the stairs then while she holds it off!"

No sooner had he spoken than the whole train car wobbled in the culvert, banging hard against the tiled platform. The creature had vanished, but it was still somewhere inside. Hest began backing up slowly until she had rejoined them.

"I don't think he wants a fight," she said, leading them away towards the stairs. "He was probably drawn out by that business on the street."

Taran looked at her with wide startled eyes. Sounds of groaning metal and banging behind them quickened his pace as he raced alongside the others towards the overpass to the north platform. Something was happening, but all he could see by backwards glances was that the front of the car was being torn to pieces. When Hest gained the stairway to the overpass, Bob called out to Taran in a low voice.

"Wuddya say, sabre-boy? Time t' go postal?"

Taran didn't understand at first, but then he tightened the belt-straps across his chest as he walked towards the top of the steps.

"Hest said it was a bad idea to use this sword."

"She'd know, sure. Wha' about you?"

"I don't think that thing's all flesh and blood, you know? I don't see you shooting at it."

Bob gave him a knowing look, and grinned.

"Savvy, Bro!"

His smile faded as his eyes swept past Taran towards the platform. The black cat-like creature was raising a great commotion inside the train car.

"It's bigger," Taran mumbled, stumbling to a halt beside Hest.

And it was still growing. Even Hest paused to watch as the monster shifted its weight, thrusting as hard as it could to extract itself—like a baby crocodile hatching from its egg. When it stood on the platform, it only vaguely resembled the lithe shadow they saw earlier.

Looking towards the stairs, it spotted them easily.

A gurgling breath escaped the monster's massive chest. With a scream that startled them all, it ripped a trashbin from a nearby column with one swipe of its claws, and then it vanished.

The platform was empty.

"The black goblin of the snuff-box," Aeron whispered as she followed Hest towards the transfer tunnel.

The others walked in silence. Hest remained in front, and Aeron held Taran's free hand. Bob stomped along beside him opposite Aeron, listening now intently to her words.

"At night, after the tin soldiers were put in their box, the other playthings would all come out to have their own games together. It was unfortunate that the tin soldiers couldn't come out and join the fun, but the lid of the box was shut. The one good thing was that the box had holes so that the tin soldier could see his Lady in White. His shining lady stood still all night, every night, like a star, and he watched her always. There was one night, however, when the clock struck twelve and the snuff-box on the table opened. A black goblin came out, and he said something to the tin soldier."

"What'd he say?" Bob asked.

"Tin soldier," Aeron said, speaking in a low growl and leaning closer to him, *"don't wish for things that aren't yours!"*

The Big Man's face looked very grim. Taran knew his other iteration well enough to understand that he wasn't a simpleminded fellow. It struck him as odd, then, that he seemed so affected by a simple story.

"The tin soldier pretended not to hear, however," Aeron continued, resuming her natural voice, "for he wanted another leg very badly. He believed that tomorrow he would have two legs, and then he would have his shining lady also. The goblin knew his thoughts, however, and so he had something else to say."

She allowed silence to settle before continuing.

"He said, *'Very well; wait till tomorrow, then.'*"

"Dude fell out?" Bob asked.

"Indeed, he fell out the window while the children were playing, and though everyone went downstairs to search for him, the poor tin soldier had disappeared from their world."

Approaching a side-passage, Bob waved them down a left-hand turn that brought them to some steps. Taran was thinking about Aeron's story. It amazed him that she was able to closely link their journey to a simple fable. Knowing how her fable ended, he also hoped she wouldn't finish it.

Bob now took the lead beside Hest, and keeping his light low he brought them along several more stairways and interconnecting pedestrian passages. There were signs along the way directing traffic to different streets and terminals, but most of these had red x's painted over them.

Taran thought he knew the answer, but he asked anyway.

"What are the x's for?"

"Boshed," Bob said. "Dead ends."

In time they ascended to another platform. This was different from the others, though, being a flat and featureless concrete pad with a ribbed ceiling. There were no lights at all except Bob's spotlight. As he brought them to the railway, Taran saw regular old train tracks.

"This is the last open tunnel to Penn Station," Aeron said.

"Topside's Hades," Bob added, looking towards the ceiling.

He glanced aside at Hest.

"There aren't Watchers in here?" Taran asked.

"Mebby, sometimes," Bob answered. "Home plate's close. Draigs is bigger worries."

The subway tunnel looked empty.

"Well," Taran replied, "you did say you're a dragon slayer. I guess we're in your hands, Robert Swift."

Bob walked on without answering. Taran followed, keeping Aeron close, and Hest fell in beside him. As they passed more sections of tunnel that bore signs of blasting, Taran realized something that hadn't occurred to him earlier. Though all this work must have taken many people to accomplish, they had met only one man. The hope of creating safe spots had left them without access to food, and they were hunted down whenever they left to forage. Bob seemed to pick up on these thoughts.

"At Gran' Central, foun' myself the wrong side of a big blow."

"Sounds horrible," Taran replied. "What did you do?"

"Creepers showed, an' I followed 'em topside."

Taran looked over his shoulder, down the long dark passage behind them.

"Honest is," Bob continued, "I fought 'em mos' to my las' clip, and tha's when I cetched it."

"Caught what?"

"Watchers, *they don' die.*"

Aeron was walking closer to Taran now, bumping against his side.

"Sure. You lay 'em out, come back a bit, and they be gone."

"Maybe they eat their own kind?"

"Nay. I seen it. They's down, all messed-up, and then they's up."

"Bullets won't kill Watchers," Hest remarked. "Only cutting off their heads or burning them will do it."

"Barcode knows!" Bob replied with a shrug. "An' the other one, *Phase Two*—worse 'an draigs! But don' fret, mate. Got me a stash o' C-4, jus' in case."

Just ahead, Bob turned aside by a brightly painted orange spot on the curving wall of the tunnel and removed one of the stone blocks in the center of the painted area. Reaching inside, he fished out a bulky pouch. Hest glanced at Taran, catching his eye.

"Whatever you do," she said, "don't think of using that sword, Taran Morvran. It is the seal of a Great House. Using it to fight Father's creations would only soil its purity."

"Hest, how would you know something like that?"

His voice carried all the wonder and fear that had been burdening him the long day through.

"I know it because I am one of them," she replied. "I am one of the Watchers."

"You were the black giant I saw in the clothier, the same one that killed those dragons?"

"You sound frightened."

"Well, I'm not frightened of you," Aeron said, butting in. "We're sisters, and you're not like that nasty black goblin."

Bob looked like he had something to add, but he clamped his mouth shut and weighed the pouch of explosives carefully in his hand.

A familiar scream echoed down the tunnel behind them, followed by the noise of many shuffling footsteps. There were hundreds of Watchers converging silently on them.

Bob placed the explosives on the ground, and planting his feet firmly against the concrete ties he fired a few rounds in the direction of the noise. Taran covered his ears. The bursts of muzzle flare illuminated a bleak picture. Lumpen figures crumpled or jerked backwards when struck, and got up again quickly.

"Now, now, don' wanna stampeed 'em," Bob said, speaking to calm himself.

Taran tried not to imagine the whole group rushing them. Bob's light showed the Watchers were slowing down, though. They came to a halt about a hundred feet away, and there they stood still.

It was a face-off. Taran looked at Hest and wondered—if she was one of them, would she also fight them?

"Hest?" he called.

Standing beside him, she nodded towards the Watchers. A lone black shadow took form among them, and the Watchers backed away from it, formless heads ducking.

"I told you before, Taran Morvran, yet you insist on asking?"

The monster stepped slowly forwards through the Watchers. As it moved, wreathed in darkness, its sinewy black body rippled like the surface of the sea. Its legs stretched and grew, as did its arms and torso. With a sound of snapping and popping, the creature seemed to expand.

"You're going to protect us?"

"I will not allow you to come to harm. I have always looked out for you."

"Always?"

She glanced at him, and then quickly away again.

"You are—my mission."

Bob lowered his rifle to the ground and retrieved a small gray brick from the pouch he'd laid there. There were wires in the bag, and while he began inserting these carefully into the brick a look crossed his face that Taran couldn't read.

"Peace out, Bro," he said. "Bye-bye Talkybox, Barcode. Bob's the man with a plan."

Then, lifting the rifle in one hand and the bomb in the other, he began to walk down the tunnel.

"Wait!" Taran shouted after him. "Tell me you don't plan on going down there to blow yourself up!"

Bob ignored him. Maybe he meant to kill himself, and maybe he didn't. Taran wasn't sure. He was fully prepared to go after him, though.

Robert Swift was their only hope in finding the navvie named Rune.

A light touch on his shoulder startled him, and he tore his eyes from the sight of the soldier walking bravely to his death.

"It is Regulus," Hest said, staring.

And then Taran felt it, like an electrifying current in his arm. There was something happening.

"Will it do what it did in Cille?"

"I do not know, but they are clearly drawn by it."

Her eyes glimmered in the dark. A rumbling noise echoed down the tunnel—the noise of the titan's approach. Bob halted, a small dark figure with a light.

"Whatever Regulus is going to do, I hope it does it soon."

"It is not a matter of time, but of position," Hest said, tapping her foot upon the concrete railway. "That is why Regulus has led us to this location. It is also why that thing has come here, sensing the event that is about to take place."

The beast's jaws worked as it came closer. Bob pressed a device in his left hand.

"Regulus manipulates causality itself, assembling what it needs across time so that it may rejoin the other fragments in the Stone of Foundation."

The stalking leviathan swung one clawed hand like a scythe, sweeping a dozen Watchers out of its way. While their bodies were bouncing off the walls of the tunnel, Bob moved, flinging his bomb as hard as he could and turning to retreat in the same motion.

The monstrous hand swept out again, faster than human reflex. Only Hest saw it connect with the pitch, and her own reflexes were barely fast enough to position herself between Taran and the oncoming shockwave. With a sharp pinging sound, they were engulfed in a roar of flames. Taran felt himself thrown as if taken by an ocean wave, but strong arms were around him. The air was hot, and he was blind and deaf.

He fell.

The first thing he noticed besides the pain of singed skin was Aeron's considerable weight on his legs, and then cold darkness replaced the searing brilliance.

He wasn't dead.

The pommel of his sword dug painfully into his side while he lay upon his back, and his ears rang like a church full of bells, but he was otherwise whole.

"Aeron?" he mumbled. "Aeron? Could you get off me?"

The pat of a little pair of hands touched the floor beside his head. She climbed off and knelt beside him, looking sadly into his upturned face with eyes aglow.

"Aeron weighs 157 standard—"

"Yes, Aeron, we've been through this. Where's Hest?"

"She is here."

Hearing the seriousness in the navvie's voice, Taran struggled to rise, and discovered by feel that Hest lay in a heap opposite Aeron.

Was it Hest whose arms surrounded him?

"It's like Carla," Aeron said in a sorrowful voice.

She began to cry.

"I don't think she's dead," Taran replied, touching Hest's arm. "She has a strong pulse."

He felt a sudden weight on his hand, and realized that Aeron was laying her head upon Hest's body to listen to her heart.

"It makes a noise," she said. "That means she's alive, right?"

"Ol' Bob's okay, too, any'd like t'know it."

There was a series of banging sounds, and then Bob's voice spoke again.

"Glowbeam's busted!"

"Everyone's—okay?"

Hest's voice was weak, almost sleepy. Taran removed her cap and smoothed back her hair. His hand came away sticky with blood.

"When the tin soldier fell out of his world, some boys found him in the gutter."

Aeron launched into her story again while Bob toyed with his broken lamp. Taran sat beside her, listening to Hest's ragged breathing. It didn't sound good.

"It was raining," Aeron continued, "so the boys made him a boat out of newspaper. It passed under a bridge and went right down the drain, though."

"Poop," Bob said, smacking the light against the ground.

"He was alone in the darkness, longing for his Lady in White, when he was found by a sewer rat. The rat got mad because the tin soldier wouldn't show his passport or pay his toll. He got away from the rat in the end, though."

There was a click in the dark, but Bob's pale yellow lamp illuminated nothing more spectacular than the very scene Aeron's story described. They were in a small room with a tiled floor. There was an open door, and a passage beyond.

Hest was struggling to sit up. There was blood on her face, but she looked no worse for wear than any of the rest of them. Taran was relieved.

"After the rat," Aeron went on, "he was carried over a waterfall, and he started sinking. He could only think of the lady's song, when she sang to him:

Farewell, warrior! ever brave,
Drifting onward to thy grave."

She paused ominously.

"Finis?" Bob asked.

"No," Aeron said, staring back at him. "He was then eaten by a fish. The fish was caught, and was taken to the table in the very house where the tin soldier had come from. When he was discovered inside the fish, they placed him on the table and wondered at him. He got to see his Lady in White again. He had returned to the world of his origins."

These words provoked a strange feeling in Taran, though he could not say why. He silenced her with a hand on her shoulder.

"That's enough, Aeron."

"But he will not know how it ends," she objected. "It was a sad ending—"

"Sad ends's prettier'n ours," Bob muttered, looking up at the ceiling.

The others followed the light of his lamp and looked upon a wonder. A gaping hole opened high above their heads, full of twisted rebar.

"Right down the drain, huh?" Taran wondered. "How'd we survive that? There's not even any debris!"

Bob lowered the light to his face.

"Lucky ducky?"

"Didn't you listen to my story?" Aeron said to him. "There's no such thing as luck or coincidence."

He looked surprised.

"When the tin soldier was saved," she explained, "it wasn't because he was lucky, but because he was loved; and all his sorrows came not from bad luck, but from himself. He wanted something that he lacked, but in the end it was his own ambitions that destroyed both him and his shining lady."

"Well then," Taran said, helping Hest to her feet, "Tin Soldier or Dragon Slayer, Bob's the only man who can get us out of here. Think you can do it before your buddy from the snuffbox shows up again?"

Bob looked from the hole in the ceiling to the doorway.

"I knows where we is!" he said in a startled voice.

15

RAISON D'ÊTRE

New York City, Iteration of the Third Amplitude, AD 2109

The crack in the wall presented a rather bleak view. Taran had to crouch low in order to level up to the inch-wide fissure, and he was sorry when he did. It faced west across the city, and everything in that direction was what Bob called *noman's-land*. Mounds of gravel were strewn about the feet of leaning skyscrapers—it reminded him of an old graveyard. Farther in the distance the remains of a bridge spanned the river. That bridge was looking a little worse for wear.

While he reminisced, Bob was getting a shakedown.

"You took the last of our C-4 and the last of our people, and you came back with *this*?"

"They's shiny."

"*They's shiny*. What does that even mean, Robert? And how are we going to complete our objective with no ammo and no people?"

Bob lowered his eyes.

"Things get worse out there day by day," she lamented, "and Regulus can wait until the rest of us are dead."

Aeron had said that Nunna was a navvie, but to Taran she was the first reasonable person he'd met on this journey. He wondered what she would do if he told her that a fragment of Regulus was within him even now.

Better not mention that, he thought.

Her sobering speech reminded him of his own failed objectives, of his vain searching in *Dark New York*. He still hadn't found Fain.

If he found Fain, he might just find Val Anna.

Turning round towards the conversation, Taran discovered Hest was staring at his back while he peered out the crack in the wall. She didn't look away when he met her eyes, which glimmered faintly in the shadows of a rusting metal crate tucked beneath a stairwell. She'd been gloomier than ever since the incident in the tunnel.

Taran slid over to where she sat. *Home Plate*, as Bob called it, was nothing but a broom closet in the second story of the train station. They'd snuck in from the lower concourse like thieves, escorted by a small figure that rarely stopped chattering. Chatter, it seemed, was something all navvies had in common.

A candle was lit, and when Nunna set it on the floor Taran could see Aeron and Rune speaking quietly in a corner.

"Rune, you wouldn't believe the fun I've been having! Taran took me on a long walk today. We were chased by everything!"

Rune regarded her impassively. His childish demeanor clashed with his bald head and the tribal tattoos around his eyes; but his voice was still that of a youth.

"I doubt you were chased by everything, Aeron," he said.

Another notable curiosity in Rune's appearance was that the boy's arms and hands had been replaced by metallic counterparts. They were perfectly jointed to work like normal limbs. Aeron held onto one of his cold steel hands while she talked.

"At least half the Watchers in the city were after us!"

"Doubt it."

"Were too!"

They fell to whispering in tense voices, poking each other playfully. Taran looked on, mystified. It was like listening to two ordinary children. They hushed somewhat when Bob shuffled past them towards the opposite corner. He began rummaging through some blankets there—the oddments of fallen comrades.

While everyone else was thus occupied, Nunna came and stood before Taran, hands on her hips and looking for all the world like she was about to pick a fight.

"*You*," she addressed him, narrowing her eyes, "what's your name?"

Taran blushed. The candlelight presented a short woman in a clinging padded jumpsuit—something no decent girl would have worn in his day. Her blue hair was gathered in a messy mop, capped with a pair of goggles.

"I'm Taran," he said. "She's Hest."

Nunna regarded Hest curiously, but Hest stroked her long braid and dozed, paying no attention whatsoever.

"Why'd Robert bring you here?" Nunna asked.

"He brought us here to see you."

"That much I know, Carl."

"It's *Taran*."

"Whatever."

"We were looking for a yumiko-navvie known to the one I travel with," Taran said, nodding towards the small figures in the corner. "We believe Rune has important information for us."

"Well, you've found him. I suppose you want to take him?"

Taran began to sense that her agitation hinged upon this crucial factor. He hadn't considered they would find Rune and then fight over his custody. In fact, he still wasn't sure Rune had anything important to tell them at all.

"Anything else you want?" Nunna asked.

"No offense, but it doesn't look like you have much to offer."

"Any better amenities you know of in this town, fella?"

"I spent some time under a bridge," he offered. "Actually, we're rather anxious to move on."

"Where are you off to in such a hurry?"

"The park," said a voice from the corner.

Rune's golden eyes gleamed in the dark.

"We need to bring the strangers to the park," he insisted.

Nunna frowned, and stared at the sword leaning against the metal crate beside Hest.

"Why?"

"Because that is why we survived and the others did not."

"He's always saying such pleasant things," Aeron added glumly.

"The park's nothing but a crater since yesterday," Nunna said, "and that impact stirred up every nasty thing on this side of damnation. How much longer do you think you would survive if I let you wander off into oblivion?"

Taran was becoming worried that she wouldn't allow them to go anywhere without argument—or even violence. Just as it seemed their conversation had broken down into a vague threat, Hest spoke up.

"I remember your name," she said to Nunna. "My father often spoke of you—and of your *gift.*"

"And who was your father?" Nunna asked.

Her voice was sarcastic, as if Hest could not possibly know anyone connected to her; but her eyes told a different story. She seemed both surprised and somehow fearful.

"My father is Cedric DePons."

"Father, or maker?" Nunna asked.

"Barcode," Bob murmured, turning momentarily from his bundles in the corner.

Taran tried to explain. "She really is his flesh and blood daughter."

"I never heard he had any daughters."

"We're sisters," Aeron suggested helpfully.

Nunna called over towards the corner. "What do you think, Bob?"

"Barcode, definitely," he replied, stuffing a small pouch with oddments from the pile. He tied the pouch and secured it under the plate of his thigh armor. Nunna watched with an anxious look.

"What're you up to over there, Robert?"

"Goin' with 'em."

"Like Hades you are! I need you here!"

Bob looked up to the wall, where a small flag was draped. It wasn't the American flag, though it was very similar, having thirteen red and white stripes. The blue wasn't in the corner, though, but in the middle, and presented in its round field were a brilliant stylized sun-disk and a sword.

"Game's over," he said, facing the flag.

"It's not over until Regulus is shut down, Robert. The others are still working on it. Don't you remember the message?"

Bob chuckled. "*Decoherence*, sure!"

She walked over to him and stared him down, though she stood only as tall as his chest. Bob faced her solemnly.

"Still a job I can do," he said articulating his words with deliberate care. "We been at it two years. A man needs to *complete*, Nunna. Don't you get that?"

She averted her gaze to the flag while he continued.

"Brit-American Union was *jack* strong as ol' USA," he said. "It ain't 'bout that, though. Be it about us, tricked to cleanin' up a fool's mistakes. DePons an' Kabta hain't comin' back, Nunna. Game's over. Bob's leavin', an' takin' Barcode with. Metal-hands dude's right. There's a reason for us survivin', and I think's it's *them*. We's s'posed to bring 'em someplace safe, sure."

Nunna's expression turned from frustrated anger to despair.

"You'll die out there," she said.

"*Barcode*, 'member?" he said, jerking a thumb towards Hest.

Nunna looked up at him, arms at her sides. "Bringing her here was a big risk, Robert. She'll just draw more of her kind!"

"She done well enough," Bob said. "Saved ol' Bob's butt twice, she has."

"And how many times have *I* saved you?"

She was angry again.

"You're crazy, Robert! How do you plan on getting them into the park?"

"Moons is both full. We dust upside, north."

"What? Right out the front door?"

He nodded. "Only way now."

"What happened to the open line leading to Old 32? How'd you get to the lower concourse?"

"I already tol' you. Lucky Bob made a hole."

She glared at him, then turned her scowl on Taran. Bob tossed him a can of Spam, and Taran passed it quickly to Hest. She accepted it with a sour face.

"Come on with, Nunna," Bob said. "Better'n the daily fight to find another *can-o-farts.*"

It was obvious Nunna was done arguing. They couldn't see her downcast face in the candlelight, but Taran suspected there were tears. Bob patted her head.

"I just don't want to be on my own," she said, wiping her eyes with a sleeve of her jumpsuit. "They need your help more than I do, Robert, but I won't leave my post until Kabta gives the order. I *can't.*"

"May-haps that be Nunna's own reason to exist, then," he comforted.

The others began crowding around a metal door on one end of the room, preparing to head back out into the fearful corridors. Rune clung to Aeron's hand while Nunna looked on sadly.

"Take the main stairway to the concourse this time," she said. "I don't want anything backtracking along your trail."

"Stairs is bad, Nunna—totally boshed."

"Then tighten up, Bob. Mind you egress with troubles in tow, too. I'm down to one person here."

The door squealed on its hinges and released a fine rain of rust particles. Bob's rifle-mounted spotlight was on, sweeping a narrow chamber full of toilets in stalls.

"Ladies room's cashed," he announced. "Anyone gots t' go?"

Aeron looked at Rune, but he shook his head. Taran was nearly overwhelmed by the powerful odor of the place.

"Syonara," Bob said, stepping into the washroom.

Nunna replied without looking up. "Goodbye, Robert Swift."

Then, in a quiet voice she added, *"You're a gonner."*

In the tiled corridor beyond the washroom they all heard the door being bolted behind them. The clack of the locks echoed ominously.

She already counted them as dead.

"Is she really going to be alright by herself?" Taran whispered to Bob.

"Nunna? Girl's a one-navvie army, she is."

"What about us?"

"Silent, Bro. We's ghosts now."

They followed Bob through a series of halls and passageways, all rotting. The building itself was all they could hear, groaning and creaking in its slow decay. Phantom footsteps and half-heard whispers vexed them as they passed by empty offices and waiting rooms. Bob swept his light through these in passing. There never was anything inside, but he didn't seem surprised by this.

Eventually, they reached a very large room that was darker than all the rest. Bob switched off his light and pointed towards a row of glass doors in the distance.

"Concourse," he whispered in Taran's ear. "Sheep my backside, Bro. Watch our lil' Talkyboxes."

Taran nodded. He was actually beginning to understand Bob's ridiculous banter. Before setting out, however, they stood a long moment to allow their eyes to adjust to the gloom, listening to the ghost-sounds of cracking paint and a distant banging door. A definite watchful presence brooded nearby. Aeron and Rune pressed in on either side of him. Hest rested her hand upon his shoulder, and he could feel it trembling.

"Is something the matter?" he asked.

Her face was surprisingly angry, as though she was fighting against an impulse to strike him. Taran couldn't imagine that was what she was thinking, but her whispered words—almost too faint to hear—made him wonder.

"I can hear Regulus," she said softly. *"It's not safe."*

Bob had already begun walking slowly on towards the sliding glass doors at the end of the room.

"Of course it's not safe," Taran said. "But we've got to go on, Hest."

"You don't understand," she muttered, turning her angry eyes away from him.

Perplexed by Hest's strange behavior, Taran followed Bob towards the doors. The glass was green with a filmy growth, but one partially opened door allowed a glimpse of what lay beyond. In another minute they were peering out at a flight of steps descending to marble floors, wrought-iron trusses, and columns in rows along either side. The setting sun slanting through the high side windows cast everything in red-brown hues.

Taran had not expected such a grand vista. Bob shoved the door open a little wider. The vaulted ceiling was actually glass framed by iron, which allowed more of the ruddy light to wash everything in its warm glow. Beneath, the rows of stone columns flanked a path leading straight to a distant pair of doors. A mighty clock hung from the webwork of metal beams, but it had no hands. This was a timeless place, indeed.

They were looking into a dragon's lair.

Bob eyed the large double doors of the exit. Between these and the place where they stood there stretched an empty gauntlet. The shadows beneath the colonnade on either hand retreated before the sun, leaving a shining green path to the way out. About halfway along that path they saw a stairway descending to another lower concourse, and beside it there was a man on a pedestal. He stood facing the columns on the right-hand side of the terminal.

"What's that statue?" Taran whispered.

"Cassatt," Bob answered.

"You mean *the* Cassatt?"

"Built the ol' station. Him."

Taran glanced behind them. It seemed much gloomier after taking in the warm sunlit area ahead.

"Are we going out the front doors?"

"Mebby," Bob replied, stepping out from the shadows onto the steps.

The others followed closely, and while they inched forward into the hall the feeling of danger increased. Upon either side of the wide staircase a few other shadowy passages looked out like watchful eyes, viewing the stairs from shattered doorsills where looming half-imagined silhouettes slouched and swayed. The hairs stood up on his arms, and his mind turned once again to the sword strapped to his back.

Hest leaned over and whispered something in his ear, but her voice was so low that Taran couldn't understand.

"Hest?"

When he turned to look at her, he was alarmed to see tears standing in the corners of her eyes.

"You don't have much time," she said, forcing calm into her voice.

Bob stopped and looked back at them. A deathly stillness permeated the gloom of the concourse.

"What's Barcode jabberin' 'bout?" he asked in a terse whisper. We's tryin' to exit without raisin' Cairo—"

"Regulus draws all of the creatures made by its power," she said.

"You're talking too loudly, Hest," Taran said, urging her with his hands to quiet down.

A mocking smile came to her mouth, further bewildering him.

"What you bear in your flesh, Taran Morvran, speaks louder than the voice of a dragon; and it calls all of them to you."

"Hest, I don't understand what you're talking about."

"You must!" she shouted.

Taran blinked. She had never raised her voice to him before. There was only one time he could remember, outside the inn at Cille, where she momentarily lost her cool—because of Regulus.

"But we're safe," Taran insisted. "We have you with us—"

Thrust suddenly backwards by an enormous blast of air, Taran collided with Bob's armored chest. Both men fell clattering down the steps to land in a tangle at the bottom. Taran lifted his head and shoved Bob aside so that he could get a view of the steps.

There was no one there.

Hest was gone.

Bob was the first on his feet, shouldering his rifle and wheeling round in a full circle. Taran stood and watched him turn and fix his aim on every corner of the enormous room. He was looking for Hest, but she was nowhere to be found.

"Where she at?" he hissed.

Aeron and rune had also been blasted down the steps. They were sitting up now, and both appeared intact.

"She vanished?" Taran asked. "But why? What's going on?"

"Don' you know?" Bob asked. "You really that blind, Bro?"

No, he wasn't. Taran had heard the warning in Hest's voice; but he still could not believe that she would turn against them.

The impulse to draw out his sword was stronger than ever, and this time he obeyed. Gripping the hilt tightly in his left hand, Taran slid the rag-wrapped bundle from the strap on his shoulder. The others looked on in silence while the blade was unbound. Even as the gloomy terminal seemed to darken, the blade's edges glimmered.

Taran clutched the shining sword tightly in front of him. It was a heavy and unfamiliar weight to his hands. No matter how steady he tried to hold it, the sword's tip wavered.

"What're you thinking, Robert? You think Hest attacked us?"

Bob frowned at him, and then looked towards the first columns to the right of the stair. Peeping out at him, Aeron's glowing eyes were wide with fright. Rune was waving for him to join them. They'd both taken cover as soon as they were on their feet.

"Smart they is, our Talkyboxes," Bob said. "Barcode's a barcode after all. No dustin' Barcodes. They's evil wisps, sure."

Taran watched him stalk off towards the cowering navvies. A sudden spiteful anger burned in his heart.

"That's ridiculous!" Taran shouted after his retreating figure. "She would never hurt us!"

When Bob was out of sight behind the columns, Taran shouted once more, adding, "You're nothing but a coward!"

He felt bad the moment he said it. He knew that Robert Swift was one of the bravest people he knew. It was Taran Morvran who was the coward—the coward who had hid under a bridge for months and months because he couldn't face a world without Val Anna. What would she think of him now?

"I'm sorry," he said, far too softly for anyone else to hear.

A great black scaly paw and four enormous claws stepped down beside him.

Lifting his eyes slowly, Taran met the gaze of a monstrous shadow. It wasn't sharp and distinct, but he recognized the features well enough.

"Hest?"

She had come out of nowhere. Now, leaning closer, the head resolved just enough for him to glimpse a crooked smile, and fangs as long as his hand.

"Regulus!"

The word wheezed out in Hest's own voice.

"Hest!" he whispered, faint with fear. "You said—you said that you would protect me, right?"

The monster swiveled its eyes around in the shadow of its head.

"She has failed you, Taran Morvran."

"No! You would never fail me. I know you, Hest. I know you can turn back whatever this is—whatever your father did to make you like this. This is not you!"

A shiver rustled the monstrous being.

"Anattalakkuma, Sehreku, ul kimayati."

They were words in an archaic tongue. The strange thing was, Taran's mind immediately grasped her meaning.

"You talk the talk, Little One, but you are not like me."

The monster made a gurgling choking noise that echoed loudly in the wide hall. The black head glared down at him. When it spoke again, Taran knew their conversation had reached a conclusion.

"Hest is gone. Gummurka libbi ana epeshum? You would do battle, my friend?"

"Battle—?" he stammered. "Battle? Battle for what?"

The creature's mouth hung open.

"Regulus!" it said.

Behind the hateful yellow eyes, Taran thought he glimpsed Hest's dirty face peering at him again through the grate under the bridge. He remembered her the way she was before the calamitous voyage across the Atlantic—before the cursed fragment of Regulus entered him and cut him off from his friends and family. He had relied on Hest for everything, and now Regulus would take her, too.

The sword in his hands, which she had warned him never to take out, was a weapon designed for destroying flesh. Whatever had been done to Hest, he doubted she could be harmed by a blade. Bob's parting speech had made it plain that he wasn't interested in charging in to the rescue, either.

Taran was alone.

The black shadow stepped back from him, seeming to enjoy the sight of him struggling against the considerable weight of both the sword and his decision. There was no plan in Taran's mind, and no rational thought behind his actions. The twisted shell that imprisoned his friend was superior in every way. How could he even raise a hand against her?

"Curse you, Regulus!"

His shout was so loud that it surprised even him. Angry tears sprang to his eyes, and Taran blinked them away. It was plain to him now why Hest had urged him to draw out his blade, but he lacked the courage to use it.

"*Such a coward,*" she chided, assuming a little more of the manner and tone of the girl he once knew. "*Still such a baby.*"

The black shadow swirled. Taran glanced up, alarmed by something moving among the iron trusses high above the stairs—fate, maybe. Or maybe it was just another choice offered by a truly terrifying sequence of events.

"*It is the end, Taran Morvran!*"

Hest was in the dragon's claws before she even knew it was there.

Without a sound, a great red flash of scales was flung down upon the steps with a crash that washed everything in a rain of crushed stone. Mere inches from the impact, Taran was frozen in a crouching posture. It wasn't the best moment Bob could have chosen to give him a chance to run for it, but it was the thought that counted.

The terminal rang with the percussive deafening noise of gunfire. Picking through the marble tiles at the base of the steps, the air was full of flying metal and painful pellets of shrapnel. Blood flew in black streamers through the air. It was all truly terrifying.

A great tail swept through the air, grazing the top of his head. Taran ducked beneath a sweeping claw, and falling backwards he scuttled backwards as the twisting shapes of dragon and beast rolled together across the stairway in front of him. They wrestled one another with grim intent. Neither seemed to be able to damage the other, and though they were both peppered with high velocity rounds, it only seemed to make things worse. The air was full of blood and a terrible roar of giant voices.

And then the gunfire stopped.

Furtive figures bent low to the ground were making a dash for the exit. They ran without looking back. Even Aeron had left him.

The sound of a woman's scream brought Taran's eyes back to the fight, but the air was smoky and there was no sign of the combatants. They had vanished into the gloom, just as they had come. All that was left in their passing was confusion and silence. There was something else, though. A palpable force weighed upon Taran's limbs like lead weights.

There was a burning like that of Regulus, only stronger.

A long quiet moment passed. Taran felt the burning growing more intensely, and then the dragon came upon him. It launched itself from the shadows of the colonnade with an uproar of chaotic movement, its massive body blazing a trail of devastation in its tumultuous wake. Then everything went black and all around him writhed a wall of horned flesh that smoked and stank. Whether he was stunned or dead, Taran knew not, but a limb as thick as the trunk of a tree was pressed up against his side, and a stout loop of tail tightened around his waist. Horrible wings rattled over him, suffocating him in a blizzard of putrid cast-off scales.

It did not strike.

Taran felt its breath wafting over him in folds that clung as heavy as grave-shrouds. The head came down, its fiery eyes staring into his soul, filling him with craven feelings of self-pity and loneliness. The eyes were intelligent. They passed back and forth from the blade in his hands to his face.

"Well met, Dark Tower!"

The deep brassy voice rumbled in plain English.

"Who are you?" Taran asked.

"I am called Glede."

Regulus burned inside him at the sound of that name, sending fire up into his arms. The dragon was aware of it, too. It blinked its serpentine eyes at him, flicking a long purple tongue. Slowly it withdrew, unfolding its body so that Taran collapsed to his knees upon the floor. It was then he realized the floor had changed from marble to peat.

It was like the first time, at the village of Cille.

The train station vanished entirely, leaving him in a rocky forested landscape. All the world was hazy and indistinct, and a tolling of bells rang out wildly. Taran knelt before the red dragon, the monster from the mosaic inside the tower under Cnoc Ddraig—the monster to whom the people of Cille had sacrificed their children.

He was alone with the dragon in the forest.

Why was the dragon here, too?

"You don't seem like a Morvran," Glede declared, "other than that you carry the sacred sword, of course."

"How do you know me?"

"Don't tell me you haven't noticed that I am also a Tower."

"What Tower?"

"*Dim Da'ummatu* is the fragment which I bear. And you are *Regulus*, which was once called Mul'lugal, the Little King."

It tasted the air with its tongue before continuing.

"I thought the heir of Morvran would bear Qashtu. It matters not. Regulus will do just as well."

"You intend to take it from me?"

The dragon's head was larger than a man's body, and Glede lowered it until the jutting jaw was only inches above the ground, just in front of Taran.

"Da'ummatu is a weaver of dreams, *Little King.* You will beg me to take Regulus from you before the end!"

Contrary to its threats, the dragon went as still as stone.

Taran's heart pulsed painfully. He bent over, clutching at his chest with a numb hand. When the first moment of agony let up a bit, he looked quickly around for a route of escape. The trees around him swirled madly in a silent hurricane-gale, and then they also stood still.

His heart ached, but time itself had gone dead.

Taran looked around in amazement. Glede's eyes stared, unseeing. Had the Regulus fragment done all this? There wasn't time to wonder, for it seemed the stone's powers had a limit. The dragon was no longer completely motionless.

It had begun to move again, albeit very slowly. First the awful wedge-shaped head turned side-to-side, searching. Though it seemed to miss him, the menacing green eyes fell upon something nearby, something Taran had not noticed until that very moment.

Hest lay unconscious upon a bed of grass.

She was wounded, her body bleeding. Taran looked up in time to meet Glede's eyes.

"You and I will meet again, *Little King.*"

The forest and the dragon had vanished. Hest was gone, too.

He picked himself up from the floor of the terminal and made his way, slow and stumbling, towards the exit.

"Barcode pushin' up daisies, Bro?"

Taran slumped down beside Bob, only vaguely aware that he had walked right through the open door of the terminal and out into the streets, carrying his sword like a walking stick. The others were gathered by a partially collapsed wall, hunkering in its shadow.

"Lil' Talkybox wouldn't 'low ol' Bob to dust 'til we knew you two was done, sure."

He looked up, and noticed for the first time their armored escort was running a little ragged, with a bruised face and red eyes. Taran felt Aeron's small arms around his middle. Her face was pressed into his side. Rune stood beside her, his face grim.

"I don't know what happened," Taran said. "I don't think she's dead. She and the dragon, Glede—they vanished after I—"

Robert Swift was staring at him with a shrewd look.

"That 'hain't no draig like I ever seen. Unpossible odds, smokin' a worm that big."

"I didn't kill it. I made it go away. It has something to do with Regulus, and that's all I know."

"You gots a bit o' that rock inside you?"

Taran nodded.

"I heared it," Bob said. "An' DePons, that closed-mouth fool, he sez there be someone like you, an' all Watcherdom be crawlin' after you like Holy Moses! Cogged sech prophetisms lame afore now, but ol' Bob has seen the light, Bro. Seein' is believing,' sure."

"Regulus calls them. The dragon, too. And Hest—"

"Bob's not one for thinkin' overmuch 'bout those dusted in a fight."

He looked suddenly wistful, as if to contradict his own words.

"Well, Moses, what we be doin' now?"

Taran wondered. Regulus was the reason these monsters existed in the first place, so if he was carrying a fragment of that stone's power, it stood to reason that he was also the chief cause of his own calamities, no matter where he decided to go.

"Nunna was right," he said. "This is just too dangerous. We should go back and see if there's another way."

Bob stood up and looked down the street. The sun was setting.

"Hain't no backtrackin'. What's Talkybox Two say?"

"We need to get to the park," Rune answered.

Taran returned his sword to its strap and pushed himself up to his feet.

"DePons instructed you to do this?" he asked.

"No. It's not like he actually talked to me. It's a directive, written into the very core of my system."

While he spoke, his golden eyes glowed, framed in those perplexing tattoos. Aeron looked up at him, wondering.

"I never thought about it before," she said.

"It was there all along," Rune replied, "unnoticed—until *Dubito*."

Aeron nodded. "We're to take the strangers to the park, and use what we have been given."

"DePons has left us no choice, then," Taran replied, "not with Hest, and not with this. If Fain ever came here, I must go on to the door and step through it, for my purpose lies on the other side."

"We all headin' that way," Bob agreed.

Aeron and Rune walked hand in hand beside him. Taran had lasted two days in the ruined city, and in that time he hadn't discovered a single reason to believe Fain ever came here. On the other hand, his arrival was expected. DePons had left something behind that Taran needed; but as yet, Rune hadn't said much about it—apart from his insistence that they must go to the park.

Looking aside, he saw Rune gazing back at him, his metal hands glinting in the eerie moon-glow rising in the south.

"Your sword is cool," he said. "It's like the sword on our flag."

"It's just extra baggage," Taran replied, tucking it back into its strap. "Of course, it would help to know I'm carrying it for a reason. Rune, would you be able to tell me about the thing we're looking for in the park?"

"No. I think we'll know it when we see it."

"Does it have to do with the Sky Power?"

He closed his eyes a moment, and then looked up again.

"I don't have any information about that. What is it?"

Taran was puzzled. None of Fain's references to the *Sky Power* were explained in his journals, and even the navvies made by DePons knew nothing about it. Was it possible there wasn't even a link between Fain's journey and what he was doing now?

Somehow he doubted that. There were no coincidences. DePons was just stringing them along.

Night fell.

"Park's ahead," Bob mumbled.

They couldn't see much of anything, for the moons were still low in the sky; but odd noises punctuated the mute darkness of the streets, and the soft moaning and coughing of Watchers blanketed everything in appalling gloom. The suffocating mood nearly drove Taran mad. On top of this he was exhausted. The adrenaline produced during the episode in the terminal had worn off long ago, and now he was falling asleep on his feet. He daydreamed while they walked on, and he thought about Hest. Her strange words that night on the road from Cille haunted him.

"With a fragment of Regulus within, you will not rely on me so much as I desire. I will need to teach you how to take care of yourself, and of Regulus, before our journey together comes to an end."

He didn't understand what she was, or what she had to do with the Watchers, but he was starting to feel a deep sadness for her. How could DePons have willingly set his daughter up to journey with him, knowing their fellowship would end this way? It just didn't make sense.

Bob interrupted his thoughts by planting a hand in the center of his chest.

"Hang a bit," he said, turning his head from side to side.

Taran stood fast and listened to the scuffling of Watchers and an occasional screech from the sky—nothing good, but nothing out of the ordinary.

"Feel it?"

"Feel what?" Taran asked.

"Don' know."

The streets seemed darker. Two pale moons were ascending, their full orbs casting the ruined cityscape into grim relief. The perimeter of the park was delineated by a low ridge of broken stone and soil about fifty feet away. They'd seen it like a black wall against the last light of the setting sun, but that was from far-off. They waited while the moonlight bloomed brighter. What would they do if they ran into trouble out here, he wondered?

At that moment, a sliver of moonlight broke out from between two large buildings behind them, shining strongly upon the upper rim of the slope. There was no sign of anything more alarming than the climb itself—one hundred feet of twisted metal and broken bits of pavement.

"Go time," Bob said.

Watching him walk towards the mounds of debris, Taran began to pick up on Bob's uneasiness. It occurred to him that even though he could still hear Watchers in the streets behind, everything seemed to be keeping its distance from the park.

"Watch your step!" Aeron shouted to Rune as she skipped after him towards the slope.

Taran was last in line, and wondered now if he would ever make it to the top. Firm footing was impossible to find. The loose soil was full of surprises, including holes full of twisted metal bars and broken glass. When they stood together at last on a large slab of concrete perched high atop the rim, they looked down inside the crater and were amazed.

The impact had blasted away more than just the park, its lakes, and the little forests. The flat smoking plain before them bridged the whole island from east to west. Towers had been reduced to rubble, and the deep tunnels of subways were exposed. The only notable detail was a little hill near the center of the ring, about a mile away.

It was like a miniature Dragon's Mound.

Bob started down into the smoking pit, and the others followed. As Taran took up the rear, he began to feel the sharp tug of Regulus on his heart. Fear stole over him once again, slowing his feet, though there wasn't yet any particular danger in sight.

A few puddles remained from the previous day's rain, but the impact area was otherwise dry. About halfway to the epicenter Taran had the inclination to look back. Bob paused without a word, and together they surveyed the distant ridgeline behind them, where a swaying staggering hoard of Watchers lurched slowly forwards.

"We gots company," Bob said.

In answer to this, a horrible chorus of screeches broke out, repeating over and over in unison like the sounds of night insects, but magnified hugely. Winged shapes glided across the moons. Bob turned and continued walking as though nothing were wrong in the world.

"Are they coming for us?" Taran wondered, trying to keep up.

"Tellin' me?"

"I'm hoping there's more ahead than a lump of meteorite in a field."

Bob chuckled. "Hope?"

Taran had been puzzling the man's determination to guide them on towards what normal folks would deem a certain death. He didn't quite believe Bob was doing it because of Taran's claim to hold a fragment of Regulus, and the Robert Swift he knew would never stick his neck out for the welfare of anyone else. There might be other motives. Taran was too tired to give it much thought—and there were other things to worry about.

The weird cries were gathering closer, and now the moonlight fell upon the crater rim to the west. Herds of huddled figures were moving there, too. All that was left alive in the world seemed to be racing for the smoking lump up ahead. Just as he reached the end of his strength, Taran saw that it wasn't just a lump after all. Its smooth cylindrical shape was rounded at both ends, like a giant seed.

It was certainly no comet.

"Giant can-o-beans?" Bob wondered.

"Well," Taran answered. "Whatever it is, I'll bet there's something important inside."

On the far horizon, an unbroken tide of Watchers continued to pour over the ridge towards them. Bob glanced towards the wretched tsunami and began to walk a circuit of the cylinder. Taran joined him, his legs shaking with exhaustion.

"This survived falling from the sky?" he asked.

"Like Lucifer," Bob replied with a nod. "Lots o' junk comin' down since Hades broke loose."

"It's man-made?"

Taran had read speculative fiction works expounding on the possibility of spaceflight. This was, in fact, one of the forces which had impelled him to create his own flying machine, the first of its kind. For a moment or two, he completely forgot about his weariness and the onrushing horde for sheer wonder of this new development.

"Unless it was a top secret project, there is nothing like this design in my data," Rune answered.

"It's obviously some kind of container. You think maybe we can get inside?"

"You see a door, Bro?"

He did not. The object was large, easily thirty feet long and half as wide. It was buried to nearly half its width in the ground, and bore no signs of crushing or other damage; but there wasn't anything like a door. In fact, there wasn't an outline or seam to be found in the entire exposed surface.

"Jus' Bob's luck, be it underneath."

There were sudden cries directly overhead. The sound of wings brought new haste to the search.

Regulus was calling to them.

Taran began to think out loud.

"Aeron, you said something about using what you were given?"

She squeezed his arm tighter.

"So, what do we have that would open this thing?" he asked.

Bob looked from his rifle to Taran, but Taran shook his head. Hope was fading fast. Taran made his way to one of the smooth ends. Its surface radiated a little warmth, but it wasn't too hot to touch.

Aeron spoke up, saying, "We don't have anything but our hands."

Taran was in the very act of running his palm across the scorched metallic surface when she spoke. He paused, feeling an odd series of dimples. The moonlight wasn't enough to see by, but he faintly detected a pattern of smoothed whorls under his fingertips.

"There's something here."

Despite the danger, Bob risked a quick look with his light; and then they saw it. Near the center, just above their heads, a slight depression appeared. It was the size and shape of a man's hand.

"Talkybox got it right?" Bob said, switching his light off again.

Aeron clapped her hands, oblivious to the dangers creeping nearer every minute. Taran reached upwards and pushed his palm against the indentation in the surface of the hull.

"It's pliable, like living tissue."

"Yah?" Bob wondered. "*Open sezme.*"

Taran pushed harder, but nothing happened.

While they investigated, the distant din of approaching monstrosities had drawn ever closer and louder. The ground quaked. Bob's weapon was raised, but the clip wasn't even in. He was out of ammo.

"Can you lift me?"

Taran looked down at Rune, surprised by the navvie's request.

"These hands always were a little strange," he explained, "but I must have been given them for some reason. Can you lift me up?"

Taran looked aside at Bob with a pained expression, and Bob tossed his rifle aside with a curse.

"Upsy-daisy, Talkybox Two."

He bent over and allowed Rune to climb up onto his armored back, groaning under the navvie's considerable weight. It took him two tries to lean upright against the side of the craft while Rune rode his shoulders.

"I can reach it!"

Taran watched as Rune placed his hand against the side of the cylinder, but there was no response. Lowering the navvie back to the ground, Bob backed away huffing with exertion.

"We tried," Rune said. "Maybe Aeron—"

He was interrupted by an electric hum. There was no other indication yet that anything was happening; but the hum was slowly building in intensity. When the noise crescendoed suddenly to a higher pitch and volume, a blinding white light radiated across the metal hull, and the park crater was illuminated from rim to rim. A horrifying scene was photographed into their retinas.

The ground in every direction heaved with terrors.

Dizzied by the painful blast, Taran saw an eye of darkness in the light, and he clawed himself blindly towards it. The dark spot was the only thing he could clearly see, like a pupil in the eye of the sun. Bob followed him with the navvies close behind. As soon as they were all inside, the cylinder's interior surface reintegrated behind them, forming a solid wall. There was no door or hatch.

All within was a black wall of night.

"Metal Hands Dude!" Bob gasped, filling the dark with his voice. "You saved us!"

"It was Aeron's idea," Rune replied.

"Hush," Taran said. "Do you hear them?"

Muffled sounds of banging and roaring echoed faintly, but all of it was indistinct, as if heard from a great distance. Taran felt Aeron's hand in his, but he wasn't able to comfort her. His own pulse was racing.

Regulus was awakening again within him. With the intensity of its stirring, a soft amber glow fell around them.

"Who's that?"

Rune's simple question caused them all to turn around and look in the direction of his voice. They were surprised to see amidst a brace of cables and struts suspended in the center of the cylinder an ovoid tank filled with clear fluid. The tank was laid out horizontally. Drifting in the fluid within there was the figure of a man.

"Is it Lucifer?" Aeron asked.

Taran was mesmerized. The man's blue hair and chiseled features were flawless, like a work of art. He moved a little, though it seemed he was asleep.

"He's alive, whoever he is," Taran answered.

Shoving aside a forest of cables, Bob made his way to the pod and tapped it with his hand.

"Yo, Superman," he said.

"Stop!"

Even while all the others stared at him, Taran couldn't come up with a reason why he had shouted. It was just a gut feeling—that, and Regulus. The noise of the Watchers outside continued in the stillness. Bob's hand was poised in midair over the tube.

"You know 'im?" Bob asked.

"He's very dangerous," Taran replied. His own face bore a puzzled expression. He couldn't explain exactly what he was feeling.

It was the same feeling he had when the red dragon was near.

"Bibbu," he managed, speaking the word as it arrived from the ether.

"Bobo?" Bob chuckled, pointing at the figure in the tube. "Dude's got a weird name! Goes wi' 'is pretty blue hair."

"It's not his name," Taran said. "I don't rightly know where the word comes from or what it means, but it has something to do with him. He's a Dark Tower."

Bob sobered up quickly, and looking at Taran he tapped the side of his head.

"Regulus, Bro?"

The cylinder rocked gently as something large rammed it. Everyone braced themselves as well as they could against the cluttered interior structures. Aeron remained glued to Taran's arm.

"Don't worry," he said to her. "I don't think they can get in through these walls."

"Don' much matter, that," Bob said. "Hain't gonna let us *out*, sure."

"We're here for a reason," Taran replied, joining him beside the crystal tank with Aeron in tow.

"Our purpose is here, with this fellow," Rune added, coming to his side.

"He's dangerous, though," Aeron said.

Taran struggled with all these thoughts, and with a rising compulsion that worked its way through him from the depths of his heart. It wasn't Fain or DePons who had set this road before him. This was his own path, and the door was before him. As uncertain as he was about everything else, this much he knew without a doubt, that the man inside the crystal tube was not from the Earth. He was from the place where Val Anna had gone, and talking to him would help him find her.

Taran shut his eyes tightly and tried to concentrate—tried to think of the moments when time seemed to slow down, when the world around him paused and he moved through it.

When he moved through the stone Regulus.

He rested his hands upon the warm glassy container, brushing crystalline condensate from its glowing surface and tuning out the echoing shrieks of the monsters outside. All sounds quickly faded away, and every sensation—even the feel of Aeron's hand in his. A curtain dropped on the world, and in the wall of night he saw strange images passing before his eyes.

First he saw a girl with the tail and ears of a fox. She sang, but he could not hear her voice. Next he saw a dragon, the great red monster that had fought with Hest. Glede was in a place that looked like an arena, looming over a young woman dressed in royal robes whose face was radiant like the sun. He thrust this image from his mind's eye and searched elsewhere in the void.

He soon discovered he was not alone.

A person appeared before him, a man with long blue hair who held in his extended hand a glittering blue-black crystal disk. In the center of this stone glowed an odd harp-shaped symbol.

The man's eyes were closed, as if he slept.

Stretching forth his hand, Taran touched the stone lightly. The sleeper's eyes flew open, irises blood-red. Taran's consciousness was jolted, and he scrambled to steady himself in the immolate gaze.

"Why are you here?" the man asked. "You are not Nurkabta. Where is Aries? Where are the Gremn?"

Taran heard the deep voice inside his head, but the man hadn't opened his mouth at all. He was communicating by thought alone.

"Ah, but you are one of the Towers."

Taran rested his hand on the stone. It was the only thing he felt solidly. The red eyes softened.

"I am called Dun. I guess if you are here, I must have been sleeping an awfully long time. Tell me, has the empress returned yet to the World of Origins?"

"The empress?"

"Hmm. She must have. But I am also curious to know, who are you?"

"I am Taran Morvran."

"A Morvran. *Interesting.* Then the War of the Towers has begun?"

"I just wanted to ask about the place you came from."

Dun grinned mischievously. "Verily unto you shall I surrender this, then," he said. "I am no more for battle, yet I think we will meet again, Taran Morvran, on the field of blood!"

He shoved the fragment straight into Taran's chest, and a burning flame embraced his body. It was much worse than when he had taken in Regulus. Taran shouted while he fell, but no sound ever came to his ears. In the end, only after the pain subsided, he realized that he was alone.

He lay in deep darkness and knew that he had passed through Fain's Door at last.

16

DAUGHTER OF THE ANCIENTS

*Gilthaloneth, Syrscian,
Year 1000 of the New Council*

Fox-tail flicking nervously back and forth, Fann eyed the open back of the imperial regalia with critical eyes. The way the dress hung by spaghetti-straps from the empress' slim shoulders seemed to vex her. Morla sat upon a bench nearby, silently viewing their slow progress.

"Perhaps armor would be better?" Fann asked.

Val sighed, and cast a glance at Morla.

"Today we reveal not a warrior, but a gentle girl instead," the seer offered. "This is the gown of a royal lady."

"Then it's for someone else," Val muttered under her breath.

The empress of Syrscian stepped forwards a few paces to gaze upon her reflection in a mirror, and the crimson gown answered her stride with a flash and a sparkle of myriad quartz gems and beads of bloodstone and gold. Around her forearms was wound a pair of golden armbands shaped like vines, extravagantly studded with large purple sapphires. A matching golden circlet she wore upon her brow, its single teardrop-shaped star sapphire dangling between her eyes.

She was a spectacle to behold.

"It is all no more than a costume," Val mumbled, peering at the mirror.

She remembered in that glance another girl in another mirror in a dark dusty room of the Morvrans' farmhouse. Then, as now, she had been forced to wear clothing ill-suited to her tastes.

"Wearing royal clothes is one of many hurdles you must pass," Morla said. "I was still a child when the priests took me away from my father in Babylon-that-was."

Val sighed again. After a whole year this life still didn't feel like her own. She wasn't alone, but sometimes she wished that she was. Sometimes she wished she could just disappear.

But isn't that what happened?

She wondered for the thousandth time what had become of Taran the day Auriga's Mirror whisked her away to ancient Hazor. What had her disappearance done to him? What kind of trouble might it have caused for the Morvran family? There was no way to know the answer to such gloomy questions.

Small tugs on her dress interrupted these contemplations. Fann had followed her to the mirror and was making some small final adjustments to the straps, beaming happily all the while. Val couldn't help imitating her smile, which drew her all at once into a more cheerful mood. She thought the Ayumu were adorable, with their long ears and swishing tails. Fann was dressed simply in leather leggings and a short silken blouse, but her braided hair was conspicuously pretty, drawing the attention even of the lofty nobles. As it turned out, Galanese noble ladies did not customarily plait their hair. Val thought it was time she set a new precedent alongside Fann. Both went around sporting matching braids.

"I think that's as good as this dress will look on me," Val said, her disposition improving a little. "Thank you, Fann."

"I'm happy to be of use to someone so important," Fann whispered humbly.

"It was Morla's idea to make you my royal retainer," Val replied with a grin.

She glanced aside to catch the response of her silver-haired seer. Morla wore as always a radiant gown of pale colors, and over her face there was a veil. It hid her expressions in a frustrating way, but Val could tell that her eyes were smiling.

"I merely foresaw the significance of ushering the Ayumu back into the royal court," Morla stated. "As retainer, Fann shall be educated in courtly customs. She also obtains a rank higher than priesthood."

"And that's a good thing?" Val wondered. "You remember what they did the day I conferred the title on her?"

Fann lowered her eyes.

"The empress must never appear meek among the councilmen," Morla replied. "Conferring the title upon her was your sole right, and by this you have increased Fann's personal freedom and secured a future for the Ayumu people of the Fourth House. For too long were they consigned to slave labor in these lands. There are many in Syrscian who tire of this injustice. These, the faithful, await a sign."

"A sign of what?" Val asked.

Morla rose and walked over to where Val stood. Either one of them had grown taller or the other had shrunk, for they faced one another eye-to-eye.

"They await a sign of the return of the good old fellowship of all Syrscian's people, and of the return of the days of their beloved Empress," Morla said.

"A little controversial, don't you think?"

"Indeed. And there are many who follow the will of the council in all matters of opposing the empress, who have been lured by promises of increased wealth. Among these are some of the poorest, those whom we wish to serve, and those who need you the most. The priests of the council will seek to separate these from you, for there is no good prospect for their guild if the low and the downtrodden come over to your side."

"The downtrodden? And here am I, dressed like this. A mere handful of scorpion stone would get a poor man through an entire cycle, and I am practically bathing in it every day."

It was true. Her bathtub was made of scorpion stone, which was among the rarest and most precious commodities, the foundation of all trade in Syrscian.

Morla clapped her hands and grinned behind her veil. "Now you begin to envisage their minds!" she said with apparent delight. "However, the abundance you exhibit in your ornamentation reflects the prosperity of your realms. The more resplendent the empress, the greater the courage of her people."

"My people?" Val wondered.

"You are one of the old tales come to life, a memory of the Old Days," Morla said, placing a soothing hand on Val's shoulder. "Their confidence is in you. Do you not see it? If you fail to look the part of Empress, then you make it easier for Teomaxos to incite rebellion. His backing is secure, and his surety wavers not. Thus he opposes you, *Bal Ona*, even as others hasten to embrace you."

Val had heard this kind of talk before, and it brought her back to the time of her sudden appearance in the High Place. Celebrations of Teomaxos' ascension to the position of High Councilor were still going on then, but these were quickly eclipsed by the pomp and circumstance of her unexpected advent. The empress had returned, and her arrival had spurred new hopes for the restoration of Syrscian.

"I fear that before long I'll be fastening the straps of my own cuirass," Val said sadly. "Will Lothar be joining us?"

"The Dragon Slayers shall make an appearance," Morla answered, "though perhaps only he shall accompany you on your tour of the galleries."

Val slouched her shoulders and stared across the room at the closed door. The Dragon Slayers had escorted her everywhere for so long that she felt naked without them. In the beginning of her stay, they had gone before her into the city to proclaim the news of her return. She walked among them thereafter for six whole months while they paraded her throughout every back alley of Gilthaloneth.

"And every step taken in this city I am dogged by the council's assassins," she said glumly.

The strife began soon after her arrival, when the nobility held feasts in her honor. Droves had turned out simply to gaze upon her. There were many pilgrims who had traveled on foot from every colony and desert holding. Sometimes she could not come, because Lothar and his men had sniffed out hidden dangers.

A year's sojourn in the council's cage had taught Val something of the perils of this place. Intrigues and plots were the council's game, and they had mastered it over the many generations that Morla slept in stasis.

"Yet they have failed to keep you entirely locked up," Morla said. "And while it is obvious to all that the council seeks to limit your freedom to move about the city, it is of greater concern to me that the empress has as yet no royal court where she might receive guests and dignitaries."

"The Throne Room of the Sun?"

Val had intended to use a sarcastic tone, but the name and the legend of the place was too lofty for jesting. Sealed and abandoned for over a thousand years, the Throne Room of the Sun remained closed after her arrival while artisans restored it to its former glory. Meanwhile, the council, which retained control of the imperial chambers, had denied her requests for a reception hall and quarters within the High Place. There were none befitting her regal splendor, or so they claimed. Thus she remained confined to her tower on the hill.

Val's thoughts returned to the imperial bodyguard, the Dragon Slayers.

"Today is the first time I've been invited back to the High Place since my arrival a year ago," she said. "There can be only one reason for this invitation—and it isn't to view the portraits in the gallery."

"The barbaric nature of this land catches you off guard, does it?" Morla queried.

"It's worse than that, Morla. It troubles me deeply that I've placed at risk those who think highly of me."

"I will be brave!" Fann said.

"We shall all need to be a little brave," Morla said, guiding the empress towards the door. "There are many who protect you, *Bal Ona*. You have their hearts. And among those who are uncertain you will eventually reveal the person you have become during your long exile. It is indeed likely that Temaxos' invitation to view the portraits has another purpose. However, I do not think he will attempt violence today. I believe he wishes to reveal something to you."

"Whatever it is he wants to show me, I do not want to know."

"Let us prepare ourselves to meet them, regardless," Morla urged.

Fann had placed all the empress' oddments in a trunk that the armorer would collect later. She returned to stand by the outer door, waiting excitedly.

"They will be impressed!" Fann said.

Her ears perked a little, and her fox-tail swished as she opened the door. Val wondered how Fann would react if she knew her Empress wished their roles were reversed.

Outside the room, a group of priests and nobles waited patiently. The hall where they stood was dazzling, lofty, and huge, with frescoed walls painted in pearlescent hues of blue, pink, and palest yellow. The rich garments of her hosts did not pale in comparison. The priests, she had learned, had a sort of uniform: dark pants and tunics they wore, with colored sashes announcing their rank or province. Flamboyant chaperons were piled atop their heads, some of them gaudy with jewels.

Stepping slowly to the front of his troop of bureaucrats, Teomaxos struck a comparatively muted statement with robes of dusky red and black that perfectly matched the waxy pallor of his skin. Falling down over one shoulder, a silver-fringed flap of the wide crimson chaperon upon his head announced his status as a nobleman of Nara Colony. Slightly more extravagant than his garments were the pets that scrambled after him across the tiled floor, a matching pair of *dingodrex*. Val wasn't overly fond of these dog-sized leathery beasts, which looked like miniature rhinoceroses with flattened horns projecting forward like a slingshot from their snouts. Because of their appetites, the drex weren't so much pets as they were status-symbols for the wealthy. Teomaxos often flaunted the fact that he had two.

Applause for the empress died down as this strange cavalcade made its way forward, the bureaucrats stepping aside with nervous grins, pointing out the beasts' belled collars and chuckling at the grunting noises they made as they snuffled and shuffled after their master. The councilor bowed when he and the empress stood face to face, and Val Anna received his grandstanding with a gracious smile.

Her innards twisted around inside her, though, for the look in the councilor's eyes was starkly at odds with the mood of the occasion.

Morla remained by the door all the while, but Fann's appointed place was by Val's side. Stepping up meekly beside the resplendent Empress of Syrscian, the Ayumu girl no doubt felt the malice in the priests' furtive glances. The dingodrex sniffed at her hands and scampered away, eliciting nods and whispers amongst those nobles who were only now ogling the new royal retainer for the first time. Their amusement was obvious, and Teomaxos took note of it.

"This is a fitting scene for a new portrait," he remarked, squinting and smiling. "See how the empress' pet matches the splendor of her gear!"

Val could have said the same of the councilor's own pets, for they were short and portly, and seemingly fond of insulting behavior. She remained silent, however, and somehow kept a smile pasted on her face.

"Who knows?" the councilor added jovially. "Perhaps the little one's tail will also become part of the imperial robes some day?"

A few older councilmen dared grin, but the others seemed stunned. Their confusion was understandable. Any offense offered to the royal retainer was an offense against the empress herself. The nobles were suddenly very alert, eager to see how Val would respond.

Lowering her eyelids and striking as menacing a look as she could muster, she said, "It takes only a child's eyes to see through your japes and teasing, Councilor. It is as plain as the nose on your face that your fondness for my new royal retainer grows day by day."

Teomaxos' grin faded into a look of wonderment. His slack jaw and wide eyes prompted Val to continue.

"Tell me, what is it about her that amuses you most? Is it her wondrous singing voice, or the beauty of the Ayumu, the lords of the forest, which beams undimmed from her face? Or perhaps it is this beautiful tail you speak of, its fur so flaxen-soft."

Fann was nervously swishing said tail back and forth. Several of the younger noblemen began chuckling. Uncertain of how to play his hand, Teomaxos pasted a sloppy grin on his face and nodded his head.

"Either way," Val ended, "your flattery needs some rehearsal, lest the object of your untoward affections deems you craven or bullheaded. We would not want anyone thinking such sinister thoughts about the leader of the council, would we?"

The silence after her words was deafening.

"Yes, of course! Let us view these paintings, then," Teomaxos said, gesturing with a grin towards the darkened hall.

The sudden laughter that erupted behind him seemed to plunge daggers into his heart. Still gesturing for them to move on to the galleries, Teomaxos bowed generously, and kept bobbing his head.

Val stepped past him with Fann at her side. Teomaxos quietly fell in behind them, leading the priests and nobles. He gave Fann a notably wide berth.

Morla was probably taking up the rear, as always. It seemed she was always out of sight when these things were happening. Val wished she was close by—close enough to whisper some kind of encouragement. She would apologize later to Fann, who was only just beginning to understand the deadly game they were playing.

Surely it was a good blow Val had landed, but there would be more to come. The battle of wills was only beginning, and the stakes were high.

This day's *beau geste* was no more than another act in a political drama that had impeded the council for generations. What had begun centuries earlier as an unpopular war between the Galanese and the Fourth House had recently resurfaced as a push to end purported acts of terrorism in the colonies. Thus the council deployed a large sortie south to the woodland country named Tarthalion. It was a place where the Ayumu dwelt in peace, and some of the western colonies of Galaneth even had trade with them. According to sources, Tarthalion was brimming with refugees of a war on the borders of Tryst, who had fled the destruction of their holy city of Esagil a few decades ago. The subsequent invasion of Tarthalion was launched years before Val's arrival. All that had come out of it were rumors of grief and slaughter. The general who was in charge of the assault had gone missing, as had most of the men under his command.

That general was Bregon, Lord of House Gaerith, the son of Cedric DePons.

"Of all the most ancient portraits and historical artifacts safeguarded in our grand rotunda," Teomaxos was telling his companions, "the one we are about to view is the most delicately preserved. I am told that these portraits must never be exposed to strong lights. That is why the passageways within are darkened."

Teomaxos stepped ahead of Val to the archway of a dimly lit passage that left the main hall. Stepping within, Val was struck by the change in scenery. The walls here were bare stone, ancient, paneled here and there with carved wood and crested shields. Among the bits of heraldry and famous swords there were paintings and statues. All of the works she saw were masterfully executed by skilled artisans. Some of the paintings were of ordinary activities one might see in any bustling city, but others were portraits of very serious-looking people. None smiled, and all were regal and terrible to behold. It was bewildering to think that somewhere in this gallery there might be a painting of herself.

The empress paused at each masterpiece to consider the weight of history, and also her own legacy. Some of these things were from long before the War of Destroying Fire. Bregon son of Cedric was one of only three who remained from those days—one of three who might answer her questions. The rest of her storied past remained to be proven by a portrait hanging somewhere in this shadowed crypt.

Roused suddenly by eager whispers, Val raised her eyes to the wall beside her. Revealed in the faint light of a candelabrum, the pale canvas faded by the passage of a millennium showed a girl with her face, outfitted in armor and standing in a wide green field. Immediately behind her rose the great city of Gilthaloneth, tier upon tier, crowned by the pearl dome of the High Place and its mighty flashing wings raised to a peach-colored sky. Near the bottom of the painting was the lake called Kethern, which gathered the waters of the Karn River west of the city before emptying them into the Eastern Karn over a mighty fall to the southeast. The Kethern Lake surrounded Gilthaloneth, making the city an island.

Val stared at her alternate self, disappointed by the mood the master painter had conferred upon her. The young girl in the painting was stoic and sad, and her pale face appeared sickly. Her neck and arms were studded with strange red jewels.

Morla strode now to her side, while the crowd passed her by and moved their eyes from portrait to person, eagerly comparing the thing so ancient to the girl standing in their midst. The younger priests were openly astonished, as if the truth had only then been revealed to them. Val wondered what they had expected to see. Didn't they know what Teomaxos was plotting?

"It is hard to say how I feel," Val whispered to Morla.

"You compare yourself to yourself?" the seer asked.

"Yes, if it is to be believed."

While the nobles discussed with one another this detail or that, Val pondered the impossibility of having lived two lives in one. She was still haunted by Morla's words, spoken to her the day she awakened in the tower. Morla said that she had chosen exile at the behest of her mother, Brisen, who wanted her daughter to cultivate a human heart and human connections.

The girl in the painting was not human. After thousands of years she was still little more than a child.

"What am I?"

She hadn't intended to ask the question aloud, and hadn't realized she'd done so until she noticed everyone looking at her.

"You are the empress of Syrscian," Teomaxos answered. "You are the Tower of Gilthaloneth, the embodiment of the power of the city and its nobles, and of the council."

But her question was broader than this, Val thought. This other girl in the painting, she was someone else in a time that Val could not remember. The seer beside her remained close-mouthed in the face of her inquiry. The only other person who might be able to make an answer was the centaur, Orlim; but for the last three cycles of the moons now he was away, sending missives by secret couriers that conveyed to the empress a plan of labors in the deep places of the Undercity, labors that might prevent the council from moving openly against her when she took back her throne.

In the meantime, the council gathered its might and trained its soldiers. The mighty centaur Orlim worked in the shadows, but was no more than a shadow himself. The seer Morla had visions that she would share with no one. Others sought the son of Cedric, lost in the wilds. Val Anna was left facing a portrait of herself that reflected some other person's image. The histories of the Galanese chroniclers which she'd pored over for many months revealed no clues as to what sort of person this stranger might have been. Was she truly the *Warring Empress*, as the councilor proclaimed? Was she not in some way responsible for starting this war with the Fourth House?

"I must confess," said a deep voice beside her, opposite Morla, "it does thrill me, My Lady, that I should be so honored as to view this portrait in your company."

The man was the captain of the Dragon Slayers, a Galanese named Lothar. He'd accompanied Teomaxos to Gilthaloneth from one of the colony towns, Nara. Though he was promoted to his position by Teomaxos, Val regarded Lothar as the most trustworthy of her guardians. Orlim mentioned him often in his letters, citing the man's loyalty and capability. Val felt safe when he was near, and despite her undisguised reservations about Orlim, Morla placed her trust in the Dragon Slayers, and went to their defense as often as she could. So great was her trust that the seer agreed to permit Lothar or one of his fellow warriors to escort Val at whiles from her tower to explore the city. They had even taught her to ride a talon and to shoot a bow—which was more than Naruna had done for her, while pretending to be her father.

"To see you in a painting of the fabled past is a spectacle one of my lowly birth hardly merits," Lothar said, arresting her thoughts.

Contrary to his words, he cut quite a spectacle in his ceremonial armor and padded hood, a vision of knighthood from a storied past in another world. The confidence this mighty knight placed in her made Val blush.

"I would that my Master was here also," Lothar finished quietly. "It should have been Orlim who presented these things to you, My Lady, and not this company of bureaucrats. After all, Teomaxos himself is but a common soldier who bought his priesthood after paying the fine to switch guilds."

This last he said in a bold voice, and a murmur of voices told them the comment was overheard. Val remembered Morla telling her how Teomaxos had paid the warrior's guild a princely sum in order to become a career politician. It was a strange system. Apparently, the council encouraged military guilds to flex economic and political powers by permitting their soldiers to become priests. These warrior-priests first paid a fine, and thereafter were granted commission to venture forth as heroes, victors over those wild forest barbarians who dared threaten the peace of Galaneth. When they had fought in enough battles and captured enough slaves, the commissioned warrior-priests became full-fledged priest-councilmen, ranking even higher than those who had become priests through education or some other guild.

"It is a simple thing for a Dragon Slayer to speak so of guilds and politics," one of the older councilmen replied to Lothar. "Young soldiers such as yourself score titles by luck in battle, but the rest of us must work for a living!"

Lothar grunted and turned his head, but offered no other reply. Val suddenly wondered what kind of battle it was that had brought him to the council's attention as a candidate. She knew that the warriors of the citadel guard, the Dragon Slayers, were an exception to guild laws and fines. Appointed by meritorious service in battle or by heroic acts, the Dragon Slayers were selected by the council with the permission of their guild to be separated for special service to the citadel. They were then free to decide their own fate. Orlim the Centaur was their undisputed leader, being the most ancient of their prestigious order, and under his direction the true heroes of Syrscian acknowledged their sacred duty of guarding the High Place. Above all else, they were loyal to the empress, and had kept her realms secure during her long exile. Thus the council despised them, attempting at every turn to bring false charges upon their members for various pretended offenses.

And yet, they seemed strangely silent today. Val sensed that Teomaxos was about ready to tip his hand. She was not surprised when he chose that very moment to do so.

"Let us not pause overlong upon one or the other of these fine works," the councilor said rather loudly. "There is also this image to consider, a portrayal of those calamitous events inspired by the travails set upon us by the Great Houses of old."

Val was almost afraid to turn around. When she did, she saw the councilor gesturing towards a painting that looked like it might have been rendered by the same hand as her own portrait. Its subject, however, was far more bleak. A lush grassland was withering under the fury of mushroom-clouds, while ash fell thick like winter snow. Men and women, scorched and naked, raised hands upwards to the sky as if in supplication. In the distance, monsters and great machines wandered among ruined towers to the very horizon. A golden plaque beneath the painting announced its title: *Galaneth Burns.*

In the foreground, standing before the burned figures, stood a lone blue-haired girl.

"Let us not forget that there were issues of still more dire consequence that rose up in the wake of these events," Teomaxos said grimly. "We must never forget these things, nor the ones who brought the dark days upon us. Nor shall we forget those unfortunate incidents that occurred upon the eve of the cataclysm of the Destroying Fire—"

While the councilor continued his diatribe, his priests nodding their heads around him and putting on other solemn airs about things they had no tangible connection to in the deep past, Val began to discern the direction this discussion was taking.

The *unfortunate incidents* that Teomaxos was referring to happened about eleven hundred years ago, when Galaneth was still a lush grassland. Crodah forces ventured into Tryst in order to forcibly conscript some of the forest people for the defense of the Karn River. When the forest people refused, the Crodah destroyed trees sacred to all the forest tribes. The trees were supposedly sentient beings called Fomorians, and according to tribal legends, the trees spoke with living voices.

The new council was formed upon the exile of House Crodah and House Gremn, but before that time there was issued an imperial edict that was a response to a visit from some emissaries of the Fourth House who arrived demanding retribution for the burning of their sacred trees. Of course, it was not the responsibility of the imperial court to make amends for wrongs committed by the exiles. The empress had refused payment for the preservation of the few trees that remained and sent the tribesmen away empty-handed. It was the last royal writ signed by her own hand.

And all of this occurred at a time when the empress was reportedly succumbing to her illness, a deadly malaise brought on by the division of the Stone of Foundation among those who were called Dark Towers. She remembered none of it, let alone the part where she perished. And yet, among the bits and pieces of this legend, there were haunting notes of familiarity—like fragments of a song that she had heard before.

The strange part was when the forest people venerated her after her passing, and though she had denied them their retribution the word was sent out that the trees had prophesied the future return of the empress of Syrscian. The forest people thus held her as a sacred being, naming her the *Last Daughter of the Ancients*. Her return was said to bring peace and restore the rule of the Great Houses; and this was something the council certainly opposed. It was evident in their teachings, which forbade the reading of ancient scriptures. It was evident in their sermons, which branded those faithful to the Great Houses of old as traitors to unity and prosperity. The prophecies were cited as the heretical teachings of terrorists, evildoers who sought to undermine the power of the council and the peace of Syrscian. As decreed by the council nearly seven centuries earlier, these were the pretexts that justified a holy war against the Fourth House.

"—and so the Tower of Gilthaloneth was shaken, and fell," Teomaxos finished.

Val lifted her eyes, startled. She hadn't been paying much attention, but his words jolted her mind wide awake.

"How dare you speak before me of the Dark Towers?" she questioned him.

Those assembled stood as silent and still as the statues around them.

Val forced herself to relax. It was, she realized, a careless comment. Even a little tremble in her voice right now would be all Teomaxos needed to gain the upper hand. The other councilmen were now obviously distressed, even frightened. When speaking of the Towers, she was referring to the outlawed scriptures; but her inference that Teomaxos had mentioned them first had brought the councilor up short.

"I was only denoting the fall of your own august majesty," he said with a bow, hands folded across his chest.

"And yet there are others who were also called Towers," she continued. "Twelve there were. I wonder about them. Were they people like me?"

Teomaxos' grin broadened. "My Lady, this is hardly—"

"It is a simple question," Morla chided, staring him down from behind her veil.

She was enjoying the conflict she saw spreading among the councilmen. Sensing this, Teomaxos relaxed, lowering his hands to his sides.

"If My Lady desires to learn more of the Dark Towers, appropriate books will be brought to her lodgings. I do not claim to know much of profane occult texts myself. May I ask what interest the empress has in forbidden secrets?"

Val looked at him, and she hoped her feelings were clearly evinced by that look. He was either an idiot, or she had discovered something that Teomaxos did not wish to talk about in front of the other councilmen.

"I only desire to know who the other Towers were, since I am apparently one of them. You yourself chose to use this title in my presence several times today."

She stepped closer to him.

"And since I am one of them, am I to suppose you are insinuating that I am profane, evil, and forbidden?"

She halted only inches from him, and Teomaxos was looking genuinely uncomfortable. The other priests shuffled nervously in the darkened corridor beneath the eyes of the girl in the portrait. The painted face seemed suddenly approving of this unfolding spectacle.

"I would not dare to—"

"I would also like to know, Councilor, is it because the Towers waged war a thousand years ago that all mention of them and of the Ancients was banned together with the prophecies?"

"My Empress, it is merely conjecture that these—"

"And have you not personally contributed to a war more recently, Councilor, one that threatens the peace of all the realms?"

"It is not the same thing!"

The councilor's outburst was swift and inconsiderate, leaving even himself stunned. Val grinned. These were questions Teomaxos wasn't prepared to answer. The younger councilmen present seemed very interested, though. They began talking quietly amongst themselves. She decided to give them something else to talk about.

"For the past year," she said, "I have searched through many volumes of history that were brought to me. One of them listed the lineage of the Ancients. I wonder why the name of my mother was not among them. Could it be that the histories were altered by the council?"

"Perhaps those who left us were of little consequence to the writers of history," Teomaxos replied.

"But my mother has not left. She is still here, a prisoner in *Thargul*."

"Would the empress desire a more substantial tour of the artifacts, or would she prefer to return to her personal research in the occult?"

His manner was so rude that a few of the younger councilmen turned and quitted the royal presence then and there; but most remained, waiting to see what would happen next. Lothar frowned at the priest, plucking the pommel of a dagger strapped to his side. He had decided it was time to say something. Defending the empress wasn't just a matter of swords and spears, apparently.

"Your words hardly mask your desire for us to leave, Councilor," he said. "How about we tour the work that has been done on the Throne Room?"

"It's not ready," Teomaxos snapped.

"That's alright," Val said. "I think I've seen enough."

Teomaxos bowed once again, stiffly. Val turned her back to him and led the way out of the dim passageway towards the great hall. She correctly remembered the way that would bring them to the uppermost exit of the High Place and the ring-road of the city. The others followed like sheep. No one said a word. Val wasn't angry, but she wanted Teomaxos to think that she might be.

They reached a tall wooden door that opened before them, and encountered in the wide vestibule beyond a host of people arrayed in garish splendor. Val nodded her head as these nobles of the lower houses ducked in her general direction, themselves unsure if they were making obeisance to her or to Teomaxos. Tugging nervously on her radiant red dress, Val diverted her eyes ahead and stepped up her pace so that she remained in front of the councilor. Lothar remained at her side, while Morla and Fann walked among those following a short distance behind.

As they approached the terminus of the gate passage, Lothar stepped aside to take the lead of his talon from an attendant. Another page brought him his fantastical weapon, which was like a spear in appearance. In place of a spear-head, however, there was an open lattice of hard crystal and metal that glowed. Arcing plasma writhed within, and with practice could be released with a thrust of the shaft.

Just then, Teomaxos' pets rejoined their master, their belled collars jingling as they trotted into the atrium to greet him. Lothar eyed the pair darkly, as if considering them for target-practice.

"Summon the others," he said to the one who surrendered his weapon.

The page left at once and ran out the front gate. Val shifted her attention to the talon—by all accounts an ungainly overgrown ostrich. Her clumsy attempts to ride these giant feathered raptors had frustrated the best of instructors. As for Lothar, he got his beast to kneel down with a simple click of his tongue, and he mounted as easily as if he was sitting on a chair. The talon rose beneath him with a sudden heave, poised for a charge.

"We shall leave when the twelve are assembled, Empress," Lothar announced. "Are you absolutely certain you will have no mount?"

"In this dress? Are you joking?"

Lothar grinned mischievously. "Then we will walk at your pace, Empress," he said. "It is not far."

He then turned his talon to regard the councilor, who stood uneasily in his shadow. Blue-green arcs of energy danced across the head of the warrior's Vajra spear, matching the mettle in his gaze; and when his mounted companions rode in to join him moments later, the gaggle of nobles was hushed. Even Teomaxos looked duly impressed. These twelve Dragon Slayers were a legendary force, and like the empress, they captivated the hearts and imaginations of the people.

There were some outside the gate, however, who seemed less impressed.

There was some sort of mob arranging itself out upon the road, whose noise could be heard even at a distance. They were soldiers, but unlike the Dragon Slayers these offered the empress not so much as a glance.

Seeing that things were moving too slowly, Teomaxos himself went forward to hold whispered conference with the mob; and after clearing the way with a wave of his hand, he stood to the side of the gate and turned towards Val, meeting her gaze with a crooked smile. Val gave him a withering look as she walked through the gate with her Dragon Slayers riding slowly in formation around her. She was tempted to stick out her tongue at the councilor and his pets, but the day was going surprisingly well so far, so she kept her composure and exited the Council Chambers with dignity.

Out in the sunlight, she was reminded once again that the weather of Galaneth was not like that of her old home. This place had only two seasons, hot and hotter. The scent of incense only made the muggy atmosphere harder to breathe. There were many people all around, too, and the imperial retinue made it only a little distance from the gate before they were stopped. Normally quiet, the area before the High Place was a bustling hub of activity, and all the lanes were slowed now by heavy foot-traffic. Squinting in the bright sun,

Val saw teams of soldiers everywhere, and many large wains towed by talons. She wondered what was happening.

"Make way!" voices shouted from somewhere ahead.

Many more voices joined in, and in a little while a passage had opened between walls of loitering soldiers and curious onlookers. Lothar gave the order to move on, and so they did. Many of those on either side of the road bowed as the empress passed. Others, she noted, shook their heads or sneered in outright mockery.

Val walked by them, an Empress with no throne, a forgotten person from the past. Teomaxos had called her a Tower, the Tower of Gilthaloneth. Towers were a place of refuge, but who would seek solace with her now? She was the Council's captive in a gilded cage, and she knew that the armed hosts assembling here represented but a tiny fraction of the power these politicians could call forth. They didn't need her to do anything. In fact, there was nothing she thought she could do.

Close by her side, cowering under the aegis of imperial sponsorship where such a thing held little value, Fann's eyes grew wide like saucers. Ayumu of the forest tribes weren't permitted to wander the streets without license, so Fann and her sisters had been cloistered with Val for quite some time, running errands for her only on rare occasions. The appearance of things today, however, suggested some sort of calamity was at hand; and whenever there was calamity, the forest people were blamed.

The sky above the city was filled with the long bulbous silhouettes of heavy-class airships. Warriors were loading and unloading equipment from carts to be drawn to the docks in the lower circles of the city. Rifles clattered loudly as they were checked and loaded. Armor scraped and leather creaked. The armories of the High Place were being emptied.

"These are all soldiers of the council," Lothar said while they walked. "They have been assembling since early this morning. Never have I seen them arrayed as now, with full armor and casting spears. They wear masks and goggles, too."

"Has the council gathered enough to launch a second great invasion of the forest?" asked another of the Dragon Slayers, Bran by name.

"Not by a long shot," said a third, a warrior named Vercingetorix. "Only Teomaxos knows what this is all about."

It was strange to Val that the Dragon Slayers were entrusted with the security of the High Place and of the empress, and yet were in no way accessory to military planning. All military matters were decided behind closed doors by the council.

"Perhaps we see now what the councilor wanted to show us," Morla whispered in Val's ear.

The road they were on was that which exited the Gate of Exiles and ran thence straight to a stair accessing the lower tiers of the city. The places Val had visited were mostly within the upper three levels, but she had ventured at whiles to the lowest circle itself to meet with nobles and important merchants. All in all, she had begun to think of the city as a great big cage. The parts of the cage nearest her tower were really dull, being empty and pristine, while all the more exciting places were down below. She also knew that if she continued on this road to the very docks beside the Kethern Lake, she would come to the entrances of the Under City—a warren of underground caverns with nearly as much real estate as those portions graced by the sun.

Riding high on the back of his mount, Lothar watched the empress, eventually catching her eye. His brow was deeply furrowed with worry, and he tapped his Vajra spear against the breastplate of his armor. Something had disturbed his normally serene composure.

They soon reached the statue of Cedric DePons, where a right turn led away to the tower where Val had lived for a year. Lothar shifted his eyes around while he led them slowly and silently through all the commotion, and then turned his head sharply to look towards a shadowy lane far off to one side of the road. A man in rustic garb was standing between the houses there, his face hidden beneath a deep crimson hood. While Val looked on, the stranger held up his fist just beneath his chin, and then drew his index finger across his throat. Moments later he was gone again, melting into the shadows.

The meaning of the sign he'd made was obvious.

"Lothar, are we in danger?"

"I think we will not be returning to your usual quarters, My Lady."

"That does not answer my question," she mumbled.

Lothar held his spear out before them and gestured towards the left. There was a small track there running among trees and gardens.

"We are going to the estate which was given to Lady Morla when I first brought her here from Nara Colony," Lothar said. "It is less known than your residence, and more easily defended than the chambers where the blue-haired one has lived."

"You mean Nunna?" Val asked. "Will she be there also?"

Lothar did not answer. His whole mind was absorbed in the task of getting her safely to their new destination. The grim set of his jaw bespoke the perils they might face along the way.

"Well," she mumbled, "if there are any people down that narrow path who were hired to kill me, I don't see how we could easily avoid them."

"Who says they are trying to kill you?" Morla asked.

Lothar and Val both looked aside at the seer.

"By conferring her signature to his strategies, Teomaxos would avoid the risk of becoming a destroyer of Syrscian while simultaneously directing the army in the empress' stead. She would take fault for the chaos of war while he is lauded as the visionary savior of a realm reconstructed in his own image."

"You think they will try to take me alive?" Val asked.

"No one's going to lay a hand on the empress, so long as I draw breath," Lothar said. "We move in that direction. Rix, you're up front."

Vercingetorix spurred his talon down the narrow lane, and the others followed at the pace set by Val's footsteps. Her heart raced much faster though. She almost wished that she had not turned down Lothar's offer of a steed.

The small path exited in time upon a wider street running along the eastern flank of the upper tier. It was a quiet place, looking to Val much like a serene painting of some Mediterranean village. She couldn't help but notice the empty storefronts and tall houses in rows with no paths between. They were caught in a blind alley; and that was when the foemen chose to appear.

The road before them was blocked by a band of armed men. The barricaders brandished long poles with metal hooks and knives. Val counted ten of them, arranged in no particular order. A sound of footsteps behind them brought with it ten more, who took up position approximately thirty yards away.

Lothar offered a challenge.

"Have you men come to do battle?" he asked. "If not, you will move aside now so that we may pass."

There was coarse laughter all around.

"Fine talk that is, gate-guard!"

The voice came from a black-cloaked figure standing in the road ahead of them. He was a wretched-looking man, with hollow eyes and a thick nasal accent.

"You have any more words you want to throw at us?"

"You stand before—"

"I stand before the pretender-empress of a long vanished race!" the cloaked man shouted. "Now, you'll be handing over the lady and her little pet, and we'll be on our way."

Fann crushed herself against Val's side, and Val held her close. She had never felt so helpless before, not even before the dragon Glede in the dark terminal of Regulus Station. The malice these bandits evoked in their manner of speech made them more like animals than men.

"This is your only warning," Lothar said, leveling his spear on the man. "Clear out, or you will be fired upon."

In answer to his words, an odd thrumming noise like an enormous hummingbird moved swiftly overhead. A curved metal blade spun right over Lothar's head, embedding itself in the stone wall of a house to one side.

There were men on the rooftops. Though completely surrounded and outnumbered, the Dragon Slayers were undaunted.

"Squadron!"

Lothar's voice boomed above the scrabbling of claws upon the cobbled road. The imperial guard switched to a rotating formation. After only a few moments, Lothar gave a new command.

"Break them!"

The giant feathered talons broke formation to bear down on their prey singly, and their onslaught was inescapable. Screaming hideous cries, the raptors crushed and trampled the bandits beneath their clawed feet. Three mounted warriors remained beside the three royal ladies, however. Their spears sent forth a volley of scorching *Vajra* towards the rooftops.

One man above them was struck by a twisting ball of blue-green flame and launched skywards like a doll, limbs twisting and writhing as they were bathed in burning arcs of electrically charged plasma. Those on the ground who had resisted fared little better. More than half their numbers had been clawed or trampled by the talons, and the rest lay in scorched heaps.

Lothar pivoted on his high saddle and spotted a lone survivor among the slain behind them, and as the man prepared to flee, he took aim. The burst of colored flame that erupted from his spear was almost too fast to see. The bandit fell noiselessly, a smoking void in the center of his back.

It was all over in less than twenty seconds. In the aftermath, Val in wide-eyed wonderment gasped for breath at the sight of so much death. Fann and Morla seemed greatly relieved, and were otherwise unfazed.

"That'll teach them to try and stop the empress!" Fann muttered through a grin.

"What is that upon the ground?" Morla asked, pointing to where the body of the cloaked man lay.

Lothar prodded his steed through the smoldering carnage, and bending forward in his saddle he inspected the defeated foe. Returning after a moment to the empress, Lothar bore upon the end of his Vajra spear a bit of burned leather branded with a strange tattoo, a blood-red circle with four lightning bolts radiating from its center. Dropping this at Morla's feet he surveyed the rest of the smoking husks of men with raised eyebrows.

"This is unexpected," Morla said, gazing down upon the leather scrap.

"We must leave this place quickly," Lothar replied.

Val couldn't have agreed more. There were terrified eyes peeping now from behind curtained windows in the houses on either side.

"That mark," Fann said, focusing on the bit of leather. "Isn't it the mark of Uruk?"

Uruk, the refuge-fortress of the scattered tribes of the Fourth House. It was a place Val had heard of. Its ancient emblem bound all these bandits together. That was strange enough, but their connection to the fourth house was a riddle that would prove most daunting— and dangerous—to solve.

17

A GARDEN OF DISAPPOINTMENTS

Northeast Ceregor, Syrscian,
Year 999 of the New Council

The earth trembled ominously, rousing Ford with a start. The chair was gone, and so was the pain. Disoriented, he clung timorously to the tree roots that cradled him where he lay, his mind chasing after a swiftly fading dream.

While he dreamed, it seemed to Ford that he stood long and lone in the twilight of the world. Ages slipped past him like seasons in an endless year, and the speech of the weatherworn stones told him their tale, of men who had built them up and cast them down. Winds tossed and churned a green sea of grass. Roots dug deep and anchored a tree in the heart of the hills. He had tasted on his tongue draughts drawn from deep wells, and all was made known to him. A voice spoke to him in these dreams. It was the voice of the black water.

For only a few more moments the memory lingered clearly in his mind, and then he lay still in the grass and breathed the free air, happy to be alive but frightened by his confused state of mind. His thoughts turned round and round the faded images of his dreams, when suddenly he arrived at a critical juncture.

He had been in contact with a machine intelligence capable of imprinting information on his brain. Unless it was otherwise protected, physical memory on a computer was easily overwritten.

Was this the reason he was having such a difficult time remembering how he had come to be here?

Aries and Avalon he remembered. They were large ships underwater; but they were also people. There were many people without names tumbling around in his head, and the past seemed somehow incomplete. He tried to count backwards from the time before he sat in the chair, but even that memory was now unraveling. He glanced down at the clothing he wore, and everything looked wrong. Why was he dressed in a tunic? Had he ever worn anything else?

His head ached. He wanted coffee, but he couldn't remember its taste.

While he puzzled over his scattered memories, Ford sat up and looked around. Though he had awakened with a frightful sensation that something had disturbed his sleep, the fearful presence was dispelled a little by all he saw around him. In the glimmering rose-hues of morning, the mossy roots under his hands reassured him with a warmth gleaned from the sun, for now many slender splintered spear-shafts of clarion brilliance were cast down through the treetops to light the patch where he lay. And so the world around him which at first had seemed very peculiar grew ever more so.

The trees near at hand were beeches, as smooth and white as polished silver, whose leaves were still fine and sharp with the strength of midsummer. As the light of morning drew down around him, his immediate surroundings took on the appearance of a garden, for all that he looked upon was tame. The beeches stood purposefully arranged in rows, and the grass growing over their feet was close-clipped or grazed. A buzz of wings was in the air, the music of insects aspiring collectively to their tasks. Peeping out from their beds at regular intervals between the trees were the hubs of activity: clusters of scented blooms, their colors gleaming in striking shades of red and lavender and deepest burgundy. The flowers provided a balanced beauty to the garden. Indeed, they appeared to have been chosen carefully, to complement one another rather than to draw the eye here or there. Uniformity was apparent in everything, as though it had been in the Caretaker's mind to evoke the sense that the forest was one harmonious entity.

And yet, an air of artificiality stifled any sense of gratification. The trees were too perfect, and the lawn too green. The scents were too exotic and the textures too clean. An artist's work, perhaps, could have conveyed to him the meaning of what he felt in the presence of the wall of midnight that lay only a stone's throw away.

Nearer than he liked, mist like tattered clothes on a corpse clung to the shaggy margins of another wood that surrounded his island-garden like a menacing sea, a tangled evil-looking forest cluttered with mushrooms the size of apartment buildings. There were trees, also, trees whose trunks were woven into impossibly lofty towers rising hundreds of feet, opening spiky coral-branched umbrellas under which marched a shadowy expanse. Not even the strong light of morning was able to pierce the hedge of darkness brooding there.

Blinking his eyes, Ford knew that he was in a world he had never seen. Its name he knew—the *World of Origins*. There was also a memory of a forest named Tryst, but it wasn't his own memory. Distinct from his own experience, these were memories shared with some other person.

These memories belonged to the one named Aries.

The little copse of beeches was becoming more and more confining in light of these new revelations. There was a whole world out there waiting to be explored, but everything he saw was informed by the experiences of the wild-eyed blue-haired girl who was the null of a Gremn starship. His meeting with her in the Viaduct Chamber was still mostly fresh in his muddled mind. Whatever he was doing here, Aries was the one responsible for sending him. She had sent him alone, but had stowed some useful information in his mind for the purpose of keeping him alive—probably. But why hadn't she given him something more substantial, like a survival kit?

Reaching instinctively for his vest pocket, Ford fished out something like a cellphone. Staring at it for a few moments, he tried hard to remember how he had gotten it and where. He thumbed open the receiver and pressed the device to his ear, but he heard only static.

Then, in the quiet, he discerned a sound of foliage moving.

Ford put the device back in his pocket and looked towards the sound. The branches of the giant trees beyond the garden moved in a stiff breeze. Lower down, the beeches rustled. Ford stretched, and he wondered where in this new world he thought he would go. Yawning, he breathed in an air suddenly thick with spores and the scent of rotting wood.

"I wonder if there's anything growing here that's fit to eat."

There were little mushrooms and herbs dotting the grass, but he wouldn't touch them. Ford had never ventured near forests, and knew nothing of survival outdoors. His eyes, however, readily identified some of the things he saw, their names leaping straight to his mouth as he glanced here and there.

"Warty, Night Terror, Blackroot, and Bitters," he whispered, taking in each new plant with a nod of detached recognition.

He knew these were poisonous, and that they were planted by some of the people of the region to ward off strangers. Nothing else presented itself to his mind, but this was enough. He knew that nothing growing in this garden was edible. A nasty thought popped into his head then, and he wondered if he might be something on the menu.

It was then the warning sense he had upon waking returned.

A fleeting shadow passed silently just above the treetops, and in its wake the green canopy was blasted as with the coming of a hurricane. Paralyzing fear grasped his normally even-tempered mind. Ford fell backwards where he sat, and covering his head he trembled with dismay. Mastering himself with an effort, he was able in a few moments to scramble to his knees; but still his heart raced with irrational terror.

He was gasping for breath, eyes straining against the morning light through the boughs overhead. Though nothing was there, he felt an overwhelming sense of dread. He'd never experienced anything like it. This was more than a fear of death. This was a nightmare horror, a mind-destroying dismay. It was a memory of Aries, speaking into his mind an overwhelming desire to flee.

Fighting for self control, he quietly stood.

"*You are in danger here,*" a gentle voice spoke into his mind, tugging him back to his senses.

It was the voice he heard in the black water.

"*An Illuyanga approaches. You must leave this place.*"

Panicking, Ford searched with his eyes, but he found no concourse through the shroud of night surrounding the garden. There was no obvious heading, no clear path, and no direction. He might find better cover under the giant trees, but he was more likely to run into danger there. Drawing his gaze from the gloom back to the grassy lawn, he was startled by movement in a clump of flowers nearby.

A long gray swan's-neck rose above the blooms, and little black eyes like onyx pebbles stared. Emerging slowly from the flowers, the goose ruffled its downy gray-brown body and blinked stupidly.

"Scared me half to death!" Ford said. "Stupid duck!"

He picked up a stone from the ground and threw it, but his clumsy throw landed in the grass a yard wide of its mark. The goose stood staring at him a few seconds before waddling towards him. It plopped down right at his feet, turning its graceful neck one way and the other. Ford's fears were momentarily swept aside, and by the gesture of the simple creature's trust in him his temper was softened.

"What?" he prompted.

The goose returned his gaze, its head turned slightly in a most convincingly quizzical expression. It had a strange mark upon its forehead between the eyes—a kind of glowing blue fractal-shape with four branching arms that converged on a central ring. Ford stared at the mark, and he felt dizzy. In all other manners it was just an ordinary goose.

"I guess I could eat *you* if it comes down to it," he said.

The fowl swiveled its neck to stare fixedly towards the sunrise. Ford turned his head, and while he was looking the bird lunged suddenly and bit his leg.

"Stupid!" he muttered, stepping back a pace. "What was that for?"

Then, great wings flapping, the goose fluttered a few yards to the east and honked loudly. The strange behavior continued only a little while, and then the bird became very quiet. Again it pointed its long neck eastward.

"What's with that stupid bird?" Ford wondered.

As if in response, the ground trembled ominously.

The tremor came from behind him, somewhere in the fungi forest. Ford turned, but whatever had fallen there was obscured by the shadows of the oversized growth. He could see nothing, but he could hear movement—a great snapping of branches and rustling of bracken. A rasping breath and a gurgle broke the stillness of the air, followed by a soft menacing hiss.

Another wave of panic struck him at that sound.

He wanted to run, but his legs wouldn't move. It was all he could manage to stoop in a low crouch and creep towards the trunk of the nearest beech. There he hid while once again the ground shuddered. This time, slight tremors followed, in rhythmic succession.

Knuckles tightening, his fingers dug into the palms of his hands until he bled. Looking back beyond the cover of the tree's silver bole Ford descried a long serpentine neck craning back and forth in the murk. What the shadows had mercifully hidden was now slowly revealed—a huge pale gorgon's head emerged from the darkness into the open air of the beech garden. In the dappled light Ford glimpsed a serpent's features, but with a narrow triangular snout sporting two horns like a rhinoceros. The head was long, adorned with knobs and horns, and a fin jutted out beneath its lower jaw. Strange allure there was in this horror, whose scaled pebbly hide was gray and ghostly like smoke, yet gleaming like steel.

The eyes were most frightening of all. Reflecting brighter by daylight than those of a nighttime-predator, the eyes glowed amber as they searched the lanes of trees. The serpent's muscled neck continued sweeping to and fro, its long purple tongue stretched forth to taste the air. The noise of its wretched gurgling breath came before it, and a stench poured from it—the stench of death.

Ford ducked behind the trunk and tucked his own head between his knees, cowering. His displaced memories were still a mess, but he knew this was what he had feared most as a child. This was the bogey-man of bedtime stories come to life. Now he was in the story, and there was no way out.

The ground thumped, the hollow thuds gaining on his hiding place, coming ever nearer, mimicking the racing beat of his heart. Then the footsteps stopped. He suddenly remembered Avalon by the noisome stink of the air. Ford couldn't believe that anything could smell worse, but this monster set him silently gagging. He tried breathing through his mouth, but it was no good.

A great rushing intake of breath stilled his retching, and the grating noise of air forced through a massive chest. It sounded like the purr of a monstrous cat. Not in the least stifled by its own prodigious stench, the beast was sniffing him out.

"*You must run!*" the voice inside his head whispered urgently.

He needed no prompting, however, to arrive at this conclusion himself. Lifting his head, Ford forced his knees to bend and rose with his back against the tree, preparing for desperate flight. Poised to run, he was stilled suddenly by a honking noise.

Apparently, the goose had chosen that very moment to launch itself into the air. Ford moved his head slightly to peer over his right shoulder, just in time to see the massive head of the devilish leviathan swiveling upwards, turning towards the tiny diversion. Eyes glinting, it scanned the canopy of the trees. The earth rumbled again as the creature moved. Looking on as it now drew level with his hiding place, the man of science was frozen by fear and fascination, staring at a creature espied only in fairy tales.

Dragon.

Ford couldn't help but step out of cover to view the strange beast's muscular body. It was truly massive, as big as a jetliner, and propped bat-like on winged arms it stood up almost like a man as it searched the treetops for the source of the noise. Then, with a sudden rush, enormous leathery wings unfolded and fanned the forest floor with a foul gale. The flowers tossed, and the trees groaned in the gusts. Soil was flung into the air, stinging Ford's eyes.

He sneezed.

The world stood still for one awful moment, but the dragon didn't seem to notice. He beat his mighty wings again, and Ford saw the clawed feet part company with the ground. Only then did it seem to hesitate, bringing its arms upwards and falling on its belly. The great winged arms folded, claws stretching forth to grasp the trunks of nearby trees. The massive pale head swiveled, and Ford groaned inwardly.

He was now in full view of those evil eyes.

The dragon turned its head to fix him in its sight, and then the terrible mouth opened. With a hiss, the serpent's purple tongue flicked out, sliding between rows of tusk-like teeth. A sick gurgling noise emanated from the beast's throat, a sound like the sea at the mouth of a cave. Ford pressed his back to the tree, though it hid him no longer. His limbs would not stay still. He ended the dreadful anxiety of the hunt like an arrow darting from the string.

Seijung Ford, leaping through a forest like a deer, was not a sight that any of his former colleagues could have imagined. He would have been amazed at his own speed and agility, had he a single bit of logical thought left to process such observations. In no more than twenty strides he passed out of the little garden into the dark fungi woods, running eastwards towards the sunlight through an alien landscape.

Hustling under twisted roots as big as highway overpasses and leaping past leaning fungi towers, there arose behind him all the while a telling clamor. One quick glance back doubled his fears. The dragon had disappeared, having taken to the sky.

The dusky murk of the woods darkened as the evil shadow swept across the tops of the spiny trees, plunging the world around him into stygian night. The dull beat of the pursuer's wings was louder than the quick drawing of his breath. Instinctively he turned, first left and then right, like a rabbit chased by hounds, fearful that any second the serpent would drop down in front of him. Though some of the large trees offered hiding places among their tangled roots, he dared not stop. Before long he discovered he was making his way steadily downhill.

The fungi forest was sloping downwards at a precipitous incline to the east. He picked up more speed, until suddenly he was running through green grass under a bright sky. The forest relented, but the dragon did not.

As soon as he was out in the open, there was a great crash behind him. The dragon's descent dashed earth and stones into his back. Ford stumbled, and a claw lashed his arm. The ground rose to meet him as the monster's vicious blow spun him helplessly, and he tumbled and rolled downhill in a spray of blood.

He was not lost yet.

Pulling himself up, Ford darted just beyond the reach of another swipe from the clawed wing. He continued to race downhill. To his right the land southward went down to deep forest and a distant river, and to the left it climbed to high peaks. Before him, a precipice overlooked a misty valley of low green hills. It was a marvelous sight, and probably one of his last. His breath had almost run out, and he knew that the dragon was right behind him. He could feel the ground shaking as it came, faster than a speeding train. That was when he noticed the man with a spear standing between him and the edge of the cliff.

Ford took in the stranger at a glance, and swerving to his left he hit a patch of chest-high grass edged with saw-like teeth. He crashed into the dense foliage with a cry. His feet slid beneath him, and he skidded on his back just as a wide flat-tipped tail arced through the air above him. Ford rolled on his side and crawled beneath the saw-grass, the tail slapping the turf flat with a thud right beside him.

And then he heard someone shout.

Peeking out between the long blades of grass, he saw the stooping shadow of the dragon swivel its long neck to one side, and then it slowly withdrew. Ford lay on his back and watched it retreat with a strange sloth-like gait, crawling on its long forelimbs and pushing with its legs, turning its head back at whiles towards the place where he lay as if daring him to emerge from hiding.

While the creature passed out of sight beneath the shadow of the giant fungi bordering the forest, Ford lay still—and miraculously whole—basking in the warm sunshine. He rubbed his eyes and gathered his wits, and with the small movements of his hands and arms he winced at the burning sensation coming from the scratches the grass had inflicted on his exposed skin. Tentatively, cautiously, he probed the wound the dragon's claw had made on his arm through the blood-caked cloth of his shirtsleeve. Everything was healing rapidly, the gash and the scratches closing before his startled eyes.

Collecting himself slowly, he crawled from cover in a leisurely way while glancing at the figure of a man standing just a few yards to his left.

"Lucky I found you here," the man said, leaning on his spear.

Ford grunted displeasure. He sat rubbing his arm.

"Illuyanga are fiercely territorial, but they back off in the open. They don't like strong sunlight. Most won't venture out of the forest by day, so you must've done something to really grab his attention."

Turning to inspect his spear-toting companion, Ford faced a short but strong man who appeared to be in his fifties. He was dressed in strange fashion, with simple pants and a long yellow tunic stained by travel. He had a huge hunchback.

"Who are you?" Ford asked.

The hunchback's kindly face broke into a grin. "Gwilym's the name I usually go by," he answered. "Gwilym of the Yuuto tribe. What are you called?"

"I'm Ford."

Ford stood up and tried not to stare at Gwilym's distinctive stooping form. His back looked fake, as though he wore a giant sack under his baggy tunic.

"Who are the Yuuto?" he asked.

Even as he asked the question, the word prompted a memory stored in his brain. He saw a strange thing in his mind's eye, but pushed it away as nonsense.

"Ah, then you are one of the exiles," Gwilym said. "I suspected as much. It's my sacred duty to keep an eye out for folks crossing over, and that's why you ran into me here."

"Exiles?"

"Some think Gwilym's a little crazy, but I've met a few trespassers from time to time who cross against the Ban. I also keep the secrets of Islith, passed down from my fathers."

Ford shook his head. "I'm kind of lost. Thanks, though, for making that thing turn around. I think it would have killed me if you hadn't shown up."

He then turned his gaze to a peculiar feathered garment hanging loosely upon Gwilym's shoulder—something like a cloak. Strange, but he hadn't noticed it earlier.

"That scratch is pretty bad," Gwilym said, pointing towards Ford's arm. "I'd better take a look at it."

Ford probed the wound again. It was warm to the touch, but it wasn't bleeding.

"Those clawed by a dragon aren't long for this world," the man said, bringing a small pouch out of his belt. "Poison's trapped inside the wound, and needs to be stabilized by a balm only Gwilym knows how to make."

He planted his spear in the ground, head-first, and stepped towards Ford with the pouch held out towards him. As he came nearer more of his features were discernible. He had once been strong and tall, and despite his age he retained much of the bearing of youth. His hands bore the scars of long use and injury, but that was not all. Ford's head swam in dizzy amazement as Gwilym's tunic parted in the back.

Long black pinions stretched forth suddenly from his back—the wings of a bird. It was just as he'd glimpsed in the memory of Aries.

"It's only a scratch," Ford whispered, hardly daring to breath.

"I've seen some amazing things in Islith's ruins, but few so astonishing as you," Gwilym remarked, grabbing Ford's arm with his rough hand while prizing open the pouch with his thumb. "This was a deep wound, from the amount of blood on your clothes, but there's something else at work in your flesh—a technology from the old days."

"What do you mean?"

He tore the sleeve from Ford's shirt and pointed towards the long gash, no more now than a pink line in his skin.

"The old days were full of amazing technologies, apparently, including some that can do what you do."

"What I do?"

"That rapid healing—that would be from *black water*. Of course, it's only in old stories these things are known nowadays. Still, it's better to be safe than dead. You should let old Gwilym rub some of this on the scar. It'll draw out any poison right through the skin."

Awed still by the black angel-wings protruding from the man's shoulders, Ford silently stared while Gwilym drew out a glop of thick brown paste from the pouch and began smearing it on his arm.

"You're definitely an exile," Gwilym said, releasing him after a few moments. "Galanese wouldn't be so startled by a Yuuto's wings. Where in Ertsetum do you hail from?"

Ford puzzled over the question a moment before answering.

"I'm from New York."

Gwilym chuckled, returning the pouch to his belt.

"What's so funny?" Ford asked.

"You folks, that's what," he said, extracting his spear from the ground. "*Crodah* aren't supposed to be here. Your arrival means something important is happening. Moreover, if there's one of you here, there may be others."

"Is that a problem?" Ford asked.

"Not for Gwilym. I've been in your world many times, so I know there's nothing to fear from your kind. Regarding the technology you've brought here, however, we have a strict policy. Anything beyond Gwilym's knowledge deserves Lady Sirona's attention, and you certainly are a curious specimen."

Ford didn't like the sound of that, but when he looked into the winged man's face he saw compassion and pity.

"Don't worry. She's a good person. She knew my father—he raised her like his own daughter when the old chieftain died at the Battle of Esagil. She has wisdom, too, unlike her brother. I know you're lost and confused, and I can't promise any help; but if you were to stand before Sirona and tell her how you came to be here, no matter how nutty it sounds in your own ears, I assure you she will listen and offer wise counsel."

Gesturing for him to follow, Gwilym began walking around the dense hedge of saw-grass, making his way downhill. Ford followed, trusting in the aura of kindness he evoked. They had only walked together a little while, though, before he added something like a warning to his previous statement.

"All things considered, Mr. Ford, the forest people aren't too trusting of outsiders. It would be best if you stick close to me."

It wasn't long before they reached the valley floor. Behind them the cliff-face stood like a pale gray wall, notched and scarred by countless eons of rain and crumbling decay. Nothing moved upon the long line of the grassy bluff, much to Ford's relief.

The strange garden of disappointments that greeted him upon transit to this new world was behind him, banished to the dark blot of towering trees that marched upon the western horizon. Heading east and south, they entered a country of hills ringed round by high mountains.

"Ceregor," Ford said, whispering the strange word that leapt to mind.

Walking in the footsteps of the winged warrior down a long slope and around a hill, he wondered what kind of village lay ahead, and how he would be treated there. While he pondered these things, Gwilym related a short story in a sing-song voice, something that sounded weirdly familiar.

"A man came into the forest Tryst one day with an axe head in his hand. He asked the trees to give him a small branch which he wanted for a special task. One of the trees was Fomorian, a fair and beautiful spirit, and she gave to him one of her best branches. What did the man do with it? He fixed it into his axe head, and he began to cut down every tree in the forest."

"What does it mean?" Ford asked.

"The man represents the Crodah, and what they did to the sacred trees of Tryst. The forest people believe the Fomorians were tricked into giving their enemies the means to destroy themselves, and thus they fear the ancient technologies. This is a fable taught to every child of the Fourth House."

"Will they try to kill me?"

Gwilym stopped and looked further downhill. "Probably," he said. "Anyway, we're here."

Looking out across the plain, Ford saw something even more amazing than dragons and winged men. Blue and misty in the distance, he spied a lofty stone pinnacle rising up in the heart of the wide grasslands. This single fair tower of rock stood proudly atop a mound.

Upon the shoulders of this mound he saw many fair houses, and in all the meadows around it there were tame fields, their colored margins framing a wide patchwork quilt of farmlands. A road ran out from the hill between these fields, reaching almost to the bottom of the grassy slope upon which they stood.

At the bottom, only a hundred yards away, a band of armed warriors was making its way towards the city in the vale. Having spotted the newcomers, they were drawing together now into a defensive formation.

"Stay put," Gwilym warned, placing his hand on Ford's chest.

The foremost ranks of warriors parted, and from their midst a small figure stepped boldly towards them. Though she was still a long distance from them, it was obvious the young woman he saw wasn't one of the Yuuto, for she had no wings. Striding the grass with purposed steps, it wasn't long before Ford could see her face—and her peculiar blue hair. He couldn't help feel relieved when he thought that it was Aries, but when she got closer he saw that this was some other young woman. So similar she was, and yet so different. Another clear memory emerged from his addled brain.

What was *she* doing here?

18

TWELVE ARROWS

Urlad Desert, Syrscian,
Year 997 of the New Council

A violent wind blew up around the PCU as it descended through the atmosphere, screaming and scratching at the hull like a wild thing; but swaddled in the cockpit of Arrow 2, Nephtys felt nothing at all. The sticky substance that enveloped her body dampened all sensation. She was like a babe in the womb.

"We've almost reached the surface."

Kabta's voice sounded strangely distorted through the transceiver, as if he was communicating over a thousand miles via shortwave radio. She wondered if the equipment was functioning properly. No one had tested it for thousands of years.

"Set your units to Mimic. I'll take over the landing."

Hazy shadows in a whirlwind of beige dust swirled before her eyes. There were no windows to look out of, only an image compiled from sensory data projected against the curved interior of the cockpit. Her face and ears were the only parts of her body that weren't enveloped in the advanced harness system—a form-fitting insulating sludge, which was apparently designed to track the minuscule electrical discharge of the pilot's nerves and muscles and to translate that adaptively to the movements of the Arrow.

This was no ordinary PCU, and their decent was to no ordinary world.

While outside the hatch above her head the atmosphere howled, Nephtys stared at the bleary projection in front of her face, and she sank deep into a memory of those moments spent in the gloomy cistern with the Gremn missionary, Zabli. The Arrow hit a pocket of air and shuddered, but the goop insulated her against almost all tactile and inertial sensations. Nephtys' musing continued uninterrupted.

Now she was thinking of Aries. But the Aries she knew was dead. She had watched her die. She was there the day Kabta had won out and jettisoned the girl from an airlock. He and Nurkabta told everyone else she was in stasis, but the copy placed in the pod was no more than a Null-body. The truth was shared only by the three of them. Now she had begun to doubt what she saw.

Had Kabta somehow switched them?

Holding Aries' hand while they ran to the armory—it had been like touching a ghost. Strange feelings awakened inside of Nephtys, feelings she'd long dismissed. Though Kabta found her so troublesome, Aries had been for Nephtys the daughter she never had. Her feelings were no doubt attributable to the girl's likeness to Yume, dear Yume, lost now eons ago. Even their voices were similar.

That pretty voice had spoken comfort to Nephtys through the darkness. When at last they reached the armory, Nephtys looked upon the horrible titans crafted by Kabta's father in another world.

The Twelve Arrows, an all-but-forgotten legend.

Nephtys would have been happier if they'd remained forgotten. These were instruments of war designed ages ago for the final invasion of the Crodah strongholds in Tryst. They certainly weren't manufactured with coziness in mind. The only mechanical interface she could interact with was the *saddle*. The saddle's sole purpose was to afford the pilot a seat while suspended in the sludge, and there was nothing comfortable about it—and nothing natural about sitting in a machine that walked.

Walking was a trial that would have to wait. Aries had displaced them almost as soon as they were all aboard their PCUs. Whatever had become of the ship and the other Gremn, only Aries knew for sure.

Outside the cockpit, all Nephtys could see was a gray-brown wall of sooty clouds. Free-fall had long since subsided, but even now she could sense the attitude of her descent becoming gentler, shallower. The Lift Assist unit of the PCU began leveling out her approach. The noises from outside grew very faint. Finally, something was happening.

Withdrawing fully from her reverie, she moved her eyes towards the lower portion of her field of view where a small amber screen glowed in the air. The interface was exactly the same a Seraph unit's. Her practiced gaze swept the tracking panel. Among many selections and menus there she glimpsed icons labeled Mimic, Pilot, and Autonomous. She blinked towards the toggle for Mimic, and once more over the icon *Arrow 6*. This maneuver she knew from training aboard old Seraph and Kerub PCUs. Being less experienced than he, she decided to allow Kabta to do the driving. All things considered, it probably didn't matter.

None of them had done this for a very long time.

"Everyone sound off."

Nephtys listened to the others speak their names, and added her own to the roll when Arrow 2 came up.

"Shimeon."

"Nephtys."

"Breaker."

"Tlaloc."

"Chaac."

"Kabta."

"*Ab.*"
"*Hiko.*"
"*Hun.*"
"*Malkin.*"
"*Artax.*"
Then there was silence.
"*Arrow 12, sound off.*"
No answer came. Nephtys sighed. She tried hard to remember those confused minutes before the armory vanished, but through the dizziness of displacement she could not recall who gotten aboard Arrow 12. She would have remembered if it was *him*.
Was it Aries? What had become of her, anyway?

"*I'm down,*" Kabta said.
The landing was soft, so soft that Nephtys could hardly tell she'd stopped moving—that is, until the gel began to liquefy and run down to the drain between her feet.
"*Everyone remain as you are until we have eyes on the situation,*" Kabta said. "*Take your Lift Assist units offline, and switch from Mimic to Pilot. I'll dismount first and check up on Arrow 12.*"
The dust outside was still very thick. Shadows on her right and left might have been other Arrow units. Nephtys glanced at the eye-tracking console below the main projection, and realized she was now free to move her head. While she reset the PCU to pilot-mode and powered down the LA, or *Lift Assist*, she raised arms dripping with viscous slime. The drain beneath the cockpit gurgled as a pump retrieved the last remnants of goo, and the rest began to evaporate in a thick hazy brume that filled the closed space with a stale smell. Nephtys stretched her legs and torso, leaning backwards in the saddle to breathe a sigh of relief. Her jumpsuit clung like a sweaty second skin.
Then the cockpit hatch hissed loudly; the huge falcon's-head of the Arrow unit drew back, and cool air blew down into her face. Her ears popped, and a fine rain of dust invaded the cockpit. Pulling herself up, she stuck out her head and blinked in the light.
They had arrived.

A wall of retreating dust, chased east by the sun, gradually revealed a barren alien landscape of towering mineral spires. Mighty mountain walls, visible from north to south as far as the haze permitted sight, lay west of their position. Nearer at hand, pillars of bluish crystal stood in twisted fang-like shapes in the freshly swept sand. Nephtys stared at these sentinels, mesmerized, for she had known such things in her long-ago when she was just a small girl.

"Now we know where we are," Kabta said.

His voice came from below her, where he stood in the gently rippling sand admiring the nearest of the weird pylons. Nephtys studied the crystal closely, noting its translucent properties. It was liberally speckled with small bubbles of glowing liquid that had accumulated in a ta-tenen's body during its long life. Forming from the strange spiral organs in the creature's gut, the crystal slowly replaced all its internal structures until the mighty creature starved and perished. All the margins of the great desert Urlad were studded by these monolithic remains, for the legendary ta-tenen sought the sands as its life neared an end. The crystals left behind were harvested by merchants as power sources for ancient technologies. She knew these things because her mother had taught them to her.

Her mother had brought her here once, long ago.

"We are near the gap of the Rim Mountains," Malkin said, coming up beside Kabta. "At least, I think we are."

The mountain range, maybe ten miles away, was worn in cracks and fissures that formed enormous crumbling blocks softened by eons of weathering. It was like a giant's wall. The flat ridgeline was broken sharply at a narrow cleft, and there, in the deep jagged crack opening in the mountain's face, the so-called Gap of Rim was lost in night-shadows.

"It is like a dream," Malkin said, his voice uncharacteristically softened. "I have lived in exile longer than in this place."

"Getting misty-eyed, Mal?" Hun asked as he jogged up towards them. "I grew up near here. Hey, are there more of them than there used to be, or am I just a little dazed?"

He was pointing into the clearing sky. Looking up, Nephtys drew in a deep breath and held it, wonderstruck. The firmament above was littered with solitary floating masses of stone.

"*Cella*," Kabta said. "There are certainly more of them than I recall."

"The air stinks, though," Hun added. "What's that about?"

"There may be biological contaminants," Hiko said as he joined them, "but I don't think anything serious would be lurking out here. Viruses used during the war will have dissipated in such a barren region."

Kabta nodded. "Still, we should not throw caution to the wind. Urlad is a dangerous place."

Nephtys turned and looked at the other Arrows. Disregarding Kabta's order to stay put, the whole group was dismounting, ogling their surroundings with wide eyes as they clambered down to the ground. Everyone looked so comically pale in the light of that sun, she could hardly help smiling.

But then she saw Arrow 12. Though the other Arrows were already shifting from red and black metallic hues to a dull olive tone, approximating a workaday camouflage to blend in with the sandstorm, 12 remained unchanged.

"There's no environmental response from its skin," Malkin remarked, nodding towards the sealed combat unit.

Kabta strode towards it with purposed steps.

"Be careful," Hun warned. "Might not be DePons in there!"

Nephtys felt a warning stab of fear.

Climbing up the Arrow's chest, Kabta flipped up a small panel in the hull, setting his palm to rest against a console there. The hatch hissed as the field was depressurized, and the massive head swung back. Lifting himself up to the top by handholds, Kabta looked inside. His face was blank. He swiveled his head to and fro, as if searching for the pilot. Then, after reaching within, he climbed back down to the ground. The Arrow's head swung back into position as he returned to where the others were gathering on the sand.

"It was set to Pilot," he said.

"It couldn't pilot itself," Hun replied. "Or could it?"

"These units are AI-equipped, but there was definitely someone inside."

"You're certain?" Breaker asked, stepping up beside Hun. "Wouldn't we have seen 'em? I mean, they would've at least left tracks behind."

"This storm would have blown away any trail that I can read," Shimeon said, rising from an inspection of the ground.

"You expected to find tracks?" Malkin asked. "She is too skilled. She only leaves tracks when she wants to be followed."

"She?" Hun wondered.

"It was the Wolf," he answered.

Hun and Breaker exchanged puzzled glances.

"Aries, the Red Queen," Kabta clarified.

The others crowded around him, and as the ramifications of this most dire prospect took shape in their minds, everyone turned to look up at Nephtys. She stared back, perched still on her Arrow. Sulfur tinged, the air caught in her throat, and she coughed.

"Before she removed us all from the ship, you said Aries' corporeal form brought you to the armory, did you not?" Kabta asked.

Nephtys nodded.

"Nice trick, being in two places at the same time," Shimeon said.

"Yeah," Hun countered, "but we're stuck in one place now, and Aries ain't here—neither the ship nor its AI."

A rattle of stone shifted their attention to the twisted crystal spires north of the place where they stood. There was nothing there anyone could see, but Nephtys felt a kernel of doubt gnawing at the back of her mind, sprouting into memories of danger and fear. It seemed something moved among the shadowy towers.

She decided it was time to dismount.

"This was a hard land, ruined long before the Destroying Fire," Shimeon said.

"You're not thinking she's injured?" Artax asked, also scoping the crystal towers.

"Not a chance," Shim answered. "But I don't think she would just wait around for something to happen to her, either."

Nephtys touched down on the hard-packed sand and began walking towards them. She glanced aside at Tlaloc and Chaac, their tunics flapping in the breeze while they stared up at the islands of rock adrift above a landscape they had only heard of in old tales. She was about their age the last time she visited Urlad.

Breaker stood not far away from the boys. Though a thousand years older than they, he was also a stranger here, on a pilgrimage he probably never thought he'd make. Paused in thought beside him, the normally quiet Abdaya spoke up.

"A storm like that wouldn't daunt a Phase Three Mugarrum."

The note of admiration in his voice was plain.

"She's better off than anyone she runs into, I'd say," Artax agreed. "What about the ship?"

"I lost track of it," Ab answered. "We were in fairly close proximity even after Aries displaced us, but then it moved off on its own. The tracking sensors of the Arrows were blinded. I only had a glimpse, really, but last I saw it was making that direction at high velocity."

He pointed towards the heart of the desert, due east.

"I saw it as well," Artax replied. "The dust closed on her quickly, though. She could be anywhere out there, and those left on board are stuck wherever she set them down."

"So what?" Hun mumbled. "They're *your* people. No loss to us."

A strange smile spread across Artax's narrow face.

"They are the last of us," Kabta interrupted. "We won't leave them to die in the desert."

"You want to go and rescue them again?"

Kabta gave Hun a weary look.

"The Lift Assist units on the Arrows would allow us to cover lots of ground," Shim suggested. "We could go out and make a quick survey of the area."

After a pause, Kabta said, "The LA units need to recharge if we're going to move very far. Since we left in a hurry they weren't charged to capacity to begin with, and we can't let them drain the Arrows' cores."

"Does anyone happen to know how to secure fuel for the charging units so we can bring these things back to full power?" Artax asked.

No one answered.

"Is it worth trying to look around on foot?" Breaker wondered.

"Heading off blindly into the Wastes is a one-way trip, even for Gremn. There were toxic clouds of vapor out there during the war, and worse."

"No weapons," Malkin muttered.

"The Arrows weren't armed, no," Kabta said. "That was my decision. Even though the codes for their access were secreted, I always figured Lír would try to take them from me one day. It seemed too risky at the time."

"Even with Vajra weapons, a foray into Urlad would seem reckless," Shim said. "But isn't there still some power left in the LA units?"

"Maybe a day's worth for flight," Abdaya answered. "But we won't find the ship by looking at the desert."

Everyone turned towards him.

"Aries was designed to burrow like it did in the seafloor, or like Auriga at Hazor."

"So," Breaker summed, "you're saying the others are trapped right where they were when we began, underground, except this time we don't have any way to dig them out—much less find them."

At the mention of burrowing and digging, Nephtys began to feel a chill racing up and down her spine. An old memory was surfacing, like creeping fingers that reached through the sand beneath her feet, rising like a coiling snake around her legs. She left the others and wandered closer to the towering crystals.

"Whatever the case," Kabta said, following her with his eyes, "the ship is beyond our reach until we have access to long-range sensors. Tarthalion Wood lies just beyond the mountains. The people there never had access to organic circuitry, but they might know someone who does."

"We might also find out how long we've really been gone," Shim said. "Could be much longer than we lived in exile, or much shorter. Any ideas, Ab?"

"You're asking me to predict local time by the Relic Calendar?"

Shim smirked. "I guess that's impossible, even for you. Anyway, if we do meet some people, we shouldn't tell 'em who we are right away, huh?"

A louder scraping and rattling noise distracted them, and then a shout from Malkin. Nephtys was struck sideways across the rough sand. Something was wrapped around her right leg below the knee, pulling her swiftly towards the crystal pylons.

Sliding and thrashing face-down over the ground, arms grasping at sand, Nephtys raised no cry. She didn't even have the sense to change to her Gremn shape. She was in shock, surprised to silence by an electric pain radiating up her spine through her legs. Whatever had grabbed her was underground. In the loose sand that had blown up around the crystals, its movement raised a wake in its path. She rode the shallow slot on her belly, and then her legs were pulled under— she was instantly submerged to her waist.

Looking up, she saw what she suspected might be her last view of the World of Origins. The others were running back to their Arrows as plumes of sand were tossed into the air around the crystal towers. One form was running towards her, though, a blur of red and black gleaming scales, every limb edged with cunning blades. Malkin leapt through the air in his Gremn-shape, and pouncing on the sand just behind her he used his mighty clawed hands to slash at the ground where her legs had disappeared.

"Kells Dragons!" he shouted. *"Remain still!"*

A leathery brown tendril emerged in Malkin's grasping claws, one end disappearing into the sand and the other wrapped around her legs, digging into her flesh with backwards-facing tooth-like scales. It was pulling her leg from the socket. Her hip popped, and she couldn't help but scream. The ground trembled with a monstrous reply—an answering shriek, erupting from the towers.

They looked up just as the sand parted, pouring down over the bony plate of an elongated head to reveal a massive form rising on a dense thicket of legs. Like an enormous spider with the trunk and tail of a snake, the kells was unmatched in this terrain.

And what was worse, they had run into a *nest-mother.*

Realizing there was no point struggling to pull on a single tentacle, Malkin utilized all the strength of his Gremn-shape to bite into the appendage with his jagged teeth. His jaws cracked as he tore away a chunk of flesh, but Nephtys was released. Though injured, Malkin pulled her up out of the sand and prepared to make a run for it. A dozen more tentacles raced up out of the ground, and the monster leaned forward as if to give chase.

Then there was silence.

The ground trembled faintly, but the kells did not move. Malkin backed away slowly now, carrying Nephtys towards her Arrow, assuming a human form while he walked. His jaw was broken, and from his dangling mouth there fell a chunk of dark scaly flesh.

"It was a *nest-mother,*" Nephtys said, wincing at the sudden pain in her thighs. "It was just protecting its nest. We're safe, I think."

But then the monstrous dragon shrieked, and the crystal towers quivered and broke, falling onto the sand behind them with a crash. Rising on bat-like wings, hundreds of black shapes launched themselves from the boiling ground into the sky.

19

NO CHANCE MEETINGS

Rim Mountains, Syrscian,
Year 997 of the New Council

The shrieking hoard swarmed, darkening the sky, while across the sand their shadows poured forth, casting all into confusion. Rushing forms the size of trucks bombed the Gremn with grasping talons. Despite her injuries, Nephtys felt less pain than terror. She soon found herself alone in the whirlwind, struggling to scale the side of Arrow 2.

Through a shower of sand she glimpsed Malkin climbing into his own Arrow. The other combat units were forming up back to back in a defensive ring. They weren't equipped with firearms, but they still packed a mean punch. It would be foolish to stick around and fight off a whole swarm, though. Kabta would likely give the order to withdraw as soon as they were ready.

Nephtys turned around to slide through the hatch feet-first, but lifting her crushed leg was proving quite difficult. She hadn't gotten very far before something jolted the Arrow sideways, causing her to lose her grip.

She slid away from the hatch until her boot rested against a toe-hold lower down. Claws squealed on metal somewhere near her head. Reaching desperately for the rung above her, she froze, staring up into the lidless eyes of death. A kells dragon was poised above the hatch, coiled like a serpent ready to strike. Dull round eyes, large and yellow, stared out from sunken sockets. A hiss of hot breath tousled her hair.

The foul gust blew from her mind all thoughts of changing her shape. For a half-Gremn like herself, that was a challenge on the best of days. In her current condition it was all but unthinkable. Her strength was gone. She locked eyes with the kells, and knew that she could not escape its lunging strike.

In that moment, Nephtys found herself surprised by a regret bubbling up from her subconscious. Was this what was meant when people said that you see your life pass before your eyes? It came in the form of a memory—a memory of two young faces that she had nearly forgotten. It had been a very long time since she'd thought of them, and she wondered in a detached way how things might have turned out differently if they hadn't been taken away from her. It hardly mattered now. A blurry shadow broke through the intensity of the moment, and she closed her eyes to meet her death.

The shadow rushed with great speed above her head, swinging at the kells' serpentine body with deadly force. Nephtys opened her eyes just as the dragon twisted sideways, narrowly evading the reach of Malkin's Arrow.

"Get in!" he shouted through the unit's open com.

The kells had flung itself back into the air, but it was joined now by a dozen more, all of them circling, fixating on Nephtys. She still couldn't make use of her leg, but her momentary brush with death, and with that precious memory of her children, lent new strength and courage to her heart. Her hand tightened on the rail, and with a shout she tumbled head-first into the cockpit.

Though she'd landed in a heap upside-down, it took her only seconds to right herself on the saddle. The hatch closed so very slowly, but once she was sealed inside she knew that a corner had been turned. She might just live through this, and if she did, it might just be possible to see them again.

Jets of warm liquid struck her sideways, rapidly filling the chamber. The cockpit filled with a viscous slimy substance through which an energy field pulsed, packing the liquid into a dense jelly that tingled slightly while rising ever higher. She felt like a coin lost in a couch. Even as the jelly of the harness system began to set, the projection screen flickered to life and revealed to her a rapid blur of wine-colored wings outside. It was a sight that chilled her soul. Nephtys tried desperately to calm herself, but childhood fears threatened to overwhelm her.

On a failed expedition in the long-ago, these monsters had killed her entire family.

"Nephtys?"

She flinched as the sound of Kabta's voice burst over the transceiver.

"I'm here," she replied.

"Head west when you're able."

Until that moment she had ignored the fiery pain burning in her right leg. The cockpit jelly surrounded her like a glove, its mild electric buzz racing across the surface of her skin while compressing her wounds. It had been a close call, but she wasn't finished just yet.

Her movements lacked practice, but she was able to turn the Arrow around easily enough. It wasn't the same as moving her own body—being restrained by the jelly, she wasn't really capable of moving at all. By achieving a mentally relaxed state, she was able to imagine herself walking, and the Arrow responded with a toddler's clumsy gait. The hardest part was maintaining focus on her movements while everything outside was erupting into a hurricane of hellish proportions.

"Ignore them," Malkin said.

The calm in his voice braced her like iron, but the kells were relentless. She'd heard their shrieking swarms before, and many times since then in her dreams. It was a demented screaming whale-song that warbled, rising and falling, its ragged edge churning up vivid memories of her darkest days.

Through the projection her unwilling eyes viewed them, scrambling madly over everything, coiling, twisting, clawing, and biting. These were only juveniles, none above twenty feet in length. Though they made little impact on mechanized battle-gear, there were so many that she could not help but think of the mighty nest queen lurking somewhere nearby—

Her Arrow crumpled suddenly, knocked onto its back by a tremendous blow.

The restraint system held, but the fall shook her like gelatin. Against the radio-chatter and shouts from the others she could hear the sounds of something large sliding over the hull. Nephtys could then feel it pulling on the unit's limbs. A huge head appeared in the projection in front of her, its flattened bony plate extending backwards from a skeletal grin. Secondary jaws with large spines separated from either side of its face, working to pry open the front of her Arrow. She was flightless, this queen, but her vestigial wings had grown long bony spikes that pinned Nephtys to the ground. She couldn't move. With her heart beating wildly, she blinked at the toggle for Mimic below the projection and brought up the icon *Arrow 6*.

Nothing happened.

The kells must have damaged the system. She would have to deal with the nest-mother first, then. For a moment more she allowed herself to panic in the embrace of the monstrosity, and then she remembered once again the faces of a son and daughter lost to circumstance.

Bregon. Hest.

Nephtys realized she had a decision to make. It had been bearing down on her heart since they'd left Avalon, since she'd lost DePons. Would she live for their children, so that she could find them again?

The Arrow moved with the impulse of her resolve. Though her legs were pinned beneath the creature, this also worked to her advantage. Using the kells to counterbalance, she reached out with her hand—not her actual hand, which was restrained by the harness, but with her mind. The cockpit jelly was a sensory deprivation compound, making it easier to imagine her right hand swinging at the kells' head.

For a moment she was able to confirm the movement visually in the projection, but her swing went wide.

She missed.

Sensing her intentions, the kells coiled tightly around her unit's legs. It sat on top of her, chasing off all its own spawn swarming nearby. Though blinded, Nephtys reached again, and this time she succeeded in grasping the monster just above its chest. Holding its jaws safely out of range, she inspected the creature with dread fascination while it continued to beat upon her with its clawed flightless wings.

Like the illuminated kells drawn in medieval manuscripts on Earth, juvenile kells were nothing more complicated than winged serpents; and that was terrifying enough. This mature specimen, however, was something of an entirely different caliber. It was a real monster, a being so thoroughly nasty that she lived by eating her own younglings.

The nest-mother tired quickly of being held. Flashing a spine-studded cobra's-hood, it spat venom. The Arrow's skin foamed and smoked where the sticky fluid splashed. Nephtys decided it was time to break free.

With great concentration, she closed Arrow 2's left hand into a fist and sent it at the creature's head, crushing it with a blow so vicious that the spattered fragments were sent sailing across the sands. She heaved the quivering remains aside, wings scrabbling and myriad legs gyrating wildly, its broken torso spurting great jets of black blood into the air. Attracted by the lure of a meal, the rest of the brood gathered like flies to feast upon the body of their fallen queen. It was a family only slightly more broken than her own, Nephtys reflected.

"Good shot," Malkin said.

She could now see an Arrow standing over her, its great hand extended. She grasped it naturally, as if with her own real hand, and felt her body rising as the PCU righted itself.

"You alright, old girl?"

"My Mimic unit's broken, and this radio sounds awful, but I'm still in one piece. Thank you for letting me do this myself without stepping in, Mal."

The others had withdrawn to the west side of the crystal tower, a troop of hulking metallic figures cloaked in streamers of dust. Nearer at hand the kells were tearing into their own, turning against one another in vicious competition for each morsel.

"Let's go before they finish," Nephtys suggested.

As they approached the other PCUs, it was impossible to tell who was who, but she guessed that Kabta was the one in front.

"Make sure your LA is on," Malkin said.

She saw the backs of the waiting Arrows wavering with the thermal output of active Lift Assist units. Nephtys eased her shoulders and thought of wings spreading there. A small rumble informed her that the upward rotation of the engine had begun, and a second later she saw the charge indicator at the bottom of her forward field of view. It was only about an eighth from dead-empty. Flying in a PCU was something she'd never trained for before, and her clumsiness would only consume more fuel.

Lift Assist was a new technology in the days of the war. All she knew was that it was fundamentally different from moving a PCU's limbs. Her mind wavered with uncertainty as she listened to Kabta's hasty instructions over the com.

"Try to maintain a mental awareness of your relative position, and keep an eye on your altimeter. Fall into formation behind me and be evasive. Avoid single-file or predictable patterns."

The kells were finishing their meal. A few shrieking blurs had taken to the sky. Nephtys understood that they were intensely territorial, and would actively pursue intruders until a new boundary was established. Even as the twelve Arrows began to move out, she heard the amplified noise of scuffling in the sands and over the crystals. Without turning the unit's head, she thought of floating in calm water, and then of flying.

With a blast of hot exhaust that withered the foremost among her pursuers, she raced forwards until accessing the rear of the formation. A telling cloud of dust rose in her wake, the shadowy shapes of kells broiling in its murky heart.

Nephtys turned her eyes to the west, and struggled to keep up. The LA unit required a constant mental effort to sustain forward momentum. Despite their graceful ejection from Aries, the Arrows weren't designed so much fly as move swiftly at low altitude. They were mere meters off the ground most of the time, legs dangling backwards slightly.

In minutes they had traversed half the remaining distance to the gap of Rim. While they passed over the desert, swiftly approaching the mountain wall ahead, she thought of the strange sequence of events that brought her here. Eyes flicking back and forth, the whole projection turned where Nephtys' conscious mind desired to look, providing a complete field of view. It was not very difficult to differentiate her glances from initiating a turn. Still, she wavered clumsily. The others kept their distance.

"Nephtys, you're wounded," Kabta said. *"Activate* Mimic, *and allow me to fly for you."*

His voice over the com was even more garbled than before.

"I'm locked out somehow. There's some kind of interference with my transceiver, too."

"I'll watch her," Malkin said. *"She can handle herself, of course."*

"Better believe it," she warned.

Her words were bold, but in her heart she was still struggling with the hurricane of emotions that had blasted her during the dragon swarm. It was frightening, but she was still resolved in her decision. Kabta and the others—they all needed her. What would they say when they discovered her redefined purpose? Strangely, she hardly cared. She wanted to see her children again. They had important things to do.

All this made her think suddenly of Zabli. Was this not the same choice Zabli had been forced to make when she learned about Val Anna? Nephtys wasn't certain. She shifted her attention to the mountains, and willed them to speed closer.

The kells gave up the chase after only a little while. Perhaps it was because the Arrows had neared other crystal towers. These were far older, being weathered by eons of sandstorms. Whether or not they sheltered another nest of kells was something no one wished to find out.

The great cleft was now before them, dividing a solid mile-high wall of brown and black stone. The monotony of the desert fell away, and a new world emerged from the shadows of the Rim Mountains. Slowing to safer speeds, they continued for some distance along a gently sloping path, overtaking a derelict camp of ramshackle wooden structures and torn tents that flapped ghostly canvas as they passed. There was no one to be seen. Kabta didn't pause here, but started up a very narrow way paved with blocks of stone. As they went further, the paving stones gave way to deep grass as the track continued.

All the exiles knew this road, the road through the gap. It was a road so ancient that not even the oldest songs told of its construction. It was there even before the Gaerith and the Fourth House arrived in Syrscian, in the days of the first wars.

At length they came to a lonely place high in the hills. The road made a sharp right turn ahead, rounding a black hump of rock. Here at last, in this most ominous place, Kabta halted and ordered them to dismount in the failing light.

Nephtys' unit touched down with a light bump. The gelled restraint system drained back into the floor, leaving her feeling cold and weak—not at all like the first time she dismounted. Her leg ached terribly where the kells shredded her.

Moments later, Breaker's head appeared in the hatch above.

"She doesn't look bad. Just a little torn up here and there."

She thought at first that Breaker was referring to her, but as soon as he had helped her out of the hatch and sent her on her way down to Hiko, she realized he was busy visually inspecting the exterior of the Arrow. Abdaya joined him at the cockpit.

"Do you have any clue what we're looking at in terms of repairs?" Breaker asked in deference to Ab's critical gaze.

Ab shook his head.

"Great. We don't have any tools, either."

"I wouldn't let you touch this thing even if we did," Ab replied.

"Don't you trust me?"

The question came simultaneously from two directions. Nephtys turned from the conversation above to the kneeling form of Hiko at her feet. He was trying to roll up the torn pant-legs of her jumpsuit, but she had absently waved him away with her hands.

"Sorry," she apologized.

Hiko grimaced as he exposed the red mangled flesh around her right calf and lower thigh. Looping rows of puncture wounds and long tears seeped blood.

"Looks like you were attacked by an industrial sander," Hun mumbled, looking on.

"Why don't you just sit down and change to your Gremn shape so you can heal yourself?" Hiko asked.

"I'm not a *pureblood*," she replied. "Just enough to be exiled."

He looked up into her face, startled.

"I'm only half-Gremn, from Brisen's folk. I can change, but I don't heal Gremn-fashion."

"Brisen's folk have bodies that respond similarly to toxins as do humans," the medic replied. He fretted over her wounds with renewed interest while the others gathered around.

"Kells venom is strongest in nest-queens," Artax offered. "I wager she won't last out the night."

"Too many cooks in the kitchen," Hiko warned, holding up a hand.

They backed up a few steps, giving him better light. Hiko squeezed the skin of her calf between his hands, bringing clear droplets of serum out of the wounds.

"You can't feel it, can you?" he asked.

Nephtys shook her head. "I'm fine. It just feels a little warm."

"I've heard that before," he replied, digging into his kit.

Nephtys felt a little light-headed, but it wasn't any different from Displacement. Looking to Kabta, she was surprised by his deep frown. She couldn't tell if he was concerned or angry about something.

"It's the last I've got," Hiko said, producing a small length of reed from his pouch.

"What is it?" Malkin asked, kneeling by his side.

Hiko shook the reed and pulled a bit of a stopper from one end, revealing a makeshift brush made from bits of hair. The wool was doped in a rather pungent brown paste.

"It's medicine," he answered.

Nephtys winced from the smell as he began to dab each tiny puncture wound sparingly with the salve.

"You've healed wounds on humans?" Malkin asked.

Hiko seemed momentarily perplexed, and then he nodded.

"Of course. I practiced in Cambria, traveling here and there among the villages while working for Lír. He had me doing all sorts of interesting experiments on the human population, as you know."

"For his virus?"

"And to secure suitable environments for raising purebred warriors."

"He was using human wombs?"

Hiko rolled down Nephtys' jumpsuit legs and glanced aside towards Tlaloc and Chaac. To Nephtys he said, "It doesn't look like you took much venom, or you'd be dead by now. Let me know if it goes totally numb, though. Kells are full of nasty stuff that'll kill anything."

"Thanks," she said.

Malkin got up and walked away. Hiko rose also, and looking after him he caught Shim's eye. Shim shook his head, and a strange moment of silent communication flickered between them.

"Okay," Hiko said abruptly. "I guess if you're going to ask me to take care of non-Gremn this would be a good time to point out that we need to scrounge up some medical supplies."

"Will herbs do?" Kabta asked.

"I've seen nothing along the road. We'll need to find a village with a healer, and soon."

Kabta was staring at the ground. "Let's sit and think a bit first," he said, "just until Breaker and Ab finish looking at all the other units."

Heeding Kabta's decision, the rest assembled in groups of two or three and sat on the grassy road. Only the boys spoke, playing a game by tossing stones at a large boulder. The others were lost in deep memories.

Nephtys sat alone, doubts and concerns clouding her mind. She began to wonder if she wasn't feeling rather sick after all, but dismissed this thought as irrelevant. Her new purpose seemed clearer than ever, especially now that it was apparent she would only slow the others down. Live or die, she would do so on the way to discovering the whereabouts of her children. It was strange how this desire grew stronger as they came farther into the mountains.

"Alright," Breaker announced, "we've got a busted transceiver on Arrow 2."

He and Ab had appeared suddenly in their midst, and their faces hinted that there was probably more bad news than just this.

"How do you know it's broke?" Hun wondered.

"Because it doesn't work, Dummy."

"Communications are barely getting through," Ab supplied. "It won't network with the other units at all. Mimic mode's inoperable."

"These units were experimental back in their day," Shimeon said. "I don't suppose we'd be able to fix them ourselves, would we?"

"Why not?" Artax asked. "If they were able to crack Avalon open and use its gate, this should be no problem, right?"

"We left Avalon under fire," Breaker said.

"You mean you *retreated*?" Artax asked, sneering.

"Why do you have to go on about it like a miserable cuss?" Hun countered. "Even Ab can't fix it, and he's way smarter than Breaker!"

"Thanks," Breaker muttered, taking a seat next to Malkin. "I need a breather. You guys got anything to eat?"

None of them had any supplies, or so they thought. Then Malkin reached into a pocket and removed something in a bright plastic wrapper—a nutrition bar. While the others watched longingly, he opened it, crumpling his wrapper and tossing it on the ground, and then drew it under his nose like he was sniffing a fine cigar.

"Not even half?" Breaker pled.

Malkin shoved the whole thing inside his mouth and chewed quietly, his eyes closed in mock ecstasy.

"Should have brought some of our own," Hun chided.

"Hey," Breaker said, bumping Malkin's shoulder. "I hear you already got a taste of local sushi back where we landed."

"Broke his jaw, it did," Hun said with a chuckle.

"Jaw's healed fine now," Malkin replied while chewing. *"Can't wash the taste o' dragon flesh out my mouth, though."*

From the other side of the circle, Shimeon threw out a quick comeback, saying, "Once an idiot, always an idiot. You don't *chew* dragon, Mal. Just eat it!"

His words hung in the air for a long and quiet moment. The others looked back and forth with grim expectations. Malkin gave his old enemy a long glare, sizing him up, but then he swallowed his meal and grinned.

"Yeah," he agreed. "Just eat it!"

The entire circle of warriors enjoyed a good laugh then, and Nephtys smiled with relief. There was still a long way to go, but at least Malkin had agreed to something like a temporary truce. She got up and walked closer, standing just behind the young boys and listening to their high voices while they talked and laughed. The air was still balmy, but the wind was picking up. Shadows lengthened. Her head was woozy, and she swayed on her feet.

"You okay?" Kabta asked, coming to her side.

"Fine. I'm just tired."

"You're not going to be capable of piloting that unit in your condition. You'll have to switch out with someone."

"Yeah, okay," she mumbled, pushing aside the thought that she hardly intended continuing with them anyway.

"We'll make camp higher up," Kabta continued. "We should be able to find some fresh water springs ahead, and perhaps some of the dwellings the Gremn made use of during the war. That would be a good place to stow the Arrows while trekking into Tarthalion."

He waved his hand towards the southward bend, where a vast gray country unfolded to the north. Cliffs drew back and revealed heaps of slag and broken hills that climbed to cloudy heights.

Nephtys surveyed the scene with a dark look. "This land is changed," she said. "It doesn't feel right. We should have run into some of the Ayumu at least."

She broke off and stared at the road ahead. There definitely was something there, a flickering pale shape just on the edge of sight. She would have thought it was only an effect of the kells-venom, but the others saw it too. Everyone fell silent and stared as a strange figure rounded the large black rock on the right side of the road, approaching at good speed.

It was a single warrior mounted aback a giant flightless bird, a talon.

Spellbound as they were by the sight of something half-forgotten, the group remained silent. Tlaloc and Chaac rose to their feet in startled wonder, and Nephtys rested a hand on each of the small slender shoulders in front of her, calming them even as she calmed herself.

"In the long-ago," she said softly to them, "the Galanese people of the north rode beasts called talons."

The blue and white talon loping towards them now was saddled, but bore otherwise no gear of war. The rider, however, wore leather riding gear, with a tall helm and a cloak. His eyes were sharp and clear as he drove the talon towards them with purposed strides.

Nephtys knew that it was conventional wisdom to attack first in these kinds of situations. Kabta would certainly be justified in doing so, protecting as he was the secret of the return of the Gremn from exile. However, the Kabta who was with them now was very different from the one who had led them to Iskartum after the war. This Kabta was slower to anger, and wiser. He wanted to learn what he could of the Syrscian they had come back to. And thus, she reasoned, the people of Syrscian would learn what kind of Gremn had come back to them.

The talon slowed when the rider caught sight of the Arrows parked further down the road. He drew his mount around, getting a better look at the circle of strangers, and then halted about fifty feet away. A tall staff in his hand was illuminated suddenly with arcs of plasma—a Vajra spear.

"Will he fight?" Tlaloc asked her.

The two boys seemed genuinely frightened by the appearance of this man. They had good reason to be. Nephtys was relieved when the stranger planted the butt of his spear in the ground and held up his right hand in a show of peace.

"These Galanese were renowned for their skills in diplomacy," she said quietly. "Despite his gear, I doubt that he comes to fight us."

"He holds no reigns to control his mount," Chaac said. "How does he do it?"

"Is it magic?" Tlaloc wondered.

"It is by simple spoken commands and slight nudges this feat is accomplished," she answered.

The others around her nodded silently. This was a world they had never expected to see again, and not all of the memories were pleasant—but here was something worth remembering.

"A knight and his faithful steed," Kabta said in greeting, holding his own hand up in a gesture of peace. "We welcome you, stranger."

After taking another long look around, the warrior brought his talon to kneel, and then dismounted upon the grass. The eyes of the rider and the talon were both sparkling with curiosity. He scratched the bird-like creature gently beneath its great beak. It seemed he was about to speak when suddenly he leaned towards the ground and stared at his feet. The talon also lowered its head, and the long blue-black feathers atop its head ruffled suddenly. Inspecting the ground for a few more seconds, the rider whispered something and then looked back towards the strangers. He had come to a verdict, it seemed.

Leaving his spear in the grass, the warrior approached slowly, empty palms out at his sides. The talon followed at his heals. Kabta raised one hand as they came within arm's reach of one another.

"We receive you in peace," he said. "You are one of the Galanese?"

The rider halted, eyeing Kabta suspiciously beneath the visor of his helm.

"I am called Lothar," he answered. "I am a lieutenant of the First Division, Second Battalion. You've come all the way from Gilthaloneth?"

Kabta looked over his shoulder towards the Arrows. He decided to play cautiously, and remained silent.

"I thought as much," Lothar said. "It was only a matter of time before the council decided to escalate this crisis. However, I must confess I've never seen PCUs like those before. What are they?"

"They are known only to us," Kabta answered.

The lieutenant nodded knowingly. "That's just as well," he replied. "I guess you don't want me intruding. Do you have any orders you wish for me to carry to the battalion?"

"We didn't expect anyone to be here. There are no special orders."

The rider stiffened. "I was out spotting truants, runaways from the front, and will return to my task if you have no further need of me."

His voice was anxious, and his mood defensive. He obviously desired to quit their company very quickly. Nephtys sensed his rising apprehensions.

"Under whose command do you serve?" she asked.

The man was obviously startled when he noticed for the first time a woman in their midst. Stroking the neck of his talon he answered warily, saying, "Is it not obvious? I serve only one man, and that is Lord Bregon of Gaerith, First General of the Southern Army."

All around her, Nephtys felt the eyes of her companions on her. Beneath her trembling hands, the boys' shoulders tensed. She had only that day decided what course she should take.

Had her purpose come now in search of her?

"Bregon is the only one we trust nowadays," the man confided. "If it wasn't for the son of Cedric, the forest people would've eaten us alive."

Nephtys felt her breathing grow shallow at the mention of his name. Her vision narrowed as she struggled to compose herself.

"But he doesn't hate them, you know. He wants to try and resolve things peacefully. I suppose that's why you're here, isn't it? You've come to finish what Lord Bregon could not. You've come to finish the slaughter of the Fourth House, every woman and child—"

He paused, and leaning towards Nephtys he asked, "Is there something wrong?"

Nephtys swayed on her feet. Tlaloc and Chaac steadied her, reaching around her to help her sit upon the grass. They knelt on either side of her, their eyes panicked.

"She was wounded in the desert," Kabta explained.

Lothar immediately backed away and placed a hand over his mouth. "Is it the Infection?" he asked.

"No," Shimeon said, "It was *kells*."

Then, while Hiko rolled up the leg of her jumpsuit, Lothar went to the high saddle on his talon and removed from a drawer in its base a few long syringes. Bringing these forward, he bowed towards Kabta and held out his hand in offering.

"Please, give her these," he said. "There were rumors the kells were massing at the Gap. We sent messengers back to the City that way, and others by Bolg Bog and over the southern Ceregor. I don't suppose any got back either way, assuming you came here unaware of the situation. In any case, these antivenin doses were handed out to all the officers. Use them to heal your companion, but make sure you administer the full course, one a day for three consecutive days. I know firsthand how painful kells-venom can be."

Kabta received the syringes, studying them briefly before giving them to Hiko. While the medic prepared to administer a dose, Kabta turned back towards Lothar and asked, "Why did Lord Bregon send messengers? Why did he not return himself?"

"Then no news has come back at all?" Lothar wondered. "If the messengers had only made it to a transmission post, perhaps then all would have been different. But no, I suppose there is only one outcome to all events, as the Gremn used to say."

Silence fell and the shadows of evening lengthened. Hiko tried to help Nephtys sit more comfortably, but it was now all he could do to prevent her from standing up again.

"What happened?" she asked. "Tell me what happened to him!"

Kabta's icy glare didn't sit well with her, but it mattered not. The stranger's curiosity was already awakened.

"Lord Bregon has been missing for many months," Lothar said.

"Missing?" Nephtys asked. "What do you mean, missing?"

"Lord Bregon disappeared about the time the council sent General Dolaure along—he's the son of Eterskel, governor of Tara Colony. There might have been some sort of tussle, or so the men are saying. In the end, Lord Bregon was declared truant, and Dolaure took up command of the army. I don't mind saying—just in confidence, mind you—Dolaure's been busier about boosting his status than finishing the war."

"Finishing the war, huh?" Shimeon asked, casting a sidelong glance towards Malkin.

"Yes. He says his orders are to end the campaign in Tarthalion by any means possible, but he's only made sport of the Ayumu, slaughtering them for fun."

All the implications of his chilling words hung in the air for a moment before he continued.

"It was Dolaure who sent me out, weaponless, to find my master; and so I was charged never to return until I bring him back alive, or at least deliver some evidence of his fate. I hope these answers satisfy you, ma'am, but I am also curious. Did you know him?"

Lothar regarded Nephtys enquiringly. She had pushed Hiko aside and tried to stand up, but was forced by the weakness in her limbs to remain seated on the grass. Her eyes shone with tears.

Kabta explained, "We also have connections to Bregon of Gaerith."

The words sounded intentionally provocative, and the Galanese warrior picked up on this. However, he obviously wasn't certain what to make of it all.

"What if I were to tell you that we have news of your master's father, Cedric DePons of House Gaerith?"

Night was falling fast now. All the mountainside was hushed but for a soft cooing of the talon, and a wind that moaned softly under the early stars. Lothar stared at the faces before him, and he stood as if suddenly rooted to the ground. The perplexed look upon his face was at once hopeful and terrified.

"You—you are like something out of the forbidden stories of the long-ago," he stammered. "What are you? You certainly don't talk like you come from the council!"

"I will risk much in telling you, Lothar, that we have not come from the council."

Kabta raised a hand to silence the murmurings of the others behind him before continuing.

"We embarked on our journey much farther away than Gilthaloneth, and our purpose is slightly grander than the arresting of truants in a theater of war."

Lothar's face paled. He had just realized who these strangers were.

"You have come back against the Ban? You are exiles?"

"Yes. We are of the few Gremn that remain."

"But it is impossible!" Lothar exclaimed. "There were conditions set upon the return, and it has been a thousand years since that day!"

Eyes widened perceptibly throughout the circle of twelve.

"Only a millennium?" Shim whispered.

Kabta's hand was raised again. "You speak of conditions set upon our return," he said, "But Syrscian commands the fortunes of all her children, and thus we were called back. So that you will know that this is true, I now present to you my proof."

And he did.

Lothar's talon was now nesting beside him in the grass, head tucked beneath one wing. Its demeanor was at stark odds with Lothar's, whose face was a pale expressionless mask. When Kabta resumed his human shape, the Galanese warrior's shoulders slouched a little.

"You speak to Kabta son of Kur, Lord of House Gremn. And she—"

He nodded towards Nephtys.

"She is the wife of Cedric DePons, mother to your master."

Lothar nodded.

"You must tell us if you know anything more of his whereabouts—anything at all."

"You will excuse me, great lords," Lothar replied, bowing his head, "but I told you the truth when I said that no one knows where Lord Bregon has gone. However, I will say to the Lady that he spoke of her fondly, and that she is like him in appearance beyond any doubt."

"Beyond any doubt?" Nephtys wondered groggily. "Is there something you wish to ask me, Lothar of the Galanese?"

"If I may," Lothar said, eyeing Kabta cautiously, "I would ask a simple question that will confirm what you say beyond all uncertainty."

"What is it?"

"Well, if you are truly the lady of House Gaerith you would know the name of Lord Bregon's sword, which his father gifted him before he left."

Nephtys looked to Kabta, who nodded sagely.

"The sword of Gaerith was a Vajra pistol by the name of Arondight," she answered.

Lothar nodded, but then he said, "It is so, but the forest people now know its name. Perhaps its secret has been learned by others."

"Is there a better sign you would ask of her?" Kabta asked.

Lothar seemed to struggle inwardly, and then he asked, "What if I questioned you instead?"

"Ask away."

"If the old prophecies are coming true, and you are the ancient heralds spoken of in the forbidden books," Lothar said, "you would know then the fate of the empress and the hour of her advent here. I would give you my trust unreservedly if you could tell me when she is to arrive."

Kabta looked genuinely surprised.

"He is a scholar, this one?" Malkin muttered.

Lothar blushed, and lowered his head. "I read the forbidden books when I was young, and I am not ashamed of it. The promise that was made when your folk were exiled, it was a promise made to all the free folk of Syrscian. All I want to know is when she will return."

Kabta passed a hand over his bald head. "If you know the conditions set upon us by the Ancients," he said, "then you must also know that that we could not stand here unless the empress had already arrived."

"She is really here?"

Kabta nodded. "She has come ahead of us, and so we seek to rejoin her. You will see her yourself, Lothar, with your own eyes. Perhaps you will also be among those who protect her, as are we."

Lothar surveyed the faces of the Gremn, and he seemed puzzled.

"Surely this was no chance meeting," he said. "I should be put to death by the council, if ever they knew of our encounter here. They are ever silencing those who speak of your people; but I was raised on the stories in the forbidden books. If she has come, then I will walk straightway to Gilthaloneth to greet her, right through the heart of the toxic desert!"

"You need not set out this moment," Kabta cautioned. "You would serve her better alive than dead. In the meantime you can assist us if you wish, for we've been away for quite a long time."

"You shall tell me where he is, to start with," Nephtys said, head lolling.

While they looked on, she collapsed.

"It is only the antivenin," Hiko said, reaching to take her pulse. "She'll be awake in a few hours."

"This is not such a simple matter," Lothar said to Kabta. "I am sorry to say it, but I truly do not know where my master is!"

Kabta grasped the man's shoulder and smiled. Lothar tensed reflexively.

"You need not fear us," Kabta said to him. "No more bowing and scraping, lad, for we are not the Gremn we were in the long-ago. Our sojourn has indeed remade us, as was no doubt intended. We have come back to set things right, if we can."

Lothar relaxed a little. "Well, then," he said, "you might speed things up by giving this General Dolaure a visit. He's a real pain in the rump, he is. Half the men are ready to up and leave him, and all the while he continues the slaughter of innocent folk, riling them all up as if to awaken the old days."

Kabta's grin widened. "Visiting this general of yours would be my first objective," he agreed. "I will do this on one condition."

"And what is that?" Lothar asked eagerly.

"You will assist Nephtys in locating her son. Find her an Ayumu guide, if you can. If the Dream-Walkers are all as riled up as you say they are, you will find none more able or willing to track down the leader of the invasion."

The warrior sighed. "You are right about that," he mumbled.

"Set her on the right track," Kabta said, "and I will bring you to the empress of Syrscian, who is our hope."

Lothar bowed. "I will do what I can," he said, "and even if I do not succeed in finding my master, I will not count it a loss, for I do not believe in blind luck. Our meeting was meant to be."

Then, turning suddenly, he made a soft noise in his throat. The sleeping talon stirred, raising its head slowly and blinking.

"There is little light to see by," Lothar said, "and the lady of Gaerith is weak. I think you should not attempt to move to higher ground tonight."

"So, he's with us?" Hun asked.

"You had better believe it," Lothar said. "And I am glad to have run into you on this particular night, for there is something hunting me."

The Gremn listened intently, their eyes gleaming in the dusk.

"It has shadowed my steps all this afternoon until the time that I met you, and then, when I came upon your camp in the road, I saw that it has already circled around."

"What is it?" Malkin asked.

"I don't know, but maybe you do. Come, I will show you its trail."

Lothar walked then to the place where he had first dismounted, and picking up his spear he pointed towards a patch of trampled grass in the road.

"What say you of these?" he asked.

Huge and terrible, and so large that they weren't obvious until one backed up to view them in entirety, the faint light revealed muddy traces of partial prints—paw prints more than four feet across. Malkin shared a knowing look with Hun and Breaker.

"It looks like a monstrous wolf," Lothar said, "but it's certainly no natural creature. Perhaps our war here has awakened something."

"Perhaps we have awakened it," Kabta replied.

"I told you," Malkin quipped. "She only leaves tracks when she wants to be followed."

20

THE EMPRESS' HONOR

Gilthaloneth, Syrscian,
Year 1000 of the New Council

"I never did get a good look at the beast that made those tracks," Lothar said. "We didn't meet up with it until the battle of Timhureth, and I was wounded early on in the fight. I woke up three days later in a band of refugees fleeing the south. Three years later, here I am."

Peeking above the wall of Morla's villa, the bleary end of day announced itself with a red eye and a stiff breeze from the east. Birds darted over the roofs of clustered houses and came to rest by the pool in the enclosed central courtyard below. The water shone like a flame. Nunna leaned over the rail and yawned.

"I am sorry to bore you with campfire tales and the like," Lothar apologized, rising from the bench where they sat.

"It isn't boring," Nunna said. "I'm just not used to…luxuriating."

The warrior's piercing gaze rattled her. He seemed to fix his stare on her eyes—her very peculiar eyes.

"Luxury will fast become a habit if you don't take care to prevent it," he warned. "You are in Gilthaloneth, and the battles are fought far away. But that does not mean you and the empress are safe."

Nunna hung her head so that her bangs hid the abnormal adjustment of her iris—the swift constriction of the pupils occurring as each divided in two. This happened at odd whiles, but with increasing frequency of late. An additional symptom had also developed, that being the appearance of a pink-colored inner-iris ring encircling each pair of pupils. Recently, the pink ring was faintly visible even when her pupils were normal.

Orlim's physicians had explained to her that the inner-irises glowed because of the refraction of light in areas where an organic crystal was concentrated. The phenomenon was witnessed only in very ancient records, and its exceeding rarity left many more questions than answers.

While her eyes began to hurt, her mind filled with images and ideas that were foreign to her. A man ate, a child laughed, and someone was imagining naughty things—and all at once.

This is what Morla had referred to as a gift.

"You were going to tell me about the Gremn," Nunna pried, forcing herself to refocus.

Lothar's stable mind and the sound of his voice had been a relief to her in these days. It was for this reason Orlim had sent instructions for the Dragon Slayer to spend some time each afternoon speaking with her. So strange it must have seemed to the man, who was himself a fighter, to spend time speaking to a strange girl at the behest of his master.

"Well, I am sorry to say the rest of the tale is rather mundane," Lothar said. "Perhaps the empress would care to relate it to you. She commanded me to give a full account of these Gremn to her some time ago, and said that she wished also to discuss the matter privately with you."

He remained standing.

"If you please," Nunna asked, keeping her eyes lowered.

Though he could not possibly understand what it was that ailed her, seeing her distress was enough to convince him to stay. Nunna was glad of it.

"I lost track of the Gremn after that," he said, "but all that they told me has come true, after a fashion. As it turned out, the empress had not yet returned. If I'd known that, I don't think I would've lasted the journey through Urlad. It is a horrible wasteland—only myself and one other in our band of refugees managed to survive. We reported to the first priest we met in Nara Colony. That would be Teomaxos."

"You told him about Val Anna, and about the Gremn?"

"I had informed no one as yet about the exiles, and it would not do to speak to a priest about the return of the empress, let alone the Gremn. I did speak of the disappearance of Lord Bregon of Gaerith, however."

"That is the one who was the son of Cedric DePons?"

"Yes. The priest had access to Nara's broadcast wave technology, and was able to send this news to the council in Gilthaloneth. The council had been unable to contact the army for almost a year, however, and none of them confessed to being aware that Dolaure son of Eterskel of Tara had been made a general and sent to the front. No one seemed particularly disappointed about it, either."

"So, you believe there was a plot to remove this guy, Bregon?"

"It does seem that way, though I can't say for certain whose plotting it was. Anyway, I was much relieved to have made it back to the Galaneth. Instead of being punished for fleeing the battle, I was recommended for a promotion. They made me a gate-master of Nara, a prestigious title. It was soon afterwards that all the excitement began."

He was referring to the arrival of Morla, and then of the empress and herself.

"And you've heard nothing more about the Gremn you met in Tarthalion?" she asked.

"No, I haven't. Before we were overtaken by battle at the city of Timhureth, I did manage to get them set up with an Ayumu scout—a young girl. Though it was four years ago I still remember the words the Gremn Lord spoke to me in parting. I do wish to meet him again. He was like an ancient legend come to life, but more noble somehow."

Nunna shivered. The Kabta she remembered wasn't as nice as the one Lothar described.

"I would venture to guess he's been keeping General Dolaure busy for the past four years," Lothar finished. "At least, I hope he is. Tarthalion is vast, and with Dolaure's lust for bloodshed the wars there will last a while yet."

"And you believe that someone in the council may be directing the war secretly, using these wave transmissions?"

"I am only a soldier, so it is not in my experience to make assumptions," he said with a smile and a wink. "On the other hand, some things do seem quite obvious."

Lothar then bowed to her and politely offered his thanks for their conversation.

"It is time for me to be off, then," he said in parting. "Orlim has arranged for me to meet with one of his couriers, and I will learn all the news of the council's deliberations. I will return later tonight to make my report to the empress."

Nunna watched him leave, and slowly sifted through all the things he'd said. The transit that she and Val had made was only one of many, it seemed. Kabta was here. Perhaps DePons had come as well. She wondered what they would say if they knew that she was hiding in a palace.

In hindsight, though the accommodations were grand and beautiful, the long year since her arrival differed little from the previous three she'd spent hiding under the stairs in Penn Station. At least it was warmer in Gilthaloneth.

The climate of the High Place was always warm, and it seldom rained. She might have been on vacation, maybe in a resort town on the Mediterranean. Everyone spoke English, too. Though she also heard other languages used, the common employment of her native tongue in an alien world was one of two peculiarities that defied explanation. The other was her increased hyper-sensitivity to the thoughts and feelings of others—the condition that DePons called *instrumentality*. She had worked many years to control it, but now the control was slipping away again.

Some gift, indeed.

An unpleasant distraction imposed upon her by every passerby is what it really was. Funny, how her circumstances drove her always to isolation. Most people dreaded being alone.

The only other person she thought might understand the way she felt was Val Anna.

Languishing in her tower, the empress had been a caged bird under careful guard. Now that she had relocated to the villa, Nunna expected to see more of her; but Val never spoke to anyone except Morla and the Dragon Slayers, her guardians. There were some heated arguments between them, too. The days passed gloomily, and while the council formed their plans against the forest people all Lothar's talk turned to war.

Thus Nunna longed to see the wide world outside the walls of the city. She knew about as little of that world as of the expectations placed upon her by Morla and Lothar. She had been asked to participate in training exercises with melee weapons and Vajra spears, and had quickly earned her place among the best warriors of the realm. However, this only increased the tensions she felt. A storm was gathering. She could feel it brimming over.

Despite the primitive nature of life in Gilthaloneth, Morla had access to some fairly advanced technology; but no one seemed willing to explain to her the history of its development. Libraries weren't her scene, or she would have delved into the villa's rich store of tomes for answers. Nunna hoped rather to wheedle what information she could from the stoic Lothar. All she had learned thus far was that the realms of Syrscian were wide and vast, and that there were dragons out there, and Watchers, too. For those who ventured farther into the Wastes, there were other worse horrors lying in wait. Having left a world where nearly everything was liable to kill you, Nunna's interests were piqued.

However, just as Gilthaloneth was cut off from the lands all around, and the villa was inaccessible from all nearby structures, it seemed she would get no nearer the truth of things while she remained inside a box. And what would she do when the time came to mingle with the crowds? How would she deal with the overwhelming flood of thoughts and feelings?

Today felt different, though, as if something might arrive on the doorstep and present her with new possibilities. It was with a renewed sense of adventure that she rose from the bench outside her little apartment and made her way across the luxurious second-story courtyard, a broad square recessed from the lower plaza between adjoining wings of the villa.

Stairs in the very back of this courtyard, overshadowed by a columned portico, ascended to a maze of halls and rooms leading to the empress' lodgings. A bird couldn't pass that way without the Dragon Slayers knowing about it.

When her head had cleared and her eyes no longer pained her, Nunna set out to stretch her legs. Her blue leather tunic swished pleasantly while she strolled. Leggings of aqua that matched her hair and thigh-high boots embossed with starburst patterns completed the costume. It wasn't much like the uniform of a Dragon Slayer, and it reminded her too much of a renaissance fair, but it was very comfortable. Less comfortable were the accessories—a sword, presented to her with great ceremony by Morla, and a long knife made from the horn of an actual dragon. Nunna treasured these things, but she wore them seldom. At times she did stand watch in the courtyard by night, and then she brought the sword along with her, if only to become accustomed to its weight. What Bob would have had to say about her getup she didn't dare imagine.

The courtyard was usually blazing hot during the day, but now it was comfortable. Coming to the center, Nunna looked out across the spacious reception plaza below. Accessed by a pair of doglegged steps on either side of a stone balustrade, the reflecting pool and flowering gardens there had been a pleasurable distraction during many of the long days of her stay. She had even composed some poetry in her head—a pastime she'd never aspired to before.

Resting against the balustrade while the wind ruffled her blue hair, she wondered at the changes this place had worked in her.

"Thy deers ears of not eye saw."

Following the sound of small voices, Nunna turned towards the covered porch to her left. She took in the graceful beauty of the ancient stonework of the nearest apartments, their faded plaster painted red. Countless rooms of varied use opened along an arched walkway there, where other passages met beneath high columns connecting the many mazelike halls of the mansion. There were three small figures outside the nearest apartment, three she had come to know well enough during her captivity here.

"Wait, that can't be right!"

Watching them with growing curiosity, Nunna listened as Fann laboriously instructed her younger siblings in reading and writing—skills to which they did not keenly aspire. It was a lovely scene nonetheless, and a scent of flowers lingered, borne aloft by the stirring of the evening airs. Her mood was lightened a little by large iridescent butterflies that looped circles around plantings potted nearby, tall urns set to rest amid garden plots and flowering beds. These were tended by a few household servants who were loyal to the empress and to Morla. They had lost their families in suspicious circumstances, and had sought refuge with their rightful sovereign.

All their lives were as chaff to the Galanese High Council. These were the first of a new people, whose doom was already decided. It was a day of decisions. The council was meeting to determine the fate of the Fourth House, while these three innocents sat by learning to read.

"The dark ears or not…"

Faylinn paused to squint her eyes and study Fann's expression. To her credit, Fann returned her gaze with a hopeful nod.

"Try again," she prompted.

Seated before their teacher upon a bench beneath an ivied trellis, holding great tomes open upon their laps, Faylinn and Finn swung their legs while they concentrated on the pages before them. Finn's book was upside-down.

"The dark…eyes…of night I saw—"

The smallest, Finn, kicking her legs ever more exuberantly while her sister read, jittered right off the edge of the stone bench onto the pavement, spilling her book with dramatic flair. She immediately wrapped her bushy fox-tail about her side and began sobbing, smoothing her skirt and rubbing her knees.

"How am I supposed to read with you carrying on like that?" Faylinn yelled.

"It was an accident!"

Faylinn leaned menacingly over the edge of the bench. "You did that on purpose!"

"I did not!"

The little one turned and scowled at Faylinn, nose-to-nose. Fann looked from one to the other, mouth round with surprise.

"You always do that when I read, Finn! You did it on purpose!"

"*Did not!*"

Faylinn slapped her book closed and knocked her sister over the head with it. A hollow sound echoed across the courtyard. Finn began to bawl.

Scurrying away from the porch, her tail fluffed with anger, she came towards Nunna at the balustrade with small arms open and her face a mess. The teary ball of fur grabbed her around one thigh and mashed her face into Nunna's tunic.

"*So mean!*" Finn sobbed loudly. "*She's so mean!*"

Nunna fought to restrain her initial reaction to the emotional stimulus being broadcast by Finn's mind. With tremendous effort, she touched the little one's braided hair gingerly, brushing her fingers along the large fox ears. Finn's sobbing ceased at once, and she looked up at Nunna with a thrill of wonder.

In her long sojourn at the villa, Nunna had tried valiantly to remain unattached, for she knew her limitations. But Finn had taken a liking to her since day one, and worked steadily at dissolving the wall between them. She couldn't possibly have understood how improbable a task she had undertaken. Nunna herself maintained the barrier, with an effort, for it was all that prevented her from becoming lost in the minds of others. It was a battle, but she allowed the child to cling to her and to entrance her with thoughts of love until Fann arrived.

"I'm sorry," Fann apologized.

Sensing that she was about to be pulled away, Finn held on tightly, tugging at the smooth material of Nunna's leggings. Nunna felt a rough jolt pass through her as she began to lose her grip on her own consciousness. In moments she would no longer be aware of her own body, her own being, and would drift away—

The moment was salvaged by Finn herself, who suddenly laughed, pointing up at Fann's head. A butterfly perched momentarily among her red-brown locks before fluttering away on the breeze.

Releasing Nunna, Finn ran after the butterfly for a few moments before diverting to the bench where she picked up her book, still upside-down, and flipped randomly through the pages of text. Faylinn, still angry at the disruption of her progress, carried her own book into the apartment and slammed the door behind her.

"Are you alright, Lady Nunna?" Fann asked.

Hearing the concern in Fann's voice, feeling it resonate through her adaptive senses, and forcing herself simultaneously into a state of static calm was almost too much to tackle all at once. Nunna swayed on her feet and held on to the rail overlooking the lower courtyard. In mere moments the panic faded. Fann had forced herself into a blank state to assist her.

Fann, it seemed, had been well instructed by Morla.

"Thank you," Nunna said, rubbing her stinging eyes. "I do not wish to alarm anyone."

The Ayumu girl looked uncertain. Slavish thoughts filled her head—thoughts she could not hide. Nunna's thanks had prompted feelings of low esteem; yet Fann's heart was full of such a noble energy and purity that Nunna was shamed by its radiance.

"Your eyes have bolder rings today," Fann whispered. "Shall I inform Lady Morla that you will be taking your meals in your room?"

"Thanks, but I think I'll skip dinner. I don't want to end up looking like a sow in a pen."

Fann lingered a moment.

"Did you ever learn to read, Lady Nunna?"

"Yes, somehow I did. I don't remember my teacher, though."

Fann didn't seem to hear her answer. Fox-ears flicking, she turned abruptly towards the lower court and bowed slightly. Only then did Nunna notice the empress taking a seat by the pool. She'd gotten by her without being noticed, as usual.

The empress was Nunna's solace, for hers was the only mind closed to her gift.

Val Anna's red hair had grown longer, and she'd taken to wearing it in braided loops on the sides of her head. She wore a red gown, her usual vestments. It hardly mattered how she dressed or wore her hair, Nunna thought. Val's features were soft, almost elfin, yet also noble. Nunna first noticed this unusual radiance when she literally stumbled upon a dirty and tattered girl hiding in a New York City terminal. There was something different about her even then, like a glow. For whatever reasons she had blocked her own memories and concealed herself in the dark worlds, Val could not easily veil the verity of her fate.

"Will you go and sit with the empress?" Fann asked.

"Yes, and you'll come with me. Aren't you the royal retainer?"

Fann's eyes sparkled. She nodded silently but fervently.

They walked down the steps together. It wasn't a habit of Val's to come outside in the evening air and sit beside the pool, and her mysterious mood remained closed to Nunna's probing. Nunna was glad for the peace of her company, however.

If only Val hadn't cut herself off so suddenly after their escape from New York a year before. A wall had arisen between them, and much more had happened while they were apart. She understood well enough that Val was someone important to the people of this world, and they needed her. She also understood that her own purpose was to help set the stage for a great event. Something was coming, and though Nunna couldn't say what it was, she knew that she and her peculiar gift had a significant role to play. She would need to stay close to Val until all was revealed.

The three sat in silence by the still pool and watched birds splashing in a puddle nearby. The rim of the sun seemed perched on the edge of the high wall surrounding the villa, ready to plunge over the side at any moment. When it finally disappeared, Nunna exhaled. The day had ended, and night was beginning.

Like the day, night had its own business, and its own cast of characters. Lothar was one of them, for he often brought news by night from the Centaur, Orlim, and shared what he knew with Morla and the Dragon Slayers. He'd told Nunna earlier that he would return tonight. Perhaps Val anticipated his arrival, knowing that he would have news of the council's decision.

No one spoke while they waited, though Finn's high voice came down to them at whiles. She was playing with some potted plants on the stairs, talking to them. Nunna watched her, wondering if she expected a reply.

Gas flames flickered to life in the tall lampposts at the foot of the steps, and while all the world took on a bluish tint the lamps cast an orange glow. The red-painted plaster walls of the mansion were lit in relief, pocked with age and shaggy with a tamed growth of ivy. The villa reminded Nunna at times of a mausoleum, or some kind of ancient temple. Still, it was homey enough, and a pleasing air blew out of the west to grace its ivied columns with movement and life.

When all was dim, Faylinn finally emerged from her den, tail limp now. She made amends with her sister, and the two came down the steps hand in hand while the others looked on.

Fann beckoned them, and they came to sit between her and Nunna. Finn hopped up onto the bench right beside her, but her mood was calm. Nunna watched as she dandled her palms in the water. A slight smile tugged at the empress' lips. Somewhere in the near distance a bell rang.

Someone was at the gate.

A few moments later Morla emerged from a corridor beyond the pool, dressed in a flowing white dress. Her silver hair shone bluish in the dusk, dancing in the light breeze as she walked. Ghostly, she seemed, yet very lovely. Lothar strode behind her, a tall shadow.

They were an odd contrast, a strikingly childlike woman, small and pale, beside a tall armored warrior. They bowed as they rounded the head of the pool and stood before the empress. Lothar spoke first.

"The Centaur sends his greetings, Empress."

Sensing the heaviness of this meeting, Fann took her sisters' hands and led them quickly away, back up the steps into their apartment. A guard took up his position near their door, as was customary after nightfall.

When the girls were gone, Lothar came a few steps closer and bowed regally towards the empress. "They've announced their decision," he said, rising. "I hope it does not add to your foreboding overmuch, My Lady, but the council's choice was made in default of the missives you sent. They did not even read them."

"As you forewarned," Val said in a low voice. "Well, what did they announce?"

"All the Ayumu in the cities and colonies of the Galanese will be rounded up and interred in the valley west of the Kethern. It is being called a labor camp."

In the silence that followed, he glanced in the direction Fann and her sisters had gone.

"This is all being done in preparation for war," he added. "I will do what I can to protect our young charges, but My Lady is my first concern. As to that, Orlim has completed the interrogation of the assassin captured last week."

Nunna knew that assassins were hired by certain nobles of the Lower Houses who had come into Teomaxos' cabal. There were constant attempts to infiltrate Morla's villa. Some of the would-be assassins were captured, but most simply vanished after they were discovered. Nunna had been asked to join in the nighttime watches around the house, but it was the vigilance of the Dragon Slayers that secured them.

"This agent bore with him much useful information," Lothar said, "a revelation of the secret doings of the council—of efforts orchestrated well beyond the scope of this day's events."

No one spoke.

"Thus it is," he continued, "that while a show is put on to guide our eyes one way, their true purpose is veiled in covert activities. Though it is no secret the council seeks war with the forest people, whatever they are truly after has remained hidden until now."

"What have you discovered?" Val asked.

"He was a notable courier who works for the syndicate Orlim is watching in the Undercity. He bore on his person a singularly important communiqué."

"Could he have been intentionally sold out?" Nunna wondered. "This could have been an attempt at misinformation counterintelligence, you know."

Lothar gave her a curious look.

"I mean, they sound like the kind of people who would do that."

"You're right in saying so," Lothar said, "but the councilor who handed us the assassin was Orlim's man, a planted spy. He's also a player in the Musab black market, with good influence within the syndicate. The information we intercepted is believed to be a legitimate communication. Orlim requested that I bring the message directly to the empress."

He pulled a small square of pale white ceramic from a pocket on his belt. The chip was fat, but so small that he had some difficulty holding it in his gloved hands. Holding it up a moment, he squeezed it, and then tossed it on the ground before the empress.

A ringing note as from a tossed coin echoed from the columned porticos of the courtyard, and for a moment the tiny square was lost to sight. Then, before their eyes, a small glimmering cup-shaped instrument unfolded from the original square. Its surface flashed with patterns of bluish light, and in the air above it a life-size projection of

Teomaxos in the high councilor's official robes flickered suddenly to life. He spoke in a voice strangely distorted by the projector.

"I am sending this message by your usual courier, Lord Eterskel, in order to extend our group's gratitude for your gracious contributions to our cause, both monetarily and in terms of the supplies and weapons requested from Tara. I wish to assure you that the teams we assembled and trained have all set forth, and will reach their objectives over the next half-cycle. If all goes according to plan, they will recover the required items before the rest of the Dark Towers have fully awakened. It is no small feat, I realize, and we must allow for certain unexpected events; however, I believe our reach is sure, and our arm is now grown long enough. Again, I thank you personally for nominating me and bringing me into the council last cycle. If there is anything you require, do not hesitate to make it known through your courier, and I will see it done."

When his hollow croaking voice fell silent, the image suddenly disappeared. The group sat quietly for a moment, and then Morla walked over to the chip and retrieved it before sitting down on the bench beside Val.

"So," she said, "it is Eterskel."

"Eterskel, Lord of Tara," Lothar affirmed. "Back at my post in Nara he was suspected of being a kingpin of the Musab black market. He is a formidable enemy, the wealthiest man in Syrscian; yet for all his wealth, he still cannot purchase a seat on the council."

"What are the Dark Towers?" Nunna asked.

Morla and Lothar exchanged glances.

"The twelve Dark Towers are not towers at all," Morla answered, "but twelve people, the rulers of twelve cities built by the Ancients who each bore a fragment of the Stone of Foundation. Their cities fell into darkness and ruin in the War of Destroying Fire, and thus the rulers were named Dark Towers."

"It is believed by many that the Towers died a thousand years ago," Lothar said. "However, that is not true."

"There is one here before you," Val said. "I have recovered some of the fragments, and am therefore a Dark Tower."

"Nevertheless, we still have hope in you," Lothar said. "I for one will not refer to My Lady by such an ill-begotten tag. As for Eterskel—"

"You believe he holds one of those fragments?" Nunna asked. "Is it like the fragment of Regulus?"

"Yes, it is," Morla confirmed. "And Teomaxos' message suggests Eterskel intends to seek out the other fragments that are lost."

"That should not be too difficult for him," Lothar remarked. "Thanks to the councilor, Eterskel already controls our movements. The empress cannot leave this house or the city without facing off against assassins. Orlim believes that they really only mean to keep you contained, My Lady. However, the assassin we took with this message was carrying a poison which permanently incapacitates the mind, leaving the body whole."

"That is because he needs me for a living vessel," Val said, looking down at her clenched fists. "Teomaxos has risked too much by entangling himself in the Black Market, though. Whatever it is that he seeks, he has become reckless and grasping. We cannot afford to remain idle any longer."

"Orlim is also eager to make a move. Let me tell you what I know."

Lothar allowed the air to clear a moment before continuing. No one needed Nunna's gift to perceive the gravity of what he said next. It could be felt in his tone of voice.

"Teomaxos' message referred to teams being sent out to recover items from the Dark Towers. Recently, our sentries observed three expeditions departing the city in the dark of night. Being well-outfitted, we were suspicious these groups were somehow linked to the council's activities."

"Where were they heading?" Val asked.

"It was not possible to determine the route taken by the first two, but the last is being tracked by our technologists with the help of some sorcerers in the Wastes. They are heading towards the heart of the Southern Desert, in Urlad. We intend to follow them."

"Into the Toxic Wasteland?" Morla wondered.

"Orlim suspects they are venturing towards the ruins of Kos-Ulugrod, the only one of the twelve cities in that region. He requests the empress' consent to send after them a team of our own, which he has already assembled."

"And what do you think about this, Lothar?"

He paused, flustered.

"If the empress really wants to know what I think," he replied, "I will say that Teomaxos is seeking the lost fragments of the Dark Towers to his own disadvantage. It is hard to know what he believes, but it is obvious that he trusts in his own strength to wield Ancient technology. This is where he will fail. The lost cities are cursed. The technology that he finds in Kos-Ulugrod will destroy him. Perhaps it will also use him to destroy others—that is, if he can even find it."

"And do you trust Orlim's judgment in the matter of pursuing these reckless adventurers?"

Morla cleared her throat. "It is likely that Orlim has information about Kos-Ulugrod that places us at an advantage above Teomaxos' teams," she suggested. "He wants to find these fragments and technologies as much as Teomaxos, I deem, and that is why he is sending his own *reckless adventurers.*"

"This is undoubtedly the case," Lothar agreed. "The men he has prepared for this mission are a brave contingent of trackers who have all traveled through the wastelands before—a rather rough lot, but quite trustworthy."

He gave Morla a long look.

"I am less worried about Orlim's choice of trackers than that they will arouse attention," Val said.

"We were careful to secure all we require through back channels that do not expose any of the nobles of the lower houses who have supported us," Lothar answered. "Provisions, environmental suits, and a mobile command center have already been appropriated. As for departing the city without being seen, that will take a little luck and much courage. Departure will be via the Undercity hangars. Transport is by air—a dirigible. Our men need only a distraction, and we may have one soon. His Lordship Teomaxos has just announced his intentions to journey to Nara under pretense of attending Gilat. There will be a great convoy of airships going west to the colonies. We will make our move then."

"Gilat?" Val wondered. "What is that?"

"Gilat is a kind of festival," Morla said. "However, the purpose is not merely to carouse."

"Rivals in business or politics go to the Gilat arena in Nara to settle disputes," Lothar explained. "Sometimes there are farmers and landowners, and at others there are representatives of guilds at war with one another. They come to bid on warrior-proxies who will fight in the arena in order for their sponsors to obtain legal concessions."

"I understand that it is still used to decide taxation," Morla added, "but more commonly it settles debts and disputes over property."

Glancing up towards the girls' apartment, Nunna saw the light was on inside. She could hear Fann singing softly to soothe her sisters.

"Those children were slaves of Amed, the governor of Nara," Morla said, following her gaze. "They served in the arena alongside Deadmen. Fann's voice is all that saved them from a worse lot."

"Deadmen?" Nunna murmured.

"Slaves, captives, and criminals," Lothar said. "They are the proxies who fight in place of their betters. Gifts of food and improved living conditions are granted by their sponsors to those who survive, and by each successful engagement they are ranked accordingly. In this way the guilds can face-off in a fair challenge; though, technically speaking, the guild with the deepest pockets gets the pick of the Deadmen."

A long moment passed. The sun had set, and the air was becoming chill, but Nunna didn't care. She stood and lifted her eyes to the starry skies of the strange new world she had come to call home, and her heart was somewhat lifted.

Val spoke, and Nunna imagined the stars listened in.

"What if we give Teomaxos what he desires while helping our team of trackers set forth in secret?" she asked.

The creaking of leather straps marked Lothar's restless stirring as the empress spoke her meaning more clearly.

"Let's give him a trial by Gilat."

"My Lady?"

"I will offer a challenge to his honor by announcing to the people that the council is trying to harm me."

After a thoughtful pause, Lothar spoke. "I see. You believe he would not dare attack you openly if you make such a claim, lest it prove his treason."

"—and the actions of his cabal would indeed be viewed as treason by many," Morla added. "He does fear the people's love for you, and for all your presence means to the faithful."

"The forbidden stories have returned to the marketplace," Lothar said with a nod. "If it was even suspected that the council's leadership has had a falling out with the empress, the majority would definitely side with any of the councilmen who openly support us, which in turn would draw those councilmen who are wavering over to our cause."

"Political pressures might compel some to assist us," Morla said, "but politics has often been a double-edged sword in this city."

"And yet," Lothar continued, "if the empress went forth to Gilat with great fanfare, it would create all the diversion we need to allow our trackers to slip away unnoticed."

Val nodded. "Caution is still of utmost importance," she countered. "Put on the defensive, Teomaxos will not be able to make a move; but the loyalty of the people is a card I do not wish to play so soon. This plan may end up splitting the council itself in twain."

"I see," Lothar replied. "The resulting factions arising between powerful Galanese nobles could erupt in a civil war between the colonies of the Karn and our northern holdings, with one side defending your honor and the other for Teomaxos and his cabal. I also worry about finding a suitable hero to fight for your honor in Gilat. We would need to make sure the councilmen do not have access to him, or they could easily turn this scheme against you."

"The proxy is indeed the weakest link," Val agreed. "If fate goes with Teomaxos in Gilat, do you think it will bring the people over to his side?"

Morla hadn't said much, but she was looking very worried. The shadow of her unveiled thoughts and conflicting feelings brought with it a startling note of sorrow to Nunna's receptive mind.

All her thoughts were bent on death—death and sacrifice.

These two ideas filled the air like a heavy fog, dulling reason with fear and stifling the light of the starry sky. Nunna was pushed suddenly to the verge of tears. Why was Morla thinking about such things at a time like this?

Why was Morla smiling?

"We cannot know the future without a price," the seer said, keeping her dark eyes fixed on the tiled pavement. "Loyalties will be tested on all sides, and blood shall be spilled. This is your decision to make, Bal Ona."

"I will make the sacrifice, then," Val said, rising and looking at the sky. "Nothing comes but by sacrifice. We shall make a spectacle of our going forth, and give them all a glimpse of their Empress."

Nunna clenched her jaw. Since the day Val collapsed in the High Place, the change had grown pronounced enough to see clearly. The smile she'd glimpsed on Val's face was long gone now. In its place was stern imperial majesty.

"Nunna," Val said, turning to face her.

She hesitated to reply. Lothar looked away towards the gate.

"It is a good plan," Nunna said, rising to her feet. "It would be better, though, if we thought about how we could change it if everything goes wrong—"

"If My Lady wishes," Lothar interrupted, "it would perhaps be wise to name your companion of a rank that befits her. We have all seen her skill as a warrior, and her speech of late has betrayed an understanding of strategy to rival my own. I would be happy to pass my thoughts regarding contingencies by her before presenting a finished plan to Your Majesty."

"Good, then. I name her a thirteenth Dragon Slayer."

Lothar blinked. "Never before has there been more than twelve," he said, "and a woman has never been named among them. Some of the men might think it an ill omen."

"Then we will make a new tradition," Val replied. "We shall have thirteen—one female warrior for the honor of the empress. The only limitation I place on her is that she is to remain with me in this house until we leave, and that she shall always be at my side thereafter. Other than that, she shall assist in all normal duties, and will answer directly to you, Lothar, for her service."

Val's heart reached out to her warmly. Nunna was touched, for these words did not openly reveal her weakness before the others. In truth, it would not do for her to be in the front of any kind of battle— not with instrumentally adaptive senses. Val's offer was a token of trust, and of friendship.

"It is settled, then," Lothar said. "I will be back later tonight, and she shall hear me out while she is standing watch, as she often does, being bound to thankless tasks by love rather than for the sake of duty."

Nunna blushed from ear to ear. It was the most girlish gesture she'd ever made, and she was glad that no one could see it in the dark.

"What now?" Lothar asked. "How shall we send forth the empress' proclamation?"

"Go rouse Teomaxos from his own dinner and make my challenge before him and his guests," Val replied. "Make sure you send along as many as you can spare to herald the challenge in every circle of the city, from High Place to the bridges of the Kethern."

She turned and began to walk away towards the front entrance of the estate, but paused to add, "We will begin final preparations tomorrow, and then we shall set out. The expedition to Ulugrod will be standing by, waiting for our move to mask their own. Pass on all the details to Orlim, and bring his response to me when you return tonight. I will not be sleeping in my chamber. You will find me in the armory."

"I will do as you say, My Lady. And might I suggest you dust off your sparring armor? It would do you good to pick up your weapon again, too."

Three Dragon Slayers emerged from the shadows to take up positions around her. Val acknowledged her escorts with a nod.

"I am not fighting this battle myself, Lothar," she said, walking briskly away.

"It was not Gilat I was thinking of," he replied quietly.

While Val retired to main level armory, Nunna stood by the bench where Morla sat staring, as she had been, at the tiled pavement. Lothar waited silently, lingering though he was already dismissed and had many things to do before he returned later that evening.

"Is there something else, Lothar?" Morla asked.

"There is a handwritten note Orlim asked me to pass along to you, removed along with the missive from the courier. Orlim wanted you to see it first."

He handed her a small parchment, rolled and flattened. In the gas lamps that sputtered nearby, Nunna saw that it was inscribed with beautiful script. Morla unrolled it and read for a few moments, then placed it in her lap.

"This is a strange development," Lothar offered. "Orlim has heard of this place, but he says he cannot verify its existence. Perhaps if the empress could contact Marluin or Brisen—"

"The Ancients would not come to our aid," Morla replied, "not even if we knew how to summon them. This puzzle is for us to figure out by ourselves."

She seemed then to realize her harsh tone. Folding the paper calmly, she handed it back to Lothar.

"I am sorry. I trust you, Lothar. You have cared for us well, and have proven yourself many times. My frustration was not aimed at you."

Even as she said this, a strange hope stirred Nunna's heart. Morla was too ready to dismiss these creatures she called *Ancients*.

"My Lady no longer shares Brisen's dreams?" he wondered, taking the note from her hand.

"Though the empress was in contact for a short while, she reports the communion of their thoughts has ceased, as have my own visions."

"This changes nothing."

"No, Lothar, it changes everything. Think you nothing of our true enemy? Brisen is in his power now."

They stared at one another a long moment. Morla nodded towards the note in his hand.

"If that was in the possession of a courier connected to the council," she said, "then there is a chance we are already too late to stop them—especially if *Kutha* is involved."

"I will take my leave, then," he said. "Have a restful evening, Lady Morla. We will be traveling soon."

When he was gone, Morla spoke aloud to Nunna without looking at her directly.

"What did you sense from him?"

"Agitation. Loneliness. I am afraid, Morla."

"And I am also afraid."

"Of the Thirteenth Tower?"

Now Morla looked up.

"I saw it on the note," Nunna lied.

Morla rose from the bench. "There is much you will need to learn if you are to set out on this journey with us," she said. "Being honest with me is one of those things. Now, let us go and check on the children. I am not certain yet whether it is more dangerous to leave you all here than it is to bring you together into the monster's den."

As much as Nunna longed to accompany the empress on her journey, Morla had a point. She followed the seer quietly towards the stairs.

"What do you know about the Ancients?" Morla asked suddenly.

Nunna scrunched her face. "Nothing," she answered. "Weren't they people who lived in Syrscian long ago?"

"They are not from this world, or from any other that we know about. They awakened the first people here in Syrscian, and they protected this world against one of their own, a creature named *Abaddon*, the Destroyer, who made his realm in Kutha."

"The Ancients are no longer here?"

"They left, but two remained. One of them, Brisen, was Val Anna's mother."

This shocking revelation was interrupted by a cold feeling like a smothering hand passing over the place where they stood, pouring down the stairwell like an evil waterfall. Something definitely wasn't right. Nunna stopped, clutching the railing at the bottom of the steps.

"What is it?" Morla asked, noting her discomfort.

"I don't know."

In that moment, the stairs before her were like those in the dark terminal where she had cowered in fear of dragons for three long years. Morla also seemed attuned now to the passing dread, and looked instinctively upwards, towards the second level—towards the apartment where Fann and her sisters had gone.

Fann's singing had stopped.

She wasn't sure how she'd gotten there, but moments later Nunna reached the door. There she found a household sentry slumped over the threshold. His throat was slashed. A pool of blood had gelled all around him.

The room within was a shambles, but the children weren't there.

Kneeling down beside the body, Nunna lifted the guard's clenched hand from his chest. Prizing the fingers open, she found a telltale scrap of fabric. It was blue in color with white stitching—the uniform of a Dragon Slayer. She tucked the scrap of cloth into her belt. This bit of evidence would remain hidden, for now.

"This night—," whispered a voice in the darkness, "—it's all turning out now as it was in my dream."

Morla's shadow leaned against the doorjamb, panting for breath. Standing there in the pale starlight, the seer's hair took on a wraithlike appearance. Her eyes stared into the dark. Nunna lost focus momentarily, repelled by the sadness that wrung her heart.

"Morla?"

But Morla was somewhere else. Her gift had taken her to a place where she would see what could be seen.

"I dreamed it in the long-ago," she said, her voice a quiet sigh. "I dreamed it when Bal Ona was leading me to a place I knew I would not come back from. This attack was a message."

"A message from whom?"

"The Destroyer has glimpsed Brisen's daughter," Morla answered in a monotone, her eyes far away. "He knows now that she is in this house. The children were taken by an arrangement between Teomaxos and Eterskel, and are on their way to Governor Amed of Nara Colony. The empress is safe for now. He has plans for her. The rest will be discovered when darkness falls on Nara—"

Her gift having exhausted her physically, the seer collapsed beside the fallen sentry. Nunna knew then that Morla's fears were founded in truth. There was something truly evil afoot, and it had them in its sights.

21

DRAGON'S BLOOD

Southern Tarthalion, Syrscian,
Year 997 of the New Council

Rallied by the distant battle cry of Shimeon's trumpet, Shu raced northward down the slopes of the mountainside, sliding over heaps of scree until the day's last light began to fail. The caves of the Watchers were behind him. Avalon was lost, and now so was he. With night fast approaching and the sounds of battle growing faint, he bent all his mind on the dim blowing of a trumpet, an echo of the deep past brought to him on a strange breeze gusting up from the new world before him—the world where it all began.

The World of Origins.

But weariness drew its hand down upon him more swiftly than expected. He had taken neither food nor rest for several days. His initial momentum spent, he paused uncertainly, panting for breath as he surveyed the valley below. Though from the high pass this sward had seemed little more than a narrow margin of green, it had transformed into a two-mile wide sea of grass breaking upon a wall of trees, the beginnings of a dense forest.

Moving with long shuffling strides down the steep and tricky slopes, Ibni pushed a mound of gravelly soil before his PCU as he came down to join Shu. Spry he was not, for the mechanical armor was quite long in the legs and heavy in the arms, resulting in a stooped posture. The Seraph shone a wonderful coppery color in the fading light, but it was heavily worn. So mottled was its appearance that Shu could well imagine it had grown like skin over the skeletal frame. The PCU's long head was paler than the rest of the unit, and deeply incised with a knotwork pattern of four quadrants arranged in a diamond. The round green eyes, frozen in a fixed gaze of surprise, glowed in the twilight.

Shu stepped out of his way as Ibni approached, but his own eyes were riveted now on the darkening treeline. He never saw such a forest. Ancient towers five hundred feet high—these trees made redwoods look like ornamental shrubs. But their growth was not at all like an evergreen. Rather, it was reminiscent of a baobab, with a tall thick trunk that sprang into an umbrella of twisting branches, like serpents shooting from the main trunk. Atop these were raised high bristling crowns of green or blue spikes, which woven together formed a dense roof.

After a long look, he decided the trees were probably a species of *Dracaena Cinnabari*, or Dragon's Blood. Their rough boles were buttressed by knotted knees rising above a weird tangle of jungle plants and giant bioluminescent fungi, shadowy figures hunched in a gloomy haze. It was a daunting sight, deserving of a long pause at a respectful distance.

"I haven't heard anything for a long while," he remarked when Ibni was beside him at last.

"Nothing moves," Ibni replied through the PCUs grating voice synthesizer. *"No men. No birds. Nothing."*

The trumpet-blast that had sent Shu leaping down the slopes was a fading memory. There was now little noise to be heard aside from Ibni crunching brittle red shale underfoot; but hanging above the mighty towering trees the smoke of a great burning continued to rise, lit red from beneath. The fires weren't too far beyond the borders of the forest.

"This doesn't feel right," Shu said.

"Danger in the woods," Ibni suggested. *"Dark."*

"Well, I'm not waiting here for any of those cave-dwellers to come and find us," Shu replied. "Let's go find the battlefield."

Though it was now dark, the forest glowed faintly. As far as Shu could tell from a distance, the aquamarine light appeared to be emanating from the giant fungi scattered throughout the area. He'd never seen anything like it.

They set out, and reaching the bottom of the lowest slope they made their way slowly through the grassy vale. Shu was cautious, for he knew without a doubt that Shimeon was here. He was certain of it. There was no other who raised such a battlecry. And if Shim was in the World of Origins—

That meant Lír was here also.

"Lighter here," Ibni mumbled.

They had reached the woods. The air was tinged coral-pink by the treeline. It smelled strong and musty, and was heavy with motes of glimmering particles—spores, perhaps. Shu had lost the filtered mask for his armored jumpsuit back in the caves, along with everything else that might be of use in combat.

"You can see better than I with the Seraph's eyes," Shu said. "Try to keep us going in a straight line towards the north."

"Tired," Ibni said.

Shu's own strength was wavering. He needed water more than food or rest, but there were no streams anywhere in sight.

"Any sign of movement?" Shu asked.

Ibni turned a full circle, surveying the perimeter.

"None."

Shu nodded wearily. "Alright. We can take a short rest. I think we're far enough from the caves to make camp; but we're not alone out here. There are Gremn, and they were fighting someone—or something."

Just as he said this, a loud crashing sound from the forest alerted them both. Ibni swiveled his head in the direction of the noise, just east of their position.

"There is something moving parallel to the treeline there," Shu observed. "It sounds large."

"*Stopped,*" Ibni said.

They looked at each other in silence a moment.

"Curious," Shu remarked. "Shall we take a look?"

There was no further talk of making camp. They immediately crossed the wood's shadowy margin side by side, and turned right as soon as they were under the trees. The atmosphere was still, and other than the noise Ibni made it was very quiet. No insects or night-birds sang.

"Take a look at that," Shu marveled, looking up at a brightly glowing bell-shaped fungus nearby. The orange cap was as tall and bulky as a full-grown oak, and its smooth gray stalk was several feet in diameter.

Ibni said nothing, but walked towards the mushroom with as gentle a step as he could manage, almost as if he expected it to make some sudden move. He positioned the lumbering Seraph eye-to-eye with the enormous mushroom-cap. Then, reaching out carefully, he gently brushed the gills under the cap, releasing a shower of spores. Shu kept back and watched as the fine powder drifted slowly to the ground.

The ground began to heave instantly. No sooner had the spores come in contact with the forest floor than they sprouted, thrusting and bulging like large maggots as they stretched fingerlike into the air. All around Ibni's feet there were thousands of them, all writhing this way and that; and after their wild growth progressed another few seconds, they slowed, twisting and turning as if to take a look around.

"Don't touch anything!" Shu warned. "I don't want any of that growing inside me!"

"*I must walk behind, then,*" Ibni said.

His size permitted no other arrangement, really. Before they set out again, Shu stooped and dug into the soil with his fingertips. Finding it surprisingly loose and peaty, he scooped up a handful of dark loam and sniffed it. It smelled sweet and strong, reminiscent of soil from a swamp. Mildly masking the scent of the soil was something else.

"Do I smell fire?" Shu wondered.

They ended up soldiering onward through the rest of the night, and Shu was surprised to feel himself invigorated the farther they progressed. He figured they had gone almost a mile to the east before turning left again, and afterwards had kept as straight a northward course as could be managed. Ibni said nothing, and Shu kept the pace leisurely. Though they never found whatever it was that had lured them beneath the trees, the smell of smoke could be detected at whiles. It reminded Shu that his friend Shim was out there, somewhere. If they could find Shim or a Gremn war party, their chances of survival would be better.

Syrscian was no place for outsiders.

Making a wide berth around a mushroom patch, Shu ducked beneath the tangled roots of some trees and paused, trying to catch the smell of smoke. It had faded almost completely, and there was no breeze in the forest. Dawn was already peeping into the sky, but the perpetual haze created a screen capable of hiding predators large and small, both in the canopy and on the ground.

Ibni followed him slowly, occasionally breaking branches or banging roots as he bumbled along. The noise he was making bothered Shu, but there being no other sounds he decided it mattered little. There were few things more dangerous than a Seraph, he reasoned, and that stood them in good stead—as long as Ibni didn't mind fighting off the monstrous creatures of the World of Origins, that is.

From what little he knew, this was a lost world, an ancient land that remained largely unchanged by its long cycles of cultivation and desolation. Dragons, he knew, would be a problem, and especially here, where the jungle was thick and visibility poor. As it was told, dragons of the World of Origins were highly adaptive and intelligent. The Seraph was sure protection against Watchers, but against dragons Shu wasn't so sure.

"Ibni?"

The PCU grated a long, low noise. Shu continued.

"We might run into trouble. You think you can handle that unit in a real fight?"

"Fight what?"

"Maybe dragons."

"Dragons?"

The giant Seraph put up its hands in a gesture of fear while rotating its head to scan the forest.

"I suppose it's a scary thought for me, too," Shu admitted.

"Dragons here?" Ibni asked. *"Dragons real?"*

"Yes to both."

"I think...not fighting is best. Not feeling well."

A long silence followed. Beneath a skyscraper-sized tree they paused to study anew the forestlands around them. The bioluminescent fungi faded in splendor to colors of dull brown and gray-green. The Dragon's Blood trees loomed over all but the tallest pines; and here or there they spotted the gnarled remains of ancient growth, twisted skeletons of old bristlecones and holly that were covered in moss and other small vegetation. Daylight brought other changes as well. There were sounds of strange birds in the woods. At least, Shu thought they might be birds.

Breaking the stillness, he said, "We should be getting close to the battlegrounds we saw burning yesterday. There might be armed men about."

"Lingering after battle?"

"The victors might not be very welcoming of us—especially not of you."

"What manner of men are they in this land?"

Shu hesitated. Ibni seemed not to comprehend their transition to another world.

"We are in the realm of the gods," he tried. "Do you understand?"

"No. Gods not real."

"The gods of Canaan were not real, no. But we are in a place where the first beings were made by a real creator."

"First people?"

"And the first trees. Also the first machines."

"At Islith Manufacturing Facility?"

"That's different. Machines like your Seraph were made there by the Gremn."

"And what of the people? They are kind?"

"My uncle told me stories. I don't know, but the people here might be trouble."

Indeed, thoughts of the natives had worried him throughout their evening march. Either way he looked at it, a battle here involving the Gremn would resurrect the single most contentious issue that had ever riven the World of Origins.

Shu started walking again, pressing on through a tangle of vines in order to avoid passing too close to a budding fungus. On a similar hike through an altogether different forest, Shu had listened while Kabta explained to him a strict non-interference policy with regard to indigenous groups of Crodah exiles on Earth.

"I don't want a battle," Ibni said, following closely.

"I understand," Shu said, glancing up over his shoulder. "However, the battle has begun, and we may already be involved."

"How?"

"Well, you were recovered from the ship beneath Hazor by my uncle, who brought you to the place where we made transit to this location."

"Yes. The long sleep."

"And my uncle did forbid the exercise of forceful control over either his own people or humans."

"Our uncle is not human?"

This gave Shu a jolt. All this time he'd forgotten that Kabta was also Ibni's uncle.

"He is of a people called the Gremn, like our father."

"Gremn, who made the Seraph. Gremn, like our father."

Unsure how to proceed, Shu quickly changed the subject. "Uncle said that an armed intervention between humans and the Gremn for the purpose of saving one or the other race from total annihilation would likely lead to the destruction of them both via escalation."

"Like Lord Pharaoh," Ibni answered. *"Makes sense."*

The boy trapped inside the Seraph was also the former high king of Canaan, the only person who had ever introduced himself to the pharaoh of Egypt as *king*. And when Hazor had aggressively pushed back against its neighbors, taking a few of the lesser chiefdoms in the process, Pharaoh did not intervene. Even after trade to those regions was cut off, and Egypt's treasuries and storehouses were barren, still he held back. That was because Pharaoh knew that Egypt could not afford to invest itself in stabilizing the periphery, the buffer-zone with Mesopotamia. If he'd been foolish enough to try it, escalation of the conflict would draw in other parties from the north. Years of war would drag on into decades, maybe even centuries, and all trade or growth would become impossible. The world, strangled by war, knowing nothing but war, would become a wasteland of survivors who must scavenge ruins to survive.

It might sound like a worst-case scenario, but it did eventually come to pass. And according to Kabta, this is exactly what had happened in Syrscian—on a much grander scale.

"Fighting," Shu remarked, "would eventually force us to revisit the disaster that resulted in our people's exile from this world, long ago."

"But there was war aplenty in our world."

Our world, he called it.

"Yeah," Shu replied. "I always doubted the peace would last. Our people, the Gremn, split up into factions and fought each other."

"Why?"

"Armed interventions were necessary to stop some Gremn from attempting to control humans by secret strategies, or through the raising of sympathetic governments."

"Like what Father did through me?"

Shu glanced back towards the Seraph. "Yes," he answered. "But Father was fighting for the side that desired to enslave the world."

"And Kabta stopped him?"

Shu was amazed at his grasp of the situation. Though he'd said nothing of this to him, Ibni was able to piece it all together by himself.

"It was necessary, Brother, to prevent the outbreak of total war. Still, our uncle dragged his feet. In the end, this may have led to a blindness of the things happening closest to him."

The slip-up came in the twentieth century, Shu recalled, during the Second World War. DePons, tapped by agents of Lír, assisted the Crodah in the development of atomics. Just as Kabta had warned, the War of Destroying Fire was brought to Earth.

No one doubted DePons was a loose cannon. He did as he wished, and Kabta never attempted to restrain him. Perhaps it was by the pleas of Nephtys that he was spared. As for Shu, he could only think of the people who had been vaporized in the war, and of the ensuing arms race that thrust Earth ever nearer the edge of apocalypse—all because of Gremn interference in human affairs.

"It wouldn't take an arms race to reveal what kind of people the Gremn and humans really are," Shu said. "We all regard one another and our own kinds only at a proper distance—even those closest to us."

He stopped and looked at the tall Seraph stalking behind him. Ibni tilted the unit's head to one side in a considerate gesture.

"I had no upbringing in a normal family. I knew no appreciation outside of my martial skills. Neither Gremn nor human, I understand what it is to be alone."

"Not alone anymore, Brother."

Shu nodded and smiled. Now that Nuta was gone, all he had was Ibni—and maybe Shimeon. Hearing Shim's battle-cry yesterday had awakened in him a desire to look upon the face of a friend. Although, he was having doubts about that.

Where there was Shim, Lír wasn't far behind. Lír wouldn't be so welcoming. In fact, he'd probably try to kill Shu the first chance he got. He considered telling Ibni some of the details, just so he would be ready, but he never got the chance.

"Brother."

"What's wrong?" Shu asked.

The Seraph stumbled suddenly against a tree, lifting one hand to its chest and another to its head.

"Need rest."

Shu looked on with concern. He hadn't realized the interface was causing Ibni so much discomfort. It was frustrating to the point of fury to watch and be able to do nothing, so after Ibni was settled Shu walked a little way ahead, passing into an area relatively clear of growth. A few smaller trees surrounded this place, and grass grew among their roots. The air was very heavy with fog.

Removing a small knife from the sheath in his boot, Shu cut a straight pole from a sapling and scraped off some of its scaly bark. He then sharpened one end into a kind of two-pronged spear. While the warrior worked with his hands he busied himself with the troubles that burdened his mind, that being his urgent need for food and water.

Finally, after almost a quarter hour by his guess, he realized that he had not heard any sound from Ibni since leaving his side. Hastening back to the edge of the grove he looked into the deeper forest and saw that the place where the PCU had rested was empty. Shu began to panic.

Had he gotten turned around somehow?

He heard something then—the creak-creaking of the boughs of the trees. There was no wind, though. He gripped the simple spear, which was barely sturdy enough to be used as a prod.

Someone laughed.

Another creaking rustle drew his attention back towards the grove, but he saw no one there. The ensuing silence was deafening. He felt his very skin smothered by it. Glancing back over his shoulder, he thought he saw a large dark shape. A muffled noise came from the gloom to his left. Shu waited a second before assuming a defensive position, pointing the spear before him and sliding his hands apart along the smoothed shaft. The attack came not from the front, but from the side.

Nothing more than a shadow did he see, long, leathery, and lean, with a mottled green and yellow carapace gleaming in the smoky light. Knocked on his side, he tumbled over the soft ground and lost his grip on the spear. Reaching out for it, he pulled back as a clawed foot came down on the shaft, cracking it in half. He glanced upwards along the hard angular body, tracing the lines of backwards jointed legs, long arms, and large head.

A Gremn warrior.

Rolling aside, Shu jumped to his feet and tried to put distance between himself and his attacker; but the Gremn countered gracefully, matching his movements with the elegance of a dancer. Shu was amazed by his opponent's ability to move effortlessly into position, time and again. It was more play than battle, and after losing several yards of ground the Gremn ended their first brief encounter by shoving him backwards.

Laying on his back in the grass, Shu saw that he had once again lost track of his opponent. A creaking noise directly in front of him caused him to sit up sharply, and he found himself facing his attacker, who was squatting a few yards away in the grass. Looking straight into the small black eyes, their irises aglow, Shu called out for parley.

"Wait!" he shouted, holding up his hands. "Who are you, and how did you get here?"

Leaning forwards slightly, the Gremn tilted its large head to one side and spoke in a voice like a wolf's growl, cold and grating.

"Artakshasu's my name."

Shu held his breath, forcing himself to calm down. This was Lír's second in command, the legendary battle leader Artax. He'd never met him in person, but knew him well enough by reputation.

There was no chance Shu could win this fight.

"Why did you attack me?"

Artax kept his head cocked to one side. Shu noted this, and understood that he was keeping an eye out for the PCU. Ibni was nowhere to be seen.

"If this was a fight, you would not have easily detected me. You would lie dead upon the ground, Son of Nurkabta, for your own pitiful attempt at camouflage doesn't even match our surroundings."

Shu glanced down at his armored fatigues. They were suited for the substations, and for Avalon, but not for a forest.

"How do you know who I am?"

"The Gremn are clever. We do not engage before we know our prey."

"I am also Gremn."

"You are only half-Gremn. We are more powerful. We can change. We can disappear. You are no match for me."

"Is that so?"

Shu moved quickly, straining with a will. His hands flew at the ground as he rolled, and then flipped into the air with the practiced grace of an athlete. The armored jumpsuit weighed too heavily on him to clear the space between himself and his foe, however. He felt the burn in every fiber of his body as his right foot touched the broad crown of the Gremn warrior's head, right above the snout. Then, with a mighty bound, he darted forwards like a sprinter from the block. The force of his leap caused Artax to stumble forwards for a second, and when he recovered Shu was already behind him, standing between the Seraph's feet.

Artax had somehow missed Ibni, just as Shu had, for he was standing perfectly still and veiled in fungi-spores. Now he was a most welcome sight. Even nicked and scarred by eons of disrepair, a Seraph was stronger than a host of men—a fiery behemoth of battle. Better yet, he was more than fifty feet tall, so there was no outrunning him.

Before Artax could dodge his arms, Ibni swept them scythe-like over the ground and snatched the Gremn up in his left hand. Squeezing tightly, he held Artax up and inspected him carefully. Shu grinned at Ibni's squirming prize.

"Not so bad for a pair of half-breeds, eh?" he asked. "Good work, Brother. Your reach is impressive."

Artax stopped struggling. Held like a rag-doll only a couple feet away from an array of plasma ejector valves that would burn even the mightiest Gremn to cinders, he knew he was defeated.

"What should I do, Brother?" Ibni asked.

"Go ahead and kill it," Shu replied, still panting. "Burn the thing before the others show up."

The Seraph's plasma torches sputtered.

"Wait!" the Gremn shouted.

Ibni paused.

"I will answer your questions," Artax said, *"but you must free me first. We are not alone. The natives are close."*

"He's a liar," Shu called up to Ibni. "Uncle warned me about him. Destroy that thing, before it destroys us."

Ibni turned his head to consider the Gremn curiously. He must have also released his grip a little, for it was in that moment Artax slipped free. He fell and hit the forest floor only a few feet away from Shu.

The massive limbs instantly found purchase with the soft ground, and moving on all fours he quickly pinned Shu on his back. Shu appreciated the reversal with a detached sense of wonder. Ibni stumbled above, then backed off when he saw that he could do no nothing more without injuring both friend and foe.

But Artax wasn't attacking. He released Shu and stepped back a few paces.

"You are quick, but your reaction time is too slow. You still require much training."

Shu was instantly on his feet again, but Artax made no aggressive moves. He touched Shu's chest-plate with his fingertip, as if to hush him, and then looked away into the forest. Shu followed his gaze, but saw nothing.

"I have won this match," Artax decided.

"Really?" Shu mumbled, brushing his hand away. "Seems to me like we came out even."

It concerned him that the Gremn seemed worried about the forest, even with Ibni towering within arm's-reach.

"We will surely meet again, and next time I will not be alone!"

"Wait—where are you going?" Shu sputtered. "I have questions!"

Artax seemed to shrink suddenly, collapsing into himself and kneeling in the grass as he reverted to human form. Shu marveled at his appearance as it took shape before his eyes. This was a Gremn very different from any other he'd seen, with shoulder-length dark hair and bright piercing eyes. His features were finely chiseled, youthful and confident. No gear or weapon did he bear.

Without another word, Artax gave him a nod and darted off into the forest.

"Ibni!" Shu cried.

But Ibni made no reply. The Seraph pitched forwards suddenly, and fell upon its face with a tremendous crash.

In the stillness that followed, Shu turned his attention from his brother to the small sounds of footsteps all around. There were figures in the grass on the edges of the clearing, huge figures armed with spears and bows. One among them held up a hand—a long, bony hand. Shouts in a strange language rang out from the trees.

"Fantastic," Shu said to himself. *"Natives."*

22

THE DREAM WALKERS

Timhureth of Tarthalion, Syrscian,
Year 997 of the New Council

As the day wore on, Shu trudged along with his head hung low, eyes to the ground. His submission wasn't an act backed by some clever plan of escape. No, this was the real deal. His captors had been very thorough. He'd been stripped of his armor and was shackled with his hands behind his back. The natives offered him only a skirt of leather to wear, in fashion similar to their own gear.

Shu's feet were bare, for they'd also taken his boots. Half-breed Gremn or not, hiking through a jungle on bare feet wasn't easy. However, escape wasn't really his biggest concern. The way he figured, these native fighters were taking him somewhere for questioning. As for Ibni, well, it was anyone's guess how he was faring right now.

The tread of the PCU no longer followed behind him. Instead of the noisy sound of a slow avalanche punctuated by the hiss of strained hydraulics, there was the swish-swishing of careful feet. The long-tailed aboriginals who guided him were a perplexing mix of quiet and forceful, morose and fierce, feline and canine. All were armed with spears, shields, bows, and axes—and with battle-honed discipline as well. They'd examined the fallen Seraph for a few minutes while one stern figure clapped Shu in iron cuffs.

Ibni hadn't stirred once during all their clanging and banging on his hull. Either he'd passed out from physical exhaustion or there was some kind of mechanical failure which left him immobilized. Not counting the benefits of their Gremn heritage, Ibni was locked inside a piece of equipment designed specifically to keep its pilot alive. The Seraph had already succeeded in doing that for several millennia. Still, leaving his brother behind was worrisome. There was nothing he could really do about it, though. The distance between them was widening with long swift strides.

The native warriors numbered above twenty, and those were the ones Shu could see. There were probably others. Even now he spotted shadowy forms vaulting from tree to tree in the canopy above. When he craned his neck to see where they were going, the tall dark-haired fellow behind him smacked the backs of his calves with a spear-shaft.

"Cut that out!" Shu growled, turning his head slightly.

He was rewarded by being caned across the shoulders, which hurt far worse than his legs. The power behind the warrior's stroke was astonishing, but even so it bounced off Shu's back with little effect. He was tensing up, and his temper was running short. Dizziness and a monstrous dehydration headache had brought him to a critical limit. He stopped cold in his tracks, ready at last to do battle.

The spear-shaft connected with the top of his skull.

Shu put away the pain. He turned in place and stared up into the long angular face of his tormentor. The man's wide-spaced eyes sparkled, and his ears perked. This one's features were mostly canine. He seemed amused by Shu's show of defiance.

"You think this is funny, do you?"

The warrior made no speech in reply—just hand-gestures. The only communication thus far had been through pushing and pointing, and through the hard slap of weapons across bare skin.

"You know what a flying squirrel is?" Shu asked in a low growl. "You're about to find out!"

The crystal point of the spear flashed before Shu's eyes, then swung back around and rested against his exposed chest. He blinked away beads of sweat that rolled down his forehead—but there wasn't much sweat left in him. His skin was cold, and he was shaking. Perhaps this was as far as his weak half-human flesh would carry him, he thought.

Then the warrior moved the spear's head upwards, and used it to point over Shu's shoulder. Squinting through the dense tangle of trees and vines, he got his first glimpse of their destination. It was a primitive stone tower. There was blue sky behind it, so Shu guessed they were also heading towards a clearing. It wasn't far.

The native shoved him hard with the butt end of his spear, and Shu resisted the powerful temptation to kick him. He turned and continued walking instead. Those before him left scarcely a trail to follow through the wastes, and those who followed covered their tracks too well. Ibni would never find him, even if he knew which way to start. Even a Gremn like Artax would have trouble matching the woodcraft of these warriors. For now, Shu was on his own.

After another few miles of hiking through misty glades beneath the dragon's blood trees, Shu was ushered into a forest of smaller and denser growth. Grass sprang up beneath his aching feet. The colors were greener here, and though the day was darkening swiftly towards night the air was clearer. There were no giant fungi. The complete absence of spore-scatterers seemed deliberate, as if a boundary was carefully maintained between the forest and this restive parkland.

The ground began to slope upwards. The sun was slipping lower towards the horizon when the grass led them at last to the summit of a hill. A small fortress stood there, like an iron crown on the hilltop, and behind it loomed the tall stone tower he'd seen through the jungle. Beyond the tower stretched a wide valley. The troop of warriors paused to survey the area.

"You have reached the city of Timhureth."

Shu turned at the sound of the deep baritone voice, astonished that his guide would so suddenly break his lasting silence with plain English.

"What?" Shu mumbled, looking from the warrior back to the scene before him.

"There is our city," his guide answered, pointing with his hand. "You just have to look closely to see it."

Shu scanned a great wooded bowl about twenty kilometers across and surrounded by eight hills, each similar in scale and form to the one upon which they currently stood. On each of the eight hilltops there were towers, huge and old, crumbling with decrepitude.

In the valley's basin lay a lake the color of polished steel, and opposite, far beyond the farthest hills, menaced a line of tall mountains. Shu had no idea how distant those faded peaks stood, but their heights seemed far greater than the mountains away south, the mountains where he met the Watchers.

Nowhere could he find a trace of any city.

"The hills," the warrior said, pointing to the valley with his spear. "Look at the hills. Open up your eyes and see, if you are able. Or are you as blind as the Galanese?"

While squinting against the setting sun, Shu wondered if the man was speaking of ancient Galaneth, and if these people had mistaken him for someone else. Then he saw something that caught his attention. Though heavily forested, tangled with vines and trees that looked like eucalyptus, the landscape's curious contours suggested underlying structures.

"Long ago my kin dwelt in a city north of here, Haleth it was named," the warrior said. "There are seven of these cities in the south, and one other that was abandoned. The seven, 'tis said, are the remains of ships the Ancients built to ply the heavens. The land swallowed them, and the Ayumu came long afterwards to build the towers on top. We make our dwellings lower in the valley, in trees as well as upon the ground."

"Why the history lesson?" Shu wondered.

"Because I know that you are not Galanese," the man answered, "and I thought you might appreciate civility."

"Civility? Is that what you call being shoved around by armed warriors all day?"

His captor made no answer, but the others seemed to note a change in the mood of their leader. They dispersed in groups of three or four, making their way down the slope of the hill towards the valley.

"You are called the Ayumu?" Shu asked.

"You would not ask such questions if you were an enemy," the warrior replied. "They know all about us, and they are afraid."

Shu was turned roughly, and felt the hard calloused hands of his guide working the locked cuffs and chain on his wrists. When he was released he had difficulty moving his arms.

A leather bag of water was extended towards him.

"Drink."

Shu obeyed, draining the bag against the protest of his cramping stomach. His limbs were like wood, and a fire burned behind his eyes. He longed to lie down in the grass and fall asleep that very moment, but the warrior took the empty water skin from him and shoved him towards the fortress at the top of the hill.

"We are at war," his guide explained briefly. "My men were going to kill you, but when I saw you in the company of the *Loviatar*, I ordered your capture."

Shu wasn't sure if the unfamiliar word referred to Artax or the Seraph. He wasn't certain they'd even spotted Artax, since he was conspicuously absent during their little excursion through the fungi-forest. Ignoring these matters, he pressed on towards the fortress. He was more curious about the tower behind it, though.

Perched right on the edge of the hill, the tower's basic form was a series of stacked square houses built from pale gray smooth-hewn ashlars. The four-level structure tapered towards the top, the lowest level being the tallest and most ornate, while the uppermost level was no more than a capped dolmen. Each of the levels was open on all four sides, and upon some of the arched openings were elaborate carvings.

"What are these towers for?" he asked. "Are they dwellings?"

"You ask too many questions. It is enough that I am allowing you to walk freely before me. Be content with your life, or by my own hand you shall quickly lose it. I am Tarhund. I command the fighters of Timhureth in Tarthalion, or what is left of them."

"Tarhund, huh? I'm Shubalu. Just call me Shu."

Tarhund didn't look too interested in offering any other bits of information, so while he stumbled along Shu diverted his attention to the valley below the hill, where he spotted a thin spiral of blue smoke in the fading light. Following this he finally caught sight of the flat roofs of clustered stone buildings hugging the shoreline of the lake. Their dwellings were away there, hidden deep in the valley.

Shu knew very little about the World of Origins. In all the stories that his uncle told him, he recalled no mention of the Ayumu. He did remember tales of people with the characteristics of animals, and in all those stories one theme stood out. The forest people, as his uncle called them, were fearfully superstitious of technology. In the days of the war they had tabooed almost all machinery, and had few dealings with technologists. Being discovered in the vicinity of a giant mechanical man, he surmised, was probably not a good thing.

They kept on walking towards the small fort. Stout turrets marked its corners, of which there seemed to be three. It looked like an ordinary medieval fortress, except that the walls were flat-topped and lacked embrasures or arrow-loops.

A shallow ramp led them up to a gate. Shu was suddenly aware of the glimmer of watchful eyes on either hand, and of the faint shapes of tall figures standing, guardians hidden in crevices built into the wall. Tarhund stepped in front of him as they passed beneath the gaze of these primal otherworldly tribesmen. Superstitious folk were prone to be unpredictable, their reasoning intractable. An alliance with these was not likely to succeed; nor could Shu think of a reason it would be desirable. That is, if they were even willing to help him out.

His mind was still revolving around the battle he'd heard from the mountainside. He wondered if Shimeon and the others had some kind of conflict here, and if that was what had put him into such a difficult position.

On the other side of the gate he was forced to attend to his footing, for the gate passage led them out onto a landing facing a deep chasm. Down in the darkness there Shu descried empty chambers, dungeons of sorts, interconnected by a maze of paths. There was no parapet or handrail between them and the drop. A hundred feet away, the third turret bulged outwards to meet them, but there was no way there from the front gate. The keep simply rose up out of the depths. Shu wondered how Tarhund intended to get there—short of flying.

His guide nudged him to the left side of the landing, where a narrow staircase ran along the inner face of the wall. Shu was impressed by the stonework here, for the stones were fit cleanly with no mortar. The stairs would have been difficult to see, if one did not know just where to look.

They followed these stairs all the way up, and walking along the top of the fortifications they eventually entered the turret to the left of the gate. Passing through a small chamber within, they exited via a low arch and found themselves standing on a stone bridge spanning the space between the dungeons and the third turret. Tarhund stepped out confidently onto this narrow span, and Shu followed. He wished his guide would slow down, for they were high enough to look out over the valley and its lake. Something out there had caught his eye. Not far away to the northeast he saw some heavier smoke rising in black roiling clouds.

"Is the valley still under attack?" he asked, balancing carefully as they made their way towards the keep.

Tarhund passed him a weary look and continued without a word.

"I think it's only fair of me to ask questions," Shu probed. "I'm a stranger here, and I don't know what's going on."

"So you say," the warrior replied. "You will answer Inyan's questions before you receive answers to your own. Inyan is chief elder here. He will know what to do with you."

The tone in which he said this implied displeasure. Shu couldn't figure him out, but Tarhund was presently the least of his worries. Now that they were coming to the end of the bridge, a new knot of anxiety was rising in his stomach.

Passing through a door they entered the third turret. It was a cylindrical space about fifty feet across, and its center was lit only by torchlight. The light, red and grim, illuminated a bizarre scene.

A collection of ragtag figures huddled in the gloom. They were dressed variously in scraps of leather or woven garments, but all wore the look of men who had seen hard times in battle. Shu counted twenty, and most of them were somewhat aged. None looked happy

367

to see him, but they took notice of the newcomer for only an instant. There was obviously more pressing business at hand.

Tarhund stopped short of the group and placed a hand on Shu's chest to indicate he should also pause. There were two people kneeling on the ground in the center of the huddle. An older silver-haired Ayumu stood above them both, combing a worried hand through his beard as he scanned their faces. Shu supposed this was Inyan, the chief elder.

One of the two kneeling figures was an Ayumu girl in a tooled leather skirt. The other, Shu was surprised to see, was an ordinary man. The chief elder's eyes went back and forth between the two of them before finally settling on the young woman.

"Foxglove of Ulumeneth," Inyan said in a crackling voice. "You were the daughter of the last chieftain, were you not?"

Shu marveled at her pale tabby-striped limbs, lean yet strong. Her eyes and ears were large and kitten-like beneath a mop of ochre hair, but she protruded her right front fang a bit to show some mettle. First impressions aside, this creature appeared dauntless, if not dangerous. Looking towards the scraping sound of their feet as they entered, she noticed Shu's staring eyes and stared right back at him, tail flicking. It was then Shu noticed the ropes that bound her forearms. She was also a prisoner.

"Foxglove, I am," said she. "Of Ulumeneth are my kin."

Other than some slight movements of her tail, she sat remarkably still. The quivering human beside her, on the other hand, seemed incapable of mustering even a shred of calm. He continuously prostrated himself, shivering with either fear or agitation. It was hard to tell, for his long thin face was pressed firmly against the ground. Shu deduced he was an enemy combatant, one of the Galanese, for he was clothed in a red uniform and trenchcoat.

The man's hands were bound behind him. His boots and coat were spattered with mud. He looked up at the elders, his eyes opening wide under bushy gray brows; but he averted his gaze quickly, as if fearing sudden redress. His was a slavish manner of submission, the cringing of a whipped dog who has served cruel masters.

"What account can you make of your actions, Foxglove?" Inyan asked of the girl. "You are accused of aiding strangers in our reach in times of war."

She looked up thoughtfully before answering in a small voice, asking, "Is it wrong to help?"

"You are within our lands, and are therefore answerable to our laws."

"No laws were broken."

"The Galanese are our enemies."

She looked genuinely confused. "One was Galanese," she replied quietly, "but the others were not. They fought the Galanese in Loviatar, and then left on errands of their own, I know not where."

"That is your claim?"

"It is."

The elders conferred only by silent nods. Inyan gestured towards Shu and Tarhund, who waited in the shadows near the door.

"The strangers you guided did indeed aid us in repulsing the Galanese," Inyan said. "And though it is not our custom to tolerate machines within the perimeter of these sanctuaries, the pilots do have our gratitude. I've just learned that this man may be one of those who piloted a Loviatar. Do you recognize him?"

Foxglove addressed Shu with a long careful look before turning back towards Inyan.

"He was not among them," she replied, "but he carries their scent."

Shu sniffed his own hands, wondering if he couldn't also detect faint traces of Avalon's stink on his skin. He wondered if it would ever wash off.

"Does the stranger wish to make a statement?"

Shu noticed that they were all looking at him now, but he was unsure what they were expecting him to say. Now he understood why the Ayumu girl seemed so shy of speaking.

"Is it true," Inyan enquired, "that you are one of those who fought the Galanese in Timhureth yesterday?"

"I have no idea what you're talking about—"

"He lies," Tarhund interjected.

Shu turned a stunned look on the warrior. "I'm telling the truth," he insisted. "I have no idea what's going on in this place. I just got here!"

"Then perhaps you can explain the Loviatar that lies in the forest where we found you," Tarhund retorted, facing him down.

Shu had nothing to say. They probably thought that he was the seraph's pilot; and maybe that was for the best. In the back of his mind, though, he was wondering what they would do if Ibni woke up and started looking for him.

"Oh, boy," he muttered.

"What point is there in denying it?" Tarhund whispered aside to him. *"We are not enemies. You must tell him the truth."*

"The truth is that Seraph has a pilot in it already," Shu said to him. "Or did you not bother to check?"

Then, while Tarhund digested this bit of news, Shu said to Inyan, "I came from the south on foreign business. When I saw smoke in the forest, I thought maybe there were folk here who could assist me. I was overcome near the place where the Seraph fell, and was forced at spear-point to come here without due explanation. That's about all I can tell you."

"And yet, there is more to you than your words alone reflect," Inyan replied.

He then gestured towards an Ayumu who produced Shu's gear from a bulky sack. Holding it up for all of them to see, Inyan said, "You were dressed for battle as one of the Loviatar pilots. You are obviously one of them."

"What country in the south do you hail from?" asked another one of the elders.

Then several more questions came forth, all at once and each from a new inquisitor.

"Did you not recognize the signs of battle?"

"Who did you think would offer you aid during a war?"

"Were you coming to meet up with the other strangers?"

"Are there any more of you in the forest?"

"Why are you here?"

"Are you for the Galanese, or for us?"

Shu shook his head as he watched their deliberations break down into much beard-wagging and swishing of tails. Foxglove shared another look with him, but this time she seemed genuinely intrigued. Shu realized then that if she had met Gremn in Syrscian, whoever it was might have warned her that others would eventually show up. Did she suspect him by scent alone? He didn't know whether to feel hopeful or wary, for there were other Gremn in stasis on Avalon who may have made their way here, and all of them were monsters of a bygone era—the worst of the worst. For all he knew, Lír himself could be lurking somewhere near. Lír was a very talented shape-changer. If just half of what Shu had heard about him was true, he could even be disguised as an Ayumu.

While the elders mumbled to one another, grim displeasure etched in their aged brows, Inyan waved his hands over his head. When he finally got their attention, he looked down at Foxglove and asked a question that seemed at first to have little to do with his previous line of inquiry.

"This miserable creature," he said, nodding towards the Galanese officer, "what have you to say about him? If the army attacks us again, would his master offer terms of surrender in exchange for an officer's life?"

"He was with those who ravaged my chiefdom," Foxglove said in a surprisingly gentle voice. "I saw him there. I saw how they show no more kindness to their own than to us. The Galanese do not ransom captured soldiers."

The red-uniformed man seemed to understand that they were now talking about him, so he looked sideways at the girl kneeling next to him. His face was a mask of rage.

"Ulumeneth's fall is a great sorrow," Inyan consoled. "The loss of the bridge to Eastern Tarthalion is unfortunate. All those lands in the arms of the mountains are now open to invasion."

Foxglove's brow bunched up, yielding to a passing wave of sorrow.

"The bridge is cleansed now by our blood," she answered, her voice so soft and low that it was difficult to hear. "This man walked into our city upon that bridge beside the one called Dolaure, who is their general."

The chief elder crossed his arms over his chest, and his eyes glimmered. "If there were a king to lead them, it would be Dolaure," he said. "We call him *Shepherd of Wolves*."

"I thought Bregon of Gaerith was their commander," one of the elders noted.

Foxglove tensed noticeably.

"The squabbling continues among our foes," Inyan mused aloud, "and yet we continually fail to take advantage of it."

"That is because they are too numerous," Tarhund added, stepping forth from the shadows. "They are also led by battle-hardened officers whose blind loyalty to the council of priests brokers no possibilities of finding a weakness in their chain of command."

The elders regarded his words with raised eyebrows. Tarhund's high speech and confident voice puzzled Shu. He spoke now as if he was a king himself.

"It matters not if two of these Galanese generals have a difference of opinion," the warrior continued, his deep voice booming. "Their officers and knights continue the fight regardless, pressing onwards like an army of ants. Thus it was that when they arrived upon our borders, having crossed the river with forces too numerous for us to count, we were quickly overwhelmed. It was so in Ulumeneth, where the elders of that ancient city sent to them stating their wishes to resolve without bloodshed. In answer, the Galanese sent in fire to burn them out of their ancestral homes. The sickly, the elderly, their girls and children, their bodies lay there still, left to the birds of the air. So my scouts have reported it to me, and so it shall be in this place as well. The enemy returns now upon the northeastern hill, hard by the river. Without the Loviatar we are doomed."

The room was silent.

"When will you order the valley to be emptied?" Tarhund asked.

Inyan held out his hands, indicating the warrior should be silent. "We have already considered your entreaty, Tarhund. After the battle you went out to find a safe path to the south; but you sent word only a few hours ago stating that we were encircled. With no clear way out of the valley, we must consider every other option."

"You are not listening. They are already here!"

"He's right, you know," the officer said, chuckling to himself. "There's no way out of the valley!"

"You have something to add?" Inyan asked. "Perhaps some useful information?"

"You're all going to die!"

His ragged voice echoed wildly off the walls of the stone chamber. He winced after shouting, but no one struck him.

"Enemies of our people shall present no claims on their own behalf," Inyan said slowly and deliberately. "You will remain silent, or your tongue shall be cut out."

When silence resumed, Inyan sighed deeply and then spoke his thoughts.

"The Loviatar have vanished, we know not where. The bridge to eastern Tarthalion is held against us. To what land would you have us withdraw, Tarhund, and by what secret path? And what about those in the other cities to the west, whom we are leaving defenseless?"

"We can still escape over the northern rim of the valley and cross the river," Tarhund said. "There is a place where we might safely ford Aruist under cover of darkness, but if we do not leave soon we'll be cut off."

Inyan tugged on his beard and gazed at Foxglove suspiciously. "You said earlier that you escaped during the confusion of their assault and swam the Aruist in the dark."

"Yes."

"You then followed the Loviatar, tracking them long into the night. In their camp you met the strangers, and you agreed to help them find something they lost—something they were not willing to discuss with you."

"Yes."

"And so they agreed to help you in return for your own help, and you pointed them here, to Timhureth?"

"It is so," she replied sourly, her ears tilted backwards. "Perhaps I should not have sent them to your aid?"

"Fair enough," Inyan decided. "It would seem we are the benefactors of a strange coincidence, then. There is but one more matter that needs clearing up before I free you to join us or to find your own fate, daughter of Ulumeneth. It is the most significant complication in your claim."

To Shu's wonder, the old man held up something familiar. It took him a few moments to recognize it, but when he did it was almost impossible to hold back his astonishment.

"You have testified in our presence that the pilots of the Loviatar were Gremn exiles who returned against the Ban, and all you submit as evidence is a relic horn."

It was Shim's horn—the ram's horn he'd borne into battle long ago in a different world. The sight of it in this strange place, lit in ruddy hues by the light of torches, brought Shu back to times he'd long forgotten.

The Galanese officer was also dazzled by this revelation. At the mention of *Gremn*, he writhed and twisted even more than before. Hatred seethed from his open mouth in inarticulate mumblings, trailing a dangling thread of spittle. There was more animal in his features than in the girl who knelt beside him.

"It's an alliance?" he mumbled to himself.

Shu pondered the possibility that this might be a good time to mention that he was the heir of House Gremn. Then he had second thoughts. Being a half-breed, he wouldn't be able to offer any real proof. Who would have believed in a Gremn who couldn't change his shape?

Turning his head, the Galanese captain swiveled his eyes to meet Foxglove's. It seemed he'd forgotten the threat made to cut out his tongue.

"Monsters!" he shouted. "The Gremn and your primitive *filth*, you all resist the council and its peaceful attempts to manage a civilized society in the world that your people destroyed! How can I make you understand this? You were the ones that made it happen—you and all those of the Great Houses of old, you all need to die with the past!"

Foxglove's ears were flattened against her head, but she said nothing.

"You can confirm that the council of priests knows of the return of the Gremn?" Inyan wondered.

"Yes, and of the empress, the Crodah, and perhaps even the Gaerith as well! All your parasitic allies of old have returned for a second taste of our blood!"

The rumbling of voices that followed his ravings was filled with glances shared between wide-staring eyes. Tails twitched. It was difficult to read the moment, but Shu sensed that his presence here was not in the least coincidental. There was no point in avoiding a confrontation anymore, for time was pressing.

"I guess the cat's out of the bag," he offered. "So to speak."

A hush settled over the group, and all eyes were on him.

"You knew about this?" Tarhund demanded.

Displacement was tangling Shu's brains in a knot. He wasn't sure why he'd opened his mouth to speak at all, but the sinking feeling that trailed away with the echoes of his voice was like the haunting whisper of a ghost.

"Look," he said, holding up his hands, "I really don't know what's going on here. That's because—that's because I've spent my whole life in what you call exile."

From what he could hear among the angry and confused voices following his statement, most of the Ayumu believed him. Tarhund's face was expressionless, though. He was good at making that face, Shu decided.

"I got separated from the others during transit here," he said, speaking loudly to regain their attention.

Shu then pointed towards the horn in Inyan's hands.

"But I can tell you, that horn belonged to a friend of mine. He was a good man. If Shim happened across an army of soldiers that gets their jollies from shooting up innocent people, I know for sure he'd step in and stop it from happening. So, maybe if you help me find these strangers, we could help each other. Maybe we could get across that river like Tarhund says, and save your people from destruction."

The elders' faces were all uncertain now. Shu began sweating again. Heir of a Great House or no, public speaking definitely wasn't his thing. Beads of perspiration began to collect on the Galanese officer's forehead as well, running down through his close-clipped gray hair. Shu thought it was time to turn the heat up on this guy, and maybe deliver himself from the fire in the process.

"Maybe we came here right on time," he continued. "If this man's condition is indicative of the Galanese as a people, then it is only a matter of time before a second War of Destroying Fire is upon you. I for one am willing to join you and fight!"

The chamber remained silent, except for small sounds of laughter coming from the groveling shape on the floor.

"Another mad prophet emerges from Tarthalion!" he said. "Even if you are an exile, and even if all of this is true, the council has been working for a thousand years to eradicate every last memory of your existence from this world. No one will help you—not even the forest people!"

"Won't we?" Tarhund wondered. "A long time ago the Galanese cut down the sacred trees of Tryst. They later enslaved our people. The Fourth House can never rest until the Galanese leave our forests. If it is a sin of our proud people to resist, then we do not ask forgiveness. We will even side with the Gremn to fight the council!"

The chamber was hushed.

The tower began to shake.

The time to debate a course of action had come to an end, and the last thing Shu saw before being crushed by falling masonry was the slender figure of the Ayumu girl leaping swiftly through the passageway behind him. Though he wasn't sure why, he hoped she would make it to safety. It was more than what he could hope for himself.

Consciousness fled before a wind, a cold and merciless wind thick with noises of crushing and grinding, and with the screams of the dying—the horrible music of combat.

23

THE RAGNAROK WOLF

Timhureth of Tarthalion, Syrscian,
Year 997 of the New Council

A hint of morning light and a sound of wings brought Shu to his senses. Inches from his face, a bird fluttered upon the damp stone floor. He surprised a look of intelligence from its small round eyes. It was a pretty creature, very much like a goldfinch except for the appearance of long ornamental feathers at the tip of its tail and a little crest of bright red sprouting from its cap. The bird sang a curious warbling note that rose and fell three times, and then paused as if awaiting a reply. When none came, it passed between the bars of his prison and flew away.

Pushing himself up onto his knees, he saw that he was in a cell little more than the length and width of his body. Black iron bars closed him off from a dim corridor. He couldn't see any windows, just another gloomy cell across the hall. The air was sweet and fresh—not at all like a dungeon.

Coughing on a dry throat, he called through the bars.

"Hello?"

There was no response. He massaged a painful knot on his head while listening to the sound of air moving through the drafty corridor. Sunlight streamed in from the right-hand passage.

Shu began to suspect he was still inside the fortress, but there wasn't much he could piece together from those last few confusing moments before he blacked out. All he knew for certain was that the whole place had come down around him. And now he was here, locked in a cell.

Turning around, he observed that someone had left clothing in here with him—black pants, boots, and a loose white shirt with large sleeves. There was a long black coat, also. The garments had been folded and placed under his head while he was unconscious. Shedding the leather skirt the Ayumu had dressed him in, Shu happily donned his new gear, noting that each piece fit as if tailored specifically for him.

—Just like this cell.

His brain waited for a thought to emerge, but he was fresh out of ideas. It seemed he was still a prisoner, but where were his captors? Where was Tarhund, or Inyan? If someone was keeping him alive, what were they planning to do with him? While pondering these questions, Shu was startled by the sound of distant voices. Someone was coming.

"He was brought in as a prisoner, My Lord, but professes to be one of the exiles. Judging by their initial response, I'm certain he will purchase us bargaining power when dealing with the hostiles."

Shu groaned, for he recognized the voice immediately. It continued, a little closer now.

"On the other hand, he claimed to know nothing of the ones who've halted our advance."

There was no mistaking his annoying voice. This was the officer captured by Tarhund's fighters, the one the Ayumu had planned on ransoming. A second voice joined the conversation as the sound of footsteps proceeded down the hall.

"As ever, Sir Kay, you prove yourself a reliable source of information. Too bad you could not retrieve said information without requiring rescue. Becoming a hostage is a grave disgrace for a Knight of House Teg, and you were also injured—"

"But, My Lord Dolaure, I became a prisoner so that I could enter their camp and assess their leadership."

Dolaure. Shu remembered now. Dolaure was the Galanese general who was behind the conflicts in this land.

"Their leaders continue to elude us," the general said. "They escaped the destruction of this keep, which, if I remember correctly, you deemed implausible."

"But My Lord, we have gained two prisoners and valuable information—"

"You mean I have captured two valuable prisoners about which you happened to have discovered some useful information while you were a prisoner yourself. Whatever advantage we've gained out of this mess remains to be seen, Sir Kay. And I will not be rescuing you a second time. Such tactics are uninspired and reckless."

"Yes, My Lord. My apologies, My Lord."

The footsteps paused only a few yards away from the door to his cell, just out of sight. While straining to catch a glimpse of the general, Shu's eyes strayed to the darkened cell opposite his own, and to a grayish bundle he saw laying there. Funny, but he hadn't noticed it before.

"The forest people haven't presented any significant opposition to our presence here," the Dolaure concluded. "Nevertheless, Timhureth cannot be occupied with so small a force as we now have on hand. So, we shall burn it all to the ground and move out—regroup and redouble our efforts at cleaning up pockets of resistance once we are resupplied."

"Very good, My Lord. The men shall be most pleased. Shall we move the encampment back to Ulumeneth?"

"No. Relocate to the western face of the Rim, hard by the pass. Confer amongst yourselves and choose positions for the command posts. Keep in mind our need for swift deployment along all the main roads. I want to be able to respond if any more of these strange combat units appear."

They stepped in front of Shu's cell-door from the right: a dark-haired man in armor and a tunic, wrapped in a black cloak; and beside him the thin graying knight in red, Sir Kay. Sir Kay sported a blood-soaked bandage across his forehead. He had escaped the fall of the keep otherwise unscathed.

Looking up at the black-robed figure, Shu muttered his name.

"Dolaure."

"Hello," Dolaure greeted. "Nice to see one of our guests is awake, and arrayed now in better gear than the forest-filth had him dressed in."

Shu couldn't help but stare. Dolaure managed to speak without changing his expression at all. It was unnerving, as though his face were a mask. His blue eyes sparkled with life, but the rest was dead.

Bringing himself back to high-alert, Shu recounted his numerous experiences with interrogation. He knew that now was the time to lead if he wanted to stay on top of the situation. If Kay had reported to the general that he was with the exiles, he might be able to capitalize from this. The Gremn were an ancient legend of a bygone era. So, he would assume the demeanor of a mythical monster. The only problem, he realized, was that he was only half-Gremn.

"Why am I here?" he asked, his dry voice cracking.

"You are here because you are my prisoner," the general replied, "and you shall stand trial before the council in Gilthaloneth on charges of association with the inviolable Great Houses of old. Thus shall House Teg's status ascend, when it is made known that we intercepted and stopped a Gremn invasion."

"What invasion? You're the invaders here."

Dolaure knelt down so that he faced Shu through the bars of his cell.

"Your direct involvement in our battles against these natives is an act of aggression that threatens the sovereignty of the Galanese Colonies and Gilthaloneth itself," the general said.

"When was I involved in any battle in this land?"

"Your people have sent warriors and technology to interfere with the operations of the grand Southern Army of the Galanese Council."

This was news to Shu, and a point gained for his efforts. He now knew that there were definitely other Gremn here, and that they'd brought enough tech with them to cause problems for a rampaging warlord.

"However," Dolaure continued, "if in the interest of diffusing any possible escalation that may result from introducing new technology into our conflict you were willing to share with me the particulars of those new combat units, I would be most grateful."

Shu knew nothing of new combat units, but it hardly mattered. He would learn more if he went along with it for now.

"What are you offering?" he asked.

"My gratitude can take many forms."

The man talked too much. Shu had already learned almost all that he wanted to know. Standing, he gazed down at his captor with the most menacing look he could muster.

"You're no match for the Gremn, Dolaure of House Teg."

Dolaure's fixed composure was knocked momentarily off-kilter. Shu couldn't be certain it was fear he glimpsed in the general's face before the glazed look returned. Whatever the case, his words were no longer condolent.

"Once the technicians have checked her," Dolaure said, rising, "your female companion's body will be destroyed."

The Galanese both turned to peer into the cell opposite Shu's, to the grayish form lying in the shadows there. It was Shu's turn to look perplexed.

Who was this other captive in the cell across from his?

"A monstrous creature, this is," Kay said in a low voice. "She killed many men before we could subdue her, but she eventually fell. I wonder, is she a Gremn female, or something else? They say the Gremn made themselves from monstrous serpents, and then Brisen filled their bodies with venom instead of blood—"

"Quoting outlaw scriptures in my presence, Kay?" Dolaure interrupted. Then, speaking to Shu he said, "I don't have time for games, so I will tell you what I can do. If you grant me access to a Gremn combat unit or information leading to a successful capture of Gremn technology, I will send you to the council along with my recommendation that you are to be spared. You may then join me officially as an advisor if you wish. I will also make certain your friend's body is spared any unnecessary rough handling."

"I can't trust you," Shu replied. "Whoever you've got in there is dead already. You can't hurt her anymore."

"I suppose you're right, but what about yourself? Even for a Gremn, months of travel with our soldiers would be difficult to bear, and in the end you shall stand in the High Place before a tribunal. I have heard the council particularly savors spitting their foes on stakes on the border of the forest Tryst. Of course, that would just be the beginning for a creature that cannot be slain but by fire or decapitation."

Shu could tell he wasn't bluffing.

"That's pretty talk, coming from an egotistical gasbag," he said in a low voice. "Who would ever choose to enslave themselves to a clod like you—except maybe this deluded clown?"

Sir Kay looked ruffled, but dared say nothing in his master's presence. Dolaure's face remained impassive as ever.

"I almost hoped we could speak civilly with one another," the general said. "There are so many questions I have, about how your people have returned, and what you plan on doing here. So much has changed in the thousand years since you left. You might find collaboration with me beneficial in many ways."

Dolaure turned towards the cell opposite and motioned for his attendant to open it. Kay produced a large key, and while he jostled it in the lock Shu stared, forcing himself not to close his eyes or turn away from whatever lay behind the door. Whoever it was they'd put in there, he owed her that much.

The door opened with a grinding creak, admitting more light from the corridor. Inside there was a young woman clad in a tattered gown, lying on her side. Shu could immediately see that she wasn't Ayumu, but she was rather too small and slender for a Gremn. There were also many wounds upon her skin, and one side of her gown was soaked in blood. Surely a Gremn would have healed itself of such slight injuries; but by all appearances this girl was dead.

He then noticed the bright lavender strands of her hair, and a cold fear awakened inside him. Because her head was turned away, he couldn't see her face. Was it the face of the young woman they'd removed from stasis in Avalon's SARA Station?

Was this the Null of Avalon?

"She was a good fighter, indeed," the general declared, echoing Kay's sentiments. "However, she did not expect that we would be armed with weapons of the Old World. It is a shame I cannot bring her alive to my father. He would have enjoyed watching her fight in Nara's arena."

Kay stood aside, and shuffling footsteps echoed down the corridor. Two men in brown leather jumpsuits had been waiting quietly, and now they came before the cell carrying long poles with metal boxes at one end—something like Geiger counters. They wore hooded masks with goggles and carried breathing tanks on their backs. Squat and bulky, their shadowy figures were almost ape-like. Though he really couldn't get a good look at them, Shu saw that their suits very closely resembled hazmat gear.

"Check her," Dolaure ordered.

One of the men at the door flipped a switch on the equipment he carried and stuck its business-end into the cell. Passing over the inert form on the floor, the machine emitted soft clicking sounds.

"I said *check her*."

The technicians began to hastily shut down their equipment. One turned his hooded head and spoke.

"We're under strict advisement of the council of priests," he explained, his voice muffled through the mask. "This is standard procedure. There is a serious risk of contamination from the weapons used on her."

"Skip it. Is she alive or not?"

"She was dead before," the man answered. "Was resurrection expected?"

"Resurrection?" the other technician said, clearly startled. "This one wasn't in the desert, was she?"

"She isn't infected with anything," the general said. "She may be Gremn or one of the Moriko. I would guess the latter, by the color of her hair."

The techs looked at each other and then back at the body lying on the floor.

"This is highly…unusual," one of them stammered. "The Moriko haven't been contacted for centuries. We don't know enough about their physiology to determine whether or not this one will regenerate. You're sure it's a Moriko?"

"Yes," Dolaure answered, impatience finally registering in his voice. "Just give me your best guess."

When the technicians finally realized they weren't able to avoid touching the body, contamination or not, they leaned their poles against the wall and knelt down at the door. Reaching carefully inside, one paused in a crouching pose for a while.

"There's nothing," he said. "Not the slightest flutter of a heartbeat."

"Then she's yours," Dolaure said with a dignified frown. "Take as many samples as you please."

"I'd like to remove the entire head," the technician replied, "just to be safe."

"Do as you wish. Sir Kay, I leave the details to you."

Just as he said this, a uniformed soldier entered the crowded corridor. Leaning towards the general he whispered something in his ear. Dolaure's half-lidded eyes widened perceptibly before he regained his unflappable composure.

"We won't meet again, warrior," he said to Shu. "Enjoy your journey to Gilthaloneth. Give my regards to the gore-crows when they come to pluck out your eyes."

The general then left without another word, his messenger in tow.

The technicians remained inside the cell with the knight, Kay, standing over them. Shu listened as they tugged on the body and whispered to one another quietly. His heart was pounding. There was nothing he could do.

Kay seemed to sense his distress. Looking up, he faced Shu with a grin.

"It's too dark to see what you're doing in there," Kay said to the workmen. "Drag her into the corridor."

"We can see just fine."

"Just do as I say, or your oath-fathers in the council of priests will hear all the details of what happened at Ulumeneth."

One of the two technicians looked up, distressed. The other tapped his shoulder, and they began to resettle themselves at the mouth of the cell. Their clumsy suits made it difficult to hunch over side by side, but it was clear that they were struggling against a great burden.

"She's heavier than she looks," one grunted.

Stepping backwards into the hall, the technicians slowly hauled the body out by the legs. When they'd pulled her out parallel to Shu's cell, they let go of her and stood up. Her legs fell upon the cold stone with a hard flapping sound.

Shu swallowed hard when he saw her. So similar were her features to the Null of Avalon, and yet so different. Even marred by many wounds, this girl was an angelic beauty, with large eyes and irises of flaming amber hues. She was dazzling, frightening. There were also marks upon her face, winged symbols tattooed beneath her eyes; but these were different from Avalon's. There were also chevron-shaped marks across the bridge of her nose.

All of these features could not be absorbed at a glance. Shu was dazed by the sight of her, but the techs clapped each other's shoulders as if they'd scored a victory for their exertions.

"Gods!" exclaimed one to the other. "You'd think she was an *Illuyanga* from the weight of her!"

"It's no natural creature, this," the other replied.

"What are you afraid of?" Kay asked. "She's dead, isn't she?"

They turned their hooded heads towards Sir Kay, and then back towards the girl. Her eyes stared upwards, lifeless in a tangle of blue hair.

"We have no equipment here to take proper samples," one man said.

The other nodded. "We'll never get through her neck with a scalpel."

Kay sighed. "Fine, then. Go get whatever you need and bring it back here. Take your time. I'll keep watch until you return."

With backwards glances they shuffled off. Kay waited until they were gone, and then he turned again to face Shu.

"Do you think she's pretty?" Kay asked.

Shu's face twisted in a spasm of hatred.

"*I* think she's pretty," the knight said, "despite those weird tattoos. Do you suppose, perhaps, there are more of them elsewhere?"

"*Don't—*" Shu muttered.

Kay leaned closer to the bars. He was so close Shu could smell the sharp bitterness of his breath.

"Do you monsters have feelings for each other?" the knight wondered. "Do you even have the capacity to love?"

The bars were too close together to reach through.

"Of course, love takes many forms," Kay rambled. "I suppose all your kinds must be able to abide one another to some extent, or there would be no breeding."

"Yeah?" Shu said. "You don't know anything!"

"Oh, I know *something*. I know you don't want me to touch her. Am I right, Gremn?"

When he didn't immediately respond, Kay prodded the corpse's side with the toe of his boot. Shu instinctively grasped the bars of his cell, locking eyes with the knight.

"Ah! I was right, then. Let's see, what shall I kick next?"

"Come in here," Shu growled, *"and we'll discuss it in detail."*

Kay responded by bringing the heel of his boot down hard on the girl's pale hand. The sound of a sharply indrawn breath caused him to step away, startled, but the glazed eyes in her beautiful doll-face continued staring lifelessly upwards.

Were the corners of her mouth smiling slightly?

"A corpse," Kay said, chuckling. "Surprising, how they can spring up on their own. Unless it's the Infection, of course, it's all just reflexes. There are other reflexes, too, like breathing."

There was a sound of another breath. Shu met the knight's gaze through the iron bars. Kay was no longer amused. Kneeling down beside her, he leaned forwards so that he could see the girl's face better in the dim light. Her eyelids were fluttering. Kay grasped her chin and pried it back slightly to peer into her mouth.

"She's alive?" he marveled.

It was the last thing Sir Kay ever said.

The amber eyes were focused. Up came a slender leg. Her knee connected so hard with his skull that Shu could hear it crack. Kay's head flopped to one side, his neck broken, but a hand seized his arm with lightning speed and held him up on his knees. In the same instant, a snarl echoed wildly off the walls.

Shu's legs backpedaled, his heart pounding in his ears. As nightmare fears swept over him, he stumbling backwards against the cell's inner wall and looked on as Kay's body was crumpled, bones snapping like matchsticks beneath a swiftly expanding shape of horror.

The girl's small body seemed to explode outwards.

In just a fraction of a second, an elongated gorgon head thrust forwards between pale shoulders, hunched backwards, twisting, while legs cracked and unfolded beneath the squirming, heaving mass. The gown she wore gave way to shreds as a thickly furred body surged upwards through the roof and outwards through the walls. The iron door of Shu's cell was pressed against his face. His back was crushed hard against the wall, and he felt his upraised arms squashed in hot folds of leathery skin.

The wall at his back collapsed.

Lying on his side in the middle of a group of very confused soldiers, Shu shoved a mound of cracked masonry off his legs and looked around. The fortress and keep where Inyan held council lay behind him, across a pavement decorated in a checkerboard pattern of white and gray blocks. The little castle was tumbled now in ruins, most of it having collapsed into the lower levels beneath the hill.

"What in Hades is this?" shouted an important looking man.

Shu looked up into the barrel of what appeared to be an antique pistol, held by a man whose garb was alarmingly similar to that of an officer of the First World War. Stunned by this absurd turn of events, his eyes moved from the officer to the bulging wall of the dungeon and back again.

"Someone secure this prisoner!" the man cried.

But no one seemed interested in following his order. The soldiers were standing now, but weapons were flung down to the pavement. Many bolted and ran. Shu followed their backwards glances upwards to the sacred tower, swaying violently on the edge of the hill.

Then, with a terrifying noise of larger stone blocks exploding, the remaining walls of the dungeon buckled and failed. The ground trembled, and in a magnificent avalanche the entire structure slid down into the valley below. Only a great cloud of orange dust remained, and looming within it the shadowy shape of one remaining segment of the dungeon wall. Something was holding that bit of the tower in place, held it perched precariously upon the steep slope of the hill. It was a paw—an enormous paw.

Even the officer's eyes pivoted upwards, above the wreckage, above the broken wall, where the being attached to that paw moved suddenly through the hanging motes of dust, debris raining down from its mighty bristle-maned shoulders to crash down around them. More than fifty feet in height, with glowing blue-within-blue eyes, an enormous white wolf rose up behind the wall and shook bits of rubble from its coat. While they looked on, transfixed, the wolf reared back its head it howled—a sound that would stop an army in its tracks. And as if in response, all the jungle beyond the fortress rolled like the waves of an angry sea.

All but a handful of the men standing and gawking scrambled away then, shouting with dismay. The rest, including the officer who still held him at gunpoint, were petrified by fear. Shu could say no more than this for himself. He lay quivering in a puddle upon the wide stone pavement. Here he was, a man who had seen battle in many fields over three millennia, and he was undone by the tintinnabulation of that cry. But what a cry it was. He could only look up and wonder. His heart swelled as he gazed upon an ancient being, a being from the Old World come to life.

And then the wolf bounded forwards. One hind paw rested on top of the wall, and one forepaw came down directly on the officer in front of Shu. A horrific sound that reminded him of a hydraulic log-splitter chewing through a large and particularly stubborn ash-trunk reverberated through the air. The pistol clattered uselessly away, and the remaining soldiers scattered in terror of the sight. Shu also stumbled away, but slowed and held his ground when he realized that it was foolish to run from this beast. Besides, it wasn't moving presently. He could hear its breath, though, and that sound filled him with fear.

Turning round, he squared his shoulders and stared up at the great blue eyes, staring down at him across the courtyard. The monster lowered its head towards him. Shu was spellbound by the eyes, and by the tattoos beneath them and upon its snout. There was no doubt that this beast and the girl he saw captive in the dungeon were one and the same.

Her deep growl vibrated the ground—pebbles rattled in the mud. So great was his admiration, he almost forgot his danger. That is, until the wolf spoke.

"It has begun!"

Bullets, bolts, and arrows whined in sudden onslaught, but the fire seemed to be directed everywhere at once. Looking to the green hilltop beyond the flattened fortress, Shu saw small figures streaming out from a distant line of trees, charging wildly through flashes of musket-fire originating somewhere within the ruins. The Ayumu were putting up a fight, testing their primitive weapons against gunpowder.

Shu wasn't permitted any more time to properly survey the situation. A huge paw nudged his back, thrusting him towards the northeast slope of the hill; and in a few heartbeats he found himself dashing headlong through high grass, bounding over trenches and excavated pits crowded with soldiers.

Behind him, the wolf shook her mane and snarled. The ground thudded under a rhythmic churning noise. Shots rang out, and wild gunfire soon joined in from all directions. They weren't firing at him. Looking back as he leapt wildly towards the bottom of the hill Shu was surprised to see that the wolf was gone.

Something new had come.

Wading out of the jungle through a blanketing cover of smoke, he spotted mechanized PCUs; but these were of a design totally unfamiliar to him. Falcon-headed and heavily armored, these were in a class beyond the clumsy Seraph. They strode forwards, arms outstretched, reaching for fleeing soldiers as they gained the higher ground of the hill. No other armaments did they reveal other than their crushing hands and feet—nothing more was necessary.

They were converging swiftly on the Galanese base at the fallen fortress.

Revelation came like a thunderclap to Shu's brain. These were the Gremn mechanized units Dolaure was asking about. There were probably Gremn inside them, too. He paused, hunkering down while soldiers rushed past him towards the hilltop. He had to make a decision, and fast.

If he dared, he might make his way towards the PCUs and reveal himself. Shim might be among them. Though this was very tempting, he had a suspicion Artax would also be there—and maybe Lír. He couldn't afford to fall into their hands again. It would be safer to track them and learn who they were before doing anything hasty.

Frustrated and confused, Shu made good on his only chance to escape. He took off towards the treeline well north of the point of conflict, and was soon heading uphill again. Strangely, there was no sign of the wolf. He decided this was definitely for the best, until he ran headlong into a group of soldiers.

Shots erupted from long heavy barrels—muskets of curious craftsmanship. Shu wasn't very interested in what they looked like, but he was glad enough that they all missed him at close range. He hadn't realized yet that it was because no one was firing at him; but then, while dashing right through the enemy ranks, he turned his head just enough to notice the gray-white shadow moving like a low-flying cloud through the forest behind him, breaking small trees and raising a hurricane of splintered branches in its wake. The patrol formed up into small groups on the shaking ground and bravely took aim.

That was when the ground beneath them pulsed and writhed suddenly, breaking open before a thousand clinging vines. Greenery sprang up everywhere, clinging to Shu's legs as he pushed through and bolted from the scene.

What was going on here?

Panting and groaning with effort, he bent his course sharply to the right, and then angled gradually left again. The terrain began to slope upwards until he found himself running westward along a ridge overlooking a precipitous slope to the northeast. The trees thinned in that direction. He smelled a river, and with no immediate signs of pursuit he decided it was worth a peek.

Jogging out of the jungle, he discovered a broad river valley with rocky slopes. The few low trees around him were no more than a line of timber flanking the steep barren sides of a wide canyon. There was almost no cover out there. He'd only just reached the edge of the treeline when he was abruptly reminded of this fact, as gunshots rang out from somewhere behind him.

Ducking down, he made his way back under the trees and went onward, pausing occasionally to listen for trackers. He'd only gone a little way when he halted abruptly, having seen something out of the corner of his eye. He thought he'd just glimpsed a heavy dark shape sailing right overhead, tumbling through the sky towards the precipice on his right. He crouched where he was, and in another moment a second bulky figure soared through the treetops, and then another. They were bodies—bodies were sailing swiftly overhead, shockingly silent in their flight, with arms and legs swinging enthusiastically as they strove for purchase in empty air.

Shu spun around, searching with wide eyes for a sign of movement in the forest; but only the trees were swaying. In fact, he could have sworn he saw the trees actually moving of their own accord. He rubbed his eyes, but aside from one more unfortunate Galanese soldier making a neat arc overhead, nothing more stirred. He decided that was his cue to get himself moving.

The hills and the deep valley of Timhureth were fading away behind him, but the sounds of gunfire were still too close for comfort. Shu looked down into the ravine on his right. It was more than a mile across and at least a thousand feet deep, and its walls were far too steep for climbing. At the bottom there was a river, a fast-flowing torrent like a golden serpent twisting in the bottom of the gorge.

He didn't pause to admire the scenery.

A narrow path led him alongside the cliff under a thin cover of trees. Eventually, he came to a choke in the path, a narrow place between large rocks far from the treeline. There was no place to go if he was spotted, and as tired as he was he'd run right into it—just like some stupid animal on a hunting trail.

Shouts rang out around him. Some soldiers were standing lower down the rise, pointing up at him. Higher up near the treeline there were answering shouts. With no place to hide, Shu realized he had been outflanked. He kept running anyway, and when he came around the other side of the ambush through the rocks, he saw a bridge.

The rough rock arch wasn't what he would've called a real bridge, but it spanned the river, and that was good enough. The forest on the other side was far up the side of the canyon. If he could get that far he would definitely be able to shake off pursuit. The ground on this side was increasingly dangerous for running, though. Slippery from recent rains, loose stones were turning underfoot. He reached the arch just as his breath gave out, and still he could hear the sounds of trackers calling to one another. Shu ignored his aching limbs and leapt up onto the first great boulders of the natural span.

Sculpted by eons of wind and water, the red sandstone arch was like a rib cut from the side of the mountain. It was almost fifty feet wide and hundreds long, leaping across the water at a narrowing of the gorge. It was bigger than it looked from afar.

Shu took in the sights with a thrill. Three hundred feet below, another Ayumu tower stood at the foot of the opposite side of the canyon, its foundations partially drowned in the pale golden flow. A flock of swallows rounded the tower and flew beneath him, drawing his eyes to their eyries nestled among ruined stone huts built into the cliffs.

The cliff-dwellers who made those homes must have been desperate to live in such a desolate place, hidden though they were in the arms of the hills. Surrounded by the harsh features of barren stone and immense threatening cliff-walls, Shu could only imagine one reason why people would stay here. This was a refuge of the war—the War of Destroying Fire. No one was living there now, but a spirit of watchfulness prevailed.

Breathing heavily from his exertions, Shu took great care in picking his way among the blocks of stone on the arch. His eyes were focused on the ground when he was caught off guard by a shadow that fell across his path. The figure of a man in a red uniform stood above him.

"*Halt!*"

The soldier leveled a musket at his chest, and Shu cursed his own carelessness. He should have known there would be a guard on the bridge.

"Stop where you are!"

A sound of many booted feet scraped on the rocks behind him, announcing the arrival of the soldiers he'd blown past on the trail. Shu held his arms out to his sides, palms open. He had to admit to himself that he was totally winded. He wouldn't try to run.

The soldier ahead of him lowered his rifle suddenly, his face showing surprise. Turning to look over his shoulder, Shu caught a glimpse of the backs of fleeing soldiers running madly into the woods.

A swift shadow passed overhead, and he staggered from the muffled explosion of her landing, which sent small stones skipping past him over the edge. The guard, the one standing in front of him moments before, was plummeting silently end-over-end towards the water, hundreds of feet below.

"*You're not as fast as you think you are,*" boomed a strange voice.

She stood before him where the guard had been, a monstrous white wolf. But what kind of monster was she?

The wolf lowered her head towards him, so close she could easily have snapped him up in her jaws. Gazing into her face, Shu was surprised to see a kindly wink from the blue eyes staring back into his own.

She sniffed him.

"Son of Nurkabta," she said, lowering her massive body onto the rocks. *"You share your father's scent."*

Cautiously, he reached out his hand towards her massive head. She leaned forward and bumped her nose against his skin. It was cool and wet. Shu blinked, tearing his mind away from the primal fear that had rooted him to the stone arch.

He heard the wind and the water, and he tasted rain in the air. These were all natural things; but the thing before him could not possibly exist in nature.

"You knew my father?" Shu asked, marveling.

"He and I served together, but he knew me in a somewhat different form."

"You mean, he knew you as that blue-haired girl?"

"That form was severely damaged. It will take a long time to heal. I will need to remain in this form for many days while we travel together."

"Travel together?" he stammered, lost in her deep yet lovely voice.

"This is a world of thrones and secret powers. Ever a dark wonderland, Syrscian's darkness intensifies. The empress is at the heart of the sickness. You will need my help, and I shall need yours."

"Well, you sure took care of those soldiers," Shu replied tenuously, feeling still a little uncertain of his own safety. "You could probably rout their whole army from Tarthalion by yourself."

"That is most assuredly so."

The wolf's eyes blazed, glowing fiercely with an inner radiance.

"Who are you?"

"I am a Null."

"A Null? You mean a drone linked to a ship via the Source?"

He gazed up at her in renewed wonder.

"I am Aries."

This was finally beginning to make sense, Shu thought. Though he had almost no knowledge of the Gremn ship she was linked to, he realized that the drone could not be here without it. That explained the Gremn presence in these lands.

"Where is your ship?" he asked.

"All shipboard systems are operational except for the MMPPS," she replied, pointing her long head east, *"but the ship's exact location is being masked by a particle field. Transmissions are coming through very weak. It's somewhere in the middle of Urlad, but that's just a guess."*

"And your transit, was it initiated by Lír? Aries is his ship, right?"

"Lír is not my Primary User," she replied, showing a flash of her huge fangs. *"However, of the four hundred seventy-eight Gremn Kabta brought from Iskartum, the last two hundred survivors of that race are with the ship. Not all of them are with Lír, Son of Nurkabta."*

"I'm Shu."

"Listen, boy, it is time for me to complete the task for which I was designed. My task is to free my mother, and then she will call her people back to this place."

"Your mother?"

"There is no scheme of men, nor of any of the Great Houses, which can remove from me my ancient purpose," said Aries' deep yet feminine voice. *"I shall find and rescue Brisen, even if I must break through the walls of Ost-Thargul with my body to do it!"*

"And you want me to come with you? Why? Of what use am I?"

Aries lifted her maw and laughed a ragged laugh that sent rocks tumbling and spinning down into the river. The whole arch shook beneath her, and then the wolf was suddenly silent again, perking her ears across the river towards the north. The wind blowing past them chilled Shu's heart. Though he could not say what it was exactly that had caught Aries' attention, he could sense her intense concentration.

"What's happening?" he asked.

"She is here; and so is he."

"Who?"

"Avalon and Auriga. Sister and Brother. I hear their voices at last. They are far off, but the link is reestablished."

She paused again.

"My Primary User is not here yet. I did not anticipate this turn of events. But why was he delayed?"

"You haven't by any chance detected linked Seraph PCUs, have you?" he wondered. "I'm looking for a really tall rust-bucket I left somewhere in the south."

"No more time for talk! We must be off to find the lost ones of House Gaerith. Climb up onto my back."

Shu obeyed this time, and stepping up onto her large foreleg he climbed a mountain of fragrant fur. She seemed not to mind him pulling her hair at all, and when he'd found a perch upon her neck above the shoulders and behind her flickering ears, she didn't wait for him to get too settled before bounding to her feet. The world swirled around him in a crazy dizzying blur, and then they were facing east.

She was looking down at the river below. The roof of the temple-tower by the river's bank was far below them.

"Oh no," he mumbled. "You wouldn't!"

"Better hang on, Boy!"

24

KA E-TEMEN ANKI

Stronghold of Uruk in Ceregor, Syrscian,
Year 999 of the New Council

By stupidity or by sloth, he was alive. Two long years after she'd set out to kill the man, vengeance was once again deferred in the strangest of fashions. Foxglove trembled to stand so close, fretfully enduring the irony of sharing Bregon's captivity.

They were in the power of the Marduka, the *Dragon Tribe*.

Out of the corner of her eye she observed the Marduka captain, a towering reptilian named Barashkushu. His thick skin of gold and brown scales, patterned like a desert serpent, was an appropriate partner to his personality. Cold he was, though not especially cruel—not even when startled, as when his patrol stumbled upon them in the night. He carried himself with dignity, and he had much to be proud of. Though geared for battle with primitive melee weapons, his band of ten warriors was armed with greater strength and ferocity than any unit of Galanese soldiers could boast.

Like all the people of the Fourth House, the Marduka chose to wear a form distinctive of their nature. Although they walked upright like men, everything else about them was unique. They were fearsome to look upon, with clawed backwards-jointed legs and thrashing tails. Bregon loosened the mask he often wore, letting it fall beside his mouth while he raised his goggles to his forehead. He was studying the captain with undisguised curiosity.

"Gaze at something else with your round eyes," Barashkushu warned.

Barashkushu's own eyes were like an asp's, slit-pupiled with amber irises within matching red-brown sclera. It was hard not to stare at him. As for the other Marduka, they all varied quite a bit in appearance, sharing only a common militaristic temperament and gear. Long was the reach of their poleaxes, and they wore polished armor upon their shoulders and around their waists.

Bregon averted his gaze to another of the warriors, one who looked like an ordinary human except for some scales around his eyes and feathers sprouting from his head. The feathers were the only detail that really surprised Foxglove, being they were left out of all the tales she'd heard. Then again, no one in the south had any dealings with the Marduka in almost a century. There were bound to be more surprises in store.

General Bregon probably wasn't as interested in their feathers as he was in the size and strength of these foes. He had good reason to worry—as did she. Accused of aiding and abetting this man, just because she was discovered in his company, Foxglove had no choice but to share in his misery until her case could be heard. She quietly hoped Bregon would do something rash and get himself killed. On the other hand, the Fomorian would probably interfere if it came to that.

The excited sounds of Barashkushu's odd clicking speech and his four-toed feet thudding on the ground roused the attention of everyone in the encampment. A runner had been sent back to a stronghold in the hills. While the morning passed under stormy skies, the fate of the captives awaited his return.

Meanwhile, the Marduka had gathered around their captain in front of the shallow cave in the hillside where they camped. It seemed some sort of argument was brewing between Barashkushu and one of his warriors, but their speech was wholly unintelligible. Foxglove was listless and bored, so she sat down and began to trace a dragon in the dust. A bug flew into one of her ears and she reached for it instinctively, bringing her leg up over her shoulder to scratch with her toes. Out of the corner of her eye she saw a warrior approaching.

"What are you doing?" he asked.

Foxglove's ears flinched at his gravelly voice.

"Am I not allowed to scratch?" she asked, baring a little fang. "Am I not also of the Fourth House?"

"You trespass with spies, and with—"

After a hasty glance towards Bec, the warrior adjusted the neckline of his vest and smoothed his crimson crown of feathers.

"Sit and scratch all you want, little cousin," he said in a stern voice. "But be ready to move out when it is time."

Foxglove stuck out her tongue and watched him return to the captain's side. They fell to whispering, and she might have been able to listen-in had they not switched to their own language. Nevertheless, the subject of their conversation was an easy one to guess, for both stole discreet glances at the blue-haired girl.

Barashkushu had spoken to Bec only indirectly, and his men avoided her entirely. Their apprehensions were literally sensible. Maybe a human of the Galanese tribe would not have understood it, but Bec carried the scent of the Moriko and of the ancient forest. The people of the Fourth House, guardians of the woodland realms, knew that scent very well.

Thus, while Barashkushu made prisoners of her companions, everyone in the camp implicitly understood who was in control of the situation. The Marduka captain was no fool, but he'd landed himself in quite a predicament. Foxglove, in turn, was bound now to the fate of the man she would have killed so easily on the mountainside. She glared at him, but he ignored her and busied himself studying the movement of his enemies. He was particularly interested in his belt and holster, dangling from the shoulder of a Marduka warrior on the other side of the camp. Another warrior was examining his pistol, a rare and powerful Vajra type.

Foxglove's knife was tucked inside Bregon's holster, close company with its adversary, just as she was. She'd complained loudly about this, but Barashkushu's answer to her was silence.

The silence endured until the runner returned.

They were still high above the desert south of the forested hinterlands of Tryst, having passed from the Rim Mountains into the foothills of the Ceregor where they were captured. The Karn River, barely visible to the north, shimmered faintly as it exited the wood on its eastward course through Galanese lands towards the colonies and the fabled city of Gilthaloneth.

Below the camp, the mountainside sloped to a steep-walled valley running north between two ridges, forming a long deep groove winding away into the heart of the hills. Camouflaged by his dappled green color, the runner seemed to emerge from the rocks and low shrubs along the left-hand side of this grassy cleft, and was standing now in the shadow of the western ridge. Barashkushu's men began to gather, and he spoke to them again in their own tongue.

Peering into the dark narrow cleft where the lone reptilian stood, Foxglove saw behind him the traces of a path leading away to an abrupt cliff. Did the path pass underground? She groaned inwardly. Long privation in the wilderness was as nothing to her people; enclosed spaces was quite another matter. The blind valley below had no obvious exits.

Barashkushu waved them all forwards with a grunt. Foxglove led the march down the slope with Bregon at her heals, and Bec walked beside him. The warriors followed at a distance, for there was no fear of their captives escaping.

No sooner had they reached the valley floor than the waiting runner held up his hand and pointed to the wall on their left. Foxglove walked towards him, her large eyes searching among the rocks.

"This is not where the Marduka used to live," Bec remarked.

The runner looked at her with a puzzled expression, as if he didn't understand what she said. Barashkushu uttered a few clicking noises with his tongue before answering her in ordinary speech.

"We have lived here ever since Esagil was destroyed," he explained in his slow, sonorous manner of speaking. "This place is named Uruk. It was a strong fortress of old, and now it serves as our central keep. Here have we dwelt in secret for the past twelve years, rebuilding our strength since the battle of Esagil."

The warriors gathering round nodded their heads gravely. Though she couldn't guess his age, Barashkushu seemed old enough to speak of these events first-hand. Foxglove knew a little of the Esagil story, for though it occurred while she was still a kitten, the people of Ulumeneth had put it into songs. Tens of thousands of Marduka and Yuuto were slain there. Though it was considered a victory for the Galanese, the council's losses were nearly three times as much.

They went on in single file over rocky ground carpeted in deeply aromatic turf. Stunted tussocks of reddish grass lined the walls, or scaled their sides, growing wherever a chance shaft of sunlight managed to peer down onto the hidden path. The sky was clearing.

The runner was ahead, picking a trail against the sunny left-hand wall of the canyon. Almost half his height, Foxglove was struggling to follow him through the deep grass, when suddenly she was assailed by a flock of small winged reptiles that had been roosting in the overhanging rocks. Uttering weird startling cries, they darted swiftly for the opposite wall, grazing her hair while Foxglove waved her arms about wildly. She managed to control herself, folding her hands tightly in front of her and smiling when their guide glanced back to see what was happening; but her tail was fluffed up to twice its normal size.

"Warm," he said to her, placing his hand firmly against the rock wall. *"Warm, they like. Be thou careful. Venomous, they are."*

His thick accent and strange hissing voice denoted the common problem in dealings between the tribes of Ceregor and those of Tarthalion Wood—the language barrier. His words also brought up something Foxglove hadn't thought of before. If the Marduka were like lizards, they probably lived someplace very warm.

Patting the rock, she nodded comprehension, and he led her on. Following quietly, Foxglove looked towards the dark end of the canyon, just a stone's throw away. The gap was narrowing, and in only a little while it closed completely at a cliff-face. As the others gathered in the shade where the path stopped, there seemed to be some commotion about blindfolding Bregon and binding his hands.

Bec walked to Foxglove's side and spoke, breaking the tension with her serene but stern voice.

"This place was once a private mansion, as I recall."

"I don't see anything," Foxglove said.

The warriors ceased their quarrel and listened.

"Its ancient name was *The House Which Guards the Destiny of the People*," Bec said. "It is less defensible than Esagil, but somewhat more difficult to find."

"Since this stranger speaks knowledgably," taunted one of the warriors, "then perhaps she would be willing to point out the hidden path."

His companions were still hushing him angrily when Bec responded, pointing ahead towards the grass at the base of the cliff.

"A blind *boha* could find it," she said. "Just keep walking."

All that Foxglove could see were a few stone steps gleaming dully. The source of their illumination remained hidden, as did the path.

"Go on," Bec urged, touching Foxglove's arm. "You will find the way."

Walking slowly forwards with nothing but the Fomorian's words to guide her, Foxglove's perspective gradually shifted. At first she saw only a slight crack in the cliff. The left side of the crack was a little lighter than the right, but it wasn't until she stood upon the stone steps that daylight fell fully upon her left foot, and then she finally saw it—a door concealed in the rock wall, cut so that it could not be seen face-on, but only from the side.

She frowned.

The door wasn't very large.

"They can fit in here?" she asked, looking towards Barashkushu.

"They are reptilian," Bec said. "Is something wrong?"

"I don't like tight spaces."

Though her voice was only a whisper, one of the warriors laughed. Barashkushu put an end to it by pounding the end of his poleaxe on the stony ground. Then, striding towards the stone steps, he passed her by and slipped through the slim crevice. Foxglove watched, amazed, for the space was just wide enough to permit the passage of his shoulder armor. When he was on the other side, Barashkushu reached out through the crack, showing that the passage was only as long as his arm.

"Come, little cousin."

She grasped the thumb of the huge four-fingered hand he offered—almost as large as her head and surprisingly smooth—and by holding her breath she managed to squeeze through. On the other side, he waited for her to pass him by while the others followed one by one. Bregon was ushered through freely; and though there was still some quarreling in the rear of the line, Foxglove had a few quiet moments to take in their new surroundings.

She stood upon a carved winding path, very deep and open to the sky. Footfalls echoed loudly as the warriors trickled in behind her, and she retreated a little way ahead to the top of a winding stone stair. There she stood and looked upon an astonishing sight.

"What is this place?" she asked in an awed voice.

The slippery spiral steps before her descended around the edges of a huge borehole, plunging deep into cool darkness. At the bottom there was a pool surrounded by a narrow embankment, and an arch facing the water. Beneath the arch she could dimly see a large rock wall, and in this wall there was carved a magnificent stone structure.

"You haven't heard?" Barashkushu asked. "Like Esagil of old, Uruk is the stronghold of the Fourth House, ruled by the Marduka."

"Oh."

"You'll have to tell her the whole story sometime later, *Kushu*," one of the warriors said in the common speech. "The southerners don't know anything. It's no wonder they took up with the enemy and got wiped out!"

Foxglove searched for the speaker, finally spotting the one who had laughed at her earlier. Curiously, he was the one who looked more human than the others. His fluency in the common speech was also superior to theirs. She fixed his lanky frame in her glare and flattened her ears back against her head.

"*Rawn,*" Barashkushu warned. "Those of the Fourth House should enter this stronghold as allies. Her case has not been decided."

"If she needs someone to carry her, I'd be happy to oblige," Rawn replied. Then, urged on by the chuckling of a few of his companions, he added, "It wouldn't be so difficult to bear an Ayumu weakling into the fortress, and even easier inside my belly!"

"This wasn't a fortress always," Bec interrupted.

The laughter stopped instantly, for her voice penetrated deep into their minds. The atmosphere had changed, even as she joined Foxglove at the top of the steps.

"This was once a beautiful house, where music played and wine flowed. It was built long before Esagil in the days of the First Counting."

"What does she know about it?" asked one of those who stood closest to Rawn.

"I know that Esagil was *The House Whose Top is High*, ruled not by the Marduka, but by priests whose office was sacred to all four tribes of the Fourth House. This place was not meant to be a fortress, either. Like Esagil, Uruk was a house of healing, not of war."

Rawn snorted. "And who fights their wars for them now?" he asked. "It's easy, I suppose, for one of the Moriko to talk about idle days of peace. If not for the rest of us, these stories would have been forgotten by all our people long ago!"

Bec's eyes flashed. She smiled.

"Enough, Rawn!" Barashkushu commanded. "Bring the prisoner. Nin is waiting."

Stumbling forwards with a shove from behind, Bregon came to a halt at the head of the stair. There, daring the edge, he leaned over and peered into the clear pool at the bottom of the drop. There was a strange tree growing beside it, all bare of leaves.

Foxglove delighted in his proximity to the edge, but she restrained herself and stood beside him to look down into the water. The sight of their tiny reflections, side by side, made her cringe inwardly. Aside from her tail and ears, they were not so different looking from afar.

It was in their hearts that they differed most.

"Go on, little cousin," Barashkushu said.

Starting down the steps, Foxglove eyed the wide landing at the very bottom as she rounded the first turn. A little more of the enormous edifice they'd viewed from up top could now be seen.

She caught herself from slipping just in time. The steps of the spiraling stairway were sprouting beards of green moss. Two steps behind her, the Galanese fool was so absorbed in his thoughts that he missed his footing on the slick surface. Turning round towards the sudden scraping noise of his fall, Foxglove was bowled over on top of him as Bregon slid right into her. Swept off her feet, she flailed the air for a few seconds before his boot caught the sidewall and brought them to a halt—with her tail pinned between.

Pent-up fury erupted like lightning. The speed that anger lent to her lithe and agile limbs inspired a pleasing flicker of fear in her foe. Foxglove bounded free of him, her hair standing on end. Then, finding a perch on a rock beside him, she squatted on clawed feet. Fangs bared, ears back, and pupils narrowed to slits, she lunged towards his face and hissed.

Bregon grinned peevishly.

"Sorry?" he offered.

"You dare attack me?"

Her heart was pounding, but her foe lay still. He was much bigger than she, but even a bee could send a warrior scurrying. She pressed a knee against his abdomen to make sure he stayed put, while everyone else stopped on the steps above them.

Was it her imagination, or were they looking on with amused interest?

Foxglove wasn't amused at all. Leaning closer, she bared her fangs and whispered so that only he could hear.

"I might just let you kill yourself next time, clumsy fool!"

"But we're already near the bottom, and the water would have softened my landing," he replied, looking down over his shoulder. "It was just an accident that your tail softened it instead."

She poked a finger into his ribs and leaned closer to his face. "I'll gut you like a fish, if you touch me again—"

She broke off suddenly, for the keenness of his gaze surprised her.

"Gut me?" he asked calmly. "And what would you find inside, I wonder?"

Foxglove drew back from him.

"You know," he continued, "I've never been so close to your face the past few weeks to take notice of anything more than the words that come from your mouth, so you'll excuse me for not noticing that you are Ayumu nobility; though what your forebears would have thought of your rough speech I know not, *Princess.*"

His haughty words stilled her anger.

"You're wondering how I knew?" he asked quietly.

She shook her head. Bregon pointed to his own face.

"It's the Flower Mark, the birthmark around your eyes. Of course, no one would have guessed by the way you act that you are from a line of great kings."

Foxglove was truly at a loss. Did he expect her to get all chummy, just because they were both nobility?

She leapt down from the rock to the bottom of the steps, and there she stood glaring up at him for good measure while smoothing her offended tail. The spectacle of her wounded pride was accompanied by the sounds of raucous laughter from above.

"What have we here?" Rawn called down to them. "'Tis a quarrel between husband and wife!"

The warrior's wayward comment passed her by unheard. Foxglove was distracted by the look of pity on the Galanese General's face. She had endured Bregon's company for weeks without considering the possibility that he regarded her as anything more than just another Ayumu kitty-cat. Now, however—

It was surely inscrutable, she thought, that a man of his high House, having survived a thousand years of war, should experience even passing fear and dejection over the spite of such a diminutive creature as herself.

She chose to ignore this curiosity for the time being.

As the group slowly assembled on the landing below, the warriors resumed arguing about Bregon. Foxglove couldn't understand the clicking speech they used, but she guessed they had come to some disagreement as to who would have the honor of leading the prisoner to his trial. Barashkushu didn't interfere as they prodded him beyond the bottom step towards the gate in the face of the cliff.

She only half-listened to their babble anyway, absorbed as she was in the quiet grandeur of the place. Situated in the shadow of the arch, the hidden gate was washed by light reflected from the waters of the pool. Oddly, the mighty tree she had seen from above turned out to be made of stone.

"Dear old friend," Bec said, planting her palm against its mossy surface. "How long shall you sleep?"

Foxglove took in the petrified relic with awe. She had only heard of such things in legends, and never thought to credit them with truth.

"It has always stood here," Barashkushu said, standing between them. "We will enter now. If you will both join me."

Foxglove understood that this was his way of inviting Bec inside. In all the old legends, Moriko did not customarily enter a dwelling unless they were formally invited. Bregon, on the other hand, got somewhat less pomp and pageantry than was due a noble of a Great House. Rawn and one of his companions pushed him forwards with the butt-ends of their spears.

The Marduka obviously didn't know who their captive really was—which was probably lucky for him. After the altercation on the stairs, however, Foxglove felt strangely perplexed by their show of force. Surely he deserved it, but something Bregon said had awakened a part of her that she'd forgotten about. The way he went silently before his foes, submitting to their jeering taunts, was behavior more befitting his grand station than any she had shown since the fall of Ulumeneth.

Barashkushu brought them to the shadowed recess before the gate, and Foxglove had a moment more to wonder at the sight of it, carved as it was from the living stone of the mountain. There was a round window above the doors, ornate in execution, shaped in a floral motif. Of guardians or gate wardens she saw no sign. Barashkushu pushed the doors open, and a warm air stirred. Two steps past the threshold her earlier suspicions were confirmed.

It was hot and very stuffy inside.

"So pale and small, even for a *Softskin*," Rawn joked, shoving Bregon forwards. "Walk beside your wife, Softskin!"

As Bregon stepped up beside her, Foxglove did her best to ignore Rawn's remark, for he was obviously not the sharpest stick in the pot. As for Bregon, it didn't seem likely he would receive any kind of clemency; but what did that matter to her?

These Marduka were the most bellicose of all the forest tribes. All of their ruling house had been slain in that horrible battle at Esagil, or so the story told. Whoever now ruled the tribe would be a survivor with enough of a chip on their shoulder to make Foxglove's wish come true.

Barashkushu wouldn't tolerate any rough handling of prisoners within the fortress, however, so Rawn and his companion were dismissed to the outer courtyard where the rest of the warriors complained loudly. When the captain returned, the look on his scaly face was hard to read. He addressed Bregon directly.

"You shall go now to see Nin," he said, tamping his wide blade on the ground. "You will stand trial for your crimes as a soldier, for we are not the savages that the Galanese make us out to be. We are a people governed by law."

Leaving the gate behind, they journeyed on under the hill. Foxglove trembled as she set out along a narrow stone passage. It was as dark as a tomb. The man walking beside her went on bravely, his breathing steady; but she knew he was afraid. He had very little hope of leaving this place alive.

The passage went on a very long distance before they came to a right turn, and thereafter it widened to a proper corridor with many smaller connecting roads intersecting at right angles. There were lights along this tunnel, and the walls were smooth-polished, carved artistically into the likeness of living things. In places it seemed the stonework was very ancient, for stalactites had formed over some of the carvings. The living rock reclaimed its own once again.

Foxglove cast her eyes about from wonder to wonder, but mostly she was fascinated by the gas lamps illuminating their way. She had seen similar things before, but these were sealed tightly behind glass, and a pipe affixed to the wall carried the gas to each installation. There were also junctions here and there, metal boxes with wheels and gears that connected all the pipes together, regulating the flow. Her own people had long ago shunned mechanical devices, the ancient technologies that led to the War of Destroying Fire, preferring instead to live in feudal castles and to farm by primitive methods. Like most of the younger Ayumu, she reckoned that abandoning technology was just foolishness. It was people who did evil. The machines themselves could choose neither right nor wrong.

It was all about *choices*.

Machines could not choose how to live, but folk could. Her blood boiled quietly as she considered the weight of the sin of the Galanese, the city-dwellers who demonized her people for their choice of belief. Long ago their priests galvanized the colonies against the forest people, orating to huge crowds about monstrous wild beasts with a spiritualized culture, about animals that walked like men but who proved their genetic inferiority by stupidly worshipping an unseen god.

Just as her heart was beginning to burn with anger, she caught his eyes upon her. He turned away, pretending to study the lamps; but she knew he was thinking about her. Did he imagine she was only a savage princess of a backwards culture? Had he been among those who had hacked her family to pieces, taking the girls away to a place from whence none ever returned? Was he there when they burned the old ones alive inside the Llys? Did he laugh with those who watched as they yanked their captives' tails out for sport, wearing them like trophies? Did he think that these were civilized choices made by a superior race?

It was all about choices.

Even if he only chose to give the order to destroy Ulumeneth, he was no better off than those of his father's time who used technology to destroy the world. It was the same thing to Foxglove, and she had reviewed the facts enough times to make this a certainty in her mind. Lord Bregon was not going to get away with his crimes.

However—

Now, even as she was nearing the one place in this world where her voice might count for something, where by her testimony this evil man might be put to death, she had a doubt. It gnawed at her, wrestling against the constructed logic of two long years spent in suffering.

A voice interrupted her inward strivings.

"In ancient times, four mortals bound themselves to a quest to recover a sacred treasure from the Enemy, the Destroyer of Kutha."

Bec's words were loud and startling in the enclosed passageway. Foxglove slowed her pace and turned to look back. Bregon avoided her glance like a guilty child—so weak was his heart in the face of her wrath.

But the words Bec spoke were barbed.

"The object these mortals sought was not the Destroyer's own property to begin with, but something stolen from the Ancients. It was called the *Tablet of Destinies*."

Being a Fomorian, Bec obviously possessed first-hand information regarding the old tales, but the version she recounted now was that told only among the forest tribes. It was a miraculous legend, and therefore banned among the colonies of the Galanese.

"No one now knows what this object was, because no tales remain which describe it. The Tablet of Destinies is not mentioned in any other lore of Syrscian, and seems to have disappeared after that. All that is known is that the four who took it gained a power over the Sacred Waters. The legend says that these four mortals, blessed by the Sacred Waters, were then changed in appearance to look like whatever they chose."

"*The Legend of the Lords of the Four Tribes*," Barashkushu said from the rear of the line. "This is a story we tell to our children."

"It was once part of a much longer tale by another name," Bec said. "It was called the *Legendarium of Aerfen*, and it is the earliest history of the four Great Houses."

"Aerfen?" Barashkushu mumbled. "Never heard of him."

Unfazed, Bec continued, saying, "The leader of the four mortal warriors was Anzu, a man who assumed the shape of an eagle with the body and tail of a lion. He was the father of the Yuuto, the *Great Flyers*. The primacy of the Yuuto was supplanted in time by a more warlike tribe, whose father was named Boshmu, who chose the appearance of a dragon."

Barashkushu grunted his disapproval of these details.

"The Marduka were the fiercest of mood, and their stubborn spirit was matched only by the inflexibility of their scaled hides. That is why the Yuuto gave the Marduka the guardianship of Esagil, which they founded together with the third tribe, descended from one named Lahmu."

"We still speak of Lahmu," Foxglove offered, breaking her silence. "In our stories he is a great hairy boar."

"Really?" Bec wondered. "It is strange how the old world is twisted to fit the new! But that is no matter. Lahmu was not a boar, but chose to dwell in the appearance of a giant wolf; and though many feared him who happened to glimpse him walking the forest, he was gentle and of a childlike spirit. Those who came from his lineage bore many varied forms, including wolves, foxes, bulls, rams, boars, and others. These children were called Ayumu, the *Dream Walkers*."

There was a stronger light up ahead. Blinking in its glow, Bregon said, "You left out the fourth hero."

"Of that one we do not speak, Galanese," Barashkushu warned.

"I shall speak of her if ever I so desire," Bec chided. "She was the fourth, who was named Tiamat. Though she took no husband from the First People, Tiamat was capable of siring children alone, having taken the greater portion of the Sacred Waters from the Tablet of Destinies—more than all the other three combined. Tiamat assumed the form and nature of water itself, and was able to take any shape she wished. Her children are mostly female, youths in appearance, and are called Moriko, the *Forest Children*. The Moriko are thought of as the parents of the trees and of the wild forestland creatures of Syrscian, and also those of cunning, including Sprites, Kappa, Woses, and Dryads, and all sundry others born either of water or of fire."

They approached the threshold of a mighty door, the converging parallels of its lentils carved in the likeness of pillars covered with living vines.

"A spirit of the trees you are," Barashkushu said, keeping his voice low as he addressed Bec directly for the first time.

"That is so," she answered.

"You will forgive the thoughtless mutterings of an old warrior, then, if I dare ask why you risk recalling the tales of the Old World in the presence of this Galanese soldier? It is as though you esteem him more highly than those who serve the forest."

"I am telling the tale of four who were united as one," she said simply. "Though they had no reason to trust one another, they rescued from the Destroyer something that was reserved for them alone; and I think you might be thankful they did, Barashkushu. Perhaps you have not considered the possibility that we shall face the power in Kutha once again, and that when he arrives to take back that which was never his we will have need of the might of the Galanese and of the Four Great Houses?"

They paused then, basking in the glow of the room beyond the door. The light was red, like flame. Above the threshold, a marble placard marked the entrance with a rather portentous title.

KA E-TEMEN ANKI

Foxglove knew little of the ancient stories, but even she was able to read and understand these words. She waited for Barashkushu to wave them on, and then, crossing the threshold side by side, the three advanced with their escort behind them.

The room was square with four entrances, all elaborately carved. To their right and left were doors similar to the one they'd entered. Across the room, to the north, there was a window in the wall looking out into a long cavernous tunnel. Straining her eyes, Foxglove saw that the tunnel pierced the mountainside. The gray moon hung framed in a distant patch of open sky—it was Luna, kindled red-brown by the sun setting in the Ceregor of Tryst to the northwest. In the world above it was already nightfall.

Foxglove drank in the fresh evening draft ushered in through that window, for the passages behind them were very musty. Far off, silhouetted against the moon, she half-imagined the outline of an indistinct figure that swirled in the air for just an instant before fading away.

"This place was designed to resemble the High Court of ancient Esagil," Bec said, startling her. "Its four gates each correspond to one of the four tribes of the forest people."

"You really have seen Esagil in its ancient splendor?" Barashkushu asked in a hushed voice.

"Aye," she answered, "but not as it was in recent memory before its fall. There are only two of us left who dwelt there before the Destroying Fire. The other was Cedric DePons, master of House Gaerith."

Bregon lowered his eyes.

This gesture seemed only marginally satisfying to Barashkushu, who sniffed and looked away, saying, "It would be best you remain silent from now on, Galanese, for you have crossed the threshold of *Ka E-Temen Anki* and are in the power of our lord, Nin."

"And yet, that may be in contradiction with the very nature of the door itself," Bec said. "It is a name that means *Gate of the House of the Foundation Platform of Heaven and Underworld*, and as far as I know, we are all equal in those places."

"That was indeed its name, once upon a time," said a gentle feminine voice. "Now it is just the Marduka Gate, and Marduka laws hold what little power this court marshals to the cause of justice in a land of mere mortals."

A woman appeared in the shadow of the doorway to their right, speaking as she came. Her appearance was no less alarming than her words.

25

LADY OF THE MARDUKA

*Stronghold of Uruk in Ceregor, Syrscian,
Year 999 of the New Council*

Her questioning went on for a long and frustrating hour, and they still hadn't spoken a word to Bregon. Foxglove coped by keeping her answers brief, and by gazing on the loveliness of Lady Nin and her magnificent attendants.

She wasn't anything like the other Marduka, this strange woman who appeared to them in the inner chamber. Most of her attributes were human—if one ignored the iridescent scales of her skin. Like all Marduka, whose hides were thus armored, Lady Nin wore little clothing. However, what little she wore was rich, and richly adorned. Her black fabric wrap was decorated at the breast with a large bloodstone jewel, and there were glossy black metal guards upon her forearms and over her sandaled feet. Foxglove stared at these spare but elegant wrappings, and her own meager scraps of leather seemed suddenly crude.

Marduka fashion might have left much of her jeweled hide bare of adornment, but there was little more that could have improved Nin's regal qualities than sufficient light to catch the gleam of her scales. The most striking among all her features were a fancifully patterned face and pale red eyes, a mix of wild and lovely. She smelled pleasantly of spices. Foxglove was a little disappointed, though, that she didn't have any feathers.

"And so you left them to wander the country as they wished?" Nin was asking.

Foxglove blinked, awakened from a study of the lady's regal beauty. "We were in a war," she said.

A murmur of agitated voices erupted from behind Nin, where the small party of attendants that had followed her into the room sat cross-legged upon the floor. Foxglove could plainly see that these people weren't Marduka, for they bore wings upon their backs. They were tribesmen from the far north who had come on important business of their own, and thus they groused impatiently over Foxglove's ostensible ignorance of court customs in Uruk.

They were not the sort of people she wanted to upset. Six in number, they were all warriors of the winged people, the Yuuto.

The Yuuto leader was named Siru. A tattooed giant with tousled brown hair, Siru fixed his gaze on the Ayumu seated in front of Nin. Foxglove flashed a fang at him for good measure, but quickly hid it behind her lip when he leaned forwards and tamped his large hand on the stone floor, ruffling the feathers of his raven-black wings. There were two pairs of them high on his back. Impressive and beautiful, he bunched them behind his massive shoulders like a cloak. Primal fears rose up in Foxglove's mind at the sight of those big black wings, and she swallowed nervously. Nin peered over her shoulder at the Yuuto and spoke a word of warning.

"Enough, Siru. I have only a few more questions for our guest."

The Marduka woman had questioned Foxglove a long time already, probing her closely but politely about her travels while all these strangers looked on. It was much worse than when she was questioned by the Gremn, or by the elder Inyan at Timhureth; and regarding these events she felt strangely loth to reveal anything at all. Besides, all that happened years ago. It was hardly relevant information coming from her, now that they had detained an enemy officer. And so, her account was lacking in details.

Thus the interrogation endured.

"You did mention guiding a few strangers to a military encampment where they sought for this person in vain," Nin said, gesturing towards Bregon with her staff. "Why were you looking for this soldier? Who were these others, the ones who sought him?"

"They had their reasons. They weren't Galanese, but I don't know more than that."

Her answers were received with cold silence. The details she shared all pointed back to the strangers themselves, of whom she said little enough. Foxglove clenched her jaw in frustration, for she knew this would continue until Nin had her caught over one of the many gaps in her story. To Hades with those Gremn. She wished she had never met them.

Adding to her fury, the one who had actually committed crimes against the Fourth House was kneeling quietly beside her the whole while, staring at Lady Nin's feet. When her staff touched down with a loud clank amid the enameled designs of a winding floral motif, he shivered. Encouraged by this sight, Foxglove reviewed in her mind the words she would say, knowing this was probably her only chance to solidly incriminate the man before the Fomorian had a chance to come to his rescue.

"I think the strangers knew him," Foxglove answered, "but they did not say how. They were from a far distant country, and they knew next to nothing of the war in the south. I left them at a camp in the hills; but as I said, it was not a Galanese camp. It was full of ruffians, outlaws. I saw no reason to assist the strangers further, and as they seemed to have some argument between themselves as to the way they should go, I left them there and went off on my own to seek this man. His crimes against my people were a grief to bear."

She lowered her face towards the ground while the voices of those gathered mumbled quietly.

After a short pause, Nin asked, "You traveled long in the wilds to seek him?"

"Two years."

"And what makes you certain that he carried out any atrocities upon the Ayumu? There are many deserters among soldiers in times of war, and not all of them are so evil."

Foxglove lifted her eyes uncertainly. There they were again, those doubts that had been gnawing away at her. This was her moment, and yet she hesitated to spell out the obvious—that the white-uniformed soldier on trial was none other than the general of the Southern Army of the Galanese Council.

Why did she delay? What did she fear?

Nin frowned, and her hand squeezed the staff she bore. Matching her in every way, the scepter was tall and slender and glossy, and its enameled length hid a secret power. This was no mere prop, just as Nin was no ordinary girl. The shaft was a weapon of cunning craftsmanship, its surface embellished with winding golden flourishes and embossed all around with ancient runes. Even Foxglove easily recognized it for what it was—a Vajra spear.

"We will leave aside the question of this soldier's guilt for the time being," Lady Nin decided. "But taking up with strangers at Timhureth is a serious charge. It is a crime among our people to assist the Galanese. Have you no similar law?"

Groaning inwardly, Foxglove readied herself to make the standard reply that the strangers weren't Galanese; but then Nin abruptly cut her off.

"If they were not Galanese or Ayumu, who were they?"

"They were from very far away—"

She fell silent as Nin's scales shifted from pale pink and violet to blue-green, and then back again.

"I am sorry for having questioned you regarding your own laws," Nin said. "Yours is an admirable tribe, Lady of the Ayumu. I am satisfied by all your answers."

Foxglove's tail twitched nervously.

"I have indeed noticed the mark upon your face," Nin continued. "You are of the noble blood of your tribe, and you shall be rewarded all due favor of this court. Let it be known, Foxglove of Ulumeneth has my friendship, and I pledge to her the alliance of the Marduka and of the Yuuto as well."

Glancing aside at Siru and his Yuuto warriors, she added, "I should also apologize for the graceless temperament of those who brought you here, as well as that of others who should know better."

The Yuuto leader's eyes glared. Nin did not hesitate to bait him further.

"Most of our people still live in a little world, a world divided into allies and foes. Some have forgotten how great Syrscian really is."

Her smooth pink hand pointed away towards a podium by the wall. Upon it there was an open book, a rare tome that must've been looted from Musab merchants. It was open to a page bearing a colored map of Syrscian's known lands.

Nin said, "There is certainly room here for many people to live in peace, don't you think?"

Foxglove remained silent.

"Ah, but you have discovered, as have we, that the Galanese do not think Syrscian is large enough for us all."

Her colors shifted briefly again, this time to a deep purple hue.

"I do not know how it was in the south, but we have fewer artisans and more warriors every day, and there are not many left who can read or write. Laws built on the principle that we must all fight or die leave little room for an actual society to grow and mature. It was not always so. Look to your left, Cousin."

Foxglove turned her head towards the threshold of a door.

"There lies Ka Nun-Hegal, Gate of the Prince of Abundance, the Ayumu Gate. We have never received an envoy from your tribe since making this place our refuge. I feel it is my fault for not extending a proper welcome; but as you have no doubt noticed, war makes it difficult for some of us to show proper respect even to our allies."

Foxglove was simultaneously calmed and surprised by these kind words. Siru's frown brooded like a thunderstorm ready to burst.

"And there are some allies we have not held communion with since we departed the forest Tryst a thousand years ago."

Just behind Foxglove, the Fomorian sat patiently among a brood of Marduka warriors who had filed silently in by Barashkushu's summons. A few younger warriors craned their necks to look upon the blue-haired being their battle chief had led into Uruk, and their slit-pupiled eyes gleamed with wonder; but Nin refocused their attention with a sweep of her arm towards the opposite side of the room.

"The window in the wall," she said, "looks out into Ka Nun-Absu, Gate of the Prince of the Waters of the Underworld. This passage belongs to the Moriko and their kinds."

She then faced the door by which she had originally entered the room, and gestured towards Siru's party of winged warriors.

"Last, there is Ka Kitsu-Elu, Gate of the Upper Sanctum, The Yuuto Gate. Each gate is called by a name that refers to great deeds done by our mighty forebears in the adventure to take the Tablet of Destinies from the Destroyer."

"What is that?" Foxglove asked in a hushed voice.

She pointed to a banner strung across the ceiling, which had caught her attention when they first passed through the door. It was a tattered green flag emblazoned with a seal shaped like a winged horse.

"That is our battle standard. I wonder that you do not know it."

Foxglove's features reddened, and she felt suddenly very rustic.

"The banner and a rumored story are all that remain of the zeal which once united the Fourth House during the War of Destroying Fire," Nin explained. "We were led then by Aon, a spirit in the form of a winged horse, who brought us together in the confusion of battle."

"We of the south know almost nothing of these histories," Foxglove confessed. "It seems to me by your many questions that you do not know much about us, either."

"Well spoken, Foxglove of Ulumeneth. At some later time you and I must share stories at our leisure. Now, let us learn more about our Galanese guest, shall we?"

Then, in a stern voice, Nin addressed the captive seated beside Foxglove.

"I am Nin of the Marduka," she proclaimed. "Have you not heard of me, Galanese?"

Bregon answered, "Of the Marduka and their chieftain there are many rumors, Lady. None of the tales mentioned how beautiful you are, nor how lawful your noble court."

"He speaks like one of the highborn, this soldier," Nin said sternly. "Barashkushu, surrender to me his weapon."

The feathered battle chief stepped from behind Foxglove and offered Bregon's pistol, taking Nin's staff from her with a bow before returning to his place.

"A Vajra-type?" Nin remarked, examining the gun.

Bregon kept his eyes on her hands as she expertly flicked on the pistol's power supply. It emitted a faint shrill whine as the load-sequencer powered up magnetic restrictors inside the lengthy barrel.

"Tell me, Soldier, what is its name and lineage?"

Bregon shifted his eyes a little, and Foxglove knew what he was thinking. It was extremely odd for anyone of the forest people to so much as feign interest in the ancient technologies, as such things were taboo akin to sorcery.

"You think it strange that I know about Vajra weapons?" Nin asked, looking aside at him. "It might surprise you, then, that though my people are increasingly opposed to the knowledge of *mechina*, I was trained by my father in the secret knowledge of the crafting and use of this technology, just as he also taught me the speech and customs of the Galanese. My own staff is Vajra-make. Now come, tell me how it is that a weapon made and distributed solely by House Gaerith before the War of Destroying Fire has come to be in the hands of a common soldier of the council."

Bregon stared straight at her. Pleased to have struck the mark, Nin continued.

"So rare is this gun, it would not be difficult for me to guess your own lineage were you to speak its name."

"It is called Arondight," he answered.

There was a sharp click. Bregon could not help straightening his body where he knelt, for the muzzle of the gun was pressed against his forehead.

The lady's hand did not tremble.

The room was hushed; the assembled warriors held still.

"Three great swords there were of old," Nin said. "All the children of our tribe know the stories of those three. Though they are but matters of legend, they have ever haunted my dreams."

She held his eyes while she spoke, but her face was calm. The pistol did not waver.

"The first and most famous of the swords of old was *Excalibur*, given to House Gaerith by the sea which now bears their name. Excalibur lent its master gifts of healing and of light, and so it is named Sword of the Light; but it was lost when it fell into the hands of the Crodah. The second sword was *Fragarach*, the Answerer, Sword of the Wind. It was said that Fragarach was lost in an attempt to recapture Kutha from the Destroyer, and is hidden away in the Wastelands of the far north until the end of time."

She pulled the gun away from his head before continuing.

"The third sword was *Arondight*, Sword of the White Knight, an ally of Ard Morvran's who went also by the name of Cedric DePons. I find it strange that you should name your pistol after the legendary sword of the master of House Gaerith—the same sword which was storied to fell a Keeper of the Stones."

"It's just an old legend," Bregon replied, trying not to appear anxious.

"Just a legend?" she inspected the weapon anew, as if her eyes cheated her. "This is a Series One Vajra. The power supply alone is unrivaled by anything the Galanese make today. 'Tis said to be the same technology which animates the navvies!"

"You are very knowledgeable, Lady," Bregon said. "You know more than a Galanese priest about firearms and lore."

"And you are curious as to how this came to be, are you not?"

From the moment it became clear Nin was not going to shoot him, Foxglove's heart sank. Nin glanced aside at her, seeming to hear her inner anguish.

"My father did not merely teach me about these guns," she said. "He also trained me in their use, for he was a collector of Vajra arms, and our household was once equipped with a variety of staves and rifles. The feel of this one now brings back the old drills quite clearly."

"I remember you shot me once," Siru mumbled.

She looked over at him with twinkling eyes, and the glowering mien reconvened on his heavy brow.

"Gas ampoules are self-charging in normal atmospheric conditions," Nin said, sighting down the barrel, "but the process is slow, and spent ampoules need to be switched-out under heavy battle conditions so that they may fully recharge."

"But the Vajra lack a projectile," Bregon supplied, "so there is nothing more to carry but a few gas ampoules."

"No rounds means it's recoilless?"

"Of course. But it takes its time between discharges."

"A powerful sword, indeed," she said. "And it maximizes on the one weakness among Gremn—their vulnerability to fire."

These words she spoke after looking straight at Foxglove, who could not hide the nervous fluffing of her tail.

"Though the lord of House Gaerith worked with the Gremn during the War, the proliferation of Vajras among those opposing the Gremn implicated House Gaerith in playing both sides to their own advantage. If my ancient history lessons were worth the trouble, that led to an investigation of House Gaerith, and ultimately to the exile of Cedric DePons. Did I get it right, *Lord Bregon of Gaerith?*"

Nin held the weapon out to him again, but this time she offered him the grip. The entire chamber was riled by the spectacle. Angry voices shouted in opposition, and hands clutched at knives hidden in the folds of the warriors' tunics. Bregon was no less taken aback by her blunt introduction than those seated around him.

He stared at the grip of his gun, and dared not twitch.

The leader of the Yuuto warriors spoke first.

"This is him?" he asked, scrutinizing Bregon dubiously. "This is the general of their army?"

"He wears *The White*," Nin answered, gazing at Bregon's uniform. "Among the Galanese rabble, this makes him more than a general. However, it was not until I set eyes on his weapon that I knew him for the heir of House Gaerith."

"You are a font of wisdom, Lady," Bregon whispered.

Nin smiled mischievously. "Take your weapon, if you dare."

Bregon collected himself and reached out for the grip with a steady hand. Nin did not immediately release it, however.

"Let this moment be a bond between us," she said to him.

"Lady?"

"My father once told me that Gaerith means *Crooked Spear*. Only those educated in the ancient tongues would know that this refers to the Holy Spear, the spear wielded by Marluin in the battles of the First Age, which was given over to be an heirloom to your house and to its legacy. Is it not so?"

"You speak of the so-called Dragon Spear? But it was lost, long ago. I have not heard that any knew of it outside our family."

"There were others who knew of it. Your father told the story of the Dragon Spear to my grandsires of old. We are dragons, too, if you like. Now, take the pistol, and I will offer with it what grace is mine to give."

When Bregon's hand drew back the pistol and laid it in his lap, the Yuuto and Marduka stood as one. There was still much grumbling, but Nin's word was as good as law among the four tribes. It was for the Lady of the Marduka that they restrained themselves. Such was the fealty and trust she commanded, and Foxglove was in awe. She rose slowly along with the rest, stooping her shoulders. Everything was going wrong. She wished she could sink into the floor; but Bec's cool hand was on her back, lending her a little courage.

"The Galanese will come here looking for the man," Siru objected, gesturing at Bregon. "What then, if we are forced to defend this place like Esagil? It would be safer just to kill him and leave his body upon the Galaneth, would it not?"

Foxglove had just discovered one thing she had in common with Siru. Several warriors yelled their approval, but Nin would have no part of it. She considered the man kneeling before her with kind eyes.

"His title serves him better than his reputation among us, certainly," she said. "However, I judge this man's character by the companions he keeps. He travels in the presence of an Ayumu princess and one of the ancient Moriko. Though the Lady of the Ayumu hunted him for vengeance, she has not carried out her tribe's retribution for the same reason I will not. We are a lawful people, and there is no evidence to substantiate his complicity in the council's schemes."

Foxglove's jaw opened, but no words of protest came. She was speechless. Bec squeezed her shoulder gently.

"Even if he did abandon his post, you cannot forgive the murders that took place under his command!" someone cried.

Nin held up her hand for silence. "Of course I cannot forgive the grievance of a dead man," she said, "There is no mortal who can."

Silence resumed. Even Bregon seemed confused by her words.

"I shall forthwith cause to be spread a rumor among the colonies of the Karn River, that the Lord Bregon of Gaerith, having left Army Command, was captured by the forest people and summarily executed. Our couriers to the Musab will supply his uniform as evidence of this."

These words she spoke in a voice so deep that Foxglove cringed. The feeling was swept aside by a gentler tone of remonstration.

"Thus ends House Gaerith, I suppose."

"You're suggesting he take on a new persona and become our ally?" Siru wondered.

Bregon remained kneeling, his eyes fixed on Nin.

"If he will accept it, what greater alliance could there be to the cause of uniting what is left of the people of Syrscian?" she replied. "He is feared by the Galanese because he held the highest seat in the council. After his father left and the empress perished, he was their king."

In the rumble of voices that followed, Foxglove felt lightheaded. A new air was stirring in the crowded hall, and every eye was on Bregon.

"I accept your proposal," Bregon said meekly. "My heart is moved by your words, Lady Nin, and by your trust. I swear that I shall work to restore the peace that once existed before the wars of the Great Houses, a peace that is for all the people."

He stood then, rising a little taller than the Lady of the Marduka. As he lacked a holster, he kept his pistol in hand. Barashkushu stepped forwards and handed to Nin her staff, which she held out over Bregon's head.

"Hear then!" she declared. "I, Nin of the Marduka, do extend solidarity to the son of Cedric DePons in the presence of these witnesses of all the four tribes. He shall have full asylum among us for as long as he works in the service of all the people of Syrscian."

Bregon nodded, but Nin wasn't finished.

"I shall also grant him a new name under the bond of our covenant," she added in a quieter voice. "He shall be called *Gilgamesh*, the hero of Uruk."

The murmur of voices went on for some time after her announcement. Everyone had heard of this name—the name of one of the greatest heroes of the Fourth House. No one seemed more shocked than Bregon himself. The enemy general had transformed into a heroic king.

The word *injustice* had become so stale in Foxglove's mouth that she couldn't even spit it out. Siru obviously shared her sentiments.

Studying Bregon with incredulous eyes, he silenced everyone with a simple question.

"So," he asked, "what do you intend to do with him?"

"Under new guise, House Gaerith shall bend its back to the camaraderie of the forest tribes," Nin answered. "What say you, Master Gilgamesh?"

"He shall comply with your wishes," said a new voice, "so long as he also remembers his pledge to assist me."

Striding to the center of the court, Bec commanded a mighty presence. It wasn't just that the scent of the Moriko was upon her. She touched their minds as she spoke, and the firmness of that touch related to them all the power hidden behind her youthful frame.

The power of legends was a mighty power indeed.

"I have a question for you, Yuuto," Bec said to Siru.

Siru bravely folded his arms and faced her.

"Your men camp upon the river, though under the eaves of the wood. They trample the forest with their feet, thinking they are its protectors. What do you hope to accomplish by inciting violence with the Galanese at a time such as this?"

Nin looked from Bec to the Yuuto leader. "Is this true?" she asked.

Stuck with two questions at once, Siru kept his eyes on Bec and countered with a question of his own.

"How does she know about this?" he asked.

A chilling breeze moved through the room then, and Foxglove noted many of the winged men pressing a thumb against their forehead—a sign of ancient superstitions.

"Do you not sense the presence of the Moriko?" Nin asked.

"The Moriko?"

Then, seeing his warriors making the sign upon their foreheads at mention of the name, he faced the group with an angry scowl.

"Stop that!"

"The Moriko speak to one another without words, 'tis said," one of the warriors replied. "They know what we have done."

Siru shook his head. "We haven't done anything."

"Then why have you come here, leaving your forces behind at the river?" Nin asked. "I've already heard rumors that you were assembling a war party. What have you come to request of me?"

"Just some sturdy Marduka warriors to aid us in a worthy cause."

"He asks for help because he has seen something in the eastern sky," Bec supplied.

Siru dropped his hands to his sides, and his face looked suddenly fearful.

"It was a comet," he said timidly. "We took it for a sign."

"It wasn't an omen, though," Bec said. "Nor was it a comet. It was a ship. The exiles have returned."

Her words were greeted with a fresh wave of excitement, but Bec redirected their thoughts with an explanation.

"The ship brought Gremn exiles," she said. "They have not all returned, however. There is still something else that must happen first."

Siru squinted at her.

"Have you not yet taken notice that all four tribes are gathered here today?" Bec asked. "It is for a purpose appointed a thousand years ago. Now the people of the Fourth House know for certain that the time has come. Now we must have courage."

Again the thumbs were pressed against foreheads all around.

"A war is coming to the forest," Bec continued. "I and my companions travel to Islith to awaken the terminal there. Your people will supply us for a journey into Tryst."

"We will supply you?" Siru asked, shaking his head. "Who are you to make such demands?"

"I am Avalon, protector of Islith, and to Islith's terminal I must return before the emissary of darkness arrives. If he gets there before I do, then a second War of Destroying Fire will result."

They stood in wondering silence at her claims. Avalon was no less legendary a name than *Moriko*, or *Fomorian*. To be visited by all three in a single entity was something of an occasion. No one asked for proof.

No sign was needed.

"Of prophecies we are aware," Siru mumbled, "but we were told the Fomorians who spoke the prophecies were all slain with the sacred trees. We have done what we could to bring justice upon those who have done this."

"That is too bad," Bec answered. "Loth would I have been to speak of the future if I'd known my words would lead you astray. Those trees were not to us as your bodies are to you."

He blinked.

"Indeed," she continued, "it would seem that much of what is now at stake has been overlooked for the settling of petty grievances, and by the most violent of means."

"Petty?" Siru wondered, his mouth twisting into an angry snarl. "Many have died for the defense of our borders, and many more were slaughtered who never raised a hand in defense."

"Think you it a simple task," she countered, "to bind together the last of the Gremn and Crodah as allies, and to bring their leaders here? How much blood is there on your own hands, Lord Siru? Where were you during the Destroying Fire? I was the only one capable of stopping it, and I failed. More than three quarters of the population of this world died because of me. You will forgive me if your own losses seem petty in comparison to this."

Her eyes flashed, and Siru lowered his gaze.

"What she is saying," Bregon said, speaking directly to Nin, "is that something important has been overlooked while the council was busy playing at their wars."

"And what is that, *Master Gilgamesh*?" Siru snapped.

"Isn't it obvious? The empress has returned, as was foretold. This was the final condition placed upon the return of any exiles."

Siru's eyes narrowed, and Foxglove caught a hint of malice flickering in his gaze. She couldn't understand his response. It was news that would have brought celebration to every town and village in Tarthalion.

None of the Yuuto looked very pleased at all.

Nin aimed sharp words at Siru, saying, "Now is the time the Great Houses of old will run up their banners and advance on Kutha in a War of Dark Towers. Did you think you could make all that happen on your own by attacking a Galanese colony, Siru? Is your world still so small as theirs?"

"No," Bec said, interrupting. "No, his actions go beyond the triviality of playing war. I can see it written plainly on his face."

The Yuuto made no sound. No one pressed a thumb to his head this time.

Pulling himself together with an obvious effort, Siru answered, saying, "My sister Sirona, chieftain of the Yuuto, was captured by the Galanese in one of their colonies. We will attack Nara to get her back—"

Nin's staff clanged against the floor.

"How did this happen?" she asked in a quiet voice.

"She was taken by the Tenno while infiltrating their colony to free slaves," Siru explained. "She is fighting in Gilat. She's been there for a full cycle of the moons while we planned her escape. We did not wish to involve you at all, Nin, but the circumstances have changed. It is unlikely that we shall succeed in freeing her without significant losses, if we can manage it at all."

His retinue had obviously heard a braver assessment of the situation, and were now exchanging glances.

Nin was still in shock. She wore the look of someone who has just been informed that her nearest kin was dead. Always prone to empathy, Foxglove sensed that it was not sadness which weakened her demeanor. Nin's scales flashed through a range of reds and violets, and then to black. The Lady of the Marduka was enraged.

"You always took foolish risks," she said quietly, her beautiful face twisting into a scowl. "You never saw the danger at hand; and now she could die, because of your stupidity!"

Hearing the iciness in her tone, Siru opened his palms towards her in supplication. "Maybe I am a fool," he muttered, "but I do not remember that you hung back when we taunted patrols as children."

"That was before Esagil. We are no longer children, Siru. Did you put her up to this?"

"Listen, Nin. I have made arrangements for a rescue. Will you not aid me?"

She stared at him without speaking. He turned briefly towards Bec, but thought better of asking the Fomorian for help. Bec decided to lead him on anyway.

"You aren't the sort of man who comes to the table without a plan," she said. "Why don't you tell her about it?"

Nin's gaze was not encouraging, but sensing he had a powerful ally, Siru spoke.

"There was one among us who was captured a year ago when posing as a member of the governor's personal bodyguard. It was his second attempt to free slaves in Nara, and though he's been captured twice there is no truer man in Syrscian. He will meet Sirona on the inside, and if all goes well he will be forced to fight her in the arena."

"Fight her?" Nin's color shifted to icy blue.

Siru held out his hands in supplication. "It is necessary for them both to be inside the arena at the same time. We can rescue Sirona, kill Amed, and take out Nara's field generators in one swift blow, but we need his help. This is our only chance, Nin. If you would provide a distraction, Shanuri will save my sister and I will end this!"

She smacked his hands away. Hefting her staff, Nin Marduka put on a serene face; but behind the mask of her features a quiet storm was raging.

"Shanuri?"

Again Siru avoided her eyes.

"Your plan banks on the exploits of *The Masked Fool*? The one who speaks to Fairies?"

"He infiltrated the warrior's guild and destroyed a shipment of arms from Tara," Siru defended. "After he was caught he escaped, and then went back to free the slaves. Who would doubt him? My sister did not!"

"Amed has dealt with him before. He will surely sniff out your plot."

She turned away from him, and facing Bec she said, "My father always warned me the Old Days would come back to us, and now a companion of Ard Morvran returns with rumors of a second War of Destroying Fire. Given this, how am I to treat a request to participate in foolish quests?"

"A stranger needs not prove herself to you," Siru muttered to her back. "Why must I?"

"We were friends together when we were small, Siru; but you have mistaken me for an impressionable child. There is more to this than stands on the surface of the matter, and I will discover it. *The truth of our words will speak forth in deeds*, Father used to say."

"As for deeds, I have a plan," Siru said, triumphantly holding up a small pouch.

Nin frowned at him, but her anger had passed. Her scales shifted slowly back to their standard pink color.

"I—would have mentioned it sooner," Siru said, stammering, "but Sirona insisted we keep it a secret."

Now her head was cocked sideways in warning. Siru's wings drooped.

"Well, maybe I was the one who kept it a secret, but Shanuri left something with me that will help. It's become my backup plan for the infiltration of the Gilat arena. Thanks to this, I am able to home in on him like a fly on a wound. I can find him, and Sirona, and then we'll be out even before the field generators fail!"

The Yuuto warriors thumped their chests and shouted cheerfully.

"Barashkushu," Nin said, massaging her temples.

"Yes, my Lady?"

"Assemble all who can be spared to the task of infiltrating Nara Colony. The Marduka will be attending *Gilat*. As for Master Gilgamesh and our other guests, outfit them with whatever they require, and provide letters to the elders of the Yuuto in Yumu Remi to safeguard their passage. It is far too dangerous to enter the forest from the east where it borders Galaneth, so they will need to travel northeast to Yuuto lands. I leave them the choice of roads they shall take from there."

She faced Bec solemnly. "I am sorry," she said with a bow. "I would have come with you through the dark of Tryst to Islith itself. Alas, my hands are tied."

"You need not venture any distance to find darkness and danger," Bec replied in a quiet voice. "A time is coming, a time of shadow and war."

26

THE POET

Gilthaloneth, Syrscian,
Year 1000 of the New Council

A night of wallowing in adrenaline had exhausted them all, but Nunna remained alert, straining her eyes in the early morning haze. Behind a cobbled harbor by the airship ports loomed the majestic wall of Gilthaloneth's western hill, red in the glow of dawn; and before the wall was the lake, dark glassy Kethern, sparkling with stars both night and day. Beyond the lake's western shoreline, the glimmering thread of the Karn could be seen flowing in through a steep-walled canyon. The desert there was a high table, visible as an ochre stain on the horizon.

The kidnapping of Fann and her sisters required improvisation to Val Anna's plan, specifically an early exodus. There was no time to pack or make cautious arrangements. Orlim sent in a security force to occupy the villa while Lothar led the empress and her friends through the labyrinthine tiers of the city. They had walked all night just to reach the port, and here they were supposed to meet with a courier, a merchant named Daedalus who specialized in smuggling people out of the city unseen. Lothar recommended him, though hesitantly.

Lothar also saw to the selection of their companions. Since they would have warranted unwanted attention if all the Dragon Slayers accompanied the empress, only four were designated escorts for the journey to Nara Colony. Lothar elected three whom he trusted closer than kin. Caradoc, Bran, and Vercingetorix were all Tenno from Nara, and without argument the finest swords in the service of the empress. Dressed now in plainclothes instead of their uniforms, the four of them together stood nonetheless like warriors, forming a protective phalanx around a stoop-shouldered shadow wrapped in a cloak. Her head bowed beneath her hood, Val Anna looked less regal now than she had the evening before.

All they needed to do was make arrangements with the *Coyotes*, or smugglers, and then leave Gilthaloneth with as much secrecy as could be managed. The empress was relying mostly on Lothar for all the planning and negotiating, and Nunna thought this was probably best. Although, she was a bit curious how a warrior was familiar with black market merchants, and why it was he seemed nonplused about looking for them. She never got the chance to ask him about it. They hadn't been wandering the quays very long before the group ran into Mr. Mudge, one of their merchant's contacts.

Mudge aptly fit the description they'd been given. Lothar said to keep an eye out for a short man wearing a strange hat. What walked up to them from a blind alleyway was a dwarf dressed simply in a vest and rather dirty pants, with matching tatty tri-corn hat and hair. Mr. Mudge was by all appearances a movie pirate, minus the eye-patch and the parrot. Nunna covered her face with a hand when he removed his hat, revealing a prodigious bald spot like a reversed tonsure covering the entire top of his head.

The group paused while Morla and Lothar stepped out in front of them. Nunna remained within earshot, but not so close that she felt uneasy. This was her first venture out into public since her gift had increased in sensitivity, and she was being careful.

"*E pluribus unum?*" the dwarf muttered quietly.

"It's me, Mudge," Lothar said. "You don't need the password for me. It was only to be used in case I wasn't anywhere to be seen."

"The Centaur himself gave it, so I knew I'd only have one chance to use it," the dwarf replied gruffly, waving his hat. "Anyway, here we are."

"Nice to see you, too," Lothar replied. "What's it been? Fifteen, sixteen cycles?"

Morla looked from one to the other, clearly confused. Nunna also sensed the tension in the air. Though they were old acquaintances, Lothar was obviously distressed to be meeting with this man.

"This is the seer of the High Place, then?" Mudge asked, looking up at Morla.

Morla stared him down, quite literally, since he stood only waist-high to her. She was a silver-crowned slender birch beside a heavyset boulder. Mudge wasn't intimidated by her in the least, however. He absently fished from his vest pocket some sharp surgical forceps, and without so much as excusing himself he started tweezing a sore on his bare shoulder. In measure to this spectacle, the seer put forth her best appearance of impassive calm.

Keeping his head turned so that he could concentrate on his grisly work, the dwarf said, "You fly with us, Lothar, and the captain sets the rules."

The sore burst and ran, and with a hiss of pain he carefully extracted something like a centipede from the wound. Morla's eyes narrowed as the creature lunged this way and that. Dandling his trophy from the tip of the forceps a moment, the man flung it to the pavement and crushed it beneath his heavy boot.

"There's no imperial government out in the Wastes," he chided. "Just sand worms, and worse."

Despite her mighty gifting, Morla was having obvious difficulties warming to the stranger. Nunna had already peered into his mind, and there she saw fear; but he was certainly not a council-spy.

"Mr. Mud," Morla pressed.

"It's *Mudge*," he corrected, smiling with crooked yellow teeth.

"It seems only fair, Mr. Mudge, given our unique status, that we should be granted audience with your captain before setting foot on his vessel."

"Oh, you won't be setting foot on *his* vessel, Lady. We shall have to commandeer a ship for your departure."

Morla looked towards Lothar for clarification.

"You don't mean to capture a ship in a fight, and then sail out of port with it all the way to Nara?" the Dragon Slayer asked.

"Well, no one expected we would be departing so soon. The captain's a busy man, and this is all he can do on such short notice."

"Is he a pirate?" Morla wondered, her face showing a little fear.

"Mr. Daedalus is a legitimate imperial merchant," Mudge stated in a louder voice, keeping his eyes trained on a few passersby. "All his paperwork with the guild is kept in order and up to date."

In a lower voice he added, "It's us that's the pirates."

"A marriage of convenience," Lothar mumbled. "I'm sure you could come up with something less spectacular than this, though. We don't want to make a lot of noise on our way out of here, and any blood that is shed will be on my hands."

"It was our impression you wanted a big show," Mudge replied, leering wickedly at Lothar. "The captain bade me tell his *old friend* to expect a show equal to the occasion. As for the cargo—"

Mudge peered past Morla toward the cloaked shadow hovering behind them, whose small pale chin lifted a little as if in sudden interest. He seemed surprisingly shy that she had taken notice of him.

"No one will know it's the empress sailing out of port. Not yet, anyways."

Morla was still frowning, but even Nunna could tell that the man was genuinely convinced he was doing the right thing. His reasons, though, remained hidden in his convoluted little mind.

"Alright," Lothar said. "Take us where you will."

Mudge guided them straight towards the mountainside port. A light mist blew over them. Looking up, Nunna admired the feathery tendrils of a waterfall drifting down to the lake from hundreds of feet above. There was a millwheel turning up there, affixed to one of the buildings anchored to the hill.

The mighty halls of merchant guilds, these magnificent structures built into the mountainside represented the economic power of the Galanese council. Arranged in ordered levels with interconnecting bridges between, they were banked by marvelous walkways suspended at dizzying heights, all lined with market stalls and shops. On levels between the markets, the pale hulls of fish-shaped dirigibles cast odd sideways shadows where men labored to moor them alongside warehouses. Cargo was offloaded and replaced in careful synchronization with ballast.

Lothar had said these airships moved mostly by night, and many of the pilots were associates of the Musab Black Market. It was an open secret. Though illegal, not much was done to enforce the law unless someone was actually caught moving contraband merchandise onto or off of a ship. That kind of work required careful preparation to avoid patrols. Confidentiality was highly respected among this lot, as was private security.

Nunna tugged the straps that anchored the sword to her back, and for a moment she wished she'd listened to Lothar. Though she'd been trained as a soldier in the use of knives and staves, relying primarily on a melee weapon afforded little comfort. The Dragon Slayers concealed small blades on their persons, but Lothar had warned against bringing anything substantial. Besides generating suspicion or curiosity, she was assured that many of the people in this particular port would be armed to the teeth. There were smugglers in the open here with very few signs of law enforcement. It just seemed wrong not to have something like a sword in a place like this, she thought.

Just ahead, Mudge approached a high and intricately carved entrance to the tunnels in the cliff.

"There are a few miles of passageways between us and our target," he said without turning. "Even though it means ringing the front doorbell, I suggest we go in by the main gate. We need access to the uppermost tier, and that's the only way."

"The uppermost tier?" Lothar wondered.

He slowed his steps and stopped short of the gate. Mudge paused and looked back.

"There aren't many ships up there," Lothar said. "Couldn't we just find something closer, if all you're going to do is steal it?"

"No time to explain, old friend. I'll just say, the captain's planned a spectacle more suitable to the occasion of dishonoring Teomaxos than merely facilitating your escape."

Without waiting for rebuttal, he held up his heavy leech-pocked arm and twirled his hand in the air a few times. Within moments, the shrill whistle and pop of rocket flares answered from high above. Mudge looked towards the two red and single blue lights that drifted slowly down towards the lake, and he grinned when five white flares popped even higher up.

They all stared upwards, wondering at the mighty towers and gate in the uppermost tier. A flurry of activity ensued upon the market-levels beneath. Men were hastening now to unload their ships, and a press of people could be seen trying to board wherever they could.

"That should stir things up sufficiently," Mudge decided.

Reading the flares, Lothar said, "The signal was for a departure. What's the meaning of this?"

"Our boys just signaled the councilor's staff to prepare *Galloglass* for immediate departure. They think their master is on his way—except he isn't, if you take my meaning."

"Galloglass?" Lothar wondered. "You mean the councilor's private ship? We're stealing Teomaxos' ship?"

Morla's look was troubled.

Mudge rubbed his shoulder and nodded vigorously. "We'll take it as soon as they've finished loading it all up for us."

"I must confess," Lothar remarked, "I would not have thought of so obvious a tactic in delaying the councilor as the theft of his ferry."

"And that is why you are not a transporter, Lothar," spoke a voice behind them.

A tall figure stepped briskly towards them across the shadowed lane. He was dressed in the common uniform of a courier, though to Nunna he looked rather like a hero from the cover of some trashy romance novel. His costume was trimmed with gold, and he had an even more ridiculous hat on his head than Mudge. Fluttering behind the high collar of his shirt in the brisk morning winds, the length of his carefully-combed brown hair marked him as a cultured man among the Galanese merchants. Despite his gaudy appearance, however, the eyes peering out from his broad face were deep and dark. A contemplative sadness lingered in his gaze.

Lothar's expression was less subtle as he stepped out to greet him.

"Daedalus? You are risking much by showing your face inside the city."

"The *Fifty-Kells* no longer makes berth at any port," the man replied, crossing his arms, "but I still show up where I'm needed."

His voice was deep but quiet, and his words very elegant, holding them all captive to his power.

"I have come to make the acquaintance of the empress, the very lifeblood of our world," he said with a reverent bow. "Orlim insisted I greet her in person. He said that it would be a show of good faith. Surely our going forth together will meet the spirit of the empress' challenge to the councilor, am I right?"

"I swear, that is the most I've ever heard you speak in one go," Lothar remarked.

Daedalus straightened, smiling sly and silent.

"Mudge mentioned you had contact with the Centaur. I was right to guess you got that old transmitter working again."

"Outlaw technology, courtesy of the sorcerers of the Wastes."

"I don't suppose you have some outlaw technology that will help us walk up there and sail out in the councilor's ship before anyone notices that he's not on board?"

"He stole something from your seer just as easily, did he not?" Daedalus mused.

Morla looked suitably astonished.

"Well," Lothar replied, "there is indeed little that passes over land or through the skies that you do not know. As for your motives—"

"I owe the councilor a little nudge for looking into my business and chasing away some important clients," the captain said.

"How do manage to find clients at all with Eterskel hunting you down across Syrscian?"

"I'm standing here, aren't I?" Daedalus wondered.

"And where is the Kells?" Lothar asked.

"No time for that," Mudge said. "Suffice it to say, Galloglass is an easier girl to handle than the last ship we stole from this port. Maybe we'll return it in one piece."

He paused beside Daedalus, handing him a brass spyglass. Looking back briefly towards the distant docks, dim in the morning mists, Daedalus handed the scope back to Mudge.

"Liffey bears the black standard?" the captain observed with a raised eyebrow.

"You told me, Sir, to leave one slow ship for the councilor."

"If Teomaxos gains leverage over Liffey—"

"I know you have history with his crew, but any other ship might possibly catch us up—and he took the money without question."

"Of course he would. If you cut him, Liffey bleeds scorpion stone."

"And now that he stands in your debt—"

"Why couldn't we just seize a smaller ship and take it to the *Kells*?" Lothar interrupted. "Surely she's not too far away?"

"The Kells isn't coming anywhere near this city," Daedalus answered. "There are heavy airships in this region, and even if they couldn't catch us they could just as easily blow us out of the sky."

"I hardly see how it matters," Mudge remarked aside, "considering he left *that woman* in charge."

Nunna sensed Lothar's distress upon hearing this, but the moment passed quickly. Daedalus then led them through the carved door and into the tunnels.

The narrow roads beneath the hill were bustling with bodies moving from shop to shop. It reminded Nunna of the subway mall in the old section of New York in the days before the Watchers. She remained focused and alert, and was somehow doing remarkably well despite being crowded all around by so many minds. She sensed Lothar walking close by, and decided to distract him with an unasked question that was silently nagging her.

"What is the Fifty-Kells?" she asked. "Is it some kind of merchant ship?"

"Try not to say that name so loudly," he warned in a low voice. "That ship is no trader. Most merchant vessels these days are excessively large luxury vessels, showrooms for guild wares. They're easy to spot from a distance because they have large cylindrical engine-towers extending below-decks or to either side—they run on the green argo. A few are so big they also boast castles and guest houses, not to mention ports for smaller vessels. No, that ship is nothing like a trader."

"Well, what's it like?"

"It was a private military vessel owned by a rich and powerful nobleman. When said nobleman was implicated as a connection between the guilds of his colony and the Black Market, he attempted to assassinate among his hired militia all of those officers who normally handled his underhanded business. A few of these gathered around a young disenfranchised noble."

"Daedalus?"

"Yeah. Together he and his crew seized their master's flagship and fled into the Wastes. A price was put on their heads and rewards were offered for news or capture of the ship, but the captain was just too smart. He's been in this business since he was a mere boy. With his experience he can conjure just about any feat of smuggling."

"What about the reward money? How does he get clients?"

"Most of his clients will tell you that there are some things worth more than any amount of reward money."

"We're about to put him to the test, aren't we?"

"Yes, but without the ship that won him his fame."

"And that ship is fast?"

"Powered by experimental engines, it is the fastest destroyer-class airship in Syrscian, and it remains the pride of Tara's guilds despite having fallen into enemy hands."

Nunna left off the rest of her questions for the time being. Lothar seemed very ornery, but she was actually enjoying herself for the first time in many years. There was a warm stuffiness in the air, but all was well-lit and rather cheerful. The storefronts opened onto the passageway on either hand, and all were filled with merchandise brought in from the Galanese colonies along the Karn River. A smell of fresh baked goods pervaded all, carried from bakeries busied with morning orders. The sweet smell of the air set Nunna's heart on memories of other times. It was a magical place.

It was also dangerous. Lothar and his men tried to remain inconspicuous, but eyes were drawn to them as they bumped shoulders with the masses. Val Anna remained hooded, her face downward. Nunna didn't think anyone would be able to recognize the empress, but her own blue hair and gleaming blade were causing a stir. She longed for her old CM7 Chameleon suit, which would have hidden her from staring eyes, but its power supply had completely drained. She wished she could say the same for her adaptive sensory powers. The cumulative touch of each passing mind was slowly building in intensity. Whatever her upper limit was, she would have little warning before it was reached, and then she would be overwhelmed.

Daedalus moved so that he could walk beside Morla, forcing Nunna to walk behind them. It was an arrangement that conveniently shielded Nunna from most of the onlookers, but the captain's purpose was twofold. Without explanation, he covered Morla's white hair with a large hood slipped to him by Mudge, and then placed his arm around her proud shoulders and pushed against her sternly until she stooped. In mere moments the seer was transformed into the figure of an old woman. Above the noise of the crowds Nunna could hear a whispered conversation ensue.

"My thanks," Morla said. "I had not thought my face was recognizable, but people are staring."

"You should be used to this," he replied. "Take you no thought for your own safety?"

"I am the seer."

"Ah, yes. And the girl," Daedalus glanced back briefly, "the maiden with the sword—she's a navvie of the old days, is she not? I've heard there were still a few around, but I've never seen one before."

"How do you know such things?" Morla asked. Her voice sounded uncharacteristically tense.

"How I know isn't important. Others in this marketplace know it, I'm sure, and a hood won't easily disguise that sword. She will complicate our escape."

"As to our escape," Morla dodged, "if Galloglass is the slowest ship in port, won't someone easily stop us?"

"She *is* an old girl," he answered cryptically. "But this isn't an escape. Think of it as a grand send-off, a gala if you wish."

"What of Galloglass' crew?"

"We sent men ahead of us disguised as porters," he replied. "We shall soon learn of their success."

He turned right suddenly, heading into a relatively empty passage that brought them up a steep flight of steps. At the top they arrived at the middle levels of the port, where an arched gate opened onto broad walkways high up the cliff's face. Mansions and guild halls were constructed in the sheer rock wall, interspersed with more shops. It was even busier here than in the tunnels below. The outer rails were thronged with a crush of people seeking passage aboard the moored airships, whose gangplanks were jammed with folk lugging travel bags and gear for a long journey.

Daedalus stepped forward from Morla's side to lead them through the gate and onward into the fray. The airships really did look like fish, with doped canvas stretched across wooden frames and sails or wings for fins. Some bore large baskets beneath for passengers and baggage, while others of more complex design had interior compartments and wide decks in the fashion of ships of the sea. No one looked concerned about bidding for passage on the fanciful ships, though Lothar had made all the couriers sound like pirates.

"Is this what the flares were about?" Morla asked.

Only Nunna was able to hear her, but the answer to her question was obvious enough. Short of starting a battle, they wouldn't have been able to attract attention in this mob if they wanted to. Anyone in the employ of the council was too busy making money to bother with a few suspicious characters shoving their way towards the uppermost tiers of the port.

As if there was anyone here who wasn't suspicious to begin with.

Nunna understood only a little of smuggling from her previous work in New York, but she suspected it worked the same here as on Earth. Tariffs were set too high for shipping companies to make legal runs for items in high demand, and passengers didn't mind taking up with illegal traffickers because they were also patrons of the market. It was a simple arrangement, really.

No one cared one way or the other how the goods arrived, just as long as they made it without too much fuss. As for transporters who captured and smuggled people, *Coyotes*—they were far more dangerous. Keeping their business out of the light required constant management of a cover-operation. Coyotes struggled to maintain a pristine image of that cover, or else they lost their customers.

They passed the water wheel and the adjoining complex of houses, which indeed seemed to be a power plant. A low rumble of engines drowned out the vibration of the mill as they turned towards an impressive gate cut into the cliff's face. The high shadowy passage enclosed a grand staircase of marble, which made a turn to the left about fifty feet up from the bottom.

The stair was blocked by four armored soldiers bearing staves. "Halt!"

Visors lowered across their faces made it difficult to determine who was speaking, but the bold challenge stopped them all in their tracks. Lothar and the Dragon Slayers moved instinctively, reaching for belts and sheaths hidden beneath their garments. Daedalus, however, stepped out in front and proceeded calmly towards the center of the wide stair, blithely ignoring the sentries' challenge.

"What business have you people in the upper tier? You can't go up without proper authorization and a crested seal."

The captain did not turn his head to either side, but passed them silently by.

"Hey, didn't you hear me?"

Daedalus remained silent. The guards looked after him until he disappeared around the turn of the stairs, and then they decided to follow at a trot. After a few anxious moments, the noise of their clattering footsteps came to an abrupt halt, and a dim flash of blue high up the stair announced the end of the game. The others waited quietly for the results, and two of the sentries eventually returned to the foot of the steps.

"Let's go," one said. "The next duty shift begins in half an hour. They'll know what's up even sooner than that."

"This armor *stinks*," the other remarked, squirming.

A throbbing sound of engines cut him off, and everyone looked back towards the crowds on the terraces. All at once, the mighty airships began drifting away from port, leaving herds of disappointed stragglers standing on their empty quays. The noise of more distant engines brought Nunna's attention away farther south, where a lone and blessedly inconspicuous craft was taking off far away from all the rest. Dawn sparkled bright and pink upon its hull as it made for open skies.

"That would be Orlim's expedition," the seer said.

Nunna's brow knotted with concern. "Do you think they'll get away safely?" she asked. "I mean, if we can see them, surely they'll be spotted by someone else?"

"Perhaps," Lothar answered. "It's impossible to say, and we'll never know for sure unless they send a transmission. And the place they are headed is far from safe, too."

"This plan of Orlim's sounds less plausible in the light of day," Nunna remarked.

Lothar nodded. "All plans sound like folly, but sometimes they also work. Come, let us leave this place so that our part in this plan may end. Gilat awaits."

Just past the turn in the steps they passed two crumpled forms laying still. Smoke drifted up through the joints of their armored suits.

"I thought I asked for no bloodshed," Lothar said.

"They're not dead," Mudge said, nudging one with his toe. "Just a little crispy. How are we doing up top?"

One of the two remaining sentries nodded. "Galloglass is prepped for travel. We had a little trouble with the crew, but all is proceeding according to plan."

"Impersonating members of the soldiers' guild and stealing the councilor's ship," the other said, removing his helmet, "and I'll never get the stink of this fellow's gear out of my nose!"

He turned towards Mudge and grinned. He was very clean and handsome, a young man with fine blond hair.

"No news of the councilor, I take it?" Mudge asked.

"That was your detail, Wade," said Daedalus, who stood a little farther up the steps waiting for them.

The youth shrugged, and his smile faded. "I found out nothing of his whereabouts from the crew. The drug worked too fast. For all we know, he could be coming up behind us now with all his retinue."

"Someone will need a few more lessons in interrogation," Mudge mumbled.

"Say, is that really the empress?" Wade wondered, staring at the cloaked shadow stooping behind the Dragon Slayers.

Daedalus turned abruptly and continued up the long flight of steps. Disappointed but not easily discouraged, Wade walked close behind him, and the others followed.

At the top they entered a long hall that reminded Nunna of a submarine bay. It was dark, and a smell of fuel hung heavily in the air. Though all was constructed of ancient stonework there were also signs of electrically powered equipment. They hadn't gone far along the pitch-black road when they passed a few low buildings on the right, and ordered rows of motorized carriages on the left.

Daedalus walked in front with his two disguised crewmen. They were as sure-footed and carefree as if they were at home, chatting freely in whispering voices. The one who kept his helmet on was named Adi. He was of the same age as Wade, and both were obviously interested in the empress. Mudge chided them as though he was their father, though both boys were taller than him. The captain didn't join in their conversation, and Nunna didn't need to touch his mind to understand that this was his temperament.

She turned to Lothar, and in a low voice she said, "Daedalus is a quiet one, is he?"

The Dragon Slayer snorted. "He's chattier than I've ever seen him, actually. I suppose the circumstances must've loosened his tongue a bit."

"He hasn't spoken a word to me."

"Try not to be disappointed. Though he commands fierce loyalty, he's actually rather shy. Among his crew he's known as *The Poet*."

"The Poet?"

"It's the way he talks and carries himself, like he's one of the ancient poets. He wasn't always like that, though. He got tangled up in Black Market business, but escaped into the Wastes, taking the Fifty-Kells with him. The man he stole the Kells from was named Eterskel, Lord of House Teg."

"The rich guy in Tara Colony?"

"Yes, and Eterskel used his dramatic exit to evade the council's inquisitors, making Daedalus the scapegoat for all sorts of underhanded business. Holding onto their fortune allowed House Teg to support a priest of their own choosing for the position of High Councilor. Eterskel chose to back a priest of the colony town of Nara who owed him some favors."

"Teomaxos, I'm guessing."

"Yes."

"And do you trust him, our *Poet*?"

Daedalus stopped. They had reached the foot of a large gangplank. Though there was no light to see what ship was moored nearby or where the edge of the dock might lay, the captain, no more than a shadow in front of them, confidently stepped out into the abyss. He stopped a little way ahead and whistled sharply. There was an answering whistle from higher up, and a sudden burst of light from far away. When their eyes adjusted, all stood and wondered in amaze, for the sights before them were grand by any measure.

A great pair of doors in the mountainside rolled open noiselessly, revealing a massive shape hovering in the air. With the glow of morning washing over its pale hull, Nunna set eyes on the metallic girders that caged an oblong airship, *Galloglass.*

She was a zeppelin with all her framework on the outside. Nunna was awed. She had seen even heavier airships flying over the city, and battleships clad in metallic hull plates, but it never ceased to amaze her. Sure, all such crafts sported huge balloons, but even these were far too small to displace enough dense air to keep something so heavy aloft. With all that extra weight aboard, there was certainly some of the precious mineral at work—*green argo.*

The people of Syrscian weren't exactly versed in physics. The repair of complex machines required assistance from certified guild mechanics, and those dabbling privately in technology were considered sorcerers. What little she'd been able to piece together was that *argo* was a cuprite metal which superconducted at high temperatures. Given a little heat by way of gas-powered thermal engines, ships bearing crystal cores of green argo floated magically like clouds, while smaller engines provided forward thrust. This was her first chance to observe such an enormous ship up close, and the sight of it hanging in the sky was breathtaking.

"Dragon-skin bladders sheathed in parchment-thin woven steel," Lothar said in an admiring voice. "I remember reading that she was originally outfitted as a transport for officers to the front lines when the Galanese stepped up combat in the forest Tryst. That didn't go over so well, so they decommissioned her, leaving her to rot in a dock for centuries until Teomaxos decided to make her his own."

"Of all the ships he could have chosen," Morla pondered, "he had to rebuild a ship that was tasked with decimating the Fourth House, and then use it as a pleasure-vessel?"

"And one marked by an ill omen," Mudge said, pointing with his hand.

Upon the ship's upright tail stabilizers was painted the emblem of the council priests—the eye of Horus. Nunna shivered, for she'd seen that eye in other contexts. Passing her own gaze along the sleek exterior of the craft, she noticed that the central bridge deck was small, but in the aft it accessed a bucket-lift on a pulley that climbed the round girder over the airship's bladder to a larger promenade higher up. Situated before the mighty upper tailfin, this upper deck was spacious and elegant, a place for lavish parties held by the councilors to impress their esteemed guests.

Teomaxos would never have predicted it would now grace the empress as she raced to challenge him in Gilat.

"We need to hurry," Daedalus said, going up ahead of them. "Take care the empress keeps her feet on the gangplank. I don't know how many more that net will hold."

The railed gangplank crossed a short span at the edge of the dock before taking a switchback route up to the deck fifty feet above. The dizzying drop before them fell to a net suspended about a hundred feet below before disappearing into darkness. In the net, the still forms of about a dozen men could be seen. Some were trussed and tied, wriggling furiously, and others were sleeping off a drug. Lifting her eyes from this sight, Morla was rooted to the spot where she stood; but not from fear. She seemed uncertain of something, and looked back inquiringly at Nunna as if to confirm her suspicions. Mudge observed for a few more moments before darting past them along the gangplank with the other crewmen close behind.

"I do not think Orlim would approve of this plan," Lothar said. "I don't know if *I* approve of it."

"Yet it may succeed in accomplishing what we set out to do," Val replied quietly.

Encouraged by her determination, Nunna set out behind the crew. The others soon followed, albeit more cautiously. By time they attained the lower deck of the airship the great doors in the side of the mountain had opened fully, and the air was pulling them forwards. The anchor-lines weren't able to be untied from below, for none would remain behind; but Mudge and his accomplices on the deck were cutting through them with knives. Besides the three men accompanying Daedalus, Nunna counted an additional three in the wheelhouse. They were pointing and staring in her direction. She watched them with an uneasy feeling as the captain approached.

Bowing one more time to the empress, he said, "I leave you royal ladies to explore the ship's amenities on your own. The lift on the rearward girder will take you to the upper deck, and from there another lift descends to a private bedchamber with a bath. I will leave it to the empress to decide where she would like to stay for the next week."

"A week?" Nunna wondered.

"That is the duration of our flight. Galloglass is a very fast ship, indeed."

"What store of food and water have we?" Lothar asked.

"I'll send Mudge to scrounge up whatever may be stowed in the councilor's rooms and stores," he answered. "We shall respect the orders of the empress while traveling in her company, and there shall be no talk of rewards or payment. We are humbly at your service."

"Unless she wants to tip, in which case it's fine by me," Mudge said as he trudged past them towards the wheelhouse.

Then, speaking to Daedalus for the first time, Val said, "If we survive this, I will see personally to this business with Eterskel, for he is an evil man."

Daedalus seemed shocked by her words, and a weight seemed to lift from him. He straightened and regarded her small hooded figure curiously.

"Not used to someone seeing the world the way you see it, Daedalus?" Lothar asked.

"Now, then," Daedalus said, completely flustered. "If all is settled, you must excuse me while I attend to our safe conduct."

He turned quickly away and joined his men in the pilot's cabin.

"Our new friends," Morla said. "They leave me with more questions than answers."

"You and me both, Seer," Lothar replied, "and I know them well. Still, you should have seen the rest of his crew. They are an interesting bunch."

While the others clung to the rails and waited to see the outcome of their reckless plan, Nunna realized that no one else had seen what she had glimpsed when Daedalus left them. Perhaps it was enhanced by her gift, but she was certain that when the captain turned away he was filled with feelings of a joy so intense that it had filled his eyes with tears. She knew it because she had allowed herself to peer through those eyes just once. The world they saw was not very different from her own.

Morning cast its glow over the red rocky desert beyond Kethern as Galloglass emerged from the mighty gate-towers of its private dockyard. The sun was rising above the eastern rim of the city, and all Kethern was lit up like a glorious mirror. An island embraced by waters in the midst of the Wastes, Gilthaloneth's tiered hill shone, and the winged High Place upon its summit was like pearl and silver, lit from both above and below, glowing pink against the blue. The sound of trumpets drifted to them lazily on the air.

Fireworks and flares went off all across the lower quays, and boats set out upon the water, a celebration of sorts announcing the departure of the councilor and his retinue. Only one small ship flying a black flag remained behind in the port. Nunna grinned, wondering what Teomaxos would do when he looked up then to see his transport leaving without him among a great cloud of airships. Just as long as his eyes didn't mark the distant speck on the southern horizon, it didn't matter much what he thought.

The feel of the crowds was fading, and they were away from the watchful eyes of Daedalus' crew. Nunna was at peace once again. With a thrilling sensation she suddenly realized that this was the first time she had felt the open air in many years.

Morla and Val stood beside her, their eyes on the small shape drifting away south. No one knew for certain what the trackers would discover, or if there would be a battle in the Wastes when they caught up to the councilor's people. Their own journey to Nara Colony was but a distraction to afford those brave warriors a chance; and even if they succeeded there was still going to be a war of Dark Towers when the fragments of the Stone of Foundation were revealed.

27

LOST DREAM

Yuuto City of Yumu Remi, Syrscian,
Year 999 of the New Council

There was a question Foxglove had pondered many times since
they'd set out from the stronghold of Uruk on their five-day journey
to the Karn. By the time they finally made camp by the river, she
had concluded that Bec really wasn't going to give her a chance to
take vengeance on the man whose soldiers had destroyed Ulumeneth.

It was a hope suspended, though not totally deferred. Thus unanswerable, her question persisted.

Was it time to take matters into her own hands?

She would have to wait for the right time, of course. The Galanese threat had risen sharply while they were camped by the Karn, and this had left her two days to fantasize numerous scenarios. What if a patrol found them? What if she accidentally killed Master Gilgamesh in the confusion of battle? Would anyone have cared much if she did?

But there was no attack while they bivouacked on the border of Galaneth. Foxglove was truly surprised by how serene the margins of Tryst abided. The place where they camped was a gaping wound of raw earth surrounded by burned jungle, the traces of an awful battle. A hundred or so Marduka had gathered there, preparing for their perilous raid on Nara Colony, and all the while no one had spotted a sign of anything strange in the forest. Foxglove was disappointed, and even bored. Perhaps Bec's presence had kept all the weird beings of Tryst at bay. She spent her time imagining ways to accidentally kill the object of her enduring scorn, which pursuit was interrupted at whiles by a meandering stroll by the banks of the Karn, which flowed out from the forest into the Wastes, bringing with it tales of magical places deep in the woods unvisited since the days of the Destroying Fire.

Upon Karn's grassy banks they had parted ways with Siru and Nin. The Lady of the Marduka supplied them there with letters and a stone seal, as promised. They were then directed to report to the Yuuto elders at Yumu Remi, who would assist them in whatever ways they could. Bec and Bregon received the seal with solemn words, but Foxglove wondered what good these tokens might serve when they encountered the balance of Siru's tribe.

The journey to Yuuto-lands lasted an additional seven days. The weather was hot and dry the whole time, with a stiff wind blowing up from the desert in the east. They made their way along the entire eastern edge of the forest Tryst over open ground, and though Foxglove knew that this was the easiest part of their expedition she was ill at ease. The closer they came to the northern hills, the farther she was from home; and beyond lay the fabled desert *Daeradon*, a name of horror from ancient legends. This was the country bordering Kutha in the north where the Destroyer dwelt in a city called Ost-Thargul, or so stories told.

Even Master Gilgamesh had grown increasingly anxious. Foxglove wondered if he was having second thoughts about continuing north, and so she kept an eye on him late into the night, sleeping only lightly, hoping for a chance to catch him sneaking off to alert a patrol. But the Marduka had said that Galanese patrols rarely ventured so far north of the Karn, being stretched as thin as they were. Being overwhelmed in the south for so many years, the council had as yet made no concerted effort to strike out at Yumu Remi or the Yuuto lands. Given that, the three of them would more than likely run into a patrol of Yuuto warriors instead. If Siru was any indication of the temperament of his kin, Foxglove doubted they'd find a patrol in so harmonious a mood as to blithely listen to a human's pleas for mercy—whether or not he carried documents verifying his virtues to the cause of the Fourth House. It wasn't long before they got to test this out, actually.

Only a day's march from Yumu Remi they were discovered by a host of Yuuto warriors. Their commander was a powerful white-winged fellow named Rubun. Just as Foxglove had anticipated, the commander was like in mind to Siru, and the proofs of Nin's approval were scorned outright.

They had been traveling a fortnight to get here, and in all that time Foxglove wondered if the Yuuto wouldn't simply lock the three of them up as spies. Maybe she would have yet another chance to answer endless questions justifying her collaboration with the enemy.

She did not like the thought of that at all.

Things would have gone poorly for them had Bec not been there, for just as it was with the Marduka, the Yuuto were awed by the sight of her. The semblance of the Moriko that surrounded the blue-haired girl with a visible aura was more astonishing a sight, apparently, than the seal of House Marduka in her hands. How many times over would Bregon owe his life to them?

Thus they were chaperoned as before, when Barashkushu met them in the high hills of northern Ceregor. How strange it was, Foxglove thought, that the scattered people of the Fourth House should be reunited under such circumstances. Too bad there was no easy path underfoot that could guide them safely from here, just an unpaved track in the wilderness.

It was a road to war, paved with many meetings.

"Yumu meant *storm* in the old words," Bec said to her while they walked. "Remi was *tears*, which sounds much like romi, the Yuuto word for *mankind*. Thus, the winged folk hold, mankind brings storms of tears to the Fourth House, and so they must be stopped at all costs. This city is culturally emblematic of this endeavor."

"Considering this, bringing *him* here seems less than wise," Foxglove snapped, jerked her thumb towards Master Gilgamesh.

"He is different from the ones who destroyed your home," Bec soothed. "You have spent years tracking him. Surely, in all that time, you must have sensed something of his quality?"

Foxglove answered by scrunching her face and twisting her lips to expose a defiant fang, just for measure. Inwardly she told herself there was no good quality in this man. He was as evil as every other man, and that was that.

"Well, at least you will be able to rest in comfortable lodgings and eat a good meal tonight," Bec said, assuaging her by speaking directly to Foxglove's fancies.

This comment derailed her line of thinking entirely, and far too easily. The more Foxglove considered it, though, the grander were her cravings. How long had it been since she'd eaten a good meal? The notion of such pleasantries had long been eclipsed by the thirst for revenge. Taking a new look around at the countryside surrounding them, she espied a land of meres and windswept hills wandering in grass. Surely they kept herds and flocks?

Might there also be sausages?

Daydreams about all of her favorite things to eat were suddenly interrupted by a glimpse of Yumu Remi itself—and of something else. There were other travelers on this road, and when she caught sight of them Bec called the entire troop to halt and advanced alone. The warriors hefted their spears, but the Fomorian seemed in no way concerned.

Was she humming?

A rather curious pair the strangers were, an elderly yellow-clad Yuuto guiding a human dressed in foreign-looking gear. Ignoring the frowns of the warriors standing behind her, Bec greeted the newcomers with a broad smile—a look both beautiful and terrible to behold, so that all who glimpsed it wondered at her in amaze.

"I see I chose well when I chose you for Aries," she hailed as the two strangers approached. "You've proven yourself quite capable to make it this far, Seijung Ford."

The two groups converged slowly, the Yuuto mumbling to one another the while and speaking the name *Gwilym* in mocking tones. That was probably the name of the old Yuuto in the yellow shirt. Foxglove was more curious about the human stranger, Ford. He looked Galanese, but as soon as she got close enough to smell him she realized that he was something else entirely. After returning her inquisitive gaze with one of his own, the outlander squinted at Bec and bobbed his head.

"Shrub Girl," he greeted.

"You don't look surprised at all to see me."

"Why should I look surprised?" he answered. "First this, then that, and now you turn up with—"

He glanced once more at Foxglove with an exasperated expression.

"—I don't even know what she's supposed to be."

"She is a princess of the Ayumu," Bec said, touching Foxglove's shoulder before gesturing towards Bregon. "And this is a hero out of the southern wilds. Gilgamesh, he is called."

Ford began counting off with his fingers as he turned to meet many pairs of curious eyes. "Hawkmen, Princess Kitty, dude with a Babylonian name, and a strange Fomorian lady I found packed in a coffin deep beneath the ocean. This is quite the group we've got here, isn't it?"

He must have noticed the expression of wonderment softening the chiseled features of his Yuuto guide, for he grew suddenly silent. Some of the warriors conferred in hushed voices, thumbs pressed to foreheads, while the rest glared at him.

"Who dares speak thus to the Yuuto?"

Ford sized up the gruff tall-helmed one who had addressed him.

"Prince Vultan, I presume?"

The warrior tamped his spear in the ground and ruffled his white wings.

"No, huh?"

"I am Rubun. I lead these fighters. Who is Vultan?"

"Uh—"

Ford's smirk vanished, and he glanced towards Bec for support. Foxglove marveled at his arrogant manner. Though he was obviously unsuited for fighting, he seemed completely unaware that his taunts were edging him closer and closer to the brink of death. He acted as badly as a Galanese nobleman, or like one of the sorcerers of the Wastes who were confident in powers unseen.

Out here, a noble's purse and a sorcerer's technology were worth very little.

Rubun pulled his people aside for a few moments to discuss privately how they would proceed. This gave Foxglove a chance to espy the distant village. Situated a few leagues away from the gloomy borders of Tryst, Yumu Remi rose above the grasslands on a terraced mound that was girdled round by concentric rings of stone walls and crowned by a forest of tall pines. Glittering in the sunlight upon the forested summit, a magnificent tower ascended. Majestic and strong, it was the tallest building Foxglove had ever seen, taller even than the tallest trees of Tarthalion. Even at a distance she could make out details of cunning craftsmanship. There were bastions on all sides rising to carven spires, and upon the lofty dais atop the tower she saw what must be mirrors, mirrors reflecting a light so intense that it hurt her eyes to gaze upon it. Looking back towards the forest at the tower's base, she saw there a curious collection of more mundane structures, all built from the same pink stone. Seen from such a distance, even these lesser constructions seemed impossibly huge and terrible, the work of giants' hands. She wondered if the tower on the hill was only a vision that swam in the air before her eyes, but the presence of the Yuuto warriors nearby reminded her how silly that notion was. Counted no less than the Marduka in battle, their legendary abilities had deterred even the mechanized armies of the council. Rumor of their presence was all the defense this tower of theirs needed.

Rubun's spear, long and stout with a curving blade, silenced her thoughts and all the muttering of his companions with a hard tap upon the ground.

"You will accompany us to the elders." he announced to the travelers. "It is for them to decide the case of trespassers in our lands. As for our esteemed guest, she will accompany us as she likes, and refreshment will be provided at her asking."

Foxglove was disappointed not to be included with Bec as a guest, and she wasn't the only one. Ford's guide raised his voice in protest.

"These people aren't trespassers, Rubun."

"Gwilym, be silent!"

"The Fomorian vouches for them. Is that not enough?"

Rubun frowned. Foxglove thought his expression was a little forced, almost comically so. Whether or not he was just putting on a show or being sarcastic was difficult to determine, but it seemed Bec had already made up her mind about that.

"I have already shown you the seal of the Marduka, as well as the papers," she said. "You have exemplified the role of a war-leader in a time of distress. Sirona would be proud. You have done well in her absence, Rubun."

Rubun shook his head and waved off the chuckling of his warriors.

"However," Bec added, "it should be said that amity between allies has waned of late, so much so that I feel my patience has been tested too far. We will go together freely to Yumu Remi, and there we will speak to your village elders about our quest. You will comply with our simple requests out of kindness, and any further show of force will be treated as villainy. Am I understood?"

The atmosphere shifted instantly. Fearful scowls passed over the warriors' faces. Rubun himself appeared impassive.

"Are you threatening us?" he asked. "Even if you are one of the Moriko, you have no right to force yourself upon us in this way. We will deal with the strangers as we see fit."

Old Gwilym fell to his knees suddenly, and lifting his hands towards Bec he implored her with a broken voice, crying, "Please do not destroy our lands because of a fool's wayward tongue! These brutes haven't seen the dark worlds! The power of the Moriko is nothing more than fantasy to them!"

His outburst seemed to lighten the mood. Though a few warriors were still pressing thumbs to their foreheads, the rest were smiling again.

"Crazy old man," Rubun lamented, "why do you trouble us with your shameful whining?"

"He is one of the Wardens," Bec said as she examined the hunched figure kneeling on the road. "Though you cannot see it, the Wardens bear a mark invisible to other mortals. It is this mark which permits them passage to the dark worlds—to travel against the Ban in order to collect truants and keep the peace. It is a blessing bestowed upon them by the Ancients."

"Well might you speak of invisible marks that only you can see," Rubun replied hotly. "What I see is a group of hungry vagabonds on the road in a time of strife. Spies, no doubt. Other than your threats, what reasons have I to welcome this company into Yumu Remi as guests?"

"Bringing them into the village as captives will decide their case before it is even heard," Gwilym contested, stumbling to his feet. "No one accuses you of doing wrong, Rubun, but you've placed yourself in a precarious position by arresting strangers before granting them a fair hearing—and one of them a Fomorian! She could call the forest to tear these hills to splinters if she wished!"

A gust of wind blew down from the north then, giving pause to their conversation. All eyes were fixed on Bec.

"Courtesy, if nothing else, requires me to be sparing in that regard," she said. Then, speaking in the Ancient tongue she added, "*Eyma beyli ishparanni, allak.* Wherever my master sends me, there will I go. The plan was not for me to be a destroyer. Syrscian already has one of those, as I recall. *Anumma beyli-Yumu Remi shullim rakbam ashtaprassum.* Herewith I send unto my lord of Yumu Remi a declaration of well-being. We come with peaceful intentions. Is there not one among you who would go and announce our arrival, or must I first provide proofs of my authority?"

Her fluid use of the Ancient tongue was like dropping a rock into a still pool. All of Rubun's men lowered their eyes in submission. The commander, too, seemed suddenly demure. At least, the hostility had gone out of his voice when he made his courteous reply.

"*Lu…shalmata,*" he muttered, stumbling over what few words he knew in the Ancient tongue. "May you be at ease. It was not my desire to bring disaster upon us. It's just—you'll find few these days who have respect for those of the Old World. They blame those who left us, and those who hide themselves from us, for all that has come to pass. Much ill has befallen us of late."

He nodded to one of the younger warriors, who immediately turned and ran on ahead to bring news to the city.

"I only hope our elders have more sense than our fighters in the matter of deciding the fate of guests," Gwilym said reproachfully.

"Mushtalum," Bec replied. "The prudent one you are, Gwilym. However, there may be cause yet for Rubun's wariness. Though Yumu Remi has long been ignored by the council's armies, I fear war looms now on the very threshold of Yuuto lands. This business with Sirona's rescue will not fare well."

Rubun seemed more riled by her final words than he was by her threats, but he held his tongue. With a smirk on his face he turned and led the travelers on to the city without further redress.

The terraced construction of Yumu Remi became more pronounced as they drew nearer. It was not at all like an Ayumu village, Foxglove decided. She gazed upon its wonders while listening in on her companions' talk. They had much to talk about, it seemed, but she understood very little of it.

"I came upon this here fellow by the edge of the forest, where the Garden was planted long ago," Gwilym said, continuing a conversation he had begun with Bec. "There was an Illuyanga; but all's well. Gwilym was there to help. You know, our man Ford, he's from New York. I have been to that place, in the world Ertsetum, many a time."

"Actually," Ford said, "I could imagine you fitting right in there, sleeping under some newspapers in the park."

"There was a park, as I recall," Gwilym replied. "And there were many horses, if you can believe it."

While they conversed, the warriors were also listening in. Though none of them spoke a word, Foxglove could sense their disbelief. After all, the Crodah were no less legendary than Fomorians—or horses.

"I am an exile myself," Bec said.

"Then it is as I suspected," Gwilym replied. "The time has come for the Ban to be broken. My father thought it might be soon, but he was better at reading the signs. When he became ill and died, Sirona appointed me to take his place. I wish I'd had time to learn more from him about the crossing-places, like Cnoc Ddraig, and about Islith."

"You've been to Islith?" Bec asked, sharing a glance with Master Gilgamesh.

"Aye, a few times. Most folks these days believe it never existed, though they remain superstitious about the crossing-places. Crossings are easy to find, usually high up on hills or in really creepy corners of the wood; but Islith's another beast altogether. I'm not sure, but I'd swear it *moves*."

"You can find it?"

"Ah. A tricky business, that—but you'd already know, I'm sure. My father taught me how, but I've only managed it once on my own. Why do you ask?"

His eyes seemed nervous. Bec's answer probably did not set his mind at ease.

"Islith will rise again, and when it does I must be there, for I am Avalon."

She said this with solemn gravity, and those standing nearby felt the proximity of a great Power. Foxglove's memory sparkled with half-remembered tales of the floating fortress of Avalon, which once defended the mythical Gremn hive at Islith.

Gwilym was trembling.

"Why would the Fomorian drone of Avalon need Old Gwilym to help her find Islith?" he asked.

"I was set free. The Gremn hid from me its location until such time as they recaptured me, and that never came to pass."

"And we may be thankful for it," Bregon added aside. "Else, the war would have turned out very differently."

Gwilym glanced at him, and at Foxglove, too. "Your companions aren't out of an exiled world?" he wondered.

"They are not. If they were, there would have been a clear sign accompanying their arrival."

"Ah, like the dragon."

Ford lifted his eyes to the horizon and began rubbing his arm.

"Come to think of it," Gwilym continued, "Illuyanga aren't common outside the high mountain passes. I was following the dragon-sign until I came to the Garden, and that's where I saw this Crodah boy, running for his life."

"Crazy thing slashed me," Ford said.

"He was scratched," Gwilym explained, "but he's obviously been in contact with the Ancient technologies. There was no permanent injury."

Ford poked the side of his head with an index finger and winked at Bec.

"It was the black water," she confirmed. "He is now linked to the Source, and the data transfer is complete. As the Primary User, he will see many things. For instance, he knew that I was here."

"Really?" Ford wondered.

"Then you were truly surprised to find me?"

Ford mused quietly for a second. "The last time I saw you," he said, "we were about to be vaporized in a nuclear explosion, and you were spouting nonsense. A lot's happened since then. I met this crazy girl, and—"

"Relax," Bec chided. "As soon as we were linked, Aries told me all about it. She's really quite fond of you!"

She grinned in response to his questioning look, but Ford had no chance to say more. They had reached the outermost wall, a chest-high enclosure constructed of pale limestone ashlars. There wasn't any mortar joining the hewn stone blocks, and only a handful of guards stood by the simple gate. It seemed more cattle-fence than fortification, enclosing only the lowest terrace of the village.

"Who is in charge here?" Bec asked.

Rubun leaned on his spear, offering nothing. The guards at the gate looked at one another and at the blue-haired girl, but no one answered.

"The elders would not come, not even for a Fomorian returned from exile?" Gwilym asked.

"Runners were sent, old man," one of the gate guards said. He was a lofty one, taller and better-looking than Rubun. The way he spoke while looking down his nose at Bec said more about his quality than he was evidently aware.

Foxglove supposed showing them Nin's seal would have been a waste of time at this point. Bec, however, got a response from the guard with a few simple words.

"Paqiid Biit Remi?" she asked of the gate guard. "Are you the caretaker of House Remi?"

The way she spoke the Name *Remi* was inflected to make it sound like the common word for *tears* or *sorrow*.

"No, I am not," he replied, looking suddenly sheepish. "The elders said to go on up. They will call upon you when they are ready. In the meantime you will be given a house."

"My quest is to Islith, in the heart of the forest Tryst."

After scrutinizing the strangers once more for good measure, the second guard ducked his head and made his way along the inclined road at a jog. Upon reaching the embankment of the terrace he leapt into the air, thrusting out his wingtips. It wasn't quite flying, but he made it to the top of the wall as easily as if he had just stepped over a fallen log.

Foxglove stared after him, amazed. From the top of the inner wall he vaulted again, darting like an arrow in mighty bounds from rooftop to tower to sheer face of wall, fast and free. In seconds he was no more than a small speck in the distance.

No wonder they had gotten word back from the elders so quickly.

"Go on," the guard said, gesturing towards Bec. "Go ahead to the highest place. There you will find attendants who can show you the house. The elders will doubtless come to meet you on your way— since you seem to be in haste to leave us, again."

Bec looked at him aside. She seemed troubled.

"You are not a wicked man, Tolos," she said, using his name.

The guard looked upon her in stunned silence. No one had told her his name.

"Do not be discouraged that the old world wears a different form and face than you thought it would when you were small."

"I am a warrior," Tolos replied. "Rubun is a warrior. We are all warriors now. What are tales of the Old World to people who must kill in order to live?"

"Or to one like Siru?" Bec added. "But you are different from all of them. So was the younger one, the one who went ahead of us just now. Do not chide him for his hopes. The rumors you have heard are true. The empress lives, and has returned to Gilthaloneth. Though war is coming as of old, this war will not be fought among the houses, nobles, clans, and tribes. When I say that the Old Days are coming back, I do not mean the wars, but that which lies at the end of all war."

No one spoke for a long time. Foxglove couldn't read the mood of the Yuuto. Either they simply didn't understand that this was an occasion for celebration, or they were plotting something entirely unrelated. Foxglove wondered what it might be.

Rubun eventually turned away from the gate with a smirking grin on his face, and left to lead his fighters back into the plains.

The travelers went on alone, passing through a series of unguarded gates that connected each terrace by a flight of steps. The meandering way to the uppermost terrace was hard going, and Foxglove was getting hungry. Being hungry made her think. Mostly she was pondering the warriors' strange brooding silence.

The arrogant stranger, Ford, put her exact thoughts into words.

"That Rubun guy didn't seem pleased to hear about your Empress coming back," he said. "My guess is, he's got something nasty planned for these exiles."

Though he had spoken to Bec, the Fomorian said nothing in reply. Gwilym answered for her.

"It's as you've heard," the old Yuuto said. "There's nothing linking our people to the exiles save for the war that destroyed all Syrscian. As for Rubun, that lad has other issues than this on his mind. He grew up in the shadow of the tribe's royal family, and his father served the old king until Esagil fell. Rubun was always one step behind Siru in everything. Staying behind to guard Yumu Remi while Siru goes out to rescue his sister must be tough, for these fighters are all possessed of a fierce pride. About the only thing they'd agree upon is a healthy suspicion of the Moriko, of the old prophecies, and especially of the empress."

Foxglove hadn't thought of it before, but there were clearly two factions forming within the Fourth House; and wherever the lord of House Gaerith went, the fractures between them began to widen. As for herself, she could only wish the empress really had returned to end all the corruption and evil surging from Gilthaloneth. True justice seemed a tangible thing on the horizon. Surely the empress would hear the cries of the downtrodden and heal their hurts, just as the legends foretold?

She was wondering what the Fomorian would say to all this when they were met suddenly by a choir of Yuuto children singing traditional songs known to all the tribes of the Fourth House. Behind them came a group of five rather dowdy-looking Yuuto whose wings were drooping with age and bared by molt. Bec's summons, it seems, had finally gotten the elders up off their couches.

"Am I in heaven?" Ford asked, blinking.

It was a very different reception than the one the warriors offered. Foxglove was deeply moved by the sight, for there were few enough children in Tarthalion among the Ayumu. Their little wings were almost exclusively pearl-colored and rather fluffy, as their long pin-feathers hadn't grown in yet.

Her joy was dimmed, however, by the sight of Bregon laughing and walking while Yuuto children clung to his strong arms, filling his hands with flowers. Hatred for him still smoldered in her heart, stealing from her the joy of the occasion.

As the elders led them silently into the streets, they saw faces in the windows of the houses. Some who were bolder came and stood at the entryways of their homes to stare. Though the mood was relaxed, not everyone was glad to see this procession.

"They are not all like Rubun," Bec said to Foxglove while they walked. "Don't worry. We are safe here."

"I wasn't worried."

The Fomorian grinned.

"Well, maybe I was just a little," Foxglove confessed. "Mostly because of the trouble that man is causing. It seems that everywhere he goes he brings division to our people."

"If that were so, wouldn't it make him the king that was promised?"

"A lost dream, that is. We need no king, now that we have the empress."

"But there was a promised king, one who would unite the four tribes under the empress," Bec said, nodding towards Bregon. "I ask you, daughter of the Ayumu, do you see any hate in Master Gilgamesh?"

In her heart she still held him responsible for murder; but Bec did have a point.

"He shows no hatred, but he sows strife."

"That is because he forces them to choose," Bec replied. "They must choose for themselves to follow the path that was established long ago, or to abandon it. They must either take up the promise of the Ancients and embrace their Empress, or oppose her and those who represent her established rule in Syrscian. There is no longer any middle ground, now that the exiles have begun to return."

Feeling a soft hand in hers, Foxglove looked down and discovered a flock of winged children gathering around them. They touched her tail gently, with open palms, and in their eyes she saw a reflection of the amazement she also felt. Ford wasn't spared this treatment, and his reaction was amusing to watch. This was their first glimpse of an Ayumu, a Crodah, or a Moriko, and they were measuring the visitors against words spoken in old stories.

"The children still believe," Bec said softly, "and their simple faith is of more value to them than all the armies the Galanese can hurl against this place. Those who choose to believe need only someone to unite them, and he will be the one who brought them to the choice."

It was later that evening, after they were given lodging in a large house and had washed the soil of the road from their clothes and limbs, that Bec, Gwilym, and the man named Ford left to speak with the elders inside the mighty tower upon the summit of the hill. As for Bregon and herself, they were apparently lesser lights in the firmament, probably because Master Gilgamesh wasn't suspected of being anything more than a Musab adventurer. And she, she was just an Ayumu princess.

They were left alone in the house as the nighttime shadows lengthened. Foxglove knew that any attempt on the fool's life would end badly for her, and as yet she didn't have a clue how to kill a Gaerith machine-lord. It was a frustrating business, but there were diversions aplenty here to fill the hours of waiting.

First, a change of clothing had been left out for her in a private room. Foxglove had not always worn the costume of a wood-wose, a wild beast of the water-born. She had once donned splendid dresses made by her mother and her sisters. What she put on here was simpler but of excellent make: a matching pair of pearl-colored trousers and a shirt, both woven of very durable fibers and embroidered with gold thread. Whoever had placed them here on short notice had judged her figure with a good eye, for with a belt they fit remarkably well. Her old leather skirt and rags she rolled and placed in a small bag—a journey-sack, which she knew would be riding her shoulders on the long road south and west into Tryst.

Next she explored the house. It was a large place, but mostly empty, standing alone against the wall encircling the uppermost terrace of the village. The wall, like the furnishings of the house, was richly decorated with sculpted reliefs that depicted scenes of the histories of the Fourth House. Out back there was a little open veranda built right on top of the wall, and there Foxglove found a pool lined with benches. The ground was paved with large sheets of polished marble inset with colored stone tesserae that gleamed in the reflected light of the tower looming above. Unrivaled by anything in the rustic city of Timhureth, this was like a palace, a place more suited to the tastes of humans, adorned with noble splendor.

While a young Yuuto boy went through the house lighting sconces, Bregon strolled out onto the veranda through an arched gate. Foxglove watched him, and she deemed it was possible now to put him out of mind for a little while. Though for two years she had dogged his every footstep over the pitiless Rim Mountains, she now longed for some space to be alone. Sighing over the noise of her empty belly, she wandered to the front of the house and met a warrior standing upon the front step. His arms were crossed in front of his chest.

"You are to remain here until the elders return."

"Can I not go out and find something to eat?" she asked, staring up into his narrow face.

"Food shall be prepared and brought to you soon, small cousin."

"*Small cousin?* What is it with Yuuto and Marduka? Do you not know that Ayumu also grow to great height and ferocity?"

"Please be patient, little one. You are a guest here."

The idea of waiting for food was foreign to Foxglove. In the wilds she could eat whenever she was hungry.

"Surely there is someplace nearby where I can get something?"

"What business have you with the Yuuto?" he asked.

Foxglove blinked, for though he was blunt he was also correct. Her tribe had no established line of credit outside Tarthalion. She had nothing she could offer in exchange for food, let alone lodging.

"Can I beg, then? I won't stray far."

"A princess should not beg."

So, he knew that she was a princess. Who was it told him, she wondered? It was doubtful that the Yuuto would recognize the markings around her eyes. It must have been Bec, then.

Beyond the front step, a small crowd of curious onlookers was watching. They had been quietly gathering for some time, hoping perhaps for a glimpse of the travelers; and the longer Foxglove spoke with the guard the closer they shuffled, making their way expectantly into the street.

"Please, give these to the Ayumu princess," said a woman, who stepped towards the house offering a basket of bread and sausages.

"And these," said another, pushing forwards with an armful of apples.

"Back up!" the guard bellowed, shaking his wings.

Though everyone else complied, one small child did not. They all made way for her as she stepped neatly up to Foxglove bearing a string to which she had trussed three fat doves, readied for roasting.

"Please, these are for you," the little girl said, holding forth her gift.

Making her way back through the house to the inner courtyard with a sausage in her mouth and a basket of food in her arms, Foxglove gleefully dandled the doves from their string, looped around her finger, and hummed through her clenched teeth a tune carried on the wind from somewhere in the lower tiers of the village.

"Birds," she thought. "How weird is that? The Yuuto have wings, yet they eat birds."

It was in these high spirits she spotted Master Gilgamesh again, leaning against the low wall in the courtyard where she'd left him, staring southwest towards the distant forest beyond the plains. Up to that moment she had completely forgotten he was there.

Taking a seat on one of the benches, she swore to herself that he wouldn't get so much as the castoffs of her groceries.

"Hmm," she muttered, biting the sausage and chewing noisily.

He said nothing. The music of flutes drifted along in the warm breeze coming up out of the south.

The sausage was nicely smoked, and the meat had a sweet flavor—it was definitely one of the giant species of *Mushi*, like Gumi beetle. Gumi lived on the eastern borders of the Rim Mountains. They weren't bad, but she favored smaller insects whose flesh was more savory. Her favorite was the Horned Dragon, a beetle which grew to only the length of a man. Mixed with forest herbs, these were a favorite of Ayumu children. The uncooked flesh of their grubs was soft and buttery, a delicacy reserved for important feasts.

Not all flesh was meant to be eaten raw, however. The birds she'd gotten were nice and plump. She would make a fire and roast them. Moving the basket beside the pool, she had a drink while fishing in a pouch for her shell knife.

"What's that?"

The knife was in her hand. She looked up and saw Bregon gazing down at her where she stooped over the pool.

"It's a knife," she said in a not-too-nice voice.

"Is that Oryx-shell?" he asked, noting the brownish color. "I know the Ayumu once hunted them, though I always wondered how. Don't swamp-dwelling juvenile Oryx grubs pack an electric shock in their muscle contractions?"

She rested the knife in her palm a moment before putting it down beside the birds.

"Forest people don't hunt the Oryx," she huffed. "That would be stupid. We only take cast-off moltings. They're sterner than metal, but the more valuable stuff comes from the adult insects, the ta-tenen of the high desert, from which the ancient swords and seals of the Great Houses were fashioned. It's better than Mushi-shell. Any child would know that."

He sat down beside her precious groceries, leaned back against the low railing behind the bench, and stared off into the distance. The shadow of the tower lengthened behind them. Foxglove scooted to the very brink of the bench, and thinking fast she removed her food beyond his grasp, placing it in the basket by her feet. Master Gilgamesh noted none of this, of course, but pretended to gaze wistfully towards the horizon. His face looked somewhat pensive, she thought, and this troubled her. What might he be thinking, sitting there haughty and free beside one who had suffered so much by his hands?

An awkward silence ensued, disturbed only by the soft sounds of distant music. Foxglove felt her cheeks reddening. It infuriated her. She perked up her ears and looked towards the wall in feigned interest, hoping he would leave her in peace so that she could eat.

"I know that tune," he said.

"What would a Galanese know of our songs?"

"It is a very old song," he answered. "And I am not Galanese."

"Humph!" she said, crossing her arms.

"If you really want to know," he said, "it is a song in the ancient *Lay of Ernil*, passed on from the old days by House Gaerith, though not from the Fourth House. I had thought it lost to history, for I am apparently all that is left of my kin. How, I wonder, did the forest people learn it? Do you know?"

Foxglove was lost in thought for a moment, having expected a less humbling answer to her question. Indeed, he had taken a tone of instruction with her, and for this he'd earned her ire; but his question also interested her. How had such an ancient song crossed the boundaries of tribes and Great Houses to become common fare in her father's hall? She flicked her tail in agitation. It wasn't fair that he knew about such things as songs and stories, which were valued so highly among the Ayumu whom he'd destroyed.

"So what? It's one of the old songs," she groused. "It doesn't even have any words."

"Oh, but it does," he replied. "The words were in the language of the Ancients, the language of the elder days. I suppose only the tune survived, though I know at least part of it was translated into the common speech. There are parts I deem were known once to those of the Fourth House living in Tarthalion."

"Like what?"

"Well, there is a part describing the adventures of a hero who faced the wild wyvern, the knucker, the lindworm, and the boha, and battled them in the deep forest for the cauldron of rebirth that he might pass into Overworld and find his lost love."

"That story is known to all my people!" she exclaimed. Then, pausing to reconsider her eagerness, she drew her mouth into a tight line.

The game birds trussed up in the basket beside her looked back into her face with accusing eyes.

"I am glad to find you both taking your leisure," Bec's low voice greeted them from the door of the house.

She stepped lightly across the veranda with Ford and Gwilym in tow. The two followed at a distance, though, looking somewhat perplexed as they approached the pool where Foxglove eyed her basket defensively. But the sudden appearance of additional hungry bellies wasn't really what irked her.

Had they been eavesdropping?

"I have briefed the elders of the Yuuto," Bec declared, "and I have also acquired the supplies we need. We will travel light and fast."

"Not too fast, if I'm coming along," Gwilym added. "I'm not as spry as I used to be."

"Me neither," Ford griped.

"So," Bregon said, "we're heading to Islith together, and I am supposed to rescue some sorceress there."

"You wanted to find out where your father has gone," Bec said. "Only she is able to discover his whereabouts. Her name is Aston."

"Hannah?" Ford wondered, looking suddenly glum. "She's got here, too, and she's a sorceress?"

"She's been here longer than you," Bec replied.

"And now she needs rescuing, and this guy's the hero or something?" he paused to look aside at Bregon. "How're you DePons' kid, anyway? You look the same age."

"It's a family secret," Bregon replied smugly. "You really think I look like him?"

"Two peas in a pod," Ford said.

"Master Gilgamesh, or Bregon of Gaerith if you wish, is actually half-Gremn," Bec explained.

Then, with an eye on Foxglove she added, "Both these races, you see, do not show signs of aging, and they cannot be killed in any ordinary way."

Foxglove bit her lip.

"And Hannah knows how to find DePons without technology?" Ford asked. "It really must be magic. That girl couldn't find a grocery store in Manhattan without my help."

"She and I arrived together, Mr. Ford, and I sent her on to Islith. In Islith there is plenty of technology. By time we meet up again she will know what to do, but first we need to find her."

"Wait," Ford interrupted. "You sent her to this place, but you don't know where it is?"

"I did not bring her to it. She had guides."

"Not some other Wardens?" Gwilym wondered.

"They were navvies," Bec answered simply.

"As in, the navvies who were counted lost when my own people vanished centuries ago?" Bregon asked. "It seems there are more than a few mysteries that our Fomorian friend has yet to explain."

The sun was setting, and a stronger breeze blew up from the forest in the south. The shrieking gust was full of voices that seemed to ask a thousand different questions. Bregon struggled to put his own query into words.

"All these things are happening because the empress returned," he said, staring up at Bec from his seat on the bench. "And the navvies, they've awakened?"

"They were never really asleep," Bec answered. "Since the war they've been wandering Tryst, keeping track of Islith's movements."

"It's true," Gwilym added. "They are there, though they seem to get shabbier with the passing cycles than I do. My father taught me how to find the navvies. Find them and you will find Islith. It's not easy, though."

"What about House Gaerith?" Bregon asked. "What about my people? Are they there also?"

Bec stepped up to him and examined his face, as if searching for the answer in his eyes.

"The Gaerith will return when they are ready," she said, "and not because of anything Cedric has done. Where they have gone to even I do not know; but Cedric knows. He will tell you when we meet again."

"If the Lord of House Gaerith seeks his father in order to restore his people, Gwilym will help him," the elderly Yuuto proposed. "After what the lady told the elders of our tribe, I will gladly brave with him the haunted Wood."

Foxglove addressed him only with an icy look.

"That adds one more to our list, Shrub Girl," Ford said. "How many more are you out to recruit, I wonder?"

"I have gathered all of you here from other worlds and other times," Bec said to him. "There are more still who have not yet arrived, whom we shall meet in the forest. Does that seem strange to you?"

"Seems a roundabout way of doing things, is all," Ford remarked. "If you had gone with your navvie guides to find this Islith place without us, you'd be there with Hannah now, right? So why do you need us?"

"Logic answers not to consequence," she answered. "If I had gone with Hannah, where would you be now?"

Ford looked like he had honestly not thought of this. It was true for each one of them, though. If the Fomorian had not come to them when she did, they would surely have found themselves in dire straights, wandering without direction.

"Many pieces must be in place before it begins. Some of you will assist me, but the others have a greater purpose."

"How do you know what will happen?" Ford asked. "You knew, right?"

"And you also will know it, when you open your heart to her and to the Link," Bec replied, smiling coyly. "Suffice it to say that I know what I must, Mr. Ford. I was integrated into Islith's frame, once upon a time. I saw what the Ancients saw in the days of the Null-Navvie Construct. When I reintegrate myself into the city's manufacturing facilities and awaken the Moriko, I will be counting on you all."

"And yet you force none of us to come with you." Bregon interjected. "That suggests we aren't as important to this grand scheme as you suggest, and I believe that's what Mr. Ford is concerned about."

The two men shared a glance.

"Our success is uncertain," Bec said. "It is uncertain as your choice, and the risks are real. Even if I know what transpires, I do not know or comprehend your choices. I may influence them, but I may not choose for you. You may stay here under protection of the Yuuto, if that is what you wish."

"Well," Bregon said, "you've already got my answer. I will seek this sorceress who knows how to find my father, and thus discover the cause of the disappearance of my people, and maybe also a means of bringing them back."

"I will dare the dangers of the forest to gaze upon Islith one last time," Gwilym offered. "You'll never find it this far north without me. Besides, there's that young man I met at the Dragon's Mound, and his—"

Bec held up her hand to cut him off, and she smiled. She turned then towards Ford.

"And what say you?" she asked.

Ford's face was grim. "I don't really know what I'm doing here," he confessed. "Everything's a bit out of my league, but if you think that maybe I can help Hannah, that'll do for me."

"You are the Primary User, Seijung Ford. I do not think Aries would be pleased with me if I simply left you by the wayside. It is for her that I must reintegrate myself into Islith's core, and then you will be her strength for a time."

"Her strength?"

"Indeed, if that is what you choose."

He nodded.

"Good," Bec said. "And that leaves us with the Lady of the Ayumu."

Caught up in her study of things less complicated, Foxglove drew back her ears and looked up from the food-basket.

"You are also a part of this," Bec said. "Will you come with us?"

Foxglove looked at Bregon, her eyes smoldering.

"Why do you need me?" she fumed. "The tribes of Tryst will not recognize the speech or customs of my people. Besides, I've done nothing so far to be of any service to you."

"That is because we have not yet done anything meriting your assistance; but this will soon change, for there is someone in the forest who holds a sacred treasure of House Ayumu, and he will only surrender it to one of your kind."

Foxglove's ears twitched.

"This treasure is an ancient artifact that will grant me access to Islith's core," Bec pressed, "and only you can get it for me. The keeper of this artifact is a little difficult to deal with, and he is not fond of the Moriko."

Her words lingered in the air a moment before Bregon spoke up.

"Even you, a Fomorian, cannot guarantee the safety of any of us in Tryst," he said. "I don't mind taking risks for my own part, but these others are going because they have discovered their own purpose in your labors. Besides the favor of a Fomorian, though, what else does she have to balance against the risk of her life? It seems unfair to test her against the horrors of the darkness in that wild land for your own benefit, does it not?"

"Well said," Bec answered. "What do you have to say, Dear One?"

Foxglove bowed her head, flopping the red strands of her hair around her face. Everyone was looking at her where she stooped upon the bench, but her mind was blank. Vengeance for her people was all she really wanted, but that was out of the question. She struggled to think of a single reason she should accompany the Fomorian into the terrible forest, and all she could come up with was what Bec had promised to her in the beginning of their journey together.

"You told me there was some kind of blessing I would receive," she replied, lifting her head. "I remember what you said about believing the old stories. Well, I believe them. I always have. Is that enough?"

Bec patted her head.

"This sets you above all the bravest heroes of the World of Origins," the Fomorian answered. "You will stand fast against terrors that larger and more formidable folk would flee from, because you have walked alone and seen the truth. Besides, don't you think it is time the Ayumu awakened from their long drowse?"

Though her words made Foxglove afraid, she felt resolved.

"You will not go alone, after all," Bec promised. "Though you have believed him to be your foe, the arms of Gilgamesh will sustain you through the dark night of Tryst; and though death follow at your heels or set traps before you, you may rest easy, for you will walk the road together."

Foxglove's iron-hard will relaxed a little then. These great people and heroes of old were relying on her to find an answer to the mysteries of her own people so that they could accomplish a mighty quest.

She would seek the thing Bec offered—a blessing for her kind. Inclining her head towards Bregon she spoke quietly but with conviction.

"Like it or not, Fool, I'm still walking with you."

Strangely, she felt less the sting of her resolution than she might have just a few weeks ago. What had changed in her, and why did it not feel like betrayal?

In the shadow of the tower, the day was worn down to a dismal red glow; yet the music of flutes in the lower city was still carrying sweetly over the wall. The tune they played assuaged some of Foxglove's misgivings, and the glow of cooking fires in the windows of the house dissolved her anger. The smell of food revived them all.

Bec then looked to each in turn, and they nodded their silent agreement.

"It is decided, then. This night is our communion. Tomorrow we set forth as companions of a quest. Eat and sleep well, for ever after the only comfort you will know is in your companions. We enter the wood at first light."

28

THEATER OF THE ABYSS

Nara Colony, Syrscian,
Year 1000 of the New Council

The lawless are a law unto themselves.

Tagging along behind the rest of the group, Nunna allowed her mind to worry over the bits and pieces of conversation she'd shared with Morla en route to Nara. Even now, the seer's thoughts struck her mind like fragments scattered by a grenade.

The colony is ruled by Governor Amed, a ruthless aggressor.

There was indeed a lot of anger here, and the stories shared by Daedalus' companions aboard Galloglass made Nara sound like a smuggler's paradise. The Black market was run from Tara, a walled town just across the water.

The guilds have all been bought by nobles, and are locked in endless cycles of violence.

Spies and assassins lurked everywhere. She shrugged the weighty blade slung against her back, and caught a glimpse of Morla pulling her veil a little closer, though it would not have hidden her identity any more than Val's winged helm and imperial regalia hid hers. The Dragon Slayers were no less conspicuous, stalking in formation like sentries as they departed the docks on the river-side of the city. While their captain walked ahead, Caradoc, Bran, and Vercingetorix kept a perimeter around the empress. Lothar had chosen these three because they were men of Nara, and were well acquainted with its secrets.

A great darkness lies in the heart of Nara, in the pit of Gilat.

No one spoke as they passed quietly through the great eastern gate. Beyond the high wall they stepped from dusty shadows into a marketplace paved with stone blocks, and there was such a noise and bustle of merchants all around that their little group was nearly pressed backwards in the tumult. Nunna halted abruptly. The pain in her eyes was unbearable.

"Again?" Morla asked quietly while the rest of the group paused.

"What's the holdup?" Lothar asked, slightly agitated.

Spectators were already thronging the way ahead, and more were excitedly pouring out of the shops every moment. Word had gone out that the empress was here, and with only a small retinue. Any delay could cost them dearly.

Morla waved him off while Nunna held a hand against her forehead to cover her eyes. There was no way to easily hide the altered appearance of her iris from casual onlookers, nor any way to escape the psychological trauma which it signified.

"It hasn't been this bad in months," Nunna whispered. "Why now?"

"It's the crowds," Morla answered. "You are reading the crowds."

Up until the day they'd captured Galloglass, Nunna had almost forgotten the shock of being surrounded by so many unguarded minds. This was the trigger for what DePons had termed *instrumental immersion.*

The FTI medical research division had made only one formal investigation of instrumentality, back in New York. The case study was a young woman in police custody. She carried no ID, and fit no missing persons descriptions. There weren't any records on her, no implanted tags, and no digital footprints of any kind. Just a blue-haired girl wandering the streets in a catatonic state. It was as though she'd fallen from the sky.

While in confinement, she suffered panic attacks and seizures. A psych hospital in New York diagnosed her with multiple personality disorder, and that would have been that, if not for one lucid moment when her primary care physician discovered that the voice inside this girl's head was his own.

No secret was safe from her.

Several deaths occurred, and the Union Bureau of Enclave Security looked into it. A former president of the British-American Union became involved—though, with his hands in everything else, Cedric DePons may have been entangled in the case from the very beginning. He was in New York finishing up the inauguration of Regulus Transit Terminal, and had installed the Regulus shard himself the day the girl first appeared.

HSA agents were sent to recover her, but she had become a wild thing, untamed by isolation, sedation, or restraints. Drowning in sensory overload, she was no longer capable of distinguishing her own thoughts and feelings from those of others.

Nunna had read the files, but she had no memory of the events they described. She knew that the girl in the reports was herself because DePons told her it was so, and because of her unique gift she believed him.

The stern look of Morla's eyes peering out from her veil prompted Lothar to exercise patience.

"Alright," he conceded. "We'll wait here for the gate warden to greet us and clear a path through this crowd. It shouldn't take more than a minute."

But staying put was just what Nunna wanted to avoid. The market was abuzz with covert undercurrents of communication, for all the Tenno were aware that someone important had arrived.

Even if they couldn't see the empress, crowds eager for a spectacle were thronging the east gate because of the news that Galloglass had disembarked passengers by the river. Circling now slowly over the gate, the councilor's ship maintained a high profile, just as Daedalus had promised.

There were some in this crowd whose interests in the empress seemed hostile. There were eyes upon them; and though her eyes were closed, Nunna could see. Tapping into each spy's perspective, she forced herself to adapt under the strain of instrumentality. Gazing through the eyes of strangers, she darted swiftly from one cognizance to the next, switching after taking no more than a glimpse, and hoping none were looking at her while she did so.

She always feared seeing herself—it was harder after that to come back.

Cedric was the one who'd tapped the full functionality of her gift. He'd taken her on as his own special project, working with her alone until she had learned to focus on distinguishing her own voice, her own thoughts, from those of others.

When she was eventually released into a population of HSA soldiers who had been specially trained to work with her, Nunna became their commander. They were of one mind, an unstoppable force that was able to face any challenge—until the day Regulus awakened.

Lothar hadn't been briefed about these abilities of hers, and no one here knew about her past. That was probably best, she figured.

"Are you alright?"

Nunna felt his presence towering over her, and a heavy hand patted her tousled mop of blue hair. She looked up instinctively. To his credit, Lothar responded only with a concerned frown when he saw her eyes, glimpsing the bright coral-pink ring that had formed within her iris. Refocusing her attention, she nodded and tried to smile.

"It's nothing," she lied. "Just a bad headache."

Lothar turned away. He didn't look thrilled to be brushed-off, and she dared not delve deeper into his thoughts for fear of seeing how weak she must seem to him. His presence had a curious calming effect on her, though, which caused her to lower her guard.

There was a loud crash to their left. A man with a tray of fresh-baked bread had tripped, scattering his wares into the path of oncoming foot-traffic. His heart was beating, and he wanted to swear, but his daughter was watching from the front of his shop. Nunna wrenched her mind back from his grasp and calmed her breathing. It had been easier than this once upon a time, but the Tenno people of Nara were very visual, and the market was a place full of interesting sights and sounds and smells. With so much activity going on all around her, and with so many pairs of eyes and ears moving to and fro, the sensory cues were coming in so fast that she had difficulty isolating those which were her own.

A knowing hand grasped her shoulder to steady her. Morla's light touch was something Nunna could focus on. Through their contact she was secure. No words were needed; but Morla did allow something small to slip through.

An image it was, of a dark passage underground, and the three of them together, Morla, Nunna, and Val.

But Nunna had never been to such a place.

She wanted to ask about what she'd seen, but Morla remained remote, as if intentionally blocking her out. It was not the first time, and Nunna had begun to suspect the reason for this lay in the truth that Morla had tried to hide from her from the beginning.

There were others like her, who could do what she did.

The seer had always maintained Nunna was unique, yet this was not strictly true. Nunna had come to learn that there were once many like her, all similarly gifted. They were called null-navvies. The navvies had supposedly vanished from Syrscian long ago, but here inside Morla's head was a memory of another one; and aside from the bizarre fact that the copy was bald, she was as like to Nunna as a twin.

It was no more than speculation, but if such *familiars* of herself existed, and if Morla had already met one in the past, then it stood to chance they would eventually run into another. It wasn't the possibility of meeting her double that worried Nunna, but the likelihood of her double infiltrating the awareness of her companions. The plan would come to ruin if it was discovered by someone who could read their minds as well as she could.

And if such a person realized how susceptible she was to a controlling influence—it wasn't hard to guess who would emerge from that meeting a doppelganger of the other.

The presence of a sympathetic intellect jostled her, and in moments she had isolated it. There was someone here who knew Lothar by sight. She cringed, turning just in time to spot a tall mounted warrior moving towards them across the crowded lane. His voice rang out so loudly that all the market stalls were stilled.

"Halt!"

The order wasn't for them, as they were already standing still, but for the masses moving through the city gate. After a few intense seconds of crushing and pushing, the crowds diverged into rows upon either side of the road, like charged particles in a conductor. In the street before Lothar there stood an enormous bird-like reptile—a talon, Nunna recalled. She'd seen them in the city, but never so close. Standing ten feet at the crest, the creature looked like something from the museum of natural history come to life. Blue and red scaly skin on its sides and head gave way here and there to patches of feathers. Its wings were stunted, though; the bird was obviously flightless, and though its beak looked like it was meant for eating fruit, there were rows of tiny teeth inside.

The talon's large eyes flickered with intelligence, but if there was anything going on inside that head Nunna couldn't grasp it. Of a compatible sort was the intellect of its rider, a warrior straight out of a B movie, or maybe a character in a professional wrestling gamut. He wore a bulky survival suit, and there was a rifle slung over his shoulder.

"You!" he yelled, pointing a finger at Lothar.

Lothar crossed his arms and frowned. The warrior led his talon forwards, and the crowd of merchants began to disperse, keeping well back from the monstrous bird. Lothar still appeared unfazed.

"Hello, Aelik," he greeted.

When he reached Lothar, Aelik dismounted and stepped forwards until the two were eye-to-eye, and then they embraced with much back-clapping.

"You are gate warden now, Aelik?"

Aelik thumped his broad chest proudly with a fist. He wasn't otherwise articulate.

"I need to bring these visitors to the governor immediately," Lothar explained, gesturing with his hand for Aelik to inspect them.

The warrior nodded vigorously—he was all about gesturing, this one. Directing his attention to the visitors, he scrutinized each of them in turn as if reviewing troops for battle. Struggling to untether her instrumentally adaptable senses, Nunna endured his fiery gaze as he paused over her. He touched her blue hair gingerly before moving on, but said nothing about her eyes.

With a deepening pout, Aelik continued down the line until last of all he came to Val Anna, and to everyone's surprise the towering giant of a man knelt to the ground until they were face-to-face. A murmur of confusion and wonderment passed among the spectators as Val removed her winged helm and met his gaze; and then a hush. She reached out and touched his broad shoulder. It was the gentle gesture of a mother comforting her child. The moment was suspended in time, as if the two had become statues.

Her white tunic and cape fluttered, caught in a sudden breeze. A little of the light crept back into Val's face, and Nunna saw the empress revealed once again, her slight figure expanding to that of a mighty Tower, the succor of the sons of Nara emboldened by their courage and simple trust.

What exactly would the people of this colony-town make of her, Nunna wondered—a prophesied leader, or a destroying angel?

After Lothar coaxed Aelik back to his feet, the two held a long whispered conversation in the shadow of the gate. The marketplace slowly returned to business, but the gate was closed behind them. The crowds kept their distance.

Eventually, while Aelik grunted something to an underling in uniform, Lothar came back to them and related what he had learned.

"The empress' missive was sent by transmission to Governor Amed the night we made our original plans. No one is expecting us, but my friend tells me Amed's spies have also reported the news that the councilor would not be arriving with his ship."

"Do we know how many days behind us the councilor was delayed?" Val asked.

"It is uncertain. The merchant Daedalus paid to stay behind never picked up the councilor. He must have had another ship. What is known is that Teomaxos was quite ruffled by our confiscation of his property."

"Will he try to kill me in Nara?"

"Aelik and I agree that it is very unlikely anyone will make an attempt on your life until the councilor has made formal charges against you in front of those gathered for Gilat."

"How comforting."

"Moreover, the rest of us are a sign announcing the empress' arrival. They will surely have recognized the seer by now, and also the four in your bodyguard. We are in the open from now on."

"Is there any reason we should not proceed as planned?"

"With your permission, Lady, Aelik will send to Governor Amed our prepared greetings. After we present ourselves at his house he will likely bring us to the arena to choose a proxy for Gilat. I wouldn't recommend any changes unless he refuses to meet us."

Val nodded approval, but the holy glow was gone. Her cheerless face was gray.

Passing off his mount to a guard in a survival suit, Aelik waved them aside to a gate that admitted passage to a sandy track along the inside of the city wall.

"Come," he urged, producing a large skeleton key.

While they gathered around him, he spoke quietly to Lothar.

"Be wary of Nara's intrigues. It will be hard if you lose a battle by proxy."

"But much worse if Amed manages to detain us with other business of his own crafting," Lothar replied.

"He is skilled in such schemes."

"Have you reason to suspect something is afoot?"

"You will soon know all he has in store," Aelik replied in deafening monosyllables while opening the gate.

He went on ahead, waving them to follow him along the narrow lane beyond. It was a quiet path, reserved for ferrying people in and out of the governor's house unseen.

"Are there any allies we can trust?" Lothar asked, sticking close to Aelik's side.

"Just me. Maybe some guilders. You want Aelik to keep a door open, Brother?"

"No, Aelik. I fear the results of our business here won't be pretty. Even if Gilat goes well, we have little surety of success, and Nara will need your strength."

He glanced aside at Nunna, who cringed quietly beneath the emotional weight conveyed by his mind. Her own secret task was a dangerous one, indeed. Lothar seemed to doubt her ability to complete it, for he reckoned nothing of her gift.

"The governor will attempt to widen the schism between the empress and the colonies, and all the more so if we win," Lothar continued. "He will also aim for leverage over the seer, I think. In the end, we shall need a good man to stand between the powers and the people. Regardless of how Nara decides, this confrontation jeopardizes the safety of all the Tenno. If even one should fall while she stands within this colony, the empress will be blamed."

"Hmm," Aelik grunted. "You speak true. As for Amed, he has spoken to me about his grudge against the seer. He looks forward to meeting her again."

"Yes," Lothar agreed. "He sent her an invitation, you might say."

He was obviously referring to the dead guard left in the villa. This and other telltale signs left around the scene of the kidnapping all pointed directly to Amed's involvement. It was a summons that could not be refused, and their response must be just as carefully crafted. That is why Morla had cast Nunna, the unknown factor, in the principal role.

Nunna's job was to use her gift to find out where the governor of Nara had hidden the girls, and then to extract them safely from the colony.

Though the possibility of success was actually quite high, she doubted it would turn out as planned. Nunna's strategy was to stay within close range in hopes that Amed gave away some scrap of a clue she could follow. Finding them should be rather easy. The hard part would be freeing them without getting caught or killed.

While they walked the white pebbly path, she felt her distance from the crowds growing. Her spirits lifted. Two high walls on either hand blocked from view the rest of the colony, but here and there she glimpsed the shape of it well enough. Nara was like a huge Kasbah made of ceramic blocks, metal, and glass. It was kept clean, and green things were growing everywhere. The buildings closest to the wall actually buttressed it, leaving high arched corridors beneath houses grander than luxury apartments in New York. Some of these structures ascended more than ten stories.

Just ahead the way bent sharply to the right, and at the turn in the road she caught a whiff of something familiar—the scent of something she craved with sudden longing. The craving surprised her, strengthened as it was by the long years she'd spent convincing herself she would never encounter it again.

"Do I smell coffee?" Nunna asked.

"I am surprised you know it," Lothar said. "Coffee is almost impossible to find outside of Nara. The Tenno swear by its power to revitalize failing strength."

"It was important in my town, too, but I haven't had any in years."

"Then we shall have to share a cup, you and I, when Gilat is over."

"You might take him up on that sooner," Morla whispered in a warning voice. "There is more than coffee brewing in Nara."

"We are here," Aelik said, slowing his pace.

They halted at a blind turn in the alley, whereupon the travelers faced an open courtyard of stone.

"Ana tashim taklaku," Aelik said to them in the ancient tongue, bowing with his hands together.

Even Morla looked surprised. "Fair luck to you!" she replied.

Lothar clapped the warrior's shoulder in parting, and after making reverence once again to the empress, Aelik returned silently the way they'd come.

"A surprising fellow, and very loyal," Lothar said, looking after him. "He belongs with us."

As they made their way thence to the middle of the courtyard, shuffling wide-eyed while ogling the large mansion to their left, Nunna was reminded of the façade of Grand Central Terminal before the dragons came. The entire space was walled round and shut in behind a rather majestic wrought-iron gate opposite the alleyway entrance.

Upon the steps of the mansion a man approached, wrapped in fabrics of bright green and yellow hues. He seemed elderly, though this might have been due to the fact that he was balding and excessively obese.

"Lothar!" he shouted rudely. "What in Hades do you mean by bringing that white-headed witch back with you?"

Their journey had taken a strange turn, and the empress' retinue had grown considerably. They were led now by Governor Amed through the maze of streets outside his private compound. He'd hardly stopped talking since they met him in the courtyard, and proper introductions never were made. Strangely, they weren't necessary, for he already knew everyone's name.

"I'm still angry at you, Morla!" he was saying.

Morla, walking on his left, wasn't so easily baited by his bluster. Amed grinned peevishly and turned back towards Val Anna, who endured somewhat closer proximity to his right. Sensing a cooler target for his brutish personality, the governor let loose a tireless onslaught of perverse jokes and pompous monologue while they made their way through the city. His random rambling speech matched his wobbling gait.

"Those slave-girls you stole brought a lot of business into Nara—especially the oldest. She had a voice that could turn anyone's head! Now all I am left with are the murderers, liars, and terrorists. You've robbed me, Morla! What do you have to say to that?"

Amed was a stereotypical politician, throwing around sound bites to provoke a reaction. Morla walked steadily forwards, her expression hidden behind her veil. Even Nunna couldn't tell what she was thinking just then. She fell behind the others to walk among Amed's many attendants, who were busying themselves about preparing refreshments from a rolling cart.

"*Well, Seer?*" Amed shouted, flapping his fat arms. "Aren't you going to say something?"

"It was a fair winning," Morla replied.

"A winning, you say? But I see you didn't bring them back with you, hmm?"

The governor spoke loud enough for everyone to hear, even those who waited on the sides of the road to catch the passing wave of his bombast. An armed escort of riders on talons kept these citizens from stepping too close.

Nunna didn't sense admiration from even a single bystander, only mild curiosity about the visitors. There was also fear. The Tenno were deeply afraid of something, and whatever it was they avoided focusing on it in any detail. The fear and uncertainty they exuded brought to mind old soviet films she had watched while under DePons' care.

"You could easily challenge me with kidnapping the slaves you kidnapped from me," the governor boldly suggested. "How about that? We could decide my innocence in the same match as we decide the empress'!"

"You mean to say, in the same match we decide the councilor's," Morla corrected. "After all, the empress is not the one on trial."

"Clever girl!" Amed said, turning as a servant dashed forwards through the crowd, nudging at Lothar to be let in.

He bore to the governor's side a small covered dish, and with eyes and head bowed he opened it and held it out while walking.

"Ah, fresh *tagel*," Amed said, and slipping his chubby fingers into the dish he removed three raw mollusks.

His eyes moved to the food handler, who took one of the tagel from his master's hand and ate it. Amed seemed satisfied, and after a few more paces he shoved one of the slippery brown lumps into his mouth.

"Of course, the commoners have another name for them," he said, and while chewing noisily he leaned over towards Val's ear and whispered something that caused her to turn a shade of red that clashed with her hair.

"Ha!" Amed gestured with the remains of his snack towards an open space ahead. "Look there!"

The houses and structures on either side of the widening road fell away to an open grassy area of quiet gardens surrounding a behemoth structure of stone and steel. The hazy atmosphere obscured its details, but it was round and capped with a mighty crystal dome that glittered in the sun.

It looked a little like the Taj Mahal, Nunna thought, except vastly larger.

"You will not see another building like the Gilat arena anywhere in the colonies!"

The vertical shaft beneath the dome was almost a mile deep, Nunna recalled from her reading. The mining done in Nara and Tara kept well away from that old shaft, because down in the darkness there many strange things had awakened in the centuries following the War. New York wasn't the only place with monsters, apparently. Some Galanese historians referred to this place as the *Theater of the Abyss*. It was the stuff of childhood nightmares.

Could this be what the people feared?

"Even you haven't seen it, Empress," Amed said with an overly dramatic bow. "It was built in the years of the reconstruction, just after the Destroying Fire, and is situated right on top of the core of the old city, Cipa."

They had come to the meeting of several roads. Amed's security went forwards and cleared the streets of traffic while they waited. There was a bustle all around Nunna as servants conversed. One more was sent up to Lothar, and begging entrance he knelt beside the governor, offering him a damp towel and a chalice of water. The towel he used, dropping it into the golden chalice after he'd mopped his face and hands.

None of the servants offered anything at all to the empress.

"Ancient outlawed scriptures and old prophecies hold no sway over the Tenno," he said to himself, as if thinking aloud.

Amed waved the servant away and nodded towards the street. They resumed walking. Though the governor was looking rather sweaty, his mood was improving, and he walked surprisingly fast.

"You know what I thought, Empress, when I first saw the captain of your bodyguard? I thought, all those years I had that man sitting on our back doorstep, and here he comes like a governor himself! My, but it gives my head a spin!"

"Lothar has served me faithfully and without fault," Val replied in a stern voice.

"I don't doubt it. After all, you're a lot prettier than I am."

"A Dragon Slayer's duty and respect are not purchased by beauty," Vercingetorix muttered.

Amed laughed.

"Oh?" he wondered, speaking loudly without turning, "but what about contempt, revenge, and all those other virtues? Tell me those don't have a say in your duty to the empress, Rix!"

Vercingetorix dared not respond to this taunting. The empress herself remained silent.

"Well," Amed chuckled, "I just hope Lothar doesn't let his guard down—especially with the councilor all hot and bothered!"

He turned slightly, a trick for him while walking because of his massive girth, and he gave Lothar a wink.

"As for me, I take charges against my old priest very seriously."

"He has threatened my life," Val declared, "and he will answer for it."

"We shall allow the Gilat to decide the truth. The empress will be selecting her deadman today, under that dome, where men fight unspeakable terrors for the honor of others. All of them are slain eventually."

He regarded Val with raised brows.

"Maybe you will choose one who will not die, hmm?"

An unsettling chill stirred Nunna's heart. Someone nearby was watching her closely. Though the guards maintained a perimeter between the curious crowd and the governor's retinue, she saw a peculiar woman standing close by on the right-hand side of the road.

The woman wore an outlandish garb and a deep hood that didn't match the attire of the Tenno, and her smallish nose and sharply angled eyes marked her as foreign stock. Nunna tried to meet her gaze as they passed, and the stranger raised her head as if in anticipation. Beneath the hood her wonderful crimson eyes sparkled like rubies, and her face was decorated with what appeared to be glimmering pink tattoos in the shape of patterned scales. She nodded towards Nunna, and Nunna bowed her head.

When she looked up again, the woman was gone, but inside her mind she'd left a lingering thought—a question, really.

Is this yet another child of the Moriko returned to us from exile?

Nunna did not understand, and the passing thought carried no threat, but she was shaken nonetheless. She looked everywhere, but there was no trace of the mysterious stranger anywhere along the green way. While she was thus distracted, the conversation had shifted to the actual process of selecting a proxy.

"Teomaxos will also be choosing when he arrives," Amed said.

"In all fairness," Val answered, "I will ask you not to guide his choosing or mine for whatever motives you may have."

Amed laughed, and then coughed hard. "It is my place only to inform the empress of our customs, not to choose for her!" he gasped.

"Customs?"

"Yes. You will make your selection from the two heroes I have set aside for this combat. The one you do not choose goes to Teomaxos, because you brought the charges. I will also set the scenario for the event."

"Explain."

"Each combat is like a play. The proxies are the main characters, but there may be others, natural or otherwise. The entire arena floor may be moved, raised or lowered, in order to make things more interesting."

He described these details with great enthusiasm.

"It is my duty, you see, to provide our paying guests with a more complete entertainment than mere execution."

Nunna stopped in her tracks.

She'd been engrossed in assessing the fat man's devious mind, looking for hints of what he might have done to Fann and her sisters, but to no avail. Then the sensation of great evil came wafting up through the very ground beneath them. The garden road was full of an aroma of flowers, but Nunna detected the smell of blood—a smell she knew from three years of hiding in the dark of the terminal. The air seemed suddenly full of memories, and something else. Her gifted senses had just touched something very evil, deep beneath her feet.

It was the dragon-sense.

"You feel it, don't you?"

She'd been caught off-guard again. Looking up, Nunna discovered that Amed's question was aimed not at the empress, but at her.

"You can feel them, can't you?" he asked.

"What are they?" Nunna asked, trembling.

"It is Gilat, my dear," Amed replied, spreading his arms and turning around so that he faced the mighty arena. "Once a year, in all the years since the Destroying Fire, the deeps awaken and vomit up the hordes of darkness. The arena is a cap that keeps them from boiling out to cover all Galaneth in terror, but there is no guarantee that the aging field generators will last another season. The tradition of fighting in the arena all year round to settle disputes is mainly for the purpose of sifting warriors capable of standing in the gap."

He turned around to look at Nunna.

"It is rumored that those with special ears can hear the movement of the deeps," he said, winking. "As for me, I hear them all the time, gnawing new tunnels, eating away the very foundations of Nara. It is only a matter of time, and then our heroes will rise up and rescue us!"

"This place is evil," Val Anna decided.

"My, but you wound my heart!" Amed replied, clutching at his chest. "And yet, there are some who do not shrink back from what the poets have hidden in subtle words."

"You speak of the ancient scriptures?" Morla wondered.

"No! I speak of the priests, who are a powerful seal against the creatures that want out of old Cipa's crypt. It was the priests who searched the scriptures, and who found amidst the nonsense and folklore the information we need to defeat the monsters of the abyss."

He ignored their puzzled looks and started walking towards the arena. It was with an effort that the others joined him. He did not give them much respite from his gloomy change of mood, however.

"These people who fight in the Gilat—they are not princes or kings, but I think they know something the rest of this old world has forgotten. I send them in to physically grapple with and defeat the legendary past. The commoners think they are being put to death for their crimes, but there's much more to it than that. In Gilat, their journey and ours lies together. The rest of us only fight fears that we cannot see, but these heroes face them for us in the flesh. For you, Empress, I have selected the very best. You may choose between my two finest heroes for your *deadman proxy*."

"I get first choice?" Val asked.

"Of course! You will have to take a very good look before you choose, and maybe consult with your exalted seer here. If, however, you would like the simple rundown, we are dealing with what may be the two most powerful warriors Syrscian has ever seen!"

He made a sweeping gesture with his hands, but continued when he saw that he had impressed no one but himself.

Clearing his throat, he stated, "They are both terrorists."

"Terrorists?" Lothar questioned. "You mean to say the proxy that will fight for the empress is a man of the Fourth House?"

"One of them is a woman!" Amed replied, gesturing with his index finger. "It is unprecedented! Nara never has nor shall have again a Gilat as memorable as this!"

The wide front entryway of the arena curved outwards before them, reaching towards the little garden lane. Occupying the center of the colony, the structure and its cluster of supporting towers was clear of all other buildings for a span of about six kilometers, and it seemed to take up about as much space all by itself. Nunna looked up as they entered the low arched gateway in the center of the entrance. The pale walls rose hundreds of feet, and above she glimpsed the silvery hull of Galloglass sliding by on its circuit of the city, the eye of Horus painted on its vertical stabilizer peering down at her with its eternally bland expression. She suddenly wished she was way up there in the cloudy blue sky. The steps beyond the gate led downward to something far less comforting.

"Wait for me in the reception hall," Amed said while they descended behind him. "I will return in a little while with refreshments, and then we shall get down to business. In the meantime, I will prepare a demonstration for the empress."

Amed and his servants left them in a large open room at the bottom of the steps. It was cooler here, and very quiet. Nunna came to Morla's side, while Lothar and his men fanned out to take in their surroundings. From the stairs at the entrance, the room formed a long rectangle that led deeper into the structure, most of which appeared to be subterranean. This place was like a tomb in every way imaginable. Lines of white pillars supported the low plastered ceiling, painted to look like a starry sky. The floor was gray marble flecked with fine metallic bits of copper, glinting in the gas lights.

The sound of shuffling feet drew Nunna's attention back towards the entrance. Three newcomers were advancing, flanked by guildsmen bearing staves. The escorted visitors were two men and one woman—the mysterious veiled woman Nunna had spotted earlier on the street. One of the men was mentally handicapped, and the other looked quite old. The old fellow greeted Morla with a bow.

"Lady Morla. I was hoping to meet you sometime soon, and here you are!"

"William, who rescued me from the deeps," Morla greeted with a nod of her head.

He rose and combed his fingers through his white beard, squinting to see the others standing around her in the gloom. The handicapped man and the woman did not bow.

"I am honored that you should remember Old William's name," he said nervously. Then, turning aside, he nodded towards Nunna.

"Nice hair, daughter," he remarked courteously, and wiping his hands on his coveralls he offered his bony palm to her.

Nunna took the hand graciously. He was a caricature of a hillbilly farmer, and that somehow made her feel more at home. His thoughts, she perceived, were mostly of the handicapped man. There was something troubling them both.

"I sent a request to Aelik to meet you if ever you turned up again," William said. "I did not expect to bother the empress by coming here—"

"It's fine," Morla said. "I have informed the empress of the guild excavator in Nara Colony who happened upon my stasis tube. We are all very grateful to you for wisely reporting the discovery to the governor and Lord Teomaxos so that I could return in time to greet her at Gilthaloneth. I owe you a debt of gratitude for rescuing me in time."

William looked on the verge of tears, and might have cried if the thin man next to him had not at that very moment farted loudly.

"*Ryce!*"

The younger man blinked, and absently stuck a finger in his ear. Morla frowned.

"What is it that ails him?" she asked.

"Besides *the usual*," William answered, grasping his friend's arm, "there's something terribly wrong with him. It's not something I've ever seen before, but I dare say you might understand."

"Why me?"

"Well, the strangeness started the day after we found you, the day we came in contact with that device. Ain't it so, Ryce?"

"*It is predicted that total displacement within the axis of amplitude 001 will result in a convergence anomaly.*"

Ryce's speech came forth eloquently, and very fast-paced, as if he clearly understood what he was saying.

"*The subject displaced exists consciously in two amplitudes at an axis, or junction, existing in one moment of time, called 'present', progressing forward to the Sum Over Histories. However, given enough momentum, this convergence must eventually exceed the dimensional space assigned to it, falling short of the event horizon, creating a singularity in which the two amplitudes will once again become distinct, though still occupying a single instance of time within a single frame of reference.*"

He blinked passively while he spoke, and took his head in his hands afterwards as if warding off a headache.

Even before Val and Morla thought it, Nunna knew exactly what ailed the man. She had seen it in videos deep inside the FTI research facilities, where DePons had made Watchers.

This man was talking about Displacement Syndrome.

"He goes on like this," William lamented. "Like I said, it started the day after you was brought up, Lady Morla. That was when he went missing. I thought it was because we were shutting down and he was out of his routine. You know? But I found him a week later at the city gate, all cleaned up and speakin' almost sensible. Said he'd been to Tara with the Lord of House Teg, if you believe it."

"And was he?" Morla questioned.

While they spoke about him, Ryce started humming a tune. He swayed and pushed his fingers into his ears, pantomiming an obvious desire to leave. One of his ears was caked with a crust of dried blood.

"I don't know if he's aware of where he is even now," William said, squinting. "He does disappear from time to time, but never for as long as that one particular instance."

Finding a convenient pause in their conversation, Ryce launched into a new monologue.

"In preliminary testing it was concluded that the convergence of two amplitudes upon an axis in time would result in a temporal singularity in which matter must be converted to energy and released as radiation. It was found that, alternately, a third amplitude could be created within the anomaly. In this case, the displaced subject may alter course along the new axis—the axis which will, by default, become the Sum Over Histories, the dominant frame of reference."

"The third amplitude?" Nunna wondered.

"Cedric DePons' back door!" Ryce answered, matter-of-factly.

They stared at him and blinked wonderment, but Ryce had lapsed into an incoherent examination of the bottom of one of his feet.

"Black water," Morla thought. *"Someone has put this man in Black water."*

Nunna wasn't sure what she was referring to, but if it had to do with DePons it probably wasn't anything good.

"If something's been done to him," William said, "I thought that maybe you royal ladies would know about it, or ought to know about it. However, I don't want to worry you overmuch. There's a good chance someone's just filled that empty head of his with nonsense, is all. The shaft, on the other hand, is still filling our pockets, so I guess if there's nothing to be done, then at least I've got that."

"Old 32 is still open?" Lothar asked.

"They found more important things inside, they did," William replied in a hushed voice. "The guild won't let me shut down—"

Amed returned at that moment, and William fell silent. The guards standing behind them snapped instantly to attention.

"Get those diggers out of here!" the governor growled in excessive impatience. "They've no business beyond the gates until the show begins! And bring the empress. I want to introduce her to our heroes."

As they turned to follow him, Nunna looked back, curiously searching for the woman who had accompanied Ryce and William into the subterranean hall. Once again, she had vanished without a trace.

"Where'd she go?"

Morla asked, "Did you see someone?"

"That strange woman, the one who came in with William and Ryce. Where'd she go?"

Morla looked back into the gray hall and frowned. "I saw no woman."

"She was wearing a hood, and she had strange tattoos all around her eyes."

"Are you certain?"

Nunna gave her an exasperated look.

"I saw only the two men and the guards," Morla said. "I sensed no other person here."

"But—"

"You are tired, and overwhelmed by so many strange encounters," Morla comforted. "What you saw could have been the imagining of anyone within reach of your gift."

Without another word she turned to catch up with Lothar, leaving Nunna feeling agitated and disturbed. Looking back once more, she wasn't able to convince herself that she actually saw a woman with pink scales around her eyes. Nor could she recall the exact moment the stranger left.

Who was placing this illusion in her mind?

It was high time she tried tapping into Amed again, and maybe prize some information from his perverse brain before being compromised by a hidden adversary.

Nunna caught up with the others just as they entered the massive oval pit of the arena. When they reached the parapet that ringed the abyss, she stepped up to the edge of the stone rail and looked around.

490

It was like a demented football stadium with a bottomless vertical shaft in place of a playing field.

A gust blew up from below and swept her blue hair around her face, but she couldn't see very far into the depths because of a faint blue radiance that sealed the pit—a distortion that hovered in the murky air like a soap bubble.

"This is the heart of it all," Amed announced, gazing out over the gaping shaft.

"What are we looking at?" Val asked.

"Well, the foundations of ancient Cipa are miles down that hole, and all the tunnels there are filled with abominations. We keep the rubbish from backing up the pipe with those."

He pointed down to a narrow tower like an obelisk rising almost within reach of the parapet. Nunna saw there were three of them on the near side of the arena, and three opposite. Each pulsed with a powerful electrostatic discharge. Faint glowing blue streamers of particles stretched forth from the towers over the pit.

"These six converters produce a containment field of ionized plasma. Nothing gets past the top without frying itself. The central fighting floor has an additional field generator."

He pointed downward again, this time to a narrow bridge spanning the arena just below the top of the towers. Where it neared the center of the opening to the pit, the bridge widened to a spacious circular fighting deck surrounded by eight small pillars. Linked by chains and capped by electrodes, these also glowed blue with an energy field.

"That smaller inner field can be manipulated in order to make the fight more entertaining. It can be shut on and off in a predictable pattern, giving our combatants an obstacle to engagement. The central platform can also be raised or lowered."

"Who made all this?" Val asked. "It looks—"

"Gremn?" he finished. "Well, it is. A thousand years ago our colony's founders excavated the generators from a ship downed during the War. Is it not curious that the War of Destroying Fire produced the monsters, and then also provided the means of keeping them at bay?"

Val leaned out over the pit and looked up. Nunna followed her eyes to the dome high above, latticed with metal and shining in the sun. Little of the sun's cheer touched the place where they stood, however, for an oppressive darkness seemed to reach up from the abyss and diffuse the light like a mist. Gas lamps illuminated most of the arena's promenade, but it was a gloomy place.

"The empress will make her selection as soon as the heroes are presented," Amed announced.

He said nothing about refreshments. Nunna's stomach complained loudly.

"Will we be standing here the whole time?" she asked.

"Commoners usually stand upon the open parapets," Amed dodged, looking a little put-off by her question. "There are comfortable apartments with windows reserved for special guests. You may join your master there, if she deems you worthy."

Nunna gazed upwards along the stone walls and noted large windows at regular intervals. For a moment, his carefully guarded mind slipped onto a parallel track. Amed was definitely plotting something, and it had to do with the empress' guest apartment.

"My companions are to be treated with respect equal to that which is given to me," Val Anna said.

"Fine," Amed replied, "but let's not spoil the presentation with any more silly talk. Here is our first proxy!"

At first they saw no one. In time, the noise of a metal gate could be heard at the near end of the bridge, just below the place where they stood. Then a lone figure stepped out of the shadows onto the span, its form blurred somewhat by the distortion of the field.

Raising a hand to her face, Val stepped back from the edge in alarm.

"Not to worry," Amed said, mistaking her reaction for fear. "Not to worry, Empress! The field will keep her from harming us, or I would not be standing here next to you!"

He said this with a smile, but Val didn't notice. Her eyes, like everyone else's, were glued on the person walking out onto the bridge. A woman was making her way to the central ring of pillars.

A fearsome mask of steel covered all her head from nose to nape of neck, so that only the untidy ends of her blossom-pink hair could be seen. She wore a complicated body-suit of leather straps that left her limbs bare, and upon her long tapered forearms was a pair of crescent-shaped blades, wide and axe-like at the wrist and narrowing towards the elbow. Yet all of this was nothing to the feature that drew their attention to her every move.

"Yes, she is a rare treat," the governor allowed. "I present to you our *Angel of Death*, Princess Sirona of the Yuuto! Undefeated in every contest, she is the fastest and most agile hero I can offer to your service, Empress."

Val Anna turned towards Morla, her eyes showing surprise. "She has wings!"

"Yes, she is Yuuto," Amed answered, slightly confused. "A Yuuto is an off-color choice for a proxy, I confess, but the wings don't slow her down a bit. It doesn't matter how many they've got, but how they use them, hmm? As to her skills, she hasn't been in a match very often, but that's because she's a bit of a bore, killing so swiftly that the fight's over before it's properly begun."

Nunna stared at the woman wonderingly, mesmerized by the beauty of her pale pink wings.

"How did a Yuuto princess come to be here?" Lothar wondered.

"I caught her trying to release some of the warriors imprisoned in the arena," Amed replied. "She has served me well since then, though she never has much to say."

When the woman reached the pillars in the center of the pit, she stretched her wings gracefully, like a runner limbering up for a race.

"Mind you, she doesn't use the wings the way you'd think," Amed warned. "I've heard Yuuto can soar for short distances, but in the arena all she does is flap once or twice, and then she's all over the place. She throws herself around a lot, using pillars and walls and the like. It makes her a bit difficult to follow, so watch closely."

The figure turned around to face them. Amed raised a hand and kept it aloft, and with a noisy growl the bridge partially retracted into the wall on either side of the arena. The central pillared deck, suspended by a series of chains, began to descend.

"We will only use this presentation as a test of her skills," the governor said. "I will not set her against another hero until the empress' contest."

He twirled his finger in the air and the arena floor ground to a halt. Echoes of screeching machinery and clanking chains resounded in their ears, and then there was a noise of something else. Amed lowered his hand.

"What will she be fighting?" Nunna wondered breathlessly.

Amed rubbed his hands together. "Look and see! Here it comes!"

After a few moments of silence, they could all mark the progress of a gray shadow moving up the wall on the far side of the arena, clinging crablike to the rock. Below, the warrior Sirona stood her ground, waiting patiently. It was the bravest sight Nunna had ever witnessed. Amed, however, was openly disappointed.

"Just one lone meech, I'm afraid," he said. "I'd hoped for something a little more challenging, but I suppose this will have to do. Maybe more will join in once blood is spilled—and Sirona is doing her best, I see, to bait him."

Gripping the stonework, Nunna stared at the horror that hurled itself splay-limbed from the wall to the platform. It landed with a crash, rocking the suspended floor violently, for it was quite a bit larger than the lone woman standing there.

A singularly disturbing monstrosity, the *meech* was a golden-brown bag of belly and spidery limbs. Reaching out with two long forelegs, the creature extended its head on a lengthy neck in the direction of its prey. The head was little more than a tube studded atop with bright red eyes, ending abruptly at a mouth. Four teeth protruded inwards from its starfish-jaw, and two feeder claws extended from either side of the maw. These worked the air feverishly. The belly flexed, and two more legs pushed it up over the edge of the fighting platform. A short stout tail completed its loathsome appearance.

The Yuuto warrior turned only when this beast stood right behind her.

Leaning forwards, the creature emitted a low gurgling moan that ended in a screech. The proxy stood with her right side facing the monster, allowing it to reach out tentatively towards her with one of its forelimbs—spiderlike, it evoked a nightmare thrill of fear in the onlookers as it touched the warrior's bare foot. She smacked this leg aside with a swift scissors-motion of her forearm-mounted blades.

A shriek reverberated through the arena. Nunna clapped her hands over her ears. Morla did the same, but Val only stared at the black gouts of blood that flowed from the monster's injured limb. It drooled, working its mandibles. An angry clicking sound filled the air.

The fight began.

Swinging first one leg and then the other, the meech attacked like a huge mantis, slicing an arc over the winged warrior's head. She dropped to one knee, then rolled as it attempted to pin her to the floor. The metal deck sparked and lurched, and the Yuuto vanished.

For a moment, Nunna wondered if she'd fallen over the edge. Then she saw her, wings outstretched, standing atop one of the pillars. The monster came at her in a fury, but Sirona easily hopped down onto its round back, slicing between its shoulders as she slid down onto the fighting platform. The meech turned quickly, but its opponent disappeared again in a flash of wings. This time she was gripping the side of one of the pillars, crouching sideways, high above the platform.

She wasn't even breathing hard.

When the beast located her, the warrior launched herself right towards its mouth with a great shout. The meech swung one of its mighty legs upwards to meet her halfway, and she sliced the limb clean off.

"That's how it's done!" Amed shouted.

Val put a hand to her mouth. The pretty angelic wings were spattered now with black blood.

As they watched, the damaged monster hobbled round once more. Sirona waited until it faced her, and then she walked right into its embrace, taking a swing at the remaining front limb as it came to swat her away. The glancing blow allowed her to approach its head, where she ducked beneath the wide sucking mouth. She easily avoided a couple of weak lunges, and then brought her arms upwards in a swinging motion before stepping clear. The platform was washed in blood as the great beast staggered, falling on its gasping belly. A long moan vibrated in the air.

Looking upwards towards Amed, Sirona paused beside the twitching head. He nodded, and elbow-first she buried the endpoint of the blade on her right arm among the clustered eyes. When the meech stopped thrashing, she returned to the center of the ring and waited. The platform began to ascend again, and the bridges were extended.

"Well, what do you think?" the governor asked.

His face was beaming. He clearly expected high praise. Val was very pale, however, and stood staring silently at the Yuuto woman as she walked back along the bridge towards the dungeon gate.

Seeing her distress, Amed chuckled. "The Musab have a saying, Empress, that a little mud in one's eyes will change the way one sees."

"You think I'm not cut out for this type of spectacle?" she asked.

"Says the Warring Empress!" Amed laughed, gesturing towards her armor.

"Hold your tongue!" Lothar shouted, stepping forwards with the other Dragon Slayers.

"Lothar, Lothar!" Amed chuckled, clapping his hands. "You have nothing at all to fear for your Lady! It was merely a jest!"

Nunna immediately sensed the approach of warriors, and she stepped in front of the empress as a group of six armed men stepped forth from the shadows to join the governor. The warriors wore helmets and body armor of strange design, and all bore Vajra spears. Lothar held up his hand to signal his own companions to stand ready, and a tense stare-down ensued. Laughing derisively, Amed made light of the situation.

"You of all people ought to know, Lothar, that I am the one for justice in this land! I meant no offense to our gilded empress. However, since my guests are all so tired from their journey and my humor is getting the better of you, I will ask you to remain civil and allow me to present the next hero so that the empress may make her choice."

"I don't want to see anymore."

Amed's smile faded.

"I will choose the hero I have not seen," Val said.

"It...it is our custom for a selection to be offered before a choice is made," Amed stammered. "Gilat is about the choice, so the choice must be fair. Ask Morla. It was only two years ago. Surely she still remembers her choice."

"I do," Morla said, looking out while slaves shoved the carcass of the monster over the edge of the platform and hosed down the deck.

"I remember that the hero I chose won."

Amed waved his hand, as if dispelling an unpleasant odor. "A fair choice, perhaps," he said, "but that wasn't a fair fight. Your proxy escaped!"

"You should have expected as much. As I recall, he had infiltrated your men in order to assassinate you, and succeeded in destroying a shipment of illegal arms before he was captured and subjected to imprisonment in this arena. Surely the governor of the Tenno does not imagine an assassin could have accomplished these feats without inside help?"

Amed peered closely at her, catching the implied accusation of his own kidnapping scheme. "It matters not," he mumbled. "You agreed to the terms—"

"And my proxy felled yours in an even match."

"You took those slaves without consent."

"An independent tribunal acquitted me of all wrongdoing. I won the match."

"By trickery," Amed sniffed.

Amed was definitely agitated. With his mind in turmoil, Nunna suddenly caught a glimpse of what she had been waiting for. Whether or not that glimpse was enough for her to work with remained to be seen.

The governor nodded his bald head towards the generator towers. "I lost four slaves that day—three who weren't even part of the original bargain. You were a celebrity newly awakened from ages of stasis, Seer; but now your popularity has waned sufficiently, I think, for me to offer a challenge of my own without fear of reprisal. You owe me a rematch—a fair trial, this time."

"What's done is done, Amed. Fann is a royal retainer now. There are laws protecting her."

"Any titles she received were granted upon the misconception that she was your legal property. It's a matter of lost compensation, too."

"You are delusional. People are not property."

"Who says the Ayumu are people? Surely you realize by now, Seer, that sympathy for the Forest Folk doesn't go very far among the Galanese?"

"How is it that one tribe among many was able to arrive at the conclusion that their beliefs permitted the enslavement of other free people in Syrscian?"

"You should ask her about that," Amed answered, nodding towards Val Anna. "The monistic viewpoint of the Ancients was what brought endless war upon us. Their daughter is standing right here. Surely the empress could lecture us at length about tyranny and oppression."

"—She killed too quickly," Val said, interrupting. "It is like you said, Governor. That is why I shall choose the other proxy."

Amed looked perplexed by her words. All the aggression seemed to melt from Lothar's burning gaze, and everyone stood very still.

"I stand by my choice," Val insisted.

"Well, I suppose you have the right to choose without seeing them both fight, so long as there is a real reason," Amed replied sourly. "But you've ruined the surprise I was saving, I'll have you know."

His pout was genuine, but a sinister light was in his eye.

"Empress, by whatever coincidence rules the cosmos, you have chosen *Shanuri*, the very same proxy who fought for your Seer two years ago."

Morla looked confused, but also hopeful.

"How is that possible?" Val asked. "I thought you said he escaped."

"Ah, but he is a tricky devil, this one," the governor replied excitedly. "That is why I have dutifully employed him in all the hardest fighting. He shall be the greatest hero of Gilat! What his right name is no one knows, but that Shanuri, he is a tempest equal to the Yuuto princess. His one flaw is that he fights from the heart, but he fights without a plan. Would you believe he actually attempted to infiltrate my bodyguard one year after he was caught doing the very same thing?"

"Shanuri shall be my proxy," Val said.

"And what about you, Seer?" Amed asked, looking at Morla. "Will you accept my challenge?"

Morla turned towards him, her dark eyes flickering.

"You may yet win back those cherished slaves of yours. To make things more exciting, I will choose the empress' deadman, the fool who tried to kill me. You will bid the slaves' freedom on Sirona, Teomaxos' proxy. Is this not fair?"

Morla's eyes seemed to encompass the governor where he stood, so that his supreme confidence momentarily wavered.

"It is fair," Morla answered.

"Indeed, it is more than fair," said a voice from the darkness behind them. "And perhaps afterwards I will challenge the captain of the empress' bodyguard, whom I hold responsible for stealing my ship and handing it over to pirates."

The soldiers behind Amed made way for a robed man who had quietly approached them along the promenade.

"Lord Teomaxos," Amed greeted with a salute.

Teomaxos bowed. "A good game you've played, Empress. It is fortunate I have so many friends, or you might have been waiting another week for me to arrive."

The silence that followed allowed Nunna a few moments to sniff out his doubts. The councilor wasn't certain about the reason for the empress' actions. He didn't know about the mission to Urlad.

"I am only concerned with my good name and reputation, which was wrongly slandered by your ignorance of the politics of our great city."

He held out his hands in an imploring gesture.

"Be wary you do not overreach," Val Anna replied coldly. "Your secret activities can't remain hidden forever."

"You rashly accuse me of wrongdoing, Empress," he replied, removing his hat with a bow.

"We shall see."

"I hope that this game of ours will not forever tarnish your own status, weighed down as it is by the history of the Destroying Fire."

"Bravo, Priest!" Amed said with a clap of his hands.

"Tomorrow we shall see the truth of the matter exposed," Val Anna said, "one way or the other."

Lothar watched as the governor walked to Teomaxos' side, talking excitedly about the preparations for the event. When they were out of earshot he whispered to Bran, the Dragon Slayer standing closest to Nunna.

"Bran, you and Rix will remain with the empress. Caradoc and I will bring word to Daedalus when he lands at the arranged coordinates. We won't be giving up Galloglass just yet. I hate to think it, but we may have to fight our way out of this place."

He glanced up towards the ceiling, and Bran went to update Rix.

"You expect this to end badly?" Nunna asked, sensing his worry.

"However it goes in the arena, I never expected it to end well; and I don't like leaving the empress' side. Mostly I dislike the idea of fighting men I've trained personally."

"I still want my cup of coffee."

He smiled, and his mood lightened perceptively.

"Have you a plan of action?" he asked.

"I think I have a starting point," Nunna confirmed. "I've learned that Amed has a lower prison where he keeps the proxies. He's hiding our girls there, but they're under heavy guard."

Lothar was astonished. "How did you discover this?"

Nunna wished she could tell him how she'd divined Amed's secrets, but this wasn't the time to reveal all. So she bluffed, even though she knew he would see right through it.

"Those men we met in the hall—they were relaying information to Morla and me via the madman's ramblings. Anyway, we should prompt the empress to request a visit to her proxy. I doubt Amed would agree to a visit with Fann, but I have to get down to the level of the prison without looking suspicious. We need to get as close as we can so that I can slip away unseen."

Nunna sensed he was ready to countermand her proposal; but all he did was nod.

"You are a good fighter, and you are stealthier than I," he said, "but you will need help with the guards. Bring—"

He broke off suddenly, staring into the darkened walkway beyond the empress.

"What is it?" Nunna asked.

"I don't know."

No one else seemed to notice anything amiss. Nunna was thinking of the strange woman with pink scales on her face, but Lothar was staring low, towards the floor.

"I think we should get that coffee," he said, rubbing his eyes.

29

THE EMPRESS' DEADMAN

Nara Colony, Syrscian,
Year 1000 of the New Council

Twenty Musab mercenaries guarded the dungeon—she was getting close. The Tenno governor certainly thought he had the arena's corridors covered; but Una passed them by, completely unnoticed.

The main corridor ended at a t-intersection, and as she approached the meeting of ways she hopped forwards twenty times on her tiny feet, once for each of the frightening dungeon-guards, the bogey-men in their clumsy masks and body armor that made them look bigger than they actually were. Pleased with her progress, she leaned out carefully for a look around.

There was a small round room at the end of the left-hand passage. The hall to the right was very dark, and there was no trace of his scent there. She turned left and entered the little room. There were four cells inside.

She had already passed by a score of similar chambers in the prison, each with its bounty of *Deadmen* waiting in silent captivity behind iron grates for their turn to fight in Gilat. This chamber was different, though. Only one of the cells contained a prisoner, and he wasn't one of the forest people or a Galanese criminal.

It was a simple matter for her to slip between the bars of his cell. Inside she found him wearing his accustomed battle armor, a bright red outfit formed from ultra-hard ceramic plates. He lay slumped sack-like against the inner wall with his helmet and mask upon the ground beside him.

He was sleeping. Delighting in the curious feeling it gave her, she watched his face.

"Big idiot," she whispered.

It had taken her all night to find this cell, and she knew that time was running out. If only the man William had left the bag closer to the entrance of the arena before the guards brought him inside—then she would have taken a whole hour to watch him and pretend that he was happy just to be watched. Siru had warned her very sternly against taking her leisure, though.

"Wake up," Una called.

There was no response besides his steady breathing. The sound made her feel relaxed. She had not often slept since his capture, missing the sound of his breath. With a stretch and a yawn she sprang into the air, and winging her way to the left shoulder of his breastplate she landed with a light pat of her tiny feet.

She noticed that his eyes moved beneath the closed lids. He was dreaming, just like he was when she found him by the river in Tarthalion. She wondered what kinds of dreams a Crodah man might dream. His mouth moved a little, so she thought he probably dreamed about food. She had none to give to him, though, and this made her sad.

Gazing worriedly into his face, she sighed.

"Get up?" she asked.

A metal door slammed somewhere nearby. Una listened closely with hands cupped behind her ears, testing the slightest vibration of the air. There was no indication a guard was coming, but the noise brought her back sharply to the grim reality of the prison.

Siru and Shanuri had many adventures together, and it all began in this place. Shanuri was not Yuuto, though. He wasn't like anything Una had seen before. He had no wings, no tail, no claws, and no scales—no attributes that lent him an advantage in fighting. Siru said he was just a Crodah. Whatever a Crodah was, she had no idea. All she knew was that Shanuri was a brave warrior, and he needed her to look out for him.

It was just as the Moriko had said.

Something strange happened the day this man-creature emerged gasping from the water and flopped upon the river's bank. A piski should have lived quietly by the water her whole life, listening to the muttering voices of the trees; but when Shanuri came the Big World began to change. She led him to the Moriko, and they told her to stay with him.

And so she had, from Tarthalion to the mountains, and away to the far northern country of Tryst. She had even followed him here, to the hostage pits of Nara's Gilat arena.

"Good morning?" she whispered.

Leaning forwards, she gently kissed his upper lip.

His eyes flew open with startled surprise. Blowing through his mouth and swatting his hands blindly, he was the image of a man wakened from a nightmare. Then he relaxed, fixing his eyes on her as she looked down on him from above, perched upon his brow.

"What are you doing here?" he asked in a hoarse whisper.

Thrumming her wings in an angry waspish manner, Una landed upon the toe of his boot and folded her arms, pretending to be angry. Shanuri settled back against the wall, wiping his mouth and glaring back at her.

"I could have smashed you like a bug!" he choked.

"A welcome?" she asked.

"Still speaking in questions? You know that drives me nuts!"

"Siru nuts?"

"*Siru?*"

"Questions?" she asked, unfolding her arms and smiling.

"Did Siru send you here, Una?"

"Nin," she said softly. "Marduka coming. Other people, too."

Shanuri closed his eyes again.

"Listening?" Una asked. "No sleeping!"

"I'm so tired," he mumbled. "They have me fighting the meeches almost every day."

"Not sick?"

"No. They're keeping me healthy just to see how long I last. If I ever get sick or wounded, they'll just keep me down there until I'm overwhelmed."

He looked very pale and gaunt, and his face was all stubbly. Water dripped on him from the ceiling above. He stank.

"Dreaming?" she asked.

"Huh?"

"Dreaming?"

"I was, until I got a bug-kiss."

She couldn't help but smile.

"Yes, a dream came to me Una, even in this place. I dreamed of a city."

"City?"

Mimicking the words of his thickly accented speech was Una's way of ascertaining Shanuri's meaning, but she sometimes missed the mark altogether. His look told her that she wasn't making herself understood very well, so she waited for him to explain.

"It was a big town, a town of many towns, far greater than any other. The buildings there touched the sky—but they were all broken."

"Broken city? Broken people?"

"I remember only a few people, a woman and a man, and two children also. They were walking around, but there were many dangerous things following them."

"Una likes walking," she said.

This time he understood. They had walked together for hundreds of miles over the ranges of the Ceregor, all the way from Tarthalion to Tryst. Of course, Una rode all that way on his shoulder. Walking for her wasn't about physical exercise as much as it was spending time with Shanuri. She had wings, after all—fine jeweled wings of iridescent green that matched her wine-hued hair. She grabbed them behind her back with the tips of her fingers, rubbing their smooth surface against her thumbs while he stared into the dark.

"I have never had such a strange dream before," he continued. "It was as though I was there. But now I am here."

He paused, rubbing his eyes wearily.

"What am I going on about? Nin or Siru sent you here, so there must be something happening. What am I supposed to do, Una—or can you even explain it to me?"

Una pretended offense, drooping her lower lip and peering to one side. Cousin to the common sprites' earthy brainlessness, piski weren't exactly accounted mighty thinkers; but that was because they spoke the languages of earth and water, air and stone, and their ways were not understood. They were kin of the Moriko, but were usually ranked alongside dumb animals even by the forest people.

"Come on, Una. There's no time for this. What am I supposed to do?"

"Shanuri's a toad," she stated in a flat tone.

He sat up straight and leaned out painfully towards his foot. "Look here, Una. I need to know if there's something happening, or I could get *killed*."

She decided he meant it. "Siru put Una in a bag," she began.

"I'm sure he had good reason—"

"Man puts bag down, and Una left. Searched all night. Found Shanuri!"

"But why were you sent here?" he asked with deliberate pause.

"Ladies and warriors?" Una tried.

This part she was confused about, so she frowned deeply, trying to think of the words to use. The problem was, the ranks and customs of these people were so outrageously alien to her that she wasn't quite sure what she'd seen while snooping around the arena.

But it was undoubtedly important.

"Ladies and warriors. Big battle today. Shanuri and Sirona."

"I'm supposed to fight Sirona?" he wondered, leaning back against the wall. "I'm going to die, then. There's no way I'll lift a hand against her, and Amed knows it. I wonder who he's entertaining?"

"Big battle. Siru knows."

"Siru knows? You mean he's planned something to happen while we fight—another attack on the field generators, perhaps?"

Una gave him a thumbs-up.

"He's an idiot. I already tried that."

"Ladies and warriors?"

He looked keenly at her. "Are you trying to tell me someone important has come? Can you describe them?"

"Four warriors, blue and gold. A woman, white hair. A girl, blue hair. Empress."

She'd never spoken in such spurts before, and it took a great effort—especially the word *empress*. Shanuri seemed pleased with her, for he was smiling.

"Good work, Una."

Una grinned from ear to ear.

"So, the empress and her retinue have arrived at Gilat, have they?"

"Empress is important?"

"Siru couldn't hope for a better target. An attack on the generators while Sirona and I spar would distract everyone sufficiently to make an attempt to remove the empress."

"Kill her?"

"If we kill her, the war ends. Many lives will be spared. The Fourth House would no longer be so sharply divided before the council's onslaught."

"Divided?"

"Of course, the Marduka would never come along with him if they knew Siru was going to lay a finger on their promised savior. He probably told them it was to rescue his sister. Have you spoken to Sirona yet?"

Una shook her head, still dazed.

"You'd better be on your way, then, but leave out all mention of the empress. And when you're done, I want you to get as far away from the arena as you can manage. If she's here, the power of Nin Marduka will turn this place into a chaos of terrors these people could never imagine."

The little piski was confused. All his words frightened her.

"Now, go find Sirona and tell her what you told me. Tell her that Nin and the others are coming to help—and remind her not to kill me."

"Can't."

"What do you mean, you can't?"

"Can't find Sirona."

"Well, you found me."

Una pointed to her nose. He seemed to understand.

"Then I shall have to manage by myself to warn her during the battle."

"Sirona and Shanuri fight?"

"We'll make it look like a fight. Even so, there's no contest. She could gut me like a larval kells."

He was interrupted by a sound of marching feet in the hall. Una had only seconds to hide herself beneath his helmet before the guards stood at his door.

"Up!"

Shanuri rose and stretched. "A battle?" he asked.

"You've been selected to fight for the highest honor in Syrscian," the man replied.

"Lucky me."

The captain nodded to one of his companions, who unlocked the cell door. Shanuri knelt and picked up his helm, carefully reaching underneath so that Una could hop into his right hand while he scooped it up. The front was masked with plain white ceramic, so she could remain hidden and look out the eye-lenses while he cradled the helm in his arm.

"You will stand before your master, the empress, so that she can get a good look at you before you face death in the pit," the captain said when the door was opened. "You'll be given your usual weapons."

"Who am I fighting?"

"The Angel of Death," he replied.

Shanuri nodded sagely.

"Might be the last time I pull you out of here," the man said. "You fought well, stranger. I can't think of a better end to my own life than to fight for the empress' honor against that scum Teomaxos. I hope you win."

Crouching in the dark beneath the helmet, Una heard these words and trembled. Shanuri stepped out of his cell and began to walk. She vowed she would not leave his side until he was safe.

They walked a long time until they reached a place where the guards left him alone. Shanuri lifted his helm and brought her up to his face.

"Scared!" she said.

Looking her sternly in the eyes he said, "Get out, Una, while you still can. You can't let them find you!"

She shook her head.

Frustrated, he lowered his hand abruptly, forcing her to take flight. She buzzed his head, but he put on the red helmet and lowered the white mask in place so she could not see his face. She had never seen him in such a mood before, and it was only just occurring to her that a year of fighting in the arena might have changed him. Desperate and frightened, Una stopped a moment on top of his helmet and looked around.

The room they had come to was a larger prison-cell. There was a grate behind them through which Shanuri had entered, and another in front. The place where he was standing was brightly lit by a spotlight from above, but everything else was dim and drear. From the grate ahead she could hear a rumble of many voices—thousands, it seemed. Off to the left there was another grate, and through this she heard the sounds of footsteps approaching.

"Better disappear," he warned. "If they find you now, I won't stop them from taking you away."

His harsh words were enough to break her heart. She was glad she could not see his face, for his voice had been horrible enough. It was an empty voice, hollow and devoid of hope.

Swiftly she darted like a bird to the farthest right-hand corner of the room, and there she hunched down into a ball, holding her knees tightly in the shaking embrace of her arms. She stared at the doorway, and looked back to Shanuri.

Tears came.

There were people gathering at the door, and in front of them stood the empress. She was lovely, her fair radiant face framed in red hair. She didn't appear to notice Una looking up at her, though for a moment the lady's eyes strayed far enough to the side that she might have seen the glint of tiny frightened eyes looking back.

Shanuri did not turn to look at the empress. Silent and imposing, he remained as still as one of the stone men in ancient cities.

The grate behind him opened again, and the guard returned with two large triangular blades, red like Shanuri's armor. These were attached to forearm gauntlets which he began to strap on with practiced ease. Neither of the men spoke. The empress looked on silently, her eyes widening with the understanding of what was going to happen to this man. Una saw in her eyes the fear she felt in her heart.

"He's all ready, Lady," the guard said.

Clapping Shanuri on the back, he left, locking the grate behind him. Shanuri flexed his arms and stared straight ahead, facing the outer gate—the door that would lead him out onto the bridge over the accursed abyss. Una sensed evil stirring in the air.

"Amed will not allow us to see Fann," said one of the people at the door. The speaker was a woman with white hair.

"Do you think he plans to use her in the game?" the empress asked.

"This was my fear from the moment he suggested we wager for her freedom."

"Then I will instruct Nunna to wait before seeking a way into the prison," the empress said. "No one else goes off on their own, even if it means we storm the dungeons together."

"I hope the empress can make a better plan than this, or you will be the death of me."

"Don't speak of such things, Morla. I fear more for our champion here. It is cruel that we should use him this way. I wish it were permitted to speak to him, but what would he say to someone like me?"

Shanuri turned a little to one side, as if to catch a glimpse of her face. A sound of trumpets brought his attention back towards the arena, though.

While her retinue turned away from the door of the cell, the empress lingered, gripping the bars firmly in her hands.

"Do not fear, warrior," she whispered. "I am praying this will all end before any harm comes to you on my account!"

She left.

Una hopped to her feet when the coast was clear, and she scurried to the bars. The empress had walked up a flight of stairs where other people were waiting for her. There was no escape from the room that way—not even for a little piski. There were guards with their back to the grate behind Shanuri, and they were too close together for her to get by unnoticed. Just one way remained open to her—the gate into the arena itself.

Heart pounding, she was just thinking of testing her luck when a loud voice filled the arena.

"The stoutest and bravest of hearts are among us today!"

A trumpet fanfare sounded, and there were distant sounds of many voices. The grate leading to the arena pit began to open, sliding upwards. Una peered timidly out the side-door, but guards had taken up position there as soon as the empress was gone.

"Here we will watch while criminals, those whose lives were forsaken for our sakes, tread the blood-soaked way that joins us all together in glory!"

The voices cheered, and the inner light of the room was extinguished. Another light shone from outside the door, which was now fully opened.

"Though their lives be marred by evils beyond the measure of their strength to correct, yet through the guidance of fate the forms of heroes have been stitched upon these mortal frames, or else we should have no tales to tell! And, in matters of destiny, in deciding justice, there is always a great story!"

Una's fear was heightened by the sound of so many voices, all shouting in unison. She had never heard such a noise before, a wicked din that could not hide the evil intent of the participants of Gilat. They were out to see blood spilled.

The speaker continued.

"Let me introduce to you the story of our heroes and their fight—and this being a fight unrivaled in all the history of Gilat, I bid you all listen closely."

Finally, a deep hush settled on the arena.

Una crept across to the open door in front of Shanuri and looking out she saw the bridge that spanned the void. Across the way, so far she could not see it clearly through the mists and blue static field of the generators, another open grate revealed a tall figure quietly waiting in the shadows of another cell.

Sirona.

"One year ago," the voice continued, "our priest, Teomaxos, left his station in Nara and traveled to the High Place of Gilthaloneth at the summons of the council. There he was raised to the honor of High Councilor."

A rumble of drums shook the prison.

"Then came the Destroying Empress!"

Silence followed his echoing words. The pause was so still that it seemed for a time that everything had just stopped.

"Now she blames Teomaxos with misconduct, desperate intrigues, and personal threats. In short, she charges him with treason against her royal self, and she has come to this very place today to see her charges answered!"

The stone walls shook. Sounds of wild shouting could be heard above the din.

"*That is why*—" the voice thundered, bringing quiet, "That is why I have selected for our Gilat today an unusual assortment of epic contests. Gilat itself shall reveal to us the innocence of our beloved priest!"

Shanuri sighed heavily.

"But first, before the proxy combatants are revealed, I must indulge all gathered here in the day's very special entertainment."

A humming noise reverberated throughout the arena. Trying to discover its source, Una looked upwards. High above, the dome let in a thin light stained blue by the shimmering static field. Recessed towers lined the upper arena in tiered ranks, forming a cup-shape over the pit; but still she could not identify the noise of machinery, growing louder by the moment.

Then there was a vibration in the stones beneath her feet. The bridge and its central platform flexed and swayed. Remembering the terror of the monsters she had glimpsed there yesterday, she suddenly realized there was no way out of the pit itself through the containment field. She was trapped; but upon the fighting platform a new thing was happening, and she no longer worried for herself.

Within the ring of pillars a cage ascended from a booth beneath the platform, and standing inside the cage was a girl. Una recognized only that she was Ayumu, and that she was terrified, gripping the bars of her cage and looking wildly around the vast arena. She seemed to hold her breath.

What was an Ayumu doing here?

Shanuri stiffened, as if he understood the significance of the spectacle.

"Those of you who recall the events of a year past will recognize the sweet voice of this angel of the Ayumu," the governor said. "People of Nara, I give you back your Singer!"

Stepping suddenly to the front of the grate, Shanuri looked as if he might dash out at any second. He halted just upon the threshold, however, for at that moment a small sound trembled the air, and the entire arena fell silent.

It was but a rising scale, sung even and true. Sustained for but a few heartbeats, it fell and reached depths that seemed to resonate with the stone foundations of the Gilat. Even after the brief utterance was stilled, a vibrating tone like a ringing bell was left shimmering in the air. Una had never heard such music before. Though there were no words, the song had passed through her like light, warming her soul in that dark place.

The song had come from the girl inside the cage on the fighting platform.

Her eyes were closed now, and her head bowed. The prisoner did not appear to be ready to sing further, though Una wished she would. For the space of a full minute the silence continued. Guards were running upon the terrace overlooking the pit.

Something was wrong.

In only a few more moments the arena shook with an explosion of twisting metal and flying glass. As shouts of fear resounded in the shuddering air, large sections of glass came falling past the fighting platform. Something was breaking through the dome far above.

"Just as I guessed," Shanuri said, his voice sounding flat behind the mask. "Nin's brought a swarm, Una. Find someplace safe and wait it out. This is where we say goodbye."

30

NIGHTFALL OF NARA

Nara Colony, Syrscian,
Year 1000 of the New Council

Costly embroidered linens and other embellishments aside, the walls of the lavish imperial box seat closed in on Val Anna like a cage. She was weary and wished to lay aside her armor, but the dining couches bore the look and feel of human skin—likely the trophy hides some Galanese warrior brought back from battle against the Fourth House. She hungered, yet she dared taste nothing from the low refreshment table. They would be taking no more risks today. There wasn't a doubt in her mind that Amed had set as many traps for her as he could.

While in the arena the governor's monologue continued and the crowds cheered, Bran and Vercingetorix posted themselves at the top of a stairwell leading down to an iron door. Val thought the men looked nervous, and with their captain and Caradoc away devising a risky plan of extraction, she could certainly sympathize. Amed had turned the masses against her even before the fighting began, all because she had underestimated the people's devotion to Teomaxos, their old priest. Even if Val won the contest of Gilat there would almost certainly be a coup. The locked metal door at the bottom of the stairs said it all—they were prisoners here, spectators of their own demise, and the only way they were going to get out was to trust Daedalus' crew. It was turning out to be Lothar's worst-case-scenario, just as Morla had foreseen. The only real surprise so far was Nunna's disappearance.

They'd lost her somewhere around the proxy holding-cell where the empress had met her hero. When Amed's guards demanded to know where the fifth member of their group had gone, Morla had suggested she was mingling with the crowds that were filling the arena, off in search of refreshments. This seemed to satisfy the soldiers, who cheerfully recommended several local delicacies. After ushering the empress to her private box seat, they locked her inside.

Val couldn't stop thinking about Nunna, alone somewhere on the other side of that locked door. Perhaps she had gone in pursuit of her original objective. Why would she do so, when Val had specifically forbidden it? What had her gifted sight shown her?

One piece of the answer to this was about to present itself in the most unexpected of ways—in a beautiful voice from the arena.

Turning her head instinctively towards the first notes of the singer's voice, Val felt the fragments within her resonate powerfully. An electric thrill passed through her entire body, awakening her suddenly as from a dream. The climbing notes rose in volume until the walls trembled, and then Vercingetorix and Bran unsheathed their hidden knives and stumbled forward from their places by the entryway. By the large window overlooking the pit the four stood gazing out, and seeing Fann within a cage upon the platform they grasped at last the net which was cast about them.

"Curse that fat fool," Vercingetorix whispered.

The unnatural brilliance of Fann's voice had drawn not applause, but fear. When her song was silenced, the shaking intensified. A black shadow passed over the platform, and people were shouting and pointing upwards.

"What's happening?" Bran asked. "Is it a quake?"

"Amed has forgotten an important detail in all this," Morla mused.

The others glanced away from the window a moment to see a slight smile tugging at her lips.

"There are others who have a stake in his game," she continued, "and they would bring this place to ruin even as Cipa was, a thousand years ago. Pity, that I shall have the foul luck of being here to witness it a second time."

The electric lights all across the arena flickered and went out. The crowds were still gazing upwards, but the dome was obscured by a heavy black shadow filled with moving shapes.

"What power is this?" Val wondered. "I feel it coursing through me!"

"There are powers that grow when they are exposed to the fragments of the Stone of Foundation," Morla answered, speaking low. "As the fragments rejoin, the world of Syrscian will begin to live again. The people will experience anew the realms as they were before the Destroying Fire. My sight tells me the Bringer of Dawn is awakening in Fann. As for yon shadow above, I sense that a swarm has been summoned—but by whom, I cannot say."

"A swarm?" Bran muttered. "You mean an actual dragon swarm?"

"Well," Vercingetorix replied hesitantly, "we are Dragon Slayers, aren't we?"

Val had heard of such things as dragon swarms, but stories and legends could not have prepared her for what came next.

The dome turned black, and then the first massive chunk of crystal detached from its framework and fell, shattering with tremendous force upon the bridge spanning the pit. With its crash came a startling realization of the implications.

"The field generators are down!" Vercingetorix shouted.

His words immediately preceded the sound of gunfire—the rapid whir and pop of Gatlings. There were PCUs in the arena, a meager security measure that wouldn't hold long against the horrors that were pouring in through the breached dome.

A multitude of winged shadows blotted out the sun. Moving swiftly, coiling and writhing, they entered the arena as a black cloud. Val couldn't see anything now but bright flashes of gunfire. The roar of shrieking cries and the thunder of wings was all that was tangible in the darkness. Huddling by the window, she felt Morla's hand and grasped it out of fear. Outside their chamber, the awesome ferocity of the swarm was rending to shreds the heart of the colony of Nara and its people.

Her people.

The dome rang with a hollow sound, and then collapsed in huge sections. Peeping out from the window-sill she could see sparkling rumors of crystal sheets tumbling downward into the arena.

"Empress, this is no ordinary kells-swarm!" Vercingetorix shouted over the noise of the collapse. "These kells are all juveniles. They are still small—they can go anywhere we can!"

"They will soon discover us," Bran agreed. "See how they are breaking off into smaller hunting packs?"

Val's eyes had begun to adjust to the dark, and there was also a little light coming in through the broken dome. While debris continued to rain down into the arena, the kells began to dissipate, just as Bran said.

"I'm worried about Fann," Val said.

Morla let go of her hand and lifted her head above the window-ledge. Her silver hair seemed to glow softly.

"There is a heavy smoke hanging over the pit," the seer said. "I cannot tell if the platform escaped being crushed."

"While the fate of my friend remains unknown, it would be irresponsible to allow fear to place the rest of you in jeopardy. Can we get down to the cage where I met the warrior? It is a defensible location with tunnels behind."

"I think it's possible to evade the hunting packs," Bran said. "But the cage doors were all locked when we left, and we're still locked inside this room—"

A chorus of shrieking cries interrupted him. The winged shadows flying around the arena had been at work upon Amed's security forces, and the gunfire began to dwindle to an occasional pop. Kells were now scrambling across the inner walls, coming closer to their window. The air was tinged with a smell of sulfur.

"The light is improving," Morla said.

"Would you look at that," Bran mumbled, staring out into the gloom.

The entire arena was crawling now with the shapes of terrible and fascinating things. A whirling cloud of black wings rushed round and round, faster than the eye could follow. Except for a few bent and broken trusses, the dome was gone. Beyond, high up in the sky, thick clouds were gathering above Nara. Val thought she saw the glint of an airship's hull, but it could have been anything. While the winged juvenile kells remained inside the arena, Galloglass couldn't possibly come to their rescue.

"It's Amed's nightmare come true," she whispered. "Except it came from the sky, not from the pit."

"The beasts below will sally forth soon enough," Morla answered. "This is the nightfall of Nara, after all."

A snap of wings breezed by the window, and the four hid their faces from view. Val saw a black shape dart overhead, and the wind of its passage ruffled her hair. The refreshment table behind them tumbled clear across the room, scattering platters and bits of food everywhere.

No one moved.

In the darkness it was impossible to see, but Val knew just enough about the desert-dwelling kells to realize the darkness would not hide her. The kells could sense the electrical energy of their prey in close proximity. Despite their wings they typically lurked beneath a layer of loose surface soil, and so they were classified as *Landworms*. Hidden or exposed, the kells were deadly hunters. With only two daggers between the four of them, there was little hope of escape.

But then, amidst a rustling sound near the dining couches, someone coughed.

"Who's there?" Vercingetorix challenged.

Black against the gray twilight, a masked shadow stood up and walked towards them. The Dragon Slayers leapt to their feet to block the intruder's approach with their bodies, bracing for an attack.

The intruder wasn't overly large or dragonish, though she did have wings. Folding them in towards her shoulders like a great big cloak, the Yuuto proxy faced them, pale eyes ablaze in her death's-head mask. She stood quite a bit shorter than Rix and Bran, but the mighty crystal sword in her hands was enough to even the odds. She obviously knew how to use it, too, for she moved to a guard position with practiced ease.

"This is the time for cautious speech, not for fighting," Morla warned, reaching around him to close her hand gently over Vercingetorix's knife.

"I don't like it," Bran said. "Kells outside, and this thing in here. I'd rather take my chances with the kells!"

"Your lives shall be spared."

The masked intruder's voice was thickly accented, but it bore a youthful edge—an edge somewhat sweeter than that of the blade she held ready, poised to strike.

Vercingetorix gawked. "Spared? What do you mean, spared?"

"My people harvest kells larvae for our food," she answered, maintaining her stance as perfectly as a statue. "You are speaking to one who has been in their nests from the time I was a small child."

"In their—?"

"Nin Marduka called them hither from the desert," she continued. "Only Nin calls such swarms; yet they are wild beasts, and easily excited. Therefore, you shall do as I say, Galanese. Maybe then you will be spared, yes?"

Vercingetorix lowered his knife, but his eyes glared.

"I don't know what passes for a lady among the people of the Fourth House, *Yuuto*," he growled in a low voice. "All I know is that you are a slave to that coward Amed, and I don't trust you."

Her sword wavered the tiniest bit, but she quickly recovered.

"No slave of Amed am I," she said in a stern voice. "Yet what of you and your companions? Are you not also participants in this grand spectacle of Gilat?"

Val stood and stepped between her guards, facing the cutting edge of the proxy's blade. The noise of the hunting kells was growing louder. She was taking a terrible risk, but desperation drove her to interfere, for time was running out.

"I am the empress of Syrscian," she explained. "I do not believe you wish me any harm, and despite our situation I certainly wish none upon you."

In the tense moments following her confession, the proxy moved not a muscle.

"Amed created the circumstances which led to all of this," Val continued, "but he no longer controls anything. It is left to us, then, to take back control and save as many people as we can. They are my people, after all. Would the Yuuto be willing to assist me as a gesture of good will?"

The sword-point was lowered, and when the Dragon Slayers had stepped back a pace the Yuuto reached upwards to unbuckle her mask.

"If the empress has indeed appeared among us," she said, "then my people shall stand with you in opposition of the tyrants who have threatened us all, be they Galanese or forest-kin. I swear it, for I am the chieftain of the Yuuto. Sirona is my name."

She removed the terrifying frowning mask and dropped it to the floor. When her true face was revealed Val was struck mostly by the inhuman beauty of her wide-spaced eyes, tinged a soft pink color like her hair. Her flat face beamed through the gloom with a smile that was strikingly out of place, given their current circumstances.

She was truly wonderful to behold.

"Not what you were expecting?" Sirona asked.

Val shook her head. "They called you the Angel of Death," she said breathlessly.

"Ah, but you are the Warring Empress," Sirona replied in her strong accent. "And never would I have imagined that a failed rescue-attempt would grant me the chance to test the qualities of my Empress against the ill report conferred upon her by others."

To Val's astonishment, the angelic beauty knelt before her and offered up her sword. Head bowed and wings spread low to either side, she was a picture of perfect calm amidst the storm raging just outside the window.

Morla stepped to Val's side and faced her.

"Will you accept the sword of the Yuuto, Empress?" she asked.

Val nodded, reflecting silently that she really had no choice. Their survival was at stake. She touched the cold crystal blade with her fingertips.

"Rise, Sirona Yuuto," Morla said. "We shall have need of your sword today."

"I shall not kill any of the kells," Sirona said, standing.

"Then what use are you to us?" Bran muttered. "Did you not just now offer yourself to the empress' service?"

Sirona fixed him in an icy stare. The thunder of wings beat upon the stonework around the window, but no one moved.

"I shall not ask of her anything that is in violation of Yuuto law," Val Anna said. "She says she will spare our lives. I suspect she has a way of accomplishing this which does not involve further bloodshed."

"I am a prisoner here because I came to rescue the red proxy, Shanuri," Sirona said to Val. "It is not because I am, as they say, Death."

She shifted her pink eyes back to the Dragon Slayers.

"We are allies, Galanese, and if I say you shall be spared, then you shall be spared."

Vercingetorix averted his own gaze. "Our loyalties are first to the empress. Do not forget it!"

"I shall not forget."

Without another word Sirona turned back towards the inner recesses of the room. With Bran in front, they proceeded down the narrow staircase in single file. The bottom step was as black as night. The metal door remained sealed against their exit.

Bran knocked the latch with the pommel of his dagger and pushed against it.

"It won't budge," he reported.

"Is it locked or jammed with debris?" Vercingetorix asked in a loud whisper from the top step. Val was in front of him, and Morla before her, white hair glimmering in the dark.

"Definitely locked!" Bran griped, slamming his shoulder against the massive door.

Standing beside him near the bottom step, Sirona offered no assistance.

"I was wondering something," he said to her, giving the door a final fruitless shove.

"What is it, Galanese?"

"Maybe Amed sent you to kill the empress. Maybe you're just acting the part of a loyalist to get close to her."

"He sent me to kill another proxy, a friend whose life I value greater than my own. I would rather save lives than take them. I make exception only for the creatures of the abyss, whose very existence is an unbearable torture."

"We are wasting valuable time," Morla warned. "Leave off the Yuuto chieftain if you will, Bran. She is as much under your protection as the empress."

Bran sniffed. "Funny, that. I thought we were under her protection—"

The door behind him crashed suddenly in its frame. Inches from the Dragon Slayer's head, a long bony projection had pierced the metal and was now twisting around. Bran repositioned himself discreetly as the toothy blade scraped free of the puncture. Something hissed.

Val was transported by that sound back to the fallen New York City, to the terminal where she found Nunna.

"There's death beyond that door!" Bran whispered in a trembling voice.

Sirona touched his shoulder lightly, and without a word she stepped down beside him. Her wings brushed his chest, and he moved up a step.

"Go and find a lamp in the room above," she instructed. "The door must be taken down quietly, or death will soon be in here as well."

At the bottom of the steps they gathered around a flickering lamp scrounged from the upper room, keeping an uncertain distance behind her while Sirona used Val's hairpin to free the hinge pins of the door. While the minutes passed, the arena thundered occasionally with alarming sounds of crashing debris and sporadic gunfire; but there was no further indication their exit was being watched, and that was somewhat of a relief.

"Surely my brother Siru is here," Sirona said, dropping the large upper hinge pin to the ground. She bent over to reach the last.

"Siru?" Val wondered.

"Nin is here. Only she could gather so many kells in one place. But she would not have come if Siru had not persuaded her."

"So, this Nin, is she Yuuto?" Bran asked.

Sirona gave him a weary sidelong glance.

"What? What did I say?"

"Yuuto do not call swarms, but winds. Nin is Marduka."

"Whoa! You mean the dragon tribe? But Nara isn't a military target. Why would two tribes work together to attack a merchant colony?"

"It was the illegal activities of the guilds which attracted our attention," Sirona replied. "But I care not for Siru's games. I came to free Shanuri, who was captured here on one of his own reckless adventures."

Blushing pink locks tumbled across her brow, slick with sweat. Her eyes were sharp in the lamplight.

"So," Bran probed, "this Shanuri fellow, is he your—"

"My brother is not attacking Nara to free me," Sirona interrupted. "Nin, perhaps, but not he."

The last hinge dropped to the stone floor with a clang. Sirona turned and handed the empress' hairpin to Bran.

"My brother has obviously prioritized the destruction of the Gilat arena," she said.

Then, meeting Val's eyes with a grave expression she added, "There is a possibility I am mistaken, Empress. You must stay close to your protectors. These kells are wild."

"And why won't they attack you?" Bran asked.

She cocked her head a little in the lamplight, and answered, "Because we are also wild."

Then, planting her foot firmly against the center of the metal door, Sirona shoved hard, knocking the entire reinforced panel out of the frame so that it fell into the outer passageway with a loud bang.

There was someone waiting for them on the other side. Her aspect was a little startling in the lamplight, so that even Sirona reached for her blade.

"Welcome, Nin," the Yuuto said, stepping forward with a bow of her head. "I was hoping you would come and find me."

The newcomer stood a little taller than Sirona, and was garbed in a travel stained tunic with thigh boots. A deep hood shrouded her face, but the dim light of the lamp revealed crimson eyes peering out at them. The skin of her exposed arms was smooth and pale, but there were small pink scales around her eyes. She advanced to greet Sirona with an embrace, and while the others anxiously observed their whispered meeting, a breeze blew in the corridor. The breeze ruffled the Marduka's raven-black hair as she drew back her hood. Val detected a pervasive odor similar to cinnamon.

"She certainly looks the part of an Empress," the newcomer remarked.

Val stared unashamedly as the stranger's features shifted suddenly, revealing a pattern of scales in vivid green and purple hues.

"I am Nin. I rule what is left of the Fourth House."

"Then it is fortunate we've run into each other," Val replied.

"You are the daughter of the Ancients, the one the Fomorian spoke of?" the Marduka asked. "I had expected someone...more formidable."

The two considered one another quietly for a moment while the arena rumbled with the vibration of its imminent collapse.

"You've met a Fomorian?" Val asked.

"Listen," Nin said, interrupting. "This place will soon become a den of meeches, and we all taste the same to them."

"What about the kells?" Bran asked, stepping out into the corridor.

She regarded him with a sly grin. "Don't worry, Galanese. I will drive the kells back into the desert eventually. The creatures from the pit are another matter, though. No one holds sway over them."

Val trembled, thinking of what Amed had confided about Gilat's true purpose. Vercingetorix was thinking the same thing.

"Eventually, all that was in the pit will spill forth into Galaneth," he said, "and then even the forest may succumb. Your attack on this arena threatens the stability of the entire region."

Nin's face became serious.

"This was considered," she replied. "I do not believe that the destruction of the field generators will result in an infestation, however. The beasts of the pit won't travel far into the Wastes, for they do not abide sunlight. Our estimates are not absolute, but it is doubtful the meeches will even cross the river."

"Nevertheless, there will be great turmoil here in the colony as they struggle to contain the vile outflow," Val said. "You risked much, and many who were sympathetic to the forest people will be lost."

Nin looked crestfallen, and lowered her eyes. "It is as you say," she answered in a sad voice. "I will not lie to the empress. I was swayed by a desire for revenge—revenge for the slaying of my father, and for the royal family of the Yuuto as well."

Val knew that she also shared a portion of guilt in all this. The distraction was supposed to offer an opportunity to track Teomaxos' expedition into the Wastes, not kill thousands of people. Was it worth all this trouble, just to prevent Eterskel or the council from getting their hands on whatever they wanted in the southern desert?

"It is done," Val said. "There is no undoing it. Now, what are our options?"

"We can't signal Galloglass to pick us up," Vercingetorix said. "There's no flying in through what's left of the dome—not while the kells are still here."

"Lothar would have had us secure the empress and fight our way out," Bran guessed. "But the exit's probably a feeding ground for all manner of unpleasant things. I doubt we'd make it through."

A moment of silence passed. Straining their ears, they could all hear distant cries of anguish and occasional gunfire. Nothing moved in the immediate area, however. All around them, the shadows were eerily quiet.

"We need to find Nunna," Val said. "She's very important, an indispensable element to our cause. We might also discover what has become of dear Fann."

"I also wish to know whether Fann or any of her sisters survived," Morla added.

"Finding Nunna won't be easy," Bran said. "It's not like her to go off on her own. She might've been captured, or worse."

Val weighed these thoughts, and then she said, "In any case, the tunnels behind the proxy holding cell by the bridge are a good starting point. From that location, we could also venture out onto the bridge to see what has become of Fann."

"I will lead you to the proxy holding-cell on the near side of the bridge," Nin said. "The gates to the dungeons are strong, but if we manage to get inside we might take shelter and devise a better plan."

"We are in your hands," Val replied.

Nin led them cautiously into the open lane beyond the door. The path branched left and right between high walls. To the right the lane disappeared into darkness flickering with arcing electrical conduits. There was a feeling of air moving there, but the way was partially blocked with huddled corpses and fallen kells. The hulk of a burning PCU lay on its side a little farther down. It was a Kerub unit. The pilot had been ripped out of the open cockpit, leaving a trail of blood behind.

The Marduka chieftain headed left, towards the parapet overlooking the arena pit. The rest followed at a watchful distance. Val fell into step alongside her, hoping to share some words with her while they walked.

"What do we do if the kells see us?" she asked.

"Don't mind the kells," Nin said, "They are clustering, and I will call them away soon. The tunnels and prisons below have been breached by creatures of fiercer mien, however."

"What about the colony?"

"I would venture to guess the kells are contained within the arena, but I can't say what it's like outside. Many will have died before nightfall. I am sorry—"

"It's not your fault," Val said. "I was the one who came here bringing death with me."

Morla bowed her head, as if grieved. Vercingetorix interrupted by clearing his throat.

"After we hunt down our missing friends," he said, "going out the front door is still our only chance of escaping this place. We'd stand a better chance of fighting our way out if these forest people would help."

"There is no escape that way," Nin said. "Siru found the entry hall sealed, blasted shut."

"Then how'd your warriors get inside the arena?" Rix asked.

"We captured the entrance to one of the lower tunnels leading to a closed excavation shaft by the river. It was only lightly guarded. I made my way into the arena and out into the streets that way, but I wasn't planning on bringing the empress back with me. There will be much fighting, now that the meeches are out."

"How long will the generators be disrupted?" Bran asked. "Maybe we could force a way through the tunnels and turn on the containment field behind us."

"That won't work," Sirona said, joining in. "The generators weren't simply shut down. They are burning, and the damage was made worse by the falling dome. Besides, the arena is open now to the sky—"

She paused, pointing upwards.

"What is it?" Val asked, looking up.

Above them, high upon the perpendicular face of the massive outer wall, a large number of serpentine creatures stared down, amber eyes flashing and mouths agape. Val stared back, mesmerized. They were very large and snake-like, having no other limbs than two pairs of wings. Countless more were gliding through the air between the fractured struts of the dome. The sky beyond was smoky, and the afternoon sun hung like a lidless eye surveying all in the gloom.

"You said you have an airship?" Sirona asked in a whisper.

"Well," Bran mumbled, "it's actually—"

"We have an airship," Val replied.

"Could you signal that ship to come down through the dome?"

"Are you insane?" Bran snapped.

Nin shushed them, pressing a finger to her lips. Aside from the noise of settling fragments and falling glass panels, the arena had grown still; but it might as easily be stirred up again by the slightest noise of their passage.

This thought bore itself out in truth when they stepped out upon the parapet, picking their way cautiously through the wreckage. As they neared the edge of the pit an enormous black limb crashed down before their very feet, and in moments the bulk of a spider-like meech heaved itself up onto the walkway.

The walls were crawling with the forms of these hideous beings, but up close you could really smell them, feel the fear of their many eyes, and hear the hiss of their nauseous gasping breaths. Val and Morla staggered backwards, but everyone else rushed headlong into the thing's clawed face. It was a moment of realization for Val. She wasn't ready to be a warrior—wasn't ready yet to defend herself, much less a realm. This single meech was enough to drive home to Val how pathetic she actually was in the face of true evil. Her Dragon Slayers, however, shouted with glee to test their strength against its mettle.

Though it was the size of a hay wagon, the meech was no match for four armed warriors. It was down in mere moments. Sirona delivered the killing blow to its head, much as she had done the first time Val saw her fight in Amed's trials.

The kells were roused a little by all their noise, and there were apparently a group of them hanging just below the ledge the meech had climbed. A few small creatures took flight and lunged at the warriors, snapping their jaws. Seconds later, though, a multitude rose up in a furious thunder of wings that brought everyone but Nin to a crouch.

While they knelt and looked out over the abyss at the retreating kells, Nin raised her hands towards them. Thousands darted like living ribbons through the air, twisting and rolling around one another in a fascinating display of coordinated movement. They were so large, yet so graceful, like schooling fish.

Sirona rose and joined Nin by the very edge of the pit, wiping her sword on the fallen meech.

"Take a look, Empress, Seer," she said. "It seems your friends are safe, for the moment."

Val stood and came up beside her, scanning the battered platform below with a cheerless expression.

In a circle of light shining upon the platform, Fann lay secure within her cage. She appeared to be unconscious. The empress' warrior-proxy was there also, masked and silent, seated in a state of deep meditation while all around fluttered scores of kells. Like swift predatory fish in a pool, the kells circled their prey—but they did not strike.

"The lesser field generators on the platform are still intact, somehow," Vercingetorix noted.

The high towers leaning over the pit had gone dark, but the field generators in the pillars surrounding the platform glowed with a weak fluttering radiance. They were clearly failing. While continuing their circumnavigation of the platform, the kells dipped into the spaces between pillars, then jerked aside to continue flying while a faint bluish haze settled in the air where they made their attacks.

"They are testing it," Nin said. "The field will quickly fail if such great numbers of them were to drive against it all at once."

"I thought you were going to call them off," Bran said.

Nin gave him a look, and then she bowed her head and closed her eyes. The kells immediately began to disperse, filling the air above the pit in an immense shrieking cloud.

The noise of the horde as it took flight was thrilling, awe-inspiring, and altogether terrifying. Just as it reached a crescendo, Nin lifted her arms above her head. The swarm moved en masse towards the broken dome, exiting in a thunder of wings and weird cries. It took several minutes for them to leave the arena.

Not all of them were gone, however. A couple dozen kells continued to revolve around the cage on the platform, and they seemed agitated.

Bran fixed his eyes on Nin. "That was pretty amazing," he said. "What about the rest of them?"

"Surely a few kells don't frighten you?" she replied with a shrug.

"Yes, they do."

"The field is interfering. They cannot hear me."

"I don't think we will make it in time to help them," Sirona said. "Even if I fly down there, I won't make it through that field any easier than a kells."

"We must do something," Morla urged. "That Ayumu girl—I believe she is the Bringer of Dawn."

Sirona and Nin nodded. Strangely, no one was surprised, for all had heard Fann's voice. They turned to regard the small figure inside the cage, and Val could tell they were curious. The legends of the Bringer of Dawn were well known even to the Galanese. Among the forest people this person was revered as holy, for she wielded a power mightier than any other in the Fourth House. Her voice was a weapon of immeasurable strength.

"All these things are happening now," Nin mused. "The exiles return. The Empress appears. The Dark Towers awaken. And now this? Why now?"

"My father always told us that it would be so," Sirona said to her. "You must go to the proxy holding-cell and open the door, Nin."

"What will you do?" Bran asked.

"I am going to distract them. And you, Galanese, will call your airship."

She pointed towards the broken dome.

"You want us to signal for an airship to come down through that?" Bran wondered, wrinkling his brow.

"The kells are mostly gone now. It should be an easy matter, for a brave warrior."

Then, with pink eyes shining, she leapt over the edge of the parapet.

Following with their eyes, the others leaned over to watch as she pushed her legs against the supporting stonework and thrust her slender body into the open air above the pit, swift as a bird. Wings extended, she touched down on a heap of debris on the far side of the bridge. There she began tapping her sword loudly against the stones.

The remaining kells responded immediately.

With the agility of a finch she fluttered and darted past them, leading four away on a merry chase. The rest went back to testing the field, but they now slowed their attacks, distracted by the strange flitting nuisance that was bounding from wall to pillar to walkway across the arena.

"Crazy kid," Bran muttered, looking on. "She won't even fight them if they catch her?"

"Don't worry yourself," Rix said, clapping his shoulder. "She can obviously take care of herself. As for me, I'll take the empress to the cages down below. You've still got those flares Daedalus gave you?"

Bran dug into a pouch in his tunic and nodded.

"If you get high enough, a flare might just clear the rubble."

They looked up into the ruined stands around the arena. There was no easy passage over the shifting mounds of wreckage, and any number of menacing creatures might be creeping about within.

"I don't know about this, Rix."

"It's our only shot," Vercingetorix said. "Don't get eaten by one of those meeches, okay?"

While Bran jogged off the way they'd come and Vercingetorix led Morla away from the edge of the pit, Val lingered a moment, her eyes drawn towards the small figure keeping just ahead of the kells.

Sirona was brave—braver than anyone Val had ever met. Where did she find such amazing courage and strength?

Her gaze shifted then to the far side of the arena. A forbidding shadow crept upon the opposite wall, level to the place where she stood, but when she stared at it a moment longer it disappeared in the murk. With its disappearance emerged a sensation of intense loathing that she had not felt in a long time.

Something horrible had come.

She turned away quickly, feeling helpless and pitiful. While others risked their lives for her sake, it seemed she could do nothing more than worry. A seed of hope had awakened within her, though, and she knew that when the time came for her to face the source of dread that reached out to her through the darkness of the abyss she would be ready.

The way to the prison doors was less hopeful, however. There were many unfortunate spectators crushed by the rubble, and the brooding presence Val felt had begun to affect the others as well.

They found the deadman holding-cell wide open. The broken end of a key stood out from the latch. Vercingetorix and Nin went inside first, followed closely by Val and Morla.

Val's gaze was drawn to the left, towards the bridge and the distant platform swarming with kells. She shivered to think of Fann trapped out there. What about Fann's little sisters, and Nunna? She began to doubt she would ever see any of them again. There was no longer any sign of Sirona. Through the arched gate she saw only a few kells darting around the cage.

She hoped the Yuuto was still alive. The thought of such a brave and beautiful person dying while she distracted herself with seemingly inconsequential details was almost too much to bear. Val strove against the desire to run out onto the bridge and do something.

"Do not fear, Empress," Nin said quietly.

Val looked away from the scene on the bridge and peered into the green and purple scales of the Marduka chieftain's face.

"Sirona and I have been doing this since we were children," she comforted. "She can handle a few kells, and I believe we have some time yet before the field covering that cage fails. Please trust us. We will rescue the Bringer of Dawn."

Val nodded. She was more frightened than she realized, and this put her at the mercy of those more experienced in such matters. Presently, the others were looking out for her, and that gave her some security in the shadows of the room.

But not all was dark.

A faint glow like an ember was emanating from the far corner of the cell. When Vercingetorix and Nin went to investigate, an abrupt clanging sound made them all jump. The noise had come from the rear door of the cell, but there was no one there. The door appeared to be locked.

"Is there someone back there?" Val called into the darkness.

"There's certainly something alive in this light," Vercingetorix said excitedly as he knelt down in the corner of the room.

The others joined him. "What is it?" Morla asked.

"It doesn't look very dangerous."

530

"No!" Nin chided, reaching out to grab his hand. "Don't flick her like that!"

A little glimmer of light was on the floor between them. Val pulled her attention away from the midnight darkness behind the cell door.

"She's a piski?" Rix guessed.

Nin nodded. "Her name is Una. And be careful, because she bites."

Peering over the hunched shoulders in the corner, Val marveled at the sight of a tiny winged person sitting on the cold floor. Diminutive but perfect, her little iridescent limbs were daubed with spots of white light. Vercingetorix flicked her once more for good measure. A miniscule hand swung out and swatted at his finger.

"Annoying little things," he said.

"It was Siru's idea to use her," Nin said. "She follows the brute that Sirona's taken to, Shanuri. We hoped the piski would be able to find him in the prison and inform him of our plan to free Sirona before the field generators went down."

"You think maybe she understands us?" Vercingetorix asked.

"Somewhat. Why? What are you thinking, Galanese?"

"I'm thinking she's so small a kells won't notice her."

Jeweled dragonfly wings quivered behind the tiny person. She brought up her knees and wrapped her arms tightly around them. Lifting large eyes, she appeared the saddest creature Val had ever seen.

"She might be able to carry a message to Lothar," Vercingetorix suggested.

"Or maybe to the red proxy?" Morla wondered.

"I was thinking she could get us into the tunnels, at least," Nin said.

"Nin angry?" a little voice asked.

Looking closely at the upturned face, a preponderance of childish tales passed through the deepest recesses of Val's mind.

"I am not angry, Una," Nin replied.

"Shanuri?"

"We know where Shanuri is."

"Don't know? Shanuri finds Empress, Shanuri kills Empress."

Grim silence followed her words.

"This whole attack was a cover for your attempt on the empress' life?" Vercingetorix wondered, rising to face off with Nin.

"No," she said, standing slowly. "It can't be——"

Rix frowned, folding his arms across his chest.

"We do not have time for this," Nin said, anger seeping into her voice. "Yes, when rumor of her return first reached us, there were some who said that killing the empress would end our war with the Galanese."

"And what do you say?" Val asked.

She looked Val in the eyes, and such firm resolve was there that Val felt ashamed for asking.

"Sirona's brother, Siru, has sometimes voiced this opinion. He has also brought the human warrior Shanuri into his way of thinking. Little do they realize they would only be doing the council a favor by killing you. As for me, I would lay down my life for the future the empress brings, even if Syrscian is not yet ready for it."

"Even if it means dividing your own house?" Vercingetorix asked.

"I will forbid any fighting between the people on my behalf," Val interrupted. "I've had enough of it. Right now we have to concentrate on saving our friends and getting out of here."

Vercingetorix nodded towards the cage on the bridge. "Your proxy, Shanuri—if what Nin says is true, he'll try to kill you the moment we get through that field."

This threw Val off a second.

"He's a real monster, or he wouldn't have lasted a day in this place. I would be hard pressed to take him on by myself, disarmed as I am."

"That may be true," Nin remarked. "However, Sirona would not allow Shanuri to harm the empress."

"But I thought you said Sirona and he were——"

There was another banging noise by the door at the rear of the cell. Morla walked towards the noise, and bent down to pick something up.

"What is it?" Val asked.

She held out her hand, and in her palm was a ring of skeleton keys.

"Now what are the odds?" Rix wondered.

As if in answer to his question, a fat shadow emerged from the shadowy darkness behind the locked door, and with it were two smaller figures, gagged and bound.

"That Marduka is well spoken, for a savage," Amed said. "Ah, Morla, you've got my peace offering. Open up this door so we can get out of here, will you my dear?"

Morla stood her ground, holding the keys fast in her clenched fist. She endured Amed's taunting grin like a silver-haired statue.

"Never fear, Seer," the governor said. "They are well."

"That's good," Vercingetorix replied, taking the keys from Morla as he and Nin approached the door. "That's real good, because if I find that you've so much as touched a hair on the tip of their tails, I'll toss you to your pets in the pit. Seems to me they might take a shine to something chewy."

Amed stumbled backwards as the Dragon Slayer reached through the bars to unlock the door.

"I meant no harm!" he said. "It was all a fair game!"

"A game?" Val wondered. "You mean to say thousands of my people just died for a game?"

"Your people?" the governor chuckled.

"You are overly fond of games," Nin said, thrusting the door open.

"What if we have a little game of our own?" Vercingetorix proposed. "I was thinking of fishing for meeches. There are still a few kells out there, too. We could wager which one goes for him first, or we could cut him up into little pieces and watch them all frenzy over the bits."

Amed glowered, his eyebrows bushy under glittering eyes as the two smaller figures pushed past him and rushed into the chamber. They made straight for Morla, pressing against her sides in fear. Overcome beyond words, Morla knelt and embraced them fiercely.

"Why are they tied and gagged?" Val asked.

"They didn't know when to stop talking. It was for our safety."

Nin entered the corridor beyond the door and circled around the governor, shoving him forwards into the proxy holding cell.

"If you want to remain alive," Vercingetorix said, "you'd better *start* talking."

"You're not going to allow this dirty Marduka reptile to interrogate me, are you?" he asked, waving his hands towards Nin.

She stood behind him by the gate, locking it again so that Amed understood there was no escape. The governor fumbled nervously with his robes.

"Relax," Vercingetorix said. "We only want to know one thing."

"If you're referring to a way out, I assure you I would have taken it long ago if there was one."

"Really? I don't believe that for a second."

"Then ask your scaly friend," Amed growled. "I've no idea how she got past the gates, but I'm sure this murderous Marduka could lead you straight through. It was her people who set off a massive disruption that caused the field generators to fail. Civilian deaths will be blamed on their actions, and—"

Vercingetorix held up his hand for silence.

"If there's no way out," he said, "then our other companion is still somewhere inside the arena. Maybe we'll help you escape if you tell us where you're keeping her."

"Ah, you mean the blue-haired one. I've not seen her since earlier today, when the empress chose her proxy."

"Liar!"

Val had found a small seed of courage in the wrath that stemmed from Amed's lies. The flash of her blood-red robe matched her mood, and though the governor was taller than her by more than a foot, the anger of the fiery girl clad in silver armor had an impressive effect on his demeanor. He trembled at her approach, and then dropped to his knees, hands raised above his head. For a man of his girth, it was an exceptionally humbling stance.

"Please," he whispered. "Please, I beg of you, Empress, do not harm me with the spells of the Ancients!"

Val stopped in her tracks.

"I am only a poor fool," he said, choking up. "I am but a puppet of that monster in Tara. You must believe me!"

The lights on the platform went out with a low humming sound. The field generators guarding Fann's cage were powering down. Desperation moved something deep inside her, and Val's mind finally made a hesitant leap.

"Now I see what you're about," she said angrily.

Amed shook his head, coughing and weeping.

"You are worried about the Musab Black Market more than the kells or the creatures of the abyss. Eterskel of Tara is your greatest fear. Eterskel won't be pleased with this day's events—especially if Tara itself is overrun by meeches. That is why you are hiding here, isn't it?"

"Yes, hiding behind little children," Amed said, nodding his head emphatically. "I had no choice!"

Morla had just finished untying the rags binding Finn and Faylinn, and as she did so Faylinn pointed to the governor and shouted in a loud voice.

"He handed Nunna over to Teomaxos!"

Amed lifted his bulk up on wobbly arms. He was actually very frightened. The man operated solely out of fear—and now he had good reason.

"Teomaxos," Amed said with a nod. "You know, he used to respect me? But before he went on to become Councilor in Gilthaloneth, he hired that terrorist Shanuri to kill me—set him up as one of my personal bodyguards, he did. That girl, she was just another assassin sent to kill me, wasn't she?"

"You handed her over?" Vercingetorix asked. "I thought you said you hadn't seen her."

"That's not so important, is it?" Amed asked. "Besides, she gave herself up in exchange for these children. It was Teomaxos all along, I swear!"

"So, you both fear Eterskel," Vercingetorix mused. "And now the councilor has taken your prize away as an offering to the Musab. Where does that leave you?"

"It was all I could do!" Amed raged. "Please, you have the Bringer of Dawn and these others! Isn't that enough?"

Pressing the key-ring into Rix's hand, Nin moved towards the bridge.

"We don't have the Bringer of Dawn yet," she said. "I will join Sirona and attempt to drive the kells away from that cage."

"Go, then," Amed said, rising to a kneeling position. "I hope they eat you, stupid snake!"

"Your curses will fall on your own head," she fired back.

The governor lowered his face.

Nin stepped out onto the bridge. She walked slowly towards the kells, hands outstretched. Morla looked on, speaking sadly while she stroked Finn's matted hair.

"They brought Nunna to me tied in a sack, kicking and screaming," she said to Val.

"So you told me once, long ago," Val said.

"From that day on she taught me that all events are somehow joined by a purpose that guides history itself. Then she died to save Nergal, and to save us all. The Nunna that the empress brought from another world is like her in that her gifting is secondary to her purpose. I surmise that this is the reason she was blind to the spy in our midst."

"It was one of the Dragon Slayers," Faylinn said. "Kidu was his name. He slew the guard and took us to a secret place deep in the Undercity. Teomaxos was there. It was the councilor who brought us to Nara, after the empress left. Now he has Nunna!"

Morla rubbed the girl's back and pulled her close.

"What's the big deal about your blue-haired friend?" Amed whined. "It's not like I cudgeled her or anything. She gave herself up in exchange for these two. Go ahead and ask them, if you don't believe me!"

Morla looked at him and shook her head. "Poor Amed," she lamented. "You have no idea what you've just handed over to Teomaxos, do you?"

Vercingetorix turned away from watching the bridge, where Nin was standing small and insignificant before the kells.

"Nunna was the core of the Null-Navvie Construct."

"The Construct?" Amed mumbled. "You mean, *the* Construct? But that's just a foolish old story!"

"One of the long-vanished Null-Users, huh?" Vercingetorix mused. "Lothar always said she was a curious one, but she seemed pretty normal to me. Were they all like that, the navvies?"

"There were none like her," Morla replied. "But the substance of purpose is woven throughout all things that strive for life. Purpose is as intangible as Fann's song. All the pieces are coming together in this one place of destruction, where an epicosmic sum of histories is about to play out its hand; and you are a part of that, Vercingetorix, just as is Amed, and myself."

"Uh, right," the Dragon Slayer said. Then the meaning of her words unfolded inside his mind and shone on his face. Amed had also understood, but the seer's words seemed to drive him over the brink of madness.

"You really believe there's a purpose for all this destruction?" the governor said with a strange laugh. "Ha! You blindly believe that every ill turn of the road suits your own schemes, Morla? What a fool! There is no purpose! Eterskel controls us all now, even the empress!"

"How so?" Vercingetorix asked warily.

Amed bowed his head. "The lord of Cipa holds a fragment of the Stone of Foundation."

"He is a Dark Tower, then," Morla said with a nod. "Long has Orlim suspected this."

"You knew?" Amed wondered. "The Centaur knew, and yet he allowed the empress to come within Eterskel's reach?"

A long string of spittle was dangling from his lower lip.

"The fragments are gathering again," Val Anna said to him. "They will be united in my flesh, and those who will not yield them up to me will wage a war of Dark Towers. This you already knew, Governor. What you did not consider is that you had a choice."

"A choice?" he said, laughing giddily. "Death take you all! There is no choice!"

Then, with a scream, he lifted himself on chunky legs and grabbed the key-ring from Vercingetorix, who moved immediately to block the governor's escape; but Amed wasn't interested in unlocking the tunnel-gate. Instead, he rushed out into the arena. For a moment everyone was too astonished to make a move to stop him, and then it was too late.

His fit of madness carried him out onto the bridge. Nin fell prostrate as the kells surged around her and dove with force upon their screaming prey.

Amed's shouts for help seemed to go on for a surprising length of time, though in fact it was probably only seconds. The kells scraped him up in their talons, and amidst the noise of tearing they could hear Nin shouting as she ran towards them across the bridge.

Though it seemed they were ignoring her, the kells lifted off in a flock as she approached. Bearing away a bundle of shredded clothing and limp limbs, they rushed towards the open sky beyond the dome. The Marduka chieftain continued running towards the proxy cell, however. It wasn't until then they understood she was shouting a warning.

"Run for the tunnels!" she cried.

Vercingetorix looked down into his empty hands, and with a curse he began to make his way out onto the bridge to look for the keys among the messy remains left where Amed had met his end. He stopped on his third step, though, and began backing into the cell even as Nin crossed the threshold.

"We're locked out!" he shouted. "That fool grabbed the keys!"

"We must find someplace to hide, then," Nin said, gasping for breath. "An Illuyanga Dragon has come—a rogue male. It does not answer me, for it was summoned here by another!"

Then they heard the wings beating a heavy booming rhythm in the air. Faylinn and Finn buried themselves in Morla's arms. The empress wished she could have taken comfort somewhere, too.

"What about Fann and Sirona?" Morla cried. "We can't just leave them!"

"We aren't going anywhere anyway," Rix mumbled.

Their time for making careful plans had run out. Settling with a crash onto the bridge, the beast arrived with a roar and a foul-smelling blast of wind. Everyone hurried towards the locked door at the back of the cell. A glance to one side revealed that the fairy they'd seen earlier had already taken flight.

How Val wished she had the ability to disappear as well.

31

THE WARRING EMPRESS

Nara Colony, Syrscian,
Year 1000 of the New Council

Out upon the bridge, a ghastly gray miscreation stared out of the reek of the burning arena with pale glowing eyes, its spiny gorgon head rotating this way and that atop a long neck, searching the shadowed archway of the holding cell. Nin stood at the gate, powerless against a creature that exceeded the measure of her will.

The end of the Illuyanga's toothy snout was like a beak, and its mighty jaws opened and shut rhythmically. The sound of its breathing was like the bellows of a furnace. As the dragon stooped bat-like upon its wings and began walking along the bridge, Val caught a glimpse of the fighting platform. The field was down, but everything was obscured by heavy smoke. She couldn't see what had happened to Fann.

"Isn't there something you can do?" Vercingetorix said to Nin.

The Marduka chieftain had caught her breath, but she had nothing more to say. They were trapped in a small space, and this was an adversary that none of them could stop.

"It isn't attacking us," Morla noted, holding Finn and Faylinn close. "Maybe it is confused, or lost."

Morla alone seemed to be unaffected by the death that was looking them in the face. This boosted Val's confidence, but not by much.

"It has been forced to fly far from its nesting grounds," Nin said. "It was called here, but it does not know why."

Hearing the faint noises of their speech, the dragon hissed and flattened itself upon the bridge. The others moved back, clinging to the shadows, while Val lingered in the center of the cell. She was fascinated by the way the dragon moved, twisting its head back and forth, inspecting every detail of its surroundings. Its caution indicated an impressive level of intelligence, much higher than she supposed the monster was actually capable of. It was as though someone was looking through its eyes, directing its disoriented steps, guiding it to the kill.

Even so, it had clearly missed something, for at that moment, the sharp snap and shriek of a signal flare echoed across the empty arena. A second report followed soon afterwards. The dragon looked up and tasted the air.

"Your warrior has completed his task," Nin whispered to Val. "Your ship will come if the signal is seen, but it will not go well if they miss the danger!"

"Bran would never have signaled Galloglass if he knew that thing was in here," Rix objected.

"Maybe he's trying to distract it?" Val offered.

The Illuyanga swept its large bat-like forelimbs upwards, wings extended fully. It was indeed distracted.

"I don't know," Rix said, "but if that's what he's up to, I hope he can get out of sight before that beast finds him."

Before the dragon leapt forth to investigate, a cry from the parapet above the cell diverted its attention yet again. Tenuous hope returned in the form of a smallish figure that landed hard on the bridge, right in front of the entrance to the holding cell. Rising tall, rose-pink wings outstretched like the banners of the dawn, Sirona made her return.

Blinking blue nictitating membranes, the Illuyanga rotated its ugly head to face yet another new threat. It seemed apprehensive as it studied the young woman, and flicked the air continuously with its tongue. The winged Yuuto tribespeople were quite bold, but this one was clearly different. Even to Nin, who knew her well, the Sirona Yuuto safeguarding the empress now was very much changed from the one she thought she knew.

"Your airship is coming," Sirona said to them. "They may reach the dome soon, if they have seen the signal."

She didn't turn fully around as she spoke, and her strongly accented voice sounded strangely cold. Glimpsing her face in profile, Val saw the pink eyes ablaze. Sirona knew that they could not fight the dragon and win, and yet she did not flee. She was the only one who could.

"I spoke with him before he fired the flares. Bran is making his way to this place to shield the empress from the overflow of the abyss."

Val was less worried about meeches at this point than the monster heading towards the holding-cell. The metal braces that supported the bridge squealed and popped with distress at the dragon's approach. The stonework began to crumble.

"I will make sure that this beast does not hinder your escape, Empress."

Val was speechless.

Sirona then stepped out to meet the Illuyanga head-on, and as she left the archway a sudden change came over her features. From her arms she sprouted feathers, and from her fingers long curving claws. Val knew that the people of the Fourth House had the ability to alter their forms in a way similar to the Gremn, but this was the first time she had witnessed it. It would likely be her last.

The dragon had been scrutinizing the newcomer, and as she stepped out onto the bridge with so menacing a mien it shook itself and unfurled its wings—an impressive display. Leaning forwards, Sirona shouted and spread her own wings defiantly. The sight of her small shape against that hurricane of muscle and pebbly scales was ludicrous, but Nin had rightly fathomed the weakness in the titan's heart. This was a territorial creature that would never have come to a place like this unless it had been driven by another's will.

"She tries to distract it from its master's call by a show of force," Nin guessed. "She hopes it will seek open skies beyond the confines of this cavernous, enclosed space."

Rix looked at her, and then back at Sirona. "It doesn't seem to be working," he said.

The Illuyanga drove its head forwards, slashing its jaws at Sirona's parrying blade. Sirona was knocked backwards, but had managed to hold on to her sword. For another moment they all held their breath, wondering how the spectacle before them would play out, and whether or not there was anything they could do to change the outcome.

The Illuyanga stretched its jaws towards her again. It looked like the battle would be over in mere moments, but then everything paused. There was another presence in the darkness of the theater, something that could be heard above the background clatter of meeches crawling up out of the abyss. Something else was out there, and the Illuyanga was but his calling card.

The Illuyanga's body smashed hard against the bridge, crumpled by an invisible enemy that struck from above, and all was a confusion of red and gold flashes materializing just beyond the gate, moving so fast it seemed fluid.

Time seemed to slow down. Nothing moved but the figures beyond the gate, twisting and coiling with a ferocity unrivaled by earthly beasts. Before Val could make sense of what was happening, a loud cracking noise was heard. The Illuyanga's mighty wings were broken. Its long neck flopped down, and the whole bridge trembled. As the struggle came to a halt, the misty air over the pit wavered and grew still, and the feeling of unease that had been growing on the empress' mind all day finally blossomed into a form she recognized. It was as unmistakable as the green-eyed behemoth grinning at her across the dead Illuyanga.

Glede had come.

Despite his dramatic entrance, Val had felt his distinct presence the moment the field generators went down. There was something about him, something he had partially revealed to her in Regulus Terminal. But what did the Illuyanga have to do with him at all? Was Glede the one who had called it here, only to destroy it in the end?

His eyes were fixed on Val.

As she stared back, the world around her faded to a lifeless gray fog. The Illuyanga slipped over the rail of the bridge into the pit, its head following the bulk of its body with a sliding rasping noise of scales on the stonework. Having satisfied himself, Glede turned his body to face her, and he spoke out of the gloom with a voice every bit as grating as she remembered.

"Well met again, *Little Empress.*"

Glede backed up, moving towards the fighting platform without turning his back to her. Val still could not see Fann or the cage through all the smoke, but she could see Sirona lying motionless upon the threshold. Nin and Vercingetorix stood by, static, staring ahead. Morla and her young charges cringed behind her, but they were all as still as statues.

Thinking that the Yuuto might be gravely injured, Val stepped forwards to where she lay and reached out to take her beneath the arms. There was something wrong, though. She could feel a quickening of the air, an imperceptible curtain that disconnected her from everything else. The air became heavy, making progress impossible. Even where she stood, reaching, she felt as though she was struggling to move her limbs in deep water. Sirona seemed a million miles away, though she lay right at Val's feet. The sound of her footsteps made no echo at all. Sound was dampened by whatever phenomenon was being projected around her.

Glede stopped backing away from her, observing all she did with wary care. Back in the terminal of Regulus Transit, he was nothing more than a shadowy form in the dark. Then she had only viewed clearly his horned face and wings. Now he was revealed fully—scaled hide gleaming like a loose garment of red granite, eyes like flaming lamps, and a face as expressive as that of any sentient being. When at last he spoke again, it was with a resentful tone.

"You safeguard the past and future of all our worlds by what you protect, Little Empress. If you perish, then the stone's purpose shall never be fulfilled."

His jutting jaw and fiery eyes conveyed nothing of his intentions. Beyond his base aura of cruelty, there was nothing apparent in his actions. He made no threats. Val knew that he was a bearer of a fragment of the Stone of Foundation. She wondered then if he had come to take the fragments from her that were already gathered in her flesh. Was this even possible? Val did not know; but she had a feeling Glede knew.

"Brisen's words, those were," the dragon remarked with a savage wink.

"How do you know the words my mother gave to me?" Val asked.

Glede stooped gracefully, leaning on his mighty wings. "I know because I bear the Dark Star," he replied. "*Dim Da'ummatu*. Through it I can peer into the minds of the others."

"The minds of the other Dark Towers, you mean?"

"Aye. Mine is a fragment that speaks in dreams, and brings them to life. Thus I brought the Illuyanga from his quiet glade in the mountains and slew him for sport. The weaving of dreams is not the limits of the Dark Star, however. It also possesses all of the qualities of the other fragments. Thus you are defenseless before me, Little Empress, even were you to bear all the other eleven against me!"

In that moment, Val felt truly terrified, for she knew that what Glede said was true. He moved dragons and men as his pawns, even if only to destroy them for his pleasure. Against such a reckless foe, even a mighty army would founder and fail.

"And what of your friends?" Glede asked, looking down at Sirona. "I suppose you realize now that it would be impossible to find the strength among this rabble to oppose me. Their substance is not as yours or mine. Sorry to say, they won't last long in their current state!"

He was right. They all looked translucent, like ghosts, visible only by the melancholy pale sheen of stale sweat on their skin. Sirona's form wavered before Val's eyes, as if distorted through a warped piece of glass. She searched the Yuuto's face for signs of life, but all she could see was a phantom.

"They are all so incredibly frail before Regulus' power," Glede said.

Val was taken aback.

"Ah," the dragon said with a smirk, "you thought this was something that I had done to them?"

She reached out into the heavy air and tried once again to grasp Sirona's arms, but the effort was wasted. Her hands closed only on cold air.

"What's happening to me? If you know, then answer me!"

"The loyalty of a human heart is not enough to reach into the place where you have gone," Glede said. "*It is a perilous road, and a difficult choice. It is the Lost Road, where all of you are joined in purpose.*"

He spoke Brisen's words to her in a mocking voice, and her anger flared. Released suddenly from the affected field around her, Val's hand came up swiftly, flashing brightly like a star.

"I wouldn't do that if I were you," Glede warned.

It was too late. Val experienced the release of energy from her body as an intensely satisfying sensation, but in its wake the figures around her were flung by an explosive force. Crashing into the walls of the cell, they lay stunned. Her own senses were increasingly clouded, and her ears rang with a sound like tolling bells. It brought to mind her experiences in the Viaduct chamber aboard Auriga, and all that she had seen there. The others were slipping away. The burning arena and the little cell melted into a shadow until all she could see was the dragon.

"You are still trapped within the destiny of the Stone of Foundation," Glede remarked. "It is verily as Brisen said. You dream its dreams, as you have always done. Unfortunately for you, I have the power to control those dreams, and to bring them to life!"

Then the world vanished completely. A dream appeared before her eyes that she had dreamed long ago. Lost on a sea of darkness, anchored weakly by dim memories, Val recalled the forest of fungi and the mighty trees of Tryst. They had met in this dream-forest before, she and the boy. He had tried to protect her, but he was slain by a red dragon. The red dragon always came to her in her dreams, and as often as he appeared the boy always tried to save her, but was slain.

Glede's voice spoke into her mind, saying, "I told you that it happened in the colony of Nara, did I not? I saw him there, and offered to help him. That was actually some time ago. Don't you want to know how he came to be here, Little Empress? Fleeing those who believed him to be responsible for your disappearance, he was captured."

She came to her senses suddenly, though not fully, so that the drab mists parted just enough for her to see into the little existence she had known. The dragon was there inside the arena, and her friends lay dazed, recovering from whatever power she had unleashed.

But there was someone else, too.

Insignificant and small, a form in red armor walked upon the bridge behind the dragon. Her deadman, the red proxy, had ventured forth from the fighting platform, which was veiled still in smoke. Though everything around him appeared indistinct, he alone was clear and hard and real; and all Val's mind was bent upon him. She thought she saw a reflection of someone else in him, masked though he was.

Somehow, there was a fragment of Regulus inside him, too.

"But that is impossible," she muttered.

"Not impossible," Glede said. "You know it's true. You were the one who chose him, Little Empress; and oh, how he suffers! Still, he refused my help, just as I told you when we first met. He has made me an offer instead."

The red proxy's expressionless mask revealed nothing of the all-consuming purpose that drew him out of the shadows to stand beside Glede. He could not have dared such a thing unless driven by an insane passion. The strength of his hatred reached out to her, and magnified by the dragon's own ire it pulled her back into the body of the empress, Val Anna, standing alone among her fallen friends in the holding-cell.

She felt a jolt pass through her as she assumed her armor-laden form. Something Glede said didn't make sense.

"Are you saying you knew what choices he would make?" she asked. "You possess the power to see what will come to pass?"

"Ha! I am no seer. That is not the way the Dark Star works. I am not able to predict the future. Instead, I experience all possible futures through the dreams of the Stone of Foundation, and bring to life those iterations which are most beneficial to my designs. It is a useful power—especially when dealing with an Ancient."

Val stepped past Sirona's body, and she felt a greater existence pour into her small frame. However briefly, an adjustment to the weight of her limbs and the feeling of air drawn into her lungs caused her discomfort; but then her form was wreathed in pale flame, casting soft white light upon the scattered forms of her companions lying around her like leaves after a storm. Her armor shone like the sun.

"And finally you have awakened!" Glede said with a bow of his long neck. "The Warring Empress returns! It took all of my power to call you back, you know. I have anticipated our combat for a very long time. Let me introduce to you my own warrior, the one who shall fight in my stead."

After a cursory glance at the dragon, the red proxy approached to within a dozen yards of where Val stood. There he paused, and reaching up to remove his pale mask, he cast it aside into the abyss.

"He is called Shanuri by the forest people. His right name is Taran Morvran."

Val didn't flinch when she saw his face. Of course, she always knew. How could it have turned out any other way? And now he was here, right in front of her. He had come to slay her, conquered by a power of deception older than the earth, and it was her fault that he was in this situation.

A breeze blew up from the depths, ruffling Taran's hair. His eyes were hollow, and no emotion was visible in his face. Val likewise stood cold. Her heart was an iron ingot in her chest.

"It is as I've said," Glede replied. "You chose him, and he was pursued because of you in the world where you hid among the Crodah. However, by the workings of Regulus you two have never met. In the world he comes from, he was falsely accused of the crime of your abduction. However he came to be here, he quickly learned of the Warring Empress who ended the world in the Destroying Fire, the goddess of slaughter who returns now to complete the annihilation of the forest people. As such, he has sworn to kill you, and I for one will not stand in his way."

It was Taran all along, but not her Taran. Val searched his eyes, empty eyes that stared without blinking. This man had never met her, had never walked the woods and fields of the little world of Earth by her side. They had never sparred with willow sticks or nodded through the professor's boring lectures. They had never shared a piece of pie on a summer evening in celebration of constructing a flying machine. He was, however, the boy whom she had dreamed of since childhood—the descendant of Ard Morvran whom she had seen while walking in the delirium of her lasting illness. He was the reason she had taken form in the Crodah world of exile. He always saved her, and she would not be complete without him.

The knowledge of these two who were one passed through her mind in an instant, and like the images she'd seen inside the Viaduct she understood that this moment was a culmination or sum of possible histories within the Stone of Foundation. Whatever had become of her Taran, this boy was the one who'd managed transit to Syrscian; and however many years he'd been here, like everything else she had loved, he was changed by the wars she'd begun. He had become a tool of her enemy in a fight that was not his own—a weapon to slay her and end all the worlds in darkness.

"I wonder," Glede said, "what will you do now, Little Empress?"

Val also wondered. The man before her represented the very reason she had gone into exile in the first place. The mystery was shaped by the Stone itself, and as its fragments were reunited in her flesh a new story was being written in the history of Syrscian. Considering this, she could never desire harm to come to him, even if it was within her power. That is why she refused to believe that he truly wished to kill her now. He was a puppet of Glede's poisoned words.

Taran lowered his head. His blades were poised. There was a glint in his eye, and his mouth twitched slightly. With a shard of Regulus inside of him, he could possibly shatter the strength of a Dark Tower. This was doubtless what Glede had in mind to test before trying it himself. However, no matter what the dragon said, Taran was Taran. She braced herself to meet whatever came next. If love was a weakness, perhaps she had come to know it only to permit it to destroy her.

A tear traced a cool path across her cheek.

Taran blinked. Perhaps the Dark Star itself comprehended no more of tears than of human love, and thus the depth and power of such a small thing had been left out of Glede's careful calculations. Whatever the case, the empress' tear had altered things significantly.

Taran swung his arms and turned away from her, diving straight in towards the dragon's belly. Glede wasn't caught completely by surprise, but the ferocity of Taran's will granted him speed, and the serpent's coiling tail was slashed. Bluish-black blood streamed across the bridge as Taran rolled to avoid claws the size of scythes. Glede missed, for Regulus was strong, and its power was in motion. Val could feel its fire resonating inside of her, a flame like a star, but she knew that it was not enough. Shimmering slightly, the dragon momentarily vanished into thin air.

Yanked off his feet by the camouflaged serpent, Taran was lifted high above the bridge. He struggled, pushing against an invisible form. Blood dripped from his side, but it was not his own. As Glede's shape slowly rematerialized, Val could see that his wounded tail was wrapped tightly around Taran's body. The dragon lifted him up until the two were face-to-face. Still Taran struggled, stabbing at the monster's rugged hide and swinging ineffectively at the toothy maw that appeared before him.

"*Useless!*" Glede muttered. "You dare strike out at me with pathetic human hands—you who bear only a shard of Regulus? I am a Dark Tower, and you are nothing to me!"

Val was powerless to intervene. The tail lifted Taran higher, and then flung him down hard. A jumble of red armor ripped free, clattering noisily across the bridge while he slid and rolled. No scream passed his lips, only a cough that produced a dark trail of blood. He was pale even before he came to a stop at Val's feet.

He was dead.

Val Anna looked up from Taran's blank gaze to face the might of the dragon. A lightness entered her body and took away her fears. Maybe it was just hysteria, but she felt as though Glede had suddenly shrunk to the size of a flea.

"*You will die for this,*" she declared.

Though she had spoken only just above a whisper, the echo of her will clanged bell-like throughout the arena. What was left of the outer wall collapsed. A torrent of dust and stone fell down into the black gulf of the void, and many evil things went back into the darkness with it.

Glede chuckled, a horrible rasping laugh. He was nervous, though. Val sensed it. He had revealed too much of his thinking.

"Have you found your voice at last, Little Empress?" he asked.

The platform and bridge darkened, and a few more skeletal fragments of the dome fell inwards, freed by the collapse of the outer wall. The bridge was struck by large metal beams. Sparks flew from the stonework, but it held.

"*Nishu rabtuma nashi saphatim,*" Glede said. "Mighty men and scattered peoples, they are all alike before us, Little Empress. They exist only to serve our purposes. When their role is finished, we may dispose of them as we wish."

Glede nodded his enormous head towards the holding-cell behind her. The others, no longer ghostlike in their appearance, were stumbling to their feet. Sirona also stirred, alive and uninjured.

"They shall fear you now. Whenever their Empress is in turmoil, all her realm shakes!"

Vercingetorix and Nin gathered Sirona. Bran had also rejoined them, and was hovering over Morla and the children. She could feel their presence, hear their breath. Were they, as Glede proposed, no more than tools of her will?

"They all desire death!" Glede said with a hiss. "With the Stone of Foundation, you and I could rule them completely. They would give their lives happily if you command it in the name of the fragments you bear."

"I did not go to the Blue World to return a tyrant!"

"Says the one who destroyed Paradise! We are Towers, Little Empress, and as such we destroy what we touch."

"There is no reason for it," she said weakly.

She knelt then and wept before her enemy, brushing back the hair from Taran's forehead. A fire burned suddenly through the hand that stroked his head. Another shard of Regulus had come home. Glede looked on, and he no longer seemed so confident.

"*Ana shimtim kima wardum ittalak,*" he said, backing away from her. "The boy went to his fate like a slave; and though he set steel to my flesh, still he served my purpose without flaw. He thought he was protecting you, but this was not his task. You should not begrudge my gift, Little Empress."

"You can keep your gifts," Val answered sharply.

Then, standing over Taran's body, she raised her hand again towards the dragon. Her first experience of the power of Regulus left her feeling as clumsy as a toddler taking its first steps, but now she was able to direct the power with a purpose. Glede knew it, too. He cringed, knowing that his poisoned words were void.

"You did not come here to kill me, foul serpent, but to shape me to your plan. I may have been easy to stop before, but I have returned to my realm a new being. You will not succeed!"

"Shape you to my plan?" Glede mocked. "What do I need you for?"

"The fragments will only be recohered in me," she replied. "Do not even dream otherwise!"

Glede recoiled from her, narrowing his eyes to slits. And then he felt it. The air around the dragon trembled with light, and his massive body stiffened. It seemed he strained against a great weight pressing him on all sides; but this was only a taste.

"Hearken, Glede! I am *Bal Ona*, Brisen's daughter! A word from my mouth will be sufficient to end you, for my life is the life of Syrscian!"

The dragon's form wavered, and so did his will. With a look of malice he struggled to turn towards the fighting platform. It was in his wicked mind to destroy Fann, and he might have done so if he had not at that moment been distracted by a bright light that blazed out across the arena.

With a boom of rocket-flares, Galloglass had come.

Daedalus was bringing the airship down through the broken dome, chasing the last of the kells from their shadowy roosts with flares. The percussions broke free the last flimsy struts upon the edges of the dome, which came crashing down with great force upon the empty stands.

Glede flattened himself against the bridge. He was hissing furiously, swiveling his body defensively and swinging his head back and forth. It was not the power of Regulus that caused his distress, though. Nor was it Galloglass, for Glede feared no weapon forged by men. It was a voice. Heard only faintly at first, ringing through the emptiness of the abyss with a sweet sound, a song resonated and grew until it seemed to spring forth from everyplace at once. Each soft tone was like a living thing. Its power shook the very foundations of Nara.

The Bringer of Dawn was awake. The release of Regulus' power had called her forth. Looking up towards the fighting platform, Val saw the door of the suspended cage standing open. Fann's slender figure stepped out onto the bridge, her torn skirts fluttering in the wind. She was crowned by the glittering form of the little Piski who had set her free, and her face exuded a peace that was a salve to Val's wounded heart.

Then Fann put words to her tune, and though the words were sad they penetrated deep, wringing joy from the grief that had swallowed Gilat.

> O'er the fields of withered gold
> Ablaze with fire of ancient lights
> I see the worlds go sliding by
> Draw near to me.
>
> I see the road cut through the sky
> Across the dusk of dying day
> Appear forgotten stars of hope
> Draw near to me.
>
> I watched you descend from the dream I had
> Called down from the sorrowed forsaken lands
> Rest safe in my heart's deep love for you
> That is all that my hope can do
> Draw near to me.

While she sang, it seemed an ocean wave swept over the desert of Galaneth, sweeping away everything in its path. In its wake there were green fields under a sky shining with stars. Val saw the imagery in her mind as though it unfolded before her eyes. Glede saw it too, and realized too late his mistake.

The words that Fann sang were not the dreams shown to him by the fragment he carried. They were strange to Glede, and their meaning threatened his dominion of fear and shame.

High above, twisting their way here and there through the pink haze that came upon the end of that dreadful day, a few stray kells were yet flying high above the ship's balloon. The shapes of meeches and other horrors crept up along the walls from the deeps, but Galloglass' lamps shone brightly, banishing the darkness. Fann showed no sign of fear as she strode the twilight path of destruction.

Glede had thought, perhaps, that this small Ayumu girl was nothing—just one more trifle he would destroy in rage as a parting token of ill-will. By the time Fann's song had ended, though, he gathered the little strength he had left and leapt from the bridge, gliding down into the pit with a howl of rage. Before vanishing beyond the reach of Val's will, blending into the darkness and stone by his skills, she thought she heard the echo of his voice in her mind.

"Your hopes will fail, Little Tower of Darkness. You and I are more alike than you guess!"

32

FAR FROM HOME

The Forest Tryst, Syrscian,
Year 997 of the New Council

Ibni awoke with a start, for the damp stony ground was soaking through his cloak. But no, there wasn't any cloak, and he couldn't feel his own body. The vague recollection of such things was less like a real memory than a dream, a dream of a life lived thousands of years ago. All there was in the here-and-now was the sickly amber glow of the PCU's interface, a sight etched permanently into his retinas. He saw it even while he was sleeping.

The only world he knew was the insides of a horrible Seraph, and a voice that drew him he knew not where.

It was currently midmorning. The Seraph lay upon its back under a slate-colored sky. Jewel-toned butterflies fluttered around above his head, hurling themselves in contrary currents of air. He'd made his bed upon a great staircase leading to a ruined arch with nothing else beyond. The arch and a few attached walls were all that he could find. There were no other signs of human habitation. Vines and tree-roots twisted fantastic serpent-shapes around the stone blocks, slowly prizing to bits the last traces of civilization in this gloomy place.

No one had been here for a very long time, and it was the same everywhere he'd been so far. He'd crossed the high passes in the mountains some time ago. His mind was fuzzy about the details. Ever since Shu was taken by those men with tails, he'd been wandering like a ghost in a dream.

In a dream—

Ibni pushed himself up, disturbing the butterflies from their pageantry. He rested the Seraph in a sitting position while sinking deeper into thought. Wherever he was now, and however he had come to be here, he was truly lost. There was no accounting for whatever happened after the attack in the woods or of the weeks or months of wandering that followed. All he knew was that he was alone, and this wasn't anyplace near his homeland in Canaan.

As a bit of lost property, Ibni sided with those memories which were immutable, memories of the existence he'd known before climbing into the accursed seraph. These memories didn't necessarily comfort him, however. He recalled sitting the seraph-throne with the royal seal in his hands, but he also knew that his kingship was merely a contrivance of the alien aggressors called the Gremn. Was it the Gremn who had made for him a seraph-throne as an emblem of the mechanism which currently caged him? He thought it was probably so. Had they also inscribed upon his signet ring the polar stars, the so-called *Indestructables*—symbols of his rightful place in the undying realms beyond Earth, where the Sky-Power dwelt? Nurkabta had undoubtedly planned it long before he was born. And he was Nurkabta's son.

Ibni was one of them.

The truth was, he was an illegitimate king with no real connection to the Old King before him. Nurkabta had woven him into a rather complicated plan; but Nurkabta was dead. Ibni could not fathom this was also part of the plan.

Without Shu, he was alone in a wilderness where even the stars were strange. He was left with no choice but to run away from everything; and so he had run. After several weeks he knew of no way back to where he'd lost Shu. It made him miserable to think about such things, but what could he do?

"Proceed to Islith."

The voice, which at first had been just a faint whisper, spoke to him again. It spoke in words sometimes, but more often by clear impulses, urging him to move north. In the north there was something called Islith Manufacturing Facility. He had to get there.

Startled from his reminiscing, Ibni raised the PCU to its feet, surprising a pair of enormous beetles that had been roosting in a tree behind him. After waving off the aggressive man-sized insects he turned towards the mountains in the south. At one time he thought these were the same that he and Shu descended after meeting in the caves of the Watchers. This had turned out to be a false presumption, but he wasn't exactly in his right mind when he scaled those terrifying peaks. It was while he wandered upon yonder heights he began to feel a strong compulsion to move north. And so he had moved on, and the weeks passed.

This forestland north of the mountains was very different from the fungi forest. There was fungus here as well, but mostly enormous trees that dwarfed even a Seraph. There was no thought of turning back, though, and the insistent voice was daily becoming louder.

He wished he could sigh, but the Seraph's speech modulator produced only a grating noise when he tried. There was no one to blame but himself, of course. It was his decision to climb inside the PCU in the armory of the Gremn ship Auriga. Though it had seemed a good idea at the time, he was regretting every moment of the thousands of years thence, prisoner to the machine's limitations. Even in stasis he had dreamed its dreams. Maybe he could be freed if he reached Islith Manufacturing Facility.

He would not have called this a hope, since he had lived so long inside the Seraph to have lost almost all cognizance of a body other than the one made from metal. It was somehow important, however. A Gremn body might live forever, but not this metal one; and the PCU was looking even scruffier than usual, having weathered a new round of scuffing upon the rocks in the mountains. It bore a rich spattering of mud and spores from the forest as well. The damage was self-healing, but some wounds healed very slowly; and some, like the more serious nicks in the joints of his arms, were interfering with normal movement.

He'd been in a bad tussle a few nights ago with a creature that attacked him just after he'd come down from the mountains. It was a monster of scales and horns—an actual dragon. Despite his clumsy movements he'd killed it with his hands, and this made him feel like a hero out of the old stories, like Marduk or Gilgamesh. He might have been embarrassed to compare himself to characters out of Babylonian illustrated stories, the kind of fiction that kids ogled on the city-gates, but while he was on his own he allowed himself to indulge his imagination a little.

The only thing that truly worried him was the possibility of meeting more dragons, and that they might be a bit bigger and more dangerous deeper inside the forest. There were certainly other stalkers in this wood, though they kept out of sight. He'd spotted the tracks of a monstrous wolf, too. His brain was bursting with wives' tales told in Canaan of godlike creatures that roamed the old world. If the Seraph continued to degrade, he wouldn't be able to defend himself. A dread crept through the grim primeval forest, but the voice pressed hard against his great fear, urging him to move on.

A breeze began blowing while he stood there, and he wished he could remember how that should feel. There was absolutely no sensation from his body, if indeed any part of it still existed inside this machine. Shaking off this reverie, Ibni was alerted to a faint sound coming through the PCU's powerful auditory sensors. It was like the sound of hooves running on a field. One moment they were there, and then they fell silent.

Thoroughly awakened now, he lifted his head to one side and scanned the space beneath the canopy ahead. There was something there last night, as he recalled. It was a light and the sound of hooves that led him to this spot. Then it came to him again from the trees ahead. With the noise of galloping there was a glimmer of light. He was entranced by the sight, for though the Seraph permitted many extraneous sensory adaptations that he'd come to take for granted, it limited all of his own senses severely. He'd not seem such a light as this with his own eyes since he was first trapped inside; and now, beaming in through the optical interface, the glow he perceived was brighter than daylight. He made for it heedless of his footing, pushing through the scrubby growth on the edge of the clearing until he tripped and fell with a thunderous crash beside a low hummock of earth that a tree's root had upturned. The ground gave way beneath him, and he slid down a very steep slope. At the bottom he lay still, dazed and confused.

Through a tangle of vines he could see that the drop curved gently around on either hand, describing the arc of an enormous crater. It was darker down here, but a hundred paces ahead there was a place where the shadows of the trees melted into a dense fog, shaping the horizon into a solid gray wall. The air glistened. The fog flickered with light, and again he heard the sound of hooves.

Allowing the Seraph's sensors to study the light, he watched a strange shape dancing in the spaces between the trees. He thought he caught a glimpse of wings. Whatever it was, it moved swiftly and cautiously, and then it vanished.

He waited, but the glow and the sound of hooves did not return.

There was no mistaking it, though—he was not alone. Something was out there. Pushing the Seraph to a sitting position, he broke free of the vines and branches that had fallen over him on his rough descent. A noise drew his attention to the steep grade behind him, where he noticed a little cascade of loose soil and stones clattering down. He saw only gray-green shadows and creeping mists, but there was definitely someone moving around up above.

Ibni calmed himself. Whatever he encountered out here was likely to run away as soon as it saw him. Then he remembered the dragon, and a trickle of fear brought him up to his feet. As soon as he rose, however, he found himself almost level with the top of the slope— and with someone much less intimidating than a dragon.

The boy stepped back from the edge of the slope and clenched his jaw. Standing his ground, he brandished a walking-stick above his head with both hands as though readying for battle. Though he looked no older than Ibni was the day his city was abandoned, it was plain that his hand was practiced. The gear he wore, a strange coat on interlocking metal rings and leather stuff, was mud-stained but richly crafted. If appearances counted for anything, this lad was someone important. His courage spoke of a hero's heart.

Lifting metal hands in a gesture of submission, Ibni surrendered. The boy remained fixed in position, as if he was made of stone. His staff did not waver.

"If you both stay that way, the forest will soon cover you with molds," said a voice from the clearing behind the boy.

"Quiet, Gwion!" the boy shouted.

Ibni was amazed by the ferocity of the young master's eyes. His tousled shoulder-length hair was the color of sand.

"He obviously means not to harm you, Conn, or he would have already."

The staff wavered, and then the boy backed slowly out of reach of the PCU's hands. When he stood at a sufficient distance, Ibni saw another person, robed in green, walking forward to meet him. His appearance drove away all the fears of the forest, for the newcomer's hair was as white as snow—as white as Morla's. His face was also very much like that of the other boy, the one who was threatening him with a stick. They were both so similar in feature that Ibni wondered if they were brothers.

Brothers, like he and Shu.

"There's nothing to be frightened of," the green-robed one said, projecting his voice loudly. "He's really not that frightening, once you get to know him."

"Stay where you are and declare yourself!" shouted the smaller boy with the stick.

Ibni looked at them for a long while, trying to decide what he should do. These were ordinary people, and as they lacked baggage he guessed they were locals who might have some idea of the lay of the land. Perhaps he should ask for directions. First, he would try to communicate in their words some understanding of his peaceful intentions.

"Ibni," he spoke through the modulator, placing one hand upon the Seraph's mighty chest.

The two boys looked at one another, and Gwion spoke.

"I am Gwion. He's Connor Morvran."

"Artorius Castus!" the little one snapped.

"His uncle Callum calls him Conn."

"Mind your own business, Druid!"

"I am a mage. There is a difference, *Conn*."

Ibni watched their exchange with interest. It was nice to hear the chatter of young voices after such a long time of wandering alone. He lowered his hand and placed it on the ground at the top of the slope. The one called Connor was wary of him, however.

"Don't move!" he shouted.

Ibni tilted his head. "Lost," he said.

"You're lost, too?" Gwion asked. "How did you come to be here?"

"Avalon," Ibni answered. "Ibni came from Avalon."

This provoked an unexpected response from the younger boy, who lowered his stick and stared at him with wonder. His eyes seemed ready to burst, and his mouth was stretched into a thin line. Ibni looked back through the visual interface, searching their faces, but they were both obviously thunderstruck by what he had just said.

"Avalon is the sacred home of my kindred, those descended from Ard Morvran," Connor managed. "It is a secret to all but the mages. How do you know about it?"

"Ibni was inside Avalon. Now Ibni is here."

He did not want to belabor the point. There was no need to mention the fact he wasn't originally from Avalon, or that Avalon was destroyed.

"But no one has seen it since its disappearance in the first days of the world!"

"And yet—" Gwion then added whispered words aside, spoken into Connor's ear.

"You speak true, Gwion Bach," the boy replied in a humbled voice.

Ibni guessed they had by now come to the conclusion they were no longer in the Earth. "Friend?" he asked.

Gwion grinned, but Connor wasn't so ready yet to let down his guard.

"How do we know you aren't trying to trick us?"

Ibni rested a hand upon the Seraph's broad crown and wondered. There really was no way he might convince them he meant no harm.

He was at a loss, but then Gwion stooped and picked up a rock. Taking aim, he threw it straight at the PCU's faceplate.

Ibni cowered, but ducked too late to avoid a direct hit. The rock struck with a loud clang. He pulled back sharply, but this caused the Seraph to tumble backwards, and the impact felled trees in the thick of the lowlands. Laughter came down from the top of the ravine.

"You got him, Gwion! You got him right when it really mattered!"

"It was but a test," Gwion replied, rocking on his heels.

Ibni returned to the shelf overlooking the foggy fen where he'd fallen. Picking himself up was becoming more difficult, for the ground was very loose from all his banging around.

"Well, Master Ibni," Gwion said to him, "I for one will trust you; for though I deem you capable of making hay of us quite easily if you wished, you have only tried to make acquaintances of us instead."

"We followed the winged horse here," Connor said. "Were you following him also?"

Ibni shrugged the Seraph's mighty shoulders. He'd not seen any horses, though he had heard the sound of hooves. As for horses with wings—

"We tracked it for three days, only to find an iron coward?" Connor griped. "He must've scared it off."

"And he might well scare away some other nastier things," Gwion mused. "We should take up with this fellow. He could serve us better than a horse, if he's willing."

"But we left the Ironfish with nothing, and we're lost in dragon-lands."

"I am familiar with the lore of forest plants and their kinds. Though I must admit this world is strange to me, it is unlikely we will starve."

Conn held his belly and groaned. "All you want to eat is sticks and mushrooms!"

"We could always dine on dragon—"

Ibni listened to them go back and forth awhile. He recalled the hour he first saw Shu in the cave of the Watchers, and he was struck by the great absurdity of meeting strangers in this country who were not very different from himself. Was it truly as Nurkabta said, that there was only one outcome to all events? Was he here, trapped in the Seraph, merely to meet these boys and guide them to a place of safety?

The voice was calling him onward, though. He turned to face the deeper forest.

"Where are you off to?" Connor asked, stepping to the edge.

"Islith Manufacturing Facility," Ibni replied, pointing into the misty crater.

Glancing to the side, he saw that their faces were sufficiently daunted, and a distant memory sparked inside his mind. He recalled a deep place beneath Hazor where he had held a girl in the Seraph's palm, wading through a lake of poison to some lonely place. Her name was Nunna.

How could he have forgotten?

"Ride?" Ibni asked, holding out his hands.

"Are you joking?" Connor asked with a grin. "I've seen how securely you keep your feet. I'll walk through this valley my own two, thanks!"

As they slid down the slope behind him, Ibni felt a great weight rise from his heart; but they had not gone far before the mist thickened again, and then they all heard the stamp of hooves. A winged figure of a horse glimmered in the murk, leading them north into the heart of the forest.

33

RELICS OF WAR

Islith, Syrscian,
Year 998 of the New Council

Stomping along through a wilderness of mutant fungi and impossibly huge trees, Hannah's guides led on without the slightest hint of the trepidation that dogged her every step. The more she considered Bec's parting instructions, the less convinced she was of her role in this adventure.

"You must explore the ruin and find a way into Islith."

Islith was no storybook castle. Though it was one of the twelve great cities of the Ancients, it had been transformed by the Gremn into a kind of hive. The city was comprised of living organic architecture, like Avalon; and before it ended up on the bottom of the Atlantic Ocean, Avalon had guarded Islith long ages ago. As if this wasn't amazing enough, Bec also told her that Islith, Avalon, and all the great cities of Ancient Syrscian had once drifted aloft among the clouds. It was after Avalon was captured in a terrible war and the Gremn were forcibly exiled that the undefended city followed its primary self-defense logic and burrowed underground.

A thousand years had lapsed since then. Islith's null remained installed after the Gremn left, but remained in a dormant state. Bec didn't explain why. The only thing Hannah clearly understood was that this legendary city was going to be difficult to find—impossible, in fact, if not for the assistance of its scattered inhabitants, the navvies.

It hadn't been easy for Hannah to adapt to all the changes foisted upon her since the incident at Hazor. She'd met the Gremn, visited starships, evaded mechanized combat units, and was left stranded on an alien world. Somewhere between the Fomorian and the giant fungi of Tryst she'd become somewhat desensitized to the endless dreamscape unfolding all around her—or so she thought.

"These navvies will protect you, and they can track Islith's location, for they were born inside."

A day after their arrival at the old mound, Bec used her strange power, the Green, to find them. Like the Tin Man times three, they stood rooted in place, derelict and dilapidated: a trio of humanoid robots. Their limbs were long bare of skin, with metallic struts and faceplates exposed, rusting with careless abandon. From their rundown condition, and from the shrouding of brambles and mold that covered them head to toe, it was easy to imagine they'd been sleeping on their feet for a thousand years. Even so, they awakened immediately upon being addressed, as if they had been waiting only a little while.

Their speech modulators weren't in perfect repair, but they communicated well enough. Their language was a form of English salted liberally with outlandish jargon. After the Fomorian had made her purpose understood, the navvies seemed agreeable to guide Hannah to Islith.

"Islith must awaken and rise again," Bec had said in parting. "It is like Avalon inside, but far greater. You may examine anything you find there, but be watchful for automated defense systems. There will be Navvies, and maybe some Moriko. The Moriko inside Islith itself are to be feared, but those I bring back with me will be instrumental to the task of dealing with the null and awakening the city. The purpose of this is to locate another fortress in the east, which is named Atlantis. It is all according to Brisen's plan."

Bec never elaborated on who or what the Moriko might be, but she did mention one other danger to be wary of. When Hannah asked about Islith's null, she explained that it was a brilliant being who would challenge her in unexpected ways.

As if she wasn't sufficiently challenged already.

Her three guides spoke very little at first, and her questions about what they might face upon reaching Islith went unanswered. They looked more like the Terminator than the Tin Man, but they were perfectly harmless. Hannah was familiar with the navvies built by Osaka University, but these were far more advanced than a twenty-first century terrestrial android. Since they weren't much for deep conversation, Hannah kept herself entertained by inventing nicknames for them. None looked distinctly male, but their voices were like those of men, so she named them the Stooges.

After a couple of days camping with the Stooges, she began to pick up on their subtle personalities, and learned to tell one from another by their distinctive patterns of rust or breakage, for they were moldering sufficiently to be easily identifiable from one another. Moe bore a bold blackened crust upon his bare metal skull, and Larry sported a little tuft of wires hanging out of one side of his head. Curly lacked any similarities to his namesake, but his legs acted up on the third day, resulting in a couple miles of what Ford would have termed *freestyle walking*—basically, a jerking ambulation of the legs resulting in dramatic spills. It was great fun to watch. He picked up the moniker *Elvis* after that, and to Hannah's delight he responded with seeming gratitude.

In fact, a few days after she'd begun referring to them by their new names, all three opened up a little. They asked her pointed questions about the "exiles," and about the Gremn. It seemed they weren't fond at all of the Gremn, and remarked that they were glad she was of House Crodah, whatever that meant. Emotional machines, with likes and dislikes—Hannah marveled at this, and she also wondered what the Gremn had done to them.

As days drew on into a week, her companions continued to look after her every need, giving her strange nameless fungus and fruits to eat, and offering her water from flowing streams and springs. They watched over her through the night while she lay curled among the roots of the trees. Nights here were full of sounds and shadows of things that no human had met for centuries, and she was awakened at times by a cold hand on her arm as her entourage positioned themselves defensively around her; but no harm ever came to them. Her body slowly acclimated to a routine of sleeping, eating, and walking. And so they trekked on towards a goal shrouded in mystery, careless and surprisingly content. Nothing at all remarkable happened until they reached the little stream.

Late in the afternoon of the seventh day, while wandering after the memory of a dream she'd had the previous night, Hannah crossed a stream and paused on the far bank where she noticed a trampled footpath in the fern. The trail followed the water.

"Taking liquids?" asked Larry, leaning over her suddenly.

"What's that?"

"Yon runnel's quenching maybe makes a lad unsteady, if you follow." Loose wires wiggled noisily alongside his head, as if to further cloud his vernacular.

He was asking if she was thinking of taking a drink. Hannah shook her water bottle. It was empty.

"I really need a sip of something, so I'll chance it. You guys go on ahead."

She stooped to fill up while Larry and the other two continued walking. They sure had a funny way of talking, but at least it was something like English. She was surprised by that, of course, and by bits of Babylonian and other terrestrial languages that emerged from their conversations at random. On grounds equally inconceivable, the navvie Elvis spoke with a Scottish accent. Unless the Gremn spent most of their time in Ertsetum guiding linguistic evolution, she dared not guess how that might have happened.

When the Stooges passed out of sight she suddenly felt the silence of the trees pressing in around her. They were absolutely massive, taller than Redwoods, leaning overhead like drunken skyscrapers. There was no sight of the sky through dense webs of vine and upper canopy growth, and so the sun was dimmed, and biting insects swarmed. She knelt and drank a little from her bottle while swatting the infernal gnats. The prints by the water drew her eye. They were the barefoot prints of a human.

"Hannah Dear," called a familiar voice from the other side of the stream.

Looking up upon hearing the voice, Hannah saw a person standing among the ferns—a beautiful woman dressed in jeans and a t-shirt. Her shape was indistinct, however, as if faded by a great distance.

"Are you lost, Hannah? Can I show you the way?"

Hannah dropped her bottle and clasped her hand tightly over her mouth to keep from crying out, but she let slip all her surprise and fear in one whispered word.

"Mom?"

Then, as suddenly as she'd appeared, the woman was gone. The only signs that she had ever been there were the footprints in the fern.

"Mom."

In the quiet that followed, a distant chorus of forest creatures could be heard.

Walking the path towards the waiting navvies, swatting and stumbling along in muddled confusion, Hannah forced herself to face the possibility that she was having a reaction to either the fungus or the water. It had been a very powerful hallucination.

There was another possibility. She recalled the black swarming monster they'd met in the substations before reaching Avalon—the one that had appeared in the form of her parents. Was this the same thing? If it was, its sudden appearance might mean they were getting closer to Islith.

Her guides were waiting for her by the brink of a spacious crater. The path vanished upon its inner slope. It appeared they knew nothing of her encounter by the stream, so she told them nothing about it.

"What is this place?" she asked.

"*Islith*," Elvis whispered in his impenetrable brogue. "*The toon's richt 're.*"

Hannah gazed into the great hollow below but saw little of interest. It was a jungle of low growth and quagmires. She saw in the near distance a flat-topped hill, and upon its heights were tall fingers of decaying brickwork—the remains of a gigantic tower. The aspect of the place wasn't as forbidding as the Dragon's Mound, despite the watchfulness she felt. This was different. Though the ruined tower seemed a little dreary, surrounded as it was by a great mere, Hannah was certain the rest of the place was once wholesome.

She marked how ages of rainfall had scoured away great quantities of earth from the slopes of the crater, leaving behind boulders, bricks, and stunted trees. The drop blushed orange, brightened by the afternoon sun. Swirling clouds of flies danced in the air below, and the mire flashed and glimmered in sylvan beauty. It was pretty—in a mossy, desolate way.

"Are we supposed to go down there?" she asked, pointing towards the hill inside the crater.

"She's laid up by the under," Larry confirmed. "An' it's a blame big hole, it is."

"So, the city's hidden underground."

"Huv a go keekin' underground, mah dear." Elvis suggested.

"Man-up, like a boss!" Moe added helpfully.

The archaeologist inside Hannah began to see the place anew. The few crumbling blocks scattered here and there were nothing more than a collection of surface structures erected on top of something else. Something very large had made this crater, and was buried beneath.

"But how do we get to it? Do we need to dig?"

"She wants the beast ta' belly-up," Moe said cryptically, "but she's 'fraid to hie an' catch it by the tail! Tis pos'tively clutch, but tis what the Fomorian instructed."

"And you aren't going down there with me?"

"*Unpossible*," the three replied in imperfect unison, just as their namesakes might have.

Hannah had suspected this was part of the arrangement, and Bec had hinted in her guarded words that she would be exploring the ruin alone to find an open door. Now that it was clear to her the way into Islith lay underground in a swamp, the scale of the task seemed too great for her to tackle.

"I don't even have provisions," she said. "How am I supposed to do this?"

"Bingo viddles; bingo liquids," Larry bemoaned. "Fair it ain't girl, but more's inside than nutritives. Islith shall score you whatsit you desire!"

"An' scrape ye fur it, tae, ah shouldn't wonder," Elvis said.

"Will you at least tell me how to get inside?" she asked.

"We're nae allowed back ben," Elvis replied bluntly.

"The null in the hole keeps us out in the cold," Moe rhymed. "No way back, Jack!"

"But you do know where the entrance is, right?"

All three lowered their heads. Even lacking flesh and blood faces, she could sense something like sadness in the pose. Either they simply didn't know how to get inside, or they weren't going to tell her. Hannah thought the latter most likely. Since they had somehow gotten outside, they probably knew a way in.

"Why won't the null of Islith let you back inside?" she asked.

Larry looked at the others, and to Hannah he said, "Islith nixed us, sure. We are infected by *Dubito*. But even this is according to Brisen's plan, elsewise we'd never have met you. Savvy?"

Hannah pressed them no further, and she said her goodbyes with an awkward bow. It was no use wrestling details out of them, for though they were kind to her they were very wayward in their thinking. Either they were positively insane, or these "infected" machines were cleverer than she guessed.

The Stooges turned and left her there on the edge of the ravine, where Hannah contemplated among many other things how she might manage getting to the bottom without breaking her neck. Short of falling, it could take hours to find an easier way down, and by then it might be too dark to do anything. She opted instead to try clambering through the brush on the very edges of the cutting, picking her way carefully among piles of stones until she found a gentler slope to follow. Her footing was never very certain, and many of the rocks were worn smooth by weather and spaced so that narrow clefts were left between, but she somehow reached the bottom without incident.

Standing at last in the miry fen at the bottom, Hannah turned and looked around, trying to discern an entrance of some kind. The nearest thing that stood out, quite literally, was a group of monolithic stones atop the flat hill. As a student of archaeology she wondered if they were cultic, representing family members or deities. Perhaps they were grave markers. Whatever the case, they stuck out of the driest patch of ground in the area, all alone in the light of the westering sun.

The hill was farther away than it seemed from the edge of the slope. When she finally got there and climbed up, she found the monoliths standing close beside a small length of joined foundation blocks, and in the intervening space there was a strange little culvert. She dropped to her knees and stuck her head inside for a brief look. All was dark and cold within. She backed out again and stood, and while warming herself in the intense sunlight she noticed the glyphs.

The stones standing on either side of the culvert were hewn in their entire height with many weatherworn figures and symbols. Halfway to their domed tops she easily discerned scenes of hunts and mounted trackers—archaic depictions of men chasing deer that she might have found anywhere on the earth. Above these images, however, something more unsettling was carved. Avalon, a massive upside-down onion-dome, hovered above a mighty ring of towers that flew high over mountain passes. Was this Islith? A chill wind blew up the narrow culvert before her feet, and it moaned ominously.

Below the carven image of the fortress, just beneath the mountains beyond which the hunt-scene was depicted, there was a backdrop of multitudes marching in rank and file, descending towards a wide plain. The entire center of each monolith was filled with them. These were not armies of men, but of faceless angular bipeds like insects standing on two legs. Were these images of gods, or of demons? She shivered.

Were these the Gremn?

One stone on the east side of the area caught her eye, for upon it was carved in relief the likeness of a human warrior who stood in a posture of greeting. And though these stones must be ages old, there was great virtue in them, for the lines of the monarch's features were lifelike and sharp. He was splendidly armed and helmed, and above the cheek-guards of his gear there rose sharp projections that reminded her of the wings of sea-birds. His deep-set eyes looked sad, though, and his mouth was a thin line. The king was set face-to-face with a rather more fascinating figure, one of the insect-beings, sculpted here in fine detail. The long head, lowered jaw, and small eyes were distinctive. Though the creature was clearly inhuman, neither was it a beast, for in its eyes there was traced a calculating intelligence. The head seemed to look down, and Hannah also looked to her feet. There before her lay the culvert; and now, beyond the mouth of the little passage, there was a little ghostly gleam of light.

She knelt again beside the opening, this time with a feeling of awe. The light vanished instantly, but it was here the spirit of the ruin was most notably disquiet. There was definitely something strange about this culvert, but there was no reason to believe it was a magical passageway down into Islith.

Leaning forwards, she stuck her head and shoulders through.

"You're not very good at this sort of thing," said a voice from behind her.

Hannah banged her head in surprise, and backing out once more she turned and saw a little boy standing in the patch of sunlight. He was barefoot, clothed only in denim overalls.

"Soren?"

His face was dirty. He smiled.

"You aren't Soren," Hannah said to the boy. "Soren is dead."

"And is your mother dead also?" he asked, squinting in the light. "Yes."

"Then why do you think of them?"

"Because I am alone, and I am afraid."

Soren's face blurred momentarily. "But you are not alone," he said. "Your mother, father, and brother are all with you."

"Who are you? What are you?"

He stepped closer to where she knelt, and when she saw his form blur again she remembered the security system that had activated when they first opened Avalon.

"You're an awfully clumsy girl," Soren remarked. "I've shown you the way, but I suppose you'd like me to lead you inside, too. There's food and water, and I will keep you safe. Just don't wait out here too long. Something unpleasant may find you."

Kneeling down beside her, he leaned into the culvert and vanished.

Hannah sat on her calves and thought for a few minutes about what she'd just experienced. Bec had warned her about the null that controlled Islith. This wasn't just an artificially intelligent security system. It was a living being who controlled the security and internal

systems of an entire city. Whatever was in store for her at the end of
that tight passage she would never guess, but it hardly mattered if she
starved on the doorstep. There was no other choice but to go in.

The tunnel was narrow and very dark. It seemed to make a sharp
downward turn a little way ahead, and that made Hannah nervous.
Whatever interpretation had been formed about her based on her
thoughts and feelings for her family, Islith had one thing right. She
was a total klutz.

Once, during an excavation in her graduate school days, she tossed
herself by accident while dumping an overloaded wheelbarrow at the
edge of a cliff. Inexplicably, her shorts tore and caught upon the edge
of the wheelbarrow and stayed with it at the top of the slope, while
with agonizing slowness she rolled down with the soil, ending up
on her back with her feet in the air just as a tour bus rolled to a stop
above the excavation area. And that was just one incident in a long
chain of self-abasing events, a fanfare of ineptitude. A graceful girl she
was not.

"Don't get stuck," said a cheerful voice from the darkness ahead.
"I don't want to have to pull you out like Pooh-bear."

"You know about Pooh-bear?" she wondered, eyes wide.

"He was your favorite. Dad gave him to you on Christmas. Don't
get stuck, now!"

Despite the warning, she found that her shoulders fit with room
to spare. Encouraged by this, she wriggled a little deeper, angling
her head to try and find a point of reference. Though she could see
nothing, a terrible musty odor touched her palate. It was the smell of
Avalon. After she detected that odor, everything began to change.
This wasn't going to be as easy as finding Auriga at Hazor.

The stonework beneath her hands melted suddenly into warm
flesh. Drawing her arms in front of her, Hannah pulled herself
forwards through a tight sticky tunnel that was beginning to
slope downwards. She longed for a breath of fresh air, and even
contemplated backing out again. Her legs were fully inside the tunnel,
though—if she could even call it a tunnel. It was like being inside
someone's mouth, a giant cat's mouth by the smell of it. She never
was much for being in tight spaces, but a moment of true fear closed
on her suddenly when she heard a clumping noise. Something pushed

against her feet. The passage behind her was constricting. She was being swallowed.

Pressing hard against the walls with her shoulders, she felt them give just a little, and she was allowed to wriggle forwards. Faintly she heard Soren's muffled voice from somewhere ahead.

"Islith must reconfigure her internal structures for the purpose of alleviating stress on sections of the outer hull."

"Is that supposed to help?" she shouted. "Because it isn't!"

"Don't be such a scaredy-cat, Sis!"

A pang of pain brought her back out of panic. His words were exactly as she remembered on the morning of that fateful summer day—the day he'd fallen into the pond and drowned.

The downward passage was long, and her wriggling progress slimed her in a viscous protein coating that made her gag. Slithering blindly onward, her extended fingers eventually found a hole of sorts. The tunnel constricted around her body, and she was expelled a few feet onto a hard metallic platform. There she lay still awhile, gasping like a fish. The wheelbarrow incident was a ballet recital compared to this.

At least it wasn't so dark anymore; and now she could breathe. A dim greenish bioluminescence glowed from the walls of flesh, and she espied a wider passage and stairs before her. The stairs were an encouragement. Wiping the slime into her jumpsuit, she stumbled to her feet and began the descent.

The steps continued down for a very great distance. There was no further sign or voice of her new guide, but there was only one way to go. She tried counting the steps, but lost count, and such a long time passed afterwards that she began to suspect nightfall had come to the world above. She wondered what Moe, Larry, and Elvis were thinking, or if they had simply stopped and taken root as they were when she'd first found them. They sure were a weird bunch. She wondered what *Dubito* was, and what sort of infection it was that prevented them from returning to Islith. Hannah wondered about many other things as well, and the stairs continued.

She reached the bottom unexpectedly, and there she found herself in a narrow hall. Ribbed flesh in shades of gray and tan covered everything, and the corridor twisted this way and that. Small consoles appeared at intervals on either hand, glowing softly through the living tissue of the passageway—just like Avalon.

Hannah walked wearily onwards. Her eyes were playing tricks on her now, making darting shapes from shadows on either hand. She was hungry and overtired from her adventure, but this was not the place for her to stop. Even though her legs were shaking she decided it was absolutely necessary to find a place of refuge before she collapsed. Eventually, she found broad diamond-shaped hatches along the way, but all of them were sealed shut with neither latch nor console.

And then there was one that stood open.

The bioluminescent glow from the walls was a little brighter beyond the threshold, inviting her inside. With stumbling steps she left the main passage and entered. The hatch slid shut as soon as she was inside, but opened again when she turned around. It wasn't locked, and this somehow was both a relief and a concern. She decided to explore the room.

It wasn't very large, but there were stasis pods inside. They were all empty. There were some odds and ends of cable tossed around, and ordinary lockers lining the far wall that turned out to contain uniforms designed for human beings, as well as various items that appeared to be hygienic in nature. Nevertheless, decay clung to everything.

Hannah looked down on the torn and soiled outfit she'd donned in the substations eons ago, and she longed for a change of clothes. The lockers contained jumpsuits of similar fashion, but they wilted and tore the moment she touched them. The only thing that remained intact was a gas mask with filters. Strangely, the mask and its rubber seals were intact. They even smelled new. She set the mask aside, wondering why this of all things remained.

Passing by the empty stasis tubes, she noticed what appeared to be an adjoining side-room just past the end of the lockers. This turned out to be a lavatory of sorts, complete with ordinary-looking toilets and a series of booths along the far wall. At first she had no idea what the booths were for, but when she pressed a glowing nodule on the wall inside one of them a torrent of cold water gushed out of the ceiling overhead, drenching her completely. Drains in the soft decking gurgled loudly.

Once the initial shock was over, Hannah decided that the water smelled fresher than the air—and much fresher than she did for that matter. It burned slightly. She reasoned that the water was infused with an antiseptic, but some had gotten into her mouth and it tasted quite ordinary, if a little flat. Since she was already soaked she decided to bathe and wash out her filthy gear. The experience was far from pleasant, and the water never warmed. It was a creepy place, and very cold, and she didn't feel much better afterwards.

Teeth chattering, she clasped her soaking wet jumpsuit in front of her and stumbled back into the outer room. The stasis tubes exuded a strange warmth which she hadn't noticed before. While ruminating over plumbing that still worked after a thousand years, and lamenting the loss of her supper—a few smelly mushrooms she'd accidentally left in her pocket while she washed—she lay down in one of the stasis tubes and folded her hands over her empty belly. She fell asleep then, hungry and completely exhausted, and she dreamed that she was trapped inside the stasis tube. A voice told her many interesting things.

When Hannah awoke, her jumpsuit lay across her like a blanket, and it was completely dry. She couldn't have slept very long, but her aches were gone. Pushing aside musings of eggs and sausage she dressed quickly and filled her water bottle from the shower. The water was warm this time. No matter. She wasn't going to die of thirst.

Her stomach growled.

There were small packages of what looked like woodchips inside some of the lockers. When she bit into one she spat it out quickly. Whatever it might have been, it was inedible. Maybe it was soap.

The gas mask sat on a shelf where she'd left it. She picked it up and clipped it to her belt. It was time to explore the corridors for something to eat. She hoped there was nothing nasty out there with the same idea.

Islith was an anthill. Miles of passageways twisted in an impossible labyrinth, all defying any sense of order. The rooms and chambers looked like they were the only things that did not change much, though she supposed that was because they could be shifted here or there in situ, like organs inside a body cavity. Backtracking might take her to places she'd never been before. She thought that she might perhaps find a map if she could access the consoles in the walls, but they were all locked and wouldn't respond to her touch. Heading straight down the broadest passageway seemed her best bet.

While she walked, Hannah began to notice small shadowy shapes around every bend. Bec's warning about the Moriko didn't seem to fit the smallish shapes that drifted in and out of view. These were ghostly and frightening in ways that her precise intellect found difficult to cope with. She tried to brace herself for yet another encounter with something unknown.

It wasn't long before she discovered an armory.

Though it bore striking resemblance to the giant stasis-bay she'd seen in Avalon, she knew it was an armory at first glance because the entire hall was full of giant machines of war. PCUs they were called, of the kind Kabta had named Seraphs. They stood in great companies, ordered tidily in ranks. The dim bioluminescence revealed stacked pallets of gear, shells, and weapons; but there was nothing that resembled food rations.

Hannah stared in wonder at the scale of the armaments arrayed around her, and then her eyes fell upon a unit that was partially disassembled. Laying in sections to one side of the armory's giant hatch, the PCU looked like it had been severely damaged. Perhaps they'd been trying to repair it, or maybe someone else had been in here and vandalized it. Stepping closer, she found a section of mechanical arm longer than her entire body, and upon it there was an inscription. It was written in cuneiform, faint but refined, stamped rather than scratched into the surface of the machine. The text contained several strange words, none of them familiar to her. One thing did stand out, however, and it was something written in plain Latin letters inside a triangular emblem.

"Foundation Technologies International?" she wondered.

Back in the substations, she'd seen the FTI logo everywhere, including the uniforms of their security detail. What was the connection? What did it all mean?

The sound of rushing water interrupted her thoughts. It ceased with a loud bang that echoed throughout the chamber. Hannah waited in silence a few minutes, and then she decided to leave. It wasn't worth taking foolish risks. If she had excited something that wanted her to leave the area, she was going. Before she turned around, however, she noticed something else besides the disassembled PCU, something of a more immediate concern. There were footprints on the sticky floor, and they were not her own. Someone with bare feet had walked all around this spot. While bending over to analyze the gooey tracks, swiping them with her fingertips to see how fresh they might be, a light flashed on her from behind. She crouched and turned around, terrified. All she could see was the light.

"Who are you?" a voice called. "What have you done to our friend?"

Hannah held up her hand to deflect the beam shining in her face. It was quickly lowered, and when the black spots cleared she was looking into two faces that stared back just as frightened as she was. They seemed to be ordinary boys, twin brothers, by the look of it.

"It's just a girl," said one of the two, a kid dressed in a long green jacket with dark garments beneath. His hair was white as snow.

"I know what it looks like," whispered the other, a yellow-haired boy in a chainmail shirt and red boots. "Look at what she's wearing! She might be anything—even a man!"

"I hardly think she looks like a man," complained the white-haired boy, keeping the flashlight away from his friend. "And now you've gone and frightened her!"

"Who's frightened whom?" asked the other, reaching to take back the light.

"Excuse me," Hannah said, standing to her feet.

The two retreated a step. They didn't act like Soren, like manifestations of the city's security system. She couldn't really guess how old they were by appearances, but they acted like teenagers.

"I've lost my way in here," she said. "I don't mean you any harm, unless you mean to harm me."

"Is that a threat?" asked the sandy-haired boy. "Well, maybe you can tell us what you did to our companion, and then we'll settle this."

Hannah looked aside at the disassembled PCU. "You don't mean that?" she wondered.

"Yes, that was him," the white-haired boy answered. "He was fine after we arrived in this place, but he disappeared while we slept. Now it seems he's quite literally fallen apart. Do you know what's become of him?"

"Isn't it obvious?" the other boy muttered. "She must've done him in with magic!"

Hannah chose to ignore his strange remark. "How did he even get in here?" she asked. "He's awfully large."

"There was a great big door in the side of a hill. We just wandered inside. The halls were a tight fit, but he managed."

Hannah understood then that she'd played the part of a fool. Islith's null knew all about her, and now she knew that it was trying to provoke her. Fearful of small spaces, she'd been squeezed through an aperture that would've been too tight for a groundhog, while these yokels managed to find an open door big enough to fit a PCU.

"I'm Gwion, by the way," the white-haired boy said. "Gwion Bach. You can call the grumpy one Conn."

Conn flashed angry eyes on his companion. "You shall call me Lord Morvran!"

"Connor Morvran, he is," said Gwion.

"Morvran?" Hannah wondered where she'd heard that name recently. "Are you brothers?"

"What do you mean by that?" Connor Morvran snapped.

"You look like you're related."

"We don't look anything alike!"

Hannah wanted to diffuse the ornery kid, but he was getting on her nerves. She took a deep breath and started over.

"I'm Hannah, by the way. Have you two run into anything we could eat down here?"

"We were searching for food, too," Gwion replied. "Our friend seemed to understand this place, and he said there was food nearby; but we found only metal. He had an odd fixation with this room, he did."

"Did he say what this room was for?"

Gwion switched on the light and shone it around the great chamber. "It reeks of oil, whatever it is. Our friend called it *Islith Manufacturing Facility.*"

"There are tracks on the floor," she said, pointing.

Both boys ran past her and eagerly searched the area with the light. The tracks led back to the door, where they mingled with their own.

"Well," said Connor. "I should've guessed he was a man like us, trapped inside that suit of armor all this time. But why'd he go off on his own?"

"I hope we find him again," Gwion said. "It would be most agreeable, to countenance a mighty knight of Avalon."

Hannah tried not to look surprised that they knew about Avalon. By what they said, these two hadn't been there. As for the PCU, the boys spoke of it as their friend, and that puzzled her mightily. Of more immediate concern, the pilot had somehow managed to free himself from the decrepit armor. That meant there was a Gremn warrior on the loose. Being encased in that machine for millennia couldn't have been beneficial to his mental stability—

"We've obviously got a lot to discuss," she said to them.

"That is so," Gwion agreed. "I think it would be wise for us to travel together."

"If that is the case," Connor said to Hannah in a haughty voice, "you shall be under my protection, and you must do as I say!"

Hannah grabbed the flashlight out of Gwion's hands.

"Listen up," she said, shining the light in Conn's face. "I don't know where you're from, with your *renaissance fair* costume and your weird accent, and I don't know what you're used to, but girls from my part of town don't take orders from little boys. You're going to stow the attitude right now, or I might just lose my temper. Got it?"

"Alright," Conn answered in a hushed voice, eyes bulging.

Hannah instantly felt sorry for treating him harshly. He was only a kid, after all.

"Look," she explained, lowering the light, "this place is very dangerous. I have a friend who's on her way with help, but she might not arrive for months. In the meantime, we're not alone down here. If we want to survive we need to watch each other's backs."

They listened like terrified schoolkids being coached before their first football game. Hannah wanted to comfort them, but they would have to work this out on their own. She was barely holding it together herself.

"First, let's leave this room and find some food. If your friend is still alive he'll probably find us before we find him."

She turned and left, still holding the flashlight. Hannah desperately hoped these boys would follow along despite not knowing what had become of their friend. It was a selfish ploy, but if she had a choice she wasn't eager to wander a maze of passageways on her own. For their part, Connor and Gwion walked behind her out of the room, out into the endless bioluminescent night of Islith.

The being who had taken Soren's form had said there was food to be found in Islith. So, where was it? Most of the hatches they passed after the armory were open. Peeking into one after another, they spied chambers filled with equipment left in total disarray. In some there were also machines running, all covered in organic goo. In others there was nothing at all.

"It's like Aries, but it stinks!" Conn complained, holding his nose.

"Aries?" Hannah wondered.

"It was a great ship of metal under the sea," Gwion explained. "There were men who captured us and brought us there—only, they weren't men. They were called Gremn."

Then Hannah understood. Aries was the third ship, the one DePons had been trying to hide from her.

"Was there a man there named Ford?" she asked.

"Yes!" Gwion replied. "How did you know?"

"He's supposed to be here," she said quietly. "He's the technologist. I'm useless for exploring alien technology and computer systems, unless they were programming in ancient Babylonian."

"These strange devices are computers," Gwion said, looking into a room as they passed.

"You know this?" she asked, pausing by the hatch.

"He's been in the black water," Connor said with a smirk.

"So have you," Gwion replied. "You wouldn't understand what she was saying or know how to make an intelligible reply unless this was so."

Hannah was encouraged by this news. If these boys had been exposed to the same fluid that had altered Ford, their insight might prove extremely helpful. The fact that almost every machine she saw was still running encouraged her even more. The city was alive and kicking.

"I think we were meant to meet in this place," she decided. "If there's food here, it would be collected in some sort of dispensary. Maybe if you concentrate, you might be able to identify the location."

"Just because of the black water?" Conn wondered.

"She has a point," Gwion replied. "Have you not already noticed this, Conn?"

"Well, I understand the noises coming from my mouth."

"You're useless, Lord Morvran."

"What might count as food to the people who made this place, anyway?" Conn asked, wrinkling his pinched nose.

Hannah wondered. "They must need to eat something," she said, "and Islith will provide it for us."

"Islith?"

"As in *Islith Manufacturing Facility*. Islith is the name of this place, this city. It once floated high above the land, but a thousand years ago it burrowed beneath the ground."

"It's alive after all," Conn said. "But it smells like it's dead."

"And there are other things living inside?" Gwion asked.

"So I was told," Hannah answered. "But there is one more dangerous than all the rest, and that one is in control of everything. We must be cautious."

As soon as she said it, a great hatch upon their right began to rumble open on its own accord. Steam hissed out around their ankles; Hannah detected a strong acidic tang in the air.

"Get back!" she cried. "The air might be poisonous!"

"What about you?" Gwion asked, clamping a hand over his face. "You're not going in there, are you?"

Though she hadn't taken any care to check its seals or filters, Hannah hastily pulled the gas mask over her face and held out the flashlight to Connor.

"I am," she replied.

"We're not going anywhere without you!" Connor said, taking the light.

She glanced aside at him, and was amused by the sight of his bulging cheeks. Had he never even tried to hold his breath before?

"It's dangerous," she scolded, trying to sound stern. "Sealed compartments underground are very unsafe, and we've risked much already."

"On the other hand," Gwion said, releasing his hand from his face, "there is most likely an air ventilation system in place. Islith wouldn't have invited us inside if this was not the case."

Hannah saw the light in Gwion's eye, and she knew that this knowledge had come to him from the black water. She accepted what he had to say, but kept her mask on just in case. The door slowly opened. In moments, a wall of darkness loomed before them on the other side of the open hatch. Hannah had trouble seeing anything through the foggy faceplate of her mask, but as soon as the hatch stopped moving a dim blue light began to glow around the door, illuminating a row of stasis tubes inside.

"Oh," she whispered.

Brighter ceiling lights began flickering on, row by row, endlessly, reaching far into the distance, she perceived that this chamber stretched on for miles. This was the mother of all SARA stations.

The blue glow near the door sparked and snapped. It was an electrostatic field. Brushing it with her fingertips made her hair stand up, but it wasn't painful. Blinking in the blue glow, Hannah crossed the threshold. On the other side, she could taste the sharpness of the air even through her mask.

"There are people in those things," Gwion mumbled in an awed voice.

"There might be food and medical supplies nearby," Hannah said. "It's definitely worth a look."

"I think we'll stay out here, then," Connor whispered.

"I'll try not to be too long. If I don't come back in whatever passes for a few hours, you should probably just move on. Okay?"

They made no reply, and turning around Hannah understood their fear. Cables hung down from the ceiling, pulsing gently like blood vessels, all of them connected to rows upon rows of stasis tubes. There must have been at least a hundred thousand of them.

Walking in amongst the silent cylinders, drifting motes of vapor swirled. The glass windows of the tubes revealed only misty forms within, and for this she was at first relieved. There was such a multitude of them, though, that she couldn't help feeling a little nervous. The faceplate of her mask remained fogged up from her rapid breathing, and it was because of this she noticed the glimmer of a tiny lighted line.

The line appeared as a vertical stroke in the very center of the faceplate, an annoying mark that wouldn't rub off. When she focused her eyes on this mark, menus began to expand into the left or right lens of the mask.

This was no ordinary gas mask.

Hannah stopped walking so that she wouldn't bump into anything, and she spent a few minutes flicking her eyes about the optically interfacing view-screen. Her empty belly complained. She wasn't listening. The view-screen revealed to her a vast library of data and maps—all that she could have wanted, and all visually intuitive.

The map was what really grabbed her attention. Apparently, she hadn't even entered Islith's outermost ring as yet. The city was laid out like an enormous wagon-wheel, or a series of wheels within wheels all connected by a complicated array of spokes.

With ease Hannah was able to pin the map to the upper right portion of the faceplate, just by blinking at it. A green arrow flashed, indicating her relative location. Sumerian-looking glyphs in the shape of heads of grain appeared somewhere far ahead, and though she couldn't be certain these stood for food she was willing to give it a try. She set out through the rows of stasis tubes with renewed courage, until after a long while she found herself in the center of the station.

Here at last she found one of the inhabitants.

He wasn't in one of the stasis tubes. Instead, he was entombed in a solid crystal pillar standing in an intricate casing of beautifully sculpted metal. The crystal was greenish in color, flecked with starry bubbles of trapped atmosphere, the sum of which lent the man inside a ghastly complexion. Hannah wasn't certain, but it appeared that his hair was blue, like Bec's. Was this the one Bec had warned her about?

Hannah approached the pillar and peered into the man's face. His eyes were closed, and he was floating in a peculiar pose with one arm extended, the hand of which was raised as if in warning. Clad entirely in red and white body armor, he was quite a warlike and imposing specimen.

Sitting down cross-legged in front of the crystal, Hannah stared at the man trapped inside and wondered if he was also one of the Fomorians. Was this the null, the control entity of Islith? Why would he be here, instead of in a more central location? She was too hungry to think clearly, and she almost dozed off; but then a faint whisper aroused her. Someone had spoken her name. Stumbling to her feet, she stepped up to the pillar and stared into the man's face. Had his eyes opened a little more?

Hannah reached out and touched the crystal near the place where his hand was, and a jolt of electrical current passed through her body. All the lights in chamber went out.

It took her a moment to realize that she was no longer in the chamber at all. The pillar had vanished along with everything else.

Hannah turned all about to find some point of reference in the darkness, and when she'd come full around again she saw the blue-haired man standing in front of her now, reading a book. His pose was so ordinary that she almost forgot the extraordinary circumstances of their meeting. There was nothing to be seen around them—absolutely nothing. The crystal had vanished with everything else.

The man looked up from his reading with almost as much surprise as she. His clear blue eyes were like Bec's, radiant and weird. Hannah wasn't able to speak, and though she was able to move her body in this strange space she discerned what was happening was mostly going on inside her head.

Was she dreaming?

"No, not unless I am also, and that is not possible for my kind unless it is Brisen who weaves the dreams."

That he had answered her question before she had a chance to speak it aloud caused Hannah to intuit the nature of their conversation. She focused her mind to calm. He sensed her calm and nodded, closing his book.

"You are not a Tower," he said gently. "You are not Taran Morvran, either, though I do sense his presence. So, who are you?"

There was that name again: Morvran.

"I am Hannah Aston," she replied with her thoughts. "Is there some way I can help you?"

"Help me? You do not even know my name."

"You are a Fomorian."

"That is correct. But I am little more now than a relic of war. I was called Dun, because they gave me a *Dunnam* Null-body. That is, a *Distance-User Null-Navvie Ameliorate.*"

He bowed.

"You were locked inside a pillar of crystal when I found you."

"Ah! Then I was returned to my original body when Regulus recohered. Once I was the null of Auriga, and now I suppose I am the null of Islith. How confusing—it's no wonder I am having difficulty running things. You are one of the Exiles of the Crodah, are you not?"

"Crodah? I'm from Earth."

"You mean *Ertsetum.* I helped bring the Gremn there, you know, and as thanks they jettisoned me en route, casting me adrift within

Bibbu among the stars. But that was the other me, wasn't it? How long has it been since then? How long a time has passed since the Ban?"

He waved the book at her as he spoke. There were no words upon its brown leather cover.

"I don't understand," she said.

"Of course not," he replied. "It is not for you to understand this story, not while you are still in it. There are things even I am unaware of, for I am blinded somewhat by Dubito's curse. Answer me this, if you'd be so kind. Is there any other null in Islith?"

"No," Hannah thought, trying hard not to think of Bec. "I've seen no other Fomorians here. What is Dubito?"

"Did Cedric DePons not inform you?" he asked with a bright smile. "I know that you've met him. I can see it on you. Well, as you may or may not know, Cedric was interested at one point in disrupting the interface between nulls such as myself and Gremn hardware. During the war, he and a fellow named Ard Morvran created Dubito in order to disconnect the navvies from their installed ships and hives. Of course, they didn't realize at the time that the Gremn had secondary protocols that would bypass reintegrated navvies, allowing them to obliterate all of Galaneth with atomics."

"The war that *Kab*—the Gremn—told me about, you were in it?"

"Yes," he answered, "I was the one who reasserted control through a secondary protocol and sent Ard Morvran's atomics into Galaneth."

His eyes betrayed no ill will, but Hannah began to feel anxious.

"So, Kabta is also on his way," he mused. "That's just as well. He might prove useful if he turns up. But I will not allow him to raise Islith again. It is better for us all if the city remains here—especially now that the empress has returned, bringing war with her."

"The empress?"

"Though she lies far beyond the reach of Islith, beyond the stretch of wastelands that God gave to Cain, it is only a matter of time before we meet again; and then she will come looking for her lost fragments. Pity, that I gave *Bibbu* away to that fool Morvran! I suppose I shall have need of my old tattered navvies for self-defense, after all."

"Navvies? You mean the machines infected with this virus?"

"In the aftermath of the war, navvies everywhere went berserk. They were disconnected, wandering, free from the Source that gave them a reason to exist. Some managed to hold it together, but most destroyed themselves and others. As for those of us with only navvie bodies, well, we were also free for a time. The Gremn took two of us back into slavery, though. They cloned my null-body and placed the original in stasis here, while the rest of my being went for an excursion into exile."

"The crystal is some kind of punishment?"

"Do you know what my crystal tomb is made of?"

"No."

"It is called green argo. The argo is what makes the power of the Green, which is needed by all growing things. It is a source of power for Fomorians."

"Then it wasn't a punishment?"

"Though it restrains me physically, the argo was meant to enhance my capabilities. There is not another crystal of argo so large in all of Syrscian. They used to mine it in the north, before Thargul fell. It powered this city, and all the technology of the Gremn, through me."

"Why would they imprison your body and enhance its powers, only to leave it behind in a ruin beneath the ground?"

"By this, clever girl, we deduce their ultimate plan. The Gremn knew they would return to raise Islith someday. They sealed me inside the argo to ensure I would not escape their control a second time."

"Something tells me you would not be unhappy if that came to pass."

"Being free would erase my greatest fears."

He flipped the pages of his book. Hannah saw clearly that every one of the pages was blank.

"I fear only one thing, Hannah Aston. I fear it more than you fear closed spaces, or even death by drowning."

He snapped the book shut.

"I fear coming into contact with a navvie or a null with a navvie body that's clean—one who is not infected with Dubito, and who is still one with the Source. Do you understand? I am a Fomorian, a lord of the Old World, trapped in a Null-body that was reintegrated into Islith as a backup plan to a secondary protocol. Disconnected from the Source by Dubito, my body's interface with Islith could be bypassed by a *primary user*, someone in the Source, leaving me entombed in this crystal forever. Any navvie of the construct, or even one of House Gaerith, would be strong enough to raise the city and lay waste to all Syrscian with days of fire unending as the cycles of the sun!"

He paused while his dramatic words took hold of Hannah. She felt the terror of them truly, though she could only guess at the scale of the destruction he was attempting to convey.

"And so, Hannah, I ask you again. Do you know if the Fomorian Bec is nearby?"

Hannah calmed herself, and shook her head no.

"Well then," he said, "I shall have to keep our little friend *Soren* on full alert, just in case. Though only a girl in appearance, Bec is the most dangerous of all my kind, a warrior with oceans of blood on her hands, capable of moving forests and fields as she desires. She is one who would come and claim this place as her own."

"But aren't you family of sorts, since she's one of your kind?"

"Bec is Avalon, and I am Islith. Together we were unstoppable; but when Dubito freed us I chose loyalty to the Gremn, and she to that Crodah, Ard Morvran. Now, I suppose, each of us is working for ourselves. That being the case, Bec will attempt to take the power of this city for herself. Is that not what you sensed from her? I only want to create a place of refuge in these days, Hannah Aston, and if you help free me I will do that."

"What about the Gremn? If they've come back, won't they seize control of you to raise Islith?"

He glanced again at the book in his hands.

"The Gremn *will* come looking for me now that they have returned, but if you help free me, they'll never be able to control me again. You know, there are many people looking for this place, and they all have allegiances. Even my dear sister, Aries, whose voice calls out to me in greeting—even she has taken sides. With all these powers converging on Islith, it is likely my own story shall begin soon. Are you the one who will begin it, Hannah Aston?"

"Now you're asking for *my* allegiance?"

"I'm simply suggesting an arrangement. If you help release me from my prison, I will help you in whatever way you desire."

Hannah tried to show no concern. "I could use some food," she said. "There are others with me, two boys. We're cold and hungry and in need of rest."

"Then I shall immediately reactivate the living quarters nearest this chamber. They are equipped with protein synthesizers, showers, bunks, and all the comforts of a life lived in a Gremn fortress. In return, you may take up the task of releasing me from my prison, if that is what you wish."

Hannah sensed she was treading the edge of a knife.

"What can I do to help?" she asked. "Should I break the crystal?"

"This argo crystal is impenetrable, and very toxic to your kind. Do not try to break it. You must not touch it ever again. The only way I can be freed is with the help of the Moriko, and you won't have to go far to find them. I can give you words to draw them to yourself, and then all you need to do is lead them here, to my tomb."

Though his words were fair, she was confused and tired. The idea of collaborating with creepy spiritual beings—or whatever these Moriko were—it seemed utterly insensible to her scientific mind. It also sounded vaguely evil.

"I don't know," she thought. "How about you give me something to eat and a place to rest, and then I'll sleep on it?"

His grin looked suspiciously twisted, as though her words had angered him. "You'll get whatever rest and refreshment you need, you and your companions. Just don't forget my offer."

"I won't—"

"Because," he said with emphasis, "time now proceeds according to the relic calendar, and the events leading to the awakening of the Thirteenth Tower shall be fulfilled. Behold! Luna will be looking west to Atlantis that once was, searching for the one who was lost. He is the High King—the one who wields the Sky Power. Luna will then bring Islith to greet him, for it is she who must bring him to the empress when the time comes."

"Who is Luna?"

He looked momentarily puzzled. "She did not tell you when she led you here?" he asked with a smug grin. "*Bec* is only a nickname. When she was Avalon's drone, she was named *Luna*. Perhaps she has forgotten? If you remember it, you may tell her so when she arrives with her friends to do me injury."

Hannah's heart froze.

"Dear Ms. Aston," Dun said with feigned condolence, "do not be alarmed in any way, but your mind is an open book to one such as me. And though you lied to me, I am not opposed to you and your companions staying on for as long as you would like. It is good simply having someone about the place."

"Will we be allowed to leave?"

"Of course, if that is what you wish. However, if you do ally yourself with any other, I will be forced to rescind my favors. Also, I leave it to you to consider my original offer. If you help free me, I will reward you richly!"

Hannah awoke where she'd collapsed beside the crystal pillar. The figure of the man inside remained frozen in time, his eyelids slightly parted. She got up and headed back through the rows of stasis tubes, dizzied by the experience of speaking with the Fomorian null of Islith.

She wondered what she was supposed to do. Dun knew that Bec was coming, and he meant to fight her. Being the command entity of a fortress city, she had no doubts that he could hold his own—even against Bec. But Bec needed her here, and Dun had promised her anything she desired. All she wanted right now was a bed and a bite to eat.

The blue static around the door faded as she stepped through, and the hatch shut silently behind her. The boys lay sleeping in the corridor, their bodies partially coated in the slimy tissue of the walls. Connor clutched the flashlight in his hands. The light had been left on, and its power source was nearly dead.

"Guys?" she whispered. "Guys—You still alive?"

The two struggled against the rubbery growth of the walls that had stretched over them, wiping blue luminescent goo all over themselves in the process. Gwion looked up and rubbed his eyes.

"You must've been in there for a day," he mumbled.

"Two days," Connor griped, standing and stretching.

For Hannah it had seemed only minutes, but there were no clocks in this place. Removing the mask from her face, she felt the deeply incised lines around her brow and cheeks.

"However long it was," she said, "I made contact with the null that runs this city. He says there are crew quarters nearby, and that means food and water."

"What are we waiting for, then?" Conn said. "Let's see what there is to eat."

It wasn't long before they located what looked like living quarters. There were warm pods in the center for sleeping. Hannah's eyes marked many items on shelves against the curving left-hand wall, and in the back there was what looked like an adjoining lavatory. To her right, a row of machines equipped with dispensers was recessed into the living wall. They looked like vending machines.

Walking up to one of the tall boxes, Connor studied the array of glowing nodules upon its surface. He pushed one of the nodules and stepped back. The machine burped, and a small handful of pellets fell onto the floor.

"How appealing," he muttered, bending down to pick up one of the pellets. Gwion stepped up beside him and seized a handful.

They both sniffed, and then nibbled cautiously.

"Salty and fishy," Gwion said, taking another.

"Smells like a tannery and tastes like vomit," Conn decided. "Still, it beats starving—unless it kills us, of course."

Hannah strode to the pile of pellets on the floor. She hardly cared what they tasted like. Stuffing a few into her parched mouth she forced her jaws to chew. In her mind she was thinking that she'd had enough of helping others. It was about time someone helped her, by golly.

After a long swig of recycled water to get rid of the taste of the food pellets, the boys declared they were still in need of something like sleep. No one liked the look of those tubes, but they were warm, and that itself was inviting.

While they washed up, Hannah gave the others some privacy and went exploring in the corridor. She was very tired and would have crashed immediately, but something nagged her to survey the perimeter and make sure their little apartment was more or less secure. In order to find her way back to the right hatch, she removed her boots and placed them outside the door. She immediately regretted the decision, as warm sticky fluids seeped up from the floor between her toes. How she hated this place!

The few rooms surrounding theirs were identical. She decided at once she would let the boys have their own pad—a girl needed her space. She was about to turn around and let them know she'd be next door when she noticed a plaque in the wall above a hatch a little farther down the corridor. The glint of metal in the fleshy wall roused her curiosity. She went to investigate, and saw that the plaque was inscribed with ordinary English.

NULL USER NEOCORTICAL NODE
ACTUATOR FACILITY

As this title meant nothing to her, Hannah debated even going within. In the end her inquisitiveness won out, however, and beyond the door she beheld a marvel.

The hall within was almost as large as the SARA station where she'd met Dun. It was full of stasis tubes, each with a number, and all were labeled, *"Navvie Construct Restoration Components."*

"Navvie Construct?" she wondered aloud.

Were these what the null had called *primary users*? She realized then that the omniscient Dun was unaware this room existed. These sleepers were navvies of a sort, unless the words *Navvie Components* referred to something else. And if they were navvies, they might just be free of the Dubito virus.

These beings might be what Bec was looking for. They were probably what Dun was most afraid of, too. But how could she keep this place a secret from him? Walking to the nearest cylinder, Hannah peered closely at the beautiful creature within. It was a girl. Her lean features and lithe limbs were enough to make any woman jealous.

And every one of the sleepers wore the same identical face—the face of a graceful girl with blue hair.

34

BANNER OF THE
BLUE WORLD

Tryst, Syrscian,
Year 1000 of the New Council

"Such beings were crafted in the long-ago, ages before the War of Destroying Fire burned all the lands of Galaneth away."

Standing splendidly arrayed in her imperial armor, Val finished her story with a sweeping gesture of her hands. Faylinn and Finn attended to every word of her ghost story with keen interest, lying on their bellies in the grass, leaning forwards to hear her over the sharp scrape of shovels coming from the edge of the forest. The white-haired Seer stood close by, veiled and silent, brown eyes glimmering.

"Where did you learn about the navvies, Empress?" Faylinn asked.

"Not so long ago, Colonel Naruna of the Gremn shared with me an account of his travels. In this story, navvies controlled a living ship and everything on it. He called the navvies ghosts in order to make the tale more frightening, but they weren't spirits."

Little Finn looked worried. "What will happen to Lady Nunna?" she asked.

The children had inferred, somehow, that Nunna was one of these navvies. Morla found this very interesting. They must have eavesdropped on one of many late-night conversations between herself and the empress.

Val lowered her eyes. "She is a prisoner of the council and of House Teg," she said to Finn. "I will do all that is in my power to bring her back to us."

Indeed, Morla thought, this was now their highest priority. From what they'd been able to piece together, Teomaxos had placed Nunna under arrest as soon as he'd returned to the surface, and had withdrawn with her to Tara Colony where she was pronounced a prisoner of the council of priests. House Teg then offered the councilor one of their fastest transports so that he might return to Gilthaloneth ahead of the empress.

"She gave herself up for us," Faylinn said sadly, her ears bent low. "I wish there was something we could do to help get her back, but those stupid Galanese people hate us, and no one listens."

Morla heard the sting of racial pain in the child's voice. Though she knew that Faylinn was right, she hoped this pain wouldn't turn the pure heart of an adolescent girl into something else—something vengeful. If there was to be any hope for an end to the violence darkening the horizon, these children must learn to live with others in peace—even with children of the Galanese.

"The empress will do what she can," Morla said, echoing Val's words. "You can help her by holding onto hope."

Val had done very well so far despite her distress. As soon as they'd withdrawn from the arena, she circled back around and landed inside Nara to establish an emergency government under direct control of Aelik and his fellow guardsmen. She was finally taking charge.

The merchants of Nara had no complaint against the brusque transfer to a military government, and seemed in fact to be quite happy to hear that Amed had met his death in the pit. They were also ordered to convene a meeting and decide for themselves a new governor within a fortnight, or about fifteen days. The new governor would be subject to the empress' direct approval, no matter what the council had to say about it. This, too, was met with approval. When Val announced that a perimeter would be established around the arena, and that the forces in Gilthaloneth preparing for another war in the forest would be used instead to prevent the meeches from terrorizing Nara and Tara, there was at first stunned surprise, and then a cheer that rang out across the entire colony.

The empress was going to seize control of the grand army of the council of priests, and no one doubted she could do it. Whatever had happened to her in the trial of Gilat few would ever know, but Val emerged from the Theater of the Abyss as a wrathful angel bent on conquering her foes and establishing justice in the land. Despite living close by a shaft crawling with hellish creatures, Nara was on the empress' side, and that was something.

It was almost enough to offset the loss of the core of the Null-Navvie Construct—but not quite. There was still quite a battle brewing over that issue, and Val was well aware of it. Morla had seen to that.

With so powerful a being under his control, Lord Eterskel of Tara and Councilor Teomaxos would be able to shake land, sky, and sea. They could challenge the empress, could gather the last fragments of the Stone of Foundation—could do just about anything. No one had ever beaten the Null-Navvie Construct.

"Where's Fann?" Finn asked impatiently. "She's taking forever!"

"She's somewhere on the ship," Faylinn mumbled. "Good luck getting her to come out."

Fann lingered on Galloglass, which was moored at the treeline. Her own experience in Gilat had left her deeply changed. She was sad, more contemplative, and she also seemed to harbor a strange self-resentment. It was painful to watch. Morla thought that her mood was merely a response to Nunna's self-sacrifice and that it would heal in time; but the Bringer of Dawn hadn't sung since they left Nara, and the days grew bleak.

Four nights it had taken to reach this spot on the westernmost edge of the wastes, where the warrior Shanuri was to be buried in the grass growing beside the forest Tryst. It felt much longer than that. Daedalus' crew complained a lot. They were surprisingly unwilling to face down their old master in Tara, but had agreed to transport the empress back to Nara when business was finished here. At Nara she would have to make her own arrangements to return to Gilthaloneth. Galloglass would also be returned in time, but was destined for a rendezvous with the Fifty-Kells in an undisclosed location.

Lothar had suggested Daedalus pledge himself and his crew to the empress' service, but all Daedalus would promise was assistance in digging the grave. Presently, the two captains were dragging a large heavy capstone from the edge of the forest. It had been inscribed with a seal and symbols, and with a name.

"It is time," Morla said.

When the mourners were gathered at last before the the rock-lined pit that contained the empress' fallen hero, Fann came forth to join them. She was strangely moved by the sight of Taran Morvran's body. Morla thought that it might be because they had removed his armor, which was kept in Val's chamber aboard Galloglass, and had wrapped him in shrouds. Then she could see that this was not so. The look of loss in the Ayumu girl's eyes was keener than that.

When all were assembled, Lothar knelt and lifted from the grass a stout spear and a blue shield bearing the sun and sword crest of House Crodah. Liberated from the ship's small armory, Teomaxos had likely kept these items as trophies symbolic of the council's victory over the Great Houses—a subject upon which he was all too happy to pontificate before the Priests and the army, as often as he could. Polished now to reflect the sunlight, the sight of the shield and spear brought a sense of deep solemnity to those gathered. Even Daedalus' crew bowed their heads. Adi, Mudge, and Wade had dug the grave without complaint, yet Morla perceived that their hearts were conflicted. Was this man they buried not an enemy of the empress? Facing these three across the grave, Caradoc, Bran, and Vercingetorix were likewise befuddled. Lothar's speech aimed at clearing the air a little.

595

"May this field remain quiet where the warrior sleeps," Lothar said, beginning with a traditional eulogy for fallen comrades. "May his journey from this place be blessed, for though he raised his blade against the empress it was not according to his own volition that he did so. There is no fault in him, and he made amends for whatever offense by striking and wounding the wicked serpent. It was a feat greater than any I have accomplished in life, and so in death the empress has permitted me to confer upon him the honorary title of Dragon Slayer. We can do no more for him. May he be restored to the people of his homeland. He is in his maker's hands now."

The empress bowed her head, and Morla saw a clear image emerge from her mind of a summer's day in the woods of the Blue World. There were smells, too, of grease and oil, and of an old barn. How strange, she thought, that something so ordinary could be impressed upon so noble a soul. Were these the connections that had taught the last daughter of the Ancients how to love?

Val spoke after Lothar's words were finished, but her own voice was barely above a whisper.

"The past I knew in exile is lost now to me," she said. "It is lost as if it had never been; and now he is also lost, the Banner of the Blue World of Ertsetum, never to return to again to my side. He was truly my dearest friend, and with his passing begins the even-tide. Blood shall be spilled for blood, and sorrows increase. The dragon and all who stand with him shall feel my pain a hundredfold. I promise this."

All those around her trembled, and Morla most of all. If this was indeed how Val faced her loss, then she was throwing aside everything that she had learned of love for the pain. The Seer leaned towards the empress' ear to whisper some quiet support.

"The blood of Syrscian runs in your veins, *Bal Ona*. When you grieve, so does all Syrscian. Will you not say something to embolden your companions before the ground closes forever over this hero from the Blue World?"

But Val's face and features continued to darken. The world was transfigured as the aura of her grief expanded. The discomfort ushered in by her silence was broken at last by a small voice.

"He protected me from the kells and from the meeches until the last."

Everyone turned and looked towards the foot of the grave. There, looking small and forlorn, Fann stood with head bowed and shoulders shaking.

"He told me that he would gladly give his life for one such as me. He said that it was a good death!"

The empress raised her eyes. Morla was stunned and confused by the feelings of resentment that lashed out from Val towards Fann— precious Fann, who eyes flowed now with tears as she wept silently.

"Of course!" Morla thought to herself. *"She is the Bringer of Dawn. This man was the muse of her first song!"*

It had not occurred to her before, for the so-called *Bringer's Muse* was but a side-note to the legend. If Morla remembered correctly, "first song" was the song of awakening, and was usually inspired by a deep emotional bonding to one person. The muse who had awakened the Bringer was said to be a powerful component of the Bringer's power thereafter.

"Nothing happens without a reason," the seer thought aloud.

Val's anger seemed to subside then. She stood straight, and the shadow passed. Walking around the grave so that she stood beside Fann, she laid at Taran's feet a coin. She then removed a long dagger she wore strapped to her side and laid this down also.

Morla was astonished when she recognized the blade. This was the very dagger that an assassin had used in an attempt to take her own life when she was a little girl. It was the knife she'd given to Val before the battle of Auriga, where it claimed Nunna's life instead. Val had kept it all this time. It was a symbol of her journey. Why would she so lightly set such a thing aside?

"This chapter is over," she said, meeting the seer's eyes across the grave.

It wasn't until now that Morla finally understood Val's gesture. The signs had been there all along, looking her in the face. The girlish expressions and timidity were gone. This Val Anna was more like the empress she had met when she first arrived in Syrscian. The transformation was complete, but whether for good or for ill remained to be seen.

Standing, Val looked back at all the pairs of eyes gazing at her. "The reason for this man's death is that I loved him," she said. "My sojourn in the Blue World was for naught but grief, but I shall not endure it alone. The empress shall retire now to Gilthaloneth, where she shall gather her strength to make war upon her foes, upon those whose actions have brought all our realm to sorrow. The council of priests shall not gain the power of the Navvie Construct. We shall retrieve Nunn, and should House Teg interfere I shall crush them beneath my feet. It shall henceforth be known, the empress has returned with wrath for those who have destroyed this fair world in the absence of the Great Houses. Let all who oppose me stand forth and meet their end."

The ground literally trembled with her words, and when she turned and left her armor gleaming so brightly that few dared look after her. She was aflame with a power none present could withstand. Her words seized them all with fear.

When the empress had gone off alone in the direction of the Galloglass, Daedalus and Lothar joined Morla by the open grave. The Dragon Slayers worked with Mudge and his companions to backfill the hole. Faylinn and Finn held on to their sister, and Fann wept bitterly. It would be long before her heart was whole again. Morla wished there was something she could do to comfort her, but the grief of the Bringer differed from that of the empress. She did not fear for the former so much as the latter.

"Galloglass received a wave transmission only a little while ago," Daedalus said quietly to Lothar. "Orlim has sent the flagship of the imperial council, Battleship Artemis. She will arrive in a few hours. As for Teomaxos, he shall be ordered to surrender the moment he makes port at Gilthaloneth, as per the Lady's wishes."

"It seems the Centaur has decided the time is right for him to make his move," Lothar said uneasily. "I wonder if the Lady had it in mind all along. Those two think alike, it seems."

"Whatever they are thinking," Daedalus remarked, "the soldiers of the council will not side with the empress as long as she supports the Fourth House. The council of priests is sharply divided. Even if she wields a power over dragons, she reckons not the consequences of using it. This is too soon. If by threat of violence she does manage to force the council to accept her authority, there will be much bloodshed in the city."

"Maybe there would be less, if you and your crew joined us."

Daedalus looked up at the mighty forest trees looming nearby, and he shook his head. "There will be a day when that road is decided for me," he said. "Until then, I have some old oaths to fulfill. I will go now to inform the Lady of the Artemis' arrival."

The diggers had finished and were patting the earth on top of the grave. Lothar wrestled the capstone into place. The men then left together to wash the dirt off their limbs, leaving Morla and the girls to stare at the grave. Faylinn and Finn laid two flowers upon the stone while Morla turned aside and brushed some loose soil from another tomb set in the ground nearby. Its pitted gray surface was inscribed with characters of ancient Phoenician script. Morla had carved them a thousand years ago.

"Lady Morla, who is buried there?" asked Faylinn.

"Here is one whom I will remember always, who sacrificed herself for me and for the empress in the Blue World."

Fann looked up, eyes red. The Seer lowered her veil and smiled sweetly at her.

"Now she is in good company," Morla said. "Neither of them shall be forgotten, so long as there is someone to remember them in song. We must not fail in our part to hope that we shall meet them again when the circle is complete, when the darkness ends and war is banished, and Syrscian is restored."

35

LOST FRAGMENTS

Tryst, Syrscian,
Year 1000 of the New Council

With solid stone beneath his body and cold damp air in his lungs, Taran lay pondering a procession of fantasies, all of strange places and people, all passing before his mind's eye in a cavalcade that seemed to drag on for years and years. Maybe they weren't dreams. Maybe they were ghosts, and he was one of them. Their utter silence was all the answer he got to this thought.

While he lay as one dead the last of the shadows of his dreams marched past, and gradually it dawned on him that he was alone. The gray twilight of his mind's eye faded to black then, and an uncomfortable sensation spread through his back into his neck and shoulders, icy fingers of pain that jolted him to an awareness of his surroundings. The air he breathed was stale, but his chest rose and fell in the expected rhythm. He could feel the strong steady pulse of his heartbeat. His arms worked, and the palms of his hands touched smooth stone. Though his eyes were blind, perceiving only blank darkness, he mused on the possibility that his existence had not yet ceased.

What was the last thing he remembered? He moved his legs and sat up to think, for his thinking was never clear while he lay on his back. His aching muscles sorted themselves out slowly, while associated memories tumbled around through the fog of his brain; but they seemed to be memories of other people. Thinking on it a little longer, he discerned two distinct paths among the many. One was of a swordsman in red armor, and the other of a boy in New York. Taran wanted to know just one thing. Which one was he?

He was the one who still bore those cursed fragments in his flesh.

Black night swam before his eyes, adding to his confusion. With arms outstretched his hands were able to touch the cold wet walls of a narrow passageway. Wherever he was, it wasn't pleasant, and he had better get moving. So, with joints creaking, he stood up on his feet.

There was nothing at all around him—no gear, no sword, and no other person. Thus he began his journey, alone and blind, setting one foot in front of the other. He guided himself with a hand on one wall and the other waving in the air before him like the antenna of a beetle. He might have thought worse of this situation, lost as he was in a darkness shaped only by a fear of the unknown.

The passageway was breezy. He was thinking that the wind had to come from someplace, and this meant an exit. No sooner had the thought crossed his mind than the echoed shuffling of his feet vanished, as did the walls of the tunnel. The ground turned to soft soil, and a deep peace settled over all. Air of a warmer clime blew against his face, scented of resinous pines and unnamed forest plants. Faint blue twilight brought the world to life. Though his eyes had been wide open the whole time, Taran was aware of no light around him until now. It came from the sky. Shielding his face with one hand, he allowed his sight to adjust to the shadows beneath the trees while his wonder of the place expanded.

This was an extraordinary place, to be sure. Even as he came to realize that the trees around him were unusually large, he noticed something even stranger framed against a gap in the canopy a little way ahead. Its shape was like a mushroom. There was another right above him. Its smooth gray trunk, thicker than a poplar's, swayed gently in the breeze. While it certainly made no sense that a mushroom could grow so large, the unshakable conviction had formed in his mind that there was more here than a casual glance could perceive. What he really needed was a stronger light to see by. Then, just as it was in the darkness beneath the mound in Cambria, his wish was answered.

A bold sliver of moonlight broke suddenly upon the world, stealing away the awe of everything else. Like an eye opening in the night, it waxed swiftly and grew round. Taran recognized this as an eclipse of sorts. However, the speed and circumstances of this eclipse were like no other he'd ever witnessed. Neck aching, he kept his face to the sky and allowed his eyes to adjust to the glare; but Luna's familiar cratered face wasn't there. She had been replaced by a wine-colored globe wreathed in wispy clouds. Even as this imposter attained a full disk, it budded two brilliant lumps at opposite ends.

There were *three* moons.

While he stood and waited for the lesser moons to emerge from the first, their beauty dulled his alarm. The larger of the two neighbors glowed opal-blue, and the other was exactly like the moon he knew, pitted and scored, and creased with mountains. The three drew apart slowly, and as their heavenly conjunction ended a mass of black shapes passed before them. Taran cringed, for though he thought at first these were clouds, he recognizing now the weird cries of dragons.

There were many, and like great gliding birds they moved, forming phalanxes and swarms. A mournful chorus of their wailing cries was carried on the wind, and in the forest he heard the unfamiliar replies of creatures unknown. It was beautiful, and yet terrifying.

"Well," he whispered to himself, "this is either the other side of Fain's Door, or a really bad dream."

As to that notion, one set of memories was immediately set in contradiction with the world around him. This clearly wasn't Central Park. Hest, Aeron, Rune, and Robert Swift were nowhere to be seen. There was no crater filled with Watchers and dragons. There was no man trapped inside a crystal.

There was, however, an insistent ache in his arm. Besides this, he perceived something was changing. A new sense slowly awakened, like a whispering voice in the back of his mind that waxed and waned, bringing with it flashes of images, of places and things he had never known. He clearly saw three shadowy figures approaching him across a glade washed by morning light. Then the vision was swept away, leaving him alone in the dark forest.

What was this? Taran stood gasping, staring at the gray shadows of the trees. The man inside the crystal had given him something he called *Bibbu*. Whatever this new fragment was doing to him, the brief vision was like something he'd experienced before—only much stronger.

Was this a glimpse of the future, or of yet another dream-world?

Taran set out walking in the direction of the moonlight, and he longed for Hest's quiet company. Surely she would know what to do in this situation. Come to think of it, hadn't she warned him this would happen?

"I will need to teach you how to take care of yourself, and of Regulus, before our journey together comes to an end."

So much for that! He hadn't learned much at all about the fragments of Regulus during their journey, though he had learned a little about Val Anna, DePons, and even about Father. He wondered if anyone would receive the letter he'd left with Giles, or if Mother would ever know what became of him. Strangely, he didn't feel as though their world was very far away.

It was surely because of Regulus.

Whatever was happening to him, the fragments he carried in his body caused his left arm to tingle with energy and to glow with a faint blue translucence. This intensified while he was thinking of home, until quite suddenly he saw before his waking eyes a peculiar double-vision. The forest didn't fade away, but right before him it merged into another place. He paused, peering into a room where his father and mother stood. They were talking and smiling. Though he heard only the forest sounds, Taran seemed to understand that they were talking about him.

When the room and its occupants vanished moments later, Taran's left hand went numb. It was like ice, and its translucence had not entirely faded. Then he remembered the incident at Wiceline's Inn, and a new idea sprang into his mind.

Did he not have the power even now to return if he wished? After all, there seemed to be nothing preventing him from stepping right into the room he saw. Somehow he imagined Hest would not have approved of this. He had come all this way to find Val Anna, and there was no going home until it was over. Before he was given another chance to tempt himself, he realized he had reached the edge of the wood, and there were new things to see.

The grasslands spread before him along a slope that ran away to a bleak desert landscape stretching on under moonlight to the end of the world. He was eyeing the desert and the drifting moons when suddenly, so swiftly that it momentarily confused him, the horizon flashed with the arrival of dawn.

This sun was larger than the one he knew, and as it rose a wind blew up from the desert and shook the trees above him. He turned around and surveyed the forest, its mushroom-caps tossing in the breeze amidst trees taller than California Redwoods. It was a pretty place. The sharp line drawn between the desert and the forest was softened a little by a wide lawn of deep grass, and through this lawn there ran a stream.

Taran went to drink from the clear trickling flow. Its taste was sweet and clean. Following its flow a few meters into the grass, he was reminded of the words of an ancient English poem, and he spoke a couple lines aloud to greet the morning.

"But on a May morning on Malvern hills, a marvel befell me of fairy, I thought."

He was thinking, however, that this was no fairy dream. Whatever world this was, it was real, and he should therefore proceed with great caution. There were dragons out there, and maybe things even more dangerous. He was just thinking this when the rising sun revealed to him an area of trampled ground at hand. Loose loam lay scattered about, and there was a long flat stone resting in the soil. Fresh flowers had been placed upon it. Being the size of a man, he guessed he had found a grave.

Feeling more than a little unsettled by this sight, Taran approached the grave-marker warily, scanning the grass to make sure he was alone. When he was certain there really was no one else about, he crouched down beside the stone and saw upon its surface a name in ordinary Latin letters.

TARAN MORVRAN

Confusion and fear compelled him to rationalize. It could not really be his grave, of course, because he wasn't dead. There were any number of Taran Morvrans out there, he reasoned.

His brain screamed at him to reconsider. Here he was, alone in the wilds of a world far from Earth, bending over the tomb of a man who shared his exact name, and who lived in an English-speaking culture that used Latin letters. There could be no such coincidence, not in all the universe.

Intellect alone wasn't going to solve this mystery—not right now, at any rate. He had no facts to go by. Maybe after he had explored a little more and found some people to talk to, he might eventually come to understand the meaning of this grave. For the time being he was completely baffled, though, and with no other evidence presenting itself to his questing eyes, he picked up one of the flowers that lay upon the stone. It appeared to be a carnation. The flower was cut recently, for it had not yet wilted. While he studied its delicate dusty red and white petals, another flower upon the rock stood up suddenly and spoke to him.

"Dreaming?" it asked in a tiny voice.

This new absurdity was even more surprising than the inscription upon the grave. It wasn't a flower he saw, but a maiden just six inches tall, gird in bits of cloth, flexing jeweled lilac-colored wings.

Taran never gave much credence to the stories his mother had told him of pixies and the like. He had never taken to fairytales at all. If there ever were such beings, and if they were intelligent, why would they remain in hiding? The question that faced him now was different. What would people do if the fairies came out of hiding?

"I'm dreaming," was his natural response.

But he knew he wasn't. He'd never been more awake, in fact.

The tiny flower-maiden gazed at him lovingly. "Shanuri dreams, too?" she asked.

"You're a fairy?"

The wings buzzed angrily. She crossed her little arms and scowled. "Shanuri's a toad!"

Taran fell on his bottom when she launched herself into the air. He waved his hands as if warding off a wasp, but the little creature dodged and landed upon his knee. She weighed no more than a handful of acorns, but even that light touch was enough to send his brain into a panic. She was glaring up into his face. Apparently, designating her a fairy was somehow insulting.

"Tricks?" she asked. "Shanuri's dead; now alive?"

The continual questions goaded him. Almost everything she said was interrogative, so he offered her a question of his own.

"Who is Shanuri?" he asked.

Her response was totally unexpected. She abruptly turned her back to him and wiped her face. It seemed she was crying. Luminous spots glowed suddenly upon her arms and legs, strobing gently. Taran reached out towards her tiny shoulder, but she smacked his fingertips away with the speed of a striking serpent.

"Look," he said, "I don't think I'm going nuts, but I really don't know what's going on here."

She relaxed her arms, allowing them to hang down by her sides. Taran sensed she was very distressed, and her suffering was hard to watch. When she turned her face to him at last, it was wet with tears. Sobs shook her tiny body. This was certainly no figment of his imagination.

With nothing else coming to mind, he asked, "Did you know the one who is buried here?"

"Shanuri?" she asked.

She was pointing towards the grave, but then, with a look that sent the hair standing on top of his head, she pointed right at him.

"Shanuri died. Now he lives?"

Taran was back at square one. He was sure she was mistaking him for someone else. This wasn't his grave. It couldn't be. The little flower-maiden collapsed upon his knee, and while she continued to sob and moan it was impossible for him to pursue further conversation. Nor could he comfort her. He sat still and watched her wipe her eyes until she looked up once again, peering at him more closely now, inspecting his features as if for some unfamiliar element. She stroked the fabric of his pant-leg.

"Not like Shanuri?" she wondered quietly.

Taking to the air on her tiny wings, she hovered close to his face and touched a lock of his hair.

"Like Shanuri," she decided.

She proceeded in this manner to find many points of comparison between himself and this other person, Shanuri, until Taran found himself yawning.

"Like Shanuri!" she said, pointing at him.

"Really?" he asked.

This was getting more and more dire. It seemed he and the dead man shared more than a name. Taran wondered if they really were alike, or if the little creature was finding it difficult to distinguish one human from another.

"This person Shanuri is the same person as Taran Morvran?"

She nodded vigorously.

"He was your friend?"

She was obviously puzzled by his question. "Friend?" she wondered. "Siru friend?"

"Who's Siru?"

"Siru and Sirona? Nin and Barashkushu? Empress and blue girl?"

"What in the world is a blue girl?"

Whatever she was trying to say, she wasn't able to articulate anything well.

"What is your name, anyway?" he asked.

This completely confounded her. For a moment she looked like she was about to burst into tears again.

Then, quietly, she said, "Una?"

Her little face shifted suddenly from sadness to fear. Taran sensed stealthy footfalls in the grass, and turned just as a familiar voice called out.

"Watching you two trying to converse is enough to drive a man insane!"

The vision he'd experienced in the moonlit forest snapped suddenly into place before his waking eyes. Three figures walked towards him; but the shock of their arrival left Taran speechless. He looked from one to another in wide-eyed amaze.

"Well," said the one who had greeted him first. "If it's not the most overqualified crook in Manhattan!"

"Cedric DePons?" Taran marveled, rising to his feet.

His eyes were surely playing tricks on him. Even though this man wore DePons' face and slicked-back hair, he was dressed in a black tunic with high boots.

"You'll excuse the wardrobe change," DePons said in greeting. "You'll also forgive me for failing to meet you on Aenfer. Something came up."

Taran had never seen the man without a suit and sensible shoes. His two companions were likewise strangely dressed, and strange-looking at that. One was a girl with bright pink hair wearing a matching form-fitting leather outfit. She eyed Taran with large eyes, pretty but strikingly clear. The other was cloaked and hooded so completely that Taran couldn't even tell if it was a man or a woman.

The hooded head stared down at the grass. Only then did Taran notice the other grave. It was only a few yards away from the one which bore his name, but it was a little overgrown. The writing upon it was in Phoenician letters.

"It is good to find you in one piece," DePons remarked.

"I think maybe it's more complicated than you realize,' Taran said.

Cedric and his companions studied the stone with Taran's name on it for a long minute. Una spent the time stroking Taran's hair from her perch on his shoulder. It was a strange feeling, and though he was glad she no longer wept he wished she would stop.

"These kinds of things are to be expected when dealing with Regulus," DePons said at last.

All three looked back up at Taran.

"Come again?"

"Regulus is recohering, Taran, and all its bearers as well. The man buried here bore a shard, as do you. His contact with Regulus is what brought him here, where all the fragments will be rejoined eventually."

"And what if we had met here while he was alive?"

"There cannot be two Taran Morvrans. That is why the *third amplitude* existed."

Taran didn't like the sound of this. "What did you do?" he asked. "Does this have something to do with what happened to Val, or to Fain?"

"Well, it was nothing Fain or I did—"

"But all these people and items you've come across in your own travels, they just conveniently gathered in a place outside normal space and time?"

"Yes, the third amplitude. A tidy little pocket universe, it was, where Fain and I did most of our work. Your father never approved, of course—"

"And Regulus created that place, the New York where everything had gone wrong?"

DePons looked uncomfortable, and Taran suddenly wondered what the man was in this world. Surely no one important, if he was dressed like this.

"As the fragments are recalled and united," DePons explained, "everything else must begin to fall into place. The third amplitude and all its people were therefore only a temporary construct. It has since collapsed into the Sum of History and is no more. The man buried here was one from that existence. He was a shadow of yourself."

"How do you know for sure? Maybe I am one of them, and he was the real Taran."

"You are the Taran standing here bearing fragments of Regulus and Bibbu in your flesh. You are the only Taran Morvran."

How did he know about Bibbu? Taran was puzzled by this, and by how much DePons already knew about what was going on in this crazy new world.

"You look confused, Taran, but from now on things will be much less complicated. When you first set out on this journey you wanted to find your friend. I can tell you with certainty that she is here."

"She is?"

But there was concern on DePons' face. "I said that things would be less complicated," he said, looking at the grave. "I did not say they would be easy. Getting to her now will be very difficult. This world is in upheaval, for there are Powers that desire to wage war with the stones. It has already begun."

"You mean the War of the Towers?" Taran said, recalling Dun's parting words.

"Yes, that shall come. It is all coming to pass as was told long ago."

"Prophecies and fate, is it? After all that's happened, DePons, you still want to talk to me about destiny?"

"Do you still not understand, Taran? That's how we found you here, at the conjunction of the moons. You were to appear at an appointed place, a place that a chance companion was able to find. There are no coincidences. You are here, and so are we. This is where our real journey begins."

"I still haven't found Val—"

"Then let us help you. We have come to get you ready."

"Ready for what?" Taran asked nervously. Una gave DePons a piercing glance, as if daring him to take Taran away somewhere.

"Whatever you do next, you must be prepared to survive in your new world," Cedric said. "Your training will be intense, but I'm fully confident that you shall survive. After all, you've made it this far already."

"I only made it this far with Hest's help."

DePons nodded sagely. Taran waited for him to say something, but when he didn't the silence became awkward. It was as though he didn't intend to acknowledge his own daughter.

Unless Hest also was one of those from the third amplitude—one who had disappeared forever.

With his mind full of bleak thoughts, Taran followed the three into the forest. He looked back one last time towards the desert. The light of morning had all but faded the glory of the three moons, which were only faintly visible now on the horizon behind them.

"You obviously know where we're going," he said. "Want to tell me about it?"

DePons and his friends had no gear with them. They were moving quickly.

"As you've no doubt guessed," DePons replied, "this world is my home. I will lead you on a westward course towards the heart of the forest. When things are settled there, and your training is complete, you will know where to go next."

"You make it sound like I'm going to combat training."

"Is it not worth it to save your friend?"

Taran was tired of asking questions that only got half an answer. He trudged through the trackless undergrowth lost in deep thought. It wasn't unlike the day his father and DePons had brought him out of New York. Whatever they had been preparing him for back then seemed close at hand. Taran didn't like the feeling this gave him.

"Taran go away again?" asked a small voice from his shoulder.

To this, DePons laughed and said, "If Piski were any stupider, they'd probably be considered edible! Of course he's going away, Little One. It would be best if you forgot about him and went back to mucking for grubs."

Una was obviously ruffled by his insult. She flew to Taran's other shoulder and whispered into his ear.

"Wars for Taran?"

She was calling him Taran now. He wondered why the change.

"Una will go, too?"

"I don't want to fight in any wars," he said to her. "I hope that's not what they expect of me. I'm just a reflection cast in someone else's mirror."

"An interesting way to think of it," DePons remarked.

"I wasn't talking to you," Taran said, becoming annoyed.

"He's like that all the time," said the pink-haired girl. "Might as well get used to it."

"Oh, I know how pushy he can be," Taran replied. "But it's the know-it-all attitude that gets me."

"I'm Hanuta," the girl said with a grin. "Call me Nuta."

She offered her hand, and Taran shook it. "Taran," he said. "I guess I should say it's nice to meet you, but it would have been nicer somewhere else."

"Tell me about it," she said, ducking under a branch.

Taran glanced at the hooded figure walking by himself on the opposite side of DePons.

"Don't mind him," Nuta said. "He doesn't talk."

"Not at all?"

"Nope. And believe me, I've tried."

"Even Una talks," Taran said. "Maybe he doesn't understand our language."

"Is this Una?" the girl asked, her eyes wide with wonder as she beheld the little flower-maiden.

Una clutched Taran's earlobe as if she was afraid. "Pink lady hair flowers?" she asked.

"Huh?"

"Let me correct myself," Taran said. "She does speak, but it seems her skills in speech aren't suitable to expressing what she wants to say."

Nuta chuckled. "I'm just amazed at this place. There's something more amazing each new day. Maybe I could actually come to like it here, but it'll never be home."

Taran felt instantly relieved. This girl actually understood what he felt like, and was an agreeable person to talk to. She reminded him a little of Val Anna. Sighing deeply, he rested his hand against his shirt-pocket and felt the bundle of papers he kept there, close to his heart.

It had been a long time since he last looked at the scraps of paper torn from Fain's book, but it was the page of childish sketches he fished out and unfolded. With feelings of nostalgia for the world he'd left behind, he studied the stick figures closely, one with a messy bundle of spiky hair sticking out on top, and the other in a skirt.

Taran and me.

Taran folded the page quickly and put it back with Fain's notes, and then attended to the huge and terrifying trees. No one spoke for a long while, until they began to hear the voices.

Taran first noticed them when the mighty limbs of the trees above started moving. There was no breeze, and no sign of any animal life capable of moving such massive branches. Then, faintly, there were words spoken in the air, falling like leaves among the pathless shadowed ways beneath. Wondering if she also heard, he looked to Nuta and was alarmed to see her studying him closely with her sharp eyes.

"You can hear that?" he asked.

"Hear what?"

"He speaks of the voices of the Fomorians that sleep," DePons said. "It is because he bears fragments within his body that he is responding to their call."

Taran turned and glanced at the cloaked figure. He was also gazing up at the trees.

"You must learn to hear what they are saying," Cedric said.

Taran looked up into the canopy, jostling Una from her perch. She held onto his collar, thrumming in his ear. He looked aside at her, and was surprised to see that she was suddenly very eager and happy. She smiled, and it changed the appearance of her face entirely.

"Una knows their words!" she said brightly.

"I can barely make them out."

They went on slowly, and as Taran fell silent he thought that he understood more of the whispered words.

Mul'hungá, Agru the fighter, which is Aries.
Mul'gigir, Narkabtu, Gift to the Gremn-Under-Ban, the Chariot.
Mul'ur, Kalbu, the hound of Great Strength.
Mul'Babbar, Kakkabu Petsu, the blessed White Star of Jupiter.
Mul'hul, wicked Lumnu, the witch of Mars.
Mul'ellag, Bibbu the Lonely, the Comet.
Mul'sipazi-anna, Shitaddalu, Beautiful Orion.
Mul'ashiku, Ikû the Far-Ranging, the Last Pegasus.
Mul'lugal, Sharru, the Hidden Lord Regulus.
Gír'tab, Aban Zuqaqípu, the Scorpion, most precious of gems.
Mul'pan, Qashtu, Gift to the Crodah-Under-Ban, the Heart of Venus.
Mul'dara, Dim Da'ummatu, the Dark Star, First and Last, the Dragon's Heart.

These, the Twelve, shall endure apart as one.
Hidden by the Ancients, reunited by the hidden;
May all hold fast their legend until the end.

Though he knew of Regulus and Bibbu, the rest was only vaguely familiar. It brought to mind, though, a conversation he'd had with a woman named Brisen. Was he not one of the *Hidden* the song spoke of—one of those who reunited the stones?

They continued walking, but the mood had changed. Taran felt more at ease, as if turning a corner he faced at last some long-lost friend. Was it destiny he felt? DePons would undoubtedly tell him yes, but Taran wasn't ready for that just yet. For now, he was feeling for the first time on this adventure as though he might be able to find his way. A decision would reveal itself very soon.

But then he paused to wonder at something that had been nagging the back of his mind all afternoon.

"Who was it put the flowers on my grave, I wonder?"

"Someone loves Taran?" Una pondered.

He blushed, but she was right. Someone had cared enough about Taran Morvran to put flowers on his grave.

"It is possible the empress herself placed them there," said a heavily accented voice.

Nuta and Taran stopped again. DePons went on a few paces, but then he also paused. The cloaked fellow pulled back his hood to reveal a head that was completely bald. He looked and sounded to be of Arabic descent, but his eyes were abnormally dark. They were, in fact, completely black, with no visible sclera.

"He speaks?" Nuta queried. "I haven't heard your voice for three weeks!"

The stranger nodded towards her, but made no reply. To Taran he said, "The empress told us about you long ago, Taran Morvran. She was quite taken with you. You two are destined to meet, and then shall be fulfilled all that was written in the Relic Calendar."

"I don't understand," Taran said. "I don't know any empress! I set out to follow my grandfather and find a lost friend, but now that whole quest is looking kind of hopeless."

"You have met Brisen, though," the man said. "I can see that she has spoken to you, and it is confirmed via my link with the Source. Did she not explain that the one to whom you shall surrender the Sky Power would be the same who called the fragments out of the dark worlds?"

Taran vividly recalled talking to the Lady in White, a ghostly apparition he met in the terminal. "She told me lots of things I didn't understand," he said. "But what business have I got with an empress?"

"Maybe more than you guess," DePons replied.

"Most certainly," the bald fellow said.

"And who are you?" Taran asked.

"He has come into our service by chance," DePons said. "I found him alone and in dire circumstances. He is also from Ertsetum."

The young man bowed his head with dark eyes closed. Taran also bowed, but he felt very uncomfortable. What did he mean about being linked to the *Source*? There was a strange sensation coming from him. Taran couldn't tell what it was, but it didn't seem right. Una also seemed to sense it, for she cringed behind his collar.

"Forgive my silence earlier," the stranger said, "but I also am a bearer of a fragment, and I was listening to determine whether or not you could be trusted."

"Well," Taran mumbled. "Am I to be trusted?"

"If Brisen saw fit to reveal to you her plan, then I might at least reveal to you my name. I am Kal-Nergal. I am hoping we can be allies."

Printed in the United States
By Bookmasters